BLACK JADE

Voyager

DAVID ZINDELL

Black Jade

Book Three of the Ea Cycle

HarperCollins*Publishers*

Voyager
An Imprint of HarperCollins*Publishers*
77–85 Fulham Palace Road,
Hammersmith, London W6 8JB

www.voyager-books.com

Published by *Voyager* 2005
1 3 5 7 9 8 6 4 2

A catalogue record for this book
is available from the British Library

ISBN Hardback 0 00 224759 3
Trade Paperback 0 00 224760 7

Set in Meridien Roman by Palimpsest Book Production Limited,
Polmont, Stirlingshire

Printed and bound in Great Britain by
Clays Ltd, St Ives plc

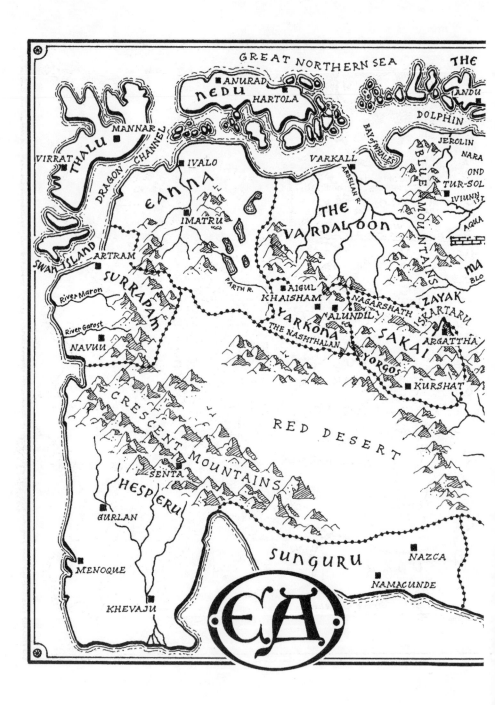

1

Each man and woman is a star. As long as we are alive, my grandfather used to say, we must endure burning if we are to give light. As for the dead, only the dead know if their eternal flame is a glory or an anguish. In the heavens they shine through the dark nights of the ages in uncountable numbers. There, since I was a child, my grandfather has dwelled with Aras and Solaru and the other brightest lights. There, my mother and father, my grandmother and brothers, have joined him, sent on by the deadly lies and misdeeds of one they loved. Some day, it is said, a man will come forth and impel the stars to end their vast silence, and then these splendid orbs will sing their long, deep, fiery songs to those who listen. Will this Shining One, with the Lightstone in his hands, cool the tormented hearts of men, the living and the dead? I must believe that he will. For it is also said that the Lightstone gathers all things to itself. Within its luminous center dwells the earth and men and women and all the stars – and the blackness between them that allows them to be seen.

The Lightstone, however, was as far from this Shining One's grasp as the sun was from mine. With the Red Dragon's ravaging of my father's castle to steal the golden cup, men and women in every land were looking toward the Dragon's stronghold of Argattha with fevered and fearful eyes. In Surrapam, the victorious armies of King Arsu stood ready to conquer Eanna and the other Free Kingdoms of the far west, and crucify their peoples in the Dragon's name. In Alonia, mightiest of realms, quarrelsome dukes and lords slew each other to gain King Kiritan's vacant throne. Across the Morning Mountains of my home, the Valari kings fought as always for ancient grudge and glory. A great rebellion in Galda had ended with ten thousand men being mounted

1

on crosses of wood. The Wendrush was a sea of grass running red with the blood of the Sarni tribes. Too many of these fierce warriors had surrendered their independence to declare for the Red Dragon, whose name was Morjin. As scryers had foreseen in terrible visions, it seemed that the whole world was about to burn up in a holocaust that would blacken the very stars.

And yet, as the scryers had also told, somewhere on Ea lived the Shining One: the last Maitreya who might bring a light so pure and sweet that it would put out this all-consuming fire. I sought this great-souled being. My friends – heroes, all, of the Quest to find the Lightstone – sought him, too. Our new quest, by day and by night, took us ever farther from the green valleys and snow-capped mountains of my homeland. To the west we journeyed, following the fiery arc of Aras and Varshara and the other bright stars of the ancient constellations where they disappeared beyond the dark edge of the heavens.

And others followed us. Early in Ashte in the year 2814 of the Age of the Dragon, a squadron of Morjin's famed Dragon Guard and their Sarni allies pursued us across the Wendrush's rolling steppe. Our enemies seemed not to care that we were under the escort of forty-four Sarni warriors of the Danladi tribe; for three days, as we approached the great, icy, stone wall of the White Mountains, they had ridden after us like shadows through the Danladi's country – always keeping at a distance that neither threatened nor invited attack. And for three nights, they had built their campfires and cooked their dinners scarcely a mile from the sites that we chose to lay our sleeping furs. When the third night fell upon the world and the wind shifted and blew at us from the north, we could smell the smoky char of roasting meat and other more disturbing scents.

On a swell of dark grass at the edge of our camp, I stood with my friend Kane gazing out to the northwest at the orange glow of our enemy's campfires. Kane's cropped, white hair was a silvery sheen beneath a round, silver moon. He stared off into the starlit distances, and his lips pulled back from his white teeth in a fearsome grimace. His large, savage body trembled with a barely-contained fury. I could almost hear him howling out his hate, like a great, white wolf of the steppe lusting to rend and slay.

'So, Val, so,' he said to me. 'We must decide what we are to do about these crucifiers, and soon.'

He turned his gaze upon me then. As always, I saw too much of myself in this vengeful man, and of him in me. His bright, black eyes were like a mirror of my own. He was nearly as tall as I; his nose was that of a great eagle, and beneath his weathered, ivory skin, the bones of his face stood out boldly. Between us was a likeness that others had remarked: of form, certainly, for he looked as much a Valari warrior as had my father and brothers. But our deeper kinship, I thought, was not of the blood but the spirit. Now that my family had all been slaughtered, I sometimes found the best part of them living on in his aspect: strange, wild, beautiful and free.

I smiled at him and then turned back toward our enemy's campfires. One of our Sarni escort, after earlier riding close enough to take an arrow through the arm, had put their numbers at fifty: twenty-five Zayak warriors under some unknown chief or headman and as many of the Red Knights, with their dragon blazons and their iron armor, tinctured red as with blood.

'We might yet outride them,' I said to Kane. 'Perhaps tomorrow, we should put it to the test.'

We could not, of course, so easily escape the Zayak warriors, for none but a Sarni could outride a Sarni. The Red Knights, however, encased in heavy armor and mounted on heavy horses, moved more slowly. Of our company, only Kane and I, with our friend, Maram, wore any kind of real armor: supple mail forged of Godhran steel that was lighter and stronger than anything Morjin's blacksmiths could hammer together. Our horses, I thought, were better, too: Fire, Patience and Hell Witch, and especially my great, black warhorse, Altaru, who stood off a hundred paces with our other mounts taking his fill of the steppe's new, sweet grass.

'Well, then,' Kane said to me, 'we must test it *before* we reach the mountains.'

He pointed off toward the great, snow-capped peaks that glinted beneath the western stars. As he held out his thick finger, his mail likewise glinted from beneath his gray, wool traveling cloak, similar in cut and weave to my own.

'So, then – fight or flee,' he growled out. 'And I hate to flee.'

As we pondered our course, mostly in silence, a great bear of a man stood up from the nearby campfire and ambled over to hear what we were discussing. He tried to skirt the inevitable piles of horse or sagosk dung, and other imagined dangers of the dark grass, all the while sipping from a mug of sloshing brandy. I drank in the form of my best friend, Maram Marshayk. Once a prince of Delu and an honorary Valari knight of great renown,

3

fate had reduced him to accompanying me into Ea's wild lands as outcasts.

'Ah, I heard Kane say something about fleeing,' he said to us. A belch rumbled up from his great belly, and he wiped his lips with the back of his hand. 'My father used to say that whoever runs away lives to fight again another day.'

His soft eyes found mine through the thin light as his thick, sensuous lips broke into a smile. Upon taking in the whole of his form – the dense, curly beard which covered his heavy face, no less his massive chest, arms and legs – I decided that it would be a bad idea to try to outride the Red Knights. No weight of their armor, be it made of steel plate, could match the mass of muscle and fat that padded the frame of Maram Marshayk.

'If we flee,' Kane said to him, poking his finger into Maram's belly, 'are you willing to be left behind when your horse dies of exhaustion?'

It was too dark to see Maram's florid face blanch, but I felt the blood drain from it, even so. He looked out toward our enemy's campfires, and said, 'Would you really leave me behind?'

'So, I would,' Kane growled out. His dark eyes drilled into Maram. 'At need, I'd sacrifice any and all of us to fulfill this quest.'

Maram took a long pull of brandy as he turned to regard Kane. 'Ah, a sacrifice is it, then? Well, I won't have *that* on your conscience. If a sacrifice truly needs to be made, I'll turn to cross lances with the Red Knights by myself.'

I looked back and forth between Maram and Kane as they glared at each other. I did not think that either of them was quite telling the truth. I rested my hand on Maram's shoulder as I caught Kane's gaze. And I said, 'No one is going to be left behind. And we *will* fulfill this quest, as we did the first.'

Just then Master Juwain, sitting with our other friends by the fire, finished writing something in one of his journals and came over to us. He was as small as Maram was large and as ugly as Kane was well-made. His head somewhat resembled a walnut, and a misshapen one at that: all lumpy and bald with a knurled nose and ears that stuck out too far. But I had never know a man whose eyes were so intelligent and clear. Like the rest of us, he wore a gray traveling cloak, though he refused to bind his limbs in steel rings or carry any weapon more deadly than the little knife he used to sharpen his quills.

'Come,' he said as he grasped Maram's wrist. 'If we're to hold council, let us all sit together. Liljana is nearly finished making dinner.'

I looked over toward the fire where a plump, matronly woman bent over a pot of bubbling stew. A girl about ten years old sat next to her making cakes on a griddle while a boy slightly older poked the fire with a long, charred stick.

'Excellent,' Maram agreed, 'we'll eat and then we'll talk.'

'You would talk more cogently,' Master Juwain told him, 'if you would take your drink *after* you eat. Or forbear it altogether.'

With fierce determination, Master Juwain suddenly clamped his knotted fingers around Maram's mug. His small hands were surprisingly strong, from a lifetime of disciplines and hard work, and he managed to pry free the mug from Maram's thick palm.

Maram eyed the mug as might a child a candy that has been taken from him. He said, 'I have *forborne* my brandy these last three days, waiting for the Red Knights to attack us, too bad. As for talk, cogent as it is clever, please don't forget that I'm now called Five-Horned Maram.'

Once, a lifetime ago it seemed, Maram had been an adept of the Great White Brotherhood under the tutelage of Master Juwain, and everyone had called him 'Brother Maram.' But he had long since abjured his vows to forsake wine, women and war. Now he wore steel armor beneath his cloak and bore a sword that was nearly as long and keen as my own. Less than a year before, in the tent of Sajagax, the Sarni's mightiest chieftain, he had become the only man in memory to down five great horns of the Sarni's potent beer – and to remain standing to tell everyone of his great feat.

Kane continued glaring at Maram, and again he poked his steely finger into his belly. He said, 'You'd do well to forbear brandy *and* bread, at least for a while. Are you trying to kill yourself, as well as your horse?'

In truth, ever since the Battle of Culhadosh Commons and the sack of my father's castle, Maram had been eating enough for two men and drinking more than enough for five.

'Forbear, you say?' he muttered to Kane. 'I might as well forbear life itself.'

'But you're growing as fat *as* a bear.'

Maram patted his belly and smiled. 'Well, what if I am? Haven't you seen a bear eat when winter is coming?'

'But it's Ashte – in another month, summer will be upon us!'

'No, my friend, there you're wrong,' Maram told him, with a shake of his head and another belch. 'Wherever we journey, it will be winter – and deep winter at that, for we'll be deep into this damn new quest. Do you remember the last time we went tramping all across Ea? I nearly starved to death. And so is it not the soul of prudence that I should fortify myself against the deprivations that are sure to come?'

Kane had no answer against this logic. And so he snapped at Maram: 'Fortify yourself then, if you will. But at least forbear your brandy until there's a better time and place to drink it.'

So saying, he took the mug from Master Juwain and moved to empty its contents onto the grass.

'Hold!' Maram cried out. 'It would be a crime to waste such good brandy!'

'So,' Kane said, eyeing the dark liquor inside the mug. 'So.'

He smiled his savage smile, as if the great mystery of life's unfairness pleased him almost as much as it pained him. Then, with a single, quick motion, he put the mug to his lips and threw down the brandy in three huge gulps.

'Forbear yourself, damn you!' Maram called out to him.

'*Damn* me? You should thank me, eh?'

'Thank you *why*? For saving me from drunkenness?'

'No – for taking a little pleasure from this fine brandy of yours.'

Kane handed the mug back to Maram, who stood looking into its hollows.

'Ah, well, I suppose *one* of us should have savored it,' he said to Kane. 'It pleases me that it pleased you so deeply, my friend. Perhaps someday I can return the favor – and save *you* from becoming a drunk.'

Kane smiled at this as Maram began laughing at the little joke he had made, and so did Master Juwain and I. One mug of brandy had as much effect on the quenchless Kane as a like amount of water would on all the sea of grasses of the Wendrush.

I looked at Kane as I tapped my finger against Maram's cup. I said, 'Perhaps we should all forbear brandy for a while.'

'Ha!' Kane said. 'There's no need that *I* should.'

'The need is to encourage Maram to remain sober,' I said. I couldn't help smiling as I added, 'Besides, we all must make sacrifices.'

Kane looked at Maram for an uncomfortably long moment, and then announced, 'All right then, if Maram will vow to forbear, so shall I.'

'And so shall I,' I said.

Maram blinked at the new moisture in his eyes; I couldn't quite tell if our little sacrifice had moved him or if the prospect of giving up his beloved brandy made him weep. And then he clapped me on the arm as he nodded at Kane and said, 'You would do *that* for *me*?'

'We would,' Kane and I said with one breath.

'Ah, well, *that* pleases me more than I could ever tell you, even if I had a whole barrel full of brandy to loosen my tongue.' Maram paused to dip his fat finger down into the mug, moistening it with the last few drops of brandy that clung to its insides. Then he licked his finger and smiled. 'But I must say that I would wish no such deprivation upon my friends. Just because I suffer doesn't mean that the rest of the world must, too.'

I glanced at the campfires of our enemies, then I turned back to look at Maram. 'In these circumstances, we'll gladly suffer with you.'

'Very well,' Maram said. Then he nodded at Master Juwain. 'Sir, will you be a witness to our vows?'

'Even as I was once before,' Master Juwain said dryly.

'Excellent,' Maram said. 'Then unless it be needed for, ah, medicinal purposes, I vow to forbear brandy until we find the one we seek.'

'Ha!' Kane cried out. 'Rather let us say that unless Master Juwain *prescribes* brandy for medicinal purposes, we shall all forbear it.'

'Excellent, excellent,' Maram agreed, nodding his head. He held up his mug and smiled. 'Then why don't we all return to the fire and drink one last toast to our resolve?'

'Maram!' I half-shouted at him.

'All right, all right!' he called back. The breath huffed out of him, and for a moment he seemed like a bellows emptied of air. 'I was just, ah, testing *your* resolve, my friend. Now, why don't we all go have a taste of Liljana's fine stew. *That*, at least, is still permitted, isn't it?'

We all walked back to the fire and sat down on our sleeping furs set out around it. I smiled at Daj, the dark-souled little boy that we had rescued out of Argattha along with the Lightstone. He smiled back, and I noticed that he was not quite so desperate inside nor small outside as when we had found him a starving slave in Morjin's hellhole of a city. It was a good thing, smiling, I thought. It lifted up the spirit and gave courage to others. I silently thanked Maram for making me laugh, and I resolved to sustain my gladness of life as long as I could. This was the vow *I* had made, high on a sacred mountain above the castle where my mother and grandmother had been crucified.

7

Daj, sitting next to me, jabbed the glowing end of his fire-stick toward me and called out, 'At ready! Let's practice swords until it's time to eat!'

He moved to put down his stick and draw the small sword I had given him when we had set out on our new quest. His enthusiasm for this weapon both impressed and saddened me. I would rather have seen him playing chess or the flute, or even playing *at* swords with other boys his age. But this savage boy, I reminded myself, had never really been a boy. I remembered how in Argattha he had fought a dragon by my side and had stuck a spear into the bodies of our wounded enemies.

'It *is* nearly time to eat,' Liljana called out to us. Her heavy breasts moved against her thick, strong body as she stirred the succulent-smelling stew. 'Why don't you practice after dinner?'

Although her words came out of her firm mouth as a question, sweetly posed, there was no question that we must put off our swordwork until later. Beneath her bound, iron-gray hair, her pleasant face betrayed an iron will. She liked to bring the cheer and good order of a home into our encampments by directing cooking, eating and cleaning, even talking, and many other details of our lives. I might be the leader of our company on our quest across Ea's burning steppes and icy mountains, but she sought by her nature to try to lead me from within. Through countless kindnesses and her relentless devotion, she had dug up the secrets of my soul. It seemed that there was no sacrifice that she wouldn't make for me – even as she never tired, in her words and deeds, of letting me know how much she loved me. At her best, however, she called me to *my* best, as warrior, dreamer and man. Now that the insides of my father's castle had been burnt to ashes, she was the only mother I still had.

'There will be no swordwork tonight,' I said, to Liljana and Daj, 'unless the Red Knights attack us. We need to hold council.'

'Very well, then, but I hope you're not still considering attacking *them*.' Liljana looked through the steam wafting up from the stew, straight at Kane. She shook her head, then called out, 'Estrella, are those cakes ready yet?'

Estrella, a dark, slender girl of quicksilver expressions and bright smiles, clapped her hands to indicate that the yellow rushk cakes – piled high on a grass mat by her griddle – were indeed ready to eat. She could not speak, for she, too, had been Morjin's slave, and he had used his black arts to steal the words from her tongue. But she had the hearing of a cat; in truth, there was something feline about her, in her wild, triangular face and in the way she moved, instinctually and gracefully, as if all the features of the world must be sensed and savored. With her black curls gathered about her neck, her lustrous skin and especially her large, luminous eyes, she possessed a primeval beauty. I had never known anyone, not even Kane, who seemed so alive.

Almost without thought, she plucked one of the freshest cakes from the top of the piles and placed it in my hand. It was still quite hot, though not enough to burn me. As I took a bite out of it, her smile was like the rising sun.

'Estrella, you shouldn't serve until we're all seated,' Liljana instructed her.

Estrella smiled at Liljana, too, though she did not move to do as she was told. Instead, seeing that I had finished my cake, she gave me another one. She delighted in bringing me such little joys as the eating of a hot, nutty rushk cake. It had always been that way between us, ever since I had found her clinging to a cold, castle wall and saved her from falling to her death. And countless times since that dark night, in her lovely eyes and her deep covenant with life, she had kept me from falling into much worse.

'The girl never minds me,' Liljana complained. 'She always does just as she pleases.'

I smiled because what she said was true. I watched as Estrella tried to urge one of the cakes into Liljana's hand. She seemed not to resent Liljana's stern looks or scolding; indeed, Liljana's oppressive care for her and her desire to teach her good manners obviously pleased her, as did almost everything about the people she loved. Her will to be happy, I thought, was even greater than Liljana's urge to remake the world as the paradise it had been in the Age of the Mother. It must have vexed Liljana that our quest depended utterly upon this wild, magical child.

'She was a slave of the Red Priests,' Kane said to Liljana. 'So who can blame her for not wanting to be your slave, too?'

As Liljana paused in stirring the stew to glare at Kane, more wounded by his cruel words than angry, Master Juwain cleared his throat and said, 'The closer we've come to Argattha, it seems, the more she has relished her freedom.'

We were, I thought, much too close to Morjin's dark city, carved out of the dark heart of the black mountain called Skartaru. Our course across the Wendrush had inevitably brought us this way. And it seemed that it had inevitably brought the knights of Morjin's Dragon Guard upon our heels.

9

As Estrella began passing out rushk cakes to everyone, Liljana called for Atara to sit down, and she began ladling the stew into wooden bowls. From out of the darkness at the edge of our encampment where our horses were hobbled, a tall woman appeared and walked straight toward us. And that, I thought, was a miracle, because a white cloth encircled her head, covering the hollows which had once held the loveliest and most sparkling pair of sapphire-blue eyes. Atara Ars Narmada, daughter of the murdered King Kiritan and Sajagax's beloved granddaughter, moved with all the prowess of the princess and the warrior-woman that she was. In consideration of our quest, she had cast off the lionskin cloak that she usually wore in favor of plain gray woolens. Gone were the golden hoops that had once encircled her lithe arms and the lapis beads bound to her long, golden hair. Few, outside of the Wendrush, would recognize her as one of the Sarni. But in her hand she gripped the great, double-curved bow of the Sarni archers, and the Sarni knew her as the great *imakla* warrior of the Manslayer Society. I knew her as a scryer who had great powers of sight, in space and time, and most of all, as the only woman I could ever love.

'Vanora, Suri and Mata,' she told me, naming three of her sisters of the Manslayers, 'will take watches tonight, so we won't have to worry about the Zayak trying to steal the horses.'

For the thousandth time that day, I looked back in the direction where our enemy gathered. As Atara knew very well, I worried about much more than this.

She sat down between Liljana and Master Juwain, and picked up a bowl of stew. Before permitting herself to taste any of it, she continued her report: 'Karimah has set patrols, so there won't be any surprises. Bajorak has, too.'

In the deepening night, the steppe's grasses swayed and glowed beneath the stars. There, crickets chirped and snakes slithered, hunting rabbits or voles or other prey. There, forty yards to our left, Bajorak and some thirty Danladi warriors sat around their fires roasting sagosk joints over long spits. And forty yards to our right, Karimah and her twelve Manslayers – women drawn from half a dozen of the Sarni tribes – prepared their own dinner. It was our greatest strategic weakness, I thought, that the Manslayers disdained camaraderie with the Danladi men. And that both contingents of our Sarni escort neither really liked nor trusted us.

'I would sleep better tonight,' Maram told her, 'if the enemy weren't so close.'

10

'Hmmph, you sleep better than any man I've ever known, enemy or no enemy,' Atara said to him. 'But fear not, we Sarni rarely fight night battles. There won't be any attack tonight.'

'Are you speaking as a Sarni warrior or a scryer?'

In answer, Atara only smiled at him, and then returned to her dinner.

'Ah, well,' Maram continued, 'I should tell you that it's not the *Zayak* who really concern me, at least not until daybreak – and *then* I shall fear their arrows, too bad. No, it's those damn Red Knights. What if they charge straight into our encampment while we're sleeping?'

'They won't do that,' Atara reassured him.

'But what if they do?'

'They won't.' Atara looked up at the bright moon. 'They fear arrows as much as you do. And there's enough light that they would still make good targets, at least at short range.'

I touched the hilt of my sword, sheathed beside me, and I said, 'We can't count on this.'

'In three days,' Atara said, 'they've kept their distance. They haven't the numbers to prevail.'

'And that is precisely the point,' I said. 'Perhaps they are waiting for reinforcements.'

'So, just so,' Kane said as he squeezed his bowl of stew between his calloused hands. 'And so, if there must be battle, we should take it to *them* before it's too late.'

For three days and nights, I thought, my friends and I had been arguing the same argument. But now the mountains were drawing nearer, and a decision must be made.

'*We* may not have the numbers to prevail, either,' Atara said. She positioned her head facing Estrella and Daj, who sat across the fire from her. 'And what of the children?'

The children, of course, were at risk no matter what course we chose: attacking our enemy would only expose them to recapture or death all the sooner. It was that way with all children everywhere, even in lands far away and still free. With Morjin in control of the Lightstone, uncontested, it would only be a matter of time before everyone on Ea was either put on crosses or enslaved.

'I can fight!' Daj suddenly announced, drawing out his small blade.

We all knew that he could. We all knew, too, that Estrella had a heart of pure fire. Her great promise, however, was not in fighting the enemy with swords but with a finer and deeper weapon. As

11

her dark, almond eyes fixed on me, I felt in her an unshakeable courage – and her unshakeable confidence in me to lead us the right way.

'We must either fight or flee,' I said. 'But if we do flee, flee *where*?'

'We could still go into the mountains,' Maram said. 'But farther south of the Kul Kavaakurk. And then we could turn north toward the Brotherhood school. We'll lose our enemy in the mountains.'

'We'll lose ourselves,' Master Juwain put in. 'Try to remember, Brother Maram, that –'

'*Sar* Maram,' Maram said, correcting him. He held up his hand to show the double-diamond ring that proclaimed him a Valari knight.

'Sar Maram, then,' Master Juwain said with a sigh. 'But try to remember that this school has remained a secret from the Lord of Lies only because our Grandmaster has permitted knowledge of it to very few. No map shows its location. I *may* be able to find it – but only from the gorge called the Kul Kavaakurk.'

For the thousandth time, I scanned the ghostly, white wall of mountains to the west of us. *Could* we find this secret school of the Great White Brotherhood? And if by some miracle we did reach this place of power deep within the maze of mountains of the lower Nagarshath, would we find the Grandmaster still alive? And more importantly, would he – or any of the Brotherhood's masters – be able to tell us in which land the Maitreya had been born? For it was said that this great Shining One might be able to wrest the Lightstone from Morjin, if not in the substance of the golden bowl, then at least in the wielding of it.

'There *must* be such a gorge,' I told Master Juwain. 'We will certainly find it, if not tomorrow, then the next day.'

'We would find it the easier,' Atara said, 'if we took Bajorak into our confidence. Surely he would know what gorges or passes give out onto the Danladi's country.'

'He might know,' Master Juwain agreed. 'But he might not know it by that name. And if we can help it, he *must* not know that name.'

He went on to say that Bajorak, under torture or the seduction of gold, might betray the name to Morjin. And *that* might key ancient knowledge of clues as to the school's whereabouts.

'If the Red Dragon discovered our greatest school so close to Argattha,' he told us, 'that would be a greater disaster than I can tell.'

The fire, burning logs of cottonwood that we had found by a stream, crackled and hissed. I stared into the writhing flames as I marvelled at the near-impossibility of this new quest. There were too many contingencies that must fall in our favor if we were to succeed. Would Estrella, I wondered, when the time came, really be able to show us the Maitreya, as had been prophesied? And if she did, was it not the slenderest of hopes that we would be able to spirit him to safety before Morjin succeeded in murdering him?

'All right,' I said, 'we cannot go south, as Maram has suggested. Our choices, then, are either to turn and attack or to lead the way into this Kul Kavaakurk and hope that we can lose our enemy before we betray the way to the school.'

Master Juwain's lips tightened in dismay because either alternative was repugnant to him.

'Or,' Maram put in, 'we could still try to outride the Red Knights. If you're concerned about me lagging and can't bear to see me make a stand against them, I could always turn off in another direction and try to meet up with you later.'

I leaned over to grasp his arm, and I said, 'No, you'd only make yourself easy prey, and I couldn't bear *that*. Whatever we do, we'll all stay together.'

'Then perhaps we should make our way to Delu and stay there until next year.'

He went on to say that his father, King Santoval Marshayk, would provide us shelter – and perhaps even a ship and crew to sail the lands of Ea in search of the Maitreya.

I stared at the sky in the west over the mountains leading to Skartaru, and in my mind's eye, I saw a great hourglass full of sparkling sands like unto stars. And with every breath that I drew and every word wasted in speculation – with every minute, hour and day that passed – the sands fell and crashed and darkened like burnt-out cinders as Morjin gained mastery of the Lightstone.

'We cannot wait until next year,' I said. 'And we are agreed that our best hope of finding the Maitreya lies in reaching the Brotherhood school.'

'In that case,' Maram said, 'our dilemma remains: do we flee or fight?'

Atara had now finished her stew, and she sat quietly between Liljana and Master Juwain as the fire's orange light danced across her blindfolded face. Sometimes, I knew, she could 'see' the grasses and grasshoppers and other features of the world about her, and other times she was truly blind. Just as sometimes she could see the future – or at least its possibilities.

'Atara,' I asked her, 'what do you think we should do?'

'Flee,' she said. 'Let's see how well these Red Knights can ride.'

She waited as my heart drummed five times, then turned toward me as she declared, 'You would rather see how well they can fight.'

I said nothing as I gripped the hilt of my sword.

'I must tell you, Val,' she said to me, 'that it is not certain that the warriors who ride with us will fight just because you ask them to.'

I pointed out across the steppe and said, 'Fifty men, Red Knights and Zayak, pursue us. And your warriors are *Man*slayers, are they not?'

'Indeed they are,' she said. Now it was her turn to grip the great unstrung bow that she had set by her side. 'And indeed they will fight – if *I* ask them. But Bajorak and *his* warriors are another matter.'

'He agreed to escort us to the mountains.'

'Yes, and so he will certainly fight if we are attacked. So far, though, we are only followed.'

'In this country,' I said, 'with this enemy, it is the same thing.'

Liljana made a show of collecting our empty bowls and serving us some succulent bearberries for dessert. During dinner she had not said very much. But now, as she often did, she cut me to the quick with only a few words: 'I think you love to hate *this* enemy too much,' she told me.

For a moment I looked down at my sword's hilt, at the diamond pommel and the smaller diamonds set into the black jade. Then I met eyes with Liljana and said, 'How should I *not* hate them? They might be the very same knights who put nails through my mother's hands and feet!'

'They might be,' she admitted. 'But would you then throw yourself upon their lances and put nails through *my* heart?'

Because I could not bear to look at Liljana just then, I returned to my vigil, staring out across the steppe at our enemy's fires. I muttered, 'How did they find us and who leads them? What do they intend?'

Kane scowled at this and spat out, 'What does Morjin *ever* intend?'

'I must know,' I said. I looked around the circle at my friends. '*We* must know, if we are to reach a decision.'

'Some things,' Master Juwain said, 'are unknowable.'

I turned to Liljana and asked, 'What of your crystal?'

'And other things,' Master Juwain continued, looking from me to Liljana, 'are better left unknown.'

Liljana reached into her tunic's inner pocket and brought out a small figurine cast into the form of a whale. It had the luster of lapis and the hint of the ocean's deep currents. Long ago, in another age, it had been forged of blue gelstei.

'Are you asking,' she said to me, 'that I should look into the minds of these Red Knights?'

Just then, out of the blackness beyond the fire, Flick appeared like a tiny, whirling array of stars. His colors of crimson, silver and blue, throwing out sparks, also pulsed in patterns that I took to be a warning. What *was* this strange being who had followed me across the length of Ea, I wondered? Was he truly a messenger of the Galadin, a little bit of starlight and angel fire? Or did he possess a will all his own, and therefore his own life and his own fate?

Master Juwain, upon glancing at Flick, turned to Liljana and commanded her, 'No, do not use your gelstei!'

Then he brought out his own gelstei: the emerald healing crystal that he had gained on our first quest. He held it up to the fire, letting the flickering light pour through its green-tinged translucency. Although it was hard to tell in the deep of night, a darkness seemed to have fallen over the crystal, as if it were steeped in shadow.

'It's too dangerous!' he said to Liljana. 'Now that the Dragon has regained the Lightstone, too damned dangerous! Especially for you.'

Maram regarded Master Juwain in shock, and so did I, for we had never heard him curse before. Liljana sat looking at her gelstei, cupped in her hands. As if she were holding a newborn, she swayed rhythmically back and forth.

'I won't believe that Morjin can use the Lightstone to taint this crystal,' she said. 'How can that which is most fair abide anything foul?'

'Surely the foulness,' I said, 'arises from Morjin himself and our weakness in resisting him. He desecrates everything he touches.'

I turned to look at the white cloth binding Atara's face. I couldn't help remembering how Morjin, with his own fingers, had torn out her eyes.

'So, every abomination, every degradation of the spirit,' Kane said, gazing at Liljana's blue stone. 'But things aren't as simple as you think, eh? Don't be so sure you understand Morjin – or the Lightstone!'

'I understand that we must fight him – and not with swords,' Liljana said.

She was a wise woman, but a willful one, too. And so she clasped her figurine between her fingers and brought it up to the side of her head.

'No,' Master Juwain called out again, 'do not!'

Once, in the depths of Argattha where the very rocks stank of rotting blood and terror, Liljana had touched minds with Morjin. And now, even as Estrella could not speak, Liljana would never smile again.

The moment that the gelstei touched her temple, she cried out in betrayal and pain. The crystal seemed to burn her like a heated iron, and she dropped it onto the grass. Her eyes rolled back into her head, showing the whites.

'Liljana!' I cried out. 'Liljana!'

It took me a moment to realize that not only I had called to her, but Maram, Master Juwain and Atara – even Daj and Kane. And then Atara sidled closer to Liljana and wrapped her arm around her back as she cradled Liljana's drooping head against her breasts. Estrella took Liljana's hand between hers and squeezed it tightly. Their little comforts must have worked a quick magic on Liljana, for soon her eyes regained their focus, and she gathered herself together and forced herself to sit up straight again. She drew in ten deeps breaths, and let each of them out, slowly. She wiped the sweat from her sodden hair. Finally she retrieved her blue gelstei. In her open hand it glinted, and she sat staring at it.

Then she cried out: 'He is there!'

'Morjin!' I called back to her. 'Damn him! Damn him!'

Daj rose up to one knee and leaned over to get a better look at Liljana's crystal. He asked, 'How, then? Where, then – *here*?'

'He is everywhere!' Liljana gasped. 'Watching, always watching.'

She closed her fist around her stone and put it back in her pocket. Atara still embraced her, and now they both swayed together back and forth, back and forth.

Although I hated the need of it, I put to Liljana the question that must be asked: 'Were you able to open the minds of the Red Knights?'

'No!' she snapped at me. And then, more gently, 'He was waiting for me, Morjin was. Waiting to open up *my* mind. To twist his soul and his sick sentiments into me. Like snakes, they are, cold, and full of venom. I . . . cannot say. You cannot know.'

I *could* know, I thought. I did know. When I closed my eyes, the bodies of my mother and grandmother, nailed to wood, writhed inside me. Only, they were not cold, but warm – always *too* warm as they cried out in their eternal anguish, burning, burning, burning . . . .

'I'm sorry,' Liljana said to Master Juwain, 'but you were right.'

Master Juwain sighed as he knotted his small, hard fingers together. 'I'm afraid it's too dangerous for any of us to use our gelstei, now.'

'And dangerous not to,' I said. 'Atara can still see, sometimes, with her gift, but without my eyes, I would be blind.'

And with that, I drew my sword from its sheath. Even in the thick of the night, the long blade gleamed faintly. The silustria from which it was wrought, like living silver, caught the stars' light and gave it back manyfold. It was harder than diamond and double-edged and sharp enough to cut steel. Alkaladur, men called it, the Sword of Sight that could cut through the soul's dark confusions to release the secret light within. The immortal Kalkin had forged it at the end of the Age of Swords, and it had once defeated Morjin. The silver gelstei was said to be one of the two noble stones; it was also said that the gold gelstei that formed the Lightstone had resonance with the silver but no power over it.

'Put it away!' Master Juwain said to me as he pushed out his palm. 'Use it in battle with the enemy, if you must, but until then, put it back in its sheath.'

I held my beautiful sword straight up, pointing toward the stars. A lovely, silver light spilled down the blade and enveloped my arm; it built around me like a luminous sea and flowed out to bathe the grasses and the cottonwood trees and the other things of the world.

'Valashu!' Master Juwain said to me.

And I said to him, 'Liljana is right: the enemy is here, and everywhere. And the battle never ends.'

I turned to look north and west, toward Skartaru where Morjin dwelled. Although I could not see the Black Mountain among the lesser white peaks leading up to it, I felt it pulling at my mind and memory, and darkening my soul. Then suddenly, my sword darkened, too. I held before me a length of gelstei no brighter than ordinary burnished steel.

'Damn him!' I whispered. 'Damn him!'

Now I pointed my sword toward Skartaru, and the blade began to glow and then flare in resonance with the faroff Lightstone – but not as brightly as it once had.

17

'He is there,' I murmured. 'There he sits on his filthy throne with the Lightstone in his filthy hand, watching and waiting.'

How could the world abide such a being as Morjin and all his deeds? How could the mountains, the wind, the stars? The same bright orbs poured down their radiance on Skartaru as they did the Wendrush and the mountains of my home. Why? And why shine at all? My eyes hurt from staring so hard as I brooded over the conundrum of a star: if it let fire consume itself, it would burn out into blackness. So it was with me. Soon enough I would be dead. A Sarni arrow would find my throat or I would freeze to death crossing the mountains. Or, more likely, one of Morjin's armies would trap me in some land near or faraway, and then I would be taken and crucified. I would descend to that dark, cold realm where I had sent so many, and that was only justice. But it seemed wrong to me, terribly and dreadfully wrong, that with my death, the bright memory of my mother, father and brothers that lived inside me would perish, too. And so those I loved most would truly die, and Morjin would have twice murdered my family and stolen them from the world.

'Valashu!' Master Juwain called to me again.

Where, I wondered, did the light of a candle's flame go when the wind blew it out? Could it be that the land of the dead was not fell but rather as cool and quiet as a long, peaceful sleep? Why should Morjin keep me in this world of iron nails, crosses and fire even one more day?

'Valashu – your sword!'

I squeezed my sword's hilt of black jade, carved with swans and set with seven diamonds. Once, I had sliced the sharp blade through Morjin's neck, but by the evil miracle of his kind, he had lived. My aim, the next time, must be true. I would plunge the star-tempered point straight through his heart. Atara had once prophesied that if I killed Morjin, I would kill myself. So, just so, as Kane would say.

'Damn him!' I whispered as I pointed my sword toward Argattha. 'Damn him! Damn him! Damn him!'

I would cut off Morjin's head and mount it on a pike for all to behold. I would hack his body into pieces and pour pitch upon them and set them on fire. I would feel the heat of the flames upon my face, burning, burning, burning . . .

'Valashu!' Master Juwain, Liljana and Atara cried out as one.

When my vision suddenly cleared, I gasped to see that my silver sword seemed to have caught fire. Blue flames clung to the silustria

18

along its whole length like a hellish garment, while longer orange and red ones twisted and leaped and blazed with a searing heat. So violent was this fire that I dropped my sword upon the ground. The grass there was too green to easily ignite, but Liljana and Daj hastened to douse it with water even so. We all watched with amazement as the flames raced up and down my sword's blade, cooled, faded and then finally died.

'Oh, my Lord!' Maram called out. 'Oh, my Lord!'

'I didn't know your sword could burn like that!' Daj said to me.

'Neither did I,' Master Juwain told me.

And neither did I. Even Kane, who had once been Kalkin, the great Elijin lord who had forged this sword with his own two hands and all the art of the angels, stared at it mysteriously. His black eyes seemed as cold as the space between the stars. He held himself utterly still.

'Like hell, that was,' he finally said. He turned to stare at me.

'Like *hate*, it was,' Master Juwain said to me. Again he pushed his palm toward my cast-down sword. 'Surely its fire came out of that which consumes you.'

Daj, who was bright beyond his years, studied my sword and asked, 'Did it? Or did it burn because Lord Morjin is gaining control of the Lightstone?'

Liljana patted his head at his perceptiveness, then looked at me as she said, 'In the end, of course, it might be the same question.'

'Whatever the answer,' Master Juwain said to me, 'it is certain that the Lord of Lies is learning the Lightstone's secrets. Your hate will not deter him. Put your sword away.'

I leaned forward to wrap my fingers around Alkaladur's hilt. The black jade was as cool as grass. But the blade's silustria still emanated a faint heat, like a paving stone after a long summer day.

'Surely this is damned,' I said as I lifted up my sword. 'As I am damned.'

Liljana slapped her hand into her palm, then shook her head violently as she waggled her finger at me. 'Don't you ever say that!'

She edged past Daj and Estrella and knelt before me, and she laid her hand on top of mine. Her voice grew soft and gentle as she told me, 'You are *not* damned! You, of all people. And you, of all people, must never think that of yourself.'

I smiled at her kindness, but she did not smile back. I let go of Alkaladur for a moment to squeeze her hand. And then I grasped yet again the sword that would carve my fate.

19

'Morjin *is* poisoning the gelstei,' I said. 'Or trying to.'

Once, I remembered, in a wood near my home, Morjin's priest named Igasho had shot at me an arrow tipped with kirax. The poison had found its way into my blood, where it would always work its dark enchantment. I wondered if this evil substance that connected me to Morjin was slowly killing me after all. As I fiercely gripped my sword, I felt the kirax burning my stomach, liver and lungs with every breath, and stabbing like red-hot needles through my eyes and brain.

'Damn him!' I said again, shaking my sword at the heavens.

In the west, clouds were moving in, blocking out the stars. Lightning rent the sky there, and thunder shook the earth. Far out on the steppe, wolves howled their strange and mournful cries. There, too, our enemy's campfires burned on and on through the night.

'And damn them, too!' I said, stabbing my sword at the Red Knights who followed us.

I watched with dread as my silver sword again burst into flame. And then something dark and dreadful as a dragon burned through my hand, arm and chest, straight into my heart.

'He is here!' I cried out as I sprang up to my feet.

'*Who* is here?' Master Juwain asked me. Now he stood up, too, and came over to me, and so did the others.

'Morjin is – he rides with the Red Knights!' I said.

'Morjin, here?' Kane shouted. His eyes flared like fire-arrows out toward the steppe. 'Impossible!'

Atara stood by my side, but well away from my burning blade. She put her hand on my shoulder to gentle me, and she said, 'Your sword shone much as it ever did when you pointed it toward Argattha, and so the Lightstone must still be there. And so, as you have said yourself, must Morjin.'

'No, he is here, a mile away across the grass!'

'Atara is right,' Master Juwain said to me. He rested his hand on my other shoulder. 'Think, Val: the Dragon would never leave the Lightstone out of his clutches, even for moment, not even to ride after you.'

'And if he *did* hunt you,' Atara added, 'he would have come out of Argattha at the head of his whole army, and not leading a couple of dozen knights.'

As lightning lit the mountains and fire sheathed my sword, my friends tried to reason with me. I could hardly listen. For I *felt* Morjn's presence too near me. The flames of his being writhed and twisted as they ever did, in shoots of madder, puce and incarnadine, and other colors that recalled his tormented soul.

'I know it is he!' I said, to Atara and my other friends.

Then Liljana moved closer and told me, 'Your gift betrays you. As mine betrayed me.'

All my life, it seemed, I had felt others' passions, hurts and joys as my own. Kane called this gift the *valarda*: two hearts beating as one and lit from within as with the fire of a star. He had also said it was impossible that Morjin should be here, in our enemy's encampment scarcely two thousand yards away. But it seemed impossible that the malice, decay and spite I felt emanating from that direction could have its source in any man except Morjin.

'Do you remember Argattha?' I said to Liljana. 'There Morjin soaked his skin with the essence of roses to cover the smell of his rotting flesh. But he could not cover the stench of his soul. I . . . smell it here.'

Liljana pointed at my sword, at the flames that still swirled up and down its length. And she said to me, 'Is that really what you smell?'

I noticed that Flick, spinning like a top in the air beyond my reach, seemed to be keeping his distance from me.

Liljana brushed past Master Juwain, and laid her hand over the steel rings that encased my chest. And she said, 'I think you hate Morjin so much that you always sense him close now. Here, in your own heart.'

I held my breath against the pain that her words caused me. My sword dipped lower, and its flames began to recede.

'There is a great danger for you here, Val,' Master Juwain said to me. 'Do you remember the prophecy?: "If a man comes forth in falseness as the Shining One concealing darkness in his heart, if he claims the Lightstone for his own, then he shall become a new Red Dragon, only mightier and more terrible."'

'But that's just it, sir!' I said to him. 'I have proved that I am not the Maitreya!'

'Yes, you have. But have you proved that you could *not* become like unto the Red Dragon?'

I watched the flames working at my sword, and I could not breathe.

'Do you not remember your dream?' Master Juwain asked me.

I slowly nodded my head. Once, in the innocence of my youth, I had vowed to bring an end to war.

'But there's no help for it!' I gasped out. 'The more I have sought

21

not to kill, the more I have killed. And the more war I have brought upon us!'

Master Juwain squeezed my shoulder, and then pointed out toward the Red Knights' campfires. And he told me, 'Killing, even at need, is an evil of itself. But killing when there may be no need is much worse. And killing as *you* feel compelled to kill, in vengeance and hate . . . that is everything you've been fighting against.'

'But there's no help for that either!' I said. I blinked my eyes against my sword's searing flames. 'Ten thousand men Morjin crucified in Galda! He is poisoning the world!'

I went on to say that Morjin would use the Lightstone to master men: their lusts, fears and dreams, even as he was trying with our gelstei. And then soon, perhaps in another year, perhaps less, all of Ea would be lost – and much more.

'You know,' I said to Master Juwain. 'You know what will happen, in the end.'

'I do not know about *ends*,' Master Juwain said. 'I only know that it is as it ever was: if you use evil to fight evil, then you will become evil.'

'Yes,' I said, gripping my sword, 'and if I do not, the whole world will fall to evil and be destroyed.'

It grew quiet in our encampment after that. The fire made little crackling sounds, and from out on the grasslands an owl hooed faintly, but none of us spoke. I stood staring at my burning sword. It was strange how the blue and red flames licked at the bright silustria but did not seem to really touch it.

Then Liljana said to me, 'Morjin has long tried to make a ghul of you. It may be that, through your sword, he could seize your will.'

'No, I won't let him,' I said. Then I smiled grimly. 'But if he does, then Kane will have to kill me – if he can.'

'Ah, Val, Val!' Maram said to me as sweat beaded on his fat cheeks. He cast his eyes upon Kane. 'Don't make jokes, not at a time like this!'

No one, I thought, not even Liljana, could read the look on Kane's face just then. He stood as still as death, gazing at my sword as his hand rested on the hilt of his own. Like coals, his black, blazing eyes seemed to burn open the night.

And then this strange man said a strange thing: 'Hate is just the left hand of love, eh? And so with evil and good. So – Val hates Morjin, even as Morjin hates him. Don't be so sure what will come of it.'

I pointed Alkaladur toward the Red Knights a mile away. I said, 'There Morjin watches us and waits. Let us end things now, if we can.'

Kane followed my gaze, and I felt his insides churning with an unusual disquiet. 'Don't be so sure he is there. The Lord of Lies has laid traps for us before, eh? Let us ride tomorrow, for the mountains, as fast as we can.'

Master Juwain nodded his head at this and said, 'Yes, surely he has conjured up confusions, somehow. Let us ride, as Kane has said.'

Maram, naturally, agreed with this course of action, and so did Liljana, Atara and even Daj. It was not Estrella's way to pit her will against mine or even to make a vote by pointing towards or away from the Red Knights. But she knew with a quiet certainty that she had a part to play in our decision. She came up close to me, heedless of my burning sword. Against the curve of the dark world, with her fine features and wisps of black hair, she seemed small and slight. She stood gazing at me, her lovely eyes looking for something bright and beautiful in my own. She was a *seard*, I remembered, gifted with finding things and the secrets inside them; a dying scryer had once promised me that she would show me the Maitreya. Since the night I had met her, it been both a grace and a torment that she had also shown me myself.

'Don't look at me like that!' I said to her. I stabbed my sword out toward the steppe. 'If Morjin *is* there, he won't expect us to attack. When we do, you and Daj will ride with Liljana and Master Juwain toward the mountains. You'll be safe there. After we've won, we'll meet up with you. And then it will all be over . . . everything. We'll regain the Lightstone, and much else besides.'

Evil, I know, speaks in the most seductive of voices. It plays to our lusts, fears, delusions and hates. There is always a part of us that wants to heed this voice. But there is always a deeper voice, too, which we might take to heart if only we would listen. As Estrella looked at me with so much trust, I heard it whispering, like the songs of the stars: that war *could* be ended; that I could grip my sword with hate's right hand; that darkness could always be defeated by shining a bright enough light.

'Estrella,' I whispered, 'Estrella.'

I would give anything, I thought, that she should grow into womanhood without the blight of murder and war.

Then she called back to me in her silent way, with a smile and a flash of her eyes. She placed one hand over my heart and the other upon my hand that held my sword. I watched as its fires dimmed and died.

'All right, we won't attack – not tonight, not like this,' I said. I slid my sword back into its sheath. 'But if Morjin *is* out there, it will come to battle, in the end.'

After that, I sat back down with my friends to finish our dessert of fresh berries. Maram brought out his brandy bottle; I heard him muttering to himself, commanding himself not to uncork it. He licked his lips as he held himself proud and straight. In the west, lightning continued to torment the sky, but the threatened storm never came. As I watched our enemy's campfires burning with a hazy orange glow, far into the night, the wolves on the dark grass about us howled to the stars.

2

The sun, at the breaking of the morning, reddened the green grasslands in the east like a great blister of flame. We rose at first light and ate a quick, cold breakfast of dried sagosk and battle biscuits. I pulled myself on top of my great, black warhorse, Altaru, as my friends did their mounts. The twelve Manslayers formed up behind us to cover our rear. Their captain was Karimah, a fat, jolly woman who was almost as quick with her knife as she was with her arrows, which she could fire with a deadly accuracy while turning in her saddle. Bajorak and his thirty warriors took their places on their lithe steppe ponies ahead of us, as a vanguard. If we were attacked from the rear, he and his men could quickly drop back to support Karimah and the Manslayers. But as he had told me the day before: 'The danger in that direction is known, and I scorn the Zayak, even more the Crucifier's knights. But who knows what lies ahead?'

As we pushed our horses to a quick trot and then a canter, I watched this young headman of the Tarun clan. Although he was not tall, as the Sarni headmen and chieftains usually are, he had an air of fierceness that might easily intimidate a larger man. His handsome face was thrice-scarred: an arrow wound and two saber cuts along his cheeks had the effect of pulling his lips into a sort of permanent scowl. Like his warriors, he wore much gold: around his thick, sunburned arms and wrists and encircling his neck. Unlike the men he led, however, the leather armor encasing his barrel chest was studded with gold instead of steel. A golden fillet, woven with bright blue lapis beads, held back his long, blond hair and shone from his forehead. His senses were as keen as a lion's, and as we pounded across the grass, he turned to regard me with his bright blue eyes. I liked his eyes: they sparkled with intelligence

25

and spirit. They seemed to say to me: 'All right, Valashu Elahad, we'll test these enemy knights – and you and yours, as well.'

For most of an hour, as the sun rose higher into a cobalt sky, we raced across the steppe. Bajorak and his warriors fanned out in a great V before us, like a flock of geese, while the Manslayers kept close behind us. Our horses' hooves – and those of our remounts and our packhorses – drummed against the green grass and the pockets of bitterbrush. Meadowlarks added their songs to the noise of the world: the chittering of grasshoppers and snorting horses and lions roaring in the deeper grass. I felt beneath me my stallion's great surging muscles and his great heart. He would run to his death, if I asked him to. Atara, to my right, easily guided her roan mare, Fire. It was one of those times when she could 'see' the hummocks and other features of the rolling ground before us. Then came Daj and Estrella, who were light burdens for their ponies. What they lacked in stamina, they made up for in determination and skill. Master Juwain and Liljana followed close behind, and Maram struggled along after them. His mounds of fat rippled and shook beneath his mail as he puffed and sweated and urged his huge gelding forward. Kane, on top of a bad-tempered mare named the Hell Witch, kept pace at the end of our short column. He seemed to be readying himself to stick the point of his sword into either Maram's or his horse's fat rump if they should lose courage and lag behind. But we all rode well and quickly – though not quite quickly enough to outdistance our enemy.

As we galloped along, I turned often to study these two dozen Red Knights, flanked by as many of the Zayak warriors. At times, a hummock blocked my line of sight, and they were lost to me, and I hoped that we might truly outride them. And then they would crest some swell of earth, and the sun would glint off their carmine-colored armor, giving the lie to my hope. They seemed always to keep about a mile's span between us; I could not tell if they held this close pursuit easily or were hard put to keep up. Fear and hate, I sensed, drove them onward. I felt Morjin's ire whipping at them, even as I imagined I heard the crack of their silver-tipped quirts bloodying their horse's sides.

'Damn him!' I whispered to myself. 'Damn him!'

After a while we slowed our pace, and so did our pursuers. Then we stopped by a winding stream to water our panting horses, and change them over with our remounts. Bajorak rode up to me, and so did Karimah and Atara. Bajorak nodded at Maram, and said, 'You *kradaks* ride well, even the fat one, I'll give you that.'

Maram's face, red and sweaty from his exertions, now flushed with pride.

Then Bajorak turned to look farther down the stream where the Red Knights had also paused to change horses. 'Well indeed, but not well enough, I think. The Crucifier's men will not break chase. Their horses are as good as yours, and they have more remounts.'

It was Bajorak's way, I thought, to speak the truth as plainly as he knew how.

'We still might outrun them,' I said.

'No, you won't. You'll only ruin your horses.'

Bajorak dismounted and came over to lay his hand on Altaru's sweating side. It amazed me that my ferocious stallion allowed him this bold touch. But then it is said that the Sarni warriors love horses more than they do women, and Altaru must have sensed this about him.

'If all you kradaks had horses like *him*,' Bajorak said, stroking Altaru, 'it might be a different matter. I've never seen his like. You still haven't told me where you found him.'

'This isn't the time for tales,' I said. I shielded my eyes from the sun's glare as I took in the red glint of our enemy's armor a mile away.

Bajorak spat on the ground and said, 'The cursed Red Knights won't move unless we do. Why, I wonder, why?'

I said nothing as I continued studying the twenty-five knights and the Zayak warriors who stood by the stream to the east of us.

'You haven't told me, either,' he went on, 'why you wish to cross our lands and what you seek in the mountains?'

At this, Kane stepped up and growled at him: 'Such knowledge would only burden you. We've paid you good gold that we might ride in silence, and that's burden enough, eh?'

Bajorak's blue eyes flashed, and so did the fillet of gold binding his hair and his heavy golden armlets. And he said, 'The gold you gave us is only a weregild to pay for my men's lives should there be battle between us and Morjin's men – or anyone else. But it is not *why* we agreed to ride with you.'

I knew this, and so did Kane. I grasped his steely arm to restrain him. And Bajorak, whose blood was up, went on to state openly what had so far remained unspoken: 'I owe a debt to the Manslayers, and debts must be repaid.'

He nodded at Karimah, and this stout, matronly woman gripped her bow as she nodded back.

27

'When Karimah came to me,' he said, looking at me, 'and asked that we should escort your company across our lands, I thought she had fallen mad. Kradaks should be killed out of hand – or at least relieved of the *burdens* of their horses, weapons and goods. Hai, but *these* kradaks were different, she said. One of them was Valashu Elahad, who had ridden with Sajagax to the great conclave in Tria and would have made alliance against the Crucifier. *The* Elahad, who had taken the Lightstone out of Argattha and whom everyone was saying might be the Maitreya.'

As he had spoken, two of his captains had come over, bearing their strung bows. One of them, Pirraj, was about Bajorak's height, but the other, whose name was Kashak, was a giant of a man and one of the largest Sarni warriors I had ever seen.

'And with the Elahad,' Bajorak went on, 'rode Atara Manslayer, Sajagax's own granddaughter, the great *imakla* warrior. She, the blind one, who has slain seventy-nine men! And so might become the only woman of her Society in living memory to gain her freedom.'

Here Bajorak's sensual lips pulled back to reveal his straight white teeth. It was a smile meant to be charming, but due to the thick scars on his cheeks, seemed more of a leer. All the women of the Manslayers, when they entered their Society, took vows to slay a hundred of their enemy before they would be free to marry. Few, of course, ever did. But those who fulfilled this terrible vow had almost free choice of husbands among the Sarni men, who would be certain to sire out of them only the strongest and fiercest of sons. As Bajorak's desire pulled at his blood, my own passion surged inside me: hot, angry, wild and pained. I glared at him as I gripped the hilt of my sword. Then it was Kane's turn to wrap his hand around my arm and restrain me.

'And so,' Bajorak said, looking at Pirraj and Kashak, 'my warriors and I agreed to Karimah's strange request. We were curious. We wanted to see if all kradaks are like *them*.'

He pointed to the Red Knights down the stream. Then his clear blue eyes cut into me, testing me.

And I said, testing him, 'Do you think we're alike? The Red Knights are our enemies, as they are yours. What is strange is that you allow them to ride freely across your lands – the Zayak, too.'

'*You* say,' he muttered. He shot me a keen, knowing look. 'I think you want us to attack them, yes?'

'I have not said that, have I?'

'You say it with your eyes,' he told me.

28

I continued scanning the glints of red armor along the river, looking for a standard that might prove the presence of Morjin.

'If *we* attacked them,' I asked Bajorak, 'would you join us?'

'Nothing would please me more,' he said, causing my hope to rise. And then my sudden elation plummeted like a bird shot with an arrow as he continued, 'But we may *not* attack them.'

'*May* not? They are crucifiers! They are Zayak, from across Jade River!'

'They are,' he said, turning to spit in their direction, 'and Morjin has paid for their safe passage of our lands.'

This was news to us. We crowded closer to hear what Bajorak might say.

'In the darkness of the last moon,' he told us, 'the Red Knights came to Garthax with gold. He is greedy, our new chieftain is. Greedy and afraid of Morjin. And so Garthax allowed the Crucifier's knights to range freely across our country, from the Jade River to the Oro, from the Astu to the mountains in the west. *They* are not to be attacked, curse them! And curse Morjin for defiling the Danladi's country!'

His warriors, savage-seeming men, with faces painted blue, braided blond hair and moustaches hanging down beneath their chins, nodded their heads in agreement with Bajorak's sentiments.

'Was it Morjin, himself, then,' I asked Bajorak, 'who paid this gold to Garthax? Does he lead the Red Knights?'

'I have not heard that,' he told me. 'Were it so, we would attack them no matter if Morjin had paid Garthax a mountain of gold.'

'It will come to that, in the end!' Kashak barked out. Blue crosses gleamed on his sunburned cheeks to match the smoldering hue of his eyes. 'Let us ride against them now, with these kradaks!'

'And break our chieftain's covenant?'

'A chieftain who makes covenant with the Crucifier is no chieftain! Let us do as we please.'

Bajorak, too, shared Kashak's zeal for battle. But he had a cool head as well as a fiery heart, and so to Kashak and his other men he called out: 'Would you commit the Tarun clan to going against our chieftain? If we break the covenant, it will mean war with Garthax.'

'War, yes, with *him*,' Pirrax said, shaking his bow. 'We're warriors, aren't we?'

Now Atara stepped forward, and her white blindfold gleamed in the strong sunlight. Her face was cold and stern as she addressed these fierce men of the Tarun clan: 'It's wrong for warriors to make

29

war against their chieftain. Can not Garthax be persuaded to return this gold?'

Bajorak shook his head. 'You do not know him.'

'I know what my grandfather, Sajagax, said of Garthax's father: that Artukan was a great chieftain who would never scrape before Morjin. Does a lion sire a snake?'

'Garthax,' Bajorak said, 'is not his father's son.'

'Have you tried helping him to be?'

It was one of Atara's graces, I thought, that she tried ever to remake men's natures for the good.

'Help *him*?' Bajorak said. 'You do not understand. Garthax quarreled with Artukan over the question of whether we should treat with Morjin. And two days later Artukan died while drinking his beer . . . of poison!'

'*Poison*!' Atara cried out. 'That cannot be!'

'No, no one wanted to believe it – certainly not I,' Bajorak told her. 'But it is said that upon taking the first sip of his beer, Artukan cried out that his throat was on fire. One of his wives offered him water, but Artukan said that this burned his lips. Everything . . . burned him. No one could touch him. It is said that he put out his own eyes so that he would not have to bear the torment of light. His skin turned blue and then black, like dried meat. He screamed, like a kradak burnt at the stake. It took him a whole day to die.'

Master Juwain's faced paled, and then he said to Bajorak, 'If what you tell is true, then surely the poison was kirax.'

Surely it was, I thought as my heart pushed my flaming blood through my veins. And surely thus I would have died, too, if only the assassin sent by Morjin had managed to bury his arrow even a tenth of an inch into my flesh.

'I do not know this poison, kirax,' Bajorak said to Master Juwain.

And Master Juwain told him, 'It is used only by the Red Priests of the Kallimun. And by Morjin.'

Bajorak's gaze flashed from Master Juwain to Kashak and Pirraj, and he made a warding sign with his finger as he cried out, 'Treachery! Abomination! If Garthax really was in league with the Red Priests, if he *is*, then . . . '

'Then his eyelids should be cut off, and he should be staked out in the sun for the ants and the yellowjackets to eat!'

These terrible words came from Atara, and I felt my heart nearly break against my chest bones to hear her pronounce the age-old punishment that the Sarni meted out to poisoners.

'He should be unmanned,' she added, 'and his parts given to the vultures!'

It was one of Atara's griefs, I knew, that when her hopes for men failed, she could fall icy cold and full of judgment, like a killer angel.

'If true,' Bajorak said, nodding his head, 'what you say should be done. But we know not that it *is* true. Only that, from what we've learned of Garthax, it *could* be.'

'Then until it is proved,' Atara said, 'he is still your chieftain. And so you must persuade him with words to break this covenant with Morjin, rather than with arrows and flaying knives.'

'*Words*,' Bajorak spat out. He looked from Atara to Kane and then at me. 'Valashu Elahad, all of you, rode with Sajagax to Tria to unite the free peoples against Morjin, with words. And what befell? Alonia is in flames, and in the Morning Mountains, the Elahad's own Valari make war with each other. And on the Wendrush! The Zayak ride openly into our country! It is said that the Marituk have allied with the Dragon, the Janjii, too! And so the Tukulak and the Usark, and other tribes, soon will. They think to choose the winning side before it is too late. They have no sense of themselves! Whatever side the Sarni choose will be victorious. And that is why we Tarun, and the other Danladi clans, must choose another chieftain, before it is too late. And we shall make our votes with *these*!'

So saying, he reached into his quiver and drew out a long, feathered shaft. With one smooth, quick motion, he nocked it to his bowstring, drew it back to his ear and loosed it toward the Red Knights and the Zayak warriors. His great horn bow unbent with a crack like thunder. The arrow whined through the air and buried itself in the grass a few hundred yards away. Not even Sajagax, I thought, could shoot an arrow a mile.

Bajorak's eyes gleamed, but he sighed. 'Atara Manslayer is right,' he said. 'Until Garthax's treachery is proven, he is still our chieftain. And so his cursed covenant will be honored.'

Much of what he had told me we had learned while in winter camp with Karimah and the Manslayers, for the Wendrush is Ea's crossroads, and news flows as freely as the great sagosk herds over its windswept plains. I had not, however, known about the Marituk's alliance with Morjin. They were a great tribe, and so this was evil tidings – but no surprise. In Tria, I had nearly claimed the Lightstone for myself; I had spoken a lie and slain a man, and as with a stone cast into a black water, these evil deeds had rippled outward to touch many peoples and many lands.

'And so,' Bajorak continued, looking from the Red Knights back at me, 'we shall not attack our enemy. They know this. It is why they ride so impudently.'

'But what if they attack *us*?' Maram wanted to know. It was a question that he could not stop asking Bajorak – and himself.

'They won't,' Bajorak told him. 'They haven't the numbers . . . yet.'

'*Yet*?' Maram called out. 'Ah, I don't like the sound of that, not at all. What do you mean, *yet*?'

'I believe,' Bajorak said, 'that these are not the only companies of Red Knights or Zayak that Garthax has allowed into our country.'

At this Maram craned his neck about, scanning the horizon. And all the while he muttered, 'Oh, too bad, too bad!'

Bajorak ignored him and looked straight at me. He said, 'Until Karimah came to me asking us to escort you, I could not imagine what these companies were seeking in our lands.'

I said nothing as I watched the Red Knights, who seemed to be waiting for us to remount so that they might renew the chase.

'But I do not understand,' he went on, '*why* they are seeking you.'

'Surely that is simple,' I told him. 'We are Morjin's enemies. Surely he would pay much gold to anyone who brings him our heads.'

I rested my hand on the hilt of my sword; I looked into Bajorak's eyes to see if he desired this gold badly enough to betray us. But I saw there only a blazing hatred of Morjin and a fierce pride.

Then Bajorak looked away from me toward our enemy. 'Perhaps they *do* want to kill you. But perhaps they are seeking the same thing as you.'

His perceptiveness vexed me, and I told him, 'We have not said that we are seeking anything.'

He smiled as best he could and said, 'No, you say little, with your lips, Valashu Elahad. But your eyes sing like the minstrels. I have never seen a man who *desires* as you do.'

'Perhaps,' I told him, 'we desire nothing more than to cross your lands.'

He pointed at the snowy peaks in the west. 'To go into the wild mountains where no one dwells?'

'Perhaps we wish to dwell there.'

He held out his hand toward Estrella and Daj. 'It is strange that you take children with you on such a journey.'

'Is it strange to want to find a place where they might come of age in peace?'

Bajorak's face softened as he said, 'No, that is not strange – if any such place exists. But if it *did* exist, surely you would not seek it in the Sarni's lands so close to Sakai.'

'We go where we must,' I told him. 'Will you help us?'

'We would help you better if you helped us.'

'We ride together,' I said. 'If our enemy attacks *you*, we will fight *them*.'

'That is good. But it would be even better if you trusted us.'

'We've trusted you with our lives.'

'Yes, but not with that which impels you to risk your lives.'

'As Kane has told you, that would be an unnecessary burden.'

'*You* say. But the greater burden is not knowing where we are going or why. It puts my men at risk. And I do not spend *their* lives as readily as I do gold.'

As the sun's light broke upon the fillet binding his forehead, I pressed my finger hard into the little zags of the scar that cut mine like a lightning bolt. And I said, 'You have pledged to ride with us, even so. Will you keep your pledge?'

Bajorak looked back and forth between Pirraj and Kashak as anger clouded his eyes. He shook his bow at me and snapped out: 'We Tarun are no pledge-breakers! Hai, but you are a hard man, Valashu Elahad. And a willful one! Let us ride then, if that is your wish!'

And with that, he jumped back on his horse, and with Pirraj and Kashak, galloped back to the bend in the river where most of his warriors were gathered.

Liljana stood with her arms thrown protectively around Daj and Estrella. And she scolded me: 'You were barely cordial to him. I've never seen you be so hard.'

I watched as Karimah returned to the Manslayers, who were getting ready to ride again. And I said, 'We know little of this Bajorak and his true intentions. And you've been able to tell me little.'

She clapped her hand to her pocket where she had secreted her blue gelstei. 'Would you have me *try* to tell you?'

'As you tried with the Red Knights?'

Liljana's heavy eyebrows pulled into a frown. 'You're hard with me, too – cruel hard. What have I done to make you so?'

The hurt in her eyes stabbed straight into me. I took her hand in mine and said, 'My apologies, Liljana. You've done nothing. Now why don't we see if we can lose these damn knights before the sun reaches noon?'

After that we set out as before and continued our race across the Wendrush. We drove our remounts too hard; I felt fire in the lungs of these great beasts and spreading out along their blood to torment their bunching muscles and straining joints. It grew hot, not quite so sweltering as in Marud or Soal, but too hot for early Ashte. The sun rose higher and shot its golden flames at us. I sweated beneath layers of wool, mail and leather underpadding. The wind in my face carried some of this moisture away, but did little to cool my sodden body. I turned to see the others working hard as well. Maram, on top of his bounding brown gelding, puffed and grunted and sweated like a pig. Kane sweated, too, for he was attired no differently. As always, though, he made no complaint. His black eyes seemed to say to me that the Red Knights following us in their thicker armor suffered even worse than we.

The riding quickly became a misery. Biting black flies buzzed around our eyes and ears. I watched Bajorak leading his more lightly-clad warriors ahead of us. Would he honor his word, I wondered? Or did he hope to use us as bait, inviting an attack by other companies of Red Knights and Zayak who would join our pursuers? Perhaps, I thought, Bajorak would then call down a host of Tarun warriors that he might have secreted somewhere among the steppe's long grasses. He would annihilate his enemy and use this incident as a reason to mount a rebellion against Garthax. And he would not care if my friends and I – kradaks, all, except for Atara – happened to be annihilated, too.

My father had once told me that a king should strive to dwell inside others' skins and perceive the world as they did. It should have been easy for me to know the truth about Bajorak, easier than it was for Liljana. But it was harder. In the shallows of the Great Northern Ocean, I had once seen an oyster which closed itself inside its shell when disturbed. So it was with me and my gift. All my life I had avoided the harsh touch of others' passions. And why? Because, like grit in the eyes, it hurt. And even more, because I was afraid. Bajorak had said that Garthax was not his father's equal. Neither, I thought, was I mine.

And so I rode on and on, watching the glints of gold about Bajorak ahead of me and turning to gaze at the red smear of Morjin's knights and the Zayak warriors on their ponies pounding

34

after us across the sunlit plain. We did not escape them all that long day. We were only three miles from the mountains when at last we stopped to make camp by a stream that flowed down from these heights. And, as with the night before, our enemy set up their tents only a mile away.

We were all tired and sore from the cruel day's work, and so none of us had much enthusiasm for tending the horses, gathering wood and water, making the fire, and other such things. As usual when the sun went down, Liljana took charge. She insisted on preparing us a hot meal, and it was good to sit down with our bowls of bloody sagosk meat, whose juices we mopped up with fresh rushk cakes. These Liljana made herself, for she had excused both Daj and Estrella from their chores. The children were so weary and worn that they could hardly hold their bowls to eat their dinners. The sun had burnt their faces, and dust dirtied their hair. Although Daj would not allow himself to whine as other children did, much less to weep, I knew that the hard riding had chafed him, nearly flaying the flesh from his legs. Estrella was in even worse condition. She sat very still, fighting to keep her eyes open. Even the slightest motion caused her to wince in pain.

'Ah, that was a day!' Maram sighed out as he worked at a piece of hastily roasted meat. 'The hardest ride we've had since Count Ulanu chased us to Khaisham.'

I remembered that day too well. It had ended with an arrow shot through Atara's lung and the death of our friend, Alphanderry. I suddenly could not bear the iron tang of my meat, and I put down my knife and bowl.

'Ah, oh – oh, my poor, poor aching body!' Maram groaned. He moved stiffly to bring out his brandy bottle, and he caught Master Juwain's eye. 'Surely, sir, this is a night for prescribing a little restorative drink?'

'Surely it is not,' Master Juwain told him, taking the bottle and putting it away. 'At least, not *that* kind of drink. I shall make us all a tea that will soothe rather than numb us.'

So saying, he found some herbs in his medicine chest and brewed up a pot of tea. The hot drink, sweetened with honey, stole some of the hurt from our limbs. Upon sipping it, Daj and Estrella almost immediately lay down upon their furs. Liljana sat between them, stroking their hair and singing them to sleep. After a while her dulcet voice murmured out above the crackle of the fire as she said to me: 'We cannot travel tomorrow as we did today. They're *children*, Val.'

35

Because her words disturbed me, I stood up to walk by the stream. I paused beneath a huge old cottonwood tree as I looked out at our enemy's campfires. Across the stream Karimah had posted sentinels who would sit on their horses all night guarding us from attack. Kane found me there, staring at their dark, ghostly forms as I listened to the water gurgling over rounded rocks.

'You shouldn't be alone here,' he told me as he stood with his hand on the hilt of his sword. His eyes searched the grass for stalking lions, no less Zayak warriors.

'I shouldn't have brought Daj and Estrella with us,' I told him. 'All on such a narrow chance.'

'You know the need,' he growled out. 'You did the right thing.'

'Did I? Or have I only stolen from them the few days of peace they might have had before . . . before there *is* no peace, for anyone?'

'You take too much upon yourself.'

'No, too little,' I said. 'Daj is as tough as a diamond, but Estrella suffers. Inside, even more than out. I . . . cannot tell you. She *sees* too deeply inside of things. There are places she's terrified to go. And it's as if *I* am taking her into the worst of these places, back into a black tunnel that has no end.'

'Is it her suffering that grieves you or your own?'

'But there is no difference!' I said. 'Especially with her, it is one.'

'She is a radiant child,' he told me. 'I have seen many moments when her joy, too, became your own.'

'Even then,' I said, listening to the stream, 'it is like drinking too much wine too quickly.'

Kane stared up at the stars, and his voice grew strange and deep as he told me, 'The *valarda* is the gift of the One. You have yet to learn how to use it.'

'It is a curse!' I said, shaking my head. 'It is an affliction, like a pox upon the skin, like a rupture of the heart.'

At this, he grabbed my arm and shook me as a lion might a lamb. And he growled out, 'You might as well complain that life is a curse. And that light is an affliction because it carries into your eyes all the ugliness and evil of the world!'

'Yes,' I said, feeling the fire inside me. 'It must have been like that for Artukan when the kirax made him gouge out his own eyes.'

Now Kane squeezed my arm so hard I thought my bones might break. 'Tell *that* to Atara, why don't you? Let her hear you damn your eyes, and hers, and see what she will say!'

I pulled away from him, and looked past the cottonwood's dark, fluttering leaves at the sky. I found the Seven Sisters and the Dragon and other twinkling constellations. The stars there were so bright, so beautiful. Which ones, I wondered, burned with the light of my father and my mother and all the rest of my slaughtered family?

'You *saw*!' I said to Kane. 'In Tria, you stood and saw with your own eyes as I struck down Ravik with my "gift"!'

'So – so I did. The *valarda* is a double-edged sword, eh?'

It was bad enough that others' dreads and exaltations should flood into me. But why, I wondered, should my passions strike into them when I lost my head – especially my killing passions?

'I *murdered* a man!' I shouted at him.

'No, you killed a Kallimun priest who would have killed Atara.'

'You don't understand!'

'Don't I? So, I've seen you kill rabbits and rock goats for food, and how many of our enemy have you sent on with that sword you wear? Killing is only killing, eh? It doesn't matter *how* we kill, only *who*.'

The stream purled in darkness, and the wind rustled the steppe's grasses, and the whispering inside me told me that Kane was wrong.

'It *must* matter,' I said. 'Just as everything we do matters.'

'These are hard times, Val. So, we must do hard things.'

'*Hard* things, yes.'

'Would it be so hard for you to tell Bajorak that we seek a great treasure in the mountains beyond the Oro River? And that in finding it, we would fight Morjin's gold with our own? Is that not close to the truth?'

I smiled at this as I listened to my heart drumming inside me. I said, 'I have learned . . . that the smallest of lies can grow, like a rat's bite beginning a plague of death.'

'We need Bajorak on our side, you know.'

'I will not lie to him.'

'But you cannot tell him the truth about our purpose! What if he is captured, eh? What if he sells our secrets for gold?'

'I trust him no more than you do.'

'Do you trust him to fight, if it comes to that? So, it would not take much, at need, for you to push him into battle.'

I ground my teeth at the fury I felt for Morjin seething inside me. How hard would it be to touch Bajorak – or anyone – with a little of this flame?

'No, I will *not*,' I said to Kane.

'No? No matter what befalls? No matter which of your friends is threatened? What else *won't* you do, then?'

I drew in a deep breath and held it until my lungs burned. And then I said, 'I will not torture. I will not sacrifice innocents, not to save you or me, or even the children. I will not use the valarda . . . as I would my sword, to strike terror or maim. And never again to kill.'

As Kane glared at me through the near-darkness, I drew Alkaladur and watched the play of starlight along its length.

'So,' he said, gazing at it, 'in such goodness, in such purity of truth, you think to fight Morjin and all his evil deeds?'

I smiled sadly as I shook my head. 'I am neither good, nor pure, nor am I renowned as an exemplar of the truth. Who, then, am I to fight evil?'

'Ha – is that not itself an evil question?'

I said to him, 'I don't understand you! Once, on top of a mountain, you told me that I could not fight Morjin your way without losing my soul!'

'So – perhaps I lied.'

'No, you did not!'

His voice softened then as he told me, 'Listen to me, my young friend: we do what we *have* to do, eh? Just don't be so sure it's always easy to know what is evil and what is not.'

And with that, he stalked off back toward our encampment.

I waited with my drawn sword, watching the world turn into darkness.

I breathed in the smells of grass and woodfire and the fresh blood of a lion's kill wafting on the wind. I sensed many things. The horses standing in their small herd nearby were all exhausted and would have a hard time when morning came. I quivered with the fear of the field mice as they looked for the owls who hunted them, and my heart leaped with the gladness of the wolves as they followed the scent of their prey. And in all this immense anguish and zest, I thought, in all this incessant struggle and striving there was no evil but only the terrible beauty of life. It was too much for me to take in, too much for any man. And yet I must, for the stars, too, had a kind of life: deeper and wilder and infinite in duration. How, I wondered, would I ever feel my mother's breath upon my face or hear Asaru laughing again if I could not open myself to this eternal flame?

Just then Atara appeared out of the glare of our campfire and walked closer to me. Then she called out: 'Val, your face – your sword!'

To be open to love, I knew, is to be vulnerable to hate.

'Morjin is out there,' I said to her. My sword glowed red like an ember as I pointed it toward our enemy. 'Can you "see" him?'

Atara drew out her scryer's crystal and stood rolling it between her hands. She said, 'Everywhere I look now, Morjin is there. It is why I am loath to look.'

'Your gift,' I told her, 'is a curse. As is mine.'

I went on to relate my conversation with Kane. She came up close to me and grasped my hand. 'No, it is just the opposite. Kane was right: you have yet to learn how to use the valarda.'

I wrenched free my hand and said, 'If I could, I would cut it out of me, the way I've cut off others' hands and carved out their hearts.'

'No – please don't say that!'

'Such terrible things I have done! And what is yet to come?'

I stared at the Red Knights' campfires, then Atara touched my cheek to turn my face toward her. And she said to me, 'I don't know what is to come, strange though you might think it. But I know what has been. And I know *where* I have been, with my gift.'

She held up her gelstei: a little white sphere gleaming beneath the white circle of the moon. 'I've tried to tell you what it is like to see as I have seen. To live. Such glory! So much light! Truly, there are infinite possibilities, the dreams of the stars waiting to be made real. I've seen them all, inside this crystal. And here, for too long, I have dwelled. It is splendid, beyond the beating of a butterfly's wings or the sun rising over the sea. But it is cold. It is like being frozen in ice at the top of a mountain as high as the stars. And all the time, I am so utterly, utterly alone.'

'A curse,' I said softly as I covered her crystal with my hand.

'No! You don't *see*! The price of such beauty has been such terrible isolation – almost too terrible to bear. But I *have* borne it, even gloried in it, because of you. Your gift. *You* are such a gift, Valashu. You have a heart of fire, and it is so brilliantly, brilliantly beautiful! Is there any ice it could not melt? No, I know – only you. You bring me back into the world, where everything is warm and sweet. I don't want to know what it would be like to live without you. You are the one being with whom I do not feel alone.'

Her hand was warm against mine. Because she had no eyes, she could not weep. And so I wept for her instead.

'Kane has suggested,' I finally told her, 'that I should use the valarda to manipulate Bajorak. Like a puppeteer pulling on strings.'

She smiled sadly and shook her head. 'Kane is so *knowing*. But sometimes, so willfully blind.'

'How *should* I use the valarda, then?'

'*You* know,' she said to me. Her voice was as cool and gentle as the wind. 'You've always known, and you always *will* know, when the time comes.'

I looked out at the millions of stars shimmering through the night. The black sky could hold their splendor, but how could any man?

'And now,' she said to me, 'you should get some rest. Tomorrow will be a long day, and a bad one, I think. Come to bed, Val.'

She pulled at my hand to lead me back to our camp. But I let go of her to grip my sword, and I told her, 'In a moment.'

I watched her walk back to the fire as she had come, and I marvelled yet again that she could find her way without the use of her eyes. I wondered then how I would ever find my own way to whatever end awaited me. I gazed at Alkaladur, whose silustria glistered with dark reds and violets. The Sword of Fate, men called it. How should I point it, I wondered, toward all that was good, beautiful and true? I wondered, too, if I would ever be free of the valarda. I had spoken of using my sword to make a brutal surgery upon myself, but I might as well try to cut away my face, my limbs and all my flesh – no less my memories and dreams – and hope to remain Valashu Elahad.

'So, just so,' I whispered.

And with this sudden affirmation, my heart opened, and my sword filled with the light of the stars. Then, to my astonishment, its substance began radiating a pure and deep glorre. This was the secret color inside all others, the true color that was their source. It flared with all the fire of red and shone as numinously as midnight blue, and yet these essences – and those of the other colors it contained – were not just multiple and distinct but somehow one. Kane called it the color of the angels, and said that it belonged far away across the heavens, in the splendor of the constellations near the Golden Band, but not yet here on earth. For most men had neither the eyes nor the heart to behold it.

'So bright,' I whispered. 'Too bright.'

I, too, could not bear the beauty of this color for very long. And so as the world continued its journey into night and carried the brilliant stars into the west, I watched as the glorre bled away, and the radiance of my sword dimmed and died.

I returned to the fire after that and lay down on my furs to sleep. But I could not. As my sword remained within its sheath, waiting to be drawn, I knew that the glorre abided somewhere inside me. But would I ever find the grace to call upon it?

3

The next day's dawn came upon the world with a red, unwelcome glare. We ate a hasty breakfast of rushk cakes smeared in jelly and some goose eggs that Liljana had reserved for especially difficult work. And our riding that morning, while not nearly so fast or jolting as that of the previous day, was difficult enough. We set out parallel to the mountains, and our course here took us southeast over ground humped with many hummocks and rocky crests. We crossed streams all icy cold and swollen into raging brown torrents that ran down from the great peaks above us. All of us, I thought, rode stiffly. We struggled to keep our tired horses moving at a good pace. Often I wondered at the need, for no matter how quickly or slowly we progressed, our enemy in their carmine-colored armor kept always a mile's distance behind us.

'Surely they don't intend to attack us,' Maram puffed out as he nudged his horse up beside me. 'Unless Bajorak is right and they are only waiting for reinforcements.'

Toward this contingency, Bajorak had sent forth outriders to search the grassy swells and sweeps of the Wendrush.

'Of course,' Maram added, 'it seems most likely that they only intend to follow us into the mountains.'

'We cannot *go* into the mountains,' I told him, 'so long as they *do* follow us.'

'Ah, it seems we cannot go at all unless we find this Kul Kavaakurk. Where is this gorge, then? How do we know it really exists?'

Maram kept on complaining at the uncertainties of our new quest as his eyes searched the folds and fissures of the rocky earth to our right. His voice boomed out into the morning, and Master

Juwain caught wind of our conversation. He rode up to us and told Maram, 'It surely does exist.'

'Ah, sir, but you are a man of faith.'

'I have faith in our Brotherhood's lore.'

'But, sir,' Maram reminded him, 'it is *our* Brotherhood no longer.'

'And that is precisely why you are ignorant of this lore.'

'Lore or fables?'

'The Way Rhymes are certainly no fables,' Master Juwain said. 'They are as true as the stories in the Great Book of the Ages. But they are not for the common man.'

He went on to speak of that body of esoteric knowledge entrusted only to the masters of the Brotherhood. As he often did when riding – or sitting, standing or even sleeping – he clutched in his hand his travelling volume of the *Saganom Elu*.

'Ah, well,' Maram said to him, 'one of the things that I could never abide about the Brotherhood was this madness for books.'

'A *love* for books, you mean.'

'No, it is more of a bibliolatry.'

'But the Way Rhymes are recorded in no book!'

'And *that* is precisely the point,' Maram said, needling him. 'The Brotherhood makes an idol of the very *idea* of a book.'

Master Juwain's homely face screwed up in distress. 'It is one of the noblest ideas of man!'

'So noble that you withhold this lore from men? Should not all that is best and most true be recorded in the *Saganom Elu*?'

Now Master Juwain's lips tightened with real pain. And he held up his worn book as he tried to explain to Maram: 'But all *is* recorded there! You must understand, however, that *this* rendering of the *Saganom Elu* is only for men. It is said that the Elijin have a truer telling of things, recorded on tablets of gold. And the Galadin as well have theirs, deeper and truer still, perhaps etched in diamond or read in starfire, for they are deathless and cannot be harmed, and so it must be with their writings. And the Ieldra! What can any man say of those whose being is pure light? Only this: that *their* knowledge must be the brightest reflection of the one and true *Saganom Elu*, the word of the One which existed before even the stars – and which was never created and therefore cannot be destroyed.'

For a while, as our horses made their way over the uneven ground at a bone-bruising trot, Master Juwain continued to wax eloquent as his ideals soared. And then Maram rudely brought him back to earth.

'What I always detested about the Brotherhood,' Maram said, 'was that you always kept secrets from lesser men – even from aspirants such as I when I, ah, still *aspired* to be other than I am.'

'But we've had to protect our secrets!' Master Juwain told him. 'And so protect those who are not ready for them. Is a child given fire to play with? What would most men do if given the power of the Red Dragon?'

I turned in my saddle to look at the Red Knights trailing us as if bound to our horses with chains. I wondered yet again if Morjin rode with them; I wondered what he would do with the unfathomable power of the Lightstone.

Maram must have sensed the trajectory of my concerns, for he said to Master Juwain: 'And so like precious gems, like gelstei hidden in lost castles, you encode these precious secrets in your rhymes?'

'Even as we encode the way to our greatest school.'

Maram sighed at this, and he sucked at his lip as if wishing for a drink of brandy. 'Tell me again the verses that tell of this school.'

Now it was Master Juwain's turn to sigh as he said, 'You've an excellent ear for verse when you put yourself to it.'

'Ah, well, I suppose I *should* put myself since you have honored me with this precious lore that you say is no fable.'

'It is not a question of honor,' Master Juwain told him. 'If I fall before we reach the school, at least one of us must know the verse. Now listen well and try to remember this:

> Between the Oro and the Jade
> Where sun at edge of grass is laid,
> Between the rocks like ass's ears
> The Kul Kavaakurk gorge appears.

Maram nodded his head as his fat lips moved silently. Then he looked at Master Juwain and said, 'Well, the first two lines are clear enough, but what about the third? What about these "ass's" ears?'

'Why, that is certainly clear as well, isn't it? Somewhere, at the edge of the steppe, we will find two rocks shaped like an ass's ears framing the way toward the Kul Kavaakurk.'

'Why *two* rocks, then?'

Master Juwain cast Maram a strained look as if he were being as dull and difficult as an ass. He said, 'How many ears does an ass have?'

44

'No more than two, I hope, or I would not want to see such a beast. But what if the line you told me was instead:

Between the rocks like asses' ears

That could mean two asses or three, and so there could be four rocks or six – or even more.'

As Master Juwain pulled at his ruined ear, the one into which Morjin's priest had stuck a red-hot iron, he gazed at the mountains to the west. And he said, 'I'm afraid I hadn't thought of that.'

'And *that* is the problem with these Way Rhymes of yours. Since none of them are written down, how are we to make such distinctions?'

Master Juwain fell quiet as we trotted along. Then he thumped his book yet again and said to Maram, 'The words in here are meant to be clear for any man to read. But the words in the Way Rhymes are only for the masters of the Brotherhood. And any master would know, as *you* should know, to apply Jaskar the Wise's Scales to any conundrum.'

'Scales?' Maram said. 'Are we now speaking of fish?'

'Now you *are* being an ass!' Master Juwain snapped out.

'Ah, well, I must confess,' Maram said, 'that I do not remember anything about this Jaskar the Wise or his scales.'

'Jaskar the Wise,' Master Juwain reminded him, 'was the Master Diviner and then Grandmaster of the Blue Brotherhood in the Age of Law. But never mind for right now *who* he was. We are concerned with the principle that he elucidated: that when faced with two or more equally logical alternatives, the simplest should be given the greatest weight.'

'And so we are to look for an *ass's* ears, and so two rocks and not four, is that right?'

'I believe that is right.'

Maram covered his heavy brows with his hand as he scanned the great wall of the Nagarshath along our way. And he said, 'I haven't seen anything that looks like ears, those of an ass or any other beast, and we've come at least a hundred and forty miles from the Jade.'

'And we've still another forty until we reach the Oro. And so we can deduce that we'll come across this landmark between here and there.'

Maram looked behind at our pursuers and said, 'Closer to *here* would be better than closer to *there*. I'm getting a bad feeling about all this. I hope we find these damn donkey's ears, and soon.'

After that we rode even faster through the swishing grasses along the mountains, and so did the men who followed us. I, too, had a bad feeling about them, and it grew only hotter and more galling as the sun rose higher above us. I turned often to make sure that Karimah and her Manslayers covered our rear, just as I watched Bajorak and his Danladi warriors fanned out ahead of us. After brooding upon Master Juwain's and Maram's little argument and all that my friends had said to me the night before, I finally pushed Altaru forward at a gallop so that I might hold counsel with this strong-willed headman of the Tarun clan.

After pounding across the stone-strewn turf and accidentally trampling the nest of a meadowlark, I came up to Bajorak. He held up his hand and called for a halt then. When he saw the look in my eyes, he led me away from Pirraj and the huge Kashak and his other warriors. He reined in his horse near a large boulder about fifty yards from his men. And he said to me, 'What is it, Valashu Elahad?'

For a moment I studied this great Sarni warrior, with his limbs, neck and head encircled in gold and his face painted with blue stripes like some sort of strange tiger. Most of all I looked deeply into his dazzling blue eyes. And then I asked him: 'Do you know of two rocks, along the mountains, shaped like an ass's ears? There would be a span between them – and possibly a stream or a river.'

His eyes grew brighter and even harder, like blue diamonds, as he stared at me. And he answered my question with a question: 'Is that where we are to escort you then?'

'Perhaps,' I told him.

His fine face pulled into a scowl, and he snapped his braided, black quirt against his hand. 'I know not of any *ass's* ears, and I care not.'

I couldn't keep down my disappointment, and he must have felt this for his eyes softened as he said, 'But there are two great rocks like unto those you describe, about ten miles south of here. We call them the Red Shields. If that is your destination, however, you would have had a hard time finding it.'

'Why so?'

'Because the Shields face east, and we approach them from the northwest. From our vantage, we will see only their edges – and the rocks and trees on the slopes behind them.'

I continued gazing at him, and I finally asked, 'Do these shields, then, guard a gorge cutting through the mountains?'

He shrugged his shoulders. 'I know not. No Sarni would ever journey into the mountains to find out.'

He turned to snap his quirt toward the mountains, and asked me, 'What is the name of this gorge?'

Our eyes locked together, and something inside him seemed to push at me, as I pushed at him. I said, 'If you've no care for gorges, you would have even less for its name.'

Now he whipped the quirt against his hand so hard that it instantly raised up a red welt – but no redder and hotter than his anger at me. He seemed to bite back words that he might regret speaking. He turned away from my gaze to look at the mountains and then behind us at the Red Knights, who had also paused to take a rest. Then his eyes moved toward my friends, grouped together in front of the Manslayers; I knew with a painful leap of my blood that he was watching Atara.

'What have I done,' he asked, 'to make you scorn me so?'

And I blurted out: 'I do not scorn you, only the way that you look at one . . . whom you should not look at at all.'

Astonishment poured out of him like the sweat that shone from his brow and beaded up on his golden fillet. And he said to me, 'Atara is a great warrior, and more, imakla! And even more, a beautiful woman. How should a man look at such a woman, then?'

Not in lust, I thought, fighting at the knot of pain rising up in my throat. *Not in such terrible desire.*

He turned back to me, and his astonishment only deepened. And he half-shouted, 'You are Valari, and she is Sarni – half-Sarni! And she is your companion in arms who has yet to fulfill her vow! You cannot be betrothed to her!'

'No, we are not betrothed,' I forced out. 'But we are promised to each other.'

'Promised how, then?'

I watched Atara giving Estrella a drink from her water horn, and I said, 'Promised with our hearts.'

I did not really expect this savage Danladi warrior to understand such deep and tender sentiments, for the Sarni beat their women when they displease them and rarely show them kindness. And so he astonished me once more when he said, 'I am sorry, Valashu, I will not look at her again. But I, too, know what it is to love this woman.'

I glared and him and said, 'My father taught me that one should not mistake lust for love.'

47

'No, one should not,' he agreed. 'But it surprises me to hear a Valari speak of love.'

'I have heard,' I told him, 'that you Sarni speak of love only for your horses.'

He patted the neck of his brown stallion as he smiled sadly. 'That is because you know little about us.'

Some hurt in his voice – seething and keen and covered with layers of scar – made me feel my way past my jealousy deeper into his being. And what I sensed pulsing inside him so fiercely was only love. Love for Atara, love for his family, for his horses or the beautiful land over which they rode, I could not tell. It didn't matter. For this bright flame filled my blood and broke me open, and I could never scorn him again.

'And you,' I said to him, 'know little about us.'

His eyes softened, and he looked at me strangely as he said, 'I have heard what the Red Dragon did to your land. What he did to your mother and grandmother.'

My eyes filled with a hot stinging, and the green grasses of the steppe beyond Bajorak's wild, mournful face grew blurry. I swallowed against the lump in my throat and could not speak.

Now he wiped at his own eyes, and his throat seemed raw and pained as he said, 'When I was twelve years old, the Zayak crossed the Jade to raid for women. They surprised us, and many were taken. My mother, my sister, too – Takiyah was her name. But they would not consort with the Zayak, and so their chieftain, Torkalax, scourged them with his quirt and gave them to Morjin. But they would not be slaves in Argattha either, and they tried to kill themselves to keep Morjin's priests from possessing them. It mattered not. The filthy Red Priests ravished them all the same. And then Morjin crucified them for the crime of trying to steal the use of their bodies from the priests. It is said that he set them in his great hall as an example to others. A gem seller who did business with my father brought us the news of their torture. And on that day my father made me vow that I would never make peace with the Zayak or with Morjin.'

Out on the steppe, a lion roared and a meadowlark chirped angrily – perhaps the same bird whose nest Altaru had destroyed. And I said to Bajorak, 'Our enemy is one and the same, and so they should be no quarrel between us.'

'No quarrel, perhaps. But the enemy of our enemy is not always our friend. Were it so, we would make cause with the Marituk, who hate the Zayak as much as we do.'

'It is hard,' I said to him, 'for a Valari and a Sarni to be friends.'

'And yet you and the Manslayer call each other "friend", if nothing more.'

I saw him searching for something in my eyes as he gazed at me. And I searched for something in him. I found it beneath his gold-studded armor in the sudden surge of his blood. It was the promise of life, the very pulse of the world and breath of the stars. When I opened my heart to him, I felt it beating strong, wild and true.

'Friends,' he told me, 'do not keep secrets from each other.'

'No, they do not,' I said.

It came to me then that I had a sort of Scales of my own, for I gave great weight to what my heart told me was true. One either had faith in men, or not. As Bajorak looked at me so openly, without entreaty or guile, I knew that I trusted him and that he would never betray me.

'The name of the gorge we seek,' I told him, 'is the Kul Kavaakurk.'

I went on to explain the nature of our quest. Only the Maitreya, I said to him, could contend with Morjin for mastery of the Lightstone. We had no idea where on Ea to search for this great-souled being, but the Grandmaster of the Great White Brotherhood in their ancient school in the mountains above us might know.

'It is a small hope,' I said to him. 'But unless the Maitreya is found, it won't matter if the Danladi or Kurmak or Valari refuse to make peace with Morjin. For Morjin and all his allies will make war against us and destroy us one by one.'

'No, that will not be,' he said. 'Morjin may indeed destroy us. But *not* one by one.'

And with that, he leaned out away from his horse and extended his calloused hand toward me. I grasped it in mine, and we sat there for a few moments testing each other's resolve. With a gladness that he could not contain, he looked at me and smiled as he said, 'Friend.'

I smiled, too, and nodded my head. 'Friend.'

Each telling of the truth, I suddenly knew, was like a whisper that might grow into a whirlwind.

'It is a strange thing you do,' he said to me, 'seeking this Maitreya instead of gold, women or war. And you, a great warrior, or so it's said.'

'I've seen enough war to last to the end of my days if I lived another ten thousand years.'

And Bajorak surprised me once more, saying, 'So have I.'

I took in the paint on his face, the saber thrust through his braided gold belt and the great horn bow strapped to his back. I said to him, 'I have never heard a Sarni warrior speak so.'

Again he smiled, an expression made difficult by the scars cutting his cheeks. And he said, 'I have wives and daughters, and I would not see them violated by any man. I have a son. I would hear him make music.'

My eyes filled with amazement as I smiled at him.

'Promise me, Valashu Elahad, that you will not tell anyone what I have told you here. For me to speak of love is one thing. But if my warriors heard me speak of ending war, they would think me mad.'

'All right,' I said, clasping hands with him again, 'I promise.'

He nodded his head to me, once, fiercely, and then turned his horse about and rode back to his warriors. And I returned to my friends, who were gathered in a circle on top of their horses between the Bajorak's Danladi and our Manslayer rear guard.

'Well?' Maram called out to me as I came up to them. 'What was all *that* about?'

Kane, however, needed no account of my meeting with Bajorak to know what had transpired. His black eyes were like two disks of heated iron as he said to me, 'So, you told him.'

'Yes,' I said. 'I had to.'

'You *had* to?' The muscles beneath his wind-burnt jaws popped out as if he were working at a piece of meat. I knew that he was furious with me. 'Ha! – we will see what comes of this. Your fate is your fate, eh? Some men wait for theirs, but you have to go rushing in, like a child into a dragon's den.'

After that we continued our journey toward the place that Bajorak had told of. Five miles we put behind us in less than an hour before pausing to water the horses at a little stream trickling through the grass. I kept a watch on our enemy, and wondered yet again why they took such pains to keep their distance from us.

'It must be,' I said to Atara as she sipped from her water horn, 'that Morjin does not wish me to catch sight of his face.'

'Perhaps,' she told me. Maram, Liljana and Kane stood next to her along the stream listening to what she had to say. 'But consider this as well: If it really *is* Morjin, he must know, or guess, our mission. It would be hard for him, I think, so terribly, terribly hard to decide between letting us lead him to the Maitreya and killing us while he had the chance.'

50

'He has little chance,' I said. 'And if he comes too close, it is we who shall kill him.'

But fate was to prove me wrong on both these counts. Just as we bent low to refill our horns in the ice-cold water, I saw Bajorak, farther down the stream, suddenly put away his horn and throw his hand to his forehead like a visor. He looked out toward the east, where a grassy rise blocked sight of the flatter country there. A few moments later, a dappled horse and a Sarni warrior charged up over the rise and galloped straight toward us. I recognized the man as Ossop, one of the outriders that Bajorak had sent to keep watch on our flank.

We mounted quickly, and Kane, Atara and I rode over to learn why Ossop returned in such haste. Karimah and one of her Manslayers met there in front of Bajorak as well, just as Ossop called out: 'They come, out of the east, and five miles behind me!'

He pulled up and gasped out that another company of Red Knights, fifteen strong, and twenty-five more Zayak warriors were quickly bearing down upon us.

I turned to look for them, but could see little more than the windswept rise running parallel to the eastern horizon. To the northwest, the Red Knights who had trailed us so far were remounting their horses. And so were the twenty-five Zayak warriors who rode with them.

'Now we've no choice!' I said, looking at our enemy. 'It's too late to attack them, and so we must flee!'

I pointed at two long strips of red rock marking the front range of the White Mountains five miles away. If these were truly the edges of the Ass's Ears – or the Red Shields – Bajorak was right that they appeared very different from this point of view.

'Hold!' Kashak called out to Bajorak. Although this huge man had a savage look about him, with his ferocious blue eyes and bushy blond, overhanging brows, I sensed in him little that was actually cruel. But he was quite capable of dealing with life's cruelties in a businesslike and almost casual way. 'Hold, I say! We agreed to escort the kradaks to the mountains, and so we have done. If we remain here, trapped between two forces and these cursed rocks, we'll be slaughtered along with them. Let us therefore leave them to what must befall.'

My heart took a long time between beats as I waited to hear what Bajorak would say to this. But he hesitated not a moment as he called back to Kashak: 'We shall not leave them!'

51

'But we have earned our gold, and our contract has been fulfilled.'

'No – the spirit of it has not!'

'I say it has.'

'*You* say! But who is headman of the Tarun, you or I?'

Bajorak locked eyes with Kashak, and so fierce and fiery was his gaze that Kashak quickly looked away.

'There is no time!' Bajorak called out, to Pirraj and his other warriors. He began issuing orders as he rearrayed his men to cover us on our left flank along the line of our flight. Then he snapped his quirt near his horse's ear and shouted, 'Let us ride!'

Without a backward glance at Kashak, he urged his horse straight toward the two red rocks five miles away. Kashak paused only a moment to regard me with his bleak, blue eyes. Freely had this Sarni warrior chosen to ride with Bajorak, and freely he might choose to ride elsewhere. But he would not desert his headman and friends in the face of battle. He said to me, without rancor or resentment: 'It always comes to this, does it not? I hope you're good at fighting, Valari. Well, we shall see.'

And with that, he whipped his quirt against his horse's side and galloped off to rejoin his kith and kin.

My friends and I took only a few moments longer to urge our mounts forward and gain speed across the uneven terrain. Karimah and her twelve Manslayers rode close behind us, like a shield of flaxen-haired women and bounding horseflesh. And behind them, scarcely a mile away, the Red Knights charged at us, and they seemed intent at last upon closing the distance between us. I heard them blowing their warhorns and felt the beating of their horses' hooves upon grassy ground; I felt, too, the beating of the heart of the man who was their master. He pushed his men forward with all his spite and will, even as my blood pushed at me with a fierce, quick fire that I had learned to hate.

So began our wild flight toward the mountains. I rode beside Daj and close to Estrella, for I worried that she might be too tired to sustain such a chase. But she kept her horse moving quickly and showed no sign of slumping into exhaustion or falling off. Master Juwain and Liljana watched her, too; they were now experienced campaigners, if not warriors, and they rode nearly as well as the Danladi to our left and the Manslayers behind us. Maram, though, labored almost as heavily as his sweating horse. I felt the strain in his great body as a bone-crushing weariness in my own.

It did not surprise me that the Red Knights seemed to gain on us. But they did not gain much: perhaps a hundred yards with every mile that we covered. And we put these miles behind us quickly, with the wind whipping at our faces, to the drumming of hooves against the ground. A mile of grassy terrain vanished behind us, and then two and three. The rocks called the Ass's Ears loomed larger and larger. This close to them, I could see more than just their edges. It seemed that Master Juwain's Way Rhymes had told true, for the rocks were indeed like great, elongated triangles of stone rising up into the sky. Behind them, layers of the White Mountains built up into even greater heights toward the clouds. Between them flowed a stream. A rocky ridge ran along the Ear to the north nearest us. A smaller ridge across the stream seemed to protect the approach to the second and southern Ear. The ground between the great rocks, I saw, was broken and strewn with boulders: very bad terrain for any horse to negotiate at speed.

Bajorak, upon studying the lay of the land here, saw its obvious advantages for defense – though he came to a different conclusion than I as to what our strategy should be. With only a mile to cover before we reached this gateway into the mountains, he dropped back to me and shouted out above the pounding and snorting of our horses: 'My warriors and I will dismount and set up behind that ridge!'

Here, with a lifetime of coordinating such motions to the beat and bound of his horse, he held out his finger pointing steadily toward the northern ridge.

'Any who try to force their way between the Shields, we will kill with arrows!' he shouted. 'You will have time to escape into this Kul Kavaakurk Gorge – if there really is such a gorge!'

As Altaru charged forward with rhythmic surges of his great muscles, I gazed between the red rocks, at the rushing stream. If this narrow gap opened into a gorge, I could not tell, for great boulders and the curves of the mountains' wooded slopes obscured it.

'No!' I called back to Bájorak. 'You have chosen not to desert us, and so we will not desert you!'

'Don't be a fool!' he said. 'Think of the children! Think of the Shining One!'

Even though each moment of our dash across the steppe seemed to jolt any thoughts from my mind, I was thinking of both Daj and Estrella, as well as the need of our quest. I did not, however, have time to argue with Bajorak – or the heart to dispirit him. For I was sure that if my friends and I fled with the children into the mountains, Bajorak's warriors would inevitably be overwhelmed, and then Morjin and his Red Knights would trap us in the gorge.

'Here is what we'll do!' I called back to him. 'As you have said, you will set up with your warriors behind the ridge – all except Kashak and his squadron!'

I quickly shouted out the rest of the battle plan that I had devised. It seemed that Bajorak might dispute with me over who would take command here. But after gazing into my eyes for a long moment, he looked away and nodded his head as he said, 'All right.'

We continued our charge toward the Ass's Ears, slowing to a trot and then a quick walk as the ground broke up and rose steeply. I turned to see that the Red Knights and the Zayak warriors had halted about half a mile behind us. Clearly, they saw that they could not overtake us before we established ourselves behind the rocky ridge. Clearly, too, they awaited the arrival of the new companies of Red Knights and Zayak that Ossop had told of.

When the ground grew too rotten for riding, we dismounted and led our horses along either side of the wooded stream. It was a hard work over rocks and up shrub-covered slopes, but necessity drove us to move like demons of speed. Bajorak and twenty-three of his warriors turned up behind the rocky ridge and deployed at the wall-like crest along its length, as would archers behind a castle's battlements. They hated fighting on foot, away from their horses tethered behind them, but there was no help for it. I led the rest of our force – Karimah's Manslayers, Kashak's seven warriors and my friends – behind the smaller ridge fronting the second Ass's Ear to the south. The trees there and humps of ground obscured our movement from our enemy, or so I prayed.

While Kashak stood with his men behind some trees and Karimah waited with her Manslaying women nearby, I turned to speak with my companions and friends. I called Liljanja closer to me. I whispered to her: 'Here is what we must do.'

I cupped my hands over her ears and she slowly nodded her head. Then she brought forth her blue gelstei, cast into a whale-shaped figurine. She held this powerful crystal up to the side of her head. With a gasp that tore through me like a spear puncturing my lungs, she suddenly grimaced and cried out in pain. Then she jerked her hand away from her head and opened it. The blue gelstei gleamed in the strong sun. As Liljana's eyes cleared, she stared at me and said, 'It is done.'

After that I called Master Juwain, Daj and Estrella over as well.

54

I said to Master Juwain: 'You and Liljana will take the children into the mountains. We will follow when we can. And if we can't, it will be upon you to find the Brotherhood school – and the Maitreya.'

'No!' Daj cried out, laying his hand upon the little sword that he wore. 'I want to stay here with you and fight!'

Estrella, too, did not like this new turn of things. She came up to my side and wrapped her arms around my waist, and would not let go.

'Here, now,' I said as I pulled away her hands as gently as I could. 'You must go with Master Juwain – everything depends upon it.'

She shook the dark curls out of her eyes and looked up at me. The bright noon light glinted off her fine-boned cheeks and the slightly crooked nose that must have once been broken. She smiled at me, and I felt all her trust in me pouring through me like a river of light. I promised her that I would rejoin her and Daj in the mountains, and soon. Then I lifted her up to kiss her goodbye.

'Karimah!' I called out, motioning this sturdy woman over to us. Despite her bulk, she came at a run, gripping her strung bow. 'Would you be willing to appoint two of your warriors to escort Master Juwain and the children into the mountains, a few miles perhaps, until they find a safe place?'

'I will, Lord Valashu,' she agreed. She pulled at her jowly chin as she looked at me. 'But no more than two – we shall need the rest of my sisters here before long.'

She turned to choose two of her sister Manslayers for this task. I quickly said goodbye to Master Juwain, Liljana and Daj. And so did Maram, Atara and Kane. I watched as a young lioness of a woman named Surya led the way up the stream between the Ass's Ears. My friends, walking their horses beside them, hurried after her and so did another of the Manslayers whose name I did not know.

A few moments later, they disappeared behind the curve of a great sandstone buttress and were lost to our view. Then I turned back toward the Wendrush to complete our preparations for battle.

4

To the sound of battle horns blaring out on the grasslands that we could not quite see, I called everyone closer to me. Karimah and Atara crowded in close, with Kashak and two Danladi warriors, between Maram and Kane. And I said to them, 'The Zayak are fifty in number, and Morjin will appoint at least three dozen of them to ride against Bajorak's men along the ridge, keeping them pinned with arrows. The rest of the Zayak, with his forty Red Knights, he will send up along this stream.'

Here I pointed at the water cutting between Bajorak's ridge and the one that we hid behind. 'He will try to flank Bajorak and come up behind him. But we shall meet him here with arrows and swords.'

So saying I drew Alkaladur; Kashak's men and many of the Manslayers gasped to behold its brilliance, for they had never seen a sword like it.

Kashak, fingering his taut bowstring, asked me: 'How do you know that is what Morjin will do?'

Now I pointed behind us, where the Ass's Ears rose up above what I presumed was the way to the Kul Kavaakurk. And I said to Kashak, 'Morjin cannot go into the mountains until he clears Bajorak from the ridge.'

'Then he might decide not to go into the mountains. Or to besiege our position.'

'No, he will be afraid that I and my companions will escape him,' I said. 'And so, despite the cost, he will attack – and soon.'

Kashak's bushy brows knitted together as he shot me a suspicious look. 'You seem to know a great deal about this filthy Crucifier.'

'More than I would ever want to know,' I said, watching the slow smolder of flames build within my sword.

56

He looked at the rocky, sloping ground over which Morjin's men would charge, if they came this way, and he said, 'Why did you ask Bajorak for me and my squadron to stand with you, when I spoke in favor of abandoning you?'

'Because,' I said, smiling at him, 'you *did* speak of this. And having decided to remain even so, you will fight like a lion to prove your valor.'

Kashak's eyes widened in awe, and he made a warding sign with his finger. He stared at me as if he feared that I could look into his mind.

'I will fight like a pride of lions!' he called out, raising up his bow.

I smiled at him again, and we clasped hands like brothers. One either believes in men or not.

A horn sounded, but the swells of earth separating us from the steppe beyond muffled the sound of it. The two forces of our enemy, I thought, would be meeting up on the grassy slope below the ridges and preparing to attack us.

'We should see how they deploy,' Kashak said to me. He pointed toward the ridge above us. 'We could steal up to those rocks and see if you are right.'

I nodded my head at this. And so leaving Kashak's men behind with Kane, Atara, Maram and the Manslayers, Kashak and I picked our way up the ridge running in front of the second of the Ass's Ears. As we neared the crest, we dropped down upon our bellies and crept along the ground for the final few yards like snakes. With the taste of dirt in my mouth, I peered around the edge of a rock, and so did Kashak. And this is what we saw:

Out on the steppe, a quarter mile away, some forty of the Zayak warriors were arrayed in a long line below the ridge to the left of us where Bajorak had set up with his Danladi. They gripped their thick, double-curved bows in preparation for a charge and an arrow duel. The ten remaining Zayak, dismounted, gathered along the stream with the two score Red Knights, who would also fight on foot. I looked for the leader of these knights, encased in their armor of carmine-tinged mail and steel plate, but I could not make him out.

'It is as you said!' Kashak whispered to me. 'It is as if you can look into Morjin's mind!'

No, I thought, I had no such gift. But Liljana did. At my request, she had used her blue gelstei one last time, seemingly to seek out the secrets of Morjin's mind – and his intentions for the coming battle. And she had, in this invisible duel of thoughts and diamond-hard will, with great cunning, let him see *our* intentions: our company's flight into the mountains with the Manslayers as an escort. That Kane, Maram, Atara and I remained behind, lying in wait with Kashak's men and the rest of the Manslayers, she had *not* let Morjin see, or so I hoped. It was a ruse that might work one time – but one time only.

Then one of the Red Knights below us raised up his arm, and another horn rang out its bone-chilling blare. The forty Zayak on their horses began their charge toward Bajorak and his warriors. And the Red Knights – bearing drawn maces or swords – began moving at the double-pace up between the two ridges.

'They come!' Kashak whispered to me.

I remained frozen to the ground, gripping a rock with one hand and my sword in the other. The entire world narrowed until I could see neither mountain nor sky nor rocks running along the edge of the gray-green grasslands. I had eyes for only one man: he who led the Red Knights up along the stream cutting between the two ridges. His yellow surcoat blazed with a great red dragon. I felt the fury of the sun heating up my sword and a wild fire inside me, and I knew that this man was Morjin.

'Lord Valashu, they come!' Kashak whispered more urgently.

He pulled at my cloak, and I nodded my head. We scuttled crab-like down the slope a dozen yards before rising to a crouch and then running back down to join our companions.

There were too few trees here to provide cover for all the Sarni. Kashak's warriors grumbled at being ordered to hide behind them, while Karimah's Manslayers almost rebelled at being asked to lie down behind some raspberry bushes. I stood with Kane, Maram and Atara behind a rock the size of a wagon. We waited for our enemy to appear in the notch down and around the curve of the stream.

'Oh, Lord, my Lord!' Maram sighed out to me. He fingered the edge of his drawn sword: a Valari kalama like the one that Kane held to his lips as he whispered fell words and then kissed its brilliant steel. 'That Kashak was right, wasn't he? It seems always to come to this.'

I looked up to my left past the stream, at the ridge where Bajorak waited with his warriors. The curve of the ground obscured the sight of most of his small force, but I knew they were ready because I could see three of the Danladi nearest us. They pulled back their bowstrings as they sighted their arrows on the Zayak who would be riding uphill against them.

'Why, Val, why?' Maram murmured to me. 'I should be sitting by a stream in the Morning Mountains, preparing to eat a picnic lunch that my beloved has made for me. Look at this lovely day! Ah, why, why, *why* did I ever consent to leave Mesh?'

'Shhh!' Kane whispered fiercely to him. 'You'll give us away!'

I smiled sadly, for Maram was right about one thing: it was a beautiful day. In the hills behind us, birds were singing. The sun rained down a bright light upon the reddish rocks and the silvery green leaves of the cottonwood trees. Below us, along either bank of the stream and up the rocky slopes, millions of small white flowers grew. Atara called them Maiden's Breath. A soft breeze rippled their delicate petals, which shimmered in the sunlight. It occurred to me that *I* should be picking a bouquet for Atara, rather than gripping a long sword in which gathered reddish-orange flowers of flame.

We heard our enemy before we saw them, for as they advanced up the stream, they made a great noise: of boots kicking at rocks; of grunts and hard breath puffing out into the warm air; of interlocking rings of mail jangling and grinding against the sheets of steel plate that covered their shoulders, forearms and chests. And of twanging bowstrings, as well, as Bajorak's warriors upon the ridge rained down arrows upon them. Steel points broke against steel armor and shields with a clanging terrible to hear. A few of these must have broken through to the flesh beneath for the air below the towering Ass's Ears rang with the even more terrible screams of men struck down or dying. I wondered if Bajorak's men were concentrating on the Red Knights or the more vulnerable Zayak warriors in their flimsy leather armor. And then our enemy rounded the curve of the stream and charged up the flower-covered slopes straight toward us.

They did not see us until it was too late. I waited until they came close enough to smell their acrid sweat, and then I shouted out: 'Attack!'

Kashak's men stepped out from behind the trees at the same moment that Karimah's Manslayers lifted their bows over the tops of the raspberry bushes. With Atara, these archers were twenty in number, and they loosed their arrows almost as one. The first volley, fired at such short range, killed a dozen of the Red Knights and the Zayak. A few arrows glanced off red armor, but many found their marks through the Zayaks' throats or chests, or straight through the Red Knights' vulnerable faces. I shouted at Kashak's men to keep to the cover of the trees, but in this one matter they did not heed me. They were Sarni warriors, used to battle on the open steppe, and they thought it shameful to hide behind trees. The second volley found our enemy better prepared; the knights covered their faces with their shields, while the Zayak warriors loosed arrows of their own at us. I grunted in pain as a long, feathered shaft slammed into my shoulder but failed to penetrate my tough Godhran armor. There was no third volley. With our two small forces so close to each other, our enemy's leader shouted out for his men to close the distance and charge into us where the fighting would be hand to hand.

With a chill that shot down my spine, I recognized this voice as belonging to Morjin. It was a strong voice, almost musical in its tone, and it vibrated with sureness and command. And with malevolence, vanity and a hunger for cruelty that made my belly twist with hot acids and pain. His face was Morjin's, too: not, however, the aged, haunted countenance with the blood-red eyes and grayish, decaying flesh that I knew to be his true face, but rather that of his youth. He was fine and fair to look upon. His eyes were all clear and golden, and sparkled like freshly minted coins. His thick hair, the color of Atara's, spilled out from beneath his carmine helm. Although not quite a large man, he moved with a power that I felt pulsing out across three dozen yards of ground. In truth, he fairly quivered with all the fell vitality of a dragon.

Was it possible, I wondered, that he had somehow regained the power to deceive me with the same illusions that he cast over other men? Or had he found in the Lightstone a way to renew himself? There was something strange about him, in the way he moved and scanned the flower-covered slopes before him. He seemed to apprehend the rocks and trees and the men standing beside them both from close-up and from far away, like an ever-watchful angel of death. His gaze found mine and seared me with his hate. The flames of his being writhed in flares of madder, puce and incarnadine – and with other colors that I could not quite behold. The burning sickness inside me told me that this *must* be Morjin.

Without warning, Atara loosed an arrow at him. But he moved his head at the same moment that her bowstring cracked, and the arrow whined harmlessly past him. He pointed his finger at her then. Atara gave a gasp, and slumped back against our rock. I could feel her second sight leave her. She shook her bow at Morjin in her helplessness and rage at being made once more truly blind.

'Kill that witch!' he shouted to his men. Now he pointed at me. 'Kill the Valari!'

'Morjin!' I shouted back at him. 'Damn you, Morjin!'

I rushed at him then even as he charged at me. But his Red Knights close by, those still standing, would not let him take straight-on the fury of my sword. A few of them crowded ahead of him as a vanguard. I cut down the foremost with a slash through his neck. Blood sprayed my face, and I cried out in the agony of the man I had killed. I was only dimly aware of other combats raging around me as Kashak's warriors and the Manslayers ran down the slopes with flashing sabers to meet the advance of the Red Knights and the Zayak. Some part of me saw steel biting into flesh and bright red showers raining down upon the snowy white blossoms at our feet. I heard arrows whining out upon the ridge above us, and curses and screams, and I knew that Bajorak's men were fighting a fierce battle with the mounted Zayak. But I had eyes only for Morjin. I fought my way closer to him, shivering the shield of a knight with a savage thrust. I felt Maram on my left and Kane on my right, stabbing their swords into the Red Knights who swarmed forward to protect their lord. The world dissolved into a glowing red haze. And then I killed another of his vanguard, and Morjin suddenly stood unprotected in front of me.

'Mother!' I cried out. 'Father! Asaru!'

I raised high my bright silver blade, dripping with blood. And then one of Kashak's warriors – or perhaps it was a Manslayer – nearly robbed me of my vengeance. A bow cracked, and an arrow streaked forth. But as before with Atara, Morjin moved out of the way at the instant the bolt was loosed at him. He must, I knew, possess some sort of uncanny sense of when others were intending to deal him a death blow. As I did, too. We were brothers in our blood, I thought, bound to each other in the quick burn of the kirax poison no less than in our souls' bitter hate.

'Morjin!'

'Elahad!'

I swung my sword at him. He parried it with a shocking strength. Steel rang against silustria, and I felt a terrible power run down my blade into my arms and chest, and nearly shiver my bones. Once, twice, thrice we clashed, pushed against each other and then sprang apart. Maram knocked against my left side as he grunted and gasped and tried to kill the knight in front of him. On my right, Kane's sword struck out with a rare passion to rend and

61

destroy. He wanted as badly as I to kill Morjin. But fate was fate, and it was I who rushed in to slay the dragon.

MORJINNN!

I stabbed Alkaladur's brilliant point at his neck, but he parried that thrust as well and then nearly cut off my head. He sliced his sword at me, again and again, with a prowess I had encountered in no other man except Kane. The flashing of our blades nearly blinded me; the ringing of steel rattled my skull. This was *not* the same Morjin that I had fought in Argattha. In his cuts and savage thrusts there was a recklessness, as if he willed himself to lay me open but had little care for his own flesh. This made him vastly more formidable. Twice he missed running me through by an inch. As his sword burned past my head yet again, his contempt blazed out at me. There was something strange, I sensed, in his hate. It was not immediate, like the blast of an open furnace, like mine for him, but rather like the sun's flares as viewed through a dark glass. It had enough fire, though, to kill me if I let it.

'Look at the Valari!' I heard someone shout above the tumult of the battle. 'His sword! It burns!'

Blue and red flames ran along my shining blade and blazed only brighter and hotter as I whipped it through the air. The fiery brilliance of my sword dazzled Morjin. Fear ran like molten steel in his eyes, and I knew that I had it within me to slay him. And he knew it, too. With a boldness born of desperation, he gripped his sword with one hand and suddenly thrust at me: quick, low and deep. I moved aside, slightly, and felt his sword scrape past the armor that covered my belly. And then, like a lightning flash, I brought Alkaladur down against his elbow. The silustria fairly burned through steel, muscle and bone, and struck off his arm. The hellish heat seared his flesh; I heard blood sizzling and smelled his cauterized veins. He screamed at me then as he reached for his dagger with the only arm that remained to him.

'Lord Morjin is wounded!' someone called out. 'To him! To him! Kill the Valari!'

I raised back my sword to send Morjin into the heart of some distant star, where he would burn forever. But just then one of the Zayak loosed an arrow at me. I pulled back my head at the very moment that it would have driven through my face – right into the path of another arrow aimed by another Zayak. *This* arrow struck the mail over my temple at the wrong angle to penetrate but with enough force to stun me. A bright white light burst through my eyes, and the world about me blurred. I felt Kane to my right and Maram beside me working furiously with their swords to protect me from the maces and swords of the nearby Red Knights. When my vision finally cleared, I saw other knights closing around Morjin as they bound his arm with twists of rawhide to keep him from bleeding to death and bore him back down the stream, away from the battle.

'Morjin!' I cried out. 'Damn you – you won't escape!'

With my friends, I hacked and stabbed at the wall of knights in front of us. On either side of the stream, arrows sizzled out and sabers flashed as the Manslayers and Danladi threw themselves at the Red Knights and the Zayak. As promised, Kashak fought like a pride of lions. In this close combat against the Red Knights, his thinner sword and lighter armor proved a disadvantage, as with the other Sarni. But Kashak made up for this with a rare fierceness and strength. He towered over the Red Knights, calling out curses as his saber slashed through wrists or throats with a savagery that shocked our enemy. He closed with one of them, and he used his great fist like a battering ram, driving it into the man's face with a sickening crunch that I heard above the din of the battle. I heard Kane, as well, growling and cursing to my right even as a howl of rage built inside me. I cried out to Morjin, in a hot, red, silent wrath, my vow that he would never get away.

And as his paladins bore him down the rocky banks of the stream, away from the high ground in front of the Ass's Ears, he screamed back at me: 'You won't escape *me*, Elahad! All you Valari! *He* is nearly free! The Baaloch is! And when he walks the earth again, we shall crucify all your kind, down to the last woman and child!'

Deep within my memory burned the image of my mother and grandmother, nailed to wood. I suddenly killed one of the Red Knights in front of me with a quick thrust of my sword, and then another. My friends threw themselves at these champions of Morjin, and so did the Manslayers and Kashak's Danladi. We had cut down more than a score of them, and their bleeding bodies crushed the white flowers about the stream and reddened its waters. Even so they still outnumbered us, for they had killed too many of us as well. And yet it was we who pushed them back, with beating sabers and long swords, ever backward down the stream and over broken ground out from the saddle between the two ridges. Through the shifting gaps in the mass of men before me, I watched as four of the Red Knights bore Morjin toward a bend in the stream where our enemy had left their horses. To our left, the Zayak who had ridden against Bajorak along the ridge were in full retreat, galloping back down toward the steppe. It would be only a matter of moments, I saw, before Morjin mounted his horse and joined them.

'Morjin!' I cried out, yet again. 'Morjin!'

I could not get at him. Swords flashed in front of me like a steel fence. I howled out my rage at being thwarted. Atara, wandering the battlefield blindly as she felt her way over rocks or dead bodies with the tip of her useless bow, moved closer to me, perhaps drawn by the sound of my voice. She held her unused saber in her hand, and I knew that she would fight to her death to try to protect me. Two of the Red Knights, like jackals, moved in on her to take advantage of her sightlessness. But I moved even more quickly. I cleaved the first of these knights through the helm, and the second I split open with a thrust through his chest. He died burning with a lust to lay his hands about Atara's throat and drag this helpless woman down into darkness with him.

I fell mad then. I threw myself at the Red Knights and the Zayak warriors, who were slowly retreating over the swells of ground that flowed down to the grasslands of the Wendrush. I cursed and gnashed my teeth and howled like a wolf; I struck out with my fearsome sword, again and again, at arms, bellies, throats, and faces. Steel shrieked and terrible cries split the air. Hacked and headless men dropped before me. The living, in ones and twos, began to break and run. One of the knights threw down his sword and begged for quarter. In my killing frenzy, however, I could not hear his words or perceive the surrender in his eyes. I sent him on without pity, and then another and yet another. And then, suddenly, no more of the enemy remained standing near me – only Kashak, Maram and Kane, who were gasping for breath and spattered with blood. Kashak's warriors, the few who hadn't fallen, gathered behind us, with the remaining Manslayers and Atara.

'They're getting away!' Kane shouted at me. He pointed his bloody sword out toward the open steppe. '*He* is getting away . . . again!'

Morjin's four paladins, I saw, were grouped around their lord, and their horses galloped over the swaying grasses, away from the mountains. They were already far out on the Wendrush, to the east. The Red Knights and the few Zayak who had survived the slaughter had mounted their horses and hurried after them, soon to be joined by the Zayak who had ridden against Bajorak.

'He *won't* get away!' I shouted. 'Let us ride after him!'

Our horses, however, were nowhere near at hand. Bajorak ran down from the ridge then and came up to us. He said, 'Six of my men have fallen and four of Kashak's. And six of the Manslayers. We are only thirty, now.'

He went on to tell that we had slain some thirty of the Red Knights and all but two of the Zayak who had followed Morjin up the stream. With the Zayak that Bajorak's men had felled with arrows, we had accounted for more than fifty of our enemy.

'But they still outnumber us,' Bajorak told me. 'And if we pursue them, there will be no surprise.'

'I don't care!'

'Morjin has the distance now!'

'Growing greater by the moment, as we stand here!'

'There may be other companies, other Red Knights and Zayak,' Bajorak told me. 'We have a victory. Morjin might not survive the wound you dealt him. You're free to complete your quest.'

'I don't care!' I shouted again. I pointed my flaming sword toward the east. 'There is our enemy!'

Bajorak slowly shook his head. 'I will not pursue him. And neither will my warriors.'

'It is *Morjin*!' I shouted in rage. 'And so he *will* survive, to kill and crucify again!'

So hot did the fire swirling about my sword grow that Bajorak stepped away from me, and so did Kashak. But Kane, with a terrible wildness in his eyes, pointed toward Morjin racing away from us and shouted, 'He *won't* survive, damn him! Kill him, Val! You know the way!'

As I met eyes with Kane, we walked together through a land burning up in flames. And yet, despite the fire and the terrible heat, it was a dark land, as black and hideous as charred flesh.

'Kill him!' Kane called out as he pointed at Morjin. 'He is weak, now! This is your chance!'

In my hands I held a sword that flared hotter and hotter as I stared out at Morjin's shrinking form. Fire burned my face and built to a raging inferno inside me. I held there another sword, finer and yet even more terrible. It was pure lightning, all the fury and incandescence of the stars. With it I had slain Ravik Kirriland. I knew that I had only to strike out with this sword of fire and light to slay Morjin now.

'So – kill him! Kill him! Kill him! Kill him!'

Father! I cried out silently. *Mother*! *Nona*! *Asaru*!

'No, Val!' Atara called out to me, stumbling across the uneven ground. She found her way to my side and laid her hand on my shoulder. 'Not this way!'

'Do it!' Kane howled at me.

Could I slay Morjin with the valarda, of my own will? Could I tell a thunderbolt where to strike?

'He is getting away, damn it! *You* are letting him get away!'

No, a voice inside me whispered. *No, no, no.*

'Kill him, now!'

'No, I won't!' I howled back at Kane.

'He crucified your own mother!'

MORJINNN!

I cried out this name with all the agony of my breath, like a blast of fire. My hate for Morjin swelled to the point where I could not control it, where I did not *want* to control it. Could I stop a whirlwind from blowing? No, I could not, and so finally the lightning tore me open. I felt all my evil rage flash straight out toward the tiny, retreating figure of Morjin as he galloped across the open grasslands. But it was too late. The sword of wrath, I sensed, struck him and stunned him, but did not kill. I watched helplessly as he made his escape toward the curving edge of the world.

'It is too far!' Kane shouted at me. 'You waited too long!'

I bowed my head in shame that I had failed to kill Morjin – and in even greater shame that, in the perversion of my sacred gift, I almost had.

'Damn him!' Kane shouted.

I lowered my sword and watched as its flames slowly quiesced. With a ringing of silustria against steel, I slid it back into its sheath.

And then I turned to Kane and said, 'If I can help it, I won't use the valarda to slay.'

He stared at me for a moment that seemed to last longer than the turning of the earth into night. His eyes were like hell to look upon. And he shouted at me: 'You *won't*? Then it is *you* who are damned!'

He watched as Morjin's red form vanished into the shimmering nothingness of the horizon. Then he threw his hands up to the sky, and stalked off up the stream where the dead lay like a carpet leading to a realm that none would wish to walk.

Neither Bajorak nor Kashak, nor even Karimah, understood what had transpired between us, for they knew little of the nature of my gift. But they realized that they had witnessed here something extraordinary. Kashak stared at Alkaladur's hilt, with its black jade grip and diamond pommel, and he said to me, 'Your sword – it burned! But it didn't *burn*! How is that possible?'

He made a warding sign with his finger as Bajorak stared at me, too. And Bajorak said to me, 'Your face, Valari! *It* is burnt!'

I held my hand to my forehead; it was painful and hot, as if a fever consumed me. Karimah told me that my face was as red as a cherry, as if I had been staked out all day in the fierce summer sun. She produced a leather bag containing an ointment that the fair-skinned Sarni apply as proof against sunburns. Atara took it from her, and dipped her fingers into it. Her touch was cool and gentle against my outraged flesh as she worked the pungent-smelling ointment into my cheek.

'Come,' I said, pulling away from her. 'Others have real wounds that need tending.'

So it was with any battle. Bajorak's men had taken arrows through faces, legs or other parts of the body, and Kashak's warriors and the Manslayers had sword cuts to deal with. But these tough Sarni warriors were already busy binding up their wounds. In truth, there was little for me and my friends to do here except stare at the bodies of the dead.

I pointed at the hacked men lying on top of the pretty white flowers called Maiden's Breath, and I said, 'They must be buried.'

'Yes, ours will be,' Bajorak said to me. 'The Manslayers and our warriors, even the Zayak, we shall take out onto the steppe and bury in our way. As for Morjin's men, I care not if they rot here in their armor.'

'Then we,' I said, looking at Maram, 'will dig graves for them here.'

Maram, exhausted and bloody from the battle, looked at me as if I had truly fallen mad.

And Bajorak said to me, 'No, the ground here is too rocky for digging. And there is no time. You must hurry after your friends.'

He pointed up the stream where it disappeared between the two towering Ass's Ears. 'Go now, while you can – ten of my warriors have died that you might go where you must. Honor what they gave here, lord.'

'And you?'

Bajorak nodded at Kashak, and then at his warriors still guarding the ridge above with bows and arrows. And he said, 'We shall remain here in case Morjin returns. But I do not think that he will return.'

I looked up the stream at the many Red Knights that we had killed. They would remain here unburied to rot in the sun. So, then, I thought, that was war. I closed my eyes as I bowed down my head.

'Go,' Bajorak said to me again, pressing his hand against my chest.

'All right,' I said, looking at him. 'Perhaps we'll meet again in a better time and a better place.'

'I doubt it not,' he said to me. He clasped my hand in his. 'Farewell, then, Valari.'

'Farewell, Sarni,' I told him.

Then I put my arm across Atara's shoulders and turned toward the mountains. Somewhere, in the heap of rocks to the west, Master Juwain and Liljana would waiting with the children for us. And Kane, I prayed, would be, too.

5

We collected our horses and then made our way up the stream into the gap between the Ass's Ears. We caught up to my grim-faced friend about half a mile into the mountains. He said nothing to me. Neither did he look at me. He rejoined our company with no further complaint, taking his usual post behind us to guard our rear. Kane, I thought, might bear a cold anger at me like a sword stuck through his innards, but he would never desert me.

The way up the stream was rocky and broken, and so we walked our horses and remounts behind us. We had no need to track our friends, for the slopes of the foothills here were so steep and heavily wooded that a deer would have had trouble crossing them, and so there was only one direction Master Juwain and the others could have traveled: along the stream, farther into the mountains. These prominences rose higher and higher before us. Although not as immense as the peaks of the upper Nagarshath to the north, they were great enough to chill the air with a cutting wind that blew down from their snow-covered crests. It was said that men no longer lived in this part of the White Mountains – if indeed they ever had. It was also said that no man knew the way through them. This, I prayed, could not be true, for if Master Juwain could not lead us through the Kul Kavaakurk Gorge and beyond, we would be lost in a vast, frozen wilderness.

For about a mile, as the stream wound ever upward, we saw no sign of this gorge. But then the slopes to either side of us grew steeper and steeper until another mile on they rose up like walls around us. Higher and higher they built, to the right and left, until soon it was clear that we had entered a great gorge. Looking to the west, where this deep cleft through the earth cut its way like a twisting snake, we could see no end of it. Surely, I thought, we must soon overtake our friends, for there could be no way out of this stone-walled deathtrap except at either end.

'Ah, I don't like this place,' Maram grumbled as he kicked his way along the stone-strewn bank of the stream. He puffed for air as he gazed at the layers of rock on the great walls rising up around us. 'Can you imagine how it would go for us if we were caught here?'

'We *won't* be caught here,' I told him. 'Bajorak will protect the way into the gorge.'

'Yes, he'll protect *that* way,' Maram said, pointing behind us. Then he whipped his arm about and pointed ahead. 'But what lies *this* way?'

'Surely our friends do,' I told him. 'Now let's hurry after them.'

But we could not hurry as I would have liked, not with the ground so rotten – and not with Atara still blind and stumbling over boulders that nearly broke her knees. Even with Maram adding her horses to the string he led along and with me taking her by the hand, it was still a treacherous work to fight our way through the gorge. And a slow one. With the day beginning to wane and no sign of our friends, it seemed that they might be travelling quickly enough to outdistance us.

And then, as we came out of a particularly narrow and deep part of the gorge, we turned into a place where the stream's banks suddenly widened and were covered with trees. And there, behind two great cottonwoods, with a clear line of sight straight toward us, Surya and the other Manslayer stood pointing their drawn arrows at our faces. Their horses, and those of our friends, were tethered nearby.

Then Surya, a high-strung and wiry woman, gave a shout, saying, 'It's all right – it's only Lord Valashu and our Lady!'

Surya eased the tension on her bow and stepped out from behind the tree, and so did the other Manslayer, whose name proved to be Zoreh. And then from behind trees farther up the gorge, Master Juwain, Liljana, Daj and Estrella appeared, and called out to us in relief and gladness.

'The battle has been won!' I called back to them as they hurried along the stream toward us. 'The Red Knights will not pursue us here!'

Daj let loose a whoop of delight as he came running down the stream, dodging or jumping over stones with the agility of a rock goat. A few moments later, Estrella threw her arms around me, and pressed her face against my chest. Liljana came up more slowly. She took in the blood on our armor and garments. She gazed at my face and said, 'You are burnt, as from fire.'

Her gaze lowered to fix upon my sheathed sword, and she slowly shook her head.

Because Surya and Zoreh were staring at me, too, I gave them a quick account of the battle. I said nothing, however, of my sword's burning or my failure to kill Morjin.

'We must go, then,' Surya told us. 'Six of our sisters are dead, and we must go.'

She turned to Atara and gazed at her blindfolded face as if trying to understand a puzzle. Then she embraced her, kissing her lips. 'Farewell, my imakla one. We shall all sing to the owls, that your other sight returns soon. But if it does not, who will care for you? Must you go off with these kradaks?'

'Yes, I must,' Atara told her, squeezing my hand in hers.

'Then we shall sing to the wind, as well, that fate will blow you back to us.'

And with that, she and Zoreh gathered up their horses and turned to begin the walk back down the gorge. We watched them disappear around the rocks of one of its turnings.

We decided to go no farther that day. We were all too tired, from battle and from too many miles of hard traveling. Surya had found a place that we could defend as well as any. Four archers, I thought, firing arrows quickly at the bend where the gorge narrowed behind us, could hold off an entire company of Red Knights. We had here good, clear water, even if it was little more than a trickle. Above the stream, the ground between the trees was flat enough to lay out our sleeping furs in comfort. There was grass for the horses, too, and plenty of deadwood for a fire.

Despite our exhaustion, we fortified our camp with stones and a breastwork of logs. Liljana brought out her pots to cook us a hot meal, while Atara and Estrella took charge of washing the blood from our garments in the stream and mending them in the places where an arrow or a sword had ripped through them. We gathered around the fire to eat our stew and rushk cakes in the last hour of the day. But here, at the bottom of the gorge where the stream spilled over rocks, it was already nearly dark. The sunlight had a hard time fighting its way down to us, and the walls of the gorge had fallen gray with shadow.

Although we had much to discuss and I desired Kane's counsel, this ancient warrior stood alone behind the breastwork gazing

71

down the stream in the direction from which our enemies would come at us, if they came at all. His strung bow and quiver full of arrows were close at hand as he ate his stew in silence.

'Ah, what *I* would most like to know,' Maram said as he licked at his lips, 'is what will become of Morjin?'

He sat with the rest of us around the fire. From time to time, he poked a long stick into its blazing logs.

'Unless he bled to death, which seems unlikely,' Master Juwain said, 'he will recover from his wound. A better question might be: what *has* become of him? If Val is right that it really *was* Morjin.'

'It *must* have been Morjin,' I said. 'Changed, somehow, yes. He is something more . . . and something less. There was something strange about him. But I know it was he.'

'Unless he has an evil twin, it was he,' Maram agreed.

'But how do we really know that?' Master Juwain asked. 'He is the Lord of Illusions, isn't he? Perhaps he has regained the power to put into our eyes the same images with which he fools other people.'

Liljana shook her head at this. 'No, what we faced earlier was no illusion. Morjin's mind is powerful – so horribly powerful, as none know better than I. But he cannot, from hundreds of miles away in Argattha, cast illusions that fool so many through the course of an entire battle. And he cannot have fooled me.'

'No,' I said, fingering my cloak, spread out on a rock near the fire to dry. I had felt the blood from Morjin's severed arm soak into it, and the red smear of it still stained the collar. 'No, he has a great strength now. I felt this in his arms, when we were locked together sword to sword.'

'Could this not, then, have been the *old* Morjin drawing strength from the Lightstone?' Master Juwain asked. 'And drawing from it as well the means to deceive you about his form?'

'No,' I said, touching the hilt of my sword, 'I *know* that he has lost the power of illusion over me. And the Lightstone is all beauty and truth. There is nothing within it that could help engender illusions and lies.'

For the span of a year, after my friends and I had rescued the Lightstone out of Argattha, the golden bowl had been like a sun showering its radiance upon us. I missed the soft sheen of it keenly, nearly as much as I did my murdered family. Since the day that Morjin had stolen it back, I had known no true days, only an endless succession of moments darkened as when the moon eclipses the sun.

'Then,' Master Juwain sighed out, 'we have dispensed with several hypotheses. And so we must consider that Morjin has indeed found a way to rejuvenate himself.'

'I didn't think the Lightstone had that power,' Maram said.

'Neither did I,' Master Juwain admitted.

'But what of the akashic crystal?' Atara asked. 'Was there no record within it of such things?'

Master Juwain sighed again as his face knotted up in regret. With the breaking in Tria of the great akashic crystal, repository of much of the Elijin's lore concerning the Lightstone, Master Juwain's hope of gaining this great knowledge had broken as well.

'There *might* have been such a record within it,' Master Juwain said. 'If only I'd had more time to look for it.'

'Then you don't really know,' Atara said, pressing him.

Master Juwain squeezed the wooden bowl of stew between his hands as if his fingers ached for the touch of a smoother and finer substance. 'No, I suppose I don't. But I spent many days searching through the akashic stone, following many streams of knowledge. One gets a sense of the terrain this way, so to speak. And everything I've ever learned about the Lightstone gives me to understand that it cannot be used to make one's body and being young again. In truth, it is quite the opposite.'

'What do you mean, sir?' I asked him.

'Consider what we *do* know about the Lightstone,' he said, looking at me and the others. 'Above all, that it is to be used by the Maitreya, and by him only. But used *how*? Of this, we still have barely a glimmer. "In the Shining One's hands, the true gold; in the Cup of Heaven, men and women shall drink in the light of the One." Indeed, indeed – but what does this really mean? We know that the Maitreya is thus to *help* man walk the path of the Elijin and Galadin, and so on to the Ieldra themselves, ever and always toward the One. And in so doing, the Maitreya will be exalted beyond any man: in grace, in vitality, in the splendor of his soul. But now let us consider what befalls when the Lightstone is claimed by one who is *not* the Maitreya. Let us consider Morjin. Clearly, he has used the Lightstone to try to gain mastery over all the other gelstei – even as he has tried to enslave men's souls and make himself master of the world. He searches for the darkest of knowledge! And so he holds in his hands not the true gold but something rather like a lead stone that pulls him ever and always down into a lightless chasm. And so he has utterly debased himself: in his body, in his mind, in his soul. He is immortal, yes, and so he cannot die as other men do. But we have all seen his scabrous flesh, the deadness of his eyes, the rot that slowly blackens his insides. All his lusting for the Lightstone and struggle to master it has only withered him. And so how can he use this cup to make himself young again?'

I considered long and deeply what Master Juwain had said as I looked through the fire's writhing flames and gazed at the darkening walls of the chasm called the Kul Kavaakurk. How close had *I* been to claiming the Lightstone for myself? As close as the curve of my fingers or the whispering of my breath – as close as the beating of my heart.

Maram cast a glance at the silent, motionless Kane standing like a stone carving above us, and he said, 'Didn't our grim friend tell us in Argattha that the Lightstone had no power to make one young again?'

I touched the hilt of my sword, and I recalled exactly what Kane had told us in Morjin's throne room when he stood revealed as one of the Elijin: that the Lightstone did not possess the power to bestow *immortality*. I told this to Maram, and to the others, who sat around the fire quietly eating their dinner.

Then Maram nodded at Master Juwain and said, 'Then it might be *possible* that Morjin has rejuvenated himself.'

'It is possible,' Master Juwain allowed. 'No *man* knows very much about the Lightstone.'

He looked up at Kane, and so did everyone else. But still Kane said nothing.

'We know,' Liljana said, 'that Morjin can draw a kind of strength from the Lightstone, as he does in feeding off others' fear or adulation – or even in drinking their blood. And so I suppose we must assume he has found a way to renew himself, if only for a time.'

'I suppose we must,' Master Juwain said with another sigh. 'Unless we can find another explanation.'

The fading sunlight barely sufficed to illuminate Kane's fathomless black eyes. He seemed, in silence, to explain to us a great deal: above all that the distance between the Elijin and mortal men was as vast as the black spaces between the stars. As always, I sensed that he knew much more than he was willing to reveal, about the world and about himself – even *to* himself.

'Ah, well,' Maram said, looking up at Kane, 'Morjin *fought* like a much younger man, didn't he? In truth, like no man I have ever seen except Val – or Kane. He has a *power* now that he didn't have in Argattha. Perhaps many powers. He pointed at Atara, and struck her blind!'

Atara paused in eating her stew to hold up her spoon in front of the white cloth covering her face. She said, 'But I am already blind.'

'You know what I mean.'

She brought out her scryer's sphere and sat rolling it between her long, lithe fingers. 'Morjin has power over my gelstei now, nothing more.'

'But your second sight –'

'My second sight comes and goes, like the wind, as it always has. Surely it was just evil chance, what happened on the battle-field.'

'Evil, indeed,' Maram said, looking at her. 'But what if it was more than chance?'

Atara shook her head violently. Then she clapped her hands over her blindfold and said, 'Morjin took my eyes and with them my first sight. Isn't that enough?'

Because there was nothing to say to this, we sat around the fire eating our stew. The knock and scrape of our spoons against our wooden bowls seemed as loud as thunder.

And then I took her hand and said to her, 'Please promise me that if the next battle comes upon us with the wind blowing the wrong way, you'll find a safe place and remain there.'

'I *should* have, I know,' she said to me, pressing her hand into mine. 'But I was sure that my sight would return, at any moment, so sure. Then, too, they were so many and we so few. I heard you calling out, to me it seemed. I thought you needed my sword.'

'I need much more than your sword,' I told her.

In the clasp of her fingers around mine was all the promise that I could ever hope for.

Maram, sitting nearby, cast us a wistful look as if he might be thinking of his betrothed, Behira. And he said, 'It vexes me what Morjin said about the Baaloch. Can it be true that he is so close to freeing Angra Mainyu?'

'He would lie,' I said, 'just to vex *me*. And to strike terror into *you*, and everyone else.'

'He would,' Master Juwain agreed. 'But as we have seen before, he has no need of lies when the truth will serve him better.'

'But how can we know the truth about this?' I asked. 'Didn't you once teach me that Morjin possessed the Lightstone for thirty years at the end of the Age of Swords? And then for nearly ten times as long when the Age of Law fell to the Age of the Dragon?

If he didn't free Angra Mainyu *then* why should we fear that he will *now*?'

'Because,' Master Juwain told me, 'that *was* then, and this is now. The first time he claimed the Lightstone, he used it in desperate battle to conquer Alonia. And the second time, to overthrow the order of the Age of Law, which everyone had thought eternal. Now that he has nearly conquered all of Ea, he will surely use it to bring his master here from Damoom.'

'If he can, he will,' I said, still not wanting to believe the worst. 'But why should we think that he can?'

Atara's hand suddenly tightened around mine as she said, 'But, Val, I have *seen* this, and have spoken of it before!'

What Atara had 'seen' we all knew to be true: that beneath the buried city of Argattha, far beneath the mountain, Morjin had driven his slaves to digging tunnels deep into the earth. And there, through solid rock, as with the lightning-like pulses that coursed along a man's nerves and through the chakras along his spine, ran the fires of the earth. Master Juwain called them the telluric currents. Their power was very great: if Master Juwain was right, the Lightstone could be used to direct them, as with the flames of a blacksmith's furnace, to touch upon the currents of the world of Damoom. And then the door behind which Angra Mainyu was bound, like an iron gate, might be burnt open. And then Angra Mainyu, the Dark One, would be set free from his prison and loosed upon Ea.

'Morjin is *close*,' Atara told me, 'so very close to cutting open the right tunnel. The *wrong* tunnel. Now that he has the Lightstone, it will be *months*, not years, before he sees clear where to dig.'

Daj, who had been a slave in the mines below Argattha's first level, nodded his head at this. 'It might be even sooner. I once heard Lord Morjin tell one of his priests that the Baaloch would be freed within a year. And that was *before* he took back the Lightstone.'

'Well, then, Morjin either was wrong or he lied,' Maram said to Daj. 'It's been more than a year since we freed *you* from Argattha.'

'Morjin didn't lie,' Liljana said, 'when I touched minds with him. He *couldn't* lie, then. He believes that he will free Angra Mainyu, and soon.'

Master Juwain rubbed at the back of his bald head as he told us: 'It has been a year and a half since we took the Lightstone out of Argattha. And in that time, Morjin must have lain long abed

76

recovering from the first wound that Val dealt him. And then, many months planning and leading the invasion of Mesh. And now –'

'And now,' Maram said hopefully, 'we've tempted him out of Argattha, along with the Lightstone no doubt, and so we've delayed the worst of what he can do yet again.'

'Perhaps,' Master Juwain said. 'But now that Val has wounded him again, he'll return to Argattha and to his greatest chance.'

'And that,' I said, looking up through the gorge at the mountains beyond, 'is why we must find the Maitreya, and soon.'

I felt my heart beating hard against my ribs. Would even the Maitreya, I wondered, be able to keep Morjin from using the Lightstone?

'Ah, well, even if we fail,' Maram said, 'must we give up all hope? If what we learned outside of Tria is true, then once before Angra Mainyu walked other worlds freely, and yet in the end was defeated. He is only one man, isn't he, even if he *is* one of the Galadin.'

At this, Maram looked hopefully toward Kane, for it had been Kane, long ago and on another world, who had immobilized Angra Mainyu so that the Lightstone might be wrested from him.

A light flashed in Kane's eyes as from far away. His gaze fell upon Maram. In a voice as harsh as breaking steel, he laughed out: 'Ha – only a man, you say! Only one of the Galadin, eh? Fool! What would you do if this *man* faced you upon the battlefield or came at you in a dark glade? Die, you would – of fright. And you would be fortunate to be dead. You have seen the Grays! They are terrible, aren't they? They nearly sucked out your soul, didn't they? And yet they are as children happily playing games in a flowered field compared to the one you speak of.'

'I wish I hadn't,' Maram said, pulling at the mail that covered his throat. '*Must* we really speak of this?'

'So, we *must* speak of it,' Kane growled out. His face had fallen fierce, like that of a tiger, and yet there was much in its harsh lines that was sad, noble and exalted. 'This one time we shall, and never again. I have heard and seen today too much uncertainty. And too much pity, for ourselves. Master Juwain has told of the fires of the earth, these telluric currents that our enemy seeks to wield. Val dreads the flames of his sword. Fire and flame – ha! I shall tell you of fire! There is that in each of us that must utterly burn away. Liljana's pride at besting Morjin: at least this one time. Maram's self-indulgence, Atara's desire to be made whole again,

77

and Val's rage for vengeance. So, and my own. The grief we all suffer from the poisoning of our gelstei. It is nothing. *We* are nothing. In the face of what comes, none of our lives matters. Except that we all *do* matter, utterly, and so long as we live and draw breath, everything that we do – every word, thought and act – must be keener and strike truer than even Val's sword. For if we fail, Morjin will use the Lightstone as we all fear and open the way to Damoom.'

As Kane spoke, he paced back and forth behind the log breastwork gripping his strung bow. His fierce eyes danced about, now flicking toward the bend in the stream, now falling upon us. From time to time, he scowled as he looked up at the darkening sky.

'And then,' he told us, '*he* will come, with fire. Who of us will be able to bear even the sight of him? For his eyes are like molten stone, his flesh is red as heated iron, his hair is a wreath of flames. His mouth opens like a pit of burning pitch that devours all things. Angra Mainyu, men call him now. He is the Baaloch, the Black Dragon – but stronger than any thousand dragons. Do you hate, Valashu? It is as a match flame compared to the roaring furnace inside Morjin – and that is nothing against the hell that torments Angra Mainyu, like unto the fire of the stars. For he has been denied the stars. Ages and ages, the Galadin have bound him in darkness on Damoom, he who was once the greatest of the Galadin, and the most fair. So. So. He will burn to take his vengeance upon Ashtoreth and Valoreth and all their kind. Ha, all *our* kind as well.

'Where will we be when Morjin delivers the cup into his hands? Wherever we are, even on the most distant isle across the seas, we will feel the earth shake and see clouds of smoke darken the air as the fire mountains burst forth. When Angra Mainyu lays grip upon Ea's telluric currents, he will not care if the very earth is riven in two. First he will free the others bound with him on his dark world: Gashur, Yurlungurr, Yama, Zun. A host of Galadin, and Elijin, too – those who still survive. They will follow in Angra Mainyu's train. He will take his first vengeance upon Ea and her peoples: we who have denied him the Lightstone for so long. In every land wooden crosses will sprout up like mushrooms. The Baaloch will breathe upon those to which Valari are nailed, and they will burst into flame. He will feast upon flesh, not as a lion upon lambs – not only – but as a master wears the sinews of his slaves down to the bone. All men will be his ghuls, ready to twitch or sing or mouth his thoughts, at his whim. When he has finished subduing Ea, not even a blade of grass will dare poke itself above the ground unless he wills it.

'And then he will turn his blazing eyes upon the heavens. They who follow him will lend him all their strength. Time nearly beyond reckoning they have had to prepare for such a day. Stars, beyond counting, they will claim. Then the Baaloch will seize the stellar currents, bound inside pure starfire. Ten thousand men, it's said, Morjin nailed to crosses in Galda. Ten thousand *worlds* will burn up in flame when Angra Mainyu makes war again upon Ashtoreth and Valoreth and the other Amshahs who still dwell across the stars on Agathad. But the Galadin are the inextinguishable ones, eh? Diamond will not pierce them, no fire can scorch them, nor age steal the beauty of their form. And so, as in ages past, ages *of* ages, Angra Mainyu will try to use the Lightstone to wrest the great fire, the angel fire, from the Ieldra themselves.'

Now Kane stood facing me, and he paused to draw in a deep breath. His eyes burned into mine as he said, 'But it is the Ieldra, not the Galadin – not even Angra Mainyu – who are given the power of creation. And so no Galadin has the power to *uncreate* any other. Angra Mainyu, though, will never believe this, just as he will not accept that any power might be beyond his grasp, not even the very splendor of the One. So. So. The Ieldra, at last, at the end of all things when time has run out and there is no more hope, will be forced to make war upon Angra Mainyu, lest the evil that he has unleashed upon Eluru spill over into other universes: those millions that exist beyond ours and those countless ones that are yet to be. But Angra Mainyu was the first of the Galadin, and the greatest, and so as long as the stars shed their light upon creation, he, too, cannot be harmed. Knowing this, the Ieldra will be forced to put an end to their creation. In fire the universe came to be, and in fire the universe and all within will be destroyed. And so Eluru, and all its worlds and beautiful stars, will be no more.'

Kane finished speaking and stood still again. For a moment, I could not move, nor could our other friends. Daj and Estrella, in their short years, had seen and heard many terrible things, but Kane's warning as to the horrible end of the War of the Stone seemed to strike terror into them. They sat next to each other, holding hands and staring at the stream. Above this pale water, Flick appeared, and the lights within his luminous pulsed as in alarm. Above him, the forbidding walls of the Kul Kavaakurk grew ever darker. Their exposed rock ran along the gorge, east and west, in layers. How long, I wondered, had it taken for the stream to cut down through the skin of the earth? Each layer, it seemed, was as a million years, and as the stream had cut deeper and deeper, the War had gone on, layer upon layer. And not just the War of the Stone, but the war of all life against life, to triumph and dominate, to be and to become greater. And not just on Ea or Eluru but in all universes in all times, without end. Were all peoples everywhere, I wondered, afflicted with war? Was it possible that all worlds and universes, as seemed the fate of ours, might be doomed?

It was Maram, the most fearful of us and consequently the most hopeful, who could not bear to think of such an end. He loved the pleasures of life too much to imagine it ever ceasing – even for others. And so he looked at Kane and said, 'But Angra Mainyu was defeated once, and so might be again. And it was *you* who defeated him!'

'No, it was not *I*,' Kane said as a strange light filled his eyes. 'And I've told you before, he was not defeated. From Damoom, he still works his evil on all of Eluru.'

'But he *was* bound there,' Maram persisted. 'And so might be again.'

'No, he will not be,' Kane told us. 'Once, on Erathe, on the plain of Tharharra long ago, there was a battle – the greatest of all battles. A host of the Amshahs pursued Angra Mainyu and his Daevas there. Ashtoreth and Valoreth forbade this violence, but Marsul and others of the Galadin would not heed them. And neither would Kalkin.'

Kane, who had once borne this noble name, stood up tall and straight as the light of the night's first stars rained down upon him.

'A hundred thousand Valari died that day,' Kane said to us. 'And as many of the Elijin. So, Elijin slaying Valari and other Elijin, against the Law of the One, and Galadin such as Marsul and Varkoth slaying all – this was the evil of that day. A victory Maram calls it! Ha! Many of the Amshahs fell mad after that. Darudin threw himself on his sword in remorse, and so with Odin and Sulujin and many others. But it is not so easy for the living to expunge the stain of such an atrocity, eh? Many there were who bore the shadow of Tharharra on their souls.'

Kane paused in his account of this ancient history before known history. He began pacing about like a tiger again in front of the fire, and his hand clenched and unclenched like a beating heart.

'And so,' he said, 'once a time the Amshahs came to Erathe;

they will not come to Ea, especially if the Baaloch and his Daevas are loosed upon it. The danger is too great. Ea is a Dark World, now – *almost* a Dark World. Here, Morjin turned from the fairest of men into the most foul. Here, even the brightest of the Amshahs might come under Angra Mainyu's spell, and how could the stars above us abide even one more fallen Galadin? And then, too, there is the Black Jade.'

Almost without thought, my hand fell upon my sword. Seven diamonds, like stars, were set into its hilt, carved out of true black jade, which might be dug up from the earth like any other stone. But the jade of which Kane spoke was the black gelstei, rarest of the rare, wrought in furnaces long ago from unknown substances and with an art long since lost. And not just *any* black gelstei.

Kane paused in his pacing to set his bow on top of the logs of the breastwork. Then he brought forth a flat, black stone, shiny as obsidian, and held it gleaming dully in the palm of his hand. And he said to us, 'This baalstei is small, eh? And yet the one that Kalkin used upon Angra Mainyu was no larger – in size. But it had great power, like unto the dark of the moon, for in it was bound all the blackness of space and the great emptiness that lies inside all things.'

He stood still for a moment as he stared up at the sky. Then he continued: 'You can't imagine its power, for in a way, the Black Jade is the Lightstone's shadow. I spoke of how the Ieldra might be forced to unmake the universe, but I say the Black Jade is the greater dread. For even men, such as Morjin, might use it to steal the very light from *this* world: all that is bright and good.'

Maram thought about this as he gazed at Kane. Then he asked him, 'But why didn't you tell us that the black gelstei you used on Angra Mainyu had power beyond any others?'

'Because,' Kane said, 'I didn't want to frighten you. So, I didn't want to frighten myself. To wield it was to touch upon a cold so terrible and vast that it froze one's soul in ice as hard as diamond. To wield it too *long* was to be lost in a lightless void from which there could be no escape. Angra Mainyu himself, early in the War of the Stone, forged this cursed stone we call the Black Jade. There will never be another like it. Long ago, it was lost. And so once the Baaloch is freed, no one will ever bind him again.'

Maram stood up from the fire to get a better look at the black crystal seemingly welded to Kane's hand. And he asked: 'If Angra Mainyu made the great baalstei, how did Kalkin come by it?'

'So, how *did* Kalkin come by it, eh?' Kane said. He spoke his ancient name as if intoning a requiem for a long lost friend. '*That* is a story that I won't tell here, unless you'd like to remain in this cursed gorge for a month, and then half a year after. Let's just say that the Lightstone wasn't the only gelstei that the Amshahs and the Daevas fought over.'

'But how was it lost, then?'

Kane clamped his jaws together with such force that I heard the grinding of his teeth. Then he said, 'That story is even longer. I can tell you only that Angra Mainyu's creatures regained it. Some say that it was brought to Ea, to await his coming.'

Again, I stared at the chasm's layers of rock, now nearly black with the fall of night. It seemed that in ages without end, on uncountable worlds, anything might happen – and almost everything had. It seemed as well that the folds of the earth might conceal many dark things, even one as dark and terrible as the ancient black gelstei.

Kane suddenly made a fist, and the small crystal seemed to vanish. When he opened his hand again, there was nothing inside it except air.

And I asked him, 'Do you believe the baalstei was brought to Ea?'

'Where else would it have been brought if not here?'

My mysterious friend, I thought, possessed all the evasive arts of a magician. Somewhere on his person, no doubt, he had secreted the black gelstei. Just as somewhere in his soul he kept hidden even more powerful things.

'You told us once,' I said to him, 'that the Galadin sent Kalkin to Ea. Along with Morjin, and ten others of the Elijin?'

Kane's eyes grew brighter and more pained as he said, 'Yes – Sarojin and Baladin, and the others. I have told you their names.'

'Yes, you have. But you haven't told us *why* you were sent here? Why, if Ea was so perilous for your kind?'

'It was a chance,' he said, looking up at the night's first stars. 'A last, desperate chance. The Lightstone had been sent here long before, and that was chance enough.'

And this supreme gamble on the part of Ashtoreth and the other Galadin on Agathad had nearly succeeded: Kalkin, in the great First Quest, had led the others of his order to recover the lost Lightstone. But then Morjin had fallen mad; he had murdered Garain and Averin to claim the Lightstone for himself. And Kalkin, in violation of the Law of the One, had killed five of Morjin's henchmen, and in a way, slain himself as well. Now only Kane remained.

'So, you see how it went for the Elijin who came to Ea,' Kane said. 'How much worse would it be for any Galadin to come to this cursed place?'

At this, Liljana's kind face tightened in anger. She patted the ground beneath her, and snapped at Kane: 'Such things you say! I won't listen to such slander! The earth is our mother, the mother of us all – even you!'

As Kane regarded Liljana, I felt a strange, cold longing ripple through him.

'Liljana is right,' Master Juwain said. 'You can't blame Ea for corrupting Morjin. Neither can you blame the black gelstei.'

And Kane said, 'The greatest of scryers foretold that Ea would give rise to a dark angel who would free the Baaloch.'

'Either that,' Master Juwain reminded him, 'or give birth to the last and greatest Maitreya, who will lead all Eluru into the Age of Light.'

For a moment, Kane stared down at his clenched fists. Then he looked at Master Juwain and said, 'I know you are right. It is not soil or even black gelstei that poisons men, but their hearts. What lies within.'

He reached down to scoop up a handful of dirt. He said to us, 'And that is the hell of it, eh? What being, born of earth, does not suffer? Grow old and die?'

'The Galadin do not,' I said to him.

'You think not, eh? So, the Bright Ones grow old in their souls. And in the end, it is their fate, too, to die.'

The brilliance of his eyes recalled the most beautiful, yet terrible, part of the Law of the One: that each of the Galadin, at the moment of a Great Progression, in the creation of a new universe, was destined to die into light – and thus be reborn as one of the numinous Ieldra.

'And as for suffering, Valashu,' he said to me, 'despite what *you* have suffered, you cannot know. How many times have you swatted a mosquito?'

For a moment, his question puzzled me. My skin fairly twitched as I recalled the clouds of mosquitoes that had drained my blood in the Vardaloon. And I said, 'Hundreds. Thousands.'

'Could you have killed them so readily if they had been human beings? Do you think they suffered as men do?'

I, who had already killed many tens of men with my bright sword, said, 'I know they did not.'

'Just so,' Kane said to me. 'The pain that men, women and children know, compared to that of the Galadin, is minuscule. And yet it is no small thing, eh? And *that* in the end, is what poisoned Angra Mainyu's sweet, sweet, beautiful heart.'

Kane's words were like a bucket of cold water emptied upon me. I sat by the fire, blinking my eyes as a chill shot down my spine. I said to him, 'I never thought to hear you speak such words of the Dark One.'

And he told me: 'Angra Mainyu was not always Angra Mainyu, nor was he always evil. So, he was born Asangal, the most beautiful of men, and when still a man, it is said that he loved all life so dearly that he would *not* swat mosquitoes. And more, that once he saw a dog in excruciating pain from an open wound being eaten with worms. Asangal resolved to remove the worms, but could not bear for them to die. And so he licked out the worms with his own tongue so as not to crush them, and he let them eat his own flesh.'

At this, Daj's face screwed up in disgust, and Maram shook his head. And Kane went on:

'Asangal so loved the world that he thought he could take in all its pain. But after he became an Elijin lord and then was elevated as the first of the Galadin, the pain became an agony that he could not escape. In truth, like a robe of fire, it drove him mad. He began to question the One's design in calling forth life only to suffer so terribly; as the ages passed into ages, it seemed to him particularly cruel that all beings should be made to bear such torment, only, at the end of it all, to die. Love thwarted turns to hate, eh?, for one of the Galadin no less than a man, and so it was with him. So, he began to hate the One. And in hating, he began to feel himself as other from the One and the Ieldra's creation, and so he damned the One and creation itself.

'And then, for the first time, a terrible fear seized hold of him. It gnawed at him, worse than worms of fire, for he knew that he had only damned himself. He could not bear to believe that he must someday die, as the Galadin do, in becoming greater. As the evil that he made inside his own heart worked at him, he could not bear to believe that *any* being, not the greatest of the Ieldra, not even the One, was greater than himself. For how could they be if they suffered to exist a universe as flawed and hurtful as ours? And so he resolved to gather all power to himself to remake the universe: in all goodness, truth and beauty, without suffering, without war, and most of all, without death. Toward this magnificent end, out of his magnificent love for all beings, or so he told himself, he would storm heaven and make war against the Ieldra, against all peoples and all worlds opposing him. So, even against the One.'

Kane stood closer to me now, looking down at me, and his face flashed with reddish lights from the fire's writhing flames.

'Do you see?' he said to me. 'It is possible to be *too* good, eh?'

'Perhaps,' I told him. I smiled, but there was no sweetness in it, only the taste of blood. 'But I'm in no danger of *that*, am I?'

'Damn it, Val, you might have *killed* Morjin!'

I stood up to face him and said, 'Yes, I might have. And what then? Would one of his priests have used the Lightstone to free Angra Mainyu anyway? Or might *I* have regained it – only to become as Morjin? And then, in the end, been made to free Angra Mainyu myself?'

'You ask too many questions,' he growled. He pointed at my sheathed sword. 'When you held the *answer* in your hand!'

My fingers closed around Alkaladur's hilt, and I said, 'Truly, I held *something* there.'

'Damn you, Val!' he shouted at me. 'Damn *you*! Would you loose the Baaloch upon us!'

I looked down to see Daj set his jaw against the trembling that tore through his slight body. Master Juwain's face had gone grave, and his eyes had lost their sparkle, and so it was with Maram and Liljana. It came to me then that our hope for fulfilling our quest hung like the weight of the whole world upon a strand as slender as one of Atara's blond hairs. In truth, it seemed that there was no real hope at all. And if that were so, why not just ask Master Juwain to prepare a potion for all of us that we might die, here and now, in peace? Was death so terrible as I had feared? Was it really a black neverness, freezing cold, like ice? Was it a fire that burned the flesh forever? Or was it rather like a beautiful song and the brightest of lights that carried one upward toward the stars?

No, I heard myself whisper. *No.*

I glanced at Estrella, who looked up at me in dread. And yet, miraculously, with so much trust. Her quick, lovely eyes seemed to grab hold of mine even more fiercely than Kane grasped my arm. So much hope burned inside her! So much life spilled out to fill up her radiant face! Who was I to resign myself and consign her to its ending? No, I thought, that would be ignoble, cowardly, wrong. For her sake, no less my own, I would at least act as if there somehow might be hope.

85

I said to Kane, 'Not even the greatest of scryers can see all ends.'

'So, I think you can see your *own* end. And long for it too much, eh?'

I shook my head at this, and told him, 'Last year, at the Tournament when Asaru lay abed with a wounded shoulder, King Mohan spoke these words to me: "A man can never be sure that his acts will lead to the desired result; he can only be sure of the acts, themselves. Therefore each act must be good and true, of its own."'

'A warrior's code, eh? Act nobly, always with honor, and smile at death, if that is the result. The code of the Valari.'

'Yes,' I said, 'better death than life lived as Morjin lives, or as one of his slaves.'

Kane regarded Daj and Estrella a moment before turning back to me. He said, 'But we're not speaking of the death of a lone warrior, or even an entire army, but that of the whole world and all that *is*!'

'I . . . know.'

'Do you really? What, then, *is* good? Where will you find truth? Do you know *that*, as well?'

'I know it as well as I can. Is it not written in the Law of the One?'

'So, so,' he murmured, glaring at me.

'Is it not written that a man may slay another man only in defense of life? And is it not also written that the Elijin may not slay at all?'

'So, so.'

'And yet you slay so *gladly*. As you would have had me slay Morjin!'

At this he gripped the hilt of his sword and smiled, showing his long white teeth. But there was no mirth on his savage face.

'You are one of the Elijin!' I said to him.

'No, Kalkin was of the Elijin,' he told me. 'I am Kane.'

I held out my hand to him and said, 'If I gave you this sword that is inside me, would *you* slay with it? What law for the valarda, then?'

'I . . . don't remember.'

His eyes smoldered with a dark fire almost too hot to bear. I felt his heart beating in great, angry surges inside him. It came to me then that there were those who could not abide their smallness, and they feared mightily obliteration in death. But those, like Kane, who turned away from their greatness dreaded even more the glory of life. How long had this ancient warrior stood alone in shadows and dark chasms, away from all others, even from himself? Was it not a terrible thing for a man to forget who he really was?

'I know,' I said to him, 'that the valarda was not meant for slaying.'

'So – you *know* this, do you?'

'Somewhere,' I said, 'it must be written in the Law of the One.'

Kane stared at me as through a wall of flame. His jaws clenched, and the muscles of his windburnt cheeks popped out like knots of wood. It seemed that the veins of his neck and face could not contain the bursts of blood coursing through him.

Then he whipped his sword from its sheath and shouted at me, 'Then damn the One!'

His words seemed to horrify him, as they did the rest of us. Daj sat looking at him in awed silence. Even Estrella seemed to wilt beneath his fearsome countenance.

Then Kane murmured, 'What I meant to say was that *Asangal* damned the One. Angra Mainyu did – do you understand?'

I looked down at my open hand. A bloody spike pierced the palm through the bones. The agony of this iron nail still tore through me, as did that of the other nails driven through my mother's hands and feet. And I said to Kane, 'Yes – I *do* understand.'

I felt the hard hurt of his sword pressing into his own hand. He did not want to look at me, but he could not help it. His eyes said what his lips would not: *I am damned. And so are you.*

'No, no,' I told him. I took a step closer and covered his hand with mine. 'Peace, friend.'

As gently as I could, I peeled back his fingers from his sword's hilt, then took it away from him. He stood like a stunned lamb as he watched me slide it back into its sheath.

'Valashu,' he whispered to me.

I clasped hands with him then, and stood looking at him eye to eye. His blood burned against my palm with every beat of his great, beautiful heart. Such a wild joy of life surged inside him! Such a brilliance brightened his being, like unto the splendor of the stars! What *was* the truth of the valarda, I wondered? Only this: that it was a sword of light, truly, but something much more. It passed from man to man, brother to brother, as the very stars poured out to each other their fiery radiance, onstreaming, shining upon all things and calling to that deeper light within that was their source.

'Kalkin,' I said to him, whispering his name. For a moment, as through veil rent with a lightning flash, I looked upon a being of rare power and grace. But only for a moment.

'No, no,' he murmured. 'You promised.'

'I am sorry,' I said.

'No, it is *I* who am sorry. What do I really know of the valarda, eh? Perhaps you were right to try to keep *that* sword within its sheath.'

His gaze, it seemed, tore open my heart. I said to him, 'If Angra Mainu is defeated, I do not believe that it will be by my hand, or yours, or even that of Ashtoreth and Valoreth.'

'Perhaps you are right. Perhaps.'

'And so with Morjin.'

'So, so.'

'Only the Maitreya,' I said, 'can keep him from using the Lightstone. And I do not believe I will ever be allowed to lay eyes upon this Shining One if I use the valarda to slay.'

Then he smiled at me, a true smile, all warm and sweet like honey melting in the sun. 'So, there will be no slaying tonight, let us hope. Peace, friend.'

He stepped back over to the breastwork and picked up his bow again. His smile grew only wider as his eyes filled with amusement, irony and a mystery that I would never quite be able to apprehend.

After that it grew dark, and then nearly as black as a moonless eve, for here at the bottom of the gorge, there was very little light. Its towering walls reduced the heavens to a strip of stars running east and west above us. But one of these stars, I saw, was bright Aras. After all the work of washing the dishes and settling into our camp was completed, with Atara singing Estrella to sleep and Kane standing watch over us, I lay back against my mother earth to keep a vigil upon this sparkling light. It blazed throughout the night like a great beacon, and I wondered how this star of beauty and bright shining hope could ever be put out.

6

I did not welcome my awakening the next morning. My battle wounds – mostly bruises from edged weapons or maces that had failed to penetrate my mail – hurt. The cold wind funneling down the gorge set my stiff body to shivering, and that hurt even more. No ray of sun warmed the gorge directly for the first few hours of the day, as we ate our breakfast and broke camp with a slowness and heaviness of motion. All of us, except Kane, perhaps, were exhausted. It would have been good to remain there all day before a crackling fire, eating and resting, but we needed to gain as much distance as we could from the gorge's entrance at the gateway to the Wendrush. And so we loaded our horses and drank one of Master Juwain's teas to drive the weariness from our bodies. Then we set forth into the gorge, winding our way around walls of naked rock deeper into the Kul Kavaakurk's shadows.

As we kicked our way over the rattling stones along the riverbank, I looked back behind us often and listened for any sign of pursuit. I sniffed at the cool air and reached out with a deeper sense, as well. I heard water rushing along its course and smelled spring leaves fluttering in the wind, but the only eyes upon us were those of the squirrels or the birds singing in the branches of the gorge's many trees. No one, it seemed, followed us. Nothing sought to harm us. The only enemy we faced that morning, I thought, dwelled within. The horror of what lay behind us in the previous day's butchery haunted all of us, even those who had not actually witnessed the battle. We feared what lay ahead in the vast unmapped reaches of the lower Nagarshath. Fear, in truth, was the worst of all our inner demons, for who among us did not gaze up at the sky and wonder if the Dark One could devour the very sun?

It was after dinner that evening when Maram finally let fear take hold of him. He rose up from the campfire to tend his horse's bruised hoof, or so he said. But I followed him and found him in the stand of trees where the horses were tethered, rummaging through the saddlebags of Master Juwain's remount. Quick as a weasel stealing eggs, he prized out a bottle of brandy and uncorked it. I ran over to him and slapped my hand upon his wrist with such force that I nearly knocked the bottle from his hand. And I shouted at him, 'What of your vow?'

And he shouted back at me, 'What of *your* vow, then?'

I clamped my fingers harder around his massive wrist as he struggled to bring the mouth of the bottle up to his fat lips. And I asked him, 'What vow?'

'Ah, what you said when we first met, that ours would be a lifelong friendship. What kind of friend keeps his friend from drinking away his pain?'

'The kind who would keep him from a greater pain.'

'You speak as if we have endless moments left to us.'

'Our whole lives, Maram.'

'Yes, our whole lives, as long as they will be. But how long *will* they be? Didn't you hear *anything* of what was said last night? Months we have, until Morjin frees Angra Mainyu, perhaps only days. And so why not allow me what little joy I can find in this forsaken place?'

I let go his arm and stood facing him. 'Drink then, if that is what you must do!'

'I shall! I shall! Only, do not look at me like that!'

I continued staring through the twilight into his large, brown eyes.

'Ah, damn you, Val!' he said more softly. 'I'll do what *I* want, do you understand? What *I* choose. And what I choose now is *not* to drink after all. You've ruined the moment, too bad.'

So saying, he put the cork back in the bottle and sealed it with an angry slap of his hand. He tucked it back into Master Juwain's saddlebag. Then he stood beneath the gorge's towering wall staring at me.

Our shouts drew the others. They stood around us in a half-circle as Maram said, by way of explanation, 'All that talk last night of Angra Mainyu and worlds ending in fire – it was too much!'

Kane eyed the poorly tied strings of the saddlebag but did not comment upon them. Then he said, 'Perhaps it *was*.'

There was a kindness in his voice that I had heard only rarely.

His black eyes held Maram in the light of compassion, and that was rarer still.

'There are only six of us against Morjin and all his armies!' Maram cried out. 'Eight, if we count the children! How can we possibly keep the Dragon at bay while we find the Maitreya?'

'We were one fewer,' Kane said, 'when we found our way into Argattha.'

'But Morjin is stronger now, isn't he? I *saw* this. So damn strong. And there is Angra Mainyu, too.'

Kane regarded him as a deep light played in his eyes. And then he snarled out, 'Strong, you say? Ha, they are weak!'

His words astonished us. I stared at him as I shook my head. He was a man, I thought, who could hold within fierce contradictions, like two tigers in rut locked inside the same small cage.

'So, weak they are,' he growled out again. 'Who are the strong, then, the truly powerful? They who follow the Law of the One, even though their faithfulness leads to their death. They who bring the design of the One into its fullest flowering, for in creation lies true life. But Morjin and his master create nothing. They fear everything, and their own feebleness most of all. So, fearing, thus they hate, and in hating chain themselves to all that is hateful and foul. Daj escaped from Argattha, Estrella, too, but how can the two Dragons ever break free from the hellhole that they have made for themselves with every nail they have pounded into flesh and every eye they have gouged out? From the very chains that they have forged to make themselves slaves? So. So. Knowing this, they would cloak their slave souls in royal robes and seek to conquer others, as proof of their power over life – and death. But the truly free can never be conquered, eh? At least not conquered in *their* souls. The stars can all die, their radiance, too, but *not* the light of the One. It is *this* that terrifies Angra Mainyu, and Morjin, too. And that is why, in the end, we'll win.'

His words stunned Maram more than they soothed him. But for the moment, at least, they drove back the demons that impelled him to find solace in his brandy bottle. He stood proud and tall staring at Kane, transformed from a drunkard into a Valari knight. And he said, 'Do you really think we can win?'

'So, we *must* win – and so we will.'

Kane, I thought, understood the nature of evil better than any man. But it was the nature of evil, the truly horrible thing about it, that understanding alone would not keep evil from devouring a man alive.

'We *will* win,' Master Juwain affirmed, looking at Maram, 'so long as we do not let down our guard. Have you been practicing the Light Meditations?'

'Ah, perhaps not as often as I should,' Maram said.

'Well, what about the Way Rhymes, then? Memorizing them would be a better balm than brandy.'

'Ah, I'm too tired, and it's too late. My brain aches almost as much as my poor body.'

'Then I'll prepare you a tisane that will wake you up.'

'Ah, what if I don't want to wake up?'

Master Juwain rubbed the back of his shiny head as he regarded Maram. He seemed at a loss for words.

It was Liljana who came to his rescue. She waggled her finger at Maram, then poked it below his ribs as she said, 'How many nights have *I* stayed up cooking and cleaning so that *you* might go to bed with a full belly? Master Juwain has asked you to memorize his verses, and so you should, for *our* sakes, if not your own.'

Everyone looked at Maram then, and he held up his hands in defeat – or in victory, depending on one's point of view.

'All right, all right,' he said, 'I'll learn these silly rhymes, if that's what you all want. It will easier than everyone nagging me all the time.'

Master Juwain's smile lasted only as long as it took Maram to add, 'I'll begin tomorrow, then.'

Kane suddenly took a step closer to him and stood staring at him like a great cat tensing to spring. I knew that he was only testing Maram, and would never lay hands upon him. Maram, however, was not so sure of this.

'All right, all right,' he said again with a heavy sigh. He turned to Master Juwain. 'What verses for tonight, then?'

At Master Juwain's prompting, I heard Maram recite:

At gorge's end, a wooded vale . . .

And so it went as we returned to our places around the fire and drank the spicy teas that Master Juwain made for us. It was much to his purpose that we should learn the Way Rhymes, too, and so we took turns intoning the verses and correcting each other when we made mistakes. We did not continue our practice quite as long as Master Juwain might have wished, for we all *were* quite tired. But when it came time to retire for the night, we took the words into sleep, and perhaps into our dreams. And that was a good thing, I thought, for the essence of the Way Rhymes was the promise that if a man took one step after another, in the right direction, he would always reach his journey's end.

The next day dawned clear, as we could tell from the band of blue that slowly brightened above us. We continued our long walk through the gorge, over loose stone and through stands of cottonwood trees that gradually showed a sprinkling of elms and oaks the deeper we penetrated into the White Mountains. Twenty miles, at least, we had travelled since our battle with Morjin and his Red Knights. None of us knew the length of the Kul Kavaakurk, for Master Juwain's rhymes did not tell of that. But here, deep in this cleft in the earth, where the wind whooshed as through a bellows' funnel and tore at our hair and garments, the gorge seemed to go on and on forever.

And then, abruptly, as we rounded yet another bend in the stream, the gorge opened out into a broad valley. A forest covered its slopes, gentle and undulating to the north but still quite steep to the south of the river. For the first time in two days, we had all the sun we could hope for; its warm rays poured down upon rock, earth and leaf, and filled all the great bowl before us. Smaller mountains, cloaked in oak and birch with aspens and hemlock higher up, edged the rim of this bowl; beyond rose the great white peaks of the Nagarshath. The valley continued along the line of the gorge, toward the west, and it seemed that our course should be to follow the river straight through it. But there were other exits from the valley that we might choose: clefts and saddles between the slopes around us, through which smaller streams flowed down into the river. Any one of these, I thought, might lead us up toward the Brotherhood's school, though the way would obviously be difficult and dangerous.

'Well,' Master Juwain said to Maram as we walked out into the valley, 'what is our way?'

And Maram recited:

> At gorge's end, a wooded vale;
> Its southern slopes show shell-strewn shale.
> Toward setting sun the vale divides;
> To left or right the seeker strides.
> Recall the tale or go astray:
> King Koru-Ki set sail this way.

Maram stood next to his horse licking his lips as he glanced to the left. He said, 'Ah, who devised these rhymes, anyway? "Its

93

southern slopes sow hell-strewn shale." Now there's a tongue-twister for you! I can hardly say it!'

'But it's not so hard!' Daj said, laughing at him. Then quick as a twittering bird, he piped out perfectly:

Its southern slopes show shell-strewn shale.

Master Juwain beamed a smile at him and patted his head. And then he said to Maram, 'The Rhymes aren't supposed to be easy to *say* but to memorize – hence the rhythm and rhyme. The alliteration, too.'

'Well, at least I *did* memorize it,' Maram said. 'Little good that it would do me if you weren't here to interpret for us.'

The Way Rhymes, of course, might be meant to be easy to memorize, but they were designed so that only the Brotherhood's adepts and masters might resolve them correctly. Thus did the Brotherhood guard its secrets.

'Come, come,' Master Juwain said to him. 'These lines are as transparent as the air in front of your nose.'

Maram pointed at the turbulent water rushing past us and muttered, 'You mean, as clear as river mud.'

'What don't you understand? Clearly, we've passed the Ass's Ears and the Kul Kavaakurk, and have come out into this valley, as the verse tells. Look over there, at the rock! Surely that is shale, is it not?'

We all looked where he pointed, across the river at the nearly vertical slopes to the south of us. The rock there was dark, striated and crumbly, and certainly appeared to be shale.

'I'm sure you're right,' Maram said to him. 'You know your stones. But does it bear *shells*? Who would want to cross the river to find out?'

Kane coughed out a deep curse then, and mounted his horse. He drove the big bay out into the river, which looked to be swift enough to sweep a man away but not so huge a beast. In a few mighty surges, his horse crossed to the other bank and soaked the stone there with water running off his flanks. Kane then rode up through the trees a hundred yards before dismounting and making his way up the steep slope on foot. We saw him disappear behind a great oak as he approached a slab of shale.

'He's as mad as Koru-Ki himself,' Maram said, watching for him. 'He'd cross an ocean just to see what was on the other side.'

A few moments later, Kane returned as he had gone, bearing a huge smile on his face.

'Well?' Maram said. 'Did you see any of these shells-in-shale?'

'Many,' Kane told him as his smile grew wider.

'I don't believe you – you're lying!'

'Go see for yourself,' Kane said, pointing across the river.

'Do you think I won't?' Maram eyed the swift water that cut through the valley and shook his head. 'Ah, perhaps I won't, after all. It's enough that *one* of us risked his life proving out those silly lines. You *did* see shells, didn't you? She sells? I mean, *sea* shells?'

'I've told you that I did. What more do you want of me?'

'Well, it wouldn't have hurt to bring back one of these shelled rocks, would it?'

Kane laughed at this and produced a flat, thick piece of slate as long as his hand. He gave it to Maram. All of us gathered around as Maram stared at the grayish slate and fingered the little, stone-like shells embedded within it.

'Impossible!' Maram said. 'I saw shells like these on the shore of the Great Northern Sea!'

'But then how did they get into this rock?' Daj asked him.

Kane stood silently staring at the rock as the rest of us examined it more closely. Not even Master Juwain had an answer for him.

'Perhaps,' Atara said, 'there really *was* once a great flood that drowned the whole world, as the legends tell.'

Kane's black eyes bored into the rock, and he seemed lost in endless layers of time. He finally said to us, 'So, the earth is stranger than we know. Stranger than we *can* know. Who will ever plumb all her mysteries?'

'Well,' Maram said, hefting the rock and then tucking it into his saddlebag, 'this is one mystery I'll keep for myself, if you don't mind. If I ever return home, I can show this as proof that I found *sea* shells at the top of a mountain!'

I smiled at this because it was not Maram who had found the rock, nor had it quite been taken from a mountain's top. It cheered me to know, however, that he still contemplated a homecoming. And so he held inside at least some hope.

'Your way homeward,' Master Juwain said to him, 'lies through this valley. Are we agreed that we must traverse it?'

'Toward the setting sun,' Maram said, pointing to the west. 'But I can't see if the valley truly divides there.'

I stood with my hand shielding my eyes as I peered up the

valley. It seemed to come to an end upon a great wedge of a mountain rising up to the west. But it was a good thirty miles distant, and the folds and fissures of the mountains along the valley's rim blocked a clear line of sight.

'Then let us go on,' Atara said, 'and we shall see what we shall see.'

A faint smile played upon her lips, and it gladdened my heart to know that she could joke about her blindness. Then she mounted her horse and said, 'Come, Fire!' She guided her mare along the strip of grass that paralleled the river, and it gladdened me even more to see that her second sight had mysteriously returned to her.

And so we followed the river into the west. It was a day of sunshine and warm spring breezes. Wildflowers in sprays of purple and white blanketed the earth around us where the trees gave way to acres of grass. It seemed that we were all alone here in this quiet, beautiful place. Our spirits rose along with the terrain, not so high, perhaps, as the great peaks shining in the distance, but high enough to hope that we might have at least a day or two of surcease from battle and travail.

And so it came to be. We made camp that first night in the valley on some good, grassy ground above the river. While Kane, Maram and I worked at fortifying it, and Liljana, Estrella and Daj set to preparing our dinner, Atara went off into the woods to hunt. Fortune smiled upon her, for she returned scarcely an hour later with a young deer slung across her shoulders. That night we made feast on roasted venison, along with our rushk cakes and basketfuls of raspberries that Estrella found growing on bushes in the woods. Master Juwain chanted the Way Rhymes to Maram, and later Kane brought out the mandolet that he had inherited from Alphanderry. It was a rare thing for him to play for us, and lovely and strange, but that night he plucked the mandolet's strings and sang out songs in a deep and beautiful voice. He seemed almost happy, and that made me happy, too. Songs of glory he sang for us, tales of triumph and the exaltation of all things at the end of time. He held inside a great sadness, as deep and turbulent as oceans, and this came out in a mournful shading to his melodies. But there, too, in some secret chamber of his heart, dwelled a fire that was hotter and brighter than anything that Angra Mainyu could ever hope to wield. As he sang, this ineffable flame seemed to push his words out into the valley where they rang like silver bells, and then up above the snow-capped mountains through clear, cold air straight toward the brilliant stars.

With the making of this immortal music, Flick burst forth out of the darkness above the mandolet's vibrating strings. At first this strange being appeared as a silvery meshwork, impossibly fine-spun, with millions of clear tiny jewels like uncut diamonds sewn into it. Strands of fire streamed from these manifold points throughout the lattice, making the whole of his form sparkle with a lovely light. The longer that Kane played, the brighter this light became. I watched with a deep joy as the radiance summoned out of neverness many colors: scarlet and gold, forest green and sky blue – and a deep and shimmering glorre. And still Kane sang, and now the colors scintillated and swirled, then mingled, deepened and coalesced into the form and face of Alphanderry. And then our lost companion stood by the fire before us. His brown skin and curly black hair seemed almost real, as did his fine features and straight white teeth, revealed by his wide and impulsive smile. Even more real was his rich laughter, which recalled the immortal parts of him: his beauty, gladness of life and grace. Once before, in Tria, *this* Alphanderry, as messenger of the Galadin, had come into being in order to warn me of a great danger.

'Ahura Alarama,' I said, whispering Flick's true name. And then, 'Alphanderry.'

'Valashu Elahad,' he replied. 'Val.'

Kane stopped singing then, and put aside his mandolet to stare in amazement at his old friend.

'He speaks!' Daj cried out. 'Like he did in King Kiritan's hall!'

The boy came forward, and with great daring reached out to touch Alphanderry. But his hand, with a shimmer of lights, passed through him.

Alphanderry laughed at this as he pointed at Daj and said, 'He speaks. But I don't remember seeing him in King Kiritan's hall.'

So saying, he reached out to touch Daj, but his hand, too, passed through him as easily as mine would slice air. Then he laughed again as he turned toward Estrella. His eyes were kind and sad as he said, 'But the girl still doesn't speak, does she?'

Estrella, her eyes wide with wonder, spoke entire volumes of poetry in the delight that brightened her face.

'But where did you come from?' I asked Alphanderry. 'And why are you here?'

'Where did *you* come from, Val?' he retorted. 'And why are any of us here?'

97

I waited for him to answer what might be the essential question of life. But all he said to me was, '*I* am here to sing. And to play.'

And with that, he reached for the mandolet, but his fingers passed through it. It was as hard, I thought, for such a being to grasp a material thing as it was for a man to apprehend the realm of spirit.

'So,' Kane said, plucking the mandolet's strings, '*I* will play for you, and you will sing.'

And so it was. We all sat around listening as Kane called forth sweet, ringing notes out of the mandolet and Alphanderry sang out a song so beautiful that it brought tears to our eyes. The words, however, poured forth in that musical language of the Galadin that even Master Juwain had difficulty understanding. And so when Alphanderry finally finished, he looked at Master Juwain and translated part of it, reciting:

> *The eagle lifts his questing eye*
> *And wings his way toward sun and sky;*
> *The whale dives deep the ocean's gloom –*
> *Always seeking, always home.*
>
> *The world whirls round through day and night;*
> *All things are touched with dark and light;*
> *The dusk befalls on light's decay;*
> *The dying dark turns night to day.*
>
> *The One breathes out, creates all things:*
> *The blossoms, birds and star-struck kings;*
> *With every breath all beings yearn*
> *To sail the stars and home return.*
>
> *The dazzling heights light deep desire;*
> *Within the heart, a deeper fire.*
> *The road toward heavens' starry crown*
> *Goes ever up but always down.*

As Kane put down the mandolet, Alphanderry looked at Master Juwain and smiled.

'Am I to understand,' Master Juwain asked him, 'that these words were intended for me?'

It was one of the glories of Alphanderry's music that each person listening thought that he sang especially for him.

98

'Let's just say,' Alphanderry told him, 'that there might be a sentiment in this song that a master of the Brotherhood would do well to take to heart. Especially if that master guided his companions on a quest through the dark places in the world.'

'Were you sent here to tell me this?' Master Juwain asked him.

In answer, Alphanderry's smile only widened.

'Who sent you, then? Was it truly the Galadin?'

Now sadness touched Alphanderry's face, along with the amusement and a deep mystery. And he said to Master Juwain, and to all of us, 'I wish I could stay to answer your questions. To sing and laugh – and even to eat Liljana's fine cooking again. Alas, I cannot.'

He looked skyward, where Icesse and Hyanne and the other glittering stars of the Mother's Necklace had just passed the zenith. In that direction, I thought, lay Ninsun, the dwelling place of the Ieldra – and the light that streamed out of it in the glorre-filled rays of the Golden Band.

'But if you could remain only a few moments longer,' Master Juwain persisted, 'you might tell me if –'

'I can tell you only what I have,' Alphanderry said with a brilliant smile. And then he added:

> The road toward heavens' starry crown
> Goes ever up but always down.

He reached out to touch Master Juwain's hand, but this impulsive act served only to brighten Master Juwain's leathery skin, as with starlight. And then Alphanderry dissolved back into that brilliant whirl of lights we knew as Flick. Only his smile seemed to linger as Flick, in turn, vanished once again into neverness.

'Ah, how I *do* miss our little friend,' Maram said, staring at the dark air.

Kane, I saw, stared too, and his dark eyes wavered as if submerged in water.

'But I wonder what he meant,' Maram continued, turning to Master Juwain. 'His verses are even more a puzzlement that your Way Rhymes.'

Master Juwain held his hands out to the hissing fire. His fingers curled as if grasping at its heat.

'It is possible,' he finally said, 'that Alphanderry sang verses of the true Way Rhymes.'

'The *true* Rhymes?' Maram said.

'Perhaps I should have said, "the deeper Rhymes". The higher ones. Just as there are verses that tell the way to many places on Ea, there are those that describe man's journey toward the One.'

He went on to explain that the path to becoming an Elijin, and so on toward the Galadin and Ieldra, was almost infinitely more difficult than merely finding the Brotherhood's secret sanctuary.

'Our order,' Master Juwain explained, 'has spent most of ten thousand years trying to learn and teach this way. But we have understood only little, and taught less. The Elijin surely know, the Galadin, too. But they do not speak to us.'

Everyone looked at Kane then. But he sat by the fire as cold and silent as stone.

'At least,' Master Juwain went on, 'the angels do not speak to *us*, we of Ea. Surely on other worlds, they share with the Star People and the eternal Brotherhood the songs that I have called the true Way Rhymes.'

'Why are *they* so favored, then?' Maram asked, looking up at the sky.

'It is not that they are favored,' Master Juwain told him. 'It is rather that we, of Ea, are not. You see, the true Way Rhymes are perilous to hear. Consider the lesser Rhymes I've taught you. If learned incorrectly or in the wrong order, they could lead one off the edge of a cliff. This is even more pertinent of the higher Rhymes that would guide a man on the journey to becoming an Elijin, or an Elijin to becoming a Galadin.'

The fear that flooded into Maram's face recalled the fall of Angra Mainyu – and that of Morjin.

'I notice that you say, "guide a *man* on this journey",' Liljana carped at Master Juwain. Her voice was as sharp as one of her cooking knives.

'It was a figure of speech,' Master Juwain told her. 'Of course women must walk the same path as men.'

'Oh, *must* we, then?' Liljana's soft face shone with the steel buried deep inside her. Then she added, 'You mean, walk behind men.'

'No, not at all,' Master Juwain said. 'You are to be by our sides.'

'How gracious of you to accept our company!'

Master Juwain rubbed the back of his neck as he sighed out, 'I meant only that our way lies onward, together.'

'Oh, does it really?'

Liljana moved closer to Master Juwain and knelt by his side. She placed her thumb against the tips of her other fingers and held them cocked and pointing at him. From deep inside her throat issued a hissing sound remarkably like that of an adder. And then, quick as any viper, she struck out with a snap of her arm and wrist, touching her pointed fingers against the lower part of Master Juwain's back.

'Your way, I think,' she said to him, 'is that of the serpent.'

'And your way is not?'

'There are serpents and there are serpents,' she told him. 'Ours is of the great circle of life, and we name her Ouroboros.'

What followed then, as the fire burnt lower and the night darkened, was a long argument as to the different paths open to man – or to woman. Liljana spoke of the sacred life force that dwelled inside everyone, and of the arts that the Maitriche Telu had found to quicken and deepen it. Master Juwain's main concern was of transcendence and the way back toward the stars. I did not pretend to follow all the turnings of their contentions and justifications, for there was much in what they said that was esoteric, legalistic and even petty. I understood that their dispute went back to the breaking of the Order of Sisters and Brothers of the Earth long ago in the Age of the Mother. And like siblings of the same family who had set out on different paths in life, they quarreled all the more fiercely for sharing a mutual language and deep knowledge of each other. Both spoke of the serpent as the embodiment of life's essential fire. Both taught the opening of the body's chakras: the wheels of light that whirled within every man, woman and child. But each put different names to these things and understood their purpose differently.

Master Juwain, noticing how closely Daj followed their argument, turned to him to explain: 'We of the Brotherhood teach the way of the Kundala. At birth, it lies coiled up inside each of us. There is a Rhyme that tells of this:

> *Around the spine the serpent sleeps.*
> *Within its heart a fire leaps.*
> *The serpent wakes, remembers, yearns –*
> *And up the spine, like fire, it burns.*
>
> *And through the chakras, one by one,*
> *Until it blazes like the sun,*
> *And then bursts forth, a crown of light:*
> *An angel soars the starry height.*

101

'This is man's path,' he said to Daj, 'and it is a straight one, though difficult and perilous. Seven bodies we each possess, corresponding to each of the seven chakras along the spine, and they each in turn must awaken.'

At this Daj's eyes widened, and he looked down at his slender hand as he patted his chest. He said, 'How can we have more than *one* body?'

Master Juwain smiled at this and said, 'We have only one *physical* body, it's true. But we have as well the body of the passions, associated with the second chakra, which we call the svadhisthan, and the mental body as well.'

'I never knew they were called "bodies". It sounds strange.'

'But you understand that a boy could never become a man until they are fully developed?'

In answer, Daj rolled his eyes as if Master Juwain had asked him the sum of two plus two.

Master Juwain, undeterred, went on: 'I'm afraid that most men do not progress beyond these three bodies, nor do they ever develop them fully. The physical body, for instance, can be quickened so as to heal any wound, even regenerating a severed limb. It is potentially immortal.'

At this, we all looked at Kane. But he said nothing, and neither did we.

'But what is the fourth body, then?' Daj asked him.

'That is our dream body, also called the astral. It is the bridge between matter and spirit, and it is awakened through the anahata, the heart chakra.'

So saying, Master Juwain reached over and laid his gnarly hand across Daj's chest.

'Then, higher still,' he went on, 'there is the etheric body, which forms the template for our physical one and our potential for perfection, and then the celestial. There lies our sixth sight, of the infinite. The highest body is the ketheric, associated with the sahastara chakra at the crown of the head.'

Here Master Juwain stroked Daj's tousled hair and went on to say that each of the bodies emanated an aura of distinctive color: red from the first chakra, orange from the second and so on to the sixth chakra, which radiated a deep violet light. The highest chakra, when fully quickened, poured forth a fountain of pure white light.

At this, Daj exchanged smiles with Master Juwain and recited:

And through the chakras, one by one,
Until it blazes like the sun,
And then bursts forth, a crown of light:
An angel soars the starry height.

'Yes, that is way of it,' Master Juwain said as his voice filled with excitement. 'When we have fully awakened, every part of us, the Kundala streaks upward and joins us to the heavens like a lightning bolt. And then as angels we walk the stars.'

Liljana scowled at this as she eyed Master Juwain's hand resting on top of Daj's head. Then she huffed out, 'The serpent does not so much break through as to light up our being from within. And then, when we have come fully alive, like our mother earth turning her face to the sun, we can drawn *down* the fire of the stars.'

Here she sighed as she shot Master Juwain a scolding look and added, 'And as you should know, the serpent's name is Ouroboros.'

She went on to tell of this primeval imago, sacred to her order. Ouroboros, she said, dwelled inside each of us as a great serpent biting its own tail. This recalled the great circle of life, the way life lived off of other life, killing and consuming, and yet continuing on through the ages, always quickening in its myriads of forms and growing ever stronger. Ouroboros, she told us, shed its skin a million times a million times, and was immortal.

'There is in each of us,' she said, 'a sacred flame that cannot be put out. It is like a ring of fire, eternal for it is fed by the fires of both the heavens *and* the earth. And our way must be to bring this fire into every part of our beings, and so into others – and to everything. And so to awaken all things and bring them deeper into life.'

So far, Atara had said very little. But now she spoke, and her words streaked like arrows toward Master Juwain and Liljana, and were straight to the point: 'Surely the spirit of Alphanderry's song was that both your ways are important, and indeed, in the end, are one and the same.'

Kane smiled at this in an unnerving silence.

And Maram willfully ignored the essence of what Master Juwain and Liljana had to say, muttering, 'Ah, I've never understood all of this damn snake symbolism. Snakes are deadly, are they not? And the great snakes – the dragons – are evil.'

Master Juwain took it upon himself to try to answer this objection. He rubbed the back of his bald pate as he said, 'Snakes are deadly only because they have so much power in their coils, and therefore life. And the dragon we fought in Argattha *was* evil, as are all beings and things that Morjin and Angra Mainyu have corrupted. But the dragon itself? I should say it is pure fire. And fire might be used to torture innocents as well as to light the stars.'

I thought his answer a good one, but Maram said, 'Well, I for one will never like those slippery, slithering beasts. Whether they be found in old verses and books, or in long grass beneath the unwary foot.'

Liljana shot him a sharp look and said, 'You're just afraid of them, aren't you?'

'Well, what if I am?'

'Your fear does neither you nor the rest of us any good. Perhaps if you had spent more time practicing Master Juwain's lessons and moving into the higher chakras, you wouldn't be as troubled as you are.'

'But I thought you scorned Master Juwain's way?'

'Scorned? I can't afford such sentiments. We *do* disagree about certain things, that's all.'

The Sisters of the Maitriche Telu, as I understood it, also taught the quickening of the body's chakras, but they numbered and named these wheels of light differently: Malkuth, Yesod, Tiphereth and seven others. Strangely, Liljana called the highest chakra, Keter, which corresponded almost exactly with the Brotherhood's ketheric body, associated with the crown chakra at the top of the head.

'You dwell too often,' Liljana told Maram, 'in the first chakra, in fear of your precious life. This impels a movement into the second chakra, in a blind urge to beget more life. And there, as we've all seen, you dwell *much* too often and wantonly.'

'Ah, well, what if I do?' Maram snapped at her.

Master Juwain, allying himself for the moment with Liljana, added to her criticism, saying, 'Such indulgence fires your second chakra at the expense of the others and traps you there. It leaves you vulnerable to lust – and to drunkenness and the other vices that aid and abet it.'

Maram cast his gaze toward the horses, where the brandy was safely stowed within the saddlebags. He licked his lips and said, 'Ah, that's what I can't *stand* about the Brotherhood and all your ways. You're too damn dry. With your damn dry breath you'd blow out the sweetest of flames in favor of lighting these higher torches of yours. And why? So you can spend your days – and nights – in anguish over a transcendence that may never come?

104

That's no way to live, is it? If I had a bottle in hand, I'd make a toast to drunkenness in the sweet, sweet here and now – and a hundred more to lust!'

Again he eyed the saddlebags as if hoping that Master Juwain or I might retrieve a bottle and rescue him from his vow. And then he shook his head and muttered, 'Well, if I can't drink to what's best in life, I'll sing to it. Abide a moment while I make the verses – abide!'

Here he held out his right hand as he placed his other hand over his closed eyes. His lips moved silently, but from time to time he would call out to us, 'Abide, only a few moments more – I almost have it.'

As Kane heaped a couple more logs on the fire, we all sat around listening to its crackle and hiss, and looking at Maram. At last he took his hand away from his thick brows and looked at us. He smiled hugely. And then he rose to his feet and rested his hands on his hips as he stared at Master Juwain and called out in his huge, booming voice:

> The higher man seeks higher things:
> Old tomes, bright crystals, angel's wings.
> He lives to crave and pray accrue
> The good, the beautiful, the true.
>
> And there he slithers, coils and dwells
> In higher hues of higher hells;
> In sixth or seventh wheels of light –
> There's too much pain in too much sight.
>
> But 'low the belly burns sweet fire,
> The sweetest way to slake desire.
> In clasp of woman, warmth of wine
> A honeyed bliss and true divine.
>
> I am a second chakra man;
> I take my pleasure where I can;
> At tavern, table and divan –
> I am a second chakra man.

As Maram sang out these verses, and others that flew out of his mouth like uncaged birds, he would strike the air with his fist and then lewdly waggle his hips at each refrain. He finally finished and

105

stood limned against the fire grinning at us. No one seemed to know what to say.

And then Kane burst out laughing and clapped his hands, and so did we all. And Atara said to him, 'Hmmph, if you had remained with the Kurmak and taken wives as my grandfather suggested, these second chakra powers of yours would have been put to the test.'

'How many wives, then?'

'Great chieftains take ten or even twenty, but it's said that only a great, great man such as Sajagax could satisfy them.'

Here she smiled at Liljana, who added, 'Our order has discovered that when a woman awakens the Volcano, which we call Netzach, it would take ten or twenty *men* to match her fire.'

'Do you think so?' Maram said with a wink of his eye and yet another gyration of his hips. 'I should tell you that my, ah, *greatness* has never thoroughly been put to the test. Perhaps I'm a fool for even considering marriage with Behira only and cleaving to Valari customs.'

'Would you rather try our Sarni ways?' Atara asked him.

'In this one respect, I would. I'd take twenty wives, if I could. And I would, ah, entertain all of them in one night.'

'*My* tribemates?' Atara said. 'They would kill you before morning.'

'So you say.'

Atara laughed out, 'And you would have them call you "Twenty-Horned Maram" I suppose?'

'Just so, just so. It would create a certain curiosity about me, would it not?'

'That it would. And you'd be happy satisfying this curiosity with other women who *weren't* your wives, wouldn't you?'

'Ah,' he said with a rumble of his belly and a contented belch, 'at least *someone* understands me.'

'I understand that if you practice your ways on the women of *my* tribe, their husbands and fathers will draw their swords and make you into *No*-Horned Maram.'

In the wavering firelight, Maram's happy face seemed to blanch. And he muttered, 'Well, I don't suppose I'd make a very good Sarni warrior. I'll have to practice on other women I meet along the way.'

Atara fingered the saber by her side. And this fierce young maiden told him, 'If you must – but just don't think of practicing on *me*.'

At this, Maram held up his hands in helplessness as if others were always conspiring to think the worst of him. His gaze fell upon Liljana, who said to him, 'I should warn you that if you brought your horns to a practiced matron of the Maitriche Telu, she *would* likely kill you – with pleasure. Perhaps you'll find a nice harridan somewhere in these mountains.'

The ghostly white peaks of the Nagarshath gleamed faintly beneath the stars. It seemed that there were no other human beings, much less willing women, within a thousand miles.

'Maram would do better,' Master Juwain said, 'to practice the Rhymes I've taught him. Now, why don't we all retire and get a good night's sleep? Tomorrow we'll journey up this valley and see what lies at the end of it.'

He smiled at Maram and added, 'Tell me, again, won't you, the pertinent Rhyme?'

And, again, Maram dutifully recited:

> *At gorge's end, a wooded vale;*
> *Its southern slopes show shell-strewn shale.*
> *Toward setting sun the vale divides;*
> *To left or right the seeker strides.*
> *Recall the tale or go astray:*
> *King Koru-Ki set sail this way.*

Except for Kane, who took the first and longest of the night's watches, we all wrapped ourselves in our cloaks and lay down on our sleeping furs. Maram spread out next to me, and I listened to him intoning verses for much of the next hour. But they were *not* those that Master Juwain hoped for. I smiled as I drifted off to sleep with the sound of my incorrigible friend chanting out:

> *I'm a second chakra man*
> *I take my pleasure where I can . . .*

7

The river wound through woods and meadows, and I couldn't help thinking of it as a mighty brown snake. No great rocks or other obstacles blocked our way. The ground was good here, easy on the horses' hooves, and provided all the fodder they needed to carry us higher into this beautiful country. By noon, the place where the valley came up against the mountain at its end was clearly visible; by late afternoon we reached the divide told of in the Way Rhyme. To the left of the mountain, the valley split off toward the south. And to the right was a great groove in the earth running between the rocky prominences north of us.

We all sat on our horses as we considered the next leg of our journey. Master Juwain, upon studying the lay of the land, turned to Daj and said:

> Recall the tale or go astray:
> King Koru-Ki set sail this way.

'Well, young Dajarian – which way is that?'

And Daj told him: 'North, I think. Didn't King Koru-Ki set out to find the Northern Passage and the way to the stars?'

'You know he did,' Liljana said to him. 'Didn't I teach you that the ancients believed that the waters of all worlds flow into each other? And that there is a passage to other worlds at the uttermost north of ours?'

As Daj looked at Liljana, he slowly nodded his head.

'Very good, then,' Master Juwain said. He smiled at Maram. 'We'll turn north, tomorrow – are we agreed?'

'Ah, we were agreed before we reached this place. *This* Rhyme, at least, was easy to unravel.'

'Indeed it was. But the Rhymes grow more difficult, the nearer we approach our destination. Let's make camp here tonight and ponder them.'

And so we did. That evening, after dinner, I heard Maram repeating the verses to the Way Rhymes as well as those of his epic doggerel that he insisted on adding to. Over the next few days, as we continued our journey, the Way Rhymes, at least, guided us through the maze of mountains, valleys and chasms that made up this section of the lower Nagarshath. Through forests of elm and oak, and swaths of blue spruce, we rode our horses up and up – and then down and down. But as the miles vanished behind us, it became clear that our way wound more up than down, and we worked on gradually higher. Each camp that we made, it seemed, was colder than the preceding one. On our fourth day after the King's Divide, as we called it, it rained all that afternoon and turned to snow in the evening. We spent a miserable night heaping wood on the fire and huddling as close to its leaping flames as we dared, swaddled in our cloaks like newborns. The next day, however, the sun came out and fired the snow-dusted rocks and trees with a brilliance like unto millions of diamonds. It did not take long for spring's heat to melt away this fluffy white veneer. We rode up a long valley full of deer, voles and singing birds, and we basked in Ashte's warmth.

And then, just past noon, we came upon a landmark told of by the Rhymes. Master Juwain pointed to the right as he said, 'Brother Maram, will you please give us the pertinent verses?'

And Maram, making no objection to being so addressed, said:

> Upon a hill a castle rock,
> Abode of eagle, kite and hawk.
> From sandstone palisades espy
> A tri-kul lake as blue as sky.

As Altaru lowered his head to feed upon the rich spring grass blanketing the ground, I sat on top of his broad back and stroked his neck. And I gazed up at the hill under study. A jagged sandstone ridge ran along its crest up to some block-like rocks at the very top, giving it the appearance of a castle's battlements.

'This is surely the place,' Maram said, holding his hand against his forehead. 'But I see no eagles here.'

And then Daj, who had nearly the keenest eyes of all of us,

pointed to the left of the hill at a dark speck gliding through the air and said, 'Isn't that a hawk?'

And Kane said, 'So, it is, lad – and a goshawk at that.'

'If I were an eagle,' I said, looking at the crags around us, 'I think I would make my aerie here.'

'If you were an eagle,' Maram told me, pointing to the north, 'you wouldn't have to climb that hill to spy out the terrain beyond it, as the verse suggests.'

'You mean, *we* wouldn't have to climb it, don't you?'

'I? I?' Maram said. He rested his hands upon his belly and looked at me. 'Surely you're not suggesting that I dismount and haul my poor, tired body up that –'

'Yes, I am.'

'But such ascents were made for eagles or rock goats, not bulls such as I.'

'Bulls, hmmph,' Atara said from on top of her horse. 'You eat enough for an elephant.'

Maram ignored this jibe and said to me, '*You* are the man of the mountains.'

'Yes,' I said, 'and so I'll go with you. And then *you* can recite for me the next verse.'

Maram sighed at this as he grudgingly nodded his head. We decided then that Maram, Master Juwain and I would climb the hill while Liljana and the others worked on preparing lunch for our return.

Our hike up the hill proved to be neither as long or arduous as Maram feared. Even so, he puffed and panted his way up a deer trail and then cursed as he nearly turned an ankle on some loose rocks in a mound of scree. To hear him grunting and groaning, one might have thought he was about to die from the effort. But I was sure he suffered so loudly mainly to impress me. And to remind both him and me of the great sacrifices that he was willing to make on my behalf.

At last, we gained the crest, where the wind blew quickly and cooled our sweat-soaked garments. We stood resting against the sandstone ridge that topped it. We looked out to the northwest, where a great massif of snow-covered peaks rose up along the horizon like an impenetrable white fortress. But between there and here lay a country of rugged hills and lakes that pooled beneath them. All of them were blue. Which one might be the lake told of in the Rhyme, I could not say.

'A tri-kul lake,' Maram intoned, looking out below us. 'Very well, but what is that? A "kul" is a pass or a gorge, and I can't say that any of these lakes is surrounded by three such, or even one.'

'Are you sure the verse told of a *tri*-kul lake?' Master Juwain asked him.

'Are you saying I misheard the Rhyme?'

'Indeed you did. The word in question is *drakul*.'

'But why didn't you correct me before this?'

'Because,' Master Juwain said, 'I wanted to give you a chance to puzzle through the Rhymes yourself. Our goal will never be won through memory alone.'

'But what is a drakul, then? I've never heard of such a thing.'

'Are you sure? Think back to your lessons in ancient Ardik.'

'Do you mean, try to remember lessons in that dry, dry tongue that I tried to forget, even years ago?'

Master Juwain sighed and rubbed his head, now covered with a wool cap. And he said, 'Why don't you give me the next verses, then? How many times have I told you that clues to a puzzle in one verse might be found in those before or after it?'

'Very well,' Maram said. And he dutifully recited:

> *The Lake's two tongues are rippling rills*
> *That twist and hiss past saw-toothed hills;*
> *A cold tongue licks the setting sun,*
> *But your course cleaves the shining one.*

'No, no,' Master Juwain said to him. 'You've misheard the final line here, too. It should be: "Your course cleaves the *shaida* one".'

'Shaida?' Maram called out. His great voice was sucked up by the howling wind. 'But what is that?'

'Think back on your lessons – do you not remember?'

'No.'

Master Juwain dragged his fingernails across the rough sandstone beneath his hand, then turned to me. 'Val, do *you* remember?'

I thought for a moment and said, 'Shaida is a word from a much older language that was incorporated into ancient Ardik, wasn't it? Didn't it have something to do with dragons?'

Master Juwain smiled as he nodded his head. And then here, at the top of this windy hill, where hawks circled high above us, he took a few minutes to repeat a lesson that he must have taught us when we were boys. Two paths, he told us, led to the One. The first path was that of the animals and growing things, and it was a simple one: the primeval harmony of life. The second path,

111

however, was followed only by man – and the dragons. Only these two beings, Master Juwain said, pitted themselves against nature and sought to dominate or master it: man with all his intelligence and yearning for a better world and the dragon with pride and fire. Indeed, because men forged iron ore into steel ploughshares or swords and wielded the coruscating fury of the firestones themselves, our way also was called the Way of the Dragon. It was a hard way, perilous and cruel, for it led to war and discord with the world – and seemingly even with the One. But out of such strife, Master Juwain claimed, like the great Kundalini working his way up through the chakras, would eventually emerge a higher harmony.

'The Star People surely know a paradise that we can only imagine, the Elijin and Galadin, too,' Master Juwain told us. 'That is, they would if not for Angra Mainyu and those who followed him. Their way, I'm afraid, is still our way, and we call it the Left Hand Path.'

Here he nodded at Maram. 'And now you have all the clues you need to unlock these verses.'

Maram thought for a long few moments, pulling at his beard as he looked out at the blue sky and the even bluer lakes gleaming beneath it. And then he pointed west at the longest of them and said, 'All right, then, surely we are to espy a *drakul* lake, and of all these waters, only that one looks very much like a dragon – or a snake. And, see, two streams lead down into it, or rather away from it, past those saw-toothed hills. They *do* look something like tongues, I suppose. And so I would say that we're to follow the southernmost stream, to the left.'

'Very good,' Master Juwain said, nodding his head. 'I concur.'

Our course being set, we hiked back down the hill and sat down to a lunch of fried goose eggs and wheat bread toasted over a little fire. Then we checked the horses' loads and led them around the base of the hill topped by the castle rock. We worked our way through thick woods, and up and down the ravines that grooved the hill's slopes. Finally we came out into the valley of the lakes on the other side. We made camp that evening in clear sight of the dragon lake to the west of us. Its two tongues, of dusk-reddened water, caught the fire of the setting sun.

It took us most of the next day to reach this lake, for we had to forge on past other hills, lakes and ground grown boggy from all the water that collected here. But reach it we did, and we began our trek through the dense vegetation of its southern shore. We paused for the night in a copse of great birch trees. We smelled the faint reek of a skunk and listened to the honking of the geese and the beating wings of other waterfowl out on the lake. The next day we walked on until we came to the stream told of in the Rhymes. We followed this rushing rill toward its source, south, and then curving west and north. The hills around us grew ever higher. In this way, over the next two days, we made a miles-wide circle and came up behind the great massif that we had sighted from the sandstone castle. And then, as the Rhymes also told, we came upon a road that snaked back and forth still higher, winding up through barren tundra toward what seemed a snow-locked pass between two of the massif's mountains.

'Ah, I don't like the look of this,' Maram said as we stood by our horses looking up at the white peaks before us. 'It's too damn high!'

'But we don't have to go *over* the pass,' Daj said, 'just through it.'

'I don't care – it's still too high. It will be cold up there, cold enough to freeze our breath, I think. And what if there are bears?'

He went on complaining in a like manner for a while before he turned his disgruntlement to the road we must follow up to the heights. It was an ancient road and seemed once to have been a good one, built of finely-cut granite stones taken from the rock around us. Some of these stones, though worn, were still jointed perfectly. But time and ice and snow had riven many of the stones and reduced the road in places to no more than a path of rubble. Below us the road simply vanished into a wall of forest and the dark earth from which it grew. We could detect no sign of where this road might come from. Above us the road led on: through the mountains, we hoped, and straight to the Brotherhood's secret school.

'Well, I suppose we should camp here for the night,' Maram said.

'No, I'm afraid we must go up as high as we can,' Master Juwain told him, pointing at the great saddle between the two mountains. 'You have the verses – give them to me, please.'

Maram nodded grudgingly, then recited:

> *Approach the wall round Ashte's ides –*
> *There wait till dark of night subsides;*
> *If sky is clear, at day's first light*
> *Go deep into a darker night.*

113

'But we *have* approached the wall!' Maram said to Master Juwain.

'Not close enough. The essence of these verses, I think, is that we must be ready to move quickly at the right moment. Now let us go on.'

And so we did. Our slog up the road was long and hard, though not particularly dangerous. As Maram had worried, it grew colder. The road passed through a swath of pines and broke out from treeline into tundra. Ragged patches of snow blanketed the side of the mountain and covered the road in several places. We had to break through the crust and work against the snow's crunching, cornlike granules. Our feet, even through our boots, smarted sharply and then grew numb. The wind drove at us from the west in cruel, piercing gusts. But the sky, at least, was a great, blue dome and remained perfectly clear in all directions. And the sun comforted us for while – until it dropped behind the sharp-ridged peaks of the mountains farther to the west. Then it grew truly cold, enough to ice our sweaty garments and find our flesh beneath them. By the time we set to making camp at the crest of the road, we were all miserable and shivering.

Maram pointed at the pass, where the road disappeared into a dark tunnel cut through the white wall above us. And he said, 'We would be warmer if we slept inside *there*.'

'We would,' Daj agreed, 'but the Rhyme says that we're supposed to wait out *here*.'

'The damn Rhymes,' Maram muttered. 'They make no sense.'

'But that's just it,' Daj said, 'we're supposed to make sense *of* them.'

Atara began unloading some faggots of wood from one of the packhorses, and she said to Maram, 'It *would* be warmer in the tunnel. If there are any bears on this mountain, I'm sure they've made lair there.'

'Bears?' Maram said. 'No, no – surely they've come out of their winter sleep and have gone down to feed on berries or trout. Surely they have. *They* at least have sense.'

He set to unloading wood and building a fire with a fervor that kept away his gut-churning fear of bears. But he must have remembered the great white bear that had attacked us on a similar pass in the Morning Mountains – as did Master Juwain and I. We said nothing of this maddened animal that Morjin had made into a ghul, for we did not wish to frighten the children, or ourselves. I prayed that no ghul-bears – nor snow tigers nor any other beasts directed by Morjin – would find us here. It was enough that we still had to fight our way through this rugged terrain and through the Rhymes that were our map to it.

We sat for most of the night by the fire. The ground here was too steeply sloped and rocky for reclining, and too cold, too. And so we made cushions of our sleeping furs and huddled together with our cloaks thrown over us as a sort of woolen tent. Estrella sat between me and Atara, and fell asleep with her head resting against my side. Maram's back pressed firmly, and warmly, against my own. In this way, we propped each up and kept away the worst of the cold.

I slept only a little that night, and Master Juwain and Kane did not sleep at all. At times, in low voices, they discussed the meaning of the Way Rhymes; at other times they sat in silence as they looked up at the stars. I kept watch on these bright points of light as best I could. But I must have dozed, for I awakened in the deep of night to the weight of Kane's hand gently shaking my shoulder. He stood above me uncloaked, and he pointed up at the constellations spread across the heavens.

'Look, Val,' he murmured. 'The Ram is about to set.'

In the biting cold, we roused the others and broke camp. This required little more work than heaping a few handfuls of snow upon the fire's coals and tying our rolled-up sleeping furs to the backs of the horses. We breakfasted on some battle biscuits and a little cold water to wash them down. And then we waited.

As the last stars of the Ram set behind the western horizon, a faint light suffused the world and touched the mountains around us with an eerie sheen. At a nod from Master Juwain, we lit the torches that we had readied for this moment. And then without wasting another breath, we set out up the road and into the tunnel.

None of us knew what we would find there. The tunnel's starkness and long straight lines were almost a disappointment. The road through it seemed good and solid, and the horses' hooves clopping against the paving stones sent echoes reverberating up and down around us. The light cast by our oily torches showed a tube seemingly melted through the mountain's rock. The curving walls and ceiling above us gleamed all glassy and black, like sheets of obsidian more than fused granite. Maram guessed that the Ymanir must have once burned this tunnel with great firestones, for those shaggy giants had once ranged through most of the White Mountains and had built through them underground cities, invisible bridges and other marvels. Surely, I thought, this tunnel must be one of them. As we made our way down its gentle slope, I could see no end to it. Who but the Ymanir, I wondered, could carve a miles-long tunnel out of solid rock?

'How I *do* miss Ymiru,' Maram called out into the cold, still air. 'He was a broody man, it's true, but the only one I've ever known bigger and stronger than I. A great companion, he was, too. If *he* were here, I'm sure he could explain the mystery of this damn tunnel and what we'll find when we come out on the other side.'

'But we have the Rhyme for that,' Master Juwain said to him. 'Why don't you recite it?'

'Ah, *you* recite it,' Maram said to him. 'My head has never worked right at this accursed hour.'

'All right,' Master Juwain told him. And then he intoned:

> *And through the long dark into dawn,*
> *The road goes down, yet up: go on!*

'Shhh, quiet now!' Kane called out to us in a low voice. 'We know nothing about this place or what might dwell here.'

His words sobered us, and we moved on more quickly, and more quietly, too. It was freezing cold in this long tube through the earth, though mercifully there was no wind. After a few hundred yards or so we came upon yellowish bones strewn across the tunnel's floor and heaped into mounds. At the sight of them, Maram began shaking. The bones did not, however, look to be human; I whispered to Maram and the others that a snow tiger must have holed up here, dragging inside and devouring his kills. This did little to mollify Maram. As he walked his horse next to mine, he muttered, 'Snow tigers, is it? Oh, Lord, they're even worse than bears!'

The smell of the bones was old and musty, and I did not sense here the presence of snow tigers or any other beings besides ourselves. And yet something about this tunnel seemed strange, almost as if the melted rock that lined it sensed *our* presence and was in some way alive. As we moved farther into it, I felt a pounding from down deep, as of drums – but even more like the beating of a heart. I wondered, as did Master Juwain, if the tunnel's obsidian coating might really be some sort of unknown gelstei. All the gelstei resonated with each other in some way, however faint, and a disturbing sensation tingled through the hilt of my sword. It traveled up my arm and into my body, collecting in the pit of my belly where it burned. It impelled me to lead on through the smothering darkness even more quickly.

'Val,' Maram whispered to me through the cold air, 'I feel sick – like I did in the Black Bog.'

'It's all right,' I whispered back. 'We're nearly through.'

'Are you sure? How can you be sure?'

We journeyed on for quite a way, how far or how long I couldn't quite tell. Our torches burnt down and began flickering out, one by one. We had brought no oil with which to renew them. And then, at last, with the horses' iron-shod hooves striking out a great noise against cold stone, we sighted a little patch of light ahead of us. We fairly ran straight toward it. Our breath burst from our lungs, and the patch grew bigger and bigger. And then we came out of the tunnel into blessed fresh air.

We gathered on a little shelf of rock on the side of the mountain. A cold wind whipped at our faces. Spread out before us, to the north and east, was some of the most forbidding country I had ever seen. Far out to the horizon gleamed nothing but great jagged peaks covered with snow and white rivers of ice that cut between them. No part of this terrible terrain seemed flat or showed a spray of green.

'This *can't* be the Valley of the Sun!' Maram cried out. 'No one could live here!'

In truth, even a snow tiger or a marmot would have had a difficult time surviving in this ice-locked land. Snowdrifts covered the road before us; this little span of stone seemed to dip down along the spine of a rocky ridge before rising again and disappearing into the rock and snow of another mountain.

'We must have made a mistake,' Maram said. 'Either that or the Rhymes misled us.'

'No, we made no mistake,' Master Juwain huffed out into the biting wind. 'And the Rhymes always tell true.'

And Maram said:

> And through the long dark into dawn
> The road goes down, yet up: go on!

'Well,' he continued, 'we went through that damn tunnel, and if we go on any farther, we'll freeze to death. There's nothing left of this road, and I wouldn't follow it if there were. And there are no more Rhymes!'

But there were. As Kane again warned Maram to silence, Master Juwain said, 'Yes, be quiet now – we have little time.'

And then he recited:

117

Through mountains' notch, a golden ray:
The rising sun will point the way.
Before this orb unveils full face
Go on into a higher place.

'Into *that*?' Maram cried out, pointing at the icy wasteland before us. 'I won't. We can't. And why should we hurry to our doom, anyway?'

'Shhh, quiet now,' Kane said to him. 'Quiet.'

He watched as Master Juwain lifted his finger toward two great peaks to the east of us. The notch between them glowed red with the radiance of the sun about to rise.

'*This* is why we were to come here near Ashte's ides,' Master Juwain said. 'You see, on this date, the declination of the sun, the precise angle of its rays as it rises . . .'

His voice died into the howling wind as the first arrows of sunlight broke from the notch and streaked straight toward us. So dazzling was this incandescence that we had to shield our eyes and look away lest we be struck blind.

'And so,' Master Juwain went on, 'the sun's rays should illuminate exactly that part of this land leading on to our destination. Let us look for it before it is too late.'

'I can't look for anything at all,' Maram said, squinting and blinking against the sun's fulgor. 'I can't see *anything* – it's too damn bright!'

'Hurry!' Liljana said to Master Juwain. She stood by her horse gripping its reins. 'If these Rhymes of yours have any worth, we must hurry. What did you say are the next verses? The last ones?'

And Master Juwain told her:

If stayed by puzzlement or pride
Let Kundalini be your guide;
But hasten forth or count the cost:
Who long delays is longer lost.

'The Kundala always rises,' Master Juwain said. 'Rises straight to its goal. But I can see no way to go up here, unless it is over the top of that mountain.'

Still shielding his eyes, he pointed straight ahead of us. And Liljana asked him, 'Are you sure you've remembered the verses correctly?'

'Are you sure your name is Liljana Ashvaran?'

118

I had rarely heard such peevishness in his voice – or pride. And then, as the sun pushed a little higher above the mountain's notch and flared even brighter, a sick look befell Master Juwain's face. I saw it drain the color from his skin, and so did Liljana.

'Well?' she said to him. 'What is it?'

And Master Juwain, who honored truth above almost all else, said, 'There is a *small* chance I may have rendered the lines inexactly. But it doesn't matter.'

'Oh, doesn't it? Why not, then?'

'The lines may have been:

> *If stayed by puzzlement or pride*
> *Let sacred serpent be your guide.*

He cleared his throat as he looked at Liljana, and said, 'To my order, of course, the sacred serpent and the Kundala are one and the same.'

'But what if the verses' maker knew the deeper way of things?' Liljana asked him. 'What if his sacred serpent was instead Ouroboros?'

'Impossible!' Master Juwain called out.

Now the sun had risen like a red knot of fire almost entirely above the notch. We could not look upon its blazing brilliance.

'Impossible!' Master Juwain said again.

He turned around toward the mountain behind us. Although the dawn was lightening it seemed to me to be growing only darker, for our hope of finding our way was quickly evaporating before the fury of the sun.

And then I heard Master Juwain whisper the words that Alphanderry had sung to us on a magical night:

> *The dazzling heights light deep desire;*
> *Within the heart, a deeper fire.*
> *The road toward heavens' starry crown*
> *Goes ever up but always down.*

'Back!' Master Juwain suddenly cried out. He pointed at the mouth of the tunnel and the snow of the mountain around it. The sun's fiery rays had set the whole of it to glowing. 'Back, now, before it's too late!'

He turned his horse to lead him into the tunnel. And Maram

shouted, 'Are you mad? It's black as night in there! I'm not going back inside unless we find a way to relight the torches!'

I reached out and snatched the reins of his horse from his hand, and followed after Master Juwain. Atara grabbed Maram's empty hand to pull him after us. Then, quickly, came Liljana, Estrella and Daj. Kane, as usual, guarded our rear.

And so we went back into the tunnel. The moment we set foot within, it came alive. The glassy walls glowed, changed color to a translucent white and then poured forth a milky light. It was more than enough with which to see. There were few features, however, to catch the eye. The tunnel's floor seemed the same cut-stone road that we had trod before. The air was cold, and lay heavy about us as we pushed on through this long scoop through the earth.

'Val, I feel sick!' Maram said to me. 'My head is spinning, as if I'd drunk too much wine.'

I felt as he did, and so did the others, although they did not complain of it. But there seemed nothing to do except to follow Master Juwain deeper into the cold air of this mysterious tunnel.

And then the air around us was suddenly no longer cold. The walls and ceiling seemed to pulse unnervingly, even if the light they shed was steady and clean. I looked back behind me to reassure Maram that everything would be all right. But even as I opened my mouth to speak to him, his form wavered and dissolved into a spray of tiny lights before coalescing and solidifying again.

'Oh, Lord!' Maram called out as he stared at me in amazement. 'Oh, Lord – let us leave this place as quickly as we can before we all evanesce and there's nothing left of us forever!'

Just then Altaru let loose a long, bone-chilling whinny. He shook his great head, struck stone with his hoof hard enough to send up sparks and then reared up and beat the air with his hooves. He nearly brained Master Juwain, and it was all I could do to hold onto his reins.

'Lo, friend!' I called to him as I stroked his neck. 'Lo, now!'

The other horses, too, began either to whinny or nicker in disquiet. And Kane called to me: 'Let's tie blindfolds around them as we did when we crossed the Ymanir's bridge over the gorge!'

And as he said, it was done. With our dread working at us like a hot acid, it did not take us long to cut some strips from a bolt of cloth and bind them over the horses' eyes.

After that, we moved on even more quickly. I tried not to look at Master Juwain's flickering form, nor that of Maram or the pulsing, hollowed-out walls of the tunnel. I pulled at Altaru's reins and concentrated on the rhythm of his hooves beating against stone. I tried to ignore those moments when this rhythm broke and my horse's great hooves seemed to beat against nothing more than air. I did not want to listen to Maram's complaint that he could find no sign of the bones that littered the tunnel near its entrance. For I had eyes, now, only for its exit. As this circle of light grew larger and brighter, we all broke into a run. Master Juwain was the first of us to breach the tunnel's mouth and step outside. I followed after him a moment later. And I cried out in awe and delight. The serpent, it seemed, had indeed swallowed its own tail. For spread out below us was *not* the rugged terrain and long road by which we had originally entered the tunnel but a beautiful green valley. And somewhere, perhaps near its center along the blue river below us, there must stand a collection of old stone buildings that would be the Brotherhood's ancient school.

8

For a long while, however, we stood on a mantle of ground near the tunnel's mouth looking in vain for this fabled school. Kane set out along the heights to our left to see what he could see, while Master Juwain picked his way along the rocks to our right. They returned to report that they could descry no sign of the school, or indeed, of any human habitation.

'Perhaps,' Master Juwain said, pointing at the folded, forested terrain below us, 'the school is hidden. The lay of the land might conceal it.'

'Then let us find a better vantage to look for it,' Kane said.

'As long as that vantage lies *lower* and not higher,' Maram said. 'It's damn *cold* on these heights.'

We began making our way down the rugged slope into the valley. We found a line of clear patches through the trees that might or might not have been part of an ancient path. After an hour, we came out around the curve of a great swell of ground, and we gathered on a long, clear ridge that afforded an excellent view of almost the entire valley. All we could see were trees and empty meadows and the river's bright blue gleam.

'Perhaps your Rhymes misled us after all,' Maram complained to Master Juwain.

Master Juwain's jaws tightened as he readied a response to Maram's incessant faithlessness. And then, from below us, through the trees, there came the faint sound of someone singing. I could make out a pleasant melody but none of the words. Although it seemed unlikely that an enemy would cheerfully alert us, Kane and I drew our swords even so.

A few moments later, a small, old man worked his way up the path into view. He wore plain, undyed woolens and leaned upon

122

a shepherd's crook as if it were a walking staff. I saw that he had the wheat-colored skin and almond eyes of the Sung. Long, thick white hair framed his wrinkled face. Despite his obvious age, he moved with the liveliness of a much younger man.

'Greetings, strangers!' he called to us in a rich, melodious voice. 'You look as if you've come a long way.'

His words caused Master Juwain to rub the back of his head as he scrutinized this old man. He said to him, 'A stranger's way is always long.'

'Unless, of course,' the old man said, smiling, 'he is no stranger to the *Way*.'

Now Master Juwain smiled, too, and he bowed to the old man. Having completed the ancient formula by which those of the Brotherhood recognize and greet others of their order in chance encounters in out of the way places, the two of them strode forward to embrace each other. Master Juwain gave his name and those of the rest of us. And the old man presented himself as Master Virang.

'You did well,' he told Master Juwain, bowing back to him, 'to find your way here. My brethren will be eager to learn why you have brought outsiders to our valley.'

He cast a deep, penetrating look at Kane and me, as we faced him with our swords still drawn. I had a sense that he could peel back the layers of my being and nearly read my mind. And Maram said to him, 'Then this *is* the Valley of the Sun? We weren't sure, for we saw nothing that looked like a school. You don't dwell underground, do you?'

He shuddered as he said this. Since the Ymanir, who might have carved the mysterious tunnel above us, had also built the under-ground city of Argattha in these same mountains, it seemed a likely surmise.

His question, though, made Master Virang smile. 'No, we are men, not moles, and so we dwell as most men do.'

'Dwell *where*, then?' Maram asked. 'I could swear that there isn't a hut or even an outhouse in all this valley.'

'*Could* you?'

Master Virang kept one of his hands inside his pocket as he looked at Maram strangely. Then he looked at me. The space behind my eyes tingled in a way that seemed both pleasant and disturbing. I found myself, of a sudden, able to make out the trees in the distance with a greater clarity. It was as if I had emerged from a pool of blurry water into cold, crisp air.

'Ah, I *could* swear it,' Maram muttered. 'We've looked every-where.'

'Indeed?' Master Virang asked. 'But did you look down *there*?'

So saying, he pointed the tip of his staff straight down the slope below us toward the most open part of the valley, where the river ran through its heart. The air overlaying this green, sunny land began to shimmer. And then I gripped my sword in astonishment, for out of the wavering brilliance a few miles away, along the banks of the river, many white, stone buildings appeared. So distinctly did they stand out that it seemed impossible we had failed to perceive them.

'Sorcery!' Maram cried out, even more astonished than I. He shook his head at Master Virang, and took a step back from him. 'You hide your school beneath the veil of illusion!'

Liljana, too, seemed disquieted by the sudden sight of the school – and even more so by Master Virang. In her most acid of voices, she said to him, 'We had not heard that the masters of the Great White Brotherhood had learned the arts of the Lord of Illusions.'

But Master Virang only matched her scowl with a smile. He said to her, 'To compel others to see what is not is indeed illusion, and that is forbidden to us, as it is to all men. But to help them appre-hend what *is* – this is true vision and the grace of the One.'

He bowed his head to Liljana and added, 'Our school is real enough, after all. You are tired and travel-worn – will you accept our hospitality?'

Although he posed this invitation as a question, politely and formally, there could be no doubting what our answer would be. All of us, I thought, bore misgivings as to how the Brotherhood's school had been hidden from us. Even more, though, we were curious to learn its secrets and ways.

And so Master Virang twirled his staff in his hand as he led us back along the path. He fairly jumped from rock to rock like a mountain goat. The rest of us, trailing our horses, moved more slowly. It took us most of the rest of the morning to hike down into the valley and to come out of the forest onto the school's grounds, laid out above the river. We walked through apple orchards, ash groves and rose gardens, and fields of rye, oats and barley. The Valley of the Sun was as warm and bright as its name promised, especially near the ides of Ashte with the full bloom of spring greening the land. A ring of great, white mountains entirely surrounded it and guarded it from the worst winds and snow.

This refuge deep within the Nagarshath range was nothing so

splendid and magnificent as the Ymanir's crystal city, Alundil, beneath the Mountain of the Morning Star. But it shone with a quiet beauty and was pervaded by a deep peace. It seemed to exist out of time and to take no part in the ways and wars of the world. We all sensed that it concealed ancient secrets. The two hundred or so Brothers who dwelled here worked hard but happily in getting their sustenance from the land. We passed these simple men dressed in simple woolen tunics, laying to in the fields with hoes or dipping candles or working hot iron in the blacksmith's shop. Others tended sheep in pastures on the hillsides or attended to the dozen other occupations necessary for the thriving of what amounted to a small town. But the Brothers' main occupations, as we would learn, remained the ancient disciplines, or callings, of the Great White Brotherhood. And each of these seven callings was exemplified by a revered master, and indeed, by the Grandmaster of the Brotherhood himself.

Master Virang, who proved to be the Meditation Master, helped us to settle into two of the school's guest houses just above the river. Liljana, Atara and Estrella took up residence in the smaller of them, while the rest of us set up in the other. There, in these steeply-roofed stone hostels that reminded me of the chalets of my home, we spent hours soaking our cold, bruised bodies in hot water and washing away the grime of our journey. It was good to put on fresh tunics, and even better to sit down to a hot meal. Master Virang saw to it that we were served chicken soup and fresh bread for lunch, and cheese and berries, too. He left us alone to eat these heartening foods, but then returned an hour later to spirit away Master Juwain to a private meeting with the Grandmaster.

What they discussed all during that long afternoon we could only wonder. Master Juwain rejoined us only at the end of the day, when we gathered with the entire community of Brothers for a feast in the Great Hall. We were so busy, however, exchanging pleasantries with the curious Brothers that Master Juwain could not find a moment to confer with the rest of us. His face seemed tight and troubled, and I wondered if the Grandmaster had given him ill tidings or perhaps had chastened him for leading our company here.

I did not have to wait long to find out the answers to these questions – and to others that vexed me even more sorely. After the feast, we were summoned to take tea with The Seven, as the Brotherhood's masters were called. On a clear, lovely night we adjourned to one of the nearby buildings. Here, from time to time, in a little stone conservatory, the Grandmaster came to dwell in solitude or sit with the Music or Meditation Masters, or others with whom he wished to speak. Indeed, the circular space where we met with them had much the air of a meditation chamber. White wool carpets and many cushions covered the floor across its length and breadth. Vases of fresh flowers had been set into recesses built into the walls. These curves of white granite were carved with various symbols: pentagram, gammadion and caduceus; sun and eagle, swan and star. In various places, some ancient artisan had chiselled the Great Serpent in the form of a lightning bolt – and of a dragon swallowing its tail. The twelve pillars supporting the dome above us also showed cut glyphs. The light from the room's many candles illumined the shapes of the Archer, Ram, Dolphin, and nine other signs of the zodiac. The dome itself was smooth and featureless save for twelve round windows letting in the light of the stars.

This radiance seemed to gather within the hollows of a goldish bowl, set upon a marble pedestal beneath the northernmost window. In size and shape, if not shimmer, the bowl seemed like unto the Lightstone itself. I sensed immediately that it must be a work of silver gelstei, for I felt the silustria of my sword fairly singing to it. It must be, I thought, one of the False Lightstones forged in the Age of Law. Once, in the Library of Khaisham, my friends and I had come across a similar vessel of silver gelstei, shaped and tinted *as* the Lightstone in a vain attempt to capture its powers. Like all the silver gelstei, though, this cup would resonate with the true gold, and so was still a very great treasure.

The conservatory's only items of furniture were three low tea tables, inlaid with tiny triangles of lapis, shell and jet, and set with little round tea cups. As my companions and I entered the room, the Grandmaster and his Brothers stood up from behind them to greet us. In Tria I had sat at table with kings, but these seven masters of the Great White Brotherhood seemed possessed of no less presence and authority.

Tallest of the Seven, and the most striking, was the Grandmaster himself. His name was Abrasax, but because the Brothers found it too much of a mouthful to address him as Grandmaster Abrasax, most of them called him, simply, Grandfather.

His age, I thought, was hard to tell. A corona of curly white hair covered his head and flowed in waves down his cheeks and chin to form a rather magnificent beard. His seamed and weathered skin made for rather a stark contrast with it, for it was as brown as a tanned bull's hide. According to Master Juwain, Abrasax's father had been a chieftain of the Tukulak tribe and his mother a Karabuk maiden taken captive as concubine. In Abrasax, I thought, gathered the comeliest features of both the Sarni and Karabuk peoples. He had the long, well-shaped head of the Sarni and a solid and symmetrical face. His muscular hands fairly radiated strength; I could easily imagine them working one of the Sarni's stiff war bows, if not the great bow of Sajagax himself. But his nose flared like a delicate and perfect triangle, and so, I guessed, it must have been with his mother and her kin. His eyes were large and liquid like a horse's eyes, full of gentleness and grace. And full of wisdom, too. And something else. In the way he looked at me, with sweetness and fire, I had a deep, disturbing sense that he could perceive things in me that others had never seen – not Atara or Kane, or even my mother, father or my own grandfather.

He motioned for me to sit opposite from him at the center-most table. I lowered myself onto a plump cushion, with Master Juwain to my right and Liljana to my left. Master Virang sat to the right of Abrasax, and Master Matai, the Master Diviner, joined us as well. The two other tables were pulled up close to ours, end to end, making for what seemed one long table. Maram and Kane took places at the one to my right, and so, across from them, did Master Okuth and Master Storr. To my left, Atara, Estrella and Daj sat facing Master Yasul and Master Nolashar, the Music Master. I couldn't help staring at this middling-old man. His hair was cropped short like that of most of the Brothers, but was as straight and black as my own. Too, he had the long nose and black eyes of many of my people. His name and quiet, alert bearing proclaimed him as a Valari warrior, at least by lineage and upbringing. But now, it seemed, he trained with the flute or mandolet instead of the sword, and made music instead of war.

As soon as we all had settled into our places, the doors opened behind us, and six young Brothers entered bearing big, blue pots of tea. They set them down before us, along with smaller pots of cream and bowls full of honey. I took my tea plain, in the Valari way, and so did Master Nolashar. But most of the others set to pouring in cream and stirring their tea with little silver spoons that tinkled against the sides of their cups. The Brotherhood makes use of scores of teas, blended from hundreds of herbs, and the one I first sipped that night was as sweet as cherries, as fiery as brandy, and as cool and bracing as fresh peppermint.

Abrasax waited for the young Brothers to finish their work and leave. He smiled at Daj and Estrella in a kindly way. Then his face fell stern, and he looked at the rest of us, one by one, and most keenly at Master Juwain as he said, 'I would like, first and foremost, to welcome you all to our school. It has been nearly a hundred years since anyone outside our order has taken refuge here, for our rules are necessarily strict and we do not usually break them. Master Juwain, however, has explained the need that drove him to lead outsiders here, and I am in agreement with his decision, as are the rest of us. As long as you abide by our rules, you may remain as long as you would like.'

His voice was deep and strong and sure of itself. But there was no pride or veiled threat in it, as with a king's voice, only curiosity and an insistence on the truth. And so, with all the candor that I could summon, I bowed my head to him and said, 'Thank you, Grandfather. If we could, we would remain in this beautiful place for a year. But as Master Juwain will have told you, we have urgent business elsewhere, and we would ask of you not only your hospitality but your help.'

Abrasax exchanged a quick look with Master Virang, and then Master Storr, a rather stout man with fair, freckled skin and eyes as blue and clear as topaz gems. And then Abrasax said, 'You shall certainly have our hospitality; as for our help in your quest, we are met here tonight to decide if we *can* help you, and more, if such help would be wise.'

His obvious doubt concerning us seemed to pierce Maram like a spearpoint, and my prickly friend took a sip of tea, and then muttered, 'The whole world is about to burn up in dragon fire, and the Masters of the *Brotherhood* must sit and debate whether they will *help* us?'

Abrasax just gazed at him. 'You must understand, Brother Maram, that a great deal is at stake. Indeed, as you say, the whole world.'

'Please, Grandfather,' Maram said, 'I'm a Brother no longer, and you should call me Sar Maram.'

'All men are brothers,' Abrasax reminded him, 'but it will be as you've asked. Sar Maram, then.'

Maram nodded his head as if this name pleased him very well – even if Master Storr and a couple of the other masters present clearly disapproved of it. Maram looked around the table at the pots of tea, and I could almost feel his fierce desire that they should contain brandy or other spirits instead.

'Few men,' he told Abrasax as he nodded at me, 'whether they are Brothers or not, have seen what we've seen or fought so hard to free Ea from the Red Dragon's claws.'

'You *have* fought hard, it's true,' Abrasax agreed. 'But ferocity at arms, even of will, can never be enough to defeat the Dragon. Even as we speak, he moves to seize his moment. Has Master Juwain told you the tidings?'

'No,' Maram grumbled, shaking his head, 'he hasn't had the chance.'

'Evil tidings we've had out of Alonia,' Abrasax told us. 'Count Dario Narmada is dead, murdered by one of Morjin's Kallimun. Baron Maruth has proclaimed the Aquantir's independence, and so with Baron Monteer in Iviendenhall and Duke Parran in Jerolin. In Tria, Breyonan Eriades has allied with the Hastars to hunt down all Narmadas of King Kiritan's sept.'

Abrasax looked at Atara and said, 'I'm sorry, Princess.'

Atara turned her grave, beautiful face toward him. 'I'm sorry, too. My father's father reconquered the dukedoms and baronies you speak of and made Alonia great again. Count Dario *might* have held the realm together. No one else is strong enough.'

'Not even King Kiritan's only legitimate child?'

Atara touched the white cloth binding her face and said, 'A woman, and a blind one at that? No, I am Atara Manslayer, now – no one else.'

'Then it must be said that Alonia is no more.'

Atara laughed bitterly. 'Morjin will hardly even need to send an army marching north to reduce her to ashes.'

Abrasax massaged the deep creases around his eyes, then said, 'Galda has fallen, Yarkona and Surrapam, too. In all lands, our schools are being found out and burned down one by one. Our Brothers, put to the sword. And yet the evilest tidings of all have come out of Argattha.'

His words piqued Liljana's intense interest, and her plump, round face turned toward him as she asked, 'And how *have* these tidings come to you, then?'

Abrasax looked deep into her eyes and told her, 'We will be as forthcoming with you as we hope you will be with us. You see, for a very long time now, we have kept a secret school within Argattha. But not five months ago, it was discovered, and the last of our order there, Brother Songya, was captured and crucified. We will try to re-establish the school, but . . .'

A silence fell over the tea tables and spread out into the room. I gazed up at the flowers in the stands and the ancient glyphs cut beneath the stone ceiling. The round windows there glistened with starlight.

'Before Brother Songya died,' Abrasax went on, 'he sent word of the excavations beneath the city. There is, as you know, a great earth chakra there – the greatest on Ea. Morjin's slaves have nearly driven tunnels straight down into the heart of it. The digging has been stopped only by a great seam of quartz that breaks picks and shovels. If Morjin had a firestone, all would be lost. All is nearly lost, as it is.'

'Do not speak so, Grandfather, ' Master Yasul said to him. The Master Remembrancer was an old man with skin as dark as mahogany and tight little curls of white hair capping his bald head. He might have hailed from Karabuk or Uskudar, but seemed so at home in this quiet room as to have been born here. 'We still have hope.'

Abrasax picked up his cup to take a long sip of tea. Then he looked around the tables. 'We must at least *act* as if there is hope. But I have said that this is a night for openness, and we cannot turn away from the truth. The Red Dragon needs only to gain a little more mastery of the Lightstone to open the great chakra. When its fires break free . . .'

His voice choked off as he looked at Master Yasul and Master Juwain. Then he said, 'The first faint flames have *already* broken free. It cannot be long before he unleashes the Baaloch upon the world.'

At the mention of Morjin's master, Angra Mainyu, the Great Beast, we all fell into a deep silence as we sipped our tea. Then Master Juwain said to Abrasax: 'But what *of* the Maitreya, Grandfather? Isn't it clear that he must be found and aided so that he can keep the Red Dragon from using the Lightstone?'

Abrasax pulled at his long beard. 'No, that is not so clear as you might wish. With your help, Valashu Elahad gained the Lightstone only to lose it to the Red Dragon. If we lost the Maitreya as well, then there truly would be no hope.'

At this, I drew in a quick breath and said, 'If fate leads us to find the Shining One, we will *not* lose him.'

I stared at Abrasax as he and the other six masters stared back at me.

Abrasax motioned toward Master Matai. He had the soft curls and golden complexion of many Galdans, and his sharp brown eyes seemed to perceive a great deal. And Abrasax said, 'Our Master Diviner believes that these are the last days of the age, and that the Valkariad is surely near.'

With reverence and longing he spoke the name of that great moment at the end of history when all men and women would ascend to becoming greater beings: Ardun into Star People, and Star People into Elijin, who would take their rightful places as newly crowned Galadin. And the Galadin themselves would become as gods in the glory of a new creation.

'The Age of Light *must* be at hand,' Abrasax said. 'Either that or the Skardarak, when all the stars shall be put out and it will grow cold and dark forever.'

He drew in a deep breath, held it and then let it out slowly in a whoof of wind. Then he said, 'And even as we see two possibilities, and only two, for the world, so we have only two choices open to us now: to entrust Master Juwain and his companions with the quest to find the Maitreya, or not. Let us now speak truthfully with one another so that we might make this choice. Master Yasul?'

The Master Remembrancer pulled at the dark folds of skin beneath his narrow jaw as he regarded me. He said, 'Valashu Elahad speaks of his desire, and that of his friends, to make a quest to find the Maitreya, but is this their true calling? They are a strange company, and we must be sure of whom Master Juwain has brought to us.'

'And who *is* it, then, whom Master Juwain has brought to us?' Master Storr asked. His blue eyes sparkled in the strong candle-light. I wondered what land had given him birth: Nedu? Thalu? Eanna? The Master Galastei ran his blunt hand through his wispy white hair and coughed out, 'A claimant to the throne of Delu, an heir to Kiritan's branch of the House Narmada, and the sole surviving son of the Valari's greatest king. Beware the pride of princes, I say. Beware their *true* purpose. And this lordless knight, Kane. All of them, of the sword.'

I rested my hand on the hilt of my sword, which I had set by my side. I looked at Kane who had taught me to wield this terrible weapon with a single-minded will to destroy any and all who stood against me.

'And then there is Liljana Ashvaran,' Master Storr said. His cool blue eyes fixed on the woman who was as my mother. 'Master

Juwain has told us little more than that she is a noble of Alonia who joined Valashu and the others on the great Quest. An unusual calling, isn't it, for one of her age, rank and gender?'

In truth, I knew of no other matron, noble or not, who had set out into the wilds of Ea in pursuit of the Lightstone.

Liljana's pretty round face grew as intense and reflective as a full moon. To Master Storr, she said, 'Why should you think that noble impulses are so unusual? Your order, I've been told, exists to quicken that which is noblest in everyone.'

Master Storr blinked at Liljana's riposte. He exchanged pained looks with Master Yasul and the others. I gathered that he wasn't used to being addressed by women – or anyone – so sharply.

Then he pointed his teaspoon at Liljana. 'Surely what is noblest is *not* the keeping of secrets from those who would help you.'

'And what secrets do you think I keep?'

Master Storr did not respond. His eyes grew even colder, like glacier ice, as he gazed at her with a greater and greater vehemence. Liljana thrust her hand inside the pocket of her tunic, and her jaw tightened in defiance. Finally, she removed her fist from her tunic and shook it at him. 'You will *not*,' she told him. 'You will not.'

'*Will* I not?' Master Storr said to her.

In answer, her soft brown eyes summoned up such an intense heat that he finally blinked and looked away.

Liljana turned toward Abrasax and said, 'Your Master Galastei tries to use *this* to read my mind!'

So saying, she opened her hand to reveal her blue crystal.

'He tries to seize control of it – and me!' she said. 'Like the Red Dragon himself!'

'No – I only wanted to know what you conceal from us,' Master Storr called out. 'As Master Matai has said, we must be sure of you.'

'Not *this* way! You have no right.'

'I *am* the Master of the Gelstei.'

'Not *my* gelstei. Would you steal my journal as well, and force the lock to read its pages?'

'I will make no apologies,' Master Storr said. 'Too much is at stake, and we must do what we must do.'

'Is that the way of the Masters of the Brotherhood, then? Is *that* noble?'

They might have contended thus all night if Abrasax hadn't finally held up his hand and said to Liljana, 'Master Storr has fought too many battles with the Red Dragon, and is sometimes overzealous in protecting the Brotherhood. You are right, forcing another's mind is *not* our way. *I* do apologize, for all of us. But Master Storr also is right that too much is at stake, and so there can be no secrets within this room.'

Liljana sat facing Abrasax. She must have perceived that of all the Seven, he studied her the most intently. She gazed back at him with all the force of her will, as if commanding him to fix his attention elsewhere. But not even Liljana, it seemed, could stare down the Grandmaster.

'Your Sisters,' he said to her, 'have always kept too much hidden.'

'My . . . Sisters?' Liljana coughed out. It was one of the few times I had ever seen her at a loss for words.

'Do you deny,' Abrasax asked her, 'that you are of the Sisterhood?'

'But why would you think that?'

'I am a Master Reader, am I not? Your chakras, each of them, give off flames – how should I *not* be able to read their colors? And to perceive that your aura shimmers like that of one who has been trained in the ways of the Maitriche Telu?'

Liljana looked at Kane and Master Juwain briefly before glancing at me. She seemed, somewhere inside herself, to cast off a heavy cloak. Then she held her head high as she told Abrasax: 'I am the Materix of the Maitriche Telu.'

The Seven, all except Abrasax, seemed to draw in a single, hissing breath. Master Yasul leaned over to confer in low tones with Master Nolashar, while Master Matai exchanged resentful looks with Master Virang. And then Master Storr called out: 'So *this* is her secret! And a dark one it is, too!'

In silence he stared at Liljana, and so did Master Matai and the others – even the gentle-faced Master Okuth.

But if they thought to intimidate or even shame Liljana, then they did not know her. The more they beamed their disapproval and dread at her, the brighter and stronger she seemed to grow. And then she told them, 'Others have called my Sisters and me "witch" before.'

'No one has called you that,' Master Storr said.

'Not with your lips, perhaps, but you say it with your eyes.'

Master Storr rubbed at his temples a moment before asking Liljana: 'Do you deny that in times past you nearly succeeded in inserting one of your Sisters into Morjin's chambers as a concubine? With the intention of poisoning him, as the Maitriche Telu once poisoned King Daimon and many others?'

'King Daimon Hastar,' Liljana said to Master Storr, 'was nearly as evil as Morjin. After his untimely death, Alonia enjoyed nearly fifty years of prosperity and good rule.'

'Poisoners,' Master Storr muttered. And then more softly: 'Witch.'

'We did what we *had* to do! When *your* ways failed to educate and uplift, *we* were left to deal with one bloodthirsty tyrant after another!'

I looked to my right to see Kane smiling savagely as his lips pulled back from his long, white teeth.

Master Storr tried to ignore him, and he snapped at Liljana: 'And your way has been poison, seduction, even the violation of men's minds!'

'No, that has not been our way – you know nothing about us!' Liljana turned toward Abrasax, and for what seemed an hour she gazed at him, and he at her. His understanding seemed to pour out from him and embrace her. Tears filled her eyes. She was the hardest woman I had ever known, but sometimes the softest, too.

Finally Abrasax rose from his cushion and circled the tables until he stood above her. He reached down to grasp her hand and pull her up facing him. With his fingertips, he wiped the tears from her cheek. And then, as we all looked on in astonishment, he bent down to kiss her moist eyelids. To Master Storr and the rest of the Seven, and to all of us, he said, 'War will come soon enough, but let us not allow it into this room. Once, we of the Brotherhood and the Sisters of the Maitriche Telu *were* as brothers and sisters. I would have it so again.'

He squeezed Liljana's hand and bowed his head to her. Then, fixing Master Storr with a stern look, he returned to his place.

The room fell quiet, and for a while, the seven Masters of the Brotherhood sat drinking their tea. Strong sentiments like invisible currents passed between them. At last, Master Storr looked at me and said, 'War, of the spirit, at the very least, Valashu Elahad and his companions must wage, if they make this new quest. Theirs will be a *dangerous* journey. And one danger we should speak of now, since Liljana Ashvaran has already hinted of it. I would ask to see the rest of their gelstei.'

I nodded my head at his request, and drew Alkaladur from its sheath. My sword's silvery silustria gleamed in the starlight. Then Master Juwain brought forth his emerald varistei. Liljana set her little blue whale upon her table while Atara sat cupping her scryer's sphere inside her hands. Kane scowled as he reached into his pocket and showed Master Storr his baalstei, cut into the shape of a flat, black eye. And then Maram gently laid his firestone, red as a ruby and as long as his forearm, on his table.

'Ah, my poor, poor crystal,' he said, gazing at the webwork of fine cracks running through it. 'Ruined in battle with that damn dragon.'

Abrasax just stared at him. '*That* battle, I think, will prove to be as nothing against the battle you still must fight against the *Red Dragon*.'

'Ah, I don't want to fight at all,' Maram muttered. Something in Abarasax's manner seemed to encourage Maram to open himself to him. 'It's nearly ruined me, you see. The madness of the world: her stupidities and cruelties. If only I had time enough for love! If only I could heal this beautiful crystal, I might find the way to heal my heart.'

'I'm not sure,' Abrasax said to him, looking around the room, 'that we all see the connection.'

Maram gazed longingly at his crystal. 'To use the red gelstei is to summon and concentrate fire. Ah, to direct it toward a single target, you see. So with love, and therefore the heart. If my heart were made whole again, I might find the great love I was born for.'

Abrasax smiled as he again stood up from the table. He stretched back his shoulders and drew in a deep breath. Then he walked around Master Okuth and Master Storr sitting at their table with Maram, who turned toward him. Abrasax held his hands above Maram's head for a moment before bringing them down over his shoulders and then his sides. And he said, 'You have a great heart, Sar Maram Marshayk. Flames fill it with a bright green radiance. But they would burn brighter – much brighter – if they weren't so concentrated here, lower down in your svadhisthan chakra.'

With that he rested his hand on Maram's belly and smiled at him.

'Ah,' Maram said, nodding at me, 'I suppose this isn't a good time for a recitation of "A Second Chakra Man"?'

'No,' I said to him, 'I suppose it is not.'

Abrasax's eyebrows pulled together in concern as he pushed against Maram's belly and told him: 'Between here and your heart chakra is where your sun makes its orbit. And a great whirl of fire it is, blazing orange with streaks of viridian and crimson.'

As Abrasax's hand continued pressing against Maram, I could almost see this fiery orb that he spoke of.

'There is nothing wrong with your heart,' Abrasax told Maram.

'And you *do* have time for love – all the time in the world. But what *is* it that you love, above all else?'

Maram glanced at me nervously, and then turned back to Abrasax as he said, 'There is a woman. Somewhere in the world, a woman who can take in my heart and, ah, *all* of me. The one whose hips and breasts swell like the mountains and seas, like the very curves of the earth: she, whose desire is as boundless as my own. Some men seek the most beautiful of women, others the kindest or the most pure. But I dream of the most passionate.'

At this Abrasax cleared his throat and said to him, 'You must be careful what you wish for. Careful even of what you whisper inside your mind. The earth listens. There are powers there that no one fully understands. Her fires feed ours, and what we create inside ourselves, we can bring into being.'

He pressed his hand against Maram's chest, then walked around the tables again to return to his cushions. He sat gazing at Maram, who wrapped his huge hand around his red crystal and lowered his eyes to study the fine cracks marring it.

'*All* of them,' Master Storr said, looking from Maram to Liljana, 'must be careful with their gelstei. Each time they use the sacred crystals, Morjin will use the Lightstone to find his way farther into them and twist their power toward *his* will.'

I gazed into the silustria of my sword, and so did my friends study their gelstei.

'Indeed,' Master Storr continued, eyeing our crystals, too, 'I counsel that they surrender their gelstei to us for safekeeping.'

At this, Maram's hand closed around the cut planes of his fire-stone while I gripped the hilt of my sword more tightly.

'Surrender *this* to you?' Maram said, holding his long, red crystal pointing at Master Storr. 'You might as well ask me to cut off, ah, more personal parts of myself so that they don't lead me into troubles.'

'I know,' Atara said, turning her sphere between her hands, 'that this came to me for a purpose.'

Kane's response was the simplest and most direct of all of us. He held up his black stone for all to see and then closed his fist around it as he called out, 'Ha!'

Abrasax sighed as he looked at Master Storr and said, 'I told you this would be the way of things, as you of all of us should understand.'

Master Storr bowed his head, but said nothing as he turned his attention back to the gleam of our crystals.

And Abrasax said to us, 'So it goes. Everywhere on Ea, Morjin finds his way into men's minds, and so gains control of their arms, voices and eyes. And no one is willing to give *them* up either just to thwart him. But I counsel you: if you use your gelstei, Morjin *will* slowly seize control of them.'

'Even my sword?' I said, holding up its blade so as to catch the room's candlelight.

'The silver gelstei,' Master Storr said to me, 'would be last of your crystals to be perverted, if indeed it truly *can* be perverted. It is possible that only the Maitreya, having gained full mastery of the Lightstone, could touch upon the silustria of your sword – and then only for the highest of purposes. But I don't really know. Therefore I, too, counsel not using it.'

Kane smiled at this as he gripped his large hands together and said, 'And have you followed your own counsel, then?'

'What do you mean?' Master Storr said.

Kane pointed toward the waist of Master Storr, and then at Master Okuth and Abrasax. 'What is it you keep inside your pockets?'

At this, Abrasax smiled at Master Storr in a knowing way, and then looked at Kane. 'You have keen perceptions – from where do they come? What is that you keep inside *yourself*?'

Abrasax's smile deepened as he studied Kane. I knew that my mysterious friend hated being singled out for scrutiny in this way. His glare fell hot with a barely-contained fury. And then he stood up to face the Grandmaster of the Brotherhood.

It took a brave man to hold Kane's gaze, as Abrasax did. I didn't need to be a reader to see the fire that seemed to leap straight out of Kane's black eyes. As the candles flickered in their stands and the other Masters drew in deep breaths or held them inside, Abrasax continued staring at Kane. The Grandmaster's eyes grew brighter, like moonlit oceans, and I fancied that I saw this radiance touch his hair and beard and spill down over his tunic in flows of scarlet, orange and other colors. And yet it was nothing against the splendor that enveloped Kane. He stood as beneath a rainbow. Its hues clung to his body like a robe of fire and slowly deepened and brightened into a shimmering brilliance. White light crowned his savage head, and so did flashes of glorre. I stared at him, awestruck. I couldn't believe what my eyes or some other sensing organ told me must be true. It lasted only a moment, this piercing vision into the heart of Kane's being. And then I blinked my eyes, and it was gone. I saw my old friend standing before me as he usually did: fiercely, willfully, joyfully – with challenge toward Abrasax or anything in the world that might try to thwart or even contain him.

The others of the Seven, with my companions, sat gazing at Kane in wonderment. Master Storr shook his head as he called out, 'No, it cannot be! Not this rogue knight!'

Then Abrasax bowed to Kane and said, 'I never thought to live so long that my path would cross yours, Lord Elijin.'

Again, Master Storr said, 'It cannot be!'

Abrasax drew in a deep breath. He looked from Master Storr to Master Matai, and then at Kane. 'It surely is. This man is no rogue knight. It is, as the Master Diviner and I have deduced, now beyond argument that one of the Old Ones of the Elijik Order journeyed with this company into Argattha. And has found the way into our valley. His name, of old, was –'

'I am,' Kane growled out, interrupting him, 'not the one you speak of. Once I was, perhaps, but now I am Kane.'

'Kane, then,' Abrasax said to him. 'But you were, were you not, sent to Ea along with eleven others of your order to find and safe-guard the Lightstone for the Maitreya?'

'So,' Kane said, glaring at him.

'And of those eleven, only one other survives – Morjin.'

'So,' Kane said again.

Abrasax and the others of the Seven sat staring up at Kane. I noticed Master Storr's hard blue eyes drilling into him as he regarded him with dread. He called out, 'If this *is* that one, then he has fallen nearly as far as the Red Dragon. How can we be sure that if we help him to find the Maitreya, he won't fall even farther?'

Kane, not deigning to respond to the Master Galastei's terrible doubt, stood as still as a granite carving.

'How can we be sure what any man or woman will do, in the end?' Abrasax asked, looking at his fellows. 'Master Juwain tells that in Argattha, Kane gave back the Lightstone to Valashu when he might have kept it for himself. Can all of us say that *we* would have surrendered it so faithfully? Surely Kane has passed the most vital test.'

His reasoning seemed to persuade even Master Storr, who inclined his head toward Kane. And Kane growled out to Abrasax, 'And what of the Brotherhood's *Masters*, then? You speak of keeping no secrets, and yet you keep some very powerful baubles hidden inside your pockets, eh?'

Abrasax smiled at Master Storr. 'Did I not tell you that we could not conceal things from one of the Elijin?'

And with that he nodded at Master Matai, who reached into his pocket and brought out a small crystal sphere that shone like a ruby. The First, he named it. Master Virang likewise showed us a stone, which he called the Second, which gleamed golden-orange in hue. And so with Master Nolashar and his bright yellow sun stone and Master Okuth's green heart stone, and then Master Yasul's and Master Storr's crystals – colored blue and purple – whose names were the Fifth and the Sixth. And then, finally, Abrasax drew forth a marble-like sphere as clear and brilliant as a diamond. It was, he told us, the Seventh: the last and highest of the crystals called the Great Gelstei.

'Your crystals,' he said to us, 'are powerful and rare, but on all of Ea there are no other gelstei like these, for they were not made on earth.'

He went on to say that only the angels, and the Galadin at that, could possibly possess the art of forging the Great Gelstei. Then he held up his clear stone and showed it to Kane. 'The Elijin who were sent here brought these with them, didn't they?'

'So,' Kane growled out. 'Nurijin, Mayin and Baladin were the stones' keepers. And Manjin, Durrikin, Sarojin – Iojin, too. And all of them killed over the years on this cursed world. I had thought the stones lost.'

He drew in a long, pained breath and said to Abrasax, 'It must have been a great work to seek these out and bring them here.'

'The work of ages,' Abrasax told him. 'Many Brothers died in this quest.'

'As *you* will die if you continue to use them.'

'The Red Dragon, we believe,' Abrasax said, 'does not yet know that we keep them. And use them we must, at least tonight. There are tests still to be made.'

He sat cupping his clear stone in his hand. It shimmered a soft white, even as the crystals of the other Masters radiated colors of crimson and orange, up through a glowing violet.

'We have questions for the girl,' Abrasax said, looking at Estrella. Then he turned to me. 'And for you, Valashu Elahad.'

The room fell quiet, and I nodded at Estrella and then Abrasax. I sat gripping the hilt of my sword as I waited for the seven Masters of the Brotherhood to test me somehow – if not in actual combat, then perhaps in a trial of the soul.

9

Abrasax oriented his long, stately body toward Estrella, sitting almost motionlessly on her cushion by her table. For a long time he regarded her in silence. His liquid brown eyes seemed to empty of all thoughts, even questions, even as they filled with a strange and piercing light. The round crystal resting in his open palm gleamed like a little star. Those of the other masters seemed to resonate with it, gathering radiance from it and feeding it back to Abrasax's stone, all at once.

At last, the Grandmaster's eyes regained their normal focus. And in his deep, strong voice, he announced, 'This girl's aura is like none I have ever seen. So pure: as if the flames of her chakras flow toward one color, in one direction. And bright it is – so very bright.'

Abrasax continued gazing at Estrella, who sat peacefully on her big red cushion gazing back at him. Estrella's happy smile seemed to warm Abrasax's heart, and his whole face pulled into a smile, highlighting the deep lines around his eyes.

'Strange,' he murmured as he looked at her. 'There is indeed something strange about this girl.'

'Then is it possible,' Master Storr asked, 'that she is truly a seard?'

Abrasax nodded his head. 'I'm certain that she is. Master Juwain has identified her correctly.'

'But what *is* a seard?' Daj asked from his place next to Estrella. It was the first time that evening he had dared to speak. 'Master Juwain tried to explain it, but I didn't really understand.'

'I'm not sure that *I* fully understand, either,' Abrasax said. 'But from the accounts in the *Book of Illuminations*, it is clear that seards are great and pure souls, gifted with being able to see deeply into all things and all people, and most especially the Maitreya. I believe that Estrella might perceive the Shining One where others could not, perhaps not even himself.'

He went on to say that where I might be the fated guardian of the Lightstone, and therefore of the Maitreya, a seard such as Estrella was his herald.

'Then, Grandfather,' Master Matai said, 'you must believe Kasandra's prophecy will prove true, that the girl will show the Maitreya?'

'I believe the prophecy. She would be drawn to him like a fire moth finding its mate across many miles.'

Although I could not behold Estrella's aura just then as Abrasax did, she seemed the brightest being in the room, and her eyes outshone even the silustria of my sword.

'It's a pity,' Master Matai said, 'that she cannot speak to us. I would like to know where she was born, and when. A seard's stars would be close to those of a Maitreya.'

'It *is* a pity that she cannot speak,' Master Okuth said. He was a smallish man who seemed to hold inside his kind green eyes whole rivers of compassion. 'For pity's sake, and her own, I would like a chance to heal her of her affliction.'

Master Juwain held up his varistei and said to him, 'More than once, before the Red Dragon regained the Lightstone, I tried to use this to heal Estrella – in vain. Of course, I am only a Master Healer; you are *the* Master Healer.'

'I believe you have done as much as any of us can do,' Master Okuth told him. 'At least until the Maitreya is found and comes into his power. *My* power is now constrained. I am entrusted with a green gelstei, as are you, but the Red Dragon knows that we keep this stone, and I do not dare to use it.'

'Then how do you propose to heal Estrella?'

'In truth, I don't. At least not here, and not tonight. But it may be that through the Great Gelstei, she could speak to us in a way that we can understand, for a short while.'

'And the cost to the girl? What if she doesn't want to speak?'

All eyes now turned on Estrella, sitting calmly as she nibbled on a cake crumb and regarded Master Okuth.

'There should be no cost,' Master Okuth said.

'Just the opposite,' Master Matai said. 'Those whose chakras have been opened by the Great Gelstei feel strengthened and enlivened.'

'And you believe that engendering speech,' Master Juwain said to Master Okuth, 'is it merely a matter of opening the girl this way?'

'It is indeed more complicated than that,' Master Okuth told us. 'Much more complicated. But let us just say that the power of the seven Openers projects through sound and resonates with the secret music that inheres in all things.'

Kane scowled at this, and looked at me. I knew that my savage friend hated it when the Brothers spoke so esoterically.

'You have my promise,' Abrasax assured us, 'that this test will leave Estrella unharmed. But will she consent to it?'

Estrella looked at him with complete trust. Then she quickly nodded her head.

'Good,' Abrasax said. 'Then why don't we begin?'

He held his hand, cupping his clear gelstei, out toward Estrella. The other Masters did likewise with their crystals. Estrella sat very straight and still, not knowing what to expect. She seemed at once curious and bemused by the powers of these seven old men and their mysterious crystals.

As we all waited, breathing deeply, the seven Openers began to luminesce. I sensed, rather than saw, the seven wheels of light along Estrella's spine scintillating in response to the gelstei's touch. The red of the First, Master Matai's stone, seemed to give its fire to Estrella's lowest chakra even as something deep inside Estrella called out to it. And this calling we all heard as a single, clear, plangent note. It played back and forth between Estrella and the gelstei. The other Masters with their stones likewise opened Estrella's other chakras, and a beautiful music poured out into the chamber's cool air. I could almost see the colors of this music. Master Storr's gleaming purple stone, I thought, struck deep chords with some secret organ of speech within Estrella's head. Master Yasul's gelstei, the Fifth, as blue as a sapphire, blazed more brightly than did any of the others. It seemed to summon a bright song from within Estrella's throat. Without warning, she began laughing out loud: a delightful sound like the tinkling of bells. And then her mouth opened as perfectly formed words began pouring from her lips like a silver stream:

'I've wanted to talk so *badly*, to tell you things, Val, Maram, Atara, everyone, to tell you *everything*, and now there is all the time in the world, but so little *time*. Now, I can speak again, and that's a miracle but it won't last because nothing does and yet everything . . .'

She continued chattering on in a like way as we all sat listening in amazement. Her voice was sweet, passionate and perfectly clear. It flowed with a musical quality, bright as the notes of a flute. It partook of Atara's diction and phrasing, and Liljana's, too, as if she patterned her speech after that of these two women whom she adored. And yet, this torrent of sound fairly soared with a wild joy that was all her own. It seemed that she wanted to cram the entire world into a few, quick, rushing breaths:

'. . . it's all so beautiful, and I'm so grateful, Val – Val, Val, Val! – so grateful to you for saving my life. For *life*. I've wanted so badly to sing with you, and Kane, our bright, bloody, beautiful Kane, and all of you, to sing and laugh: to laugh at Maram and his silly, stupid, wonderful jokes. To weep with Atara. No eyes, no tears, no hope, it seems, but love – love, love, love! There is *so* much to say. But so little, really, only one thing, and I should be glad I can speak again, almost as I did inside, not in words but in a kind of music that gives birth to words. Do you know what I mean? It's like the singing of the birds: so pretty, so pure, so *here* . . . and now, and yet always and forever. This beautiful, beautiful thing – it sings *me*! I am so happy! And so I can't help singing, too, to the birds and the sky and the world, and everything sings back, in rubies and rainbows, in songs to the sun, and sometimes even in silence. *The* silence. It's pulling me back, soon, too soon, but don't feel sorry for me, please! These fires that the old men's gelstei lit inside me flare like little suns, but soon they will fade, I can feel it, quickly burning out but never quite *out*. Because *it* always blazes, even in dark things: black gelstei and burnt crosses and hate. Val! – even in the dead! In your father and mother, and mine, wherever they are, because no one is ever *really* dead and there is a light that always shines, *the* light, the light, the light . . .

As the candles' flames cast dancing shadows on the room's graven walls, we all sat regarding Estrella. At last, she seemed to run out of things to say. She sat peacefully on her cushion with her fingers laced together. I could not tell if she had fallen quiet for a moment or had returned to the deeper silence of the mute.

And then Abrasax nodded his head and said to her, 'That was remarkable.'

'Yes, remarkable,' Master Storr agreed. But his voice swelled with a patronizing tone, and he seemed to regard Estrella as if she might be simpleminded. He said to her, 'I'm sure that we were all touched by your . . . enthusiasm. But I'm not sure that any of our questions has been answered.'

143

'But you haven't asked me any questions yet!' she said to him. She smiled at him, and then laughed softly, and I felt her voice box vibrating like the strings of a mandolet.

'You must know, child, what we wish to know.'

Estrella looked at the Brotherhood's seven masters, who studied her every expression. She said, 'I think you want to know everything.'

Even the sour, serious Master Storr smiled at this. 'No, not *everything* – at least not tonight. But we would like to learn more concerning the Maitreya. Can you not tell us anything about him?'

'But I already did!'

Master Storr rubbed at his eyes and stared at her. 'To speak once again after so long a silence must be a strain on you. On your throat, on your lungs . . . even on your mind. I'm not sure that we all understood what you said.'

Her response to this was to smile at him as if she felt very sorry for his inability to apprehend the most simple of things.

'And so,' Master Storr continued, as his face reddened, 'we still have questions that we would –'

'But why don't you just *ask* them, then?'

Master Storr drew in a long breath as he squeezed his fingers around his purple crystal. And he said to Estrella: 'You are a seard – this seems beyond any doubt. But how is it that a seard can recognize the Maitreya?'

'How should I know,' she said, 'since I haven't recognized him yet?'

'But you must have some idea!'

Estrella brushed back the dark curls from around her eyes and glanced at Abrasax. 'How do you recognize the Grandfather when you meet him walking down a path?'

'But I *know* him! I've known him, now, for nearly fifty years!'

'I've known the Shining One for fifty thousand years. As long as the stars have shined. Really, forever.'

Master Storr waved his hand in the air, and shook his head. He seemed to give up hope of understanding anything that she told him.

And then Master Matai steered the questioning along a different tack as he asked her, 'Can you tell me where you were born, and when?'

'I'm sorry, but I don't remember. Perhaps it was in the Dark City.'

'In Argattha? But didn't anyone ever tell you how old you are?'

144

'No, I don't think they did. Does it matter?'

'It might help in corroborating the Maitreya's horoscope.'

'But if you've drawn up his horoscope, you already *know* how old he is and where he was born!'

Now it was Master Matai's turn to throw up his hand in frustration.

Then Abrasax said to her, 'Estrella, do you have any idea where the Maitreya might be found?'

With a quick, glad motion, she nodded her head.

'Where, then?'

And she told him, 'Here.'

'Here?' Abrasax said. 'Do you mean, on Ea? In these mountains?'

'No, *here*, with us in this room, I hope. He *is*.'

Abrasax's eyebrows pulled together. He seemed as mystified by Estrella as were Master Matai and Master Storr. He asked her, 'But who is the Maitreya, then?'

Without hesitation, she looked at me and said, 'Val is.'

My heart suddenly pounded inside my chest with hard, painful beats. I did not want to believe what I had heard her say.

And neither, it seemed, did Abrasax. He said to Estrella, 'You were with Valashu in Tria when it was finally proved that he could *not* be the Maitreya. And now you are telling us that he is?'

'Yes, he is,' Estrella said smiling at me. She turned to look at the table to the right of mine. 'And so is Maram.'

'Sar Maram Marshayk!' Abrasax said.

Maram's eyes widened in astonishment as he patted his over-stuffed belly and belched.

'Yes, he – he *is*!' Estrella said. 'And Master Storr, too.'

The Master Galastei shook his head as he looked at Abrasax. And then Master Okuth, sitting next to him as he held out his green crystal, announced, 'The girl is tiring, and so we should conclude the test.'

'The girl is more than tired,' Master Storr said. 'She suffers from delusion.'

'No, only from *confusion*, I think,' Master Okuth said. 'We know that the Red Dragon, in making her mute, did mischief to her mind. Our gelstei have let her summon up words but it seems have not undone the harm. There is *something* about her words and our understanding of them, and vice versa, that doesn't quite go together. It is like oil and water.'

'Her words,' Master Storr said, speaking in front of Estrella as if she were only one of the room's ornaments, 'are as unreliable as thin ice over a pond. I do not see how we can trust her to recognize the Maitreya.'

Liljana, sitting next to me, had finally had enough of Master Storr's rudeness. She leaned over to the table next to her, and threw her arm around Estrella as she said, 'You speak of words, and yet fail to use them precisely. Kasandra prophesied that Estrella would *show* the Maitreya, not merely recognize him.'

'I'm not sure I see the difference,' Master Storr said.

'I'm not sure you *do*,' Liljana said, drawing Estrella closer as she glared at Master Storr. 'And so *who* is deluded?'

At this, Abrasax held up his hand as if to ask for peace. He said, 'And I'm not sure that words, or any understanding of them, will help Estrella fulfill the prophecy. Her mind might or might not have been harmed, but *not* her eyes and certainly not her heart.'

'Then why don't we,' Master Storr huffed out, 'conclude the test as we had agreed?'

Abrasax inclined his head at this, and said to Estrella, 'Are you willing?'

'Yes, I am,' Estrella said, nodding back to him. She slumped on her cushion, slightly, and rubbed at her eyes. 'But I *am* tired. I'd like to talk and talk all night, and maybe you'd understand, but I'm so *so* tired, and it was all so bright and warm inside, but now its getting cold, and it hurts, and so will you please give me back the silence?'

'But there is more,' Master Storr said, 'that she might tell us and –'

'*Please* – it hurts!' Estrella said. 'It hurts, it hurts, it hurts . . .'

Abrasax regarded her only for a moment before bowing his head to her. Then he closed his fingers around his clear gelstei, which seemed to quiesce and lose its light. The other Masters took this as a cue to put away their stones. Estrella immediately sat up straighter. I felt her plunge into a deep, silent pool. Her face lit up with a smile of contentment that spoke more than entire rivers of words.

Then Abrasax motioned to Master Storr, who reached down by his side. He lifted up a cracked, ebony box and showed it to us. He called for Estrella's table to be cleared. After Liljana and I helped Masters Nolashar and Yasul move tea cups and plates to our table, Master Storr stood up and stepped over to set the box in front of Estrella. With great reverence, he opened it. One by one, he took out various artifacts: a glass pen, a jade spoon, a chess piece (the white king) carved out of ancient ivory, a plain gold ring. He stood gazing at the items gleaming faintly on the table.

'One of these things,' he said to Estrella, 'once belonged to the last Maitreya, Godavanni the Glorious. Can you recognize which one? Or, that is, *show* it to us?'

His face hardened into an iron-like mask, so as not to give hint which item this might be. So it was with the other Masters. They hardly dared to breathe as they waited to see what Estrella would do.

As quick as the beating of a bird's wings, she clapped her hands together. Her face brightened as she smiled with delight. Then, without hesitation, her hands swept forward and closed around the wooden box.

'Excellent!' Master Virang cried out. 'Most excellent!'

'A seard, indeed,' Master Nolashar said.

Master Storr's lips tightened as if someone had forced a sour cherry into his mouth. He looked from Estrella to Liljana, and said, 'You didn't, Materix of the Maitriche Telu, teach this girl to read minds, did you?'

In answer, Liljana only glared at him. Master Storr clearly didn't like what he must have seen in *her* mind, for he turned away from her and stared at the box cupped in Estrella's hands.

'It is known,' he announced, 'that Godavanni kept three song stones inside this box. The stones have long since been lost, and perhaps the songs as well, but at least we still have *this*.'

Estrella set the box back on the table, and smiled at him. And then Abrasax said to Master Storr, 'This is enough, do you agree? I believe the girl *will* show us the Maitreya.'

Master Storr rubbed his jaw as he stood eyeing the box. 'I am coming to believe that, too. But the question that must be answered above all others is: can Valashu Elahad lead her to him?'

And with that, he turned to regard me.

'Tell me where he might be found,' I said to Master Storr, 'and I will lead Estrella there, along with the rest of my friends – and even yourself if you don't trust me.'

'Bold words, Prince Valashu,' Master Storr said. 'We have heard how you put yourself forward as the Maitreya, with great boldness, and claimed the Lightstone for yourself. To what purpose, we must wonder? You would have made yourself warlord of a grand alliance, commander of a hundred thousand swords, a king of kings – is it your hope now that finding the Maitreya will help you claim this authority?'

The look of scorn on Master Storr's face made me grind my teeth. Wrath filled my heart then, and to the seven old masters gazing at me I said, 'What man can say in truth that his purpose is as pure as damask, unstained by any desire for the good regard of other men or influence upon them? Who can declare that every act of his life has flown straight and true as an arrow toward a single target? Did you, Master Storr, Master of the Gelstei, join the Brotherhood solely out of a love for knowledge and service, with no thought at all of excelling and being recognized for your efforts? Do you never doubt if your study of the gelstei conceals a deeper urge to control and wield them? You have heard a great deal about me, it seems, but know very little. I am of the sword, as you have said. I would break it into pieces, if I could. All swords, everywhere. There was a time when I wanted nothing more than to enter the Brotherhood, as you were privileged to do, to play the flute and spend my life making music. But I had duties: to my family, to my father, to my land. To all lands. Fate called me to recover the Lightstone, with the help of my friends, and then to see it stolen by the Crucifier. Was there not one moment when I desired to lead armies against him and see *him* cut into pieces? Do I never long, now, by force of arms to cut the Cup of Heaven from his bloody hand? If I said no, you would hear the lie in my voice. Hear, then, the truth: six brothers I had, and I would have shouted in gladness if any of them had become king of Mesh before me. A mother, father and grandmother I had, and they are all dead because of me. Four thousand of Mesh's bravest warriors, too. Everyone knows this. I am an outcast, now. And so I cannot hope to be king of Mesh, let alone lord of a great alliance. All that remains to me is to try to stop the Red Dragon from doing the worst. It is why I think and feel and breathe. I do not dare even to hope that a time may come when I can cast *this* into the sea and take up the flute once more.'

So saying, I lifted up my sword, and looked at the seven Masters who regarded me. Master Storr stared at me with his cold, blue eyes, and I sensed that he saw only my fury to defeat Morjin.

Abrasax, however, saw other things. He studied me from across our table as he pulled at his beard. 'We know there were signs that you were the Maitreya.'

'Yes,' I said, 'there were signs.'

'But you ignored, didn't you, the even stronger sign of the truth inside yourself?'

I held my breath in disquiet that he could read me so keenly.

Then I said, 'Yes, I always knew. But I didn't *want* to know. I wanted . . . to make everything right. And so I claimed the Lightstone.'

And upon this crime, destruction and death had followed like an evil wind. Abrasax, I thought, understood this very well, as he understood me. He had no need to act as my accuser and judge when I had already condemned myself so damnably. But he was not ready to see me act as my own executioner. I felt forgiveness pouring out of him, and something else, too: an admonition that hatred of myself could destroy me more surely than any weapon or poison of Morjin's. Abrasax's eyes were soft yet unyielding upon my face. Looking into these deep, umber orbs made me want to trust him without question.

'I didn't know,' I told him, 'who the Maitreya is. Or *what* he is. And despite what Estrella has told us tonight so beautifully, I still don't.'

I looked over at Estrella to see if my words disappointed her, but she just smiled at me.

'Master Juwain,' Abrasax said, 'has given an account of the akashic crystal that you found in the little people's wood. It is too bad that it was broken: you might have gained the knowledge that you sought. But there are other crystals.'

I looked across the room at the golden, False Lightstone resting on its marble pedestal beneath the window; I looked at the seven Masters of the Brotherhood who kept hidden the Great Gelstei. I said, 'Do you possess an akashic crystal, then?'

'No, we don't,' Abrasax told me. 'But there is this.'

So saying, he drew forth a book from beneath the pile of cushions behind him and showed it to me. Its cover seemed made of some shiny, hard substance like lacquered wood. Bright golden glyphs shone from it, but I could not read them, for they were of a script unfamiliar to me. Abrasax laid the book on our table. He opened it, and my eyes fairly burned with surprise, for its pages were like none I had ever seen. Abrasax riffled through them, and I thought that there must be thousands of them, each thinner than a piece of rice paper and as clear as a window pane. It seemed that Abrasax's strong fingers must easily rip or fracture these tinkling, tissue-like wisps. When I expressed my fear of this, he smiled and said, 'The pages are quite sturdy. Here, try turning them yourself.'

I put my thumb and finger to one of the pages; it felt strangely cool to the touch and as tough as old parchment.

149

'I read this long ago,' Abrasax said. 'After speaking with Master Juwain earlier, I asked Brother Kendall to retrieve it from the library that we might make reference to it tonight.'

'You read it *how*?' Maram called out. 'The pages have no letters!'

'Do they not?' Abrasax asked him with a smile. 'Perhaps you are just not looking at them right.'

And with that, he opened the book to a page he had marked, and he held his hand over it. Then Maram gave a little gasp of astonishment, and so did I, for the clear crystal of the page suddenly took on an albescent tone as of the white of an egg being fried. Hundreds of glyphs, like little black worms, popped into view and crowded the page in many columns.

'Sorcery!' Maram called out to Abrasax. He thumped his hand down upon our table near the book. 'I would accuse you of sorcery, as I did Master Virang, but I suppose that you'll just tell me, ah, that you're only helping me to see what was already there to see?'

Abrasax exchanged smiles with Master Virang, then turned his attention back to Maram and the book. 'No, this time the explanation is simpler, for the writing was *not* there to see. Only one who possesses the key to the book can unlock it and bring the script into sight.'

'But you made no move to unlock it, unless waving your hand like a conjuror constitutes such. Where is the key?'

Abrasax pointed his finger at his forehead and told Maram, 'Inside here. Each book is keyed to open to a phrase, which must be memorized and held inside the mind or sometimes spoken.'

'Like one of the Way Rhymes?'

Abrasax nodded his head at this. 'The Brotherhood must protect its secrets. And its treasures.'

'But I never heard that the Brotherhood kept such treasures!' Maram said as he regarded the book in wonder.

'Neither,' Master Juwain said, studying it as well, 'did I.'

'But what *is* its secret?' Maram asked. 'Obviously, the pages are made of some sort of gelstei – what sort, and how do you make it?'

'It is called the *vedastei*,' Abrasax informed him as he ran his finger down the page's glyphs. 'And I did not say that *we* made this – only that we protect it. And cherish it for what it contains. It is *that* knowledge, of the Maitreya, that concerns us now.'

He cleared his throat and pressed his finger at the writing near the middle of the page as he read to us: '"He is the Shining One who dwells in two worlds; he is the light inside darkness, and the life that knows no death."'

Against one of the windows above us, I saw Flick spinning about in a whirl of silver lights. I remembered how, in Tria, the Galadin had sent this luminous being to bring me word of the Maitreya, in verses that I now recited to Abrasax:

> The Shining Ones who live and die
> Between the whirling earth and sky
> Make still the sun, all things ignite –
> And earth and heaven reunite.

> The Fearless Ones find day in night
> And in themselves the deathless light,
> In flower, bird and butterfly,
> In love: thus dying, do not die.

I finished speaking and nodded at Abrasax. He tapped his book as he said to me, 'Do not these words concord with your verses and what Estrella has told us tonight?'

Without warning, Maram thumped his hand upon the table, rattling our cups. He looked at Abrasax and grumbled out, 'Estrella said nothing of *two* worlds. I, for one, know *this* world, and that should be enough, shouldn't it? And yet you of the Brotherhood are never satisfied unless you can speak of another.'

Abrasax's response to this was to flip through the pages of the book. He must have found the passage that he was seeking, for he suddenly nodded his head. He said to Maram, 'These words were written by Master Li of the Avasian Brotherhood.'

'The Avasian Brotherhood? Ah, I've never heard of such.'

'That is because,' Abrasax said, without further explanation, 'it existed on *another* world, that of Varene, many ages ago. Now listen, for this bears most pertinently on the matter of the Maitreya.'

His eyes gleamed as he pulled at his fluffy white beard. Then he read to us:

'"Two realms there are: the One and the manifold. The first is causeless, inextinguishable, infinite – and some say as blissful as the sun's light on a perfect spring day. The second realm is created, and all things that dwell there suffer, age and die. It is all nails and fire, beauty that fades, a few moments of sweetness and noble dreams. Some call this the world and others hell. It is man's path to strive ever upward, toward the heavens, toward the sun. But to go beyond the world toward the One, we must go beyond ourselves. It is almost like dying, is it not? A newborn ceases to exist in becoming a child, as a child does in becoming a man. And as all men must do if they are to walk the path of angels. And then, the greatest death of all when the Galadin perish in their bodies and die into light in the creation of a new universe. Who has utter faith in the goodness of such a sacrifice? Who would not fear that such a path might lead to the utter obliteration of one's being?"'

Abrasax finished reading and looked at me. 'And yet we must not fear. Overcoming fear is the cardinal task of any warrior, be he of the sword or the spirit. Many fail. Even the angels.'

He paused to take a drink of tea and moisten his throat. Then he said to me, 'In Tria, you learned the truth of Angra Mainyu, didn't you?'

I shrugged my shoulders at this. I glanced at Kane. 'Can any man know very much about the Galadin?'

'We know *this*, I think,' Abrasax said. 'Angra Mainyu, and too many of his kind, came to dread the Galadin's fate. And so he clung to his form as a leech does to living flesh. And so rather than becoming infinitely greater in giving himself to the universe, he tries to suck the blood from all things and take the universe into himself – and so becomes infinitely less.'

I considered this for a moment, then asked him, 'And the Maitreya?'

'The Maitreya is sent to heal those such as the Dark One and to keep others from falling as he has.'

I remembered the blood rushing from my father's lips as he died, and all the thousands of men lying still upon the reddened grass of the Culhadosh Commons. I felt Morjin's baleful eyes nailing me to a fiery cross, and all the while my heart drummed with a dreadful sickness inside my chest. And I said to Abrasax, 'Is that possible?'

'It *must* be possible.' He glanced over at Estrella sitting happily at her table. 'The Maitreya, in great gladness of life, is sent to show all beings the shining depths of themselves that can never die. And that, ultimately, the two realms are one and the same.'

Maram seemed not to like what he was hearing, for he knocked the bottom of his tea cup against the tiled table as if to announce his annoyance. He caught Abrasax's attention and asked him, 'Are you saying that when we when pass into this infinite realm of yours, that some part of us keeps on shining? And that therefore, there is no true death?'

'That,' Abrasax told him, 'is my belief.'

152

Maram gazed into his empty teacup as he muttered, 'And therefore, I suppose, there is nothing to fear.'

'You understand, then,' Abrasax said, smiling at him.

'I understand that there is *nothing* to fear, and that is precisely what I *do* fear: the great, black void at the end of life that swallows us all. You say this neverness is full of light. The Shining Ones, if we're to believe you, say this in their gladness. Ah, all your books say it, too. But who, I ask you, has ever returned from the land of the dead to tell of it?'

Abrasax seemed to have no answer to this; for a moment he turned his attention to sipping his tea. Then his eyes grew hard and bright, and he called out: 'Master Virang! Master Matai! Master Storr!'

He issued instructions for a repositioning of the tables and of everyone in the room. Atara, Estrella and Daj moved over to join the rest of our company at our two tables, while the Seven took their places with Masters Yasul and Nolashar at theirs. The artifacts still resting there were put back into the treasured ebony box – all except the ivory chess piece. This carved, ancient 'king', four inches long, Abrasax set precisely at the center of the table. Then he and the other masters once again brought forth their seven round crystals. They sat in a circle holding out these stones around the chess piece.

'I must now say more about the Great Gelstei,' Abrasax told us. 'Is there anyone who does not remember the account of creation in the *Beginnings*?'

'Do you mean,' Daj piped in, 'how the Ieldra sang the universe into existence?'

He beamed with pride at his recently acquired knowledge as Abrasax smiled and nodded his head at him. And then Abrasax said, 'The account in the *Saganom Elu* is poetic and magisterial, and certainly true. But not all has been told there. Exactly how, we might ask, *did* the Ieldra bring the One's design into its full flowering?'

He looked at Kane and added, 'You must surely know.'

'So – I have forgotten, if ever I *did* know.'

Abrasax smiled sadly, and then he told us that many books in the Brotherhood's library contained knowledge as to this arcane subject. He related an amazing story, part of which had been revealed to my companions and me the year before in the amphitheater of the Urudjin outside of Tria: 'Seven colors there are, and they create all the beauty of the world and all that we

153

see. And the seven notes that we summon out of trumpet or mandolet ring out the melodies of all music. So with the seven Openers and the creation of the world. The gelstei that crystallized out of the primeval fire were infinitely greater than these little stones that we of the Brotherhood are privileged to keep. And they opened up all the infinite possibilities of life. For as the Ieldra sang, the great crystals vibrated like the strings of a harp, and brought into being and form all things.'

Maram gazed at the gelstei shining in the Masters' hands. He asked, 'Are you saying that *these* stones partake of the power of the mythical gelstei?'

'They are *not* mythical,' Abrasax told him. 'They exist somewhere, out in the stars, beyond Agathad.'

'But do they still have the power to create?'

'Yes – and to *uncreate*. Even as these stones do.'

He nodded at Master Matai, whose red crystal lit up like a glowing demon's eye. Then Master Virang's stone, the Second, flared with an orange fire, and so with the other Masters' gelstei in a progression of hues. As Abrasax's clear stone spat out a fierce white light, the crystals all began pouring forth sound as well. It might have been called music, but the harsh tones and shrills that vibrated from the crystals filled the chamber with a terrible stridor more like a wail of death than a song. It built louder and ever more jangling upon ear and nerve until I felt compelled to throw my hands over my ears. I watched in amazement as the ivory of the chess piece seemed to lose its substance and began wavering in the candles' soft light. And then, suddenly, with a skreak like breaking metal, it vanished into thin air.

'Sorcery!' Maram cried out. He moved over to the Masters' table, and rudely wedged his body between Master Yasul and Master Storr. He ran his hand around the table's bare surface where the chess piece had sat.

'It's gone!' Daj cried out. 'The king is gone – but *where*?'

'Ah, gone into nothing,' Maram muttered. 'Into hell. It would seem it has been annihilated, like a man's soul when life's candle blows out.'

The seven Masters seemed to meditate upon their gelstei. And Abrasax said to Daj, and to Maram, 'Wait.'

A few moments later, with a chiming like that of struck bells, the chess piece winked back into plain view. I sat blinking my eyes. Maram reached out to snatch it up with his fat fingers before it disappeared again.

'More sorcery!' he cried out. He gripped the carved ivory hard in his hand as if to reassure himself that it was real.

And Abrasax said to him, 'Don't be so sure you know what existence is – or isn't.'

Maram waved his hand at this. '*I* think you must have somehow hidden from our sight what was there all along. And then caused us to see it once again.'

Abrasax held out his hand to take the chess piece from Maram as he shook his head. He showed us all the gleaming white king.

'No, that was not the way of things,' he said. '*This*, for a moment, was truly unmade. But our gelstei, being small, possess only a small power. We of the Seven possess even less. It is *not* the province of man to unmake things.'

'So,' Kane growled out. His black eyes seemed to grow even blacker, like two bits of neverness that might swallow up not only a chunk of carved ivory but entire worlds.

'And it is not,' Abrasax said, looking from Kane to Maram, 'the province of the Elijin, or even the Galadin. To the Ieldra, and only to the Ieldra, is given the power to create and uncreate.'

'I wish the Ieldra would just *uncreate* Angra Mainyu,' Maram said. 'And Morjin – and every other evil creature in the world.'

'That is not the way of things, either,' Abrasax told him, giving him back the chess piece. 'The Ieldra, according to the One's design, sing the universe into creation. But once it *is* created, no single part may be unmade. *All* is necessary. Nothing may be subtracted just because it seems to be hateful or bad.'

I sat watching Maram twirl the chess piece between his fingers, and I said, 'If Morjin got his hands on those gelstei of yours, he'd try to use them to subtract *us* from the world. And much else that he hates.'

Abrasax nodded his head at this. 'And with Angra Mainyu, it would be much worse. Once freed from Damoom, he would try to use the Lightstone to seize the greatest of the Great Gelstei and unmake the Ieldra themselves. He would, I think, fail. But out of his failure would come cataclysm and fire, and he would cause the Ieldra to have to destroy all things.'

I turned to look out the chamber's windows up at the faraway stars. And I said, 'But why? I don't understand.'

'I'm not sure I do either,' Abrasax said with a heavy sigh. 'At least not completely. It seems to me, though, that the Ieldra abide the evil of the world because out of it, sometimes, comes great good. But once *all* is fallen into darkness, forever, what would be the purpose of making everything suffer without redemption or end?'

What, indeed? I wondered, as I thought of my mother hanging all broken and bloody from a plank of wood.

As Maram continued playing with the chess piece, Abrasax looked at me and said, 'I think we have an answer to both Sar Maram's question and yours. If this king can return from the realm of the unmade, then so can a prince vanquish his fear of death – and so in dying, will not die. But only, I believe, with the help of the Maitreya.'

'If you *do* believe that,' I said to him, 'then for love of the world help us to find him!'

At this, Master Storr's fingers closed around his gelstei, and he said, 'It is for love of the world – and much, much else – that we must be sure of you. Wine poured into a cracked cup not only is wasted but helps destroy the cup.'

'I will not fail!' I half-shouted at Master Storr.

'Bold words,' he said to me. 'But what if you *do* fail?'

The room fell quiet as he and the others of the Seven sat regarding me. And then Master Okuth said, 'If the Maitreya is slain or falls into Morjin's hands, then we see no hope of Angra Mainyu ever being healed. And so no hope for Ea and all the other worlds of Eluru.'

'The risk is great beyond measure,' Master Virang said to me. 'And not just to the world, but to yourself. If *you* fall into Morjin's hands, or fall as his master did, then –'

'But we have to take the chance!' I cried out. 'Or else we might as well be dead already!'

For a while everyone sat quite still. The smell of various teas steeping in hot water filled the air. Then Abrasax looked at me with unnerving percipience, and said, 'Your manner, Valashu, the fire of your eyes, all you have dared and done – this bespeaks the attainment of the highest Valari ideal. And yet I think you find your valor in being drawn to that which you most dread.'

I said nothing as I tried to return his relentless gaze.

'You would wish,' he continued, 'for others to see you as fearless, as you would like to see yourself. But you fear this neverness that Prince Maram has told of so terribly, don't you?'

I could hardly look at him as I nodded my head and said, 'Yes.'

'And you fear, too,' Abrasax said as the others of the Seven bent closer to me, 'that Morjin will be the one to damn you to exile in this lightless land?'

Yes, yes, yes! And as I feared, so I hated; and as I hated, my heart ached with a black, bitter wrath that poisoned my blood and darkened everything I held inside as beautiful and good. How I longed to take a sword to this dreadful disease that consumed me! But I could not, as I might rid myself of a rotting limb, simply cut it out.

'And most of all,' Abrasax said, looking at me deeply, 'you fear your hatred of Morjin.'

'It is killing me!' I called out.

The fury that poured out of me beat against Liljana, Master Juwain and the others sitting close to me with the force of a raging river. It caught up the seven Masters, as well. Their faces fell ashen and sick, and Master Storr gripped the edge of his table as if to keep himself from being swept away. And then Master Juwain placed his hand on the center of my back, and I drew in three long, deep breaths.

'You see,' Abrasax said to me, 'your hate is a terrible thing, and we fear it, too.'

'I'm sorry,' I finally gasped out. 'I would have done better to have been born a lamb or made a gelding!'

Abrasax's smile was like a cold bucket of water splashed in my face. And he said, 'Do not mistake lack of passion for virtue. We must celebrate all the passions, as we do life itself.'

'Even hate?'

'Yes, even that. The virtuous man is *not* one who doesn't hate, but he who is in full control of it, as he is all his passions, directing it toward a good end – *and by good means.*'

I traded dark looks with Kane then, for Abrasax had pierced to the heart of the conundrum that tormented me. Then I looked back at the Grandmaster and said, 'Too often it seems that if I don't give back Morjin evil for evil, he'll win. And if I *do* fight this way, evil will *still* win.'

'It is difficult, I know,' he told me. 'But you must find the way to make use of these blazing passions of yours, even the ugly and evil inside yourself, toward a higher end – even as the One does in creating the world. Pour fire the wrong way against a lump of coal and it will burn up and crumble into ashes. Wield fire as the earth does, however, as the sun and stars do, and you will make a diamond. *This* self-creation is the path of the angels; it is their fundamental duty and test.'

He came over to my table to pour some tea into my cup, and his steady gaze seemed to remind me that I held the keys to two opposing kingdoms inside my heart: either the wild joy of life or the rage for death.

Master Storr, who had recovered from my carelessness, pointed his finger at me and said, 'We've all felt this passion of Prince Valashu tonight. With it, in Tria, he slew a man. How long before he slays again?'

'Never!' I cried out inside the cold castle of my mind. And then, to Master Storr and the others, I said, 'I have vowed never again to use the valarda this way. And Morjin lives because of this!'

It might have been more accurate to say that Morjin had survived our last battle because of my hesitation – or because I could no more control my gift than I could a thunderstorm.

'It is strange that Morjin left Argattha at this time,' Abrasax said to me. 'Indeed, there is something very strange about your encounter with him. I must believe that it is for the best that you did not slay Morjin with this secret sword of yours. All my understanding of the Law of the One is that the valarda is to be used only for the highest of purposes.'

Yes, I thought, it should be. To sense in others their deepest desires, to dream their dreams, to share with them my own – how I had longed for this! Yet too often the valarda had been a curse. I felt my heart pressing up against my throat as I said, 'All my life, I have suffered others' passions. And now, it seems, I have learned to inflict mine upon them – even to slay.'

Abrasax regarded me a moment before saying, 'Surely you must suspect that your sentiments and passions, as powerful as they are, are *not* sufficient to kill another person?'

I looked at him in alarm and waited for him to say more.

'Haven't you ever wondered,' he asked me, 'at the true nature of the valarda?'

'Only as long as I could think and feel!' I told him.

'Then haven't you ever sensed that your openness to others is only the beginning of openness to much more? Indeed, I believe it leads to the *identity* with others, ultimately with the entire world. As with the Maitreya.'

'But I am not the Maitreya!'

'No, you are not,' he told me. 'But already you have wielded some of the power that must be his. Through him would flow the great soul force, the deepest fires of the world. Such a force, Valashu, can be used either for great evil or great good.'

He went on to say that, ultimately, this angel fire could be used to destroy whole universes, as the Ieldra were sometimes forced to do, or to create new ones.

He finished speaking and poured himself yet another cup of tea. And I said, 'If what you've told us is true, then the Maitreya would possess the valarda in much greater measure than I.'

'Perhaps. But I should say rather than possessing the valarda, the Maitreya, in his essence, *is* valarda, for he would be as a window letting in the light of all things.'

Above us, the twelve round windows filled with the faint sheen of the stars. The dome above us seemed to catch the exhalations of the Seven as they looked at me.

'The Maitreya,' I said to Abrasax, and to everyone, '*must* be able to draw forth the light from the Cup of Heaven. And we must find him before Morjin does.'

Master Virang's discipline was meditation, not mind-reading, but I sensed that he exactly echoed Abrasax's thoughts as he asked me, 'Do you seek the Shining One to keep Morjin from using the Lightstone or for more personal reasons?'

'Both,' I told him truthfully.

Two flames, I thought, burned inside my heart. The first was reddish-black, and would destroy me if I let it. The other flame was as blue as the sky and connected me to all the lights of the heavens.

'If we are to help you, we must be sure of you,' Master Storr told me again. 'Sure, at least, that you can use the valarda for good, and not ill. Will you allow us to test this?'

I nodded my head as I looked at him. 'If you must.'

'Good,' Master Storr said. 'Then please stand up.'

I did as he asked, and moved off to the side of the tables beneath the chamber's dome. The Seven gathered around me. Each of them held one of the Great Gelstei out toward my chest.

'Ah, just don't make *him* disappear,' Maram called out from his cushion below me.

Abrasax smiled at this as his open hand showed a little colored sphere. So it was with Master Yasul, Master Matai and the others of the Seven. Each of them, especially Master Storr, gazed at me intently. I felt their eyes pierce me like hot needles at many places through my body. Their hands, now glowing with the radiance of their crystals, seemed to reach inside me and open me to the whirls of light up and down my spine.

'It burns, does it not?' Abrasax said to me. His eyes filled with concern for me even as his crystal flared with a white luster. 'Your belly is where you feel it, isn't it? All your hatred of the Red Dragon?'

Deep within my belly, down behind my navel, the red flame raged hot as molten stone. For a moment, I perceived it as Abrasax did: as red as burning blood and shot with streaks of orange darkening to black, like smoke. I sensed that it would soon kill me, if I let it.

'There is a saying,' Abrasax told me. 'Words as old as the stars: "If you would be freed from burning, you must become fire."'

With that, the crystals of the Seven glistened in a rainbow brilliance. Wheels of fiery light whirled along my spine in colors to match the hues pouring from their crystals. The red flame in my deepest part built hotter and hotter. It might, I knew, burn up the whole world with my hellish hate if I let it. It consumed me, now, almost, being drawn up into my chest with every beat of my heart. But there, too, gathered the other flame, pure and blue, like Arras and Solaru and the brightest of the stars.

If you would be freed from burning, you must become fire.

I closed my eyes then, and I felt the hot flickers of the red flame feed the blazing of the blue. I *willed* this to be. It grew brighter and brighter. *I* did. My whole being, out from my center into my arms and legs, feet and hands, fairly shimmered and sang with a surging new life. And then, in a rush of joy, a fountain of violet flame seemed to shoot up through my belly, heart and throat, flaring to pure white as it filled the bright, black spaces behind my eyes. For an endless moment I *did* disappear, into a fire so brilliant that it touched the whole world with an infinite light.

At last, I returned to myself. I sensed a quickness of breath and rushing blood inside Abrasax, and I opened my eyes to see as he did. And I gasped in astonishment. For the auras of the Seven and Atara and Kane, and all those in the room, impinged on each other, and flowed, swirled and shimmered in a cloud of light. This living radiance seemed to be drawn to me as water to an opening in the earth and to change hues as it brightened into a numinous and dazzling glorre. I drew my sword then, and held it pointing up toward the apex of the dome. Alkaladur, too, blazed with this perfect color.

'Fire, indeed,' Abrasax said.

Then he put away his gelstei, and so did Master Storr and the others, and the auras of everyone gathered there vanished from my sight. But my sword's silustria continued burning with an ineffable flame.

160

'Do you see?' Abrasax said, to Master Virang and Master Storr. 'Do you see? It is as Master Juwain told about Prince Valashu.'

Everyone watched as the glorre illuminating my sword slowly faded to a silvery sheen. I sheathed Alkaladur as I looked at Abrasax.

'That is enough of testing for one night,' he said, smiling at me.

Master Storr looked down at Maram swigging his tea and said, 'But what of the others?'

'Valashu is their leader,' Abrasax told him. 'As he goes, so go they. If he can overcome the worst of himself as he has here tonight, then I believe that they will, too.'

'You speak of him,' Master Storr said, eyeing me, 'almost as if *he* is the Maitreya!'

'No, Valashu is not the Shining One,' he said. 'But I believe their fates are interwoven, as threads in a tapestry. Surely it is upon the Prince of Elahad to lead the way to him. Do you agree, Master Matai?'

The Master Diviner, standing across from me, smiled at Abrasax. And then, in turn, as Abrasax queried the other masters, each of them gave his assent. Even Master Storr reluctantly nodded his head.

'I suppose we must trust Valashu and his friends,' he affirmed.

In the end, I thought, either one has faith in another or not.

'Yes, we must trust them with all our power to trust,' Abrasax said. 'And give them all our help. All the signs point one way.'

'Ah, but *which* way?' Maram asked as he fingered his beard. 'That is the question of the moment, is it not?'

Abrasax smiled at this, then called out, 'Master Matai – will you show us the parchment?'

The Seven moved back over to the empty table, and my friends and I gathered around them. Master Matai produced a large, yellowed parchment, which he unrolled and laid upon the table for all of us to examine. On its glossy surface were inscribed a great circle and various symbols marking the position of the planets and stars at the hour of my birth. It was, I saw, a copy of my horoscope, which Master Sebastian of the school in Mesh had prepared scarcely a year before.

Master Matai ran his finger over a hornlike glyph representing the sign of the Ram, and he said, 'As Master Sebastian and Master Juwain elucidated in Mesh, Valashu's horoscope is nearly identical with that of Godavanni. Valashu's stars, as they determined, are those of a Maitreya.'

'Then you should not blame him,' Maram half-shouted, 'for having believed that he might *be* the Maitreya!'

Master Matai shot him a sharp look and shook his head to silence him. And then he went on: 'As we say, the stars impel; they do not compel. There are always other signs. And there are other stars.'

'I'm afraid I still don't understand,' Master Juwain said, resting his elbows on the table to examine the horoscope, 'where Master Sebastian went wrong.'

'That is because he didn't,' Master Matai said. 'On all of Ea, there is hardly a better diviner, especially when it comes to astrology. No, Master Sebastian made no error, at least of *commission*. But it must be said that an *omission* has been made, and a critical one at that.'

So saying, he brought forth a second parchment and unrolled it on top of mine.

'Always, at the end of ages, the Maitreyas are born,' he told us. 'And at the end of *this* age, the last age that will give birth to the Age of Light, or so we hope, the stars are so strong. I have studied this for years, and for years I believed the Maitreya's star would rise over the Morning Mountains. But I have found a brighter one that rose in another land. Twenty-two years ago, now, at the same time that the Golden Band flared as it never had before and has done only once since.'

I glanced at the date that Master Matai had inked onto the parchment: the ninth of Triolet in the year 2792 – the same day as my birth.

Master Juwain studied the symbols inscribed in the great circle, and he asked, 'And for which land has this horoscope been prepared?'

'Hesperu. In the Haraland, in the north, somewhere below the mountains, to the east of Ghurlan but west of the Rhul River.'

'Hesperu!' I wanted to cry out. I could think of few lands of Ea so far away, and none so difficult to reach.

'But we *can't* journey there!' Maram bellowed. 'It's impossible!'

'So, it would be difficult, not impossible,' Kane said, his eyes gleaming.

He went on to tell us that we could complete our transit of the White Mountains and cross the vast forest of Acadu. And then choose between two routes: the southern one through the Dragon Kingdoms, or the northern route across the Red Desert.

'Oh, excellent!' Maram said. 'Then we'll have our choice between being put up on crosses or dying of thirst in the desert.'

I turned to look at Maram. I didn't want him to frighten the children – and himself.

'But think, Val!' he said to me. 'Even if the Maitreya *was* born in Hesperu, he might long since have gone elsewhere. Or been taken as a slave or even killed. It's madness, I say, to set out to the end of the earth solely according to another astrological reckoning.'

I waited for the blood to leave his flushed face, and then I asked him, 'But what else can we do?'

'Ah, I don't really know,' he muttered. 'Why must we *do* anything? And if we *do* do something, wouldn't it be enough to work in concert with the Brotherhood? Surely the Grandmaster has alerted the schools in Hesperu to look for the Maitreya. Let *them* find him, I say.'

Master Juwain looked over his shoulder at Maram and asked him, 'Have you forgotten Kasandra's prophecy?'

'You mean, that Val would find the Maitreya in the darkest of places?'

Hesperu, I thought, under the terror of King Arsu and the Kallimun, no less Morjin, seemed just about the darkest place on Ea.

'There is more that you should know,' Master Matai said as he pressed his finger against one of the symbols inked onto the parchment. 'The Maitreya's star, I believe, will burn brightly but not long.'

I looked at Maram as he looked at me. Sometimes decisions are made not in the affirmation of one's lips but in the silence of the eyes.

'But we'll die reaching Hesperu!' he moaned. 'Oh, too bad, too bad!'

And with that he hammered his fist on the table behind him hard enough to rattle the teacups and to shake from them a few dark, amber drops. 'Why can't I have at least one glass of brandy before I'm reduced to worm's meat? Are there no spirits in this accursed place?'

'There are those that you carry inside your hearts,' Abrasax told him with a smile.

Maram waved his thick hand at Abrasax's attempt to encourage him, and he turned toward me. 'Can't you see it, Val? It's madness, this new quest of ours, damnable and utter madness!'

'Then you must be mad, too,' I told him, 'to be coming with us.'

'*Am* I coming with you? Am I?'

'*Aren't* you?'

'Ah, of course I am, damn it! And that's the hell of it, isn't it? How could I ever desert you?'

We returned to our original tables then. Abrasax began a long account of how one of the ancient Maitreyas, on another world during the age-old War of the Stone, had sung to a star called Ayasha to keep it from dying in a blaze of light. We drank many cups of tea. Finally, it grew late. Through one of the windows, I saw the stars of the Dragon descending toward the west. And yet Kane still sat spellbound as he listened to Abrasax's flowing voice, and so did Daj and Estrella. But whereas Kane could remain awake for nights on end, and perhaps longer, the children began yawning with their need for sleep.

'I think that is enough for one night,' Abrasax said. He closed the crystal-paged book from which he had been reading. I sheathed my sword, and my companions hid away their gelstei. 'Tomorrow you must begin preparing for a long journey, and we must help you.'

He turned to look at Atara, Daj and Estrella, and all the rest of us, one by one. At last he rested his gaze on me. 'I believe with all my heart that you will find the Maitreya, as has been prophesied. And I also believe that what will befall then will be ruled by *your* heart. Remember, Valashu, creation is everything. It is what we were born for.'

He stood up slowly, and stepped over to the pedestal holding up the cup of silver gelstei. After lifting it with great care, he brought it back to our table and set it down. And then he enjoined us: 'Escort the Shining One back to us, here, and we shall help him, too. We shall place this in his hands, if not the true gold. And then we shall see who is truly master of the Lightstone.'

After that we went back to our hostels to rest. For hours I lay awake with my hand on the hilt of Alkaladur, by the side of my bed. A bright flame still blazed inside me. I wanted to pass it on like a strengthening elixir to Atara, sleeping in the little house next to mine, and to Estrella, Liljana, and everyone. I couldn't help hoping that we might bring something beautiful into creation, even though I knew that before us lay an endless road of blood, destruction and death.

10

We spent the next days resting and preparing for what Maram kept calling our 'mad quest'. In the warmth of the brightening spring, we feasted on good, solid food to build up our bodies against the trials that would soon come. We tried to strengthen our minds and spirits as well. Master Juwain passed many hours in the school's library studying maps and reading accounts of the lands that we must cross. Liljana held counsel with Abrasax in an unprecedented effort to combine the resources of the Sisterhood and Brotherhood. Master Nolashar taught Estrella and me secret songs to play on our flutes and drive evil humors away. We all sat in the stone conservatory with Master Virang, who guided us through meditations so as to enliven our auras. This unseen radiance, like an armor woven of light, might protect us against the malice and lies of the Red Dragon – against even cold and hunger and the depredations of our own despair.

After nearly a week of this practice, the other masters joined us in these meditations, and the Grandmaster, too. The Seven brought forth their crystals and used them to quicken our chakras' fires. As Abrasax told us, this would help open us to the angel fire and greater life.

'That is the power and purpose of the Great Gelstei,' he told us one fine morning with the larks singing in the nearby cherry orchard. 'At least, the purpose of *these* small stones that we are privileged to keep. We use them with you as we believe the Star People do: in the creation of angels.'

'Ah, yes,' Maram said as he patted his overstuffed belly and let loose a rude belch, 'I *am* rather like an angel, aren't I? Five-Horned Maram will become Maram of the Golden Wings. Soon, soon, I know, lesser men will have to bow to me and address me as "Lord Elijin".'

Abrasax shook his head in reproach for his sarcasm, and told him, 'You need not worry about taking on that burden just now. The Way is very long – long even for the Star People, and we have rediscovered only part of it.'

He looked at Kane as if in hope that he might say more about this ancient path that human beings walked toward the heavens. But Kane just stared at the conservatory's stone walls in silence.

'I must say,' Maram grumbled out, as he pressed his hand against his belly, solar plexus, heart and throat, 'that I feel little different than I did before we began this work.'

'That is because,' Master Storr chided him, 'your fires are blocked and trapped within your second chakra.'

At this, Maram shot Master Storr a belligerent look, and wantonly waggled his hips. Master Storr stared back at him in disdain.

Abrasax, however, was kinder. He smiled at Maram and said, 'Give it time.'

'Ah, time,' Maram muttered. 'How much of it do I have left before the candle burns out?'

He sighed as he stood up and gazed out the conservatory's window at the setting sun. Then he turned to Abrasax and said, 'You seem to have had all the time in the world, Grandfather, and yet that hasn't kept old age from snowing white hair on you, if you'll forgive me for speaking so bluntly.'

Abrasax smiled at this. 'I will forgive you, Sar Maram, but things are not always as they seem. Just how old do you think I am?'

Maram gazed at Abrasax, and I could almost hear him mentally subtracting ten years from his assessment in an effort to repay Abrasax's kindness: 'Ah, seventy, I should guess.'

Abrasax's smile widened. He said, 'I was born in the year that the Red Dragon destroyed the Golden Brotherhood and captured the False Gelstei. That was –'

'2647!' Maram cried out. 'But that is impossible! That would make you a hundred and forty-seven years old!'

'Please, Sar Maram – a hundred and forty-six,' Abrasax said with a grin. 'I won't have my next birthday until Segadar.'

'But that is impossible!' Maram said again. He looked from Abrasax to Kane. 'Only the Elijin are immortal and –'

'We of the Seven,' Abrasax said, interrupting him, 'have *not* gained immortality – only longevity. And other things.'

'Ah, *what* things?' Maram asked with great interest.

In answer, Abrasax stepped over to him, and he laid his long, wrinkled hands on Maram's sides along his chest. And then he lifted him as he might a child, straight up into the air. Maram, although obviously no angel, did for a moment appear to be flying. He whooped as he beat his arms like wings. I blinked my eyes in disbelief, for with all the eating he had been doing during the past week, he must have weighed twenty stone.

Abrasax set him down, and Maram stared at him as if he, too, couldn't believe what had just happened. He said to him, 'You look like an old bird, but you're as strong as a bear!'

'Thank you, I think,' Abrasax told him.

Maram clasped Abrasax's hand as if to test its strength. Abrasax squeezed back, and Maram winced and coughed out, 'Did I say a bear? A bull, you are, a veritable old bull. And all *this* from the work you do with your little crystals? What other, ah, *powers* have you gained?'

Abrasax smiled at this and said, 'What powers would *you* most like to gain?'

'Do you need to ask? A bull has only two horns, but I have five! A veritable dragon, I am, and oh how I burn! And so I would strengthen those fires that burn the most pleasurably.'

'There is more to life, Sar Maram, than pleasure. And there is more to pleasure than this little tickle in the loins that you pursue so ardently.'

'Yes, there is beer and brandy,' Maram said. 'And that which bestirs me down there is no little thing – it is more like dragon fire!'

Abrasax said nothing to this as he studied Maram with his keen eyes.

'Pure dragon fire, I tell you! And I can direct it as I will, no matter what Master Storr says about me being blocked!'

'Can you? Then perhaps you wouldn't mind if we put it to the test?'

'What kind of test?'

'One that should prove more enjoyable than one of your drinking duels.'

'Truly? Truly?' Maram smiled as he considered this. 'Then when do we begin?'

Abrasax stepped over to Master Okuth to murmur something in his ear. Master Okuth bowed, excused himself, and left the room. We waited with the other Masters around the tea tables for him to go about his business, whatever it was. Half an hour later, he returned. He produced a small vial containing some dark, reddish substance, which he poured into Maram's cup of tea and stirred with a little silver spoon. Then he gave the cup to Maram to drink.

'Ah, I must say,' Maram called out, sniffing his tea, 'that this potion of yours seems suspiciously like blood.'

'It is a tincture made from the pineal gland of the adil serpent,' Master Okuth told him. 'It will help dissolve your blockage so that the kundala can rise within you.'

Maram sniffed it again. 'Are you sure it won't poison me? Ah, like a snake's venom, paralyzing me?'

'It will only paralyze your resistance.'

I gazed at Maram, waiting for him to drink, or not – as did Kane, Master Juwain and Liljana. The Masters of the Brotherhood studied him as well. And then Maram, challenged once again to drink as part of a trial, shrugged his shoulders and downed the red-tinged tea.

'Aach!' he cried out, coughing. 'Ohhh – oh, my Lord, that was vile!'

He looked to Master Okuth for sympathy for his sufferings. But Master Okuth just looked at him sternly as he brought out his small, green heart stone. The other Masters held out their gelstei as well, and they beckoned for Maram to stand up and gathered around him.

Then Abrasax instructed Maram: 'You must try visualizing that which you most love. Hold this image inside yourself, and let it call to you.'

'Ah, you mean visualize *her* whom I love. Make *her* call to me.'

'No, Sar Maram,' Abrasax said. 'I do *not* mean that. We have other potions and other exercises designed for the realization of fancies and dreams. You have told us that you are a man of this world. There is *something* in this world – something that you've held in hand and heart – that you love above all else. Hold it in your heart now. And in your mind. Let it call to your life's deepest fire and draw it upward, even as the kundalini strikes upward, toward the heavens.'

Maram smiled at me then, and I understood that he took great satisfaction in keeping secret whatever it was that he found most to love. Was it Behira, I wondered? The Galdan brandy that Vishakan, chief of the Niuriu, had once poured for him? The smell of the earth on the most perfect day of his life? I thought that I would never know.

Then Maram closed his eyes, and the Great Gelstei of the Seven began to sing to Maram in a rainbow of fire. The Masters worked their magic upon Maram for most of an hour. Finally, there came a moment when I felt something inside of Maram break open. I sensed a great gout of flame moving up from his first and second chakras into his third, fourth and higher ones, as with companions passing from hand to hand a bright torch. Hotter and hotter it grew, like the sun in Soldru. At last Maram opened his eyes, and looked straight at me in triumph. He let out a shout of delight that shook the stones of the dome above us. His face seemed to light up as with fireworks as he cried out, 'It's as if the ecstasy of my loins is burning throughout my whole body and brain! You were right, Grandfather: *this* is more enjoyable than beer, or even brandy!'

'Even more enjoyable,' Atara prodded him, 'than women?'

'Ah, perhaps, perhaps.' Maram breathed deeply and raggedly as he held his hand over his heart. Then his eyes glazed with doubt. 'But it's almost *too* pleasurable, if you know what I mean.'

Liljana, whose Maitriche Telu possessed other means of igniting the body's fires, said to him, 'And now you know why my sisters are dreaded.'

'Dreaded or desired?'

Liljana pointed her finger at him as she shook her head. 'It's good that we've taken shelter here rather than at one of our sanctuaries. If you weren't careful, my sisters would kill you with just such pleasure.'

'Truly? Well, I must die sometime, I suppose, and I can think of no better way.'

Whatever fate awaited us on our quest, however, during our final days at the Brotherhood's school, we had only thought and feeling for more life. As the spring quickened and the warm sun poured down its light into the valley – and the Seven continued pouring their gelstei's radiance into us – we gained strength like the new shoots of the cherry trees fairly singing with sap. My companions and I all felt more vital. We found ourselves needing less sleep, and during our waking hours we seemed more awake. Although we did not gain the miraculous regenerative powers of Kane, whose flesh I had once seen regrow a severed ear, Abrasax told us that we might bear up beneath insults and wounds that would kill lesser beings.

'But it is your spirits, I believe, that will suffer the greatest trials,' he told us one fine morning. It was to be our last day in the Valley

169

of the Sun, and we had gathered with the Masters in the cherry orchard beneath a tree covered in snowy blossoms. 'The Lord of Lies will attack them, and more, try to drink your very souls. We must speak of this now. If your path is to take you through Acadu, there is one danger that you must avoid above all others.'

Maram's face blanched while Master Juwain sat on the white-petaled grass with his hands folded like a closed book. And Master Juwain said, 'And what is that, Grandfather?'

Abrasax looked at Master Juwain for a long moment as his lips pressed together. Then he said, 'I would like to give you a full account of this. Would you be willing to come with me into the library?'

'Of course,' Master Juwain told him.

'Estrella,' Abrasax said, turning toward the girl, 'there is a book that I believe will tell more than I can about this danger. It is, in a way, lost in the library's stacks. Would you help me locate it?'

Estrella smiled as she nodded her head.

The rest of us, curious as to how this new mystery might unfold, stood up and followed Abrasax as he led us toward the library. This building rose up near the center of the Brotherhood's grounds, and was made of the same white stone as every other building in the valley. Tall pillars fronted it. Its rear wall fairly pushed into the side of a hill. Although larger even than the great hall, it wasn't nearly so grand as the library of King Kiritan's palace – to say nothing of the vast, burnt-out Library of Kaisham.

We followed Abrasax and the other masters up the seven stairs leading to the doorway and into the library's single room. There, sitting at long wooden tables, a dozen Brothers bent over reading old tomes; a dozen more worked hard to preserve the knowledge of the oldest and most fragile of them, transcribing words onto new paper with ink-blackened quills. This scratching sound filled the quiet room. The many dusty, crumbling books stacked on the shelves along the four walls seemed to await renewal at the Brothers' hands. I counted some seven thousand of them. As we learned, every one of them had been indexed and accounted for. I did not understand how one of them could have been lost.

I looked in vain for the marvelous, crystal-paged books like the one from which Abrasax had read that night in the conservatory. I wondered if the Brothers might keep them locked away some-where in a cabinet, but Abrasax did not say anything about this.

He led us straight across the room to the far wall. Between two of the great shelves rising six feet above our heads, there hung a tapestry depicting one the greatest events of Eaean history: King Julamesh giving the Lightstone into the hands of Godavanni the Glorious. With great care, Abrasax moved aside this tapestry to reveal a small door set into the wall's stone. Without a word of explanation, he opened the door, which swung inward on creaking hinges to the passage beyond.

'Ah, secret doors and dark passages,' Maram said with a nervous cough. 'This reminds me too much of Argattha. Where are you taking us, Grandfather?'

Abrasax paused to turn and smile at us. 'Why, into the library.'

'What do you mean?' Maram said, waving his hand at one of the ink-stained Brothers hard at work on a book. 'What do you call this place?'

'It is only the reading room,' Abrasax told him. He turned to step through the doorway into the passage beyond. '*This* is the library.'

We followed him down an unlit stone corridor. A soft radiance suffused the opening twenty yards ahead of us. The Masters passed through this opening, out into the chamber beyond, and then so did I. I shook my head in disbelief. My belly fairly fluttered up into my throat as if I had jumped off a cliff into a pool, for I found myself gazing out into a vast, open space so deep that I did not want to look down for its bottom. I gathered with my friends and the Masters in a sort of loggia affording a view of this immense cavern. It was good that stone railings had been built at the edge of the loggia; otherwise it would have been easy for anyone, sick with the heights, to step off the edge and plunge downward.

'Oh, Lord!' Maram said as he looked out over the railing. 'Oh, Lord!'

The loggia proved to be part of the uppermost tier carved into the rock of this cylindrical pit and running around its circumference. It seemed half a mile, as a bird might fly, straight across to the tier's other side. There were many, many tiers: two hundred eighty-four, as Abrasax told us. Bands of rock separated each tier, and glowed with a pearly substance that could only be some sort of gelstei. It provided a soft, white light that illumined the entire library and its many books.

There must have been millions of them. Each tier, twelve feet high, contained ten shelves which had been carved as even deeper recesses into the cavern's solid rock. As with any library, books packed each shelf. Abrasax led us out of the loggia into the first tier, and I ran my hand across the bindings of the old books. All were of leather and paper, and seemed no different from any of the other books that I had read. And they were all, in this section of this tier, as I could see from their titles, copies of various versions of the *Saganom Elu* or commentaries upon it. I had never dreamed that so much could have been written about this Book of Books, neatly arrayed on smooth, granite shelves curving off nearly to infinity.

'I can see,' Master Juwain said to Abrasax, 'how a book might become lost here. If all the levels contain as many volumes as this one, there must be more than thirty million books!'

'There are forty million, ten thousand and forty-three,' Abrasax informed us with a smile. 'To be precise.'

'But that is more than the Great Library held!'

'It is. But we Brothers have had longer to collect our books than did Khaisham's Librarians.'

'But how *did* you acquire so many, Grandfather? And where are the crystal books that you call the vedastei? And who built your library, and how was it made?'

Master Juwain had other questions for Abrasax, which Abrasax tried to answer as he led us back into the loggia, and then down a flight of stone stairs connecting to a loggia on the second tier.

'None of us,' Abrasax said, nodding at Master Storr and Master Yasul, 'has been able to determine who built this library. When our order established itself here in the Age of Law, Grandmaster Teodorik discovered the library much as you see it today. It is possible that the Aymaniri – they call themselves the Ymanir now – melted out this cavern with firestones even before they built Agarttha. Or it might be older still: much, much older. Some of us believe it might be a wonder from the Elder Ages.'

'But the books,' Master Juwain said, 'cannot date from the Elder Ages!'

We had passed down to the eighth tier, and Master Juwain's hand swept out as he pointed outside the loggia at ancient tomes recording the *Epic of Kalkamesh*, the *Gest of Nodin and Yurieth* and other famous narratives, which were very much part of Eaean history.

'No, you are correct,' Abrasax said to Master Juwain. '*These* books we have gathered from across the world like any others. But it may be that the vedastei are not of this world.'

He led us down ten more tiers, and the sound of our boots slapping against stone steps vanished into the immense open space of the library.

172

I could almost hear Maram formulating his complaints as to the inevitable climb back up the many stairways. He must have wondered, as did I, if the library's makers had indeed been angels who could simply fly from tier to tier. It would have required hours, I thought, to retrieve a book from the lowest tiers and make the arduous climb back up into the reading room. As I watched Master Yasul and Master Virang follow Abrasax effortlessly down the stairways, it came to me that Brothers had endless hours and years to go about their work – and nearly bottomless stamina.

We made our way down to the twentieth and then the twenty-fifth tier. Here the books of leather and paper gave way to those made from crystal. Abrasax told us that most of the books on these levels, as far as the Brothers had been able to determine, were of poetry and songs. At last we came out into a loggia on the thirty-third tier. Abrasax led the way out onto this narrow curve of stone. We walked in near-silence past shelves of the marvelous vedastei. I could not guess at their subjects, for I could not read the script engraved into their colored and lacquered covers.

'Ah, I've never seen so many damn books!' Maram murmured to me. 'Not even in the Great Library.'

We moved through two more of the twelve loggias on this tier. Then we came out upon a section of shelves, all of whose books bore the same title. Abrasax pulled one of them off its shelf, and he traced his finger along the golden characters etched into its blue cover. Then he said to us a single word: 'Skaadarak.'

'Do you mean, the *Skardarak*?' Master Juwain said to him, carefully pronouncing the name of the great doom at the end of time when the universe would fall into a final dark age.

'Perhaps,' Abrasax said. 'You see, we have been able to translate the book's title, but its contents remain unknown to us.'

He opened the book and flipped through its hundreds of fine crystal pages. They remained as blank as sheets of ice.

'But can't you just unlock it?' Maram called out.

'We cannot. We have tried, and we shall continue to try, but we have been able to discover keys for only a fraction of the vedastei.'

He went on to tell us that the Brothers had discovered word keys for perhaps three thousand of the vedastei, and most of these were located on the higher tiers.

'All these books,' he said as his hand swept along the shelf, 'are a mystery to us.'

He looked out over the stone railing down into the glowing pit that made up the rest of the library. 'The books below this level remain unread, and all are vedastei, going down to the one hundred and twenty-first level.'

'And below that?' Master Juwain asked.

'Below that, there are no books.'

'But you said that there were two hundred and eighty-four levels?'

'There are, indeed. And most of their shelves stand empty.'

'But why? Did the library's makers hope to acquire so many more books?'

'We don't know,' Abrasax said. Then he held up his precious vedastei. 'Just as we don't know what lies within this book.'

Master Juwain nodded his head at this, and said, 'If the vedastei were truly written in the Elder Ages and brought to Ea, then how is it you believe that one of them might tell of some danger of the Acadian forest of *our* time?'

Master Yasul, the Brotherhood's greatest remembrancer, answered for Abrasax, saying, 'It may be that some of the vedastei were not actually *written*. With a few of the books that we have managed to open, we've had the experience of the text changing upon different readings, according to different knowledge that we were seeking and different questions that we held in our minds. Indeed, it might be more accurate to say that we don't read the vedastei as much as *they* read us.'

He went on to say that the vedastei might somehow transmit the Akashic Records, which was a sort of memory of all that had ever occurred in the universe.

'Ah, there are certain *things* that should never be recorded,' Maram said as he eyed the book that Abrasax held in his hand. 'And never read by another, if you know what I mean.'

Abrasax smiled at Maram. 'You needn't fear that anyone will learn of your exploits in *this* book – unless it is your valor in facing the unknown.'

Abrasax put it back on its shelf, then turned to Estrella, who stood with Daj near the railing as they looked out into the library. He said to her, 'We have reason to believe that one of these books entitled, *Skaadarak*, contains the knowledge we seek. Would you be willing to try to locate it for us?'

Estrella looked at the book-stuffed shelves opposite the railing, and she made a motion with her fingers and cocked her head. And Daj translated for her, saying to us: 'Estrella would like to know how many of these Skaadarak books there are?'

'Nearly three hundred,' Abrasax told us. Then he showed us the place where the first of the books in question was shelved, and he moved along the tier a dozen feet and tapped his finger against the spine of the last of the books, gleaming a dark red on one of the middle shelves.

Estrella smiled as she nodded her head. Then she began walking slowly in front of the shelves of books. What she was looking for she could not say, and we could not guess, for the covers of the books were all etched with the same fine script. At last, she came to a halt. Her eyes beamed brightly as gazed at the line of books just above her head. Then her hand darted out to grasp one of the vedastei there. Abrasax helped her pull it off the shelf. Its cover, carved with brilliant red glyphs, shone as black as obsidian.

'A seard, indeed,' Master Matai said, bowing his head to her.

Master Storr, however, looked at Estrella doubtfully, as if she might have picked this book at random with the hope that no one would ever know the difference.

Abrasax lifted back the cover to show us its clear, empty pages. And Master Juwain asked him, 'But if you don't possess the key, how will you ever open it?'

'A seard,' Abrasax said, smiling at Estrella, 'might be able to find more than just *things*. We have elucidated, over the centuries, hundreds of keys to these books, and many are related to another or are even nearly identical.'

He drew in a long breath, and then recited:

> To gain the gelstei's mastery,
> To free the perfect memory
> From Heaven's ageless library,
> The perfect word will prove the key.

'Estrella – can you tell us if any of these words are close to the ones we seek?'

But Estrella just shook her head as she stared at the book.

'But what of this rhyme, then? Listen:

> The Master Reader sought the key
> To Heaven's unbound folio;
> A million words he spoke, then he
> Said, 'Open' – and it was so.

Estrella held out her hands helplessly as she again shook her head.

175

And Maram groaned, 'This could take all day!'

So it went for the many other keys that Abrasax wished to test as he recited to her verse after verse. She seemed to warm to only a couple of them. Although it did not take Abrasax *quite* all day to run through his list of rhymes, it took long enough. We stood there for what seemed hours packed together on a ribbon of stone between the tier's shelved books and the railing that kept us from plunging down nearly half a mile to the library's lowest level. Our legs grew crampy, and we shifted our weight from foot to foot even as Abrasax's deep voice spilled out into the immense cavern.

'But this is impossible!' Maram finally called out to Abrasax. 'We might as well set monkeys to scribbling on paper in that room of yours upstairs in the hope that one of them will eventually chance upon the right rhyme.'

'Nothing is impossible, Sar Maram,' Abrasax said. 'Estrella has indicated that two or three of the rhymes might lead to the key to this book. We've had less to go on with other keys and other books. There are references to be checked, permutations of words to be made. In time –'

'But how much time do we *have*?' Maram said. 'Aren't we supposed to set out tomorrow? I, for one, want to get this mad quest over with as soon as we can, if we truly must go off questing again. Can't you just tell us what kind of danger we must avoid in Acadu without giving a complete account of it?'

Abrasax sighed as he traded looks with Master Virang and Master Matai. He said, 'I suppose I'll have to.'

He drew in a long breath as he pressed his finger against the scarlet characters graven into the book's cover. And then he told us, 'I believe that *Skaadarak* is the root word of two others: the Skardarak, when all will grow dark forever. And a place of darkness in Acadu that the people there call the Skadarak.'

In the quiet of the library's endless stacks of books, this word seemed to hang in the still, musty air. We all waited for Abrasax to say more. Then Maram finally called out, 'But what *is* the Skadarak, then?'

'It is,' Abrasax said, 'a blackness of the earth's aura so abysmally black that light cannot escape it. There is a dark thing there, like a hole through the world's soul. It blackens the very earth.'

'A *thing*?' Maram cried out. 'What kind of *thing*?'

Abrasax looked at the book in his hand, and then at Master Storr. He said, 'Unfortunately, we don't really know. We have only

176

stories and our reading of the earth's aura. Those whom we have sent into Acadu to shed light on this mystery have not returned.'

'Oh, excellent!' Maram said. 'I suppose this dark mystery of yours swallowed them up as with the Black Bog?'

'I believe,' Abrasax said, 'that what lies near the heart of Acadu is worse than the Black Bog. You see, it calls to people.'

'Oh, excellent, excellent!'

Master Juwain thought about this, then asked, 'But what could have caused the Skadarak? An opening to one of the Dark Worlds? Some sort of gelstei?'

'I know of no gelstei,' Master Storr said, 'that has such power.'

'But what of the black?' Master Juwain asked, looking at Kane.

And Master Storr said, 'I've never heard of a black gelstei that can call to people as the Skadarak is said to do.'

Liljana, ever the most practical of our company, said to Abrasax, 'If you know where this place is, then surely we can avoid it. If it calls to us, then we won't listen.'

Abrasax nodded his hoary head and told her, 'North of Varkeva near the Ea River it lies, or so we believe. We also believe that each of you has the power *not* to listen. And that, in the end, is the heart of our battle with the Red Dragon and the Dark One bound on Damoom.'

He let out a long sigh as he turned to Master Juwain. 'You, Master Healer, over the years have most counseled turning a deaf ear to Morjin's words. And why? Because it is you who most wants to hear them.'

Master Juwain rubbed at his bald head a moment before saying, 'Yes, I'm afraid you are right, Grandfather. I've always thought that the Red Dragon, as with any man, would intimate what he really knows in what he says or writes. The secret knowledge that he *must* possess, you see.'

'That which you speak of is a dark knowledge,' Abrasax told him.

'And how could it be otherwise, for how can we truly understand the light without the knowing of the dark?'

'I think you've always been too curious about this dark.'

'Yes, you are right. It is my vice.'

'Promise me, then, that you will continue to fight against it.'

'Very well, Grandfather.'

Abrasax smiled at him, and said, 'All of you, as you approach the Skadarak, will grow more vulnerable. Especially through your gelstei.'

He turned to look at Atara. 'You, Princess, must be careful of what you see in your crystal, if you really must look. Morjin will try to build a perfect world and show it to you. And trap you within it. Thus has he seduced kings and even wise men.'

Atara stood up straight and stiffly, and a coldness came over her as she gripped her scryer's sphere and said, 'The Lord of Lies gave up the power to seduce me when he took my eyes. But I shall take your counsel to heart, Grandfather.'

Abrasax sighed again, and then addressed Liljana and Kane, and each of us, in turn, warning of the ways that Morjin might strike at us through our crystals and our weaknesses to twist us to his will as he had so many others. Then he patted the black book that Estrella had found on its shelf, and he told us, 'I will take this back to my chambers and meditate upon it. Perhaps I will find the key that will open it, and be able to tell you more.'

I said nothing as I looked at Abrasax and promised myself that whatever the Skadarak truly was, and wherever it lay, I must lead my companions away from it at all costs.

'Go now,' Abrasax said to us. 'Go and sit outside in the cherry orchard or walk in the sun, as you will. Enjoy this day in peace.'

And so we did. We all left the library as we had come. Abrasax retired with his book to his chambers, and the other Masters left us alone to go about their business. That afternoon, my companions and I wandered the grounds of the school making our good-byes with those of the Brothers whom we had come to know. They gave us gifts: jars of apple butter and rare teas and spices for our food, and other such things to sustain us on our journey. We went to bed early that evening and awoke just before dawn on the twenty-third of Ashte. The sky was a clear and luminous blue that promised fine weather for travel.

Abrasax and the rest of the Seven gathered in the yard outside the stables to see us off. As the cocks crowed and new season's insects let loose a noise of buzzing and clicks, the Grandmaster apologized to us for being unable to unlock the book that told of the Skadarak.

'I remained awake all night,' he told us, 'but some of the books have taken months or even years to open – those that we *have* been able to open.'

'It's all right, Grandfather,' I said. 'Surely the Skadarak can't be any worse than Argattha, and we survived that.'

I regretted my words almost the moment that I spoke them. I felt Atara stiffen inside as if awaiting a mortal blow. Although she had truly survived Argattha, even as I had said, something within her had died.

'Try to remember,' Master Virang said to me, 'that the Skadarak will only be one of the dangers you face, and perhaps not the worst. It is a long way to the end of your quest, and you must armor yourself against the Lord of Illusions' assaults.'

'We would have a better chance,' Master Juwain said to Master Virang and then Abrasax, 'if you would come with us to Hesperu. Will you reconsider your decision?'

It seemed almost silly to think of these seven old men setting out on a perilous journey through Ea's wilds. But then I recalled how easily Abrasax had lifted Maram off the ground and Master Virang's ease at climbing steep hills, and I thought that it would be the essence of wisdom for any or all of them to accompany us.

'I'm sorry,' Abrasax told us, looking out into the valley, 'but our place is here.'

Then his eyes grew mysterious and deep as he tried to explain: 'Just as the body has higher chakras and realms of being, so does the earth. It is in these realms, above all others, that we must battle the Red Dragon's evil – and we can only do this from a place of great power, where the earth's fires burn the brightest.'

Master Juwain bowed his head in acceptance of this, and Abrasax took his hand and said, 'Just be sure to keep *your* fires burning, and we shall look forward to your return with the one who burns the most brightly of all.'

He smiled then, and clasped each of our hands in turn and kissed our brows, even Kane's. And then he told us, 'Farewell, and may you walk in the light of the One.'

I climbed on top of Altaru, whose coat was like a black sheen in the early morning light. He drove his hoof into the earth impatiently. My friends mounted their horses, too; our remounts and packhorses, heavily laden with supplies, were strung out behind us. A young student had also brought out a couple of nags from the stable. Master Storr and one of his adepts, a Brother Lorand, would be accompanying us so that they might show us the way out of the valley.

Our slow ride toward the mountains took only a few hours, and we savored each of them, drinking in the warmth of the sun and the sweetly scented air. Flowers grew in sprays of pink and purple along our way. From somewhere in the woods around us, a lark piped out its high, tinkling song. Never in my life, I thought, had a day seemed so lovely and bright. Kane rode his big brown horse beside me, fairly beaming out his fierce will to triumph against any odds. And yet I was keenly aware that our high spirits could not last. Whenever the shadow of such doubts fell across my heart, all of Kane's assurances of victory, as well as my own fierce hopes, seemed utterly in vain, the foolish longings of desperate men who refused to admit defeat.

We made our way back to the tunnel as we had come, winding back and forth up a steep slope. The horses' hooves kicked at loose rocks and sent them rattling down the road. Just outside the tunnel's entrance, where an arch of precisely cut stone invited us inward and onward, we paused to take a drink of water and eat some currants.

'Ah, here we are again at another entranceway,' Maram said, squinting at the sun in the east. 'But it's well past dawn, isn't it?'

Master Storr's fair skin was flushed from our ride, and he ran his fingers back through his wispy hair. He smiled at Maram and said, 'The sun at dawn at the ides of Ashte is only one of the things that animates the tunnel's gelstei. There is the light of the Seven Sisters, conjuncting the moon. And there is this.'

He removed from his pocket a crystal about as long as his finger. It was opaque, with a reddish patina that reminded me of rust.

'What is it?' Maram asked. 'One of your secret gelstei?'

'It's a key,' Master Storr told him. 'And yes, it is a gelstei.'

He pointed it toward the tunnel, and we watched as the dark circle before us filled with a milky white light. I felt a pulsing, as from deep inside the tunnel's rock – and along my veins as my heart began beating more quickly.

'Well, why don't we go inside?' Master Storr said. 'The way in is easy enough.'

'Ah, I don't like this,' Maram said. 'I don't like this at *all*. We can find our way *in* easily enough, it's true. It's finding the way *out* that worries me.'

Master Storr handed the crystal to Brother Lorand, a reedy young man with a long, narrow head and a serious look stamped into his face. And Master Storr instructed him, 'Hold your concentration as I've taught you. We wouldn't want to leave Brother Maram behind.'

His rather pitiless smile, showing his small, yellowed teeth, did nothing to reassure Maram, or the rest of us. But Master Storr was not a cruel man – only a cautious, difficult and guarded one. As we set forth into the tunnel, he explained to us certain of its secrets that he had so far withheld: 'There are seventeen such tunnels

180

throughout this part of the White Mountains, as far as we've been able to determine. The Grandmaster thinks it most likely that the Aymaniri built them. But Master Yasul and I are more inclined to believe that they are a work of the Elder Ages, like the library. All that we have really divined of them is that they connect to other tunnels through other mountains.'

'But connect *how*?' Maram asked. 'And how can that be possible?'

Master Storr regarded Maram with his hard blue eyes and said, 'How should that *not* be possible? All things are connected in their deepest part, in their hearts, to each other. That is why we call the One as we do, and not the Two or the Three.'

This was almost the first time we had heard Master Storr make any attempt at humor, and we all smiled at him. Then Maram continued his questioning: 'If all things are connected to everything, then that really explains nothing. How is it that I should still be standing in this lost valley in your company, as pleasant as it is, instead of enjoying a glass or two of good Meshian beer with my beloved, merely at a click of my fingers?'

So saying, he snapped his middle finger against his thumb, and looked about as if disappointed that this rude gesture hadn't magically transported him from the valley.

Master Storr kept on staring at him, and said, 'The key, of course, is in discovering *how* things are connected. We know, for instance, that Ea touches upon other worlds in places of power such as the Vilds or where the earth fires have been disturbed or concentrated.'

'Such as the Black Bog? Kane told that in our passage through that accursed swamp, we were walking on other worlds.'

'So you were – and Dark Worlds at that. The Black Bog is known to lead into such places, just as the ocean, toward the North Star, flows into the seas of the worlds where the Star People dwell.'

'Then you believe the legend of King Koru-Ki?'

Master Storr's eyes gleamed as he said, 'All worlds are connected by water, on the physical plane, as they are by the aethers on the others.'

'But that still doesn't explain the tunnel.'

Master Storr, I thought, did not like Maram's impatience to learn the truth of things, and a note of irritation crept into his voice:

'As I've said, there are other ways of making these connections. Whoever built this tunnel must have forged a gelstei that opened up the earth chakra over which the tunnel was built. And so directed its fires to open other chakras in other places so that a passage might be made.'

'Then is it possible to pass to other *worlds* this way?'

'Not through this tunnel, at least so far as we've been able to discover. But there may be other tunnels through other mountains somewhere on Ea that lead to the Star People's worlds.'

'But might it be possible,' Maram asked, 'to pass to another part of *this* world through this tunnel? Ah, perhaps to journey to Hesperu in a click of a moment?'

Again, he snapped his fingers, and again Master Storr looked at him with disapproval. He said to Maram, 'There are no tunnels like these that we know of in Hesperu, or indeed outside of the White Mountains. But if you discover any such on your journey, you must be sure to let me know.'

'I shall, I shall,' Maram muttered as he looked into the tunnel's glowing mouth. 'But I still don't understand how walking into *here* will result in our walking out *there* – when 'there' is not just one other tunnel, but any one of seventeen.'

'Haven't you been listening to anything of what I've told you?' Master Storr asked him. 'There is really only *one* tunnel, interconnected in its seventeen parts. But connected how? Geometrically, yes, certainly, in ways that we don't fully understand. But we know they are also connected through thought and will. This is the key, Sar Maram. When you were looking for our school and went back inside the tunnel, which the sun had brought to life, its gelstei sensed your desire to reach us, and so brought you out into our valley. If you had willed a different destination and held it strongly enough in your minds, you would have found that place instead.'

'Ah, but what if the tunnel came alive, and we willed *nothing*?' Maram's voice boomed out and disappeared into the curved, pulsing walls of gelstei ahead of us. 'Because we were frightened or confused?'

'That is an experiment we haven't wanted to make,' Master Storr said. 'Presumably, you would eventually come out into one lost valley or another.'

'But what of Morjin then? Aren't you afraid that he will learn to control the tunnel's gelstei?'

'He might know nothing of it,' Master Storr said. 'He is not omniscient, you know. Now, if you will, please forbear and let Brother Lorand learn the ways of these tunnels.'

None of us, I thought, was pleased at the prospect of Master

Storr utilizing our circumstances to teach his young student, but that was the way of the Brotherhood. In truth, however, there was little danger of Brother Lorand guiding us wrongly, for Master Storr guided *him*, holding his concentration on the rustlike gelstei even as he encouraged Brother Lorand with a ready smile or a kind word. Our passage through the tunnel was much as before. We lined up in order behind Master Storr; I took the lead of my companions, followed by Atara, Liljana, Daj and Estrella, with Master Juwain and Maram riding closely behind this irrepressibly joyful girl. Kane, in the rear, kept a close watch on what Estrella watched, gazing into the flowing hues of the gelstei on the walls in hope that she might discover something of note. The horses, which we had blindfolded, clopped along nervously as each of us fought the spinning sensation in our heads and the sickness that crept into our bellies. Maram moaned to see Master Storr waver like a ghost and then reappear a moment later. It seemed that we walked a long time and an even longer way over the road's cold stones. But in the end, as Master Storr kept promising Maram, we drew closer and closer to the spot of light at the tunnel's end.

We came out, as before, into a valley – but a very different one than the Valley of the Sun. Below us, down steep and heavily wooded slopes, ran a long, deep groove between two ridgelines of jagged mountains. It was higher here, and colder, and crusts of snow whitened the rocks above the treeline. The blueness had fled from the sky, to be replaced by a solid sheet of grayish-white clouds.

We stood by our horses on the rocky ground outside the tunnel, trying to catch our breaths as we scanned this rugged terrain. Maram leaned across his knees as if he might lose his breakfast. And then he pointed down into the valley as he gasped out, 'But which way *is* that? I can't see the damn sun! North, I would guess, but it seemed that we were walking south, or perhaps east.'

Master Storr came up beside him and placed his old hand on his shoulder. And he said, 'It is north by west. The line of the valley curves off due west, just around the base of that domed mountain. It will take you down into Acadu.'

'Are you certain of that? What if we get lost?'

'Would it reassure you if I taught you a Way Rhyme to guide you?'

'Ah, is that really necessary?'

'No, it is not,' Master Storr said, smiling at him. 'From here, you can't help but walk straight into Acadu, but you'll have to find your own way through the great forest, as your circumstances will determine.'

He embraced Maram then, and me and the others as well. And he told us, 'You must undertake this quest with only one end in mind. But if you *should* come across any new gelstei on your journey, I would be forever grateful if you would return them to our school for study. You seem to have a knack for finding gelstei – let us hope that also holds for finding the Maitreya.'

As Abrasax had, he enjoined us to walk in the light of the One. Then he gathered in the reins of his horse, and with Brother Lorand, moved back into the tunnel.

'Well,' Maram said to me as we looked off into this new valley, 'shall we get this over with?'

I nodded at him, then turned to pull on Altaru's reins and go down into the dark forests of Acadu.

11

For the rest of the morning, we worked our way down into the valley. The going was rough. The road here, as ancient as any I had ever seen, had mostly disintegrated into a long, twisting slip of broken rock and dirt. Near the bottom of the valley, where a river rushed between steeply cut banks, the forest swallowed up the road altogether. We had to take care where we stepped, lest a rock hidden in the undergrowth or a root turn an ankle or hoof. We moved slowly, from need, guiding our horses over this bad ground. And yet a greater need drove us like a match flame slowly growing hotter inside us. We each knew that our quest had little chance of success in any case, and none at all if we wasted a week coddling ourselves – or perhaps a day or even an hour.

After a quick lunch of ham and cheese sandwiches, washed down with a bubbly apple cider, it began to rain, and this added misery to the difficulty of our descent. As we came down near the river and the ground flattened out, Maram let out a grunt of thanks – and then he began cursing as the rain suddenly drove down harder in stinging sheets that made him, and all of us, squint and shiver as we hunched down into our cloaks.

'I'm tired and cold,' he complained late in the afternoon. 'And I'm getting hungry again, too. Why don't we break for the day, and see if we can roast up some of that lamb the Brothers packed for us before it rots?'

Kane, however, insisted that we plod on another hour before making camp, and so we did. But by the time we found a level spot above the river and began unpacking the horses, Maram had grown quite surly with hunger – and fairly wroth when he discovered that every twig, stick and log that he could find rummaging around in the woods was soaking wet. As the day darkened into night, he spent another hour fumbling with matches and strips of linen, trying to get a fire going. He finally gave up. He sat on a large, wet rock feeling as sorry for himself as he was ashamed at failing the rest of us. Then he took out his firestone and held it between his hands as he might a dead child.

'Oh, my poor, poor crystal!' he moaned. He nudged the pile of wood beside him with his foot. 'If that damn dragon hadn't ruined you, I'd turn this damn kindling into char with a *real* fire.'

'It might help,' Atara said, sitting down next to him, 'if you used paper for tinder instead of linen.'

'Paper? What paper?'

At this, we all looked at Master Juwain, who said, 'Tear up one of my books? You might as well tear off my skin and try to get a fire out of that. Only if we were dying from cold would I consider it.'

'Ah, well, it wouldn't matter anyway,' Maram said, kicking his woodpile again. 'The problem is not with the tinder – these damn logs are soaked to the core, as am I.'

We brought out two large rain cloths, and propped them up with sticks. Then we all sat around in a circle beneath them staring at the heap of sodden wood through the dying light. Liljana had taken Daj under her cloak, and Atara likewise sheltered Estrella. We listened to the rain patter against pungent-smelling wool and break against the leaves of the trees towering above us.

Atara oriented her soaked blindfold toward Maram's crystal, and she said, 'Do you remember the prophecy concerning your firestone?'

'Do you mean, that it will bring Morjin's doom?'

'Yes. But I can't see how it ever will.'

'That's because you've no faith that it will be made whole again. I *know* it will,' Maram said. He sighed as he pointed his crystal northwest, toward Argattha. 'And *then* I'll make a fire such as has never been seen on Ea, I swear I will. *Then* I'll roast Morjin like a damn worm!'

'Ha!' Kane said, coming over to clap him on the shoulder. 'You can't even roast a little lamb for our dinner! Well, it will have to be cold cheese and battle biscuits for us tonight, then.'

And so it was. We sat in the driving rain eating these unappealing rations with resignation. Our two cloths did not keep this slanting deluge from soaking us. Maram complained for the hundredth time that we should have brought tents with us, and for the hundredth time Kane explained that tents were much too bulky and heavy for our horses, which were already weighted down with our supplies. In truth, they could not carry enough oats and food to take us even half the way to Hesperu; this arithmetic reality of constant subtraction would compel us to replenish our stores along the way, and Kane bitterly resented this necessity.

'But there's no help for it,' Maram said.

'No help, you say? *I* say we could jettison certain stores to make room for more food.'

Maram cast Kane a suspicious look and said, 'I hope you don't mean the beer and the brandy!'

Kane turned up his wrists and let the rain gather in his cupped hands. 'It seems we won't lack for drink, at least until we reach the desert.'

'Brandy,' Maram said, 'is *not* just drink – it's medicine. And one that is badly needed on such a night. We could all use a little of its fire.'

Master Juwain, however, was not quite ready to concede this need. He said to Maram, 'Why don't you practice moving the kundalini fire up your spine, as Abrasax taught you. That would warm you better.'

'Ah, a woman would warm me better still,' he moaned. 'If only I had a good tent against the rain, and my sleeping furs were dry, I'd crawl inside with her, wrap my arms around her poor, cold, shivering body, and then, like flint and steel, like a match held to a barrel of pitch, like a poker plunging into a bed of coals, I'd –'

'Maram,' I said to him, 'I thought you'd learned to redirect this fire of yours?'

'Well, what if I have?' he said. 'I *could* redirect it, as you say, if I wanted to – I'm sure I could. But why should I want to? It's too hard, too uncertain, too . . . unnatural, if you know what I mean. I'm a man who was born to live on the earth, not the stars. And it's been too long since I held a woman in my arms, much too long.'

And with this lamentation, he tried to settle in to sleep for the night as best he could. And so did the rest of us. But it rained all that night, and we awoke to a dull gray light fighting its way through the gray clouds above us and slatelike sheets of rain. We fought against the ache of our cold, stiff limbs to get under way and continue on down the valley. The squish of the horses' hooves against mud and soaking bracken was nearly drowned out by the rushing of the river and the unceasing rain.

By mid-afternoon, however, this torrent had let up slightly. And then, as the valley gave out into lower and flatter country, it dried up to a stiff drizzle. So it was that we at last entered the great Acadian forest. This vast expanse of woods stretched from Sakai in the northwest five hundred miles to the borders of Uskadar and Karabuk in the southeast. We proposed to cross it, east to west, along a route through its northern part less than two hundred miles long. This would take us well to the north of Varkeva, Acadu's greatest and only real city. And north, as well, we hoped, of that dark place of which Abrasax had warned us. Master Juwain had brought with him a map of Acadu, little good that it would do us. It showed Acadu's few main roads, but these we could not take. Into the map's tough parchment was inked the position of the few bridges across Acadu's rivers, but we would have to find fords or ferrymen to help us along our way.

It did not distress me to set out into this strange woods without any path to guide us. Maram often envied my sense of direction, even as he called it uncanny, even otherworldly. I had been born knowing in my blood east from west, north from south, with all the certainty of a ship's pilot steering a course by the stars. Even on such a dark, sunless day as this I had no trouble leading my companions due west.

The openness of the woods here made my task all the simpler. We needed no road or game track to wend our way beneath the great oaks and elms, for the ground of the forest was remarkably free of shrubbery, deadwood or other entanglements. Grass grew in many places, beneath the trees and in clearings where they had been cut down. Antelope and sheep, in goodly-sized herds, grazed upon the grass. Atara drew an arrow and pointed it toward one of these fat sheep, whose spiral horns curling close to its head resembled a helmet. But then she lowered her bow as she thought better of killing it.

'We have uncooked lamb wrapped in store already,' she said, 'and who knows if we'll be able to cook tonight – or tomorrow?'

At this observation, not meant as a jibe, Maram's face pulled into an angry pout, but he said nothing.

'At least,' I said, 'it seems we won't lack for meat here. I've never seen a wood so rich with game.'

And that, as Master Juwain informed us, was not due to any natural bounty of Acadu but rather the design of man. From one of the books in the Brothers' library, he had learned that the Acadians, many of them, disdained the hard work of farming such crops as potatoes or barley, and therefore farmed animals instead. Each autumn, when the forest floor grew bone dry, they would set fires to burn out the undergrowth. Grass grew in its place, and animals such as sheep and antelope – and deer, wild cattle and even a few sagosk – grew fat and strong upon the grass.

Indeed, the whole of this great wood teemed with life. As we rode our horses beneath miles of an emerald-green canopy, racoons and squirrels scurried out of our way, and we saw foxes, wood voles and skunks, too. Many of the trees were like old friends to me, and it gladdened my heart to see the oaks, birch and hickory standing so straight and tall. Other kinds, holly and chestnut, were rarer in the Morning Mountains and in other lands through which I had journeyed. And there were trees that I had never laid eyes on before, two of which Master Juwain identified as hornbeam and hackberry, with its bushy, drooping leaves that looked something like a witch's broom, or so he said. Many bees buzzed in fields of flowers: day's eyes, dandelions and sprays of white yarrow. There seemed to be few mosquitoes about, however, or any of the other vermin that had so tormented us in the Vardaloon. It was truly one of the loveliest forests I had ever beheld.

And yet, from the moment I set out to cross Acadu, I felt ill at ease. What little we knew about this lost place, I thought, would be enough to disquiet anyone. It seemed that many years ago, twenty-three 'kings' had held sway between the two great, lower ranges of the White Mountains. Now Morjin claimed it. Not being willing to commit any great force to subdue this wild country, the Red Dragon instead had sent into its vast reaches corps of assassins and his Red Priests, to murder, maim and persuade, to terrorize the scattered Acadians into submitting to his will.

This danger, however, was known and quantifiable, even if we presently had no news as to our enemy's position or numbers. What vexed me more was the *unknown*: rumors of strange beasts that could suck the life out of a man's limbs with a flash of their eyes and even turn a man into stone. Had Morjin, I wondered, also sent cadres of the terrible Grays into Acadu? Worst of all, I thought, was the dread of the dark place called the Skadarak that Abrasax had warned of. Even the glory of the orange hawkweed over which we trod and the burst of scarlet feathers of a tanager flying across our path could not drive this foreboding from me. I could almost smell its blackness, like a fetor tainting the perfume

189

of the periwinkles and other flowers around us. It seemed to whisper to me like an ill wind, to call to me faintly and from far away.

As we made camp at day's end, I sensed that none of my friends felt the pull of this place – at least not yet. They set to work drawing water and building our rudimentary fortifications out of wet logs with good cheer. This diminished somewhat when Maram yet again failed to make a fire. But the rain finally stopped, and the patch of blue that broke from the clouds just before dusk promised better weather for travel the next morning, and we all hoped, drier wood.

For all the next day, we journeyed as straight a course west as I could guide us. We encountered no people – only some rabbits, deer and chittering birds – and that was to our purpose. A few low hills rose up to block our way, and we had no trouble skirting them. The sun, pouring down through the numerous breaks in the trees, warmed us. It dried out the woods, as well. That night Maram finally succeeded in striking up a fire: a good, hot, crackling one. But when Liljana unpacked the leg of lamb to roast it, she wrinkled up her face as she sniffed at it and said, 'Whew – it's gone bad!'

Kane came over to test it with his nose, and said, 'It's a little off, it's true. But I've eaten worse. Why don't you roast it, anyway?'

'And poison the children?' she asked him as she rested her arm across Estrella's shoulder. 'Will *you* care for them if they fall ill?'

She told him that he could roast the lamb if he wished, and eat it himself as well. But as none of the rest of us was eager to put tooth or tongue to this tainted flesh, Kane picked up the lamb's leg and flung it far out into the woods. He said, 'I'll not feast in front of the rest of you. Let the foxes or racoons have a good meal. *They*, at least, aren't particular.'

Liljana, undeterred, set to preparing us what she called a 'good meal' anyway: fried eggs and rashers of bacon, wheat cakes spread with apple butter and some freshly picked newberries for desert. We went to bed warm that night and with full bellies. Even the howling of wolves from somewhere deeper in the woods did not disturb our sleep.

Just after daybreak we set out again toward the west. Atara, bow in hand, determined to take one of the woods' wild sheep for our dinner, or perhaps a deer. But all that morning, strangely, we saw no game larger than a skunk. The wind through the trees reminded me of the faroff whispering that I had first sensed upon entering Acadu. It carried as well a faint reek of rotting flesh. Altaru smelled this stench before I did; the twitching of his great, black nostrils and a nervous nicker from within his throat alerted me to it. We walked on two more miles beneath the maple and hackberry trees, and it grew stronger, nearly choking us. And then, a hundred yards farther along, we came out into a grassy clearing littered with the carcasses of sheep. They lay in twisted heaps. There were thirty-three of them, as I quickly counted. All had been killed with black arrows fired through their bloodstained white wool.

'Oh, Lord!' Maram called out in a muffled voice. He held his scarf over his mouth and nose. 'The poor little lambs! Who would slaughter so many and leave them here to rot?'

It was a question that almost needed no answer. The black arrows, as Kane quickly determined, were Sakai-made and stamped with the mark of the Red Dragon.

'Hmmph,' Atara said, walking around the edge of the massacred herd. 'Morjin's men must have arrows in abundance, to waste so many leaving them this way.'

'It's not waste at all,' I said, suddenly understanding the purpose behind this dreadful deed. 'At least, not waste as Morjin's men would count it. Surely they left the arrows as an advertisement.'

'A warning, you mean,' Maram said. 'And it's all the warning *I* need to flee this district.'

Kane, sniffing at one of the sheep and testing the rigidity of its limbs, said to him, 'These beasts are three days dead. Whoever did this is likely long gone.'

'So *you* say,' Maram grumbled.

'What is strange,' Master Juwain said, 'is that none of the scavengers have gone to work here.'

No, no, I thought. I reeled before the fire that sucked in through my nose and burned through my blood. *It is not strange at all.*

Liljana, as well as Kane, dared to uncover her face in order to take in the stench of the rotting sheep. And she said, 'I think these arrows were poisoned with kirax. It taints the flesh so that when it turns, it gives off an odor like burning hair. If I can smell it, so can the badgers and bears.'

On the lips of many of the sheep, I saw, black blood drew swarms of buzzing flies. I guessed that the sheep had gnashed their jaws together in a maddened frenzy that severed tongues and broke teeth, so great was the agony of the kirax.

'Let's leave here,' I said, 'as quickly as we can.'

'Very well,' Master Juwain said to me. 'But we'll have a difficult choice to make, and soon. How far into Acadu do you think we've come?'

'Forty miles,' I said. 'Perhaps forty-five. If your map is right, we should find the Tir River in another five miles or so.'

'And how do you propose we cross it?'

'Come,' I said to him, and to the others as I remounted my horse. 'Let's go on to this river, and then we'll see about crossing it.'

As we rode through a patch of oaks, the soft wind in our faces drove away the stench of the murdered sheep. Despite Kane's assurances to Maram, Kane scanned the woods about us with his sharp black eyes, looking for the sheep's killers, and I did, too. After about four miles, the air grew more humid, and we heard the rushing of water through the trees. We pushed through some dense undergrowth to find the Tir River raging through the forest in full flood.

'Abrasax said that the snows had been deep this past winter,' Master Juwain sighed out. 'We must be at the peak of the spring melt.'

I gazed at this torrent of churning brown water, which sloshed and spilled over the Tir's muddy banks. The river would sweep even the horses away if we tried crossing here.

And so we set out along the band of denser vegetation close to the river. Every quarter mile or so, we would force our way back through the bracken and trees to look for a place where we might ford the river. But the Tir, it seemed, swelled swift and deep all along its course. And so instead we set our hopes on finding a ferry.

At last, after a few more miles, we came upon a clearing planted with new barley. A farmhouse, built of stout logs, sat near the center of it. In the yard outside the house, a few chickens squawked and pecked at pellets of grain. I saw no barn to shelter cows or draft horses; the sty by the side of the house was empty of pigs. I thought it strange to see no one about doing chores or working in the fields on such a fine spring day.

'Perhaps they've fled this district, as I've proposed we do,' Maram grumbled. We stood by our horses at the edge of the clearing, looking at the house. 'Perhaps we should go inside and see if they've left behind any stores that we might, ah, appropriate.'

'Don't you think,' Atara said to him coldly, 'that we might at least knock at the door before plundering these poor people?'

It seemed the wisest course. But then Kane cast his piercing gaze across the clearing, and pointed at the house. He said to me, 'Do you see those crosses cut into the walls and the door?'

I strained my eyes to peer at these darkenings of the house's wood that looked like black, painted crosses. I knew suddenly, however, that they must be arrow ports. When I remarked upon this, Kane smiled grimly.

'So, it would be wisest if only *one* of us knocks at the door,' he said. Then he looked at Maram and smiled again.

And Maram looked right back at him as if he had fallen mad. 'You *can't* think I'm just going to walk up to that house under the aim of arrows, can you?'

'It was your idea to enter it,' Kane reminded him.

'Ah, well, perhaps we should ride on, then.'

'At least,' Kane said to him, 'call out to whomever might be holing up inside the house. Of all of us, you have the loudest voice, eh?'

And so Maram cupped his hands around his mouth and bellowed out a greeting that fairly shook the trees above us. Through the silence that befell upon this blast of Maram's breath, a woman's voice, shrill and faint behind the dark cross of one of the arrow ports, called back to us: 'Go away! We don't talk to strangers here!'

'But we're only poor pilgrims!' Maram shouted back to her. 'And we would only ask a little of your hospitality!'

'Go away!' this unseen woman shouted again. 'The Crucifiers have already taken everything, and we've no hospitality to give!'

'But at least tell us if we might find a ferry nearby to take us across the river!'

'Go away! Go away! Would you kill me, too? Please, go away!'

The anguish in the woman's voice told of great loss, perhaps of a husband killed trying to protect this little homestead or a daughter carried off. I placed my hand on Maram's shoulder and said to him, 'For mercy's sake, let's do as she says and not torment her!'

Maram nodded his head at this as a watery sadness crept into his eyes. I heard him mutter, 'Oh, these poor people – too bad, too bad!'

We turned to skirt the house and its fields, into the forest along the river. From the darkness through the trees, crows cried out their raucous caws that seemed a warning. Soon we came to another farm where a ragged man stood hoeing his field; when he saw us approach, he dropped his hoe and ran inside his house. He, too, shouted out that we should go away, and told us to return to whatever land we called home. We came upon two more farms whose houses and fields had been burnt to the ground, and then another where the bodies of a young girl and boy lay on top of splinters by a woodpile. Their homespun tunics were bloodstained and torn. An axe, encrusted with black blood, had been dropped on top of a tree stump nearby. Their father, or so I guessed he was, remained close to them: for planted into the loamy, black earth in front of the house was a roughhewn cross onto which a man had been nailed. I thought this man had been young, like myself, but it was hard to tell, as both the cross and the body attached to it had been burnt to a black char. It was a hideous thing to see, and I pulled Estrella closer to me to cover her face with my hand; I held her slender body next to mine as shudders of sorrow tore through her and she wept without restraint.

'Oh, Lord!' Maram called out, nearly weeping, too. 'Oh, Lord, oh Lord!'

But Daj, who couldn't have been more than eleven years old, stood dry-eyed staring at this terrible sight as if he wanted to burn the memory of it into his brain.

Then Liljana covered his face, too, for she would not suffer him to look upon such sights: he who had already seen too many terrible things in Argattha. And she said, 'I would like to know how many Red Priests Morjin has sent into this accursed forest.'

'So, not many,' Kane growled out. 'Surely the Crucifier could not afford to send very many to subdue such an out-of-the-way land.'

'His men might be few in numbers,' Master Juwain said, gesturing at the trees around us, 'but they have no lack of wood with which to work their abominations. The terror they've unleashed, I think, is something that takes no count of numbers.'

I nodded my head at this as I swallowed against the knot of pain choking up my throat. I forced out, 'Let us bury them, then.'

Of all my companions, only Kane thought to gainsay me. But then his eyes met mine as he looked deep inside me. He finally said, 'All right, then, but let's be quick about it.'

The rich bottomland here was soft from the spring rains. We had no trouble digging in it, though it took us longer than Kane would have liked to excavate three rather deep graves. When we had laid the three murdered Acadians beneath three neat mounds, I said a requiem for the dead, praying their souls up to the stars. And then it was time to go.

But Kane, standing guard with his bow in hand, motioned me

closer to him. He murmured, 'Look off past that elm to the south of the fields. There's a man standing in the woods there who has been watching us.'

Through the trees perhaps a hundred yards away, I saw the cloaked figure of a man. He stood facing us and appeared to bear no weapon more fearsome than a staff; neither did he move to arm himself or flee when it became obvious that we had espied him.

'Surely he can't mean us any harm,' Maram panted out as he hurried up with his bow. 'Else he would have attacked us while we were engaged digging the graves.'

The mystery of this man's identity was soon to be solved, for he began walking straight toward us. He seemed utterly unconcerned to stride right into the bow-range of three strange archers. He pushed through the charred shoots of barley, using a long, unstrung bow as a sort of staff. He was an old man, I saw, with straggles of gray-white hair hanging down from his square, block-like head. His unkempt beard was colored likewise and spread out across a florid face that looked as strong and weathered as a piece of granite. Though not tall, he was thick in the arms and chest. His old eyes were grayish-green and care-worn, like the home-spun cloak that covered his sturdy body.

'Thank the stars!' Maram said to me as the man approached us. 'His eyes are as human as yours, and so he can't be one of the Grays!'

And then the man stepped closer and held out his open hand to us as he called out in a rough voice, 'My name is Tarmond. And whom do I have the pleasure of making acquaintance?'

'My name is Mirustral,' I said, giving him the Ardik form of my name, which meant 'Morning Star'. I nodded at Kane, and then told the man one of Kane's many names, saying, 'And this is Rowan Madas.'

In turn, I presented each of my other companions, telling Tarmond the names that we had settled upon for our journey. This slight deception pained me, but there was no help for it. We could not simply march right into the heart of the Dragon Kingdoms giving out our true names to all whom we encountered.

'From what lands do you hail?' Tarmond asked as he gazed at Atara's long blonde hair. Then he looked from Estrella to Maram, and then back at me as if trying to solve a puzzle. 'Few strangers other than the Crucifiers journey through our forest these days, and none in such a strange company as yours.'

195

'And yet *you* were willing to walk straight up to us "strangers" under the aim of our arrows. Is that not a strange thing?'

Tarmond looked Kane up and down as if he didn't like very much of what he saw.

And then Tarmond thumped his hand across his chest and told him: 'I do not fear your arrows. To a man such as I, whose sons the Red Priests have murdered, whose daughters have been taken as concubines, an arrow through the heart would be a blessing.'

So great was the sorrow that poured out of him that I had to harden my own heart against it lest I begin howling out in anguish.

'We have heard,' I said to him, 'that the Red Dragon has sent priests into your land.'

'They are everywhere,' Tarmond told us. 'And yet they are nowhere, as well, for they go about in secret or in disguise, and turn even good Acadians to their cause. Some say the Red Dragon himself has given his priests cloaks that render them invisible.'

And with these words, he looked at the burnt cross rising up above us as if one of these secret priests might be standing wraith-like beside it.

Liljana stepped up to Tarmond and grasped his hand. She said, 'Do you not fear that one of us might be a priest in disguise?'

A slow, grim smile broke upon Tarmond's lips. 'The Red Priests do not bury those they murder or crucify. And they do not weep for the dead.'

Here he looked at Estrella and then at me.

'You *might* be priests, or their acolytes,' he said, 'but that would be a deception greater than any I have seen.'

'Then you have not seen all of the Lord of Lies' deceptions,' Kane growled out as he continued to eye Tarmond suspiciously.

A shadow of doubt darkened Tarmond's face as he looked at Kane. 'You seem to know more of the Crucifier than is good for a man.'

'So, perhaps I do. As you say, his priests are everywhere, and they have no sympathy for a company of pilgrims such as us.'

Tarmond gazed at the scarred and nicked crossguard of Kane's sheathed sword. He said, 'Pilgrims, then, who are well-armed.'

Liljana, who was better at dissembling than I was, said to Tarmond, 'I am of Tria, and so is Master Javas. The boy and girl are my nephew and niece. Rowan and Mirustral are knights who guard us, as is Basir. Mathena is one of the warrior women of Thalu – you may have heard of them. We seek the Well of

Restoration, said to lie in the Red Desert. It is also said to bestow wisdom along with healing.'

She went on to tell of Master 'Javas' and his quest for knowledge, and of Estrella's desire to be healed of her muteness; Atara's blindness, of course, was evident, though it obviously puzzled Tarmond that she should be able to move about so freely and bear a bow as if she could actually aim arrows at any target. I thought that the story that we had concocted to explain our company was a poor one. Although it contained elements of the truth – for surely the Maitreya could gather a healing radiance within the well of the Lightstone – I knew that people could always sense a lie.

'I've never heard of this Well of Restoration,' Tarmond said. 'But if you're bound for the Red Desert, then you've a long journey ahead of you, and a hard one.'

'It would be less hard,' Liljana said to him, 'if we could find a way across the river. Surely there must be a ferry nearby.'

'Indeed there is,' Tarmond said, motioning with his thumb over his shoulder. 'Four leagues back down the river. But the ferryman, Redmond, is friends with the Crucifiers, and you can expect no confidentiality from him, if it's confidentiality you seek.'

And with that, his eyes fell upon the hilt of my sword. To cover its bright diamond pommel and the seven diamonds set into its black jade, I had fashioned a crude jacket of buckskin, as of a good leather grip.

'I do, however,' Tarmond said to me, 'know a fisherman who used to run a ferry. He might be willing to take you across the river. His name is Gorson, and he is of my village.'

He told us that his village lay only another league and a half farther on upriver. He was returning home to it, he said, after a journey some twenty leagues to the south.

'Come,' he said to us, 'why don't we walk together and share a little bread, and perhaps a few stories, too. It's been at least ten years since I've talked with anyone from outside these woods – except, of course, the cursed Crucifiers, and they lie.'

Kane, as I would have guessed, was loath to join company with this unknown old man, even for a walk of five miles. But if we were to gain the services of the fisherman, Gorson, it seemed that we would need Tarmond to present us to him and perhaps persuade him. And so Kane reluctantly nodded his head to me.

'All right,' I said to Tarmond. 'We'll accompany you to your village. What is its name?'

197

'Gladwater,' he told us. 'Named in happier times, when the Emerald King reigned in this part of Acadu.'

We set out away from the burnt-out farm and its stench of char and death. I was glad indeed to enter a swath of elms and maples, whose three-lobed leaves fluttered in the breeze. It was good to breathe in the scent of the day's eyes and periwinkles and to listen to the chirping of the kingbirds. It was good, too, to listen to Tarmond talk, in his rough old voice, for he was a man of passion and wisdom, who had seen a great deal in his long life. The tale that he told was an old and sad one, in a way the very story of Ea itself.

Long ago, he said, in the time of the Forest Kings, there had been peace in Acadu. Of course these kings had possessed less power than King Danashu of Anjo, even less than any of his dukes or barons. It didn't matter. For in those years, Uskudar, to the south, had been a divided realm and the Red Dragon still slept, and Acadu had no other enemies. And above all else, Acadu had a single law, and this was the Law of the One, for the Acadians were at once the freest and most devout of peoples.

But at last the Dragon awakened, and so did a mysterious darkness deep within the heart of Acadu. The Forest Kings, attuned to the songs of angels of the woods, no less the Law of the One, began to hear other voices. They quareled with each other and called up armies to battle to the death. Then warlords overthrew the kings, and tribal chieftains rebelled against the warlords; clan opposed clan, until the only safety was to be found in one's family or village, and anarchy spread. During the Dark Years, Tarmond told us, Acadian killed Acadian until a land rich in people and goodness became poor.

And then, under the guise of helping this torn realm, the Red Dragon began sending missions to Acadu: mine masters to search for new veins of gold; moneylenders to give out coin and restore a long-ruined trade; soldiers to protect whatever village or demesne requested their aid. And he sent in as well the Red Priests, to minister to the spirits of the miners, moneylenders and soldiers, and to any Acadian who desired instruction in the Way of the Dragon.

'It was the accursed Red Priests,' Tarmond told us as we walked through the woods, 'who brought these evil times upon us. They promised that if we Acadians followed the Way of the Dragon, we would gain riches, even immortality. But it is the Law of the One that immortality is the province of the Elijin and Galadin.'

Here I looked at Kane, but my silent friend only glared at me with his black, ancient eyes.

'Some there were,' Tarmond continued, 'who said that the word of the Priests was abomination, and that they should be put to death. The Keepers of the Forest, they called themselves: the greatest huntsmen of Acadu. They began hunting down the priests as they would stags or boar. But the Priests are no easy prey. Morjin sent in more soldiers to protect them, along with the moneylenders and miners. And he sent the Shadow Men, who have neither eyes nor hearts. It's said that they can freeze a man's blood with the whisper of their breath and suck out his soul before they eat him alive.'

At the mention of these demon-like men who could only be the dreaded Grays, Maram shuddered and wiped the sweat from his neck. And he said to Tarmond, 'And did no other Acadians join in this rebellion?'

Tarmond smiled sadly and said, 'Many did – of course we did. We still do. But the fiercer we fight, the more bestial the Crucifiers become and the more terrible their deeds.'

'But is there no one of royal lineage,' I asked, 'who might rally an army against your invaders?'

Tarmond shook his massive head. 'In Varkeva, Urwin the Lame calls himself Waldgrave but he is under the spell of Arch Yatin, the reddest of the Red Priests, if you know what I mean. Any leaders of true heart and stout bows, the Priests find out and murder as they come forth.'

'But how?' I persisted. 'The Priests are few and your people are many.'

'Not so many as you might hope,' Tarmond said. He rubbed the deep creases cut into his weather-beaten skin. 'And they are afraid. And *not* of just the Red Priests, but of each other. You see, no Acadian can know who has joined the Order of the Dragon, and who has not.'

With a heavy sigh, as he drove the tip of his bow into the forest floor in rhythm with his heavy steps, Tarmond told us of this secret society of men and women who had given their allegiance to the Red Dragon. They were the deluded and the depraved, Tarmond said, who believed the Red Dragon's lies. They participated in the Priests' secret rites of sacrificing innocents and drinking their blood; some aspired to be anointed as acolytes and even become Priests themselves. As Tarmond spoke of the elevation of one Edric, a man of his district, to this exalted if vile rank, I thought of Salmelu, my fellow Valari who had betrayed his own people and nearly murdered me with an arrow tipped with kirax.

'It is fear that undoes us,' Tarmond said. He suggested that we stop by a stream and take a bit of lunch, and so we did. He shared with us a loaf of bread and a mutton joint stowed in his pack; we cut wedges of cheese for him from a fresh wheel sealed in red wax, and gave him handfuls of raspberries, too. 'A man's own brother might be a spy for the Order of the Dragon; a woman might surrender up her own daughter if pressed hard enough. Few there are who can face the Red Priests' fire-irons or being mounted on a cross.'

I chewed at the tough mutton as I regarded Tarmond's worn yew bow; although he bore no sword, there was steel inside him. I said, 'And yet you fight the Priests, don't you?'

'What else is there to do?' he said, brushing crumbs from his beard. 'We fight, but too late and too few. And we do not fight as one. I, myself, was chosen to journey to Riversong, Greenwood and other villages, in order to speak in favor of electing a true Waldgrave to raise an army. But these days, no one will trust anyone from another village, and few enough from their own.'

He stood up and shouldered on his pack again. 'We're good people, we Acadians, with good hearts. But too afraid.'

After that we began walking through the forest again. We passed by farms whose occupants might have known Tarmond, but they called out no greeting to him. With each rebuff or stare of shamed silence, with every suspicious look these freeholders cast at us, I heard Tarmond mutter to himself: 'We're a good people, we are – at heart, a good, strong people.'

Soon we neared Gladwater, at the juncture of the Tir and a much smaller river that ran into it. It was a tiny village, as Tarmond described it, with a mill, a granary, a dock for a handful of fishing boats, a couple of dozen houses and little else. Its largest building was the longhouse, built of great oak logs, at the edge of the woods. In good times, the villagers of Gladwater used it as a meeting place where they might take ale and good company together; in bad times, they might take shelter behind its thick timbers and throw open the shutters of the longhouse's arrow ports.

'We're almost there,' Tarmond said to us as we pushed through the rather thick bracken in this part of the forest. He pointed through what seemed an endless expanse of trees ahead of us. 'Through these maples and over a rise, and we'll come upon the longhouse. I'll stand you all to a glass of good ale, the children excepted, of course.'

At this offer, Maram's eyes gleamed, and a new strength seemed to course through his legs. He breathed in deeply and said, 'We must be close – I can hear the river.'

So could I. Through the green wall of trees before us came the sound of rushing water. I smelled the moistness in the air. And then the wind shifted and I smelled something else, too, which pleased me less well: the reek of death. Altaru let loose a terrible whinny, and I had to grip his reins to keep him from rearing up and striking out with his hooves.

'Ho, friend,' I said to him, stroking his neck. 'Quiet now, quiet.'

Tarmond, I saw, had frozen like a piece of stone as he stared into the woods. And then he said, 'I'm old and my senses have dulled, but there's a foulness in the air.'

Upon the wind came a high, faint keening, as of a child calling out to his mother. I closed my eyes as waves of pain and fear broke inside my chest.

Tarmond placed his hand on my shoulder and asked me, 'Would you climb to the top of this hill with me?'

I nodded my head. Then Kane and Atara came forward with bows in hand, and the four of us hiked up the easy slope to the top of the rise. We stood behind the trees looking down at the muddy brown Tir and the little village built on its banks. It was much as Tarmond had described. But the smoldering ruins of two of the houses sent up plumes of dark smoke, and carrion birds circled in the air above.

The great timbers of the longhouse were the cured trunks of trees, and its three stone chimneys sent up curls of smoke. Men surrounded it. Although their round shields showed a repeating motif of small, painted red dragons, these were surely no Ikurian knights or Dragon Guard or any of Morjin's best soldiers. Mercenaries, they must be, I thought. Their leader was a stout man wearing full armor, gripping a broadsword in his hand. A yellow surcoat, emblazoned with a rather small dragon, draped from his shoulders to his knees.

'It is Harwell the Burner!' Tarmond gasped out in a fierce whisper. 'From Silver Glade, five leagues from here. He was one of the first of us to join the Order of the Dragon. It is said that Arch Yatin himself knighted him in reward.'

Without another word, Tarmond strung his bow, whipped an arrow from his quiver and fitted its feathered shaft to his bowstring. He stared down at Harwell as he made ready to draw his bow.

'Hold!' I whispered to him. 'This is no way to protect your people!'

'What other way is there?' he whispered back. 'Do you *pilgrims* intend to take part in our fight?'

Kane's dark eyes fairly shouted out a great 'no' as he stared at me. Then Daj came running up from behind us, distracting our attention from the longhouse. His slight form bounded over branches and fallen trees with all the grace of a young buck. He gasped out, 'I want to *see*.'

He knelt beside me in the bracken and looked down at the men besieging the longhouse. Four of the soldiers stood guard by a wagon bearing black-coated buckets and two barrels of what looked to be pitch. The other soldiers were busy with axes and hammers, nailing wooden planks together. One of their constructions was nearly finished: a sort of small wall of wood, three feet wide and six feet high, with handles nailed into its back and struts near its base to keep it from falling over.

'What is it?' Daj whispered to me.

'It's a mantelet,' I told him. I explained how a soldier might stand behind it and work it closer to his objective, using it as a shield against arrows or other missiles. 'It would seem that they intend to fire the house.'

Toward this end, one of the archers suddenly ignited a cloth wrapped around the tip of one of his arrows. He loosed it in a low, flaming arc that found its terminus at the longhouse's roof. The arrow buried itself in the roof and continued to burn. But the wooden shingles, moist from the recent rains, were not so easy to set on fire.

From one of the dark crosses cut into the house, an arrow hissed forth. It struck into the bark of one of the trees that Harwell's archers stood behind.

'When the mantelets are completed,' I said to Daj, 'the soldiers will go forward and soak the house in pitch.'

And then, I thought, the house's timbers would burn like matchsticks.

'Back!' I whispered. 'Let us hold council.'

I laid my hand on Tarmond's shoulder and urged him back down the hill a few dozen yards. Liljana and Maram came up to join us. I quickly explained to them what was about to befall on the other side of the hill.

'I don't like what we saw of that house,' Kane growled out. His black eyes drilled into mine. 'And I like what I see now even less.'

Just then the breeze died to a whisper, and from below our hill, the muffled wail of a baby filled the air.

'We can't just leave those people to the Crucifiers!' I said to Kane.

'People die!' Kane snarled. 'That's the way of the world! There are only four of us. Five, if we count this old man.'

The look on Tarmond's face told me that I could indeed count on him to fire his arrows straight and true.

For the hundredth time, I thought of King Mohan's words to me: that no one could see the results of a deed and thereby judge its virtue. A deed, I thought, was either right or wrong. I said to Kane, 'We might not live even to reach the Red Desert. But we are alive now to help these people.'

'It's not our fight!' Kane growled at me. 'Would you risk everything for the sake of strangers?'

The acridness of smoke recalled the ruins of my father's castle and all those who had been butchered or burnt inside. I said to Kane, 'It *is* our fight! And these villagers *are* our people – all people are!'

Kane was not a man easily to accept defeat, but he stared at me for a few long moments, then finally bowed his head.

I looked at Maram then, and the fire in my heart leaped into his. He said, 'Ah, I suppose that if I *do* flee, I'll be the only one?' He drew his sword in a burst of bravura and ringing steel that I prayed no one would hear. His smile warmed me like a draught of brandy.

Atara had strung her bow and stood with an arrow in her hand. She said that she had 'seen' four archers on the far side of the longhouse, hiding in a grove of trees.

I sent Kane on a long flanking maneuver: through the woods around the house and into the grove of trees sheltering the archers that Atara had descried. Tarmond walked beside me as Maram, Atara and I led our horses up to the top of the rise. I stationed Tarmond behind a stout maple. Maram and I drew forth our longbows and strung them. And then we waited.

A coldness burned through my belly as if I had drunk a gallon of ice-water.

'My hands are sweating!' Maram whispered to me. 'I'm no good at this!'

'You took a third at the tournament,' I reminded him. 'You're one of the finest archers in the Morning Mountains!'

'But we're not *in* the Morning Mountains. And this is different – we're shooting at *men*. They can shoot back!'

When enough time had passed to allow Kane to reach the grove of trees on the far side of the longhouse and deal with the four archers there as only Kane could, at last I hissed, 'Ready! Targets!'

Atara could work her recurved bow from a kneeling position, but Maram and I had to stand along with Tarmond to draw arrows and sight upon our targets below. These were four archers standing behind trees with their backs to us.

I whispered, 'Draw!'

As one, we held stiff our left arms as we drew the feathered shafts of our arrows to our ears.

'Loose!'

The crack of our four bowstrings seemed as loud as a thunderclap; our four arrows shot out through the air. Tarmond's and Atara's struck dead true at the center of two of the mercenary archers' backs. They cried out in their death agony. My man, perhaps sensing my murderous intent, moved just as I loosed my arrow, which drove through his armor off center and perhaps pierced a lung. He, too, cried out a hideous, bubbling scream. Maram's arrow missed altogether, thudding into the trunk of a tree.

'Oh, Lord!' he moaned to me. 'I told you! I told you!'

'Mount!' I shouted at him as I dropped my bow.

The screaming of the three stricken archers had alerted Harwell and his men. This large 'knight,' whose gray hair flowed out from beneath a conical helm, turned about and pointed at us as he cried out, 'We're under attack!'

Four of his mercenaries immediately covered themselves with their shields but the men working on the mantelets were slower to take up theirs. One of these Atara killed with an arrow through the throat; Tarmond, at the same moment, loosed an arrow that buried itself in the remaining archer's chest.

While Tarmond continued firing arrows at them, Maram, Atara and I mounted our horses and we charged down the gentle slope through the trees upon our enemy.

Harwell had the presence of mind to form up his mercenaries in front of the wagon, so that it might protect their backs and provide cover against arrows being loosed from the longhouse behind it. They stood in a line of ten men, locking shields as they faced us. As we pounded closer, I caught a whiff of terror tainting the air. The mercenaries' eyes were wide with astonishment; they had no spears with which to withstand a charge of mounted

204

knights. They must have been utterly mystified by Atara, with her white blindfold and her great Sarni bow, firing off arrows as she bounded down the slope straight toward them.

'**Aieeuuuu**!'

A terrible cry suddenly split the air; it was something like the roar of a whirlwind and a tiger's scream. And then Kane, like a tiger, like a veritable whirlwind of steel and death, burst from around the side of the wagon and fell upon the mercenaries' rear. He chopped two of them apart with his sword almost before they realized that they were under assault by this new and maddened enemy. This proved too much for Harwell's remaining men. All at once they broke, running off in different directions toward the woods.

This made it all the easier to kill them. Atara fired an arrow at point black range with such force that it pierced a mercenary's mouth and drove straight through the back of his head. While Kane set to work with his sword and Maram ran down another man, putting his lance through his back, I drove my lance at a great, red-bearded mercenary. He was quick enough to get his shield up; my lance point struck into the painted wood and then snapped as the mercenary threw down his shield. I drew my sword then. The mercenary tried to meet my attack with his sword, but like the rest of his companions, he was of little prowess and could not stand against a real knight. I swung Alkaladur, and my shining sword cleaved through his poor armor, and through flesh and bone. Then I killed two other mercenaries nearby with a coldness like unto that of an executioner. I hated this mechanical butchery almost even more than the maddened fury I bore inside toward Morjin.

Soon the battle was over. I turned to see Maram, leaning over the side of his horse, pull his lance from the neck of the dead Harwell. Maram's face had fallen a ghastly gray, but it seemed that he had taken no wound. Neither, I was overjoyed to see, had Atara. She climbed down from her roan mare and began retrieving arrows buried in the bodies of the three men she had killed.

'. . . six, seven, eight,' I heard Kane muttering as he stood over a dead mercenary counting the bodies of our enemies. 'Nine, ten, eleven – all here. Did you take out your four archers?'

'Yes,' I told him. 'And you?'

'Indeed – it was as Atara said: there were four of them, spread out. Their attention was on the house, and they didn't notice me coming out of the trees.'

He patted the hilt of his dagger; I hated the smile that broke upon his savage face.

After that, Tarmond walked down the hill toward us as the doors of the longhouse opened and the villagers of Gladwater began pouring out.

12

Tarmond, I saw, clutched at his bloody shoulder, from which the broken shaft of an arrow protruded. He said to me, 'The fourth archer shot me just as I shot at him.'

His deeds, no less ours, were the wonder of the villagers, who gathered around us. There were twenty-five of them: mothers and grandmothers, children dressed in poor woolens and a few bent old men. For a while, we traded stories with them. The only man of fighting age was a broad-shouldered woodsman, who had a thick beard and shaggy dark hair. From between a gap in his reddened teeth, he spat a stream of an evil-looking liquid. He was dressed all in green. Tarmond presented him as Berkuar. As this rough, rude-looking man took in Tarmond's wound, he said to him, 'That was some fine arrow-work I saw today, old friend.'

He turned toward me and my companions and added, 'You used the sword and the lance well, I suppose; I am mostly unfamiliar with those weapons. We of the forest rely on these.'

So saying, he held up his longbow, and he touched the sheath of his long knife.

'The Crucifiers, too, bear swords,' he said, staring at me. He stepped forward and poked a dirt-stained finger into the opening of my cloak where my mail showed through. 'And armor, as well, though nothing so fine as this steel. You say you are knights bound for the Red Desert?'

We told him the same story that we had prepared for Tarmond, and he told us his. Berkuar, it turned out, was one of the Keepers of the Forest, or the Greens, as they were called. He had come to Gladwater to test a young man named Taddeum for recruitment into his society. But one of Taddeum's rivals, Grimshaw, had betrayed them, calling Harwell and the mercenaries down upon

Gladwater. In the battle that had ensued, Harwell's mercenaries had slain nearly every fighting man in Gladwater – and many others – and threatened to burn down the entire village as punishment for sheltering Berkuar. We had come along just in time to witness the survivors' last stand inside the longhouse.

'It's a terrible choice we had,' a middling-old woman named Rayna told us. 'Fire or the cross. Of course, sometimes the Crucifiers put you on the wood and then set it on fire anyway. I was ready to slit my daughter's and grandson's throats, and my own as well.'

Here she wrapped her arm around the shoulders of a young woman giving suck to a newborn as she showed us the dagger strapped to her belt.

And then she told us, 'We owe you our lives, and we would make a feast for you, if we could. But there is no time. What happened here will be reported, and then the Crucifiers will come here by the score – perhaps even the Red Priest called Vogard or Arch Yatin himself. We have time to bury our dead, perhaps, but then we'll all have to take to the forest.'

It pained me to think of these poor people hiding among the trees, and living wild and hunted. But it seemed that there was no help for it. Rayna, for one, however, had no pity for herself – only an immense gratitude to be still alive. As she put it, she was an Acadian, one of a tough and resourceful people who had thrived off the bounty of the forest for thousands of years and who would survive for many thousands more.

One of those who *hadn't* survived, though, was the riverman, Gorson. He had died, it seemed, defending his boats from the Crucifiers. It turned out that the flatboat he used in secret to ferry his countrymen across the Tir was unharmed. Tarmond told us that we should take it as our reward, if we could manage to work it ourselves.

'I would come with you, if I could,' he told us. Then he gripped his wounded arm. 'But an arrow-shot old man is no companion for a band of pilgrims such as yourselves. And my place is with my people.'

As he spoke, Liljana and Master Juwain, with Estrella and Daj, came down the hill trailing their mounts and our packhorses. Master Juwain was of a mind to help the five villagers wounded in the battle, and Tarmond most especially. But these hard people of Gladwater preferred to tend to their own.

'I could heal them quickly,' Master Juwain said to me in a low voice as he took me aside. '*If* I could use my gelstei. If I can't, I suppose they'll have to draw arrows and stitch themselves. I'm afraid they've had too much practice at this for a long time.'

As we made ready to go down through the ravaged village to the river, Tarmond spoke a few low words to Berkuar. Then he told us, 'The woods beyond the Tir are thick, with only a few paths through them. And thirty miles from here, you'll come to another river, the Iskand. Berkuar is willing to show you the way through the woods and a ford across the Iskand, if you're willing to let him.'

The rest of us were more than willing to accept this woodsman as our guide, but Kane scowled at Berkuar, and took me by the arm as he pulled me away from the others. And he snarled at me: 'Trust this dirty stranger to lead us true? No, I say! What if Berkuar was in league with the Crucifiers? These Acadians are quick to betray their own, eh? What if their attack was staged solely to lure us to the rescue?'

I looked at Kane as if he might have been maddened by bad drink. 'Does that seem likely, or even possible? That Berkuar tricked the Crucifiers, as well as us? And why should Berkuar have thought that we would help the villagers?'

I looked over at Berkuar, standing like a bear next to Tarmond. He seemed almost as suspicious of us as Kane was of him.

'I don't know!' Kane snarled. 'So, he is *willing* to guide us through Acadu. But guide us *where*, eh? Maybe into a trap, where his confederates will capture us and torture out of us all that we know.'

I told him that if Berkuar was our enemy and had wanted to trap us, he had only to lead Harwell and the mercenaries against us in the wild land across the river. And then I clapped him on the shoulder and added, 'You've grown too suspicious, my friend. I think you've let the evil of these woods get to you.'

Then I walked back over to the others and said to Berkuar, 'We've taken counsel, and would be honored if you would guide us.'

I bowed to him, but he seemed to have no knowledge of this gesture – or indeed, of manners of any sort. He spat again on the ground and said, 'Let's be off, then. There's no time to lose.'

We said goodbye to Tarmond and the other villagers, then turned to follow Berkuar around the longhouse. We passed through the band of trees, where four archers lay with their throats slit open like gaping red mouths. The short walk through Gladwater's streets revealed other grisly sights. The dead were everywhere, in front of neat, wooden houses and blocking our way down the streets. We could not step carefully enough to avoid them. My boots, I saw, were soon stained a reddish-brown from tramping through the bloodied mud.

We found Gorson's boats tied to a dock jutting out into the river. The flatboat he had used for ferrying was a huge construction, more like a raft with low rails than a true boat. It was hard getting the horses aboard it, especially Altaru, for he had experience at being floated on top of water, and he hated being so shipped. As I pulled him on board, he drove his hoof into the boat's deck with such force that it seemed he might stave it to splinters. But the boat was sturdy enough to bear up even in a raging river. After we urged on the other horses and ourselves as well, we cast off and let the current take us out into the Tir. Kane and I, with Maram and Berkuar, pushed the boat cross-current with the aid of long poles that we stuck down into the river. It seemed a clumsy means of navigation, but it sufficed to take us across to the other bank.

As promised, the forest here was thicker than in the part of Acadu that we had so far crossed. Few people, it seemed, lived nearby to burn out the undergrowth, which grew in low walls of bracken, buttonbush and other shrubs. It would have been diffi-cult to force our way through such a tangle. We were fortunate, I thought, to have a guide who led us onto a path through the woods running almost due west.

We did not travel very far that day, for it was growing late, and we were all weary. We set to making camp in a clearing where there was a stream and good grass for the horses. Berkuar seemed amused at Kane's insistence that we fortify our camp with the usual fence of deadwood and logs. He did not say why. He was not a talkative man or a particularly friendly one. But he joined in the work at day's end willingly enough, gathering wood for our fire and then helping Liljana prepare our dinner. This was an enor-mous ham that one of the villagers had given us. As Liljana turned it on a spit, fat dripped down into the fire and popped and crackled. The sweet-salt smell of roasting meat made my mouth water.

After dinner, when Kane was apportioning hours for the night's watches, Berkuar brought out a bag of reddish-brown nuts and offered one to Maram, who would stand the first watch. When Maram asked what they were, Berkuar replied, 'We call them barbark nuts. You hold them in your mouth, beneath the tongue, and they give you wakefulness as well as strength.'

So saying, Berkuar loosed a stream of red spittle at the fire, where it caused the flames to smoke and writhe as it hissed away into vapor.

Maram looked doubtfully at the hard, shiny nut in Berkuar's dirt-stained hand. 'Does it, ah, gladden the spirit as well? Like brandy?'

'It does – but without the stupor. And it makes a man as strong in the loins as a bull.'

'Give me one, then!' Maram said, snatching the nut from Berkuar's hand. He opened his mouth and made ready to pop it inside.

'Hold!' Master Juwain said. He sat across the fire between Liljana and Estrella. 'Remember your vow!'

'My vow was to forsake brandy and beer.'

'In spirit, it was to forsake all intoxicants. And what do we know about these barbark nuts, anyway? I've never heard of such before.'

Berkuar's teeth shone red as he grimaced at Master Juwain. Another man might have patiently described the classification of the barbark nut with other botanicals, and its harvesting and preparation – or explained that its use among the Acadians had a long and honored history. But that was not Berkuar's way. He reached into his leather bag and cast a handful of nuts down into the dirt. He said, 'Chew them or not, as you wish.'

Then he picked up a waterskin and stalked off down to the stream.

'A strange man,' Master Juwain said, coming over to examine the nuts. 'I hope this barbark, whatever it is, hasn't addled his wits.'

At dawn, however, Berkuar greeted the morning with a mighty stretch and clear blue eyes. He helped us break camp with a rude good cheer. He moved with a sort of animal grace and power that reminded me of Kane. He seemed to have little liking or care for Maram or me, or indeed, any other human being. His passion, I sensed, was for flower and leaf, for the rabbits that darted across our path and the deer browsing on bracken – and even the squirrels scurrying along the branches above us. His wide nostrils quivered in the breeze as if he were breathing in all the scents of the forest and much else as well. He padded along almost soundlessly in his soft leather boots. He was a quiet man, as far as conversation with others was concerned, but often as noisy as a chittering bird. Indeed, he liked to talk to his winged friends, as he called them, trilling out notes with his thick tongue or imitating their calls. His whistles, as songlike as those of any songbird, were a marvel to hear. While passing through some oaks, he let loose a succession of shureet-shuroos indistinguishable from the voices of the scarlet tanagers that sang back to him. I had a strange sense that he was communicating to them secrets that neither I nor my companions were meant to hear.

While we were resting in another clearing later in the morning, Maram tried to make conversation with him. He moved over to me and rested his hand on my shoulder as he said to Berkuar, 'Mirustral, too, can talk to animals. He's always had a way with them.'

This indeed piqued Berkuar's curiosity. He wiped his greasy fingers in his beard, then pointed toward a robin that was standing nearby on the forest floor. 'What does yon bird say to you, then?'

I let the morning breeze wash over me. I saw a dragonfly near some goldthread and a fritillary fluttering all orange and glorious in a patch of dandelions. From somewhere deeper in the trees, a bobcat screeched out in anger. Once, I remembered, when I was a boy running free in the forests of Mesh, I had loved the wild so much that it seemed I had a covenant with these animals, indeed, with all life. Why, I had wondered, did it seem that man was too often evil and nature good? Who could look out into the woods on a perfect spring day and fail to be astonished at the beauty of the world and the way that all things seemed to beat with one heart and share a secret fire?

I finally I told Berkuar, 'The robin is hungry, as robins always are. Especially in the spring. She is listening for a worm to take back to her hatchlings.'

'*Listening*?' Berkuar said as we watched the robin cocking her head, this way and that. 'But how could you know that?'

'Mirustral *knows* things,' Maram said as he squeezed my shoulder. 'And the animals know that he knows. It's the way that he calls to them.'

I looked up at Maram and shook my head in warning. It wouldn't do to tell Berkuar, or any other stranger, too much about my gift of valarda.

Now Berkuar seemed suddenly very interested in me. He pointed up past the crowns of the trees at the blue sky. There, a hawk soared above us and called out its harsh, screaming *kee yarr*. And Berkuar said to me,

'Let's hear you call to that hawk, then. Not many can do well the cry of a red-shouldered hawk.'

'Neither can I,' I said. 'I've never been able to mimic animals.'

'Then how is it that you can call to them?'

In answer, I stood and turned my face to the sky. I looked up at the hawk even as he looked down at me. In the meeting of our eyes was a shock of recognition, like the flash of a lightning bolt. It seemed as if the hawk and I had known each other for a million years and would be as brothers for a million more.

'Come!' I whispered in the silence of my heart. 'Ashvarii, come to me!'

It was said that if you called out an animal's true name, he would do as you asked.

Again, the hawk gave voice to its screaming hunting cry; I felt this sound deep within my own throat. Suddenly, without warning, the hawk pulled back his wings and dived straight down toward me. I held my arm straight out. At the last moment, it seemed, the hawk's wings beat the air in a feathered fury as he settled down onto my forearm and wrapped his talons around my cloak and the steel mail buried beneath it.

Daj and Estrella came running to witness this little miracle, and Maram's eyes widened in surprise.

The hawk turned his bright black eye toward me. Ashvarii, my grandfather used to call this kind of hawk. He was a beautiful bird; true to his name, his feathers were rufous around the shoulder, and his wings were barred black and white. Five thin white bands marked his black tail. Nature had designed this sleek bird to hunt along the wind, flying as straight and true as an arrow. He looked at me for a long moment, as if to ask me why I remained so heavy and earthbound? Then he cried out again, and in a burst of muscles and feathers, pushed off my arm into the air. He flew up and up, toward the crowns of the trees.

'Strange,' Berkuar said, looking at me in a new light. 'Very strange.'

It occurred to me that I had not called animals in this way for a long time. It gave me hope that the lies and killings of the previous year hadn't completely sullied me. Would Ashvarii have come to me if I were forever tainted with hate? How was it possible, I wondered, to hate at all in sight of such a great being?

And then a shadow fell over my eyes as it came to me that Morjin would hate this bird solely because it claimed a realm that could not be his and flew so wild and free.

'Strange,' Berkuar murmured again. 'We of Acadu do not summon these hunting birds as you have done, but it is said that

213

in other lands they practice such arts. Is that *your* bird then, trained from a hatchling?'

'I've never seen him before,' I told him. 'And that bird belongs to no one and nothing except the sky.'

After that we resumed our journey to the west. We did not come across the hawk again. But the woods were full of other birds: warblers and ravens, sparrows, shrikes and starlings. We saw many four-legged animals as well, and many of these were deer. That evening we feasted on a young buck killed by Berkuar. He spent most of an hour washing its still form in fresh water and chanting over its spirit before he would allow us to dress and cook it. Maram, it seemed, had developed a liking for this strange man and his ways. He was overeager to take the first watch; he even offered to stand Master Juwain's and my watches, as well. The night passed peacefully, with Daj and Estrella curled up in each other's arms between Atara and Liljana in front of the fire. Toward midnight, the wakeful Berkuar called out to a great horned owl somewhere in the woods. The owl's deep, hooing answer seemed as natural as the wind, but it disturbed me even so.

Just before dawn, I came awake to the urgent press of Kane's hand. He knelt over me, gripping his strung bow as waves of anger poured out of him. When my eyes finally cleared, he bent his head low and whispered to me, 'There are men, all around us, in the woods.'

As I roused myself up and grabbed for my sword, Kane whipped about and drew an arrow. He fit it to his bowstring, which he pulled back, aiming the arrow straight at Berkuar standing guard by the wooden fence that protected our encampment. I quickly woke the others, even Daj and Estrella. Atara and Maram armed themselves, too, then joined Kane and me as we stood facing Berkuar.

'So, you've led us into a trap!' Kane snarled at him.

The day's first light barely sufficed to show the gray trunks of trees all around us and the bracken low and grayish green along the forest floor. The morning mist filled the silent woods. Between the trees, I saw, through the swirls of mist stood men in a great circle around us. There must have been more than thirty of them. They wore long, hooded cloaks and bore bows and arrows, which they pulled back on almost invisible strings. They seemed to be waiting for a signal or call.

'Kill me,' Berkuar said to Kane, 'and you'll die with a dozen arrows in you – your friends, too!'

Maram, crouching low as if he hoped our flimsy fortifications would be enough to shield him, cried out, 'Is it the Grays, then? No, no – there are too many for a company of Grays, and the Stonefaces bear knives, not bows, don't they?'

'We are the Greens,' Berkuar told him. Then he turned to Kane. 'We are the Keepers of the Forest, and it is upon us to keep the enemy out of Acadu. If you are one of them, then this is indeed a trap.'

'We've told you who we are!' Kane said as he tightened the tension on his bow.

It was a rare man who could stare down Kane in all his fury, but Berkuar seemed unconcerned with the prospect of his imminent death. He said to Kane, 'You've told of a quest to find the Well of Restoration and names that I do not believe are yours.'

'We killed your enemies!'

'You killed that traitor, Harwell, and his cursed Crucifiers, and they *were* our enemies. But were they really yours, as well? Or did you arrange the attack on Gladwater and sacrifice them to win my confidence? The Kallimun have done more deceptive things, and worse, to try to win their way into the trust of our society.'

The mist thinned to reveal the men surrounding us. Kane finally blinked his eyes then. But he did not loose his arrow. I felt his consternation, like an acid, at being confronted by a man even more suspicious than he was.

'Val,' he whispered to me.

He nodded at me as if to confess that his own evil mistrust had brought these men down on us. With his eyes, he sought my forgiveness and looked to me to put things aright.

Then Berkuar let loose a whistle like that of a goldfinch. Kane turned his attention back to him and to the Greens, about thirty of them, who slowly began advancing upon us through the woods like a tightening noose.

'What is your name?' Berkuar asked me. 'The one you were born with?'

I hesitated only a moment, then said, 'Valashu Elahad. Of Mesh.'

Then I gave him the names of my companions and the lands that had birthed them, as far as I knew. Estrella could not tell of her origins, and as for Kane, no one knew what name his father and mother had spoken on the hour of his birth – perhaps not even Kane himself.

'And what of this Well of Restoration then? Do you really seek it?'

My breath rose and fell as I looked into Berkuar's blue eyes, now gray in the early light. His breath, too, came quickly, like a bird's, as he looked back at me. There dwelled within me, I knew, a great power: that if I told the truth, utterly and completely, with all my heart, men would believe me.

'We seek the Lightstone,' I said to him. 'Or rather, the one who can wield it who is called the Maitreya.'

As quickly as I could, in a low voice that he strained to hear, I told him of our struggles against Morjin and of our quest to faroff Hesperu.

'What is he saying?' one of the Greens beyond our encampment called out to us. This proved to be a big man named Gorman, who was as thick and shaggy as a sagosk. 'Give the word and we'll fill him with arrows!'

'Let us kill them all, anyway, and be done with it!' another said. This man, almost as tall as I, was thin and angular like a piece of overly whittled wood.

'Kill the summoner?' a third Green cried out. 'Didn't you see how he called down the hawk? Would you have him call down a dragon upon us?'

Berkuar ignored them and continued to regard me strangely. At last he said to me quietly, 'That hawk's heart was as true as my own, and I cannot think that such a bird would have given his trust to our enemy. I believe you. And I believe your story, incredible as it is, though it seems that I haven't heard the tenth part of it.'

So saying, he motioned for his fellow woodsmen to lower their bows, then stepped straight toward me within reach of my sword. He paid this terrible weapon no heed. Then he embraced me, clasping me to his hard, hairy body with all the strength of a bear. His lips pulled back to show his barbark-stained teeth. It was the first time I had seen him smile.

After that, I persuaded Kane to help me tear open our wooden fence, and we invited the thirty Greens to share breakfast with us. Most of these grim men remained wary of us, though they were inclined to accept my friendship with the hawk as a powerful – and good – sign. Then Berkuar told them of what had befallen in Gladwater and of our part in the battle at the longhouse; they hadn't known of this for they ranged the wild lands west of the Tir. A few of them had wives and children in Gladwater, though, and were overjoyed to learn from Berkuar that they still lived. They came up to me and clasped my hand in thanks. They even thanked Kane for his savage knifework in the grove behind the longhouse. They appreciated prowess with the knife almost as much as with the bow and arrows.

And so on that misty morning we made together a small feast. Fires were lit from the wood of our fortifications. Venison was roasted, and stories were told. Berkuar respected the need to keep at least part of our past and our present quest a secret. Who knew better than this embattled Acadian how even the hardest of men might break and betray his friends if nailed to a cross or threatened with seeing his children tortured?

Between bites of blackened deer meat Berkuar said, 'These are the worst of times, and strange, too. There are bad things in the deep woods. I've heard stories of woodcutters whose minds the Crucifier has seized and forced like puppets to his will so that they chop down friends and family with their axes – and I believe them. There are the ones you call the Grays. They freeze men's blood like winter does water, and steal children from their beds. Something, in the woods to the far west, turns men to stone. And then there is the Skadarak.'

I shivered to hear Berkuar say this word. Seeing this, he went on.

'It is,' he said, 'a bad, bad place. There, the trees grow black and twisted, and the animals devour their own young. Pass nearby it, and it draws you without your knowing you are being drawn. Take the wrong path through the forest, and it will capture you like a fly in a spider's web. And then the Dark Thing will devour you.'

'But what it this "Dark Thing"?' Maram asked him.

'It is the Skadarak,' Berkuar said simply, staring at Maram. 'Haven't you listened to what I've said?'

He went on to explain that in the Skadarak, the forest itself was like an living entity: ancient, powerful and malevolent.

'We've been advised,' I said to Berkuar, 'to avoid this place.'

'And good advice that is. But if you're journeying west to the Red Desert, it won't be so easy to avoid.'

'Why not? Do you not know where it lies? Can't we bypass it?'

'I know where it lies,' Berkuar said. 'But how *will* you bypass it? To the north of the Skadarak, in the hills, you'll find the mineworks. There the Red Priests and the soldiers are as thick as flies on a flayed ewe. To the south, for a hundred miles, are the Cold Marshes. And to the south of *that* lie the lands around Varkeva, where the armies of Urwin the Lame and cadres of Red Priests, the Grays, too, would likely discover you – and likely blame you when the news of what happened at Gladwater gets out.'

I thought about this as I took a bite of deer meat, which was charred black on the outside and bloody red inside, the way the Greens liked to eat it. And I said, 'But you who wear the green must range your land freely, if you're to fight your enemies as you do. How would *you* cross Acadu then?'

Pittock, the tall, angular man I had noticed earlier, answered for Berkuar, saying, 'If we were journeying west, we would cross the mine lands where the hills are most broken, or pass south of the Cold Marshes. But we do not journey as you do.'

'What do you mean?' Maram asked him.

'We can climb walls of bare rock where we have to. We've no horses to whinny and snort, and leave tracks in the ground as deep as a pond,' he explained. Then he looked pointedly at Maram. 'And we don't trample the bracken as loudly as an ox – we go on foot, as silent as deer and nearly as invisible as weryan.'

'Weryan?' Maram said. 'What is that – I've never heard of such an animal?'

'That is because no one has ever seen one,' Pittock said mysteriously – and maddeningly.

Berkuar was no help in telling anything more about these 'invisible', and probably fantastical, beasts. But then, as his jaw set and he seemed to come to a decision, I looked upon him as a guiding angel, for he said, 'There *is* a way through the wild woods, north of the Cold Marshes yet just south of the Skadarak. A narrow way. I know I can find a path through it.'

'Are you sure?' Maram asked him. 'We were warned not to go near that place, and this doesn't seem very much like avoiding it.'

Berkuar shrugged his shoulders then spat into the fire. 'You have your choice then: the likelihood of keeping an arm's distance from the Skadarak against the near certainty of being discovered by the Red Priests.'

'Oh, excellent!' Maram said, looking up past the branches of the trees toward the sky. 'Why am I always so fortunate as to be given such wonderful choices?'

I tried not to laugh as I looked at Berkuar. 'If you would guide us past the Skadarak, we would be fortunate indeed.'

'I will guide you past it,' Berkuar said, 'all the way to the mountains where Acadu comes to an end.'

He smiled at me as we clasped hands to set the seal of our new fellowship. Then he choose out Gorman, Pittock and a dark, hard-looking man named Jastor to accompany us as well.

'But what of the rest of you?' Maram asked as his hand swept out toward the thirty other Greens eating their breakfasts around the other fires. 'Whatever dangers we'll find between here and the mountains would be better met with thirty extras archers than with three.'

'Perhaps they would,' Berkuar said to him. 'But we've dangers of our own to deal with. And vengeance to be meted.'

Here he looked at a lean, gray-haired man named Tarl, whom I took to be one of the Greens' captains. A series of whistles, like that of two singing larks, passed between them. Then Berkuar said, 'My men have the survivors of Gladwater to look after. And the enemy to look for. The Red Priest called Edric sent Harwell and the Crucifiers into the woods near Gladwater. He'll be hunted down and killed like the snake he is.'

So, I thought, as I sipped from a mug of tea that Liljana had brewed for us, one or more of the Greens *would* find Edric, perhaps leading a company of Crucifiers through the woods against Riversong or some other village along the Tir. They would surprise him through the trees and kill him with arrows. And then Arch Yatin would send other Red Priests and soldiers, in greater numbers, to crucify and slay in vengeance of their own, and the cycle of death would grow only greater and would go on and on. Who was I to stop it? I, who had brought so much death and destruction down upon my countrymen and those whom I most loved? Truly, I hated war as I hated Morjin himself, but there would be no end to it until the Shining One was found and claimed mastery of the Lightstone. Toward this single purpose I must direct all my will, for I could see no other hope.

And so I swallowed my bitter tea, and looked at Tarl and the other Greens in silence. In an hour, after breakfast, they would journey on east to seek their fate, while my friends and I, led by Berkuar and his three fellow woodsmen, would try to force our way deeper into the darkest of woods.

13

We moved at a good speed through the woods all that day. A few miles farther on, we forded the Iskand, as Berkuar had promised, and came out into more open woods again. Many people lived in this part of Acadu, spread out between the Iskand and the great Ea River, and Berkuar and his men knew many of them. But they chose paths that led around and away from the villages and even the small farms breaking the forest. Although we might have replenished our supplies and so conserved them, Berkuar agreed with Kane that we should keep our presence in Acadu a secret, if that was any longer possible. In any case, he and his fellows mostly disdained the soft, farm foods that he might have requisitioned from his countrymen, choosing instead to depend on their bows to put meat on the table, so to speak. Freshly-killed deer, boar and wild sheep, nuts and fruit such as blackberries and apples – this was most of what the Greens liked to eat.

As Pittock told us proudly, the Greens' culinary preferences gave them great stamina and strength, like unto that of roving wolves. He and the others padded along besides our horses through bracken or over old leaves at a pace better managed by four legs than two. But Pittock's two legs, as Pittock told us, were as hard as wood and his breath was like the west wind itself. The Greens could walk thirty miles without stopping, at need, pause for a few bites of bloody venison, and then walk thirty more.

That afternoon, in a district full of cherry orchards all snowy with white blossoms, we came to the Ea River. Berkuar knew of a ferryman who took us across it. Maram, thankful at putting this great water behind us, wanted to give the ferryman a gold piece for his efforts, but Berkuar discouraged such largess. He pointed out that the ferryman was likely already suspicious that we weren't really 'pilgrims' at all, and it wouldn't do for him to think that we were rich as merchants, too.

After traversing some miles of farmland to the west of the Ea, the farms thinned out as the forest gradually thickened. Soon, the ground rose into a more hilly country, where the woods grew even wilder. We chose a good spot to camp for the night beneath some mighty oaks and by a stream that gurgled down from these low hills.

'The mines are not far from here,' Berkuar told us as we unpacked the horses. He pointed into the wall of trees to the west. 'Twenty miles yon way, the hills rise higher, and there the Crucifier's men dig for gold. The line of hills runs thirty miles south, toward the Skadarak.'

'And what is the length and breadth of that place?' Master Juwain asked him as he unfolded his map and smoothed out the creases.

'No one knows with certainty,' Berkuar said. 'But if we make a great roundabout along these hills, as we must if we're to avoid the Crucifiers, for fifty miles, we'll come to the Cold Marshes. There we'll turn west again along the lower edge of the Skadarak.'

Master Juwain then put to Berkuar the very question that a very nervous Maram obviously trembled to ask: 'But if you don't know the precise dimensions of the Skadarak, how do you know there is a way past it, between the marshlands and it?'

'Because,' Berkuar said, 'my father once ventured that way and lived to tell of it. Unless the Skadarak has grown these past years, we'll find the same way that he did.'

'Unless it has *grown*!' Maram cried out. 'Do you have reason to think it has? Oh, I don't like the prospect of this at all, not even a dram's worth of spit!'

This proved to be a cue for Jastor and Gorman to spit thin red streams at the ground, both at once, for they chewed the barbark nut as did Berkuar and the merciless-looking Pittock. This gaunt man, whose cheeks were carved with scars, stared at Maram and said, 'Berkuar has told us little more about you than that you are a knight of Mesh, which is said to lie in the Morning Mountains, wherever that is. Do the knights of your land then make such complaint when compelled to face dangers?'

'I was born in Delu,' Maram told him. 'And, yes, we Delians, being more reasonable, as well as more civilized, *do* make complaint

221

where complaint is called for. As it is when facing not just dangers, but sheer madness.'

Maram took a sip of water from his cup and swirled it about in his mouth as if he wished it were brandy. And then he added, 'And as for dangers, you can't imagine. I, myself, have stood against the siege of a great city and fought the Lord of Lies' Dragon Guard lance to lance in a great battle. And crossed the earth's highest mountains and fought a fire-breathing dragon and –'

I reached over and laid my hand on Maram's knee to silence him. Berkuar, according to the Greens' way, had told his three fellow woodsmen what they needed to know about us, and nothing more. He, himself, knew very little. But later that night, with the moon brightening the leaves of the trees above us, I joined him by the fortifications of our encampment, and we spoke of many things. I told him what I knew about the Maitreya. He, being a devout man in his crude, violent way, had memorized many passages from the *Saganom Elu*, though he could not read. He surprised me, reciting to me words that cut me to the heart:

> *About the Maitreya*
> *One thing is known:*
> *That to himself*
> *He always is known*
> *When the moment comes*
> *To claim the Lightstone.*

'If this is true, as it *must* be,' he said to me, 'then since the Crucifier now keeps the Lightstone, the Maitreya would likely not even know himself as he really is. So how will you, Valashu, recognize him?'

And I told him, 'This is not written in the *Saganom Elu*, but it is true nevertheless. The Maitreya is he who will abide, at all times, under any circumstances, in the One. He will look upon all with an equal eye. And in his heart, like fire, will blaze an unshakeable courage.'

'Such valor,' Berkuar said, gripping the leather wrappings of his bow. 'Such impossible grace. I believe it must be so. But a million men live in Hesperu. You can't search out every one and look into his eyes to find this fire.'

'No,' I said, 'we cannot.'

Then I told him of Kasandra's prophecy that Estrella would show us the Maitreya.

222

'I see,' Berkuar said as he sucked on a barbark nut. 'Now I understand why you've brought *children* with you.'

'It seemed the only way,' I said.

'The only way,' he murmured as his eyes caught the gleam of the moonlight. 'Yes, I believe there *is* a way – there must be. This must be the time, then. The Shining One *will* come forth! I never dreamed that I might live to see such a day!'

In all the miles of our journey from Gladwater, I had not seen Berkuar so excited or happy, or indeed, known that he was capable of such exaltation. I relieved him of his watch then. But he told me that he wouldn't be able to sleep, and so we stood there by the log fence for the next two hours, gazing out into the shimmering woods as we spoke of dreams close to our hearts.

In the morning we set out with a soaring of our spirits that seemed to rise up past the crowns of the trees and spread out like a flock of swans beneath the deep blue sky. The day grew pleasantly warm, and we were full of good food, and none of our enemies seemed too near.

But it is not the way of the world for such contentment to last. Day passes into night; bellies grow empty; clouds darken the sun. As we made our way along the line of hills, south and slightly west, the soft spring wind shifted and began to blow from the north, and the air fell steadily colder. Even so, we made good distance, journeying perhaps thirty miles by the time we stopped to make camp that evening. The drizzle that began sifting down from the gray sky at dusk, however, promised worse weather later that night, and it was so. A cold rain began to fall from a nearly black sky. It smothered our two little fires, and soaked our garments. Berkuar suggested abandoning our encampment to take shelter beneath the thick foliage of a basswood tree, and this we did. Kane didn't like giving up the protection of our wooden fence, but he liked even less the prospect of the children catching the cold of death.

For most of the night, Maram prayed aloud for respite from this icy deluge. His invocations, like thunder, boomed out above the great sound of water striking leaf, rock, log and our sodden wool cloaks, and running in torrents over the earth. Our rain cloths provided us little protection. I could do little more than wrap around my neck the white, wool scarf that my grandmother had once knitted me. And wait. It seemed that I had the very heavens to thank – or perhaps Maram – when the rain softened to a drizzle again just before dawn.

The sky, however, did not clear. It grew even colder. After a miserable breakfast of old venison and cheese, we set out as quickly as we could, fairly jogging beside our horses in order to generate a little heat in our benumbed bodies. The wind died, and that was good, but with this quietening came a stifling stillness, as if we were all being smothered by a wet blanket held over our faces. Five miles of dripping woods we passed through, and then ten more, and it seemed that we must be drawing nearer to the Cold Marshes and the corridor of forest where we would turn west past the Skadarak.

I sensed this place somewhere in the forest beyond us. With every yard of slick ferns and dead branches clutching at my legs, it seemed, with every furlong we passed deeper into these wild woods, we drew closer to it. I felt it as a cooling of my blood, which seemed to grow thicker and heavier, like honey in winter. I heard it as an unwanted whispering in my mind: fell words of torment and despair, memories of nails and swords driven through flesh, and dreams as dark as rotting corpses. It almost stole away my breath. In the creeping dread that built inside me, I felt Morjin's presence. I felt him close to me, as I always did now, but here in these dark, damp woods, it seemed that the very foulness of his flesh tainted the air. When we made camp that evening and Liljana expended great efforts to cook up a succulent rabbit stew, I found that I couldn't eat a single bite. It was as if a great fist were driving into the pit of my belly, pressing my innards against my spine.

'You should eat *something*,' Liljana said to me as I sat by the fire with Maram and Master Juwain. She stood over me with a bowl of stew clutched between her hands. 'To keep up your strength.'

I was afraid that Liljana might continue to harangue me; instead, she gave the bowl to Daj and came up behind me. Her fingers, warm from the fire, pressed into various points on my neck, head and face. In scarcely half an hour, she touched away enough of my sickness that I could eat. I smiled at her in gratitude and surprise, for I hadn't known that her hands held such magic. It saddened me that she could not smile back.

Later that night, however, as I lay near Maram and Kane trying to sleep, the sickness crept back into me. I dreamed dark, bloody dreams. The veil between earth and the otherworld of the dead seemed to grow as thin and transparent as gossamer. I knew, in some ever-aware corner of my mind, that the Skadarak had something to do with Morjin and the Dark One whom he served. I tried to warn myself of this. There was a danger I did not see, my heart whispered. I came awake trying to give voice to this foreboding. Without quite knowing what I was doing, I pulled open my sticky eyes and called out, 'He is coming!'

My cries woke everyone. I sat up to see Maram grabbing for his sword, even as Atara and Berkuar threw back their cloaks and swept up their bows, along with Jastor and Pittock. Daj and Estrella rubbed their eyes as they instinctively moved closer to Liljana's soft form.

Kane was already on his feet, moving at speed the few yards toward our encampment's fortifications where Gorman stood watch. Gorman's bow, fitted with an arrow, swept around in a great circle as he scanned the woods all about us.

'What is it, Valashu?' he asked me.

'I . . . do not know,' I told him.

I stood up even as I slid Alkaladur from its sheath. The trees rose tall and straight in the quiet woods, and the bracken lay like a heavy blanket covering the ground. It was too dark to see very much. The moon's light could not easily pierce the covering of clouds and leaves above us, though it did impart to the air a glimmer of gray. Nothing made a sound or moved in the perimeter around us. And then, from behind an old broken tree, jagged and standing as high as a man, something moved even as a grating, old voice called out to us: 'I've been traveling a long way, and would beg food and fire of you!'

'There!' Gorman suddenly pointed into the woods.

His fellow Greens came over to him and peered into the ghostly gray trees near us. Kane did, too, but then quickly turned his gaze in other directions, searching the surrounding woods – as did Berkuar. Both of these old warriors, I thought, were wise to the ways of ambuscade.

'Just a little bread,' the voice called out to us again. 'And a little meat, and salt to sweeten it, if you have it.'

I came over to Gorman and saw a man limping closer to us. He leaned over his walking stick and moved slowly as if in pain; his cowled robe made his face impossible to see.

'Stop!' Kane cried out to him. 'Stop and show yourself!'

The old man, if that he truly was, shuffled closer as if he hadn't heard him.

'Stop! Pull back your cowl! We've arrows aimed at you, and we'll loose them if you don't do as I say!'

Gorman, Jastor and Pittock pulled back the strings of their long yew bows. Berkuar stood to their right, farther along our fence, as he held out his bow and looked for assault from behind us. Atara, I noticed to my disappointment, had put down her bow and had drawn her sword instead.

'It's all dark,' she murmured.

The old man took another step toward us.

Maram asked, 'What if he's so old he can't hear us?'

Even Kane, I thought, would hesitate to cut down a deaf and weaponless old man.

From behind us, where Master Juwain waited with Liljana and Estrella by one of the fires, Daj suddenly burst forward and leaped upon the fence. He pushed up his head just high enough so that he could look out over it. Then he shouted, 'He's coming! The Dragon is coming!'

An old, sick heat burned through my blood like a stroke of lightning. I felt inside flames flaring with the hues of madder, puce and incarnadine. I looked out at the old man, digging his stick into the black earth as he stepped even closer. And I cried out, 'It is Morjin!'

The Greens needed no more encouragement to loose their arrows. Berkuar let fly his arrow, as well. At a distance of ten yards, even in the near-dark, these renowned archers could not possibly miss. But miss they did. Their arrows whined harmlessly past the old man and skittered through the bushes deeper in the woods. They moved immediately to draw new arrows from the quivers slung on their backs.

The old man, however, moved even more quickly. In one blinding motion, he stood up like bent steel snapping straight, pulled off his cloak, and flung it at Kane's face as he burst into a sprint toward our fortifications. I had a moment to take in the flying golden hair and fine, furious face of Morjin. He must be mad, I thought. He couldn't hope to clear our wooden fence without being met by our swords. And if he was slow getting over the top, he would be met by more arrows as well.

'Lord of Lies!' Master Juwain suddenly cried out from behind me. 'Lord of Illusions! Val, beware – the woodsmen do not wear warders!'

His warning came a moment too late. Just as Morjin drew a sword and leaped at the fence, I heard Gorman cry out: 'Hai, a dragon – a dragon is upon us!'

'A werewolf, too!' Pittock shouted. 'He burns! The fire!'

Just as Morjin pulled himself to the top of the fence, I moved to thrust my sword through his chest. Then an arrow sang out and slammed into my back. I felt it drive my cloak and the mail beneath into the muscle along my spine. It drove my breath away, as well. I gasped at the pain of it, giving Morjin enough time to jump down upon me. Kane threw himself forward to slay him, but another arrow sizzled through the night and pierced his shoulder, causing him to drop his sword. He cried out like a maddened tiger then, not so much in hurt, but in rage at losing the use of his sword arm. It took him a moment to reach for his knife. And in that blink of an eye, as the breath burned like fire in my lungs, Morjin struck out at me.

My eyes fixed on Morjin's sword: a slender piece of steel stabbing like a snake for my throat. I did not see the rest of our company, including the children, wrestle with the illusion-maddened woodsmen and with Berkuar's help subdue them. I didn't see Atara standing helplessly behind me with her sword dipping this way and that.

It was Maram who saved me. At the last moment, he managed to bring his sword down upon Morjin's shoulder just as Kane knocked into Morjin from the other side. Kane's good hand clamped on to the hilt of Morjin's sword and ripped it from his grasp. Maram drove his huge body against Morjin, bearing him down to the ground. Then Kane threw himself on top of Morjin, too, as I lifted back my sword to drive it through Morjin's head.

'Kill him!' Kane cried out. His scream was like that of an animal. 'Kill him, now – what are you waiting for?'

I fought to breathe against the knot of flame choking my throat.

'Kill him!'

I aimed the point of my sword straight toward Morjin's forehead. He waited, looking up at me with his fearful golden eyes. There was something strange about them. The light of the nearby fire filled them with a ghastly orange glow, but little radiance of their own seemed to illuminate them from within. I smelled Morjin's fear of death, sickly and terrifying, but it had little of the foul reek of the decaying flesh of the great Red Dragon whom I had faced in Argattha. There was something strange about *this* Morjin, I thought. He did not struggle beneath Maram's great weight, little good that it would have done him with only one arm. The other I had cut off at the Battle of the Asses' Ears. He should have thrashed like a furious snake and spat venomous words at me; he should have beamed all his black, bottomless hate at me. Instead, for a moment, in his soft, amber eyes, there was nothing except confusion and pain.

'Rope!' I called out. I held back my sword, looking down at Morjin as I waited. 'Berkuar, bring me a rope!'

'Val, what are you doing?' Maram puffed out into the moist night air. 'Kill him, as Kane said!'

'No, I cannot!' I told him. 'This is not Morjin!'

I stared down at this immortal man with his glorious golden hair all dirtied and snarled in the clasp of Kane's savage hand. Something about him called to me and suggested that he was even younger than I.

'That is, it *is* Morjin – but somehow it is not. I can't explain.'

Berkuar went over to the snorting, stamping horses to fetch three ropes. Two of these he used to bind Pittock and Gorman; there was no need to likewise secure Jastor, for he sat in the mud with an arrow in his chest. It seemed that either Pittock or Gorman, firing arrows in the wild panic of illusion, had killed him.

The third rope we used to bind Morjin – or rather, the creature that we called by that name. Maram and Kane stood him up and pressed his back to the wooden fence while Berkuar looped the rope around his chest, belly and thighs, and fastened it to some sturdy logs behind him. Maram's sword had cut through the mail covering Morjin's shoulder, which oozed a dark, red blood. But Morjin seemed to pay this wound no notice. All of his attention turned upon Berkuar.

'He wears no warder!' Master Juwain called out again. 'Berkuar, do not believe what you see or heed what you hear!'

I gave Daj a thick, clublike piece of wood and posted him to stand guard over Gorman and Pittock. Then Berkuar advanced upon Morjin. He struck the edge of his bow across Morjin's face, bloodying his mouth. He said, '*This* fooled me with his first illusion, and so I missed my mark. But I've a warder of my own: my father taught me meditations against the evil eye.'

Some men, as I knew very well, were able to defeat Morjin's illusions of their own will, without the aid of the gelstei called warders.

Kane stood eye to eye with Morjin, looking at him strangely: with loathing and dread but no hate. The arrow that one of the Greens had loosed at Kane stuck out from his shoulder. My grim friend burned with a fathomless will of his own: to command the veins in his torn shoulder to stop bleeding even as his fury drove back the waves of pain that would have vexed a lesser man. He stood straight as a young knight, paying no more attention to the arrow than he would a bird perched there.

'I should draw that arrow,' Master Juwain said to him. 'And you, Val, let's get your armor off and see how bad the wound is.'

I could feel the blood dripping down my back where the arrow had pushed the links of my steel mail into my flesh, but neither the mail nor the arrow had lodged there. And I could feel something else. I studied the way that Kane studied Morjin. My sword flared white then, and I knew a thing.

'So,' Kane muttered, 'so.'

I said to him, 'You knew. At the battle, when I cut off his arm, you knew who he was.'

'So – what if I did?'

'You knew *what* he is, didn't you? Tell us, then.'

'What is there to tell, eh? This isn't Morjin, as you've guessed. But it *is* Morjin, too – as you've also guessed.'

'I don't understand,' I said, shaking my head. 'How can he be both?'

'Because he is an abomination!' Kane snarled out. 'The filthiest and most evil of abominations!'

He explained then how Morjin, with the aid of a green gelstei, must have made this motherless creature from his own flesh and brought him to a blighted manhood under the vile tutelage of his hand and mind.

'He is a droghul!' Kane told us. 'Of all the kinds of ghuls, the worst, for he has no mind of his own, and never had.'

'I didn't know such things were possible,' Master Juwain said as he brought out his varistei and stared at it.

'So, to the Elijin, the Galadin, too, such things are possible – though long ago forbidden.'

Kane scowled as he tried to flex the fingers of his right arm that fairly dangled beneath his wounded shoulder. Then he stepped forward and with his left hand grasped the droghul's hair, and slammed his head back against the branches of the fence.

'Speak!' he snarled out. 'Do you deny who you are?'

The droghul's face fell as still as a piece of carved marble – and as beautiful. This, I thought, was no illusion that the ancient, decaying Morjin wished men to see but rather the very grace and glory of his youth that had enchanted all who looked upon him.

'I do not speak,' he said to Kane with contempt in his eyes, 'when *you* command it.'

'We should not let him speak at all,' Master Juwain said. 'Of all his weapons, only his tongue is left to him, and it has cut down more men than a thousand swords.'

Master Juwain, as always, spoke the truth. But I knew that a part of him yearned even more than I did to listen to Morjin's golden voice: like a finely-tuned lyre that could let flow the sweetest and most compelling of music, reaching deep inside all who heard it to excite their fears, lusts, vanities and darkest of dreams.

'Is it true what Kane said of you?' I asked the droghul.

'I do not speak when you command it either,' he said. 'But since you ask with such earnestness, Valashu Elahad, I will tell you, yes, it is much as *Kalkin* says it is, though he cannot hope to understand.'

The droghul smiled at me, and for a moment, I almost forgot who and what he was. I felt a great, churning emptiness in his belly, and I asked him, 'Are you truly hungry, or was that just part of your ruse?'

'I'm always hungry,' the droghul said to me.

'So what if he is?' Kane shouted. 'Let him be hungry, then!'

'No,' I said. 'He should be watered and fed.'

'But, Val, think of what *this* has done to you! Let him suffer, I say!'

The loneliness that burned in the droghul's eyes, as vast as the heavens on a clear night, told of a suffering that I could just barely apprehend. I said to Kane, 'He will suffer the more if he has strength to do so.'

It was a simple thing to say that our captive should be fed, but none of us wished to put a cup to his lips or hold a crust of bread to his mouth that he might gnaw on it. Kane continued scowling at the droghul. Finally, Estrella picked up a waterskin and walked toward him. But I took it from her and performed the repulsive task of tending to the droghul myself.

Then I steeled myself to question this strange, dreadful being. I knew that it would be dangerous. And I knew that Morjin's creature would tell me things that I didn't want to hear.

14

tara, perhaps sensing my distress, came closer to the droghul and stood before him. It was she who asked of him one of the questions that vexed me: 'How did you find us?'

And this bound man who was almost Morjin said to her: 'How do *you* find anything at all now since I took your eyes?'

At this, Atara remained silent as she oriented her blindfolded face toward the droghul and clenched an arrow in her fist.

The droghul said to her, 'The world grows darker and darker, doesn't it?'

Then his gaze fell upon me, and through the veins of my neck a fire burned as my sword flared in my hand.

I said, 'He'll always find me now. It's the kirax, isn't it?'

He said with a smile, 'Our blood is one, and so how should I not find the beating of my own heart?'

'Our blood is *not* one!' I shouted at him. 'My lineage is of noble kings, while you call the Dark One himself your father!'

'I am *your* father,' the droghul said to me. 'As I've told you before, all that you are now is because of me.'

Despite the coolness of the night, my hand oozed a hot sweat that slicked the hilt of my sword. I could not bear the hatred in the droghul's eyes, so like Morjin's – and so like my own.

'You're the Lord of Lies!' I said to him. 'You're the Crucifier!'

'I am your brother,' he told me. 'If I had two arms and I wasn't bound with rope, I would embrace you to me!'

The nearness of this droghul of Morjin sent the acids of revulsion to eating at my belly. I aimed my sword at his throat. It would be a simple thing to put an end to his lies, here and now. But Morjin, the immortal and real Morjin who must at this moment

231

dwell three hundred miles away in the dark hole of Argattha, *he* would remain untouched – or would he?

I commanded my arms to lower my sword; I drew in a deep breath and said, 'I speak to you as if you *are* Morjin. But you are a ghul, aren't you, a droghul? Morjin moves your mouth and puts words into it. He moves your arms and hands. If that is so, is your hurt also his? When I cut off your arm, did Morjin feel the pain of it himself?'

The droghul shuddered as I said this. For a moment his eyes cleared, and a strange being stared back at me as through a great emptiness. Then the amber of these golden orbs seemed to grow all fiery and red as the droghul's face hardened with lines that I knew too well. His smile became as Morjin's smile: bright, prideful, anguished and cruel.

'Does a puppeteer,' he said to me, 'feel pain when a puppet's wooden arm is snapped off?'

'A better question might be,' Atara said from beside me, 'if a *man* feels anything at all when he puts his thumbs into another's eyes or pounds nails through her hands?'

'I *do* feel,' the droghul said. He looked Atara and then back at me. 'Valashu *knows* how his agony has become my own.'

'You feed on it, don't you?' I said to him. 'The way your priests drink their victims' blood?'

'Suffering makes us greater – I have spoken of this in the letter that I wrote to you.'

'Then you must not mind,' I said to the Morjin who dwelled so far away, 'any suffering that you have brought upon this flesh that is yours.'

'It is *you*,' he said to me, 'who severed my arm with that cursed sword of yours. But that begs the question: can a puppet truly suffer?'

As he spoke, the muscles along his jaw tightened and began to tremble. He ground his teeth together. The light of the fire showed a terrible hate eating up his eyes. Then he shook his head, and his lips pulled back in an anguished grimace. The being that then looked out at me might have been the real Morjin or only his droghul – I could not tell.

'I *do* suffer,' he said to me again. 'All that is flesh does. And I suffer most when *he* comes for me.'

'When *who* comes for you?' Master Juwain asked him, stepping closer.

'When the Dragon comes.'

'But are you *not* he, made from his own blood and flesh? Did he not stamp his mind into yours and shape yours as his very own?'

'I don't know,' he told Master Juwain. 'I have no memory of what I was, before I *was*. And now . . .'

'Yes?' Master Juwain asked him.

'And now it is like this: the whole world is a cavern cut out of black rock; there I dwell with the Dragon. In the instant that I do or say or think anything that is against the Dragon's will, he comes for me, with fire. It is like being dipped into a vat of burning *relb*. If I displease the Dragon a little, then there is only a little burning – let us say he takes only my feet and legs. But if I defy him or try to, then he burns me down to the bone until nothing is left except darkness – and the Dragon. He always *is*, do you understand? There is no escape. For in the end, *I* am the Dragon!'

There was a fire in his words as he said this; in his terrible eyes blazed his will to devour Master Juwain, and all things.

'I should not have asked you,' Master Juwain said, looking away from him. A sick look tormented his face as if someone had forced him to eat ordure. 'We should not let him speak.'

'Master Juwain is right,' Kane said to me. 'Don't listen to this thing – he's only trying to play upon your pity so that you don't slay him, as you must.'

But I gave the droghul some more water. Then I asked him, 'But when the Dragon sleeps, as sometimes he must, is your will your own? Can you speak the truth of your heart?'

'I don't know,' he said. 'I can never be sure which words are mine or which are his. I can't be sure when I am I, or I am he.'

'But who *are* you, really?'

'Who is anybody?' he asked me. 'I am that I am.'

His face softened as he said this, and his eyes emptied of hate. They were like deep golden waters that called to me. Tied to the fence in front me stood a young man who seemed of an age with myself. There was an innocence about him and an eagerness to live. I couldn't help feeling the joy of his heart as it beat like a great, red drum with the very sound of life itself, which was the same in all beings, whether lion or squirrel or man – or even the droghul of a man.

What *was* a man, truly, I wondered? What was it to feel and breathe and be? If I asked myself this question, if I looked past all the moments and memories of my life for the true Valashu Elahad, what would I find? Wasn't there always a deeper and truer self looking back at me? And at the very center, like a perfect jewel buried within the petals of a rose, was there not a brilliant light that illuminated all that I ever thought or felt or did and was always aware of me? A single light, the same light blazing forth in a butterfly or a bird or a man, even a droghul, always watching, always knowing, shining like a star and . . .

'Valashu!' Master Juwain called to me as from a thousand miles away. 'Do not look at him so!'

When I looked for this splendid light inside the droghul, as the droghul himself must look, peeling back the petals of the rose, I saw only the golden eyes of Morjin looking back at me.

'No!' I gasped out. 'No!'

I forced myself to turn my head; it seemed almost as difficult as it must be to pull one's own hands off the nails of a cross. When I looked back at the droghul, there were tears in his eyes. It made me want to weep with the anguish of what Morjin had done to his own flesh.

'Your pity will yet undo you,' Kane growled out to me. 'But remember that this droghul led those filthy knights against us, and killed too many of Bajorak's warriors. And somehow followed you across Acadu in order to murder you.'

At that moment, the droghul's face seemed as tormented as that of the true Morjin. I sensed that it must cost Morjin a great deal to control the droghul from so far away – and even more to twist the Lightstone to his own evil purpose.

'That *is* why you followed us, isn't it?' Kane said to the droghul, stepping closer to him. 'Or did you have a deeper ruse?'

In answer, the droghul only stared at him.

'Damn you!' Kane shouted. 'You'll speak when *I* command it, I swear you will!'

So saying, he began tearing deadwood out of the fence near the droghul and piling it around the droghul's legs. Then he called out, 'So, do you really wish to know what it is like to burn? Do not think that anything of you will remain. When you die, *you* die, and that will be the end of things, eh?'

'Kane!' I said. 'Enough!'

I placed my hand on his shoulder, a little too near the place where the arrow pierced him. He winced at this, even as I winced, too. I looked at the droghul, at the dark light of terror that ran through his eyes. I smelled the fear running out of the pores in his skin.

'I *will* die,' the droghul said to me. 'Since I failed with you, I will surely die.'

'That is upon me to decide,' I told him, wrapping my hand more tightly around my sword.

'No, it is not. *He* gave me life, and he can take it away.' The droghul closed his eyes for a moment as he drew in a long and tortured breath. Then he looked at me and said, 'And he will take it. He will command me to die so that you might know there is no hope.'

'There is always hope,' I said as I touched the scarf that my grandmother had made for me.

'Not always,' the droghul said with a smile. 'Without my leave, you'll never get past the Skadarak.'

I nodded at Berkuar and said, 'Our companion knows the way.'

'He may know the way that once was, but the Skadarak has grown.'

'We will find a way through it,' I said to the droghul, 'and go on.'

'On to search for the Maitreya? Perhaps I *should* let you pass.'

'You have great power over men,' I said to him. I looked at my sword doubtfully as it flared bright silver. 'Perhaps over the gelstei, too. But you've no power over the earth itself.'

'Don't I?' The droghul stood up straighter against the pull of the rope binding him. 'I am Lord of the Lightstone, am I not? And thus Lord and Master of the earth.'

Again, I looked at my sword blazing so brilliantly. And I said, 'No, not yet, you aren't.'

The droghul smiled without humor as he said, 'No, not yet – it's true. But soon, and then utterly and forever.'

Kane, not wishing to hear such proud speech, made a fist as if to strike the droghul. Again, I laid my hand on his shoulder.

'Until then,' the droghul said, 'I *am* master of the gelstei, and that is why you'll never get past the Skadarak. *He* knows.'

The droghul aimed his eyes at Kane, who pulled away from me and stared out over the fence toward the dark forest to the west. He would not look at me.

'It is the Black Jade,' the droghul said. 'The great black gelstei.'

He went on to tell of the War of the Stone and of the glory of *his* master, Angra Mainyu. He claimed that Angra Mainyu wanted only to vanquish the Great Lie and bring about a new creation – and to take his rightful place in it as the one called the Marudin. But the Galadin, he said, grew envious of him. And so Kalkin had stolen the greatest of the black gelstei to use against him: the very same stone that had defeated Angra Mainyu at the Battle of Tharharra. And then the Galadin bound the brightest being in all Eluru on the black wasteland of Damoom. With this crime, a doom was laid upon the Black Jade: that it would betray Kalkin and bring Damoom's darkness down upon Kane's soul and those of all who followed him.

'Kalkin tried to flee the vengeance of the Black Jade,' the droghul told us. 'He brought the crystal here, to Acadu, in hope that such a beautiful place might help him escape the crystal's pull. But he might as well have tried to flee from his own damned eyes. The Black Jade only darkened everything around it – even all of Ea, as we all have seen. In despair, Kalkin cast the crystal away. Here, in Acadu, it has dwelled for thousands of years. And so become the Skadarak.'

For a moment I thought that Kane had heard nothing of what the droghul had said. He stood staring at the droghul with eyes as empty as dry wells. Then he burst into a fury of motion, turning to stalk over to the fire and grab up a flaming brand. He came back over to the droghul and cried out, 'Speak one more lie, and you'll die in fire!'

'I will speak what I must speak,' the droghul said, 'whether you threaten me or not. But I speak the truth.'

'No, you lie!' Kane shouted. 'Others like you, at Angra Mainyu's command, poisoned my wine with poppy. And then when I slept, the Black Jade was stolen from me and brought here to aid him!'

Kane's face, like that of a snarling animal, was terrible to look upon. I was afraid that it might be *he* who lied, while the droghul told the truth.

And the droghul said to me: 'Even if you escape the Skadarak now, in your persons, you won't escape it in your souls. Look on Kane! Look on me and behold yourselves! Soon, very soon, the Dragon will use the Black Jade to make anyone he wishes into a ghul.'

'Damn you!' Kane roared out. 'Damn you!'

He moved to thrust the brand at the droghul, but I stepped between them and tore it from his hand. For a moment it seemed that I looked upon a legendary beast. Kane, as ever, shook with all the rage of a lion; his eyes flashed as fiercely as any eagle's while his long white teeth seemed as powerful as those of a shark. And then my eyes cleared, and I remembered who this dangerous friend of mine really was.

'Why trade words any longer with the Lord of Lies?' I said to him. I breathed deeply the night's dark air, hoping it would clear my mind of much of what I had seen and heard. 'Let us tear off a rag and bind his droghul's mouth.'

'And what then, eh?' Kane said as he glared at me. 'Will you leave him tied up here for the bears to eat?'

We could not leave him as Kane had said. But neither, I thought, could we drag this bound and hateful creature all across Ea, and we certainly could not free him. That seemed to leave us only one choice.

I stood before the droghul and gripped my sword with both hands. How many men, I wondered, had I slain? Although I had kept no count of the numbers, the faces of each one burned inside me. One more, surely, would poison my soul only a little more. And yet I had never put sword to a bound and helpless man. I knew that Kane would be glad to execute the droghul in my stead. But it seemed that the duty was upon me.

'Free me,' the droghul said to me. He cast a beautiful smile at Atara. 'Lead me to the Maitreya, and your woman shall be restored.'

'You do not have that power,' I told him.

'I have the Lightstone,' he reminded me. 'And so I have all the power in the world.'

'No.'

'Free me, and you shall be elevated to your rightful place. For you, Valashu, there will be no death.'

For a moment, the hilt of my sword seemed to soften, and then buckle as it came alive and writhed like the coils of a snake. I nearly cast it from me. I said to the droghul, 'You lie – as ever, you lie.'

'Is *this* a lie: that you know my heart as no other man ever has? Even as I know yours?'

'No, no.'

The droghul, with his soft, golden eyes looked at me in all the terror of death – and something more. Something deep and beautiful inside him called to me. It was a plea to be as brothers. And yet something else, dark and vile, denied him this brotherhood and shouted down to me that he would be satisfied only with my submission, flattery and adulation.

'How can I kill him?' I said to Kane – and to myself.

'So, Val, so – give me your sword and I'll give you his head!'

I hesitated. I remembered Kane once telling me how Morjin

had a sense of how he might have been noble and great, and still might be.

I said to him: 'There is good in you – I can feel it!'

As I spoke these words, a darkness fell over his eyes. His whole body jumped against his bonds and then shuddered. I had sense of hard scales and burning *relb* and terrible, black claws seizing hold of his heart.

'There is good in you!' I insisted again.

'Is there?' he asked me. His voice had fallen hard as ice.

My eyes locked onto his, and the whole world seemed to disappear. 'Yes,' I said.

'Damn you, Elahad! Do not look at me that way!' he snarled out. 'Always, you and your kind presume too much!'

'But it is the will of the One!' I told him.

'The One be damned!' he shouted at me. 'Do you want to know about the One? Then I shall tell you.'

He drew in deep breath, and then let it out in a torrent of words that was more like a fiery blast than true human speech: 'The One calls all things into being, from worms to men to myself. We are given freedom of will – those who do not surrender it to someone greater. But because *being* itself, in this hell that is the world, is cruel and hard, some few of us, the truly great ones, *will* ourselves to be even crueller and harder. Some call this evil. Some men – and Master Juwain and his order are among these – teach that the strong and the great do evil only out of ignorance, in the mistaken belief that we are doing good. At the worst, they say, *our* kind are cruel despite knowing what we do is evil, as if there is no help for it. No one wants to know the truth: that the One made this to happen when he made this hell for me to live in and gave me my perfect will to *be* the Red Dragon. I do what I do *because* it is evil. I *like* it.'

He paused to let these words pierce me like so many nails. His eyes were as hard as hammers; all the light seemed to have gone out of them, leaving only black iron in its place.

He continued. 'I *love* it that men fear me as the Crucifier, for I was born to this calling as others were to be sculptors or minstrels. It is my art. I have written of this. About how the One, above all else, wishes for me to create the greatest and most beautiful of all possible things.'

He looked at me as he licked his dry lips. His throat, I sensed, was parched. But his eyes no longer held any plea that I should

238

give him water, nor would I have obliged him by so much as spitting into his mouth, even if he had begged me.

He smiled as he looked down at his remaining hand, sticking out from beneath a turn of rope. He said to me, 'With these fingers I have torn the liver from a young boy's belly and ate it as he screamed.'

I took a step back from him, shaking my head. Master Juwain again called for the droghul to be gagged. Daj, I saw, standing over Gorman and Pittock, had dropped his club and clasped his hands over his ears. I sensed in Atara a gladness that she was blind and could not look upon the droghul's face. Kane, however, stared at this dreadful being as if entranced. Estrella simply looked at him, and listened. I could not bear for her to hear another word. I raised back my sword. I noticed that all the light had gone out of it.

'Yes, kill me,' the droghul said. 'Do you think *he* cares? Do you think *I* do?'

Again, I hesitated. For a moment, I wasn't sure who was speaking to me, the droghul or Morjin.

'What do my eyes tell you?' he asked me. 'Do they beg for mercy? Damn you! You, who are damned as I am! What did the eyes of all those you killed with that filthy sword say to you? Can you not hear their voices? Listen!'

I stood holding Alkaladur back behind my head as I looked into the droghul's hateful eyes. I felt, rather than saw, my sword's silustria beginning to glow a hellish red.

'How many have *I* killed, Valashu?' he asked me. 'How many stars are there in the sky? And each one, as it must have been for you, said *this* to me: "I die for you. I give you my life that yours might burn brighter." *This* is my will. I tear a living heart from a man's chest, and this feeds me. My hunger is vaster than all the oceans of the world. I drink the blood of a woman's cut veins, and I *do* grow, vaster, brighter and brighter – as bright as all the stars from Ea to Agathad. And the whole of creation sings to see its purpose fulfilled.'

Now I could see the flames running along my sword. It seemed that there was only one way to extinguish them.

And still the droghul spoke to me. The words poured out of his mouth, clear and lovely in their tone, but they burned me like poison: 'And some deaths, Valashu, feed us more than others, don't they? You know of which deaths I speak. Your brothers –'

'Stop!' I cried out. The diamonds set into the hilt of my sword cut into my clenched hands. 'Be silent!'

'Your brothers died beyond my sight, it's true, but *you* saw them at their end, didn't you? Your father, too. Your grandmother, though, and your mother –'

'No!'

Kane, standing beside me, could bear the droghul's talk no longer. Almost quicker than thought, he lunged forward and smashed his fist into the droghul's mouth. This mighty blow would have felled an ox; it stunned the droghul, but only for a moment. His eyes clouded as with concussion, but soon cleared as they filled with desire to destroy Kane – and me. He spat blood and teeth at my face. When he spoke again, his words were no longer so beautifully formed.

'I must tell you, Valashu. *I* must. I've written you that your mother never cried out for mercy, and that is true. But she called for you.'

'No,' I murmured. The heat of my flaming sword burned my hands, but I could not let go of it. Neither could I move it forward, not even an inch. 'No, no.'

'When I put the nails in,' the droghul said, 'her thoughts were of you. Her last words, too. Shall I tell you?'

'No!'

'I shall,' he said. His eyes seemed redder than my sword, and blood stained his lips. 'She lives in me, now, you know. She speaks, always, as she spoke that day. She said –'

NO!

'Valashu.'

I listened stunned as the timbre and rhythm of the droghul's voice changed into a perfect mimicry of my mother's. If I closed my eyes, it would have been as if my mother stood bound and tormented before me. I hadn't known that Morjin, or his droghul, possessed this power.

'Valashu,' he said again in my mother's beautiful voice. It held infinite love for me and all the pain in the world. 'Why did you leave me to die?'

What is it to hate a man? It is grinding teeth and burning skin and nails driven through the eyes. It is a tunnel of fire. Its heart beats with a rage to inflict all your agony upon him, increased ten thousandfold. And then to destroy him, utterly, expunging him from existence so that nothing – no word nor gleam in his eye nor hair upon his head – remains.

'Morjin!' I shouted out. My breath blasted out and seemed to shake the leaves of the trees all about our encampment. 'I'll kill you – I swear I will!'

Inside my heart the valarda flamed red and terrible, with a fury greater than even that of my sword. It came to me then that if I struck out with it, Morjin might feel a mortal hurt even through his droghul.

'No, Val!' Atara suddenly shouted at me. 'Remember your promise!'

I had promised myself that I would never again kill with the valarda. Could I keep this unkeepable covenant? I would, I told myself, I must – or die. But many times I had killed with my sword, as I must kill many more. The droghul might truly have good in him, as all men did. But he was evil, too, almost as twisted and evil as Morjin himself, and so he must be destroyed.

'Valashu.'

With all the fury of all the sinews of my body, with hate blackening my eyes, I swung Alkaladur down upon the droghul's head. The speed of the blade slicing through the air caused the flames to flare up and whisper with a burning wind. It sent out a sudden and bright light. I knew then that I could not kill the droghul this way. At the last moment I checked the blow, stopping the edge of my sword half an inch above his head.

'Damn you, Elahad!' he roared out.

I pulled back my sword. I said, 'We'll take the droghul with us through the Skadarak, to help us find the way.'

At this, the droghul's eyes filled with something black and vile. It was all of Morjin's malevolence made as real and palpable as iron smeared with dung.

'It was good to make your mother die,' he told me. 'But when I kill *you*, when I tear out your heart and eat it, I will sing with joy!'

I could not bear the fear fighting through the droghul's implacable face. Fear and hate, hate and fear – it seemed the whole of the droghul's existence. And then a light flared inside him, and it seemed that there was something he hated even more than me. He clenched the fingers of his single hand into a fist. He shook his head back and forth, and twisted and pulled against the rope cutting into his chest. Then his eyes, his glorious golden eyes, fell upon me. A clarity came into them. It was as if he looked straight into my heart and smiled. For a moment, as fleeting as a breath, I had a sense of an eagle beating his wings against the wind and screaming out that he was free.

'Elahad!'

The droghul's mouth opened wide, showing his reddened teeth.

And then, as the hate came back into his eyes, as a poison worse than kirax flooded through him, his jaws snapped shut with such force that I felt his teeth bite off his tongue and break. His eyes rolled back into his head, and a bloody froth bubbled from his lips. He screamed. I felt every fiber along his neck and limbs twisting in agony. His whole body thrashed like a speared fish; from some dark source, it gathered up a power so great that his spasms shook the whole fence to which he was tied. He raged and lunged and screamed; unbelievably, he pulled up a great wooden log half-rooted in the ground and lunged at me as the fence fell apart. He spat blood into my eyes, straining at the rope that still held him tied. He cried out with such a terrible and keening pain that I thought my eardrums would break. And then he died.

'Morjin,' I whispered. I hated the burn of water filling up my eyes. 'Morjin.'

The droghul lay in the mud beneath my feet, twisted and tangled up in the rope still attached to the log. I swung my sword and cut the rope. Master Juwain came forward and held his hand to the droghul's throat to make sure that he was really dead. But I knew that he was.

After that, Kane used an axe to cut the droghul into pieces. He insisted that we bury each one in its own hole dug into the moist forest floor. We buried Jastor as well. With the droghul destroyed, it seemed safe to untie Pittock and Gorman.

But we would never really be safe. While Maram let loose a cheer that we had slain yet another monster, Atara walked off by herself a dozen yards into the woods. Dawn had come an hour since, and filled the trees with a smothered gray light. She stood beneath an old oak with her hand on her blindfold, shaking her head. I could almost feel the coldness that fell upon her whenever she was gifted with a vision. And then her words chilled me even more as she told us: 'This droghul was only the first. There will be two more, each more terrible and more powerful, as Morjin gains power over the Lightstone.'

That was all she said to us. That was all she *would* say, no matter that Maram cajoled her and told her that it wasn't fair that she should reveal only part of the future. But that was the way of things with scryers, who had their own code and lived with mysteries that no one else could understand.

'Well, I hope never to see a droghul again, despite what you prophesy,' Maram said to Atara. He stared off into the woods to

242

the west. 'If we go that way, I think our passage will be bad enough.'

He looked to me then as if I might relent in our choice of routes through the Acadian forest. But I shook my head and dashed his hopes. Although the day was cool and gray and promised ill weather for travel, I said to him that we must take no terror from what the droghul had told us, and go on undeterred into that dark swath of woods called the Skadarak.

15

We did not, however, venture forth that morning or afternoon. The encounter with the droghul had exhausted all of us, and Kane and I had wounds that must be tended. Mine was the lesser of these. In the coolness of the damp morning, Liljana and Master Juwain helped me remove my armor and its leather underpadding. The force of the arrow that either Gorman or Pittock had fired at me had split the leather and the flesh along my spine as well. At least, as Master Juwain told me, the wound was not very deep. As I sat on a fallen log shivering at the mist that horripilated my naked skin, he cleaned it and rubbed in one of his foul-smelling ointments before sewing it shut. After that I could not sit up straight – much less move – without a sharp pain like that of a sword stabbing through my back.

As for Kane, Master Juwain was able to draw the arrow only with difficulty, for its barbed head caught up in his veins and tendons. Master Juwain determined that the arrow had torn the nerve chakra lying between the round of Kane's shoulder and his chest. Master Juwain's gray eyes clouded with concern, and he bit at his lip; he said that such a wound was much worse than it looked, for the fires of feeling would not be able to flow in and out of Kane's arm. Most men, suffering such an outrage to their flesh, would lose the use of their arm, which would wither and hang limp by their side.

'Perhaps,' Master Juwain said, taking out his green varistei, 'I should try to heal you with *this*. Although I must tell you that I am afraid to use it.'

'Ha, put your crystal away!' Kane said to him. He looked down at his arm, resting in the sling that Master Juwain had fashioned to support it. 'I've healed *myself* of worse wounds than this.'

Gorman and Pittock came forward to apologize for loosing arrows at us. It proved to be Gorman's arrow that had pierced Kane, and Gorman said to him, 'Forgive me, but I *saw* a dragon leap the fence and trample you to the ground. I loosed the arrow to keep it from rending you with its claws, or so I thought.'

He pounded his fist against his head as if to punish himself for his eyes' betrayal. Pittock likewise told of how he had 'seen' a flaming werewolf grab hold of me. As he put it, 'I'd heard that the Crucifier was also called the Lord of Illusions, but I never thought he had such power.'

With the droghul dead, Master Juwain reiterated his opinion that Morjin was unlikely to be able to inflict illusions upon either Pittock or Gorman – or any of the rest of us. To be safe, though, Master Juwain gave Pittock his warder to wear, as Atara gave hers to Gorman and Liljana draped her blood-red crystal around Berkuar's neck. Master Juwain's mind was as strong as a diamond; Liljana's was perhaps even stronger, and should be proof against any illusion so long as she didn't open herself to danger by using her blue gelstei. As for Atara, eyeless in eternity, Morjin had no power to make her see anything at all, for she had no power in this herself.

We spent the afternoon resting, drinking hot teas and later eating a thick venison stew that Liljana prepared for us. I dreaded going forth into the Skadarak with Kane having the use of only one arm. What monsters, I wondered, would we find to fight there, and how would we fight them with the mightiest of us hardly able to wield his sword?

Other questions vexed me as sorely. I kept thinking of what the droghul had said to me. Finally, that night as we all sat close to the fire, we had a chance to speak of this.

'You've told that Angra Mainyu's people poisoned you with poppy and stole the Black Jade,' I said to Kane. He sat to my right with his bad arm cradled in a sling. 'But why, then, was it brought to Ea?'

His black eyes grew even blacker as he glared at me. He snarled out, 'So, do you think I know *everything*?'

At this, Master Juwain, ever a peacemaker, cleared his throat and began speaking in the most reasonable of voices: 'In answer to this question, I believe that we should consider the prophecy of Midori Hastar: that Ea will give rise to the greatest and last Maitreya. We all pray that this is so, even as the Baaloch and his kind must dread it. It's likely, is it not, that the Dark One sent the

Black Jade here to help defeat this Maitreya or prevent him from ever coming forth?'

'I should think that it is likely,' Liljana said, for once agreeing with him. 'And so it makes good sense that the Galadin must have then sent the Lightstone to counteract the power of the Black Jade.'

Kane only stared into the fire. Although he made no response to this hypothesis, his silence seemed to confirm the spirit of what Master Juwain and Liljana had said.

'What *I* wonder at,' Maram called out into the cool evening air, 'is what the droghul said about a doom laid upon the crystal. Was this only another lie? If it wasn't, who laid such a doom, and how?'

Kane waited a long few moments as he sat watching the crackling fire. Then he said, 'The droghul spoke truly in this, though he twisted the truth to make a lie. The Daevas themselves laid the doom in their zeal to execute Angra Mainyu's will. It was *they* who poisoned the crystal. The black gelstei contains the great darkness itself, eh? So, it will drink in all that is dark from any who try to wield it, and who is darker than the Daevas who follow Angra Mainyu except the Dark One himself?'

Even from three feet away, I could feel Kane's heart moving against his chest bones like an animal trapped in a small, lightless room.

'But is it possible,' Maram persisted, 'for Morjin to use the Black Jade as the droghul has said? For him to make people into ghuls?'

Kane's words, as he turned to Maram, were more chilling than the dank night air: 'So, it is possible.'

He drew in a deep breath, as did I, and Atara sitting on my other side. And then he continued, now speaking in a more kindly tone: 'But first, he would have to master the Lightstone.'

'Master it or merely gain more power over it?' Maram asked. 'If Morjin could do to *us* what he did to his droghul, through the Black Jade, then it should found and destroyed.'

It took a few moments for Maram to realize the implications of his words. Atara oriented her face toward him, and said, 'Are you suggesting we search for it and destroy it?'

'*Am* I suggesting that?' Maram said as if speaking to himself. His audacity seemed to astonish him. 'Well, we're close to it, aren't we?'

'That we are,' Kane said holding out his good hand as if to feel the air. 'And if we get too much closer, the Black Jade will destroy *you*.'

He went to say that we couldn't just go strolling into the heart of the Skadarak and pick up the Black Jade from the ground, then smash it with an axe into pieces.

'It was brought here *long* ago,' he told us. 'It would be buried deep under layers of earth.'

'Unless perhaps it was left in some sort of cavern,' Maram said.

'*That* is one cavern I wouldn't walk into, and neither would you.' Kane smiled at Maram, but the coldness in his eyes only made Maram shudder. And Kane continued, 'No, I'm certain that the earth has swallowed up the Black Jade. We would have to dig for it.'

Berkuar considered this as he chewed at one of his barbark nuts, then spat into the fire. 'The Crucifier's men mine for gold not far from the Skadarak. What if they've gone into it to mine for something else?'

'No, they would not dare,' Kane said to him. 'And they would not succeed if they did. Morjin would know this. So, it would be as if the Black Jade and the earth have become as one.'

He told us that the black gelstei had surely poisoned the very earth, even as the earth fed the crystal with its own dark fires.

'If you knew all this,' Master Juwain said to him, 'why did you wait until now to tell of it?'

'Because I didn't *know*.' Kane stared up at the trees beyond the remade fence surrounding us. 'There are many dark places on Ea, eh? I haven't visited them all, and until the droghul spoke of the Skadarak, I knew no more of it than you.'

'But from what we discussed with Master Storr in the library, you must have suspected.'

'So – so what if I did? I think you suspected it, too.'

Master Juwain considered this as he rubbed at his bald head. Then he said to Kane, 'If Morjin's men would not go after the Black Jade, then what about Morjin himself – or one of his droghuls?'

'No, he wouldn't dare, either,' Kane said. 'One must be careful in employing a dragon as an ally, eh? So with the Black Jade. The Lightstone *might* give him a measure of power over it, but not over the very earth of which it has become a part – not yet. It would be the earth that would devour him.'

He sighed as he looked at Master Juwain, and then added, 'But Angra Mainyu, if he were freed – he *would* dare. So, and he would claim the Black Jade for himself.'

247

I took a sip of tea and watched the fire's light playing in the black mirrors of Kane's eyes. I said to him, 'The droghul spoke of a Great Lie and of Angra Mainyu's struggle to become the Marudin. That word is strange to me – do you know what he meant?'

'I do,' Kane told us. His sigh was almost indistinguishable from a growl. 'I've spoken of this before – part of it. Of how Asangal fell into evil out of his love for the world and so became Angra Mainyu. So, and fell even more out of fear and hate. He hated most of all his inevitable end in becoming one of the Ieldra, and cursed the One who had made things so. He cursed creation itself. But death is only part of life, eh? – just as suffering carves hollows in the soul to leave room for joy. You said this once yourself. Angra Mainyu denied this. He called this truth the Great Lie. He vowed to make anew the whole universe in a new creation. *He* would, himself, although he was only of the Galadik order and had no such power.'

Kane paused to take a drink of his tea. Then his eyes fell upon me as he continued, 'But power he seeks as a bat does blood. All the power of the Ieldra, and more. And he said the greatest part of the Great Lie was that the Galadin should die in becoming the Ieldra. For he believed that there could be *another* order, beyond that of the Galadin; he called this order the Marudin: they who would not have to die into light, but who would touch all things in light, even as the rays of the sun fall upon the earth. One, and only one, was destined to rule this order as *the* Marudin. And so rule creation itself.'

He reached into his pocket and brought forth the oval-shaped baalstei that he always kept close to him. 'I've said that the Black Jade is no greater, in size, than this little trinket that I took from that damned Gray. You've seen the seven gelstei that Abrasax and his brethren keep – they are no larger. But the first of the great gelstei that crystallized out of the angel fire at the beginning of time were immense beyond imagining. Immense in power, too. The Ieldra used them to create Eluru. Somewhere, in the stars around Ninsun, the first gelstei still dwell. So, Angra Mainyu would try to use the Black Jade to wrest the power of these crystals from the Ieldra, even as he once tried during the War of the Stone.'

Kane sat staring at the little black gelstei resting in his palm. Estrella and Daj edged up close to him, waiting to hear if he might say anything more. Maram took a swallow of tea, while Berkuar spat yet again into the fire. I listened as the wood there popped and hissed.

'Perhaps,' I said, 'we *should* find the Black Jade and destroy it.'

'No, Val,' Kane murmured to me, 'that is not possible

I went to bed that night telling myself that fighting through Morjin's forces to the north or wading through the Cold Marshes to the south would be much riskier than facing whatever darkness we might find in the Skadarak. But in truth, I didn't really know. And a deeper truth whispered like fire in some far corner of my mind: that I desired to look upon the darkest part of the world and know that the light I held inside would be bright enough to guide me through it.

We set out the next morning toward the west. Although it was late in Ashte, no hint of summer's warmth worked its way into this southern wood. It grew even colder, and the drizzle thickened into a sort of sempiternal gray cloud that enveloped us like a wet blanket. I blinked my eyes against the moistness there, while Maram licked beads of water from his mustache. We plodded along, yard by yard, through the dripping bracken.

Berkuar took the lead, with me close behind, followed by Atara, Master Juwain, Liljana and the children. Maram accompanied Kane, who, despite his wound, insisted on guarding our rear. Berkuar deployed Pittock and Gorman far out in the woods, to our right and left, to cover our flanks. Gorman, on our left, was also to look for sign of the Cold Marshes and give warning if we were about to wander into boggy ground or even quicksands. I led Altaru, the better to keep pace with Berkuar – and to feel solid ground beneath my boots. Then, too, the pain that sliced through my back with every step was slightly less in walking than in having to sit up straight in a jolting saddle.

According to Berkuar's reckoning, we should reach the Cold Marshes after only ten or fifteen more miles, and so it proved to be. We smelled this vast expanse of stagnant water and rotting vegetation long before we saw it. Through the trees wafted a stench that recalled the fetor of the Black Bog. The cloying air seemed to make it worse. Particles of drizzle caught up the reek and deposited it in our nostrils, in our hair and upon our garments. It made breathing itself a nasty trial.

'Whew!' Maram said as he fanned his hand before his face. 'If it smells this bad here, in the woods, I don't want to know what it would be like to cross these damned Cold Marshes.'

Berkuar called out to him: 'No one crosses the Cold Marshes. Now be quiet, lest you call down a demon upon us!'

Berkuar believed, as did his fellow Greens, that the souls of sorcerers and other evil beings were doomed to linger in the cursed

249

places of the world such as the Cold Marshes. These demons could even take form as werewolves and other beasts that might devour a man or suck out his blood.

'Demons!' I heard Maram mutter from behind me. There came a slap of a hand against flesh. 'That's the fourth mosquito I've sent on in the last half mile, and I've hardly seen one in all of Acadu. Ah, I'm getting a bad feeling about all this. Does no one else remember the Vardaloon? The mosquitoes *there* were worse than any demons.'

The closer we drew to the pungent reek of the Marshes, the more numerous Maram's least favorite insect grew. They did not descend upon us in clouds and choke our nostrils, as in the Vardaloon, but it seemed that every bush we brushed past disturbed dozens of the little black beasts. They winged through the air as they found their way unerringly to us and settled soft as snowflakes on our hands, brows and hair. Their whine was a torment in our ears.

'You didn't warn us of this,' Maram grumbled to Berkuar as he slapped at his neck. 'Now I know why no one crosses the Marshes!'

Berkuar only smiled at Maram, and then he spat into his hand. He rubbed this juice of the barbark nut over his cheeks and forehead. This vile, red substance seemed to drive away the mosquitoes.

A sudden trill from our left alerted Berkuar that Gorman had found something. We veered off toward Gorman, whose green cloak rendered him almost invisible against the green leaves of a bearberry bush. We walked as quietly as we could through the trees, here mostly oak and chestnut. As we drew nearer to Gorman, we saw what he saw: that the forest seemed to give out a hundred yards ahead of us. He led on past a gnarled, old oak until he stood upon some high ground, beyond which the forest dissolved into a dense grayness. We joined him there. Below us, in a great, ill-drained depression for miles to the south, stood a great swamp. Drowned grasses and a few lonely trees poked above this still water. A green slime floated upon it, and pockets of mist clung to it like tattered garments on a leper.

'The mosquitoes are bad here indeed,' Berkuar said to Maram. 'But that is not why no one crosses the Cold Marshes.'

A man on stilts, he said, would have trouble finding the bottom of this stinking mere, through which swam lizard-like beasts that could bring down even our horses. And there were quicksands, too.

'Even the birds, I think, don't like to fly over it,' he told us. 'Our path lies around it to the north, but cleaving as closely as we can.'

'Ah, and cleaving close to these damn mosquitoes, too,' Maram said as he brushed at his ear. 'They will be worse tonight. Can't we at least put a few miles between us and this swamp?'

'A few miles,' Berkuar told him, 'might take us into the Skadarak.'

'Well, then, we're damned to the left and damned to the right,' Maram said. He slapped a mosquito off his red nose. 'But better the demon we know, I suppose, than the one we don't.'

For the rest of the day we worked our way around the edge of the Cold Marshes. We could not follow a straight course, for in places the high ground above the Marshes was rocky and broken, and in other places swampy arms of water seemed to reach deep into the forest, blocking our way and diverting us farther to the north. We all grew irritable: from the constant whine and sting of the mosquitoes, from the chafe of our soaked garments and from the smothering gray air. And there was something else. At first no one articulated this, but I could feel something calling to my companions from far away, even as I could feel it in myself. It was like a voice murmuring intimations of great pleasure, and even more like a sick urge to waste gold coins in a game of dice. In its intoxicating hold on us, which worked its way into us like a perfume sweetening skin, was the promise that all our suffering would soon end and our dreams be fulfilled.

Pittock, as hard-looking and reticent as any man I had ever seen, was the first of us to remark on this. When we broke for the day to make camp, he stared off through the trees to the north and announced, 'We're close to it – I know we are. It's as if there is an itch in my bones that I can't quite scratch. I would like to go on that way, though I know that is madness. My uncle was lost to these woods, and now I know why.'

Berkuar stood near him, looking north, too. And he said, 'That thing of Morjin spoke truly, in this at least. The Skadarak has grown.'

He went on to say that on the morrow, we must try to hug the Cold Marshes even more closely lest we wander into it.

Daj, holding up a piece of firewood as he might a sword, thrust it out ahead of him and asked, 'But how will we know if we've entered it?'

It was a simple question – the question of a child. And it was

251

a good question, too, for it held the very essence of our predicament.

That night passed slowly, with no break in the great bank of clouds that pressed down upon the earth. As Maram had warned, the mosquitoes came out in greater numbers. So did the bats who ate them; they whumped through the air, as dark-shaped as any demons. But they were not the kind of bats that drank blood – at least not human blood. Pittock and Gorman, standing guard over us with their bows at the ready, looked out into the dark air for any sign of werebats, werewolves or even worse things.

As I was trying to sleep, I overheard Gorman grumble to Pittock: 'That droghul fooled you into thinking you saw a werewolf; just don't let your eyes fool you into mistaking a deer for a dragon.'

'My eyes?' Pittock said. 'There's nothing wrong with *my* eyes. It's *your* eyes I worry about.'

'I have the eyes of a hawk,' Gorman told him.

'Is that why you killed Jastor?'

'You blame *me* for that? It was your arrow that pierced him!'

'*Was* it my arrow?' Pittock said. 'At the Battle of the Drowned Oaks, I gave you five arrows to replace the ones you wasted. I know it must have been one of these that killed Jastor.'

'You *know* this, do you?'

'You've always been a wild shot,' Pittock muttered.

'At Oxfarm I put an arrow in the eye of one of the Crucifiers at fifty yards!'

'A lucky shot. At the Battle of Sleeping Lake, you put an arrow into poor Thorgard's belly.'

'How can you speak of that?' Gorman half-shouted. 'Thorgard came out of the trees before Berkuar's call, and it was deemed an accident of battle. No one else holds me accountable for this!'

'Well, Thorgard was my cousin, wasn't he?'

The two men argued on in a like manner for a while, until Berkuar rose up to put an end to their dispute. He sent them both off to their beds, standing watch in their places. But Gorman chewed at one of his barbark nuts for most of the next hour and muttered to himself, while Pittock lay awake by the fire staring into its red flames.

We all, I thought, slept poorly that night, even Estrella whose repose was usually as easy and natural as a spring wind. More than once, I heard her whimpering as if tormented by some dark dream from which she could not awaken. Even Liljana, singing a soft lullaby as she lay next to her, could not soothe her.

The cool, gray morning brought no relief in the weather. We all moved stiffly, as if the drizzle had worked its way into our bones. I could hardly sit to eat the goose eggs and cakes that Liljana cooked for breakfast, so sharp was the pain stabbing into my back. Although Master Juwain redressed my wound and pronounced it free of infection, it seemed that hot acids were eating into my flesh. Kane, as usual, made no complaint of any hurt, but the look on his face was of a bear disturbed from his den and ready to bite anyone who crossed his path.

We set out west, edging the stinking marshlands. Soon, however, we came upon a great inlet of slimy water and had to circle north. Two or three miles farther on, some rotten, limestone hills blocked our way back to the Marshes and forced us to cut through the woods. It was there, in the oaks, elms and willows nearly a hundred feet high, that a mist came upon us. It sifted through the dogwoods and lesser vegetation, and enveloped us in a smothering grayness. In only moments, it seemed, it thickened, and we could not see the tops of the trees; a short while later we had difficulty making out the trees themselves.

'I can't see our way!' Berkuar called out to me as he held up his hand. I walked up close to him and his woodsmen, and everyone else drew up behind me. 'Perhaps we should wait here until the mist clears.'

I stamped my boot down into some wet old leaves. The ground about us was low and boggy. I said to Berkuar, 'We might have to wait days – and this is no place to make camp.'

Berkuar shook his head. 'The mist is too thick; we'll wander apart.'

'We won't wander,' I told him. 'If we must, we'll rope ourselves together as we did in the Black Bog.'

'A good plan,' Berkuar said, 'but I can't see ten feet in front of my nose, and so we'll still wander.'

'No, we won't,' I said pointing off ahead of us. 'West is *that* way.'

I was as sure of this direction as I was of the difference between my right hand and my left.

'I'm sure west *is* that way,' Berkuar said. 'But will you be able to keep us on course after another mile?'

'Val will be able to,' Maram said, coming up to us. Then his faith in me seemed to evaporate. 'Unless of course he *loses* his sense of direction, as in the Black Bog.'

'If I lose my way,' I said, 'I'll tell you, and then we'll make camp on the spot. Now let's leave this place.'

None of us wished to spend another night as we had; we all told ourselves, I thought, that another ten or twenty miles of hard walking should take us well past the Skadarak.

'All right,' Berkuar said, 'but let us then set course west and south, that we can be sure to remain close to the Marshes.'

It took us a while to rope the horses together. Then I pointed my nose southwest into the mist and set out in the lead through the moist, still forest. Birds sang out to us unseen. We came upon a channel of reeking water, and that reassured us. After that I turned us almost due west. It was strange and unpleasant moving nearly blind through the silent trees, but did not seem particularly dangerous. The ground remained low and flat. The worst of things were the mosquitoes and the occasional dead tree or sharp stump that were difficult to perceive until we nearly tripped over them. But the forest floor grew clearer and more open as we proceeded, and that reassured us even more, for Berkuar had told us that the undergrowth should thin out along the western reaches of the Cold Marshes. I felt my sense of direction sharp and strong inside me; it was as if the iron in my blood pointed our way unerringly like a weather vane in the wind. I had no doubt that soon we would put both the Marshes and the Skadarak far behind us.

'This isn't so bad, Daj,' I heard Maram call out. It seemed that he was trying to reassure the boy – or himself. 'You should have been with us in the Black Bog. Ah, perhaps you *shouldn't*. There, Val disappeared like a wraith, and I thought I'd lost him forever. There, too, time ate up the moon – a whole month of moons in a single night. There was a dragon, too, I think. Kane later told us that for a few moments out of time we were walking on the Dark Worlds, perhaps even Charoth. I have to believe him. *That* night was ten times longer than this day, and I thought it would never end.'

'I wish this mist would end,' I heard Daj say to him. 'It's nearly as dark in day here as it was in the mines of the Dark City.'

'Do not speak of *that* place,' Maram said to him as he slapped his neck. 'At least there were no mosquitoes there. As for that, though, I haven't been bedevilled by them nearly so badly this last hour, and so we must be drawing near the end of these damn Marshes – mustn't we?'

Maram's question alarmed Berkuar, who called for a halt. He stood beside me sniffing the air. Then he said, 'I can't smell the Marshes.'

'Neither can I,' Maram said. 'Hurray, hurray!'

Berkuar looked at me through the mist and said, 'We can't have come that far. The marshlands should still be to the south.'

'Perhaps a shift in the wind has carried off the stench,' Master Juwain offered.

But there was no wind – only the stillness of the silent wet woods. 'Are you sure of our course?' Berkuar asked me. 'Perhaps we've veered to the north.'

'Does one of your arrows veer,' I asked him, 'or does it fly straight?'

Gorman, who had walked off a dozen yards to look for mosses growing on trees or other sign of north, suddenly straightened up and called out to us, 'Look at this sapling! Oak, it is, and white oak at that. Its bark has gone black, and it's as twisted as an old man!'

We noticed then that something was wrong with the trees around us, for their trunks, too, were blackened and twisted as with some disease.

'This is a bad place,' Gorman said. 'Let us flee it as quickly as we can.'

'And flee into a worse place?' Berkuar asked him. 'Let us remain here until the mist clears so that we can see what is about us.'

He cast no more aspersions on my leadership, but argued strongly for waiting, whatever my sense of direction might say. We finally reached a compromise: if the mist did not clear by noon or soon thereafter, we would push on to the west.

'But how will we know when it's noon?' Daj asked, looking up into the blinding mist.

Although my sense of direction, I thought, was nearly inviolate, my sense of time was not. And so I said to Daj, 'We'll have to guess.'

And so we waited. Maram and Berkuar built up two little fires, around which we all gathered to keep warm. An hour passed, and then another, and I was sure that noon had passed as well. Daj was the first of us to notice a soft wind blowing through the woods and the thinning of the mist. Maram cried out that we were saved, but his celebration proved to be premature, for as the wind sucked away the mist and the air began to clear, we had a better view of the woods all around us: in every direction, the trees grew all stunted and twisted, with blackened bark and a brownish rust that blighted their leaves. Old oaks, which should have been as tall and stately as kings, grew only twenty or thirty feet high. Many were, as Gorman had said, bent like crippled old men. Few bushes and

255

no flowers grew out of the forest floor; I put my hand to this dark gray ground, and it seemed too warm, as if the earth itself were burning up with fever.

'The accursed forest,' Berkuar said, looking at me. 'We've surely wandered into it.'

I said nothing because I could no longer deny that I had led us into the one place that Abrasax had warned us we must not go.

16

For a while, as we waited near the fires and the mist grew thinner, Berkuar stared at me. Maram, I knew, did not like the accusation in his eyes because he came to my defense, saying, 'It's not Val's fault.'

'Did I say it was?' Berkuar asked him. 'The Skadarak might well have grown so that it would be impossible *not* to wander into it. All that matters now is how we will find our way out.'

This proud woodsman did not say what was obvious: that he had become lost in the mist, and could not tell north from south. Neither did his sharp eye for mosses and the like give hint of direction, for none such grew on these diseased trees.

Above us the clouds still gathered so thick and gray that no glow of white marked the position of the sun. Gorman told us that it was often this way in Acadu, in late Ashte, for weeks on end.

'*That* way is west,' I said, pointing straight ahead of us. I drew my sword, which glowed faintly when I pointed it toward my right. 'Do you see? Argattha should be to the north of us here, and Alkaladur confirms this.'

Once, my shining sword had led us to Argattha where the Lightstone resided.

'Let us go on,' I said.

'If you're wrong,' Pittock said, 'we could walk straight into the heart of the Skadarak.'

'Yes, that's true,' I told him. 'But so long as we walk *straight*, eventually we'll come out on the other side. Now let's be off.'

We smothered the two fires with some stinking muck and resumed our hike toward what I was sure was west. The walking was easy here, with no bracken or bushes to trip us up; with the lifting of the mist, the drizzle dried up, too, and it grew cool rather than cold. The afternoon's journey might even have been pleasant but for the horror of the blighted woods and our dread of what had made it so. It was a dark wood, to be sure – darker even than the Vardaloon. The trees about showed but little green. They grew black like burnt firewood, and their worm-eaten leaves showed shades of brown and blood-red. But the worst of it, I thought, came not from the omnipresent clouds blocking the sun or the blackening of tree bark; rather, it felt like something from within was stealing their life and dimming their essential light.

As it was with the trees, so it was with us. We walked on into the woods, and we all felt a gradual dampening and draining of our life fires. The earth itself seemed to call us down into herself, and her voice was long, dreadful and deep. By the end of the day, we had to struggle to keep our limbs moving. It was like trying to fight our way out of a lake frozen with slush.

'I'm cold,' Maram grumbled as we trudged along. 'I'm tired and I'm hungry, too. And thirsty. Surely this is a night for a little brandy?'

'Remember your vow,' I said to him. My voice, even to myself, sounded as raucous and repetitive as a parrot's. 'The brandy is to be used only for medicine, and there's nothing wrong with you.'

'Is there not? My whole body feels like one big bruise.' He paused as his glazed eyes took in the darkening woods around us. 'Ah, besides, it's not my body that really needs medicine, but my soul.'

We found no clear brook or stream upon whose banks to break our journey, and so we made camp that night in the middle of the featureless forest. Maram was keen enough to build up a great fire, but Kane had to drive him – and Gorman and Pittock – to gather deadwood for our fortifications. In truth, there seemed no need. Mostly to frighten Maram into activity, Kane spoke of maddened panthers or bears made into ghuls, or even demons that might come for us in the night. But for all that afternoon we had seen not a single animal larger than a worm. We had seen no sign of men, either, nor did we expect to, for who would be foolish enough to enter such a doomed wood? Kane warned that after our encounter with the droghul, Morjin might send a company of soldiers after us or even the second droghul that Atara had told of. But as a despondent Maram pointed out in a heavy voice, 'Why should he bother, when this damned dark place will do his work for him?'

Master Juwain led us in a light meditation, and that seemed to ward off the worst of the gloom eating at us, at least for a while. I restated my belief that we could simply walk out of this wood whenever we chose. Liljana's response to our predicament was more practical: she willed herself to set to cooking us the best meal she possibly could. We sat down late that night to roast venison and cakes sweetened with some of the apple butter and jams that the Brothers had given us. We had figs for dessert, and then Liljana brewed up some rare mugs of coffee.

This feast should have been enough to stuff any man, but Maram ate as for three, cramming food into his mouth with a gluttony that was excessive, even for him. He had the grace, however, to compliment Liljana's cooking and the cunning to extol her sacrifice in working hours late into the night for the sake of our bellies and bodies, to say nothing of our spirits: 'Ah, bless you, Liljana, bless you. No one else could have summoned up such delicious fare in such a place, and no one else would even have tried. I'll go to bed a better man tonight.'

His words brightened Liljana's spirits more than could any of Master Juwain's meditations. She even insisted on staying up late to clean the pots herself so that we could get a good night's rest, and this was no little thing considering that she had little water for the task. She went to work contentedly, almost happily – that is, until she discovered that Maram had appropriated a jar of strawberry jam and consumed all its contents himself. She found this cast-off container in some leaves at Maram's place by the fire. As she held up the empty jar and shook it at Maram, her mood instantly fell from good will toward all men into a rare and shocking fury: 'How can you have gobbled all this down in one meal yourself? Don't tell me there wasn't enough else to eat!'

Maram stammered out, 'I . . . I, ah, I ate as I always eat! Do I need to ask your leave to have a little jam?'

'You ate *all* the jam – there is no more!'

'Ah, no more *strawberry*, perhaps, but we've jars of blueberry and cherry, and apple butter, too.'

'But strawberry was Daj's favorite! You *knew* this, and you ate it all, even so.'

'Well, I'm sorry,' Maram said. 'Believe me, I can't tell you how sorry I am.'

'You're sorry you got caught, that's all,' Liljana shrilled at him. 'You've no more care for Daj than you do for me – else you would have saved at least a *little* jam.'

Daj, awed by Liljana's rage, stood beside her and looked up at her as if she had transformed into a she-wolf.

'You're a hog,' she said to Maram. 'A great, fat hog of a man, and you've no care for anyone or anything except what's in the trough in front of you!'

Such words can put poison in the soul; in truth, they can poison the soul of the one who utters them, as well. Liljana stood with her hands on her hips, glaring at Maram as he glared back at her. Finally, he muttered something about having to comb down the horses, and stalked off away from the fire.

I took Liljana aside and pressed her hand into mine, trying to draw off some of her fire. I said to her, 'You, of all of us, must keep us together, not drive us apart.'

My words seemed to calm her, but only slightly. She said to me, 'All that I said to Maram was true!'

'Yes, it was true,' I told her. 'But you must know that you shouldn't say it precisely because it *is* true.'

'I *do* know that,' she said, glancing down at the ground. Then she looked at me. 'Thank you for reminding me. The Materix before me – Anahita Kirriland – warned me that I could be as murderous as Morjin if provoked, and I've always known she was right. But that Maram provokes me so! Sometimes I think he hates me!'

'No,' I said, smiling at her. 'He regards you as he would his own mother.'

'Do you really think so? But sometimes he has so little *respect*.'

'Don't you think he knows that? Don't you think he knows who he is and wishes to be better, as we all do?'

Liljana's face softened as I said this, and she might have smiled if Morjin hadn't stolen from her this grace. She returned to the task of washing her pots with a lifting of her spirits, if not exactly good cheer. And I went off to speak with Maram.

I found him thirty yards away from our camp, sitting in the dark on a log near a blighted tree. At my approach, he gave a jerk and thrust his hand under his cloak. He moaned out to me, 'Ah, Val, Val – that woman hates me!'

'Of course she doesn't hate you,' I said, stepping closer. 'She's just not herself – none of us are.'

'No, I think she's *too* much herself, if you know what I mean. Oh, too bad, too bad.'

Maram's self-pity swept over me in waves that made me sick in the belly. As he opened his mouth to bemoan his fate for the thousandth time, something else swept over me as well: a blast of brandy-tainted breath.

My sudden fury shocked me as I shouted to him: 'You've been drinking!'

'Ah, well, so what if I have!' he shouted back.

'Where's the bottle then?'

From beneath his cloak, Maram withdrew a bottle of brandy, unstoppered and half-full, judging from the sloshing sound of its contents. The sight of it further inflamed my fury. I lashed out with my fist, knocking his forearm and dislodging the bottle from his hand. It bounced off the log and fell to the forest floor, where its dark brandy ran out onto the ground.

'What have you done?' he cried out.

He lunged for the bottle as if hoping to rescue at least a few drams of brandy. But I caught hold of his arm and jerked him up short.

'What have *you* done?' I yelled back at him. 'Your vow –'

'My vow be damned!' he cried out. 'As we're all damned in this damnable woods!'

For a moment, I wanted to slap the despair from his face. But then the outrage and sense of betrayal that poured out of him stilled my hand. I made a fist again, and bit my own knuckles. And I said to him, 'I . . . am sorry. Please forgive me.'

Then it was my turn to go marching off into the woods. As my boots squeezed the moisture from mildewed old leaves, I tried breathing deeply, as Master Juwain had taught me. I tried meditating upon the brilliance of the rising sun, as he had also taught me in one of his light meditations. Nothing seemed to help. I leaned against the trunk of a twisted tree, and I could not calm the beating of my heart, which jumped in my chest like a hare fleeing a ravenous predator.

'Morjin,' I whispered. 'Morjin.'

I knew that somehow he was attacking us, through the Black Jade. This cursed crystal called to me through the blackened forest. The very earth beneath my boots seemed to despise me, and promised soon to rot my flesh and bones.

How was it possible, I wondered, that I had nearly struck my best friend? The dark earth of the Skadarak called to the darkest part of me:

Valashu.

I had impulses. All people do. I wanted to run in terror from the beast snapping its jaws at the back of my neck, even as I wanted to pretend that Liljana was my mother and fall weeping into her lap. Whenever I looked at Atara, my arms trembled to crush her to me and kiss her beautiful lips, to carry her off and fill her with the seed of our child. The wound in my back was an outrage that demanded protest. All the wounds that I had taken since I was a child, to my body and my soul, gave voice to agony. The pain of the kirax burning up my blood was a fire I could never escape. It made me want to scream at the immense torment of life. My fingers ached to tear out Morjin's liver and cast it to the dogs, as my tongue tingled to taste his blood. As the night deepened and I stood alone in the lightless woods, I wanted to free all these impulses and a hundred more as I might uncage rabid rats – even the darkest and deadliest impulse of all.

Sometime after midnight, I returned to our camp. Master Juwain sat by one of the fires with his eyes fixed upon a page of the *Saganom Elu*. He seemed to be reading the same lines over and over again. Atara was by herself near the other fire, seeking knowledge of another sort. When I sat down beside her, her whole body gave a start, and her fingers fumbled to find my hands and face.

'What's wrong?' I asked her.

'It's all dark, now,' she told me.

The heart of this brave woman sent out pulses of fear.

'We'll find our way out of here,' I promised. 'Tomorrow, we will.'

'It won't matter if we do,' she said. 'It's all dark as if there will never be light again. As if there never *could* be light again.'

I tried to lift her fingers toward my lips but she pulled her hand away from me. The coldness that flowed out of her would have frozen the very rays of the sun.

'Atara,' I whispered.

'No, don't say anything,' she whispered back. 'Go to bed and gather some strength for tomorrow. Let me be alone.'

As she wished, I said goodnight to her, but I could not go to sleep. I left her sitting silently by the fire, eyeless in eternity.

As I paced about near the quiet forms of Daj and Estrella, I brooded over all the ways that I might kill Morjin. Once, Atara had warned me that his death would be my own. My fate seemed to be hurtling toward me like a great black stone cast by a catapult. I could not step aside to save myself. It made me sweat with a sick, black fear, but I almost didn't care.

Much later my pacing carried me over to the western edge of our encampment where Kane stood leaning out over the fence.

He faced the black forest to the west. Where Master Juwain had stared at the same verses in his book, Kane simply stared – at nothing.

'Valashu,' he finally said to me. His voice rolled like a deep and distant thunder. 'Why are you here?'

'I keep thinking of Morjin,' I confessed to him.

'So do I,' he told me. 'And of Asangal.'

'Why do you speak of the Dark One by that name?'

'I was trying to remember what he was like before . . . before.'

I listened to the sound of a drunken Maram snoring by the fire, and I asked, 'What was he like, then?'

'I think he was much like you.' He turned so that the flames of the fire licked at the centers of his black eyes. 'He thought about death too much, too.'

He stood staring at me as the world upon which we stood pulled us even deeper into night. His dark gaze seemed to grab hold of me and pull me into a flight of stairs that twisted down and down through a hole in the black earth, on and on, and deeper and deeper, forever.

'Asangal feared it,' he told me in a deep and almost dreamy voice. 'So, and fearing it, he denied it.'

And in denying it, as Kane said, Asangal had gone on to fight what he called the Great Lie with every breath in his body. The results we could see and feel all around us, in the poisoned earth of the Skadarak and in our souls.

'But Valashu,' he said to me, 'a man, before he becomes one of the Elijin, *must* overcome his fear of death – do you understand?'

The Elijin, he went on to say, were destined to become Galadin, even as the Galadin themselves were doomed to die into greater beings. Some, such as Ashtoreth and Valoreth, found glory in this becoming. But for others this distant fate, if feared, would fester and grow over the ages into a crushing torment.

'Do you understand why?' Kane said to me.

I thought I understood very well why. And so I spoke to him Morjin's words to me – now my words to myself: 'Because who can bear the thought of being erased? Who can bear the neverness of night without end?'

'So, who *can* bear that?' he snarled out. 'But that is not the worst of things – no, neither the deepest dread nor the worst.'

'What could be worse than that?'

In answer, he bent down and scooped up a handful of moist earth. His hand tightened around it and he said, 'As a man lives, on and on, he takes more and more of the world into himself. If he lives truly, he opens himself to great beauty, all the glories of the earth. So, he *creates* these glories, eh? And in creating, as a father with a child, he comes to love what he puts his hand to, more and more deeply. And so he hates being sundered from it in death.'

I thought of Atara's beautiful blue eyes and the children that Morjin had taken from us when he had gouged them out. Worms of fire ate at my own eyes, and I said, 'He killed her, a part of her, even as he killed my mother and grandmother, forever. Damn him – and damn death then, too!'

Kane shook his head at this as he took my hand and pressed a clod of earth into it. 'Morjin speaks thus, and so Angra Mainyu, but you must not.'

'How should I speak, then?'

He shook his head again and said to me, 'So, the One means death to be a gift, not a curse. Why? Because in living forever, a man would want to behold all things, taste all things, drink in the whole of the world and create his own. But man, even though he be a Galadin, is only ever a finite being, eh? And so this lust for the infinite would grow vaster and vaster in a sick heat and consume him in a terrible flame. Then, despite his love for the world, that which was sweet would become bitter; the new would too-quickly grow old; things of light would fade in darkness, and the bright, green shoots of love turn into a twisted and blackened hate. Then a man will say "no" to all of creation, and most of all to himself.'

He looked about our encampment at the reclining forms of our friends. In a low voice, he told me, 'So, Val, so – there are a thousand ways to hate life, but only one way to truly love it.'

And with that, he clasped his hand around the clod of dirt cupped in mine, then returned to his vigil, staring out at the dark and silent woods.

The morning came only a few more hours after that, but it seemed to take forever for the trees around us to brighten to a sort of blackish-gray. Maram groaned upon being awakened, and complained of a terrible headache; we all moved as if we had drunk wine poisoned with poppy. Setting out into the woods was a torment of heavy limbs nearly drained of purpose, and spirits as confused as a flock of birds at an eclipse of the sun. Here, I knew, the very earth was sick and had gone mad. Soon it became clear that we were hopelessly lost. I drew my sword in order to light our way, but its silustria gleamed only dully in whatever direction I pointed it, and then faded with the miles so that it seemed it would never gleam again. My sense of direction, strangely, remained strong, and I led us on and on, five miles across the poisoned earth and then two more. Due west called to me through the sodden gray woods as clearly as a bell. Why, I wondered, did it seem that we were only working our way deeper and deeper into the Skadarak?

Because here, a voice inside me whispered, *your sense of direction has been twisted.*

For a long while, I did not want to heed this deep voice. But then, around noon, with Atara stumbling over tree roots and the children staring out at the stunted oaks with dark, empty eyes, I called for a halt. While Pittock and Gorman went off to look for sign of direction, I turned to Berkuar and said, 'This wood *is* cursed. Here, north seems west, and west turns south and then east. And all directions, it seems, lead ever and only one way.'

'Toward the Black Jade,' he muttered.

'It is calling me,' I told him.

'It's calling all of us,' he said, wiping the sweat from his forehead. He moved his jaw as if to spit, and then swallowed a gout of barbark juice instead.

Just then a great, bellowing shout sounded from farther in the woods. I turned to look past the blackened trunks of the trees at Pittock and Gorman. Gorman stood backed up to an old elm; Pittock had thrust his long knife into his belly, and stood there beside him, pushing and twisting the knife in deeper.

'Pittock!' Berkuar cried out. 'Damn you, Pittock!'

He drew his own knife and set out bounding through the woods straight toward them.

I followed him a moment later, and so did Kane. But we could do nothing. Before we could draw within ten yards, Pittock ripped his knife free from Gorman's body and let him fall dying to the ground. He shook his bloody knife at the forest and shouted out, 'He killed my cousin, so damn him, and his father and mother – and damn the whole world for whelping them and all their line!'

And with that he turned his long knife upon himself, thrusting it up beneath his ribs into his heart. He died slumping down toward the ground, and leaving bloody marks as he clawed at the bark of the elm tree.

'It was their old quarrel,' Berkuar said, going forward to stand over his two men. He spoke these words with an acceptance of the inevitability of murder, and I hated him for that. 'Let's bury them then.'

Only Estrella wept for these two ill-fated woodsmen or had the kindness to look for flowers to put on their graves. In the blighted forest, she found none.

It took all our will to get out shovels and dig two long holes and lay Gorman and Pittock in the earth. There seemed no point to interring them this way. In truth, there seemed no point to anything.

'We're lost,' Atara said as she fumbled for the reins of her horse. She was the last of us I would have expected to give voice to despair. 'I can't see our way out of this.'

'That's because there *is* no way out,' Maram muttered. He glowered at Master Juwain and snarled, 'Tell me if you know of any Way Rhymes for *this* place!'

But Master Juwain only shook his head at this and gripped the leather binding of his useless book.

'It may be,' I said, 'that the only way out is in.'

'No, Val,' Kane said to me.

'If it's the Black Jade that is truly calling us,' I said, 'then let us answer this call. We'll find the dark crystal and destroy it.'

At this Kane drew his sword and thrust it down into the ground. 'Can you destroy the very earth to which it's welded?'

'It might be that with the crystal destroyed, the earth here would have less power over us.'

'Can't you see,' Master Juwain said to me, 'that Morjin would want you to think like this?'

'I can see it well enough,' I said to him, hating the hauteur in my voice. 'We'll destroy the crystal even so, and someday, Morjin himself.'

The dark fire that filled my eyes then easily ignited the coals inside Kane. A savage smile split his face as he gazed at me and said, 'So – perhaps this *is* the only way.'

Estrella stepped up to me and grasped my hand. I was sure that she wanted to tell me that she would help me find the Black Jade. Then she shook her curly hair away from her tear-filled eyes as she looked up at me with a terrible fear.

Daj, speaking for her, came up to me and said, 'Do we *have* to go looking for this crystal? *Why* can't there be another way?'

Master Juwain rested his rough old hand on Daj's head and said to me, 'Abrasax told us that we mustn't listen to the call of this crystal. You agreed to this, Val.'

266

'If I did, then I was a fool.' I closed my eyes against the dark, hateful drumbeat of my heart. 'You see, I don't know how *not* to listen.'

I opened my eyes to gaze at Master Juwain in silent accusation. 'Well, first and last,' he told me, 'there are the Light Meditations.'

'Did they help Gorman or Pittock?' I asked him. 'Have they helped you?'

The sick look on Master Juwain's face told me that these meditations had availed him little.

'The truth is,' I told him, 'I *must* listen. How are we to destroy evil if we don't understand it?'

If the logic of my words failed to persuade Master Juwain, the force of my will bent him to our new course. A gleam came into his gray eyes as he nodded his head to me and told me, 'In truth, I don't know how not to listen either.'

And so without a backward glance at the graves of Gorman and Pittock, we resumed our journey. After another few miles, we paused in order to look through the twisted trees that trapped us. Liljana passed around a waterskin. Master Juwain walked off into the woods to look for a way out of them, or so he said.

Just as it came my turn to drink, I noticed Liljana pat her tunic's pocket with a sudden and rare panic, and then thrust her hand inside. And she cried out, 'My gelstei! It's gone!'

'Are you sure?' I called to her. I hurried over to her, and so did Kane and Maram.

'It *is* gone!' she cried out again.

'Ah, it must have fallen out,' Maram said to her. 'Perhaps while you were sleeping.'

She pressed her lips together, then hissed at him, 'It did *not* fall out! I would never let that happen. And so it must have been taken out.'

She stared at him with a dark and deadly look.

Just then Master Juwain came to Maram's defense, saying to Liljana, 'I'm afraid it *did* fall out. I found it late last night while you were snoring.'

With that, he took his hand from his pocket and held up Liljana's little blue figurine.

'But why didn't you wake me then?' Liljana shouted at him. 'And why did you go the whole day without telling me?'

She came up close to him, and her hand darted out as quick as the head of a striking snake. But Master Juwain proved quicker, for he snatched the crystal away from her, out of her reach.

267

'Master Juwain!'

Maram and I both called out his name together. Then we hurried up to Liljana and grabbed her arms to keep her from thrusting her fingers into Master Juwain's throat or some other deadly vulnerable chakra.

'Give it back to her!' I shouted at Master Juwain.

'But I was only trying to keep it safe,' he huffed out. 'And to keep *her* safe. In these woods, so dark, the temptation to use it must be very–'

'Give it back to her!' I shouted again.

He stared straight back at me as his fingers tightened around the crystal so hard that his whole arm trembled. Then he seemed to will himself to extend his fist and drop the figurine into Liljana's outstretched hand. She immediately thrust it deep into her pocket as she glared at him.

'*You*,' she said to him with an acid contempt, 'tried to use it, didn't you? To look inside Morjin's mind?'

'His mind,' he said as if intoning a magic word. His eyes glazed over as if dazzled by a bright light. 'What do we really know of it? He was an Elijin, once, but is he so different than mortal men in his mentations? Perhaps. Perhaps. I know that his words strike us as evil, even mad, but there must be a logic beneath it all. If we could discover the source of his onstreaming intelligence, which I admit is great, then we might discover the whys and ways of the great Red Dragon. The whys and ways of much more. The secrets he keeps! He has knowledge unknown to men. Perhaps knowledge of the mystery of mind itself . . . or at least his own. What if one could dive down and find the currents that give rise to it? I can almost see it! They would form up, each individual thought, like waves upon the sea. At times, one must swell larger than another, and drown it out, and then another and another – an infinitude of digressions, distractions and side-thoughts, as with any other man. But always, the deeper logic, revealed through analysis of perceptions, indications and manifestations, these endless technics and deductions, you see. There *must* be a way to peel back the waves to understand how they birth each other and impinge on each other, even overwhelming and annihilating as they ever form and reform, ever shaped by the source of all waves: the way that the very mind of the One forms thoughts, and causes all things to burst into creation. Morjin *must* seek this deepest of secrets, the final one, shining like a perfect jewel, which lies beneath

268

the endless layers and depths of watery waves, down and down and –'

'Master Juwain!' I cried out. I grasped hold of his arm, hard, and shook him. Then his madness for pure thought left him, at least for the moment, and his eyes cleared. And I asked him, 'Did you use Liljana's gelstei?'

He shook his head, then admitted, 'Almost I did. If Liljana hadn't been so suspicious of me –'

'*Me*, suspicious of *you*!' Liljana cried out.

I called out, 'This dispute must end here and now. Or else we'll all end up like Gorman and Pittock.'

I thought that Master Juwain wanted to argue with me, but then he bit his lip and nodded his head. Liljana only scowled at him – and at me. Then she turned to stomp off back toward the horses.

After that, I led us deeper into the woods. No one spoke, and we walked on into a terrible silence. The trees of the Skadarak began thinning out and grew ever more stunted and blackened with the disease that blighted them. Some sort of stinking, greenish-black fungus clung to the forest floor and fouled our boots. We were hard put to encourage the horses to set their hooves down into it and keep them moving forward. As for ourselves, it was a misery to keep going on and on, but there seemed no help for it. For a deep voice, I sensed, sounded inside all of us. It promised us endless fascinations and sweet drink to quell the fire of existence; in truth, it promised us everything. It kept calling to us in a dark and dreadful tone that none of us could resist.

How, I wondered again, could I *not* listen? I tried putting my hand to my sword and bringing to my mind all the light that was inside it. It was not enough. I listened for the sound of Atara saying yes to a marriage troth and heard our children playing happily in the yard of a little house by a stream, and that was not enough either. I remembered promising my grandmother that I would not let my burning for Morjin's death destroy me, and still the fell voice called me on.

We came to a place where the trees would not grow, nor would any other living thing. The ground before us was bare and blackened, littered with many bones, mostly human. I felt a strange, sick heat emanating as from the center of the earth.

Altaru suddenly reared up and whinnied as he struck the air with his hooves. I stroked his neck and murmured to him: 'Ho, friend, peace – it will be all right.'

I told him that we were both strong enough to walk straight into this black hell and walk out again. I could listen to the voice of the Skadarak, just a little, and take from it the knowledge to undo it. It could have no power over me, for only I, in the end, had power over myself.

'So,' Kane said, staring out into this swath of death-scorched earth.

His black eyes seemed perfectly to mirror the blackness before us. The rest of our company looked at me then to see if I would lead us into it.

'It's all right, Estrella,' I heard Daj whisper. He stood with her by their horses, holding her hand as she blinked back the tears from her eyes.

I knew then that if I took one more step and set foot into this wasteland, I would never find my way out again. There are some holes so black and deep that there can be no escape. It didn't matter. The Black Jade, I told myself, must be dug up and destroyed. I turned my face toward the heart of the Skadarak.

No, a voice whispered to me. *No.*

My eyes lost themselves in a great, blackened bloom of hate. The kirax burned me; I could feel Morjin trying to make me into a ghul. The One be damned, I thought, for shaping my fate so. I knew that even if by some miracle I *did* escape this place, it would leave its evil sear in my soul. I would have no more mercy for anyone else than I did myself. I would put to the sword my enemies, even though they begged quarter of me; I would torture captives with heated irons to make them tell me their secrets; any and all who opposed me I would slay with the bright fire of valarda.

And then another, even darker thought came to me: I didn't care. Morjin had spoken of three levels of evil, but I knew that there was a fourth: simply not caring if one's actions were evil. I would do what I must do, what I wanted to do, and the world be damned. There seemed no help for it. I steeled myself to take the final and fateful step.

No.

I looked at Berkuar, who seemed more than willing to follow me into this black hell. But I could feel his raging resentment at me for leading him here; I knew that he would be thinking that this was a trap and that I had betrayed him after all. Treacherous people were always keen to suspect others of treachery. And weren't the Greens veritable demons of treachery, as Gorman and Pittock had proved? Truly, they were, and so very soon, at the first

270

sign of Berkuar moving against me, I would have to draw my sword and cut him down. Likewise I must slay Kane, for I knew that he would be heeding the same dark call as I and would be compelled to put his sword into me before I fell upon him. Maram I must send on, here or perhaps in the desert, because someday his selfish ways would get us all killed. Master Juwain was doomed to fall beneath my blade, too, for I knew that very soon he would be tempted again to look into Morjin's foul mind. And Atara. Wouldn't killing this poor, tormented woman be a mercy? It would be the hardest thing I'd ever had to do – one quick stab through the heart – but in a way, the kindest, too. What one must do out of love, I thought, occurs beyond good or evil. I *must* kill Atara, as I would kill *for* her a thousand times a thousand times – even as I would gladly die for her. And I *would* soon die, by my own hand, for I was truly damned for even thinking of killing the one I most loved. But before I took my sword to myself, I must stab and hack to pieces all my enemies. They were everywhere. For war was everywhere and would never end. My part in this eternal war would grow only deeper and more murderous as my enemies became greater in power and numbers. And here, in the heart of the Skadarak, dwelled my most terrible enemy of all. He must be slain. All things born of this damned and twisted earth must be slain, and most of all the treacherous earth itself. I had not made the world so. But I must take my part in its unmaking, slashing out with my unquenchable sword through the flesh of all who opposed me and the blackened skin of the earth itself, feeling the heat of their blood flowing like red lava, killing all that lived in order to fulfill my fate, killing and killing . . .

Valashu.

The whispering of my soul had fallen so faint and faroff that I could scarcely hear it. The dark, fell voice of the Skadarak called to me in a thunder like that of a fire mountain bursting in two. How, I wondered for the hundredth time, could I not listen to it?

'Mother,' I whispered. 'Ashtoreth.'

Did the woman who had given me birth truly dwell with the Galadin beyond the stars? Could she hear me call to her, or was she as deaf and doomed as I was?

'Mother,' I whispered again. And then another name, that of an old friend, came almost unbidden to my tongue: 'Ahura Alarama.'

With this simple movement of my breath past my lips, Flick appeared. This being of twinkling lights whirled before me, and his colors quickly brightened and solidified into a form I loved very well. In a click of the fingers, Alphanderry stood between me and the bone-strewn circle of black earth.

He seemed every inch my companion of old: His curly black hair was tangled like a mop, and flopped down over his soft brown eyes. His skin glowed with rich browns and golds and the underlying tone of glorre. His voice, too, sounded out all bright and full of his great gladness of life. He did not wait for the stunned, soul-sickened Kane to bring forth his mandolet and accompany him. He simply sang to us. He smiled, and his sensuous lips parted, and from deep within his throat sounded a beautiful song. It rose, like the wind, and built higher and higher, and ever more lovely like the very songs of the stars. In its pure and golden notes was praise of all life – even of ourselves. We listened until tears sprang into our eyes. And still Alphanderry kept singing, like an ocean emptying itself, singing and singing. . .

'Valashu,' I heard a voice whisper to me. It was the voice of my blood, the very sound and soul of my throbbing heart. 'West is *that* way.'

I turned to face to my left and slightly behind me. Beneath the shield of Alphanderry's immortal song, my sense of direction lived again. Or rather, I could feel it within me once more: bright, steady and warm, for some things can never really die. I heard my fate, my true fate, calling me on. If we set forth through the trees behind us, we could walk straight out of the Skadarak.

La sarojin yil alla valhalla . . . .

As Alphanderry continued to pour forth music into this desolation of blackened trees and bone-cursed earth, I came to hear *all* of myself more deeply, and I remembered who I really was.

'Atara,' I called out to my blind, beloved companion who stood near me. I called the names of all my friends beside me. 'We cannot go into *that*,' I said, pointing into the heart of the wasteland. 'Let the Black Jade lie as it has. There are some things beyond the power of any man.'

For a moment, the whole world seemed to stop and hang poised on the point of a sword's blade. Maram wiped the sweat from his brow, and Master Juwain rubbed at the back of his head. Liljana closed her eyes as she fought a terrible battle with herself. Kane stared into blackness. His whole body trembled as with a tiger about to spring.

'Kane!' I called to him as I laid hold of his arm. 'Kane!'

Then he looked at me, and his eyes flashed with triumph. 'So,' he said to me. 'So.'

Liljana murmured, 'There are some things beyond any *woman*.'

Master Juwain said, 'You're right, Val. Why should we invite it to destroy us?'

He moved over to Liljana and took her hand in his. 'I'm sorry that I borrowed your gelstei. It will never happen again.'

'I'm sorry that I yelled at you,' Liljana told him. And then, 'If I should die along this journey, I want you to take my gelstei and keep it safe.'

They bowed to each other and embraced each other. At this, Berkuar laughed out in relief and spat happily upon the ground before us. Then Maram said to me, 'But we're still lost, aren't we? How can we ever find our way out of here?'

'We are not lost,' I told him. I drew Alkaladur and pointed my shining sword in the direction my blood whispered to me: the direction of my fate. 'That way will take us out of the Skadarak, and on to the desert and Hesperu.'

'Are you sure?' Maram asked me.

I closed my eyes a moment to listen to Alphanderry's strong, clear voice and the even deeper one that sounded within me. Then I looked at Maram and told him, 'Yes, I'm sure.'

I pulled gently on Altaru's reins and pointed my great, trusting horse toward the west. We walked through the nearly-dead forest over blighted, blackened ground. Alphanderry, like an angel, walked with us. And in all the miles of the seemingly endless Skadarak, he never ceased singing his beautiful, inextinguishable song.

17

And so we moved away from that terrible place. We journeyed all that day and the next as well, into the west. Daj did not ask how we might determine when we had left the Skadarak, for we all knew that in a way, we never would. But there came a time when trees grew tall and healthy about us again, with bright green leaves that fluttered in a fresh, clean wind. The dreadful call of the Skadarak faded into a murmur and then seemed to die. Alphanderry left us then. Our shimmering friend simply vanished back into the nothingness that had birthed him. We were all sad to be left alone again, but we hoped that something of Alphanderry's song would continue to sound within us, as a charm against the darkness that had no end.

We mourned for Pittock and Gorman and felt keenly the loss of their bows, for despite their failings, they had been fine warriors. We did not speak of this. We did not speak of the worst of what had befallen us in the Skadarak, neither to each other nor even to ourselves; we were like murderers reentering the company of good men and ashamed of our deeds. When we came to a little stream, we spent some hours washing the stench of the dark woods from our clothing. We bathed in the cold water and scrubbed at our naked skin until it was raw, but it seemed that the evil that clung to us could not be washed away.

Only once did I give voice to the terrible doubt that now ate at my bones. We had crossed another stream and were setting our course when I took Kane aside and said to him, 'I'm tired, so damn tired. I haven't the heart for this any more.'

'What? What's this?'

'Perhaps you should lead us,' I told him.

His eyes flared with anger, and astonishment. '*I*, lead us? Ha,

I'm no leader! Men obey me – they do not follow. The duty is upon you.'

'But I nearly led us to our doom!'

'So? I've been near to doom a thousand times. That's just the way of life, eh? In the end, you led us out of that cursed wood, and that's all that matters.'

'Is it? I am –'

'You're a star, Valashu. In the end, a bright and beautiful star. You followed its light, and so did I. And so now it's now, and now we're here in this beautiful place. A million miles might lie ahead of us; I won't hear any talk of what lies behind, do you understand?'

He squeezed my arm then, and I felt some of his inexhaustible strength flow into me. I bowed my head to him, and he smiled at me.

But it is one thing to agree to lead others and quite another to keep them moving forward when their hearts as well have nearly given up all hope. After the passage of the Skadarak, Atara fell into a silence so deep and cold it seemed that she had almost lost the power of speech. Her second sight did not return to her. I felt some deep part of her desperately looking for me to show her a way out of her darkness.

As for Maram, he tried to take solace in words. The next morning we set out into a forest chittering with many birds, and he sang almost as brightly as they did. But I sensed the falseness of bravado in his great, booming voice. I knew that he was trying to rally himself for a battle with his old demons – either that or trying to forget.

And so I said to him, 'One day, when our grandchildren are happily married, we'll sit with glasses of brandy in our hands and wonder that we once came so close to despair.'

'Do you really think so?' he asked me. 'But what if we fail?'

'We *can't* fail, Maram – at least we can't fail each other. And that is why, in the end, we'll win.'

He smiled at this. 'Brave words, my friend, and thank you for them. But I don't know – I just don't know.'

We continued our journey through the warm, open woods, and sometimes Maram's singing swelled with true hope, and sometimes it didn't. This I had learned in the Skadarak: our hearts were always free. Not even the Maitreya, I thought, could save a man who didn't want to be saved.

For two more days, we traveled into the west toward the

mountains. Ashte had passed into Soldru, and so finally did the clouds above us pass on to the east. The sky cleared, allowing the strong Soldru sun to rain down its bright rays through the glowing, green leaves above us. Arum and marigolds showed their colors in glades covered with grass. Through the occasional breaks in the forest's canopy, we caught glimpses of a great wall of white peaks that grew larger and larger.

At last we came into a thinly-populated part of Acadu that Berkuar seemed to know quite well. He guided us onto game paths and old, narrow roads. Here we might have moved more quickly, but I called for an unhurried pace. We were all worn from our journey, and Daj and Estrella most of all. They were as tough and uncomplaining as any children could be, but in the end they were still children. We stopped more than once so that they might play by a stream or pick apples from an orchard of one of the farmers who had made a homestead in these lonely woods. One of these, a stout freeholder named Graybuck, invited us to a feast of roasted ham, mashed potatoes and fresh greens picked from his fields. He insisted on plying us with some of his homemade beer, even Maram, whose vows he waved away.

'Beer is the only fit drink for friends,' Graybuck told us, holding forth at table in his long room with his wife and five children. He turned his heavy, red face toward Maram. 'Surely you can put aside your vow this one time to make toast in the company of *friends*?'

'Ah, surely I can,' Maram told him. 'A vow is sacred, it's true, but what is more sacred than friendship?'

I said nothing as I watched Graybuck's eldest daughter, Roseen, fill Maram's mug with a frothy brown beer. I bit my lip as I watched the way that Maram watched this plump, young woman go about her business, as if he would rather have had her for dessert in place of apple pie or other sweets.

'To the Keepers of the Forest,' Graybuck said, holding up his mug and nodding at Berkuar. 'May they the drive the Crucifiers from our woods.'

He went on to tell of the depredations of Morjin's soldiers who had raided down from the mine lands to the north. He praised us for having the courage and good guidance to have passed by the Skadarak unharmed, and so avoided these men that he hated.

'They've feared your bows,' he said to Berkuar, 'and so few have dared to come into the deep woods here, though I heard that last year they burnt Finlay's farm not twenty miles from here and carried off his daughters. But if you're journeying south, as you must, you'll find the forest full of soldiers. They've set up a garrison at Nayland, between the Cold Marshes and the mountains.'

'But what if we didn't go around the mountains,' I asked him, 'but across them?'

'Cross the mountains?' Graybuck said to me. 'Not with horses and children. There are no passes over them.'

Kane sipped at his beer as he eyed Graybuck. Then he said, 'No passes at all?'

'Well, there is a narrow gap about thirty miles from here, but it is cursed.'

'Cursed, you say?' Maram called out. 'Cursed *how*?'

'It's said that there is something there that turns men to stone.'

'Turns men to stone!' Maram cried out. Then he belched and muttered, 'Oh, excellent, excellent!'

'Surely,' Master Juwain said to Graybuck, 'that cannot be true. Surely it is just a legend.'

'I don't know about that,' Graybuck said to him. 'I've heard people tell of kin lost to this Stonemaker. They call it the Yaga.'

'The Yaga,' Maram muttered again as he gazed into his empty mug.

'But hasn't anyone,' Master Juwain asked, 'ever ventured into this gap to disprove the legend?'

'Would you venture into the Skadarak to disprove that it could capture a man as a spider's web does a fly?'

Master Juwain said nothing as he looked me and rubbed the back of his bald head.

'We keep well away from that part of the mountains and the westernmost reaches of the woods,' Graybuck told us. 'And you will too unless you want to stand like a statue for the rest of your days. Now it's late, and I've an acre of weeds to pull up tomorrow. And so I'll say goodnight.'

Later that evening, after Maram returned from the barn and helping Roseen to milk the cows, as he put it, we held council at the edge of Graybuck's apple orchard, where we had made our encampment. All the way from the Brotherhood's school, we had argued as to our course toward Hesperu, and it had come time to make our final decision.

'So, nothing has changed,' Kane said to us. 'We've two routes to Hesperu: through the Dragon lands or across the Red Desert.'

'Six hundred miles through Sunguru the long way?' Master

Juwain sighed out, shaking his head. 'It's bad enough that we have to venture into Hesperu.'

We all agreed to this. However fierce the heat of the Red Desert, it could not be so dangerous as exposing ourselves at every village and town in the heavily populated Sunguru along a course of six hundred miles.

'Then if we're to go into the desert,' Kane said, 'we still have two choices: across the mountains or around them.'

But to go around them, as Graybuck had said, we might very well have to fight our way past the garrison at Nayland. And worse, at the point of the Yorgos range of the White Mountains, where they gave out upon the border between Uskudar and Sunguru, we would find fortresses and yet more garrisons of the armies of both King Orunjan and King Angand.

'But couldn't we just slip around them?' Maram said. 'Better the danger that we *do* know than this stonemaking Yaga that Graybuck told of.'

'But it might turn out to be no danger at all,' Master Juwain said. His gray eyes fairly glowed with curiosity. 'The Brotherhoods have investigated many other reports of people being turned to stone, and they all proved false.'

'Ah, I don't know, I don't know,' Maram muttered. 'Perhaps there's another pass that Graybuck is unaware of.'

We all looked at Berkuar as he rubbed at his heavily bearded jaw then spat into the fire. He said, 'Graybuck is right: there are no passes through the mountains other than the gap.'

Maram gazed at Berkuar and asked, 'Are you sure?'

'As sure as you are of your nose on your fat face.'

'Ah,' Maram said, 'you know this country well, don't you? What is your belief about this Stonemaker?'

'I've never gone into the gap, so I can't say truly,' Berkuar told us. 'But my grandfather once saw something at the mouth of the gap that might have been a man of stone – he came within a quarter mile of it before he turned away.'

Master Juwain offered his opinion that this was likely some natural rock configuration or even a stone carving that the ancients had made. He restated his desire to explore this mystery.

'I know the way to the gap,' Berkuar told us. 'I'll take you there, if that is what you decide.'

He turned to look at me then, and so did Master Juwain and Maram. I drew my sword and watched as the silustria glowed glorre when I pointed it toward the west. I said, 'Surely Master

278

Juwain is right that this Yaga is only a legend. But even if he's wrong, I'd rather venture through the gap than fight our way south. I'm tired of killing.'

Atara and Liljana agreed with this, and so did Kane, and even the children. Finally, Maram bowed his head to the consensus of our company and groaned out, 'Well, we survived the damn Stonefaces and so I suppose we can slip past this Stone*maker*, whatever it really is. But I have a bad feeling about this.'

In the morning we said our farewells to Graybuck and his family and set out again toward the mountains. For the first few miles we bushwacked through a wood thick with buckthorn, sumac and many flowers. Then we came to a road that led north and slightly west. For the rest of the day, as the ground rose before us, we slowly rode up this deserted road through an archway of great elms, oaks and sycamores. We passed an old woodcutter and a couple of hunters, but saw no sign of the Dragon's men or any other people. We made camp that night on the bank of a stream that cut the road. For dinner that night we ate part of a boar that Berkuar had killed. Maram downed nearly an entire ham by himself. It was astonishing how much my friend could eat when one of his hungers came upon him.

The morning found us working our way up along the stream. The ground rose ever higher and grew rockier, as well. The tall trees mostly blocked our view of the mountains, but we could almost smell the snow and ice of these great peaks in the cooling and freshening of the wind that blew down from them. At last we came to a granite mantle of ground where only a few shrubs and a single black locust grew out of the cracks in the rock. We stood beside the rushing stream looking at the wall of mountains before us; they were so close it seemed that we should be able to reach out and touch them.

'There's the gap,' Berkuar said, pointing at a place where the mountains' contour seemed broken in two. 'The stream leads up into it.'

'What's its name, then?' Maram asked him.

'It has none that I know,' Berkuar said.

'Then I shall name it the Kul Kharand,' Maram said. 'Unless anyone objects?'

I smiled at this because *kharand* was the ancient Ardik word meaning the fulfillment of one's dreams. I loved Maram for fighting so hard to remain hopeful.

It took us two more hours to climb up to the Kul Kharand. We walked our horses along the stony north bank of the stream. Their iron-shod hooves rang out against hard granite. If anyone guarded this pass, I thought, they would hear us coming a mile away.

At last we came out into a great bowl of stone-strewn ground where the trees grew thin and far between. Berkuar was the first of us to espy the statue set there, sculpted with his arm lifted and his hand cupped back toward the gap as if beckoning travellers toward it.

'That must have been the man that your grandfather saw,' Maram said to Berkuar.

He did not add what his rigid face said so plainly: that Berkuar's grandfather had possessed the good sense to refuse the statue's invitation.

We advanced toward the statue under the cover of Kane and Berkuar, who stalked up the rocky slope gripping strung bows nocked with arrows. It was a statue in smooth stone of a young man of medium height, rendered naked, with exquisitely fine muscles carved about a slender frame. A smile almost as lovely as Alphanderry's graced the features of the statue's face which was wonderfully expressive and lifelike.

'Remarkable,' Master Juwain said, examining the statue. He held out his hand toward it. 'Truly remarkable work.'

The stone was unusual, as dark as obsidian and as smooth as marble, with strange reddish striations running along its grain.

'Look,' he said, 'not a chisel mark upon it!'

'Is that supposed to encourage me?' Maram asked him.

'Only the ancients could have made such a sculpture,' Master Juwain declared.

'I don't know,' Berkuar said, spitting a gout of red barbark juice toward the base of the statue. 'It could be possible.'

'Yes, it *could* be,' Maram said. 'But there's another possibility, isn't there?'

'Your stonemaking Yaga?' Master Juwain asked him.

'Yes, *my* Yaga, if you want to call it that. Do you remember Ymiru's purple gelstei? What if this Yaga keeps a purple gelstei and uses it to turn men into stone?'

So saying, he smacked his hand against the statue's face, and then immediately cringed back from it as if fearing that it might come to life.

'I've never heard of the purple gelstei,' Master Juwain said, 'being used this way.'

He looked toward Kane, who said, 'So, I'm not sure that it *could* be used this way.'

He paused to draw in a deep breath, and the look of relief on Maram's face instantly gave way to dread as Kane added: 'But neither am I sure that it could not.'

'No one seems sure of anything,' Maram muttered. 'Well, *I* am sure of one thing: I should never have left Mesh. I should have married Behira, I know I should have. Then I might have, ah, feasted on roasted boar and drunk the sweetest of brandy in contentment to the end of my days, few though they might have been. If ever I'm to return to my beloved's arms, I think we'd better find another way through these mountains.'

Kane, at last, had heard enough of Maram's worries and complaints. He pointed past the statue into the gap and growled out, '*This* is our way! You'll find your beloved, whoever she is, wherever she is, through here!'

At this, Atara stood by her horse orienting her face toward the gap. A coldness seemed to strike into her heart and spread out into her limbs.

I walked over and placed my hand on her cheek, gently turning her toward me. I asked her, 'What do you see in this gap?'

And she told me, 'I see nothing – nothing at all, now.'

'But you're afraid to go into it?'

'I'm afraid to go into it,' she admitted. 'But then I'm afraid to go into the south, east or north, too. There is darkness in all directions.'

It was a scryer's answer, a useless answer, and I ground my teeth in frustration. Then I drew my sword. When I raised it past the statue toward the gap it glowed a bright glorre.

'We'll go on then,' I announced. I turned to Berkuar and said, 'You've guided this far, at great cost, and we owe you great thanks. But the ground ahead of you will be as unfamiliar to you as it will be to us. We should say farewell.'

'What? And leave you to the Yaga?'

No argument that I could fashion was enough to persuade Berkuar to part company with us. He hadn't deserted us in the Skadarak, he said, and he certainly wasn't about to turn tail now.

'If you'll have me,' he said, 'I'll come with you at least as far as the desert.'

I smiled as I clasped hands with him, and watched Kane and my friends do the same. Then, with Berkuar walking to my right and Kane guarding our rear, I led the way into the gap.

We followed the stream up into the mountains. This sparkling water fell over smooth stones on a winding course between the two great mounds of rock to either side of us. The gap seemed about two miles at its widest, narrowing in places to no more than half a mile. Trees grew sparsely here; a few of them were silver maples, which I hadn't seen in this part of Acadu. The air was good and clear, and full of the songs of warblers, swifts and other birds. In the bushes along the stream, the honeysuckle hung heavy in bloom and sent out a thick and pleasing sweetness. If ever a Stonemaker had dwelled here, I thought, he had chosen a splendid place to do his work.

As we made our way higher, we saw more of the mysterious statues. They seemed planted at random in the ground along either side of the stream. Most were solitary figures, standing by a tree or kneeling near the stream, but a tableau of four of them, perched on a rocky prominence, were posed tightly together, back to back as if guarding the four points of direction. Most had been carved into the shapes of men: slender youths and bent old grandfathers leaning on stone staffs; dignified graybeards and handsome gallants and thick-thewed brutes who had the look of warriors. We saw sculptures of only three women, one of them cradling a baby in her rigid arms. All the statues were naked. And all were made out the same strange stone that we had seen in the first statue but failed to find anywhere in the rock of the gap.

'Wondrous work,' Master Juwain said again. 'Truly wondrous work.'

Truly, it was. And yet, I thought that some of the statues were less wondrous than others. That day and the next, the deeper that we pushed into the mountains, the more the faces of the statues disturbed me. The expressions carved into them were realistic, yes, but *too* realistic. A few showed smiles like that of the statue at the mouth of the gap, but too many betrayed the rawest of passions: astonishment, rage, disgust, hatred or terror, as rendered in the rictus of clamped jaws and eyes nearly popping from their heads. It was ugly work – but not ugly as Master Juwain was ugly, with a sheer magnificence that transcended into a paradoxical beauty. No, I thought, the ugliness of *these* statues struck terror into the soul and made one feel sick to be alive.

Maram obviously felt as I did, and worse, for he kept muttering to himself as he walked along, muttering and belching and chewing at a barbark nut that he rolled in his mouth. Finally, on the third day of our mountain passage, as we followed another stream through the gap's western part, he seemed to have had enough. He gazed at one of the statues, then spat out the nut and a stream of red juice along with it. And he announced, 'I think the maker of these sculptures was mad. And I'll fall mad, too, if I have to look at them much longer.'

To soothe himself, he started humming a cheerful tune; when that failed to lift his mood, he broke out into the new rounds of what had become his favorite song:

> Through higher man burn mortal fears
> Of being bound in lower spheres;
> In flesh and blood and woman's breath
> He apprehends the seal of death.
>
> And so he dwells in castle's height
> Where all is purity and light,
> But in his dry, transcending zeal
> Forgets to live and dream and feel.
>
> In woman's cry of ecstasy
> I find my immortality;
> With every kiss, caress and thrust
> I sing eternal praise to lust.
>
> I am a second chakra man;
> I take my pleasure while I can
> From maiden, matron, harridan,
> I am a second chakra man.

'Quiet!' Kane finally barked out to him. 'Quiet now, I say! You sing loud enough to wake the dead!'

'Well, what if I do?' Maram snapped at him. 'Do you think it matters? Do you think that if there's any Yaga skulking about, he hasn't heard us rattling up this gorge long since?'

We walked on a few more paces, and the horses' hooves struck out a great noise of metal against bare stone. Kane's sharp eyes scrutinized every bush, tree and rock about us. So it was with Master Juwain, Liljana and Berkuar. This great hunter gripped his bow with a white-knuckled force. I held my drawn sword as I cast about with my seventh sense for sign of the Stonemaker or any other living thing. And Maram let loose a great gout of song yet again:

> The higher man seeks higher things . . .

283

As we were rounding a bend in the stream, Maram espied a particularly striking statue. He broke off singing to walk up to where it stood perched on a shelf of rock. It was a sculpture of a woman, tall and large, with legs like tree trunks, huge hindquarters and hips, and great, pendulous breasts. Its face was hideous. The eyes were fierce, the pock-eaten nose twisted, the mouth cast into a rage of passion. Long strings of stone hung down from the misshapen head. Its maker had posed it with its stony arms held out as if to welcome a demonic lover.

'Oh, my Lord!' Maram said, gazing at this sculpture.

Berkuar came up near him gripping his bow, and he said, 'She's so ugly, she must have turned *herself* to stone.'

'Ah, I don't know,' Maram said. He stepped right up to the statue and laid his hand upon its rounded belly. He slid it freely over the smooth stone. 'Look at these hips! What magnificent thighs! Have you ever seen such breasts? If she were real, can you imagine what mighty children she would bear a man?'

As Daj and Estrella hung back from this terrifying thing, Liljana stared up at it and said, 'Ages ago they made such sculptures of the Great Mother. Though I've never seen one with a face so forbidding.'

'The eyes are the worst of it,' Berkuar said with a shudder. 'Truly, they're cold enough to turn a man to stone.'

'Ah, I don't know,' Maram said again. 'There's something about her eyes. Cold, yes, I suppose, but can't you see how they conceal a great fire? What kind of maker could have sculpted such strange, deep eyes?'

His brow suddenly furrowed with perplexity. He moved close up to the statue as he peered into its eyes and breathed into its dreadful face.

'Strange, very strange,' Maram muttered. Then he announced: 'It looks like there's a thin layer of stone enamelled over some sort of gem, like amethyst, I don't know, but if I can just chip it away with my knife then –'

As he was reaching for the dagger on his belt, his voice suddenly choked off, and I felt the breath freeze in my lungs. I felt my own eyes rigid as stone, for I could not credit what they beheld: the statue's arms seemed to soften and change color to a dusky gold as they came alive and tightened around Maram, crushing him against its breasts. Maram stood gasping and struggling to move, his arms pinioned helplessly against his sides. The statue – or whatever it really was – seemed possessed of an insane strength.

It lifted Maram off the ground as easily as I might a child. Its stonelike lips pulled back from long white teeth and red gums in a terrible smile. Its eyes began to clear. The enamel carapace dissolved into a brilliant violet that I finally understood to be of pure gelstei.

'The Stonemaker!' Berkuar shouted out. 'It is the Yaga!'

He lifted up his bow and sighted his arrow on this demonic thing. Kane, standing twenty yards farther back, called to him: 'Hold your arrow! You'll hit Maram!'

But Berkuar ignored him. In a sudden snap of releasing tension, this great archer loosed his arrow. It flew straight and struck the Stonemaker's neck. But the point broke against the stony skin there, and the arrow glanced off, skittering into rocks beyond.

'Back!' I heard Atara cry out. 'Liljana, Master Juwain – help me get the children back behind the trees!'

The Stonemaker let loose a deep, belly-shaking laugh, almost dulcet and pleasing in tone, but terrible in its promise of torment. She turned her violet eyes toward Berkuar.

'Back!' Kane called to me as he sprang away from it. 'Val – get yourself behind a tree!'

I stood frozen on a slab of naked rock gripping my sword in both hands. If the Stonemaker could move as it did, I reasoned, then her facade of stone must be thin enough that I could cut through it to the living flesh beneath. But I was too far from Maram to strike at the thing that embraced him.

'Back, I say! Back, Val!'

The Stonemaker fixed her gaze upon Berkuar, who whipped another arrow from its quiver. He never had time to nock it. The Stonemaker's eyes came alive with a hideous, incandescent light. Berkuar's face lit up with a violet glow as he froze motionless with his arrow trapped inside his hand. I watched in horror as the flesh of his hand, face and neck turned to stone. Even the thick hair of his face and head grew grayish black and hardened.

'Back, Val, back!' the Stonemaker said to me in a sweet, mocking voice. 'Go hide behind a tree – if you have time!'

She began to turn her ponderous head toward me.

I believe I never moved so quickly in all my life as I did then. I fairly flew across the rocks and took shelter behind a great oak tree. I stood with my side pressed against hard bark. If the Yaga sought me out behind the curve of the tree, I would stab her through the throat before I died.

'Ha, ha – you're quick, little man, and you may have your little

285

life, if that's want you want,' she sang out. 'I've meat enough for ten years, and anyway, it's this great dragon of a man I want.'

I heard Maram grunt in terror. There came a sound as of stone-hard boots scraping against rock. The Yaga seemed to be walking away from us. Then I heard her sing out a song in mockery of Maram's beloved doggerel that she must have overheard:

> Alone I've dwelled nine hundred years
> In mountains, deserts, stinking meres,
> Regaling travelers where I can
> While waiting for my dragon man.
>
> No scholar, magus, king on high
> If they be cool or soft or dry;
> My man is molten earth's desire,
> Whose loins are full, whose blood is fire.
>
> He comes for me, most mighty snake,
> A mighty, raging thirst to slake,
> Make live inside my honeyed womb
> The Marudin's immortal bloom.
>
> I am a maid of angel's seed,
> An unfilled well of burning need;
> My time has come to mate and breed –
> I am a maid of angel's seed.

Her voice died off into the soft wind, and so did Maram's cries. I stood stricken with a terrible fear that my best friend would be finally and forever lost.

18

When it seemed safe, we gathered near the form of the petrified Berkuar, nearly frozen ourselves with disbelief over what had just occurred.

'Well, now we know,' Master Juwain said, running his hand across Berkuar's head, 'that it *is* possible to turn a man into stone.'

I turned my stare from Berkuar to Master Juwain. It was the only time in my life that I wanted to strike him.

'If it's possible to do this,' Liljana said, rapping her knuckles against Berkuar's hardened hand, 'is it possible to change him back? As the Yaga seemed to change herself back?'

None of us knew. But it was clear that if there was to be any help for Berkuar, we must somehow persuade the Yaga to do this work.

'In any case,' I said, coming to a decision, 'we cannot abandon Maram. Our only course is to go after him.'

I looked up through the gap at the sun where it descended like a knot of fire toward the west. 'We have less than two hours of day left to us.'

'But what about the children?' Atara asked. 'Wouldn't it be better if I waited with them here? At least until you determine where that thing is taking Maram?'

I looked at Daj and Estrella, who fairly clung to Atara's side. I did not want to remind Atara that she was in no state to protect them.

'All right,' I finally said. 'But let Master Juwain and Liljana remain here, too. Kane and I will move more quickly by ourselves.'

It was a hard decision, and none of us were happy with it. But it seemed the wisest course for Kane and me to track the Yaga to her lair, and then decide what must be done.

'I doubt if she'll return,' I said to Liljana. 'But if she somehow flanks us and comes back here, you must try to use your gelstei against her mind.'

Liljana nodded her head in assent of this dangerous plan.

Then Kane and I, bow and sword in hand, set out at a trot higher up into the gap. It was not difficult to track this monstrous woman. She crushed down low-growing vegetation and left large, deep prints in the ground between the trees where it wasn't so stony. In our race up along the ground above the stream, we tried always to stay near one great tree or another so that we might duck behind it at the first hint of a flash of violet, for we could think of no other way of protecting ourselves against the Yaga's terrible eyes.

About a mile from where we had left Berkuar standing like the stone sculpture that he had become, the tracks veered off to the right, higher up toward the northern wall of the gap. We followed them, snaking around trees and climbing up old, scarred rocks past great boulders. We came upon a shelf of ground cleared of trees. And there, in the middle of this windswept patch of rock, stood a house like none I had ever seen. It was rounded like a dome heaped up from the ground. Its curving walls and roof seemed made of many thousands of white bones. An evil-looking substance, all hard and red like petrified blood, cemented them in place. A chimney of bones poked out from the roof, but from our vantage, I could see nothing in the walls that looked like a window. The door – a great, rounded work of stone – looked to be almost impossible to move. I felt waves of Maram's fear emanating outward from the house even at a distance of fifty yards.

'So,' Kane said, 'even if we get up close to it, what then? It looks like we'd need siege engines to break down those walls, eh?'

I nodded my head, grinding my teeth together. Then I said, 'If we wait until dark, it might be too late.'

Neither of us knew what this monstrous woman wanted of Maram. Her song suggested that she might have found in Maram a long-desired mate, but this did not seem possible.

'What *is* she?' I whispered to Kane. 'I've never heard talk or tale of her like.'

But Kane only stared at me in silence as he shook his head.

An image of another monster flashed in my mind. 'Do you remember Meliadus? This Yaga sang of being of angel's seed, and she has something of the look of him, does she not? Do you think it's possible that Morjin might have sired a daughter as well as a son?'

'It is possible,' Kane growled out. 'The Beast has committed every abomination, every degradation of the human spirit.'

'You told us that the Marudin was to emerge from the Galadin and go on to rule a new order of beings,' I said to Kane. 'But the Yaga sang of the Marudin as if she intended to give him birth – with Maram the father!'

I peered out again from behind the tree in order to take a longer look at the house. There came a scurry of movement from around its side, and I noticed a large, gray rat darting out from a crack in the rounded wall. The crack zigzagged vertically through the heap of bones; it seemed that an earthquake might once have rent the house nearly in two.

'That might be our chance,' I said to Kane, tapping my finger against his bow. 'Perhaps we can aim an arrow through it.'

'As Berkuar aimed an arrow at that beast?'

'If she's planning what I fear she's planning,' I said, 'her skin must soften sometime. And even if it does not, she must sleep sooner or later. There's a chance that I might be able to squeeze through the crack and kill her before she can open her eyes.'

'You're as mad as she,' he said to me. 'Mad to think you could force your way into her house without awakening her. So, you'll need help.'

He took out his black gelstei and stood staring at it. 'I might be able to steal the fire of her eyes.'

Even here, hundreds of miles from Argattha, I could feel Morjin's shadowy presence and sense him watching us as from the very eye of black gelstei that Kane held in his hand. I said to him, 'It is too dangerous!'

'So, that it is,' he growled out. 'And dangerous *not* to try.'

I scanned the bone-littered ground around the house. It would be madness, as we both knew, to expose ourselves in the light of day to the Yaga's stare anywhere in this zone.

There seemed nothing to do now except to wait for the fall of night. And so wait we did.

How was it possible that an hour spent wandering through a glade with one's beloved on a spring afternoon could pass as quickly as a heartbeat, while *this* hour – with the wind whooshing through the gap and the light slowly bleeding away from the stones and trees around us – seemed to go on for an entire month? As I stood behind the tree with Kane, wondering what was occurring inside the house, I listened to my own breathing and I counted the beats of my heart. It grew darker. From somewhere behind us, through the trees came the harsh hooing of an owl. I looked up and watched the bright constellations wheel into the sky.

'How long,' I said to Kane, 'must we wait?'

'So,' he said with a cruel smile, 'a bride and her groom, on their wedding night, might not sleep until nearly dawn.'

'But we cannot know what she truly intends. What if she *has* taken him for meat?'

'So,' Kane murmured. 'So.'

I looked down the blade of my darkened sword. I said, 'I will not wait, not another moment. Come, let's at least steal up close to the house and see what we can see.'

Kane nodded his head at this. And so we came out from behind our tree. Smoke poured out of the house's bone-made chimney in a plume limned dark as a blacksnake against the still glowing western sky. A thin, yellow light leaked from the crack in the wall. We began stalking across the stony ground straight toward it.

Kane, from ages of discipline and need, moved with the grace and quiet of a big cat. I pushed forward nearly as silently; my father had taught me to hunt sharp-eared deer in the forests of Mesh, and his lessons still lived in my muscles and bones.

We came up closer to the house. The crack, I saw to my dismay, was too small for me to force my way through it, even if I removed my armor, clothing and several layers of skin. Even a skinny child would have a hard time of such a passage.

'Oh, my – oh, my Lord!' I heard Maram groaning from within the house. 'Oh, my, oh, oh, oh!'

We moved toward the sound of his heavy, pained voice, which flowed like burning air from the crack. Over stones and hardened earth, taking exquisite care, we drew up next to the house. I gripped my sword in one hand while I rested the other against the bones of the house to steady myself. Then I drew in a deep breath and pressed my eye to the crack.

'Oh!' Maram moaned out again. 'Oh, this is too much, too, too much – oh, my Lord!'

Through the thick wall, the house seemed all to be one large, circular room, like the felt dwellings of the Sarni. On the far side, a hearth of stones held a bed of glowing coals, and a great steel cauldron – shiny and new-looking – hung bubbling over it. I had a clear line of sight toward the stone door, barred with a great beam of what appeared to be petrified wood. Two statues stood framing the doorway. Parts of them were broken off: arms and a leg, and a missing head. The crack allowed only a partial view of Maram, who lay on a large stone bed at the other half of the house. He had been stripped naked. From his great shoulders and hairy chest had been torn round, red wounds that oozed blood. Ropes, possibly made of twisted hair, bound his arms back behind his head. I could not see his legs. Neither could I see the Yaga. But I smelled her: a foul, thick stench of bloody breath and sweating skin that might never have been washed. It poured from the crack and sickened me.

'Oh – oh, Lord!' Maram moaned. 'This is the end – surely the end!'

Kane's hand fell upon my shoulder. I stepped aside so that he might have a look through the crack as well.

'Oh, oh, oh, oh!'

Then I heard the Yaga, from somewhere within the house, call out to Maram, 'You're strong, my beautiful man. The strongest yet. We'll see if you're the one, we'll surely see.'

Then she broke into song again, chanting out her love poem to Maram:

> *Alone I've dwelled nine hundred years*
> *In mountains, deserts, stinking meres,*
> *Regaling travelers where I can*
> *While waiting for my dragon man.*
>
> *No scholar, magus, king on high*
> *If they be cool or soft or dry;*
> *My man is molten earth's desire,*
> *Whose loins are full, whose blood is fire.*
>
> *He comes for me, most mighty snake,*
> *A mighty, raging thirst to slake,*
> *Make live inside my honeyed womb*
> *The Marudin's immortal bloom.*
>
> *I am a maid of angel's seed,*
> *An unfilled well of burning need;*
> *My time has come to mate and breed –*
> *I am a maid of angel's seed.*

291

And so my suitors stop on by,
Enchanted by my violet eye;
I turn to stone the small, effete:
Unworthy mates but good for meat.

To feed my fiery, fecund forge
I fill my red, rapacious gorge;
The blood of men, most potent wine,
Exalts new life and makes divine.

With love I seize and shred and skive,
Put lips to flesh, eat men alive,
Then suck sweet marrow from their bones
And roast on coals their empty stones.

I am a maid of angel's seed,
An unfilled well of burning need,
On life's red flame I fondly feed –
I am a maid of angel's seed.

Kane pulled back from the house and looked at me. In the faint starlight, his face seemed grimmer than ever. He slashed the edge of his hand across his throat. Then he pointed back towards the trees as if telling me that we should make our escape before it was too late.

But it was already too late. The Yaga suddenly broke off singing, and I heard her sniffing the air. And then she called out: 'Is that you, little man? I *know* it is. You smell so sweet – almost as sweet as my Maram.'

I heard a shuffling of hard feet, and I quickly stepped to the side of the crack. The stench of the Yaga grew stronger, and her voice louder and clearer as it poured from the jagged crack: 'Don't be so shy, Valashu Elahad. Why don't you show yourself so that I might look upon your sweet, sweet face?'

'So that you can turn me to stone?' I called out to her. 'As you did my friend?'

'Ha, ha!' she laughed out. 'I've no desire to turn *you* into stone, though I'll surely oblige you if you linger.'

'Val!' I heard Maram shout from inside the house. 'Val! Val!'

'Let Maram go!' I called out. 'And change my friend back as he was!'

'I *could* change that hunter back, indeed, indeed I could. But he would be good only for meat then, and you don't eat your friends, do you?'

'Val!' Maram cried out yet again. 'She's telling the truth! She makes men into stone, then brings them back here! When she unmakes them, they are dead!'

'Sweet Maram,' I heard the Yaga murmur. 'I haven't made *you* into stone yet, though you're harder than any man I've known, the hardest yet. Now be quiet while I talk with Valashu, or I'll have to give you another kiss.'

'Leave him alone!' I shouted. 'And how do you know my name?'

'My father told me that you might pass this way.'

'Morjin? Is he truly your father then?'

'Indeed he is. It was he who named me Jezi, which means the lovely one. And I am so very, very lovely, don't you think?'

I said nothing to this, then called back to her: 'If Morjin is your father, he would not let you tell me to go away.'

'You're beginning to vex me, little man. Do you think my father has power over Jezi Yaga?'

'If he is able to speak to you from afar, then surely he has power.'

'Ha, ha – great power, it's true. But I no longer do as he commands. We settled that long ago. When he couldn't bear the defiance in my eyes, he tore them out with his own fingers. But then I bit off his thumb and defied him all the more.'

The stench of Jezi Yaga's loathing drove into my belly and made me want to vomit. I gasped out to her: 'Such hatred – for your own father!'

'Ha, ha,' she laughed out again, 'my father commanded that I should be his bride. But he was *not* my dragon man, no, no, he was not, even though he calls himself the Great Red Dragon.'

'Abomination,' Kane muttered beside me. 'Every filthy thing, every degradation.'

'Is that you, Elijin?' Jezi called out. '*You* speak of abomination?'

'So, I do,' Kane said to her. 'Morjin used a varistei, did he not, to bring you forth?'

'The greenstone,' Jezi Yaga said. 'Ha, ha – he *did* use it this way. And he wanted to use it to breed a new race out of my sweet, sweet womb.'

'So, the Marudin.'

'The Marudin, the Marudin,' she sang out. 'The Great One who will defy even the Dark One. But *my* father is not to be *his* father. When I told him that, he took my eyes and gave me these pretty

293

purple stones in their place. He said that since my heart was stone, I should turn to stone any man who tried to love me. My skin can be hard as stone when I make it so, and therefore no one can kill me with sword or arrow. But my heart is never stone – if it were, I would die. As I nearly *did* die. He cursed me, my sweet father did, then cast me out. And so it's been ever since. I've looked all across the world for my dragon man. I've looked upon so many men these many, many years. One day, I shall find him.'

A moan from Maram returned me from the horrible past to the even more horrifying present. He called out, 'Leave me – leave me alone!'

'Yes, Valashu,' the maddened being inside the house said to me. 'Leave us alone. Go off to kill my father, and I will thank you for it. But leave me alone so that I might test the strength of the snake.'

'We won't leave without Maram!' I shouted.

'Will you not?' she shouted back. 'You vex, little man! You vex me.'

Her voice faded, and I heard her feet shuffling against rough floor stones. And Maram cried out, 'No, please don't bite me again – no!'

'You vex me!' Jezi Yaga called out. 'You vex me!'

Just then Maram let loose a terrible scream. It froze me motionless, as if I were a piece of ice standing with my fist clenched around my sword in the dark of the night. It took all my will to keep myself from whipping about and looking through the crack into the house.

'Val!' Maram shouted to me. 'Go away, or she'll eat me alive! Go, and save yourself!'

I could think of nothing else to do. It would be folly, as both Kane and I knew, for Kane to try to put an arrow through the crack. He brought his lips up close to my ear and whispered, 'Let's go back to the others while we still can.'

And so we did. We retreated as we had come, past trees and rocks, down the sloping ground toward the stream. When we drew near the place where Jezi had turned Berkuar to stone, I called out into the darkness so as not to give alarm: 'Atara! Master Juwain! Liljana! We return!'

It took our friends, drawn up with the horses near the stream, only moments to determine that we did not return in triumph. I quickly described Jezi Yaga's house and Maram's imprisonment. I gave an account of our exchange with Jezi. When I finished, Atara cried out, 'Oh, but this is terrible, terrible! I should have seen it! And I should see a way out, now, but I can't!'

I stepped up beside her, and put my arm across her shoulders. I said to her, 'Don't give up hope just yet. I have a plan.'

I bade Liljana, Master Juwain and the children to gather around me. Then, to the sound of the stream pouring over dark rocks and crickets chirping in the bushes, I told them what we must do.

'Daj,' I said, looking through the star-pierced darkness at this brave boy. 'Will you come with me?'

Daj stood up straight as he nodded his head. He told me, 'I'd do anything to help Maram.'

Kane drew out his black crystal and said, 'Perhaps I should come with you, too.'

'No,' I said, 'it will be better for you to protect the others, if you can. And to take them to Hesperu, if I do not return.'

After that, we made ready the horses and prepared to leave. I took off the gold medallion that I had worn since King Kiritan had called the great Quest, and I draped it around Berkuar's neck. I said a quick prayer for his spirit. Here he stood, dead upon the earth instead of in it, and here he might stand for a thousand more years.

While Kane set off with others further into the gap, I led Daj back up the slope toward Jezi Yaga's house. We came up behind the same oak tree that had given Kane and me shelter. Daj fairly clung to its bark as he looked out from behind the tree. In the strong starlight, the house gleamed like the heap of bones that it was.

'You must wait here until she's gone,' I said to him, 'then squeeze through the crack and cut Maram free with your sword. Don't try the door – you won't be able to move it, and the Yaga may look back and see you.'

'Don't worry,' he whispered to me as he shuddered. 'I don't want to wind up like Berkuar.'

He paused, breathing deeply to quiet the pounding of his heart, as Liljana had taught him. Then he said, 'I wonder if it hurts to be turned into stone?'

'Don't think about that,' I said to him. 'Do you have your sword?'

He smiled as he showed me the small sword that I had given him.

'All right,' I said. 'After you're out, keep to the high ground, and keep yourselves unseen. We'll meet you in the desert.'

I embraced him as I would any other warrior who was dear to

me. Then I walked out across the gleaming rocks and bones of the open ground toward the house. I positioned myself halfway between the great door and the few trees at my back. I cupped my hands around my mouth as I drew in a deep breath. Then I shouted out: 'Jezi Yaga! Daughter of angels and mother of the Marudin! Let Maram go! We have in our keeping a varistei that you may use to help make your son! We will give it to you if you let Maram go!'

From the house came the sound of Maram moaning and then the much louder voice of Jezi Yaga shouting through the walls: 'Do you tell the truth, little man? Do you tell the truth?'

I stood on the hard ground listening for the sound of the stone bar being thrown back from inside the door. I told myself that I *would* exchange Master Juwain's green gelstei for Maram. I would give up my sword and all my possessions – even my life.

'I think you *do* tell the truth, sweet man,' Jezi called out to me. Her piercing, musical voice rattled the very bones of her house. 'My father told me that you hate to lie.'

'Let Maram go!' I shouted to her, 'and I shall let you have the green varistei!'

'Do you take me for a fool, Valashu Elahad? I will never let my dragon man go!'

'Then you will never have the gelstei.'

'Will I not? Will I not?' At last I heard the harsh grating sound of stone grinding against stone.

I dared not wait a moment longer. With one quick glance toward Daj's oak tree, I turned and fled across the dark, uneven ground into the shelter of the trees. Behind me I heard the great stone door of Jezi's house grind open and then slam shut.

'Where are you, little man?' she called out to me.

She could not see me, but surely she could hear me, as I could her. Her great weight of driving legs and hard feet rattled broken rocks. It was perilous ground in the dark of night, for both of us. As I leapt down the slope from rock to rock, past boulders and around trees, over gulleys and across rotting logs, I prayed that I wouldn't stumble and fall.

For a while I ran downhill and then up again over a dark hump of ground. I listened for the noise of Jezi Yaga pounding after me. My breath burst from my lungs, and the owls hooed in the trees, and beneath the tempest of these sounds, I listened and ran and listened ever harder. I no longer heard her. I had staked everything on my being able to outdistance her, so I ran on and on, into the night.

296

I thought of Daj, the rat-boy, as they had called him in Argattha. Sly as any rat, by now he would have cut Maram free with his sword. Maram, despite his wounds, would be strong enough to force open the great door, or so I prayed. I prayed that he and Daj would then make their escape along the high ground of the gap, out into the desert.

I smelled this vast expanse of burning sands and wasted land long before I laid eyes upon it. The wind from the west blew warm and hard through the gap, carrying the scent of desert plants into my nostrils, and I ran for many miles over cracked and broken ground toward it. The air grew even drier. Few trees grew in the hard, stony soil that bruised my feet even through my boots.

But I ran on even so. The arrow wound in my back became a knot of burning pain. A worse fire tormented my blood. I could not hear the footfalls of Jezi Yaga; it seemed that I had left her far behind. But I knew she was still pursuing me, for I felt her presence as a dreadful sensation like a sucking at my guts.

I sensed her drawing closer to me. How, I wondered, could this be? I didn't know where her impossible speed came from. I couldn't guess how she had remained alive all these years, or how she could see. I waited to feel the skin along the back of my neck hardening into stone. Like Daj, I couldn't keep myself from wondering how badly it would hurt.

And then I turned panting and driving hard around a great mound of rock and almost ran straight into Kane and my other companions. Kane stood behind his horse aiming an arrow in my direction; I saw through the gloom that he had affixed his black gelstei to his forehead, as of a third eye.

'Quick . . . away from here!' I called. 'She . . . must . . . have . . . guessed where . . . . And taken a shortcut.'

I caught my breath and added, 'Hurry – the sun will be up soon!'

Already, in the east, the sky through the gap behind us glowed with red light that devoured the stars.

And so hurry we did. I had thought my friends would already be beyond the pass, but Master Juwain explained that Atara had turned her ankle on the rocky ground and so had been forced to ride. In the darkness, they had not been able to move quickly.

For a mile we worked our way up a swell of fissured rock. And then, at the top, we had our first view of the great Red Desert. The wall of mountain to the north still blocked a line of sight in that direction, but to the west and south, for as far as the eye

297

could see, a seemingly endless expanse of flat, scrub-covered ground opened out toward the horizon. Only a last short slope, no more than a quarter mile in length, led down into it.

It vexed me that the ground of this slope was so stony and broken that we still could not ride – at least no more quickly than Atara rode. Jezi Yaga, I thought, might be quick over short distances but could never outpace a horse. I wondered at the range of the purple gelstei that were her eyes. How far out in the desert must we gallop, I thought, before we would be safe?

We were never to find this out. For just as we had descended a short way down the slope, I heard a great pounding of footsteps and then a jolly laughter from behind us. I whipped my head from left to right, wildly looking about for any cover. A single boulder, not even large enough to shelter Estrella, stood out from the ground.

'Valashu Elahad!' Jezi Yaga's rolling voice called out. 'Sweet man! I'm coming! I'm coming!'

I moved quickly to help Atara down from her horse, then positioned her behind this snorting beast. The rest of us likewise took shelter behind our horses. Then we waited.

'Sweet man! Sweet man! Did you think you could escape my lovely, lovely eyes?'

A moment later, Jezi Yaga appeared at the top of the slope above us. She stood smiling with her hands planted on her huge, round hips. Her great breasts hung nearly to her waist and shook as she let loose great peals of laughter. She lifted back her blocky head in order to shake her hair out of her glowing, violet eyes.

'Come out from behind your beasts, that I might see you better!' she shouted to us. 'Must I turn them to stone, too? I've no liking for horseflesh, for it's not as sweet as man.'

I crouched behind Altaru's great, trembling body, and I stroked his neck and prayed that he could not understand Jezi Yaga's cruel words. It would be a simple thing, I thought, for Jezi to charge down the slope and find us out behind our horses once she *had* turned them to stone.

'Come out! Come out!' she called to us. 'Come out and bring me the greenstone! I've no liking to have to chisel it from your hand!'

Master Juwain, I saw, slightly behind me, cringed in back of his horse as he made a fist around his varistei. He called out, 'Take my crystal then, but let us be!'

'I will take it! I will take it! But I will *not* let you be!'

298

Just then the sun rose through the gap behind Jezi Yaga, enveloping her in a ball of red fire. It sent rays of light streaking straight at us like arrows. I felt its heat on the mail of my legs, which the legs of my horse could not quite cover.

Liljana, standing behind her horse near me, called out, 'I must try!'

I looked over to see her bring her blue gelstei up to the side of her head. A moment later, she flung the little figurine down upon the ground as she cried out: 'He is still there!'

Kane, to my right, touched the smooth, black gelstei glued to his forehead, and growled out, 'So, Valashu, if I fail, remember your sword. Remember the valarda.'

Then he looked up the slope toward Jezi Yaga. He had only a single moment to cry out: 'Damn him!' before his eyes closed and his grip upon his horse's saddle broke. I felt the life drain from his limbs as of water being sucked into dry sand. Then he fell to the ground. Never had I seen this great warrior lie so still.

Jezi Yaga turned her head toward him. Her eyes grew brighter.

I closed my eyes as I looked for the killing sword of valarda inside me. But whether because of my promise or because I didn't hate Jezi as I did her father, I could not find it.

I looked down to see the skin along the back of Kane's hand changing color and hardening. I hated it that I could think of nothing to do.

Then there came a booming in the distance like thunder. It took me a moment to realize that it was a voice, a great human voice full of wrath. I could not make out what words echoed through the mouth of the gap, but I knew with a great leaping of my heart that they belonged to Maram.

'My man!' Jezi cried out. 'My dragon man!'

The hardening of Kane's body suddenly ceased. I risked looking over the top of my horse's saddle. A streak of brilliant red fire split the air. The fire grew even more incandescent and merciless as it fell upon Jezi Yaga's naked back. With my eyes, I followed the line of this flame from the top of the slope. There, on a shelf of rock, stood Maram. The ruby light that spilled forth from him dazzled my eyes so that I could not see clearly, but I knew that he gripped his hands around his firestone.

'My man! My man!' Jezi called out to him. Her words came out more slowly now, for it seemed that she was having difficulty forming them. 'My sweet, sweet dragon man!'

She stood as still and steady as a statue. She had turned her head halfway toward Maram. But it seemed that she could move it no farther. The skin across her neck and back had hardened into a carapace of stone. As the fire continued to fall upon her, the stone grew thicker. I sensed that instinct had driven her to protect her body from the fire.

'My man. My . . . beautiful man.'

Those were her last words. The flames from Maram's firestone burned straight into her, melting the stone that she made of her own flesh. A thick, glowing lava ran down her back and sides, and dripped in bright red splashes upon the ground. In order to assuage the anguish of Maram's red-hot flame, or so I sensed, Jezi hardened layer upon layer of herself, deeper and deeper, until even her muscles and bones began to petrify. At last, the power of the purple gelstei worked its way into the deepest part of her being. I felt the life leave her then, for as she had said, she must surely die if ever her heart turned to stone.

After that, I came out from behind Altaru and called up to Maram that Jezi Yaga was dead. He must have understood, for the fire pouring out of his red gelstei suddenly ceased. I walked up the slope toward the statue of Jezi Yaga as he walked down to us, with Daj close behind him. He came closer, and I ground my teeth together to see what she had done to him. He was entirely naked, even down to his bloody feet. Blood still oozed from the bites that she had taken out of his chest, from his shoulders and belly, his hindquarters and legs, too, and nearly every other part of him.

'I knew you wouldn't abandon me,' he called out to me. 'You saved my life again, old friend.'

'Even as you saved mine,' I said, smiling at him as I clasped his hand.

He gripped his other hand around his firestone. I saw to my amazement that not a single crack marred its ruby interior.

'But how?' I said to him. 'How did this happen?'

While Estrella stood over Kane's still form, Master Juwain and Liljana helped Atara walk up to us. Then Maram looked at his red crystal and explained: 'I told Jezi that all my, ah, powers of love and life, my very potency, were bound up in this. I persuaded her to make it whole it again. And so with the touch of her eyes, she healed it.'

He reached out to touch Jezi's face, and he ran his fingers across her cheeks. As when he had first seen her, a thin layer of stone covered the purple jewels of her eyes.

300

'Amazing,' Master Juwain said, examining the firestone. 'I didn't know the purple gelstei had such powers.'

'In anyone else's hands, so to speak,' Maram said, 'I doubt if it does. Jezi, though, has had a thousand years to learn its secrets.'

Master Juwain considered this a moment, before his attention turned to more immediate things. He examined Maram and said, 'But what happened to your boots and clothes?'

'She burned them, too bad,' Maram told us. 'She said that I would never have need of them again, since I was to remain inside her house forever.'

He went on to tell of how Daj had forced his way through the crack in Jezi's house, and like an angel of mercy, had freed him. Daj stood basking in Maram's gratitude. It was nearly the proudest moment of his life.

'But what about your armor?' I asked Maram.

'Gone,' he told me. 'Jezi softened the steel and reformed it into a cauldron. She told me that she would put me in it, piece by piece, if I failed her.'

I could think of nothing to say to this, or to the torment that he had suffered. Then Liljana asked him, 'But if she wanted a child from you, why take bites and weaken you?'

'I think she was testing me,' Maram muttered. 'Testing my strength and the, ah, juiciness of my body, as she put it. My very blood. Then, too, old ways die hard, and I don't think she could help herself.'

Liljana looked him up and down, and said, 'At least she didn't bite off that unruly snake of yours.'

Maram's face flushed bright red beneath the rising sun as he covered himself with his hand and groaned, 'Oh, my snake – my, poor, poor, mighty snake!'

'That should be the least of your concerns,' Master Juwain said to him. 'We've got to see to those wounds of yours. They are many, and deep, and no animal's bite is as poisonous as a human being's.'

'All right,' Maram said, 'but first I want payment for what this monster did to me. Daj, hand me my dagger!'

Daj, who bore Maram's sword and dagger, moved to comply with his command. But then Atara, divining Maram's intentions, rested her hand on Jezi Yaga's face and called out to him: 'No, let her keep her eyes – please.'

Maram looked at me, and I nodded to him. Then he bowed his head to Atara as he muttered, 'All right then, I won't chisel them out. But it seems a pity to let a dead hunk of stone keep two of the great gelstei.'

After that, we walked down to the horses so that Master Juwain could tend to Maram and the stricken Kane as well. The sun rose higher above the gap, and its heat poured down upon us. I wondered how it had been for Jezi Yaga, dying beneath the hellish heat of Maram's firestone. I wondered if after all these years of doing monstrous deeds she could still be considered human. She stood all huge and stony above us, twisted about with a look of betrayal and anguish chiselled into her grotesque face. I decided that once, somewhere within her, there had lived a woman, and a beautiful one at that. And so I said a prayer for her spirit. Then I turned my eyes upon the great desert opening out to the west. Even at midmorning, the air had grown sweltering, and soon my friends and I might well wish that we, too, were made of stone.

19

We bore Kane's heavy body down the long slope to more level ground, where we laid one of our sleeping furs on the rocky earth, and him on it. While Liljana and I set to erecting one of our rain cloths to shield out the fierce sun, Master Juwain mixed some bluish powder into a cup of water and then held up Kane's head and managed practically to pour it down his throat. It did not revive him, but it seemed that a little color returned to his ashen face. Then Master Juwain went to work on Maram. He cleaned Maram's wounds then daubed one of his pungent-smelling ointments into them. He bound them with clean bandages. After Maram donned his spare tunic, he lay down next to Kane, moaning and cursing because he could find no position in which one or more of his bitten parts did not press the hard ground beneath him.

'Oh, oh,' he murmured, rolling from side to side. 'This is worse than the arrow wounds I took outside of Khaisham – the worst yet. Please, Val, shoot an arrow through my heart and let me die!'

We held council then as we decided what to do. With Atara injured, Maram missing pieces of skin and Kane lying as one dead, it seemed that we should retreat back into the gap, where we might recuperate by the stream. But we had no good way of carrying Kane, and as for Maram, he was loath to set foot again anywhere in that cursed valley that Jezi Yaga had terrorized for so long. I think he feared that she might somehow return to life. It was Atara, though, who persuaded us to go on, saying, 'Already we are well into Soldru, and the desert will grow only hotter these next two months. We should cross it as soon as we can, or go back into Acadu and wait for autumn. But my heart tells me that if we *do* wait, we'll come into Hesperu too late.'

'If we actually reach Hesperu,' Master Juwain said. 'Which we won't if we have to cross the Crescent Mountains in winter.'

We agreed that if Kane survived and Maram could bear to ride, we must go on.

'I'll *have* to bear it, though I don't know how I will,' Maram moaned again, resting his hand on one of his fat hindquarters. 'I'm not going back into that valley of stone, and I'm certainly not going back to Acadu. I haven't sacrificed so many precious pieces of myself to go *back*, do you understand?'

I smiled to hear him speak such brave words, and I prayed that his courage wouldn't fail him in the miles to come.

'All right,' I said, 'then we'll wait here until Kane revives.'

Master Juwain, who had removed the black gelstei from Kane's forehead, rested his hand on top of Kane's white hair and looked at him with deep concern. 'I'm afraid I have no knowledge to help him.'

I came over to touch my fingers to Kane's fierce face. Despite the heat of the day, his skin was cool. I said, 'He *will* recover – I know he will. He cannot die.'

We all gathered in a circle around Kane, and we laid our hands on top of his chest. Try as I might, I could not feel the beat of his heart beneath my hand. It surprised me to see Liljana nearly in tears over the reduction of this mighty warrior, for she had often had harsh words with him. Estrella gazed at him with a fierce concentration. Whereas most people have trouble holding an object within their consciousness for very long, Estrella often took delight in dwelling with the flowers by a stream or in playing my flute for hour after hour. And more, she seemed able to love those things so completely that it was as if the object dissolved into her consciousness, and her consciousness into it, and so became as one. So it was now. I felt her love for Kane like a gentle flame within his heart. I felt Master Juwain's love as well, and Atara's, and that of the rest of us, for that was my gift. It was also my gift to strike deep into Kane's heart with the fire of my own. Strangely, when I opened myself this way, I found Estrella smiling at me. It almost seemed that she was waiting for me to pass this fire to her so that she might concentrate it into an irresistible force that would warm every fiber of Kane's being.

After a while, however, Maram could not hold the deep silence that had fallen over us. He shifted positions yet again as he pulled his bandaged hand away from Kane. Then he muttered, 'If Morjin could do this to Kane, he could do it to the rest of us, or anyone,

304

once he gains full control of the Lightstone and the Black Jade. I think he'll be able to find us, anywhere in the world.'

I looked about us, out into the desert with its baked, red earth and sparse covering of tough-looking plants. I could see many miles out into the barren land to the north, south and west. And so anyone approaching from those directions could certainly see us beneath our white shelter flapping in the wind. In our passage across the desert, I thought, we would find neither shelter nor cover against the eyes of our enemies. I wondered with dread if Morjin could somehow see us or sense our whereabouts.

'He *knew* we were caught in the Skadarak,' I said to Maram and my other companions. 'And Jezi Yaga had been warned to look for us.'

'Warned by the second droghul?' Master Juwain asked. 'Do you think he is close?'

We all looked at Atara then, but she said nothing as she sat behind the silence of her blindfold.

Liljana, after gazing at the blue figurine that she took out of her pocket, looked up at me and said, 'Every time we use our gelstei *he* knows this. But can he really see us? You once said, Val, that you thought he couldn't.'

'That was before he stole the Lightstone,' I told her. 'Now, I don't know.'

I did not give voice to what I most feared: that now and forever more, Morjin would always be drawn to the kirax burning inside me like a vampire bat to blood.

'How is it, I wonder,' Master Juwain said to Maram, 'that you were able to use your stone without Morjin seizing control of it?'

'Well, in truth, I think he tried,' Maram said. 'I certainly *felt* him trying to wrest the firestone from my hand, as it were. It's strange how things fall out, isn't it?'

'Strange – how so?' I asked him.

'Well, he tried to pour so much power into it that it would burst apart in my face. But this only gave it more fire.' Maram turned over on his side to stare at his ruby crystal. 'It's been so long since I wielded this, I don't know if I could have continued burning that monster without his help.'

'Surely he fears your stone,' Master Juwain said to him. 'Surely he remembers the doom that was laid upon it.'

Would Maram's red gelstei, I wondered, truly lead to Morjin's undoing? I leaned over to run my finger along its smooth length as I said to Maram, 'It's a miracle that the Yaga made this whole

305

again, for I never thought it could be healed, as you always hoped. It gives *me* hope that somehow, in the end, we'll defeat Morjin.'

'Ah, then you've come to believe in the prophecy?' Maram said, smiling at me.

'I believe in *us*,' I said, smiling back at him. 'And in you. If you hadn't come when you did . . .'

I said no more as I looked out from beneath our sun cloth, up the slope where Jezi Yaga stood like a gargoyle guarding the mouth of the gap.

'Ah, well, I *did* come, didn't I? As I always will, if you need me. But let's not congratulate ourselves too soon. We still have hundreds miles of desert before us, and without Kane, I don't see how we can ever make it.'

Once, as Kane had told us, he had crossed the southern part of the Red Desert, and so he knew of the wells and water holes that we must find if we were to survive.

'Don't worry about Kane,' I told him, looking down at Kane's still form. 'Does the sun rise in the morning? Does the forest fail to turn green in the spring?'

There seemed little to do then except wait. We all sat beneath our paltry covering, shifting about as the sun rose higher and the shadow cast by the cloth shifted as well. By noon, it had grown very hot. We sweated, and we drank from our waterskins to replenish ourselves. Flies came to feed on our sweat and bite us. Our horses stood chewing up what forage they could find. Out in the desert, lizards scrambled over sun-baked rocks. The burning air sucked the moisture from my eyes.

We sweated and suffered through the afternoon. While the others dozed, Estrella and I kept watch over Kane, who did not stir. I kept a watch on the wavering desert, looking as always for sign of our enemies.

I think I had never looked forward so much to the coming of the night. After endless hours, the sun melted like a gout of burning red steel into the horizon in the west. The desert grew beautiful then. The day's last light touched the mountains behind us with a starkness that unveiled their deeper life. The air cleared, and the sky fell a deep and glowing blue. After a while, the stars came out in their glittering millions. It grew so cool that I drew on my cloak. Liljana, now awake and tending to Kane, covered him with his cloak and helped Master Juwain pour some tea down his throat. He slept, on and on, as the stars brightened and the hyenas gave voice to their eerie cries far out in the desolate land around us.

It was just before dawn, with the rocks of the desert nearly as cold as ice, when Kane finally opened his eyes. He looked at me through the light of the little fire that Maram had made out of some dead yusage. He smiled as his hand found mine and squeezed my fingers with a pitiful weakness. Then he murmured to me, 'So, Val – so.'

Liljana set to making him some broth, which she insisted that he must drink. But Kane would have none of it. 'Meat,' he murmured again. 'I must have meat.'

In our stores, Liljana found a little ham, which was going bad, and some dried venison, which had fared much better. But Kane would have none of these either. He let his leonine head roll to the side so that he could better look at me. And he said, 'Val – bring me fresh meat.'

Maram could aim an arrow straighter than I, most of the time, but he could scarcely move to draw a bowstring and was in no shape to hunt. And Atara, who might have been the finest archer in the world, was still completely blind. And so when the sun came up, I took up my bow and walked out into the desert. I gripped in my hand my brother Karshur's favorite hunting arrow, the one he had given me when I had set out on the great Quest. Around my neck hung my lucky bear claw, torn from the paw of the great beast that had nearly killed Asaru – and myself. It brought me luck that morning, or so I thought. Only three miles from our encampment I came upon a small herd of gazelles with their long, spiral horns and swishing black tails. I put Karshur's arrow through the heart of a young buck. I slung the dead animal across my shoulders and bore him back to our camp. Liljana took charge of the butchering, announcing that she would make a fine roast of its ribs. But Kane wouldn't wait for this feast. He called out to Liljana, saying, 'Bring me my meat, just as it is.'

I had watched lions eat raw meat before, but never Kane. At first, as he nibbled at the gobbets that Liljana cut for him, he was so weak that he could hardly chew. He seemed, however, to gain strength with every bite. Soon, he was tearing into red flesh with his long, white teeth, swallowing in huge gulps and calling for more meat. Sounds of deep delight rumbled in his throat; blood smeared his hands and mouth. His black eyes began filling with some of their old fire. And still he worked at the gazelle's meat, downing an entire leg and the liver and then calling for more.

I could scarcely believe that a man could eat so much, but then reminded myself that Kane was scarcely a man. After he had filled his belly, he lay back to digest this feast. Then he stirred a few hours later to begin eating again. So it went through the course of that long, hot day. By the afternoon, he was able to stand on the stony earth beneath a blazing, white-hot sun; in the early evening, he began pacing about our encampment as he cast his bright eyes toward the south, east, north and west. He drew his long sword and began his nightly practice, stabbing straight out into the hearts of imagined enemies, slashing and slicing the gleaming steel with a renewed ferocity that tore apart the air. And still the deep, red fire of life blazed hotter and brighter inside him. When full night fell upon the earth and the lions roared out in the distance, Kane turned his savage face toward the wind and roared back at them. He thrust the point of his sword straight up toward the stars, and raised back his head in a long, triumphant howl to the heavens that it was good to be alive.

After that, he rejoined us for some tea. As his hand closed around his cup, his powerful body rippled with a restlessness that drove him to pace about, circling the fire again and again as the earth does the sun.

'So,' he growled out, 'I must thank all of you for tending to me. I can tell you little of what happened – the truth that can be told is not the *deepest* truth, eh? And I had fallen so deep. So, the Black Jade in the Skadarak nearly sucked out our souls. *My* black gelstei nearly sucked out my life. Morjin made it so. It nearly turned *me* into ice. He came for me then. He sucked out my blood, and when that wasn't enough, the very liquids of my throat and eyes. There was a blackness – only a cold blackness, and nothing more.'

He drew out his black gelstei and stared at it a moment before shaking his head and putting it away again.

'How is it then,' Master Juwain asked him, 'that you are still alive?'

'Ha! – the next time I use my stone, I might *not* be, eh?' Kane's lips pulled back in a terrible smile. 'From what you've said, it seems that Maram forced Morjin to turn his attention away from my little bauble. Then too . . .'

His voice died into a deep rumble as he looked at me.

'Then, too,' he went on, 'there is always the fire, eh? The light. It is *hard* to put it out. Especially with the lights of my friends shining through me like seven suns.'

He turned his bright smile from me as he met eyes with each of us. He looked at Estrella for a long time. And then he said,

'Enough of that. We've other things to speak of. Liljana – how much food do we have left? How much water?'

With much relief, we turned our talk from Morjin and his darkening of our gelstei to the more practical concerns of our quest. Our plan to cross the desert posed considerable problems of logistics. Our horses and remounts would be able to find only so much forage in such a sere land, and if they were to bear us on their backs, the pack horses must bear on *their* backs much grain to feed them. But they could not carry all the water that we, and our mounts, would need to reach the streams and rivers of the Crescent Mountains. Therefore everything depended upon us finding the water holes that had quenched Kane's thirst so long ago.

'There should be a well fifty miles from here,' Kane said, pointing out into the dark land to the west. 'We'll find a low line of red hills, two miles in length, and the well just to the north of them.'

'But will we be able to draw water from it?' Master Juwain asked.

'If it hasn't gone dry,' Kane said. 'And if its owners allow it.'

Once, he said, the clans of the Taiji tribe had held sway throughout the southeastern lands of the Red Desert. Kane had bought water, and other necessities of life, from them. But all the Ravirii tribes hated outsiders, even pilgrims, and sometimes refused to trade water for gold. If times were hard and the hot winds of war maddened them, they would even put wayfarers to the sword, taking their lives *and* their gold.

At the look of concern on Maram's face as he told us this, Kane clapped him on the arm and said, 'Don't worry – the Ravirii are great warriors, it's true, but therefore they respect nothing so much as even greater warriors. And who are greater than the Valari, eh? If it comes to swords, once they see our kalamas at work, they'll leave us well alone.'

Two hours before dawn, in the coolest part of the night, we set out to the west. It soon became clear that Maram was to have a horrible time of it, for he could hardly ride. Because it tormented him to sit in his hard leather saddle, he took to standing in his horse's stirrups. But the constant, rocking abrasion against his torn thighs proved almost as bad. When he could bear the pain no longer, he dismounted and walked beside his horse. Among the few parts of his body that Jezi Yaga hadn't bitten, as he told us, were the soles of his feet.

After a while, the sun came up over the mountains in the east and touched the desert with a golden-red glow. This 'wasteland', as I saw, turned out to be full of life – but spread out sparsely across huge distances. That morning I saw snakes slithering through the knife grass, and horny toads, and sandrunners hopping along as they looked for insects to scoop up in their yellow bills. Other birds winged through the air: rock sparrows and gambels and hawks. We came across a lone, black-maned lion feeding on the carcass of an antelope. Fifty yards away, a pack of hyenas waited for the lion to finish his feast, as vultures circled high overhead.

As it grew hot, we all donned the hats that Liljana had made for us: rather ridiculous-looking constructions that might have been cowls hacked off of robes. They would help protect our heads and necks from the ceaseless sun. I sweated streams of salt water beneath my hat, cloak and my armor. Soon it became clear that I could not go on this way. I could cast aside my cloak, but that would leave my armor exposed to the sun's fierce rays. The rings of steel mail would quickly heat up like the metal of a skillet and roast me inside. Kane had warned me that I would not be able to wear my armor across the desert, but I had not wanted to believe him.

'You must divest yourself of it,' he told me, riding up beside me. 'As I must, too.'

'Must I?' I said, touching my finger to my burning, jangling mail. How many times, I wondered, in how many battles had it saved me from being pierced by arrow, spear or sword? 'I'd feel naked without it. A little farther – let's see if we can bear it.'

We rode on deeper into a burning plain dotted with clumps of ursage and thornbush. The wavering air heated up even more. So did I – so did we all. The horses sweated profusely; never had I seen so much water pour from Altaru's sleek black hide. Flies descended on us in buzzing, black clouds. Sweat now ran inside my armor in rivers; it seemed as if I were swimming in a hot, salty bath. Sweat worked its way down my forehead and stung my eyes. The others suffered as badly, or worse. I could almost feel the sweat soaking through Maram's many bandages and working salt into the red rawness of his wounds.

'Ah, oh!' I overheard him grumble to himself. 'Maram, my old friend, you're supposed to marvel at the One and all the One's works, but tell me truly: if *you* had made the world, would you have filled it with such horrible heat and these bloody damn flies that take pieces out of a man? No, no, it's too much, a child could see that – too, too damn much.'

When the sun grew too fierce, in the terrible heat of the after-noon, we broke to take shelter beneath our sun cloths and rest. I finally removed my armor and the sodden leather underpadding, and stowed this heavy mass of accoutrements with one of the packhorses. I donned a long tunic that covered me from neck to ankle. I forced myself to go water the horses before partaking of any of this vital liquid myself. It was astonishing how much a thirsty horse could drink. In nearly all our journeys, there had always been some river or stream for our mounts to try to empty. Now, as we held leather buckets to their frothy lips, they *did* empty them, with such alarming rapidity that we had to pull the buckets away and ration them. We were only slightly kinder to ourselves.

When Daj handed me one of our waterskins, I drank enough to ease some of the parch of my throat, but not enough to really replenish me. With every fiber in my body crying out for moisture, it seemed that there wasn't enough water in all the world to fill me.

Kane, turning east to orient himself on the white mountains of the Yorgos range, said to us, 'We've made good distance today, and so we should reach the first well tomorrow. There we can drink as much as we'd like.'

'If the well isn't dry,' Maram said, licking his puffy, much-bitten lips. He kicked at a clump of brown ursage and said, 'Everything about this land is dry and growing drier by the mile.'

'Ha – you think this is bad?' Kane called out to him. He stood squinting up at the sun as if challenging this bright white orb to take the water from him. 'In the deep desert, there is no water. Nothing grows, and so nothing lives. The winds drive the sand into mountains. The Tar Harath, they call that place.'

He looked toward the northwest, and a strange burning filled his eyes.

'If there is no water there,' Maram asked him, 'then how will we cross it?'

'We won't,' Kane said, pointing almost due west. 'Our course lies well to the south of the Tar Harath. There'll be water enough, if we don't waste what we have and keep ourselves strong enough to reach it.'

Strength, however, Maram now lacked, for Jezi Yaga had bled much of it out of him. In the late afternoon, with the heat abating slightly, he dozed in his saddle and several times nearly fell off. Dusk found us still plodding along, for we had to take advantage of the first evening hours to gain as many miles as we could; in the cool twilight Maram fought to keep his eyes open and his hands fastened around the reins of his horse. At last I took pity

311

on him and gave him the bag of barbark nuts that I had removed from the pocket of the cloak draped around Berkuar's petrified body. I hated to see Maram put tongue to any intoxicant, but if the barbark juice would help him to remain awake and ease his pain, so much the better.

We finally encamped on a little swell of ground affording a fine view in all directions. Maram struck up a little fire, and Liljana brought out her gleaming cookware, made of galte that the Ymanir had forged for her out of the ores of the White Mountains. None of us had much stomach for the hotcakes and roasted gazelle that she prepared for dinner. But she, like Kane, insisted that we must keep up our strength. I tried to eat with a grateful smile, but found myself longing for pears, plums and other succulent foods instead.

Kane, having 'slept' more than long enough beneath the evil enchantment of his black gelstei, stood watch through most of the night.

Maram thought it strange that we had seen no sign of man since setting foot in the desert. But as Kane told him: 'I once wandered here for forty days, and my only companions were the lizards and snakes.'

'Wandered?' Maram moaned. 'I don't like the sound of that!'

'Don't worry,' Kane said. 'Our course is set and is nearly straight. Now get yourself a little sleep, and heal those ugly wounds of yours.'

Our journey the next morning was much the same as that of the previous day, save that it seemed even hotter. Maram sweated the scabs off his wounds, and Master Juwain had to cast away his bloody bandages and make new dressings. I grew very alarmed at the rapid and inexorable disappearance of our water. As I calculated things, we would arrive at the first well with our waterskins less than half full. If the well proved dry, our situation would fall grim.

'If the well proves *full*,' Maram said to Kane, 'it's likely to be in use, isn't it? By the Taiji, as you call these people? They'll see us coming from miles away. I only hope they greet us with alms instead of arrows.'

Maram, I knew, felt even more vulnerable than I at losing his armor.

Kane waved off his concern, saying, 'The Ravirii tribes know nothing of arrows, as they haven't any wood to make them. Their weapons are the lance and sword. And they don't wear armor, either.'

His words encouraged Maram, a little, and for a while it seemed he sat up straighter on his horse. When Kane finally descried the hills that he had told of rising red along the horizon, Maram let his hand rest upon the hilt of his sword. He licked his lips and swallowed against the dust, then said, 'If there *is* water there, I'd fight a very dragon to claim it.'

Late that afternoon we drew closer to the last, low hump of a hill. I looked hard to make out anything that seemed like a well, but the perpetual shimmer of the desert distances stymied me. The horses' hooves kicked up a cloud of dust that billowed into the air like a great, waving banner. We all waited for Taijii warriors to ride out to greet us – with either salutations or swords.

But no one did. Maram, who could blow as fickle as the wind, chose to take this as a bad sign, saying that surely this proved the well must be dry. We rode closer to the place toward which Kane had pointed us. At last I saw the well: a circular wall of stones built as if erupting from the very ground. All around it was nothing except ursage and bitterbroom, spike grass and thornbush and the red rocks of the desert.

I fought the urge to press my heels into Altaru's sides and gallop straight up to the well. We continued our slow ride in good formation. I saw signs of old encampments everywhere: the blackened rocks of firepits and rubbish heaps full of bits of broken horn, charred wool and cracked, sun-bleached bones. When we had drawn within a dozen yards of the well, I noticed Altaru's nostrils quivering as if he had caught scent of water; he nickered happily and dug his hoof into the earth. I knew then that the well was full. Maram, though, couldn't quite believe our good fortune, and so I told him to go see for himself.

He fairly flew off his horse and ran up to the well. After bracing his hands on its rim, he stuck his head down into it and called out a great, echoing shout of relief. Then he jumped back, grabbed up the leather bucket attached to a long rope tied around the well, and heaved the bucket down in. There came a muffled splash. Maram cried out again.

'Oh, joy!' he called out. 'Oh, mercy and sweet succor! There is hope for us yet!'

In the hours after that, we pulled up many bucketfuls of sweet, cool water. We all drank to our deepest content. We let the horses quench themselves, too. We washed the dust from our faces and sticky old sweat from our bodies. All our waterskins we filled. Liljana was keen to set out her pots so that she might wash our soiled and stinking clothing, but we finally decided against this. It wouldn't do to waste the well's water, even if it did seem inexhaustible.

We slept contentedly that night if not very long. Again, we roused ourselves well before dawn and made our preparations for the next leg of our journey. After leaving some coins by the well to pay for the water that we had taken, we set out into the cool desert. The stars, twinkling brightly, pointed our way. We all dreaded the rising of the sun. That day was very much like the ones that had preceded it: clear, hot, dusty and dry. As Maram had said, with every mile that we rode toward the west, the desert grew even drier. Here the hardy grasses yielded to ursage and thornbush, and the herds of antelope and gazelle vanished, to be replaced by a few scrawny ostrakats and wild asses who ran away at our approach. The flies, however, still filled the air in abundance. They buzzed most fiercely around Maram and swarmed around his bandages, drawn by the smell of blood.

For two days we rode straight across the cracked red earth toward the second well. We sucked down the water from our leather containers, and the burning air sucked the water from us. I looked to the sky for any sign of rain, but the immense blue dome above us showed only a few wispy white clouds, drifting toward the north. Kane told us that in the Red Desert, it never rained in the month of Soldru, nor in Marud or Soal.

We found the second well with mounds of sand blown against its stone walls. As we all feared, it proved dry.

'It's been many years since I came this way,' Kane said, 'so it shouldn't be a surprise that *one* of these wells has failed us.'

'No,' Maram said, rubbing at one of his bloody bandages, 'I'm not surprised either. Why should anyone be surprised by his fate?'

'Take heart,' I said to him. 'The next well will be full.'

'Full of sand, most likely,' Maram muttered. 'And what then?'

'It *won't* be full of sand,' I said to him. 'Believing it will be will only make our journey harder and thirstier.'

Maram sighed as he wiped the sweat from his eyes and stared out into the hot, ruddled plain to the west. He said to Kane, 'How far then, to the next well?'

'Eighty miles,' Kane said, looking that way, too. 'Perhaps ninety.'

'Ninety miles!' Maram groaned. 'Will our water take us that far?'

Liljana licked her dusty lips and said, 'If we're careful. And careful we'll be as long as I'm in charge of the water.'

With a heaviness pulling at us, we resumed our journey. We rode long into the night before we encamped by a great outcropping of stark, red rocks. Our dinner that night was meager: battle bread and dried apples and a few handfuls of old nuts. Liljana told us that the body requires much water to digest its food. The Ravirii, it is said, eat no meat when they are unsure of their water, and when it falls very low, they do not eat at all.

For the next three days, we pushed on into the deeps of the desert. The Soldru sun grew ever brighter as the angle of its searing rays steepened toward the height of summer. The air grew hotter and even drier. We did not make good distance, for the children had a hard time of things, and Maram weakened by the mile. Master Juwain kept changing Maram's bandages, and came to fear that he would soon run out of cloth to bind his wounds. He confided to me that they were not healing as they should. Maram needed rest, shelter and fresh food, all of which, in this terrible journey that seemed to go on and on forever, were denied him.

'I'm concerned about Maram,' Master Juwain said to me one night beneath a white, crescent moon. 'And not just about his wounds.'

'Don't worry, sir,' I told him. 'He's much tougher than even he knows. In the end, he'll come through.'

For part of those three days, we plodded across a wide, gravel-covered pan. The stony ground bruised the horses' hooves and jarred our spines. Nothing grew there, not even ursage or bitter-broom. We saw only a few beetles scurrying along; even the lizards seemed to have fled this terrible terrain. No sign of the Taijii or any other Ravirii tribe could we find anywhere in the empty miles around us.

Late on the third day, one of our remounts and two of our pack-horses collapsed and died. It seemed that we had made their burdens too great while giving them too little water. We all feared that soon we would share their fate.

And then on the fourth day out from the dry well, the desert broke up into a series of long rocky ridges running north and south. It was all torment and treachery to work our way over these fractured, knifelike formations. At the top of one of them, late in the day, I caught wind of a faint sensation that I dreaded almost more than any other. And as we crested the next ridge, farther to the west, Kane came up to take me aside. He pointed out into the wavering distances and told me that he thought he had descried a flash of a white cloak and the bound of a white horse. I sat up straight as I held my hand to my forehead; if a rider was moving along the western horizon, the dust and glare hid him from my sight.

'So, I think we are alone no longer,' Kane said to me. 'That might have been one of the Taiji.'

'Or someone else,' I said, pressing my fist into my belly.

Kane turned his attention from the burning horizon to me. He looked at me deeply and said, 'Morjin?'

'Or his droghul, at least.'

'Are you sure?'

I closed my eyes as I let the currents of hot air sift over me. My blood seared my flesh like molten lead. Then I looked at Kane and said, 'No, I'm not sure. Since the Skadarak, Morjin seems to be everywhere – and inside me most of all.'

'In the desert,' Kane said, 'it's easy to mistake a mirage for a mountain. Perhaps you're only suffering a mirage of the soul.'

'Perhaps,' I said to him.

'Well,' he told me, looking out into the west again, 'if it *is* the droghul, fate will find him soon enough. But let us keep our swords ready tonight.'

Kane and I said nothing of our discovery to the others, for we had no choice but to continue toward the next well. Our water-skins were nearly empty. It didn't matter if the droghul – and all the armies of the Red Dragon – stood between us and it.

We camped that evening within sight of a stark, lone mountain rising up out of the lands to the south of us. I had little appetite for the food that Liljana set before me; it hurt to swallow the water that she rationed into my cup. A sickness began eating into my belly. Late in the night, as I stood guard with Kane, looking out at the moonlit land to the west, I opened myself to feel for the droghul's presence; the exercise of this strange sense of mine was something like sniffing the air for the taint of rotting flesh or listening for a hideous scream along the wind. All of a sudden, a wave of agony swept over me. I cried out as I grabbed at myself below my heart and fell writhing down upon the ground. The others woke then and gathered around me. Liljana feared that I might have been stung by a scorpion or perhaps the even more deadly black-ringed spider. Maram, though, took one look at my face and said, 'Ah, surely this is some magic of Morjin's. Surely it is the working of the Black Jade.'

It was Master Juwain who apprehended the real cause of my torment – and my great peril. He moved quickly to draw my sword and place it in my hands. He knelt by my side as he told me: 'Shield yourself, Val. Now, before it is too late!'

I tried to grip the seven diamonds set into my sword's hilt; the shimmer of my sword's silustria in the starlight seemed to envelop me like a silvery armor. I fought to breathe. With the valarda I had reached out blindly, as of an open hand into a hornet's nest; now I withdrew this hand of my soul and made it into a tight fist that I pressed over my heart.

'Val.' Atara knelt above me and pressed her cool lips against my forehead, whispering my name.

Her deep regard for me, along with the radiance of my sword, proved a magic of its own. After a few moments, I was able to open my eyes and look at her. With Kane's and Maram's help, I sat up. 'Thank you, sir,' I said to Master Juwain. Then, 'Thank you all. I . . . almost died.'

'Died?' Maram said to me. 'But you haven't slain anyone, not for many miles! Died of *what*?'

'Died of death,' I said to him. I pointed out into the desert. 'Somewhere, near here, there is so much death.'

That was all I was willing to say then. After that I tried to sleep but could not. I failed even to meditate, as Master Juwain prescribed for me. I dreamed terrible waking dreams. Two hours before dawn, when it came time to rise and break camp, I could barely force myself to climb on top of Altaru. With my friends on their horses behind me, I rode toward the still-shadowed lands to the west as if moving into a black cloud.

Dawn brought a glowing beauty to the harsh, sculpted terrain of the desert at odds with the ugliness that I knew lay ahead of us. The sun rose higher and flared ever hotter and more terrible. As we approached the third well, I nearly retched to espy a dark cloud hovering low in the sky a couple miles ahead of us. It was not a rain cloud. We drew closer, and the cloud broke up into hundreds of vultures circling above an outcropping of red rocks. Atara, I thought, was lucky that she could not see them.

Soon many tents came into view. Perhaps forty or fifty people lay on the rocky ground between the tents and the single, central well. They did not move. We shouted out to scare off a few hyenas who had already gone to work on them, then rode up ever closer. I feared we would find slashed throats and pierced bellies, but I could see no mark on any of the bodies, a few of which were stripped naked. They were, I thought, a tough-looking people. The men, though slight of stature, seemed hard as whipcord, with curly black hair and beards, dark skins and chiselled features as stark as the desert rocks around them. The folds and fissures of one old woman's face could only have been burnt by a lifetime of wind and sun. I tried to look away from the rictus of agony stamped into the countenances of a young boy and girl who lay near her. Kane dismounted and found more of the dead inside the tents. By the time he had gone about the encampment, making a count of them, I was ready to retch up the little water that I had drunk an hour before – either that or to kill whoever had killed these poor people.

'Sixty-four,' Kane said, walking up to where I sat stunned on my horse. His eyes picked apart the jumble of rocks farther away from the well. 'We might find more of them out there.'

So many dead, I thought, as I stared through the burning air. I wondered what their names were. I wondered how it was possible to slay so many innocents so wantonly just to strike vengeance into the enemy.

'Oh, Lord!' Maram said. 'Oh, my – too bad, too bad!'

The rest of us dismounted. Master Juwain examined a young man whose body and limbs were covered in a dusty white robe. He said, 'He is nearly twelve hours dead.'

'Dead of what then?' Maram asked him.

Maram, I saw from the dread that worked at his face, knew well the answer to this question. So did we all.

'Poison,' Master Juwain said. 'I'm not sure which one.'

Liljana joined him kneeling beside the man's body. After shooing away the flies, she sniffed at his open mouth and ran her finger over the whites of his eyes. She said to us, 'I believe it is zax. It is a slow poison but a certain one.'

'Who did this?' Maram suddenly raged, kicking at the ground. 'Who would poison all these people to get at us?'

It was a question that answered itself. It came time to tell of the rider that Kane had seen the day before, and this I did. When I had finished, Maram drew his sword.

'It *is* the droghul,' he said. 'It is surely the second droghul.'

He offered his opinion that the droghul must have ridden into the encampment last evening and either charmed these simple desert-dwellers or enchanted them with one of his illusions. And then somehow managed to pour his evil poison into the well.

Liljana confirmed that the well was indeed poisoned, walking over to lean down into it and sniff its water far down in the dark earth below. Atara stood looking at nothing; I wondered if she had seen this terrible moment in one of her visions.

318

Kane went about collecting waterskins, from the tents and the many horses that stood about not knowing what to do. He pried them from the very hands of the dead. All the skins were empty. It seemed that the droghul must have poured their water into the sand.

'So,' he said, gripping his fists around one of the skins. 'I'd hoped we'd find at least a few of them full of untainted water.'

Maram brought his sword up to his face and stared into its mirror-like steel. I heard him murmur: 'Ah, you're thirsty, aren't you, my friend? *Very* thirsty, and that's a very bad way to die, isn't it – the very worst?'

I asked Liljana how long our remaining water might last if we were *very* careful, and she slowly shook her head. Her voice trembled and nearly cracked as she looked at the children and forced out: 'Another day, perhaps.'

'And the next well?' I asked Kane.

'So. So,' he said, gazing into the burning land to the west. 'It is another seventy miles.'

'Seventy miles!' I wanted to cry out. We could not make such a distance in a single day, not with our horses worn to the bone and Maram nearly ready to drop from loss of blood. I could not let into my mind the meaning of Kane's words; the horror of what had happened poisoned my soul and nearly paralyzed me. Death was suddenly upon us. A short while before we had been looking forward to drinking our fill of cool, sweet water, and now we found ourselves sentenced to die. So it always was. Death always hovered behind one's neck like a great, black vulture, watching for its chance and waiting.

I knew better than to entertain such thoughts, or even to think them. Some of my despair overflowed into Maram, who said, 'That droghul did his work well. Now it's time to do our work *as* well.'

He began to contemplate the point of his sword in a way that struck fear into my heart.

'No, Maram,' I said, stepping over to grip my hand around his arm. 'We're in a bad way, it's true, but we can't give up hope.'

'Hope?' he cried out. 'What hope is left even to give up?'

I rubbed my eyes, which seemed as dry as my brain and every other part of my body. I tried to think; it was like trying to see my way out of a cloud of dust. I tried to think as Morjin would think. Finally, I drew my sword and swept it in a circle toward the desert around us. 'The droghul has journeyed on, and so he must have water. It may be that we can find his tracks and ride after him.'

'To appropriate his water?' Maram said. 'Even if we could overtake him, it wouldn't be enough.'

'It *might* be enough,' I said.

'If we *did* overtake him,' he said, 'he would poison his water before letting us have it.'

'He would,' I agreed, 'if he hadn't already poured all his poison into the well.'

'Then he would empty his water onto the sand. Do you think Morjin would care if his damned droghul dies of thirst?'

I shook my head and told him, 'It may be that we could take him before he does this.'

'Take him how?'

'Even a droghul,' I said, 'must rest sometime. We might be able to take him while he sleeps.'

'Do you really think that's possible?'

'It *might* be possible,' I said. 'The droghul must have been sent to meet us here. And so he might know of water that we do not.'

'Do you think he would just *tell* you where this water is, then?'

I looked over at Estrella, staring down at a fly-covered boy about her age. Her dusty face, I saw, almost concealed the anguish and suffering that she did not want me to see. I said to Maram, 'There must be a way – there's always a way. We can't just lie down and die.'

'No – can we not?' Maram looked around the well at all the bodies splayed there. He dropped his sword with a loud clang. With a great, heavy sigh, he sat down on a long slab of sandstone, and then collapsed back against it. 'Ah, my friend, this is surely the end, and since I'm in such fine company, I think I *will* just lie here and die.'

I could find no words to rouse him. It would take a horse, I thought, and a rope tied around his ankles to drag him from that spot. Just as I was contemplating such desperate actions, I overheard Liljana scolding Daj. It seemed that while the rest of us had concerned ourselves with other matters, Daj had gone about the dead stripping them of jewelry, which he had piled up on top of a sheepskin. Most of this was of gold, but a few silver bracelets and rings, set with bright, blue stones that I hadn't seen before, flashed in this mound of yellow.

'What are you doing?' she shrilled at him. 'Are we thieves that we rob the dead?'

Daj finished pulling a necklace off an old woman, and said to Liljana, 'But they won't need it where they're going! And we might need it to buy water or food, in case our coins run out!'

Liljana's round face flushed a hot red. I saw that she was ready to shame him for such an ignoble act, but I felt her check her natural inclinations. As she looked at me knowingly, her eyes softened with forgiveness. I could almost hear her thinking that Daj had learned to do almost anything to survive in the black pits of Argattha, and he would apply those lessons in the desert, and everywhere else we went. This little rat-boy would be the last of us to give up and die.

Liljana bent down and kissed Daj's head. Then she began to explain why we must not take the jewelry. At that moment, though, Kane let out a great shout. He pointed to the mound of rocks to the south of us as he cried out, 'Val! Maram! Arm yourselves! We are attacked!'

I looked toward the rocks expecting to see the droghul – and perhaps a company of the Dragon Guard – charging at us. But two horseman only came flying from around the edge of a great red standing stone. Both wore long, dust-stained robes. The one in the lead howled out a curse or a challenge, or perhaps both. His bearded face was as sharp as a flint and hard with hate; he pointed his saber at Master Juwain. The man behind him, I saw, could hardly be counted a man, for his smooth face showed a boy only a couple years older than Daj. He, too, bore a saber, which he held back behind his head as he whipped his horse straight toward Kane.

I was slow to move, not because of hunger or thirst or weakness of limb, but only because I had seen enough of death for that day – and for the rest of my life. I dreaded what now must befall. It seemed, though, that I had no choice: when death came screaming out of the desert like a whirlwind, who could think to stop it?

And so, with the sun beating down at me like a war hammer and the first horseman pounding closer, I went forward to do battle yet again.

20

I waited on broken ground as my adversary pounded nearer. His face – dark and fine-boned – contorted with wrath. He must have thought that he would easily cut me down and make vultures' meat of me. But my father had drilled me, and all my brothers, in standing with sword at ready to meet the charge of armored knights. This man, though, was no Valari knight. His sword was shorter than mine, and only thin cloth covered his limbs. He fairly oozed overconfidence and a rage to kill. From the cast of his body and the angle of his saber, I saw his error in strategy; I sensed how he anticipated that at the last moment I would cringe in fear of being trampled, allowing him to slash his sword into me. I knew that I could fend off this cut and strike a death blow of my own. And then, as he whipped his horse forward and his dark, anguished eyes met mine, I knew that I could *not*.

'Well-poisoner!' he screamed at me. 'Well-poisoner!'

My father had also taught me a strategy, little-used because it was dangerous. I used it now. I stood fast, as if frozen with fear, as my adversary's horse practically drove its hooves into me and snorted into my face. At the last moment, rather than trying to avoid the sword slash by pulling backward, and to my left, I leaped to my right, past the front of the horse and toward its other side. As the sweating beast pushed by me, I reached up with my hand to grasp my startled adversary's arm, held almost straight out to counterbalance the sword gripped in his other hand. I jerked on his arm, hard, and pulled him flying off his horse. He hit the ground with a loud crunch that I feared broke his back. He lay stunned, coughing blood and gasping for breath. I stood with my boot stamped down on his sword arm as I brought the point of Alkaladur within an inch of his throat.

'What are you waiting for?' he managed to cry out. His eyes were dark pools of hate. 'Kill me! Better to die by the sword than by poison!'

I pressed down with my boot against his wrist until his fingers relaxed their grip upon his saber. I looked down at him and said, 'We are not poisoners!'

But the man wasn't listening to me. He spat out a mouthful of blood as he called out, 'Turi, my son! Kill the white-hair if you can, or die on his blade! Don't let the poisoners capture you!'

Just then Maram finally came up to help me. The man I had unhorsed tried to drive his neck up into my blade even as Maram kicked him back to the ground and then fell on top of him, pinning him against the rocks. I turned to see his son whip his horse toward Kane, standing thirty yards away. It seemed that he had already made one pass at Kane and was about to make another.

'Don't kill him!' I shouted at Kane.

I was nearly certain that he *would* kill him, even if his opponent was only a boy, for I had never seen Kane suffer an enemy a chance to wound him or cut him down. But Kane surprised me. This time, the boy did not charge past him, but reined in his horse as he swept his sword at Kane's head. With a ringing of steel, Kane easily parried this stroke, and then another, and yet another. He stood in the hot sun fending off the boy's saber with his sword as if giving him a fencing lesson.

'Call off the boy!' I said to the man beneath Maram. Struggle though he might, he could hardly move, for Maram must have outweighed him by ten stone. 'Call him off before he gets hurt! We are not well-poisoners, but we know the one who is!'

Seeing that our attackers were only two, the others came over to help Maram and me. Atara stood holding Estrella's hand. My fallen adversary looked at her and marveled: 'You bring the blind with you! And children, too!'

His hate softened to suspicion and then puzzlement. From beneath Maram, he gasped out, 'Who are you then, and who is this well-poisoner?'

'We'll tell you, happily,' I said to him. 'But first call off your son.'

He turned his head to shout out: 'Turi, enough! But keep ready to fight again!'

Turi, I thought, had already had more than enough combat for one day. He seemed so tired that he could hardly raise his sword against the tireless Kane.

I said to Maram, 'you're crushing this man – let him up!'

I still worried that the fall had broken something inside my adversary, but this tough desert man had little trouble sitting up. He sucked at his bitten tongue and spat out a mouthful of blood before saying to me: 'My name is Yago of the Soah clan of the Masud. My son is Turi. And who are you?'

While Kane stood eyeing Turi, and Turi him, the rest of my companions gathered around Yago. I presented myself as Mirustral and Kane as a knight called Rowan, and everyone else according to the names that we had chosen to use on our journey. I told Yago that we were pilgrims who sought the Well of Restoration.

'Pilgrims, you say?' He looked at me as his black eyebrows pulled together in doubt. He pointed his sharp chin toward the jewelry that Daj had collected and said, 'Pilgrims pay gold to pass through our lands, they do not collect it. In truth, they no longer pass this way at all.'

'We were afraid,' I said, looking at the bangles and bracelets mounded on the sheepskin, 'that the hyenas would take your kinsmen into the desert and their possessions with them. We collected their things that such a treasure might not be lost.'

I told myself that this was true in spirit; at least I hoped that Daj would want it to be true.

'Treasure it is,' Yago said, regarding the pile of jewelry. 'Where did you think to take it?'

'Nowhere,' I said. 'We've burdens enough to bear, and little water to keep us and our horses bearing them.'

Liljana showed him our waterskins, which were nearly empty, and reiterated that we sought the Well of Restoration, not jewels and gold.

Yago pulled at his beard as he regarded the bodies around us. He said to me, 'Well-poisoners you cannot be, to leave yourselves so little water. But if pilgrims you really are, you've found instead the Well of Death.'

We told him a little of our journey then, and he told me of his. It seemed that the lone mountain to the south of us was sacred to the desert tribes, who called it Ramah, the Pillar of the Sky. Yago and his son had made a pilgrimage to it in order to seek visions.

'My son and I,' he told us, 'journeyed from the hadrahs in the southeast to stand beneath the great mountain. And then we rode on here to find the Ayo poisoned.'

He explained that the dead around us were of the Ayo clan, whose people often camped at the well at the beginning of summer.

Kane nodded his head at this as he stared at the mountain to the south. 'You say that you are of the Masud tribe? What happened to the Taiji, then, who once claimed this well?'

Yago's eyes grew bright with astonishment. 'You know of the Taiji? It has been long, past my grandfather's great-grandfather's time, since they dwelled here. But the Taiji are no more.'

His face burned with pride as he continued: 'Long ago, we of the Masud came up from the southern hadrahs, while the Zuri came out of the pans to the west. Each tribe took half of the Taiji's lands, leaving the Taiji with only sand to eat and air to drink.'

He spoke of the annihilation of the Taiji as one might the slaughtering and division of a chicken. He spared little more sentiment for the sheep baahing in the scrub outside the encampment, or indeed, for the poisoned people of the Ayo clan whose bodies were rotting in the sun.

'The dead are dead,' he told us. He licked his dry lips. 'Soon, we too will have only air to drink, and we will join them.'

'But you must know of other wells?' Maram said to him. He wiped dusty beads of sweat from his face.

'Yes, I know,' Yago said calmly as he pointed across the blazing sands to the west. 'The nearest well lies that way, seventy-five miles. It belongs to the Zuri. Do you think to claim it from them?'

'We left gold coins at the first well that we came to,' Maram said, pointing to the east.

'That is good,' Yago said. 'And the Zuri will take your coins – your horses, weapons and clothing, too. They do not abide pilgrims.'

'But there must be other wells!' Maram said. 'You must know where we can find water!'

Yago smiled grimly at this and said, 'We'll find all the water we wish in the Hadrahs of Heaven, when we rest with the dead.'

'But what about the hadrahs in the southeast that you told of? Where there are trees and enough water to grow wheat and barley?'

'They are two hundred miles distant,' Yago said. 'This time of year, there is no water along the way. We cannot return there.'

'But we can't just lie down and die!' Maram said.

I couldn't help smiling as Yago turned to look at his saber, which Maram now gripped in his hands. Yago said to him, 'No, I won't die here. If you'll give me back my sword, I'll ride after the well-poisoner and kill him before the sun kills me.'

'But what about your son?' I said, looking at Turi, who still sat watching us from the back of his horse.

Yago shrugged his shoulders. 'The dead are the dead. He'll ride with me. No Ravirii of any tribe can suffer a well-poisoner to live.'

I looked at Maram and said, 'Give Yago his sword.'

Maram did as I asked, and Yago's fingers closed gratefully around the hilt of his saber. I said to him: 'We'll ride with you, too. It might be that we can persuade the Poisoner to tell us where there is water.'

Yago's fatalistic smile played upon his lips again. He pointed to the west and said, 'Nowhere, in all the Zuri's lands, will we be allowed to drink their water. Toward dead south, if we rode that way, we would find the Vuai, who are worse than the Zuri. And to the north lies the Tar Harath, where there is no water.'

I turned to the east, scanning the broken country over which we had ridden. I knew that we couldn't make the return journey to the first well with the little water that remained to us. Then I looked to my left, at the highlands some twenty miles to the north-east. These mountains were stark and reddish-brown, showing no hint of snow or ice-cap. But mountains, as I knew, often called down the rain of passing clouds. And so I said to Yago, 'What of that way?'

And Yago told me, 'I don't know – that is the country of the Avari, and no one ever goes there. It is said that the Avari kill any man of any tribe who trespasses, and drink his blood.'

'Then it seems,' I said to Yago, 'that we have no choice but to pursue the Poisoner.'

'The dead are the dead,' he intoned, looking out into the waste-land to the west.

'And the living are the living,' I said to him. 'And as long as we're still alive, there is still hope.'

Yago shook his head as if marveling at the foolishness of outlanders and pilgrims. Then we went to work, stripping the dead of their jewelry, which Yago insisted we wrap in sheepskins and bury at the base of the red standing stone. The poisoned Ayo we could not bury, for there were too many of them and the ground was too hard to dig out graves.

'We'll leave them for the hyenas,' Yago said. 'Others of the Ayo clan might find their bones.'

'And their jewelry?'

'They might find that, too. But if they fail, better that the Zuri, if they come here, *don't* find it.'

After that we had a hard labor of gathering up boulders to heave down into the well and render it useless. Thus did we protect any who would come here after us, even the Zuri. As Yago said, not even the Zuri deserved to die by poison.

Just before leaving the well, Yago checked our horses' loads and announced, 'They carry too many *things*.'

'Only the necessities,' Liljana told him.

'In the desert,' Yago said, 'pots and pans are not needed. You might as well bring with you lumps of lead. You must leave them here, or kill even more horses.'

I felt Liljana's keen disappointment at facing once again the prospect of jettisoning her precious cookware. I said to Yago, 'In the miles to come, we might have need of her pots. Is there no other way?'

'No, there is not.' Then he opened the pack where I had stowed my armor, and he grasped the mail and shook it so that its links rattled. 'All this metal! You and Rowan must leave your armor here, too.'

Kane scowled at this dictate, and I shook my head. I said to Yago, 'In the country beyond the desert, we might have to fight battles. We will need our armor.'

'If you bring it with you,' he told me, 'you might not reach whatever country you hope to find. If you would survive in the desert, you must follow the desert's ways.'

I considered this for a long few moments, and so did Kane. Finally, we consented to Yago's harsh logic, and we left our armor with most of Liljana's pots, buried behind some rocks. I thought it a miracle that he allowed her to keep a single, small kettle, for boiling water for tea and coffee.

In the heat of the afternoon, we set out after the droghul. It seemed mad to let the sun simply roast all the juices out of us, but we had already spent too much time by the well. The droghul, by now, would be miles away. And every hour that we waited would only sweat more water out of us.

Yago found the droghul's tracks outside the encampment; I thought it a fine work of tracking to make out the faint hoof marks in the hard, gritty ground. We followed them, riding as quickly as we dared. Turi, after exchanging a few brusque words with Daj and Maram, kept his desert pony close to his father. And his father kept close to me.

'Tell me,' he said as our horses worked against the sun-baked turf, 'of the well-poisoner.'

327

And so I did. I began with an account of the Red Dragon's recent conquests, news that had reached even the isolated tribes of the Red Desert. I said that Morjin wished to bring down his iron fist upon all lands, and toward that end had sent his Red Priests into every kingdom of Ea. He had other agents, too. I tried to tell something of the droghul, without detailing the droghul's hellish gestation or how Morjin moved his mind. I settled on explaining that Morjin had chosen several men who looked like him to send out and act in his stead. It was close enough to the truth.

Yago thought about this as he pulled at his beard. We rode on in near-silence toward the west. The air grew brutally hot, and then hotter. For the next few miles, the country flattened out a little, and the hardpack gave way to scattered sweeps of sand. A few red rocks and clumps of hardy ursage poked out of it. Lizards took shelter there from the blistering sun; so did the flies. These buzzing black beasts must have caught Maram's bloody scent, for they swarmed around him, and worked at his wounds where his bandages had come loose. I could almost feel them biting their hard mouthparts into his already-raw flesh. Maram's lips pulled back in torment, but he uttered no complaint. It made me proud to see him riding on so bravely. Yago took note of his determination, too.

'You pilgrims are tough,' he said to me as his eyes found mine. 'Almost as tough as we Ravirii. I find it strange, though, that the Red Dragon would set a poisoner upon a band of pilgrims.'

I tried to respond to his blazing curiosity as coolly as I could. I told him that Master 'Javas' was of the Brotherhoods, whose quarrel with Morjin was ancient. 'And Kane,' I told him, 'once took up the sword against the Dragon, and so is hunted.'

'And you, Mirustral?' Yago said to me. He caught me with a long, searching look.

'I have quarrel with the Dragon, too,' I told him. 'I had hoped that we would find no evil of his in the desert. It's said that the Ravirii will not abide him or his people.'

'Is that truly said?' Yago asked me. 'I had thought that few even knew of the Ravirii.'

'Few do. But it's told that the Dragon fears to send his armies into the desert.'

Yago let loose a long, dry sigh. 'That may change. He certainly does not fear sending his agents here, nor his bloody priests.'

At this news, Kane's ears pricked up, and he called out from behind us: 'The Kallimun, here? Then the Red Priests dare to go about openly?'

'They don't dare to ride through the Masud's lands,' Yago said to him, turning in his saddle. 'Rohaj, our chief, expelled the embassy sent to us and told them not to return on pain of death. But it's said that there are priests among the Idi and Sudi in the far north, and perhaps among the Yieshi, as well.'

He told us that the Yieshi tribe dwelled to the northwest of the Zuri, between the Tar Harath and the Crescent Mountains.

'And the Zuri?' I asked him. 'The Vuai?'

'It's said that the priests have their stingers buried deep into Tatuk, who is chief of the Zuri, and into Suhu and many of the Vuai.' Yago turned back and stared at the barren country to the southwest, which the Vuai claimed. 'The priests are like scorpions – in the desert, there are many poisons, yes?'

For another mile or so we followed the droghul's tracks, pressed so deeply into the sand that they seemed to point like wagon ruts straight into the west. Then Yago nodded toward a dome-shaped mound of sandstone to our left and announced, 'That is the Ar Nurum. It marks the end of the Masud's country and the beginning of the Zuri's.'

'It would seem,' Master Juwain observed, 'that the droghul has no fear of riding into it.'

'He would fear well enough,' Yago said, 'if Tatuk learns of what he has done. Red Priests or no, I cannot believe that even the Zuri would abide a well-poisoner.'

Upon these words, something inside me tightened. I felt my heart beating hard, pushing heated blood up into my head; my ears started ringing as with the sound of distant bells.

'Hold!' I called out raising up my hand. I brought Altaru to a halt, and turned to see Atara and Liljana and the rest of my companions draw up their horses behind me. Yago sat on his smaller pony casting me a puzzled look. And I said to him, and to everyone: 'We cannot go on.'

Yago looked at me as if to ascertain if the sun had deranged my senses. 'But if we're to avenge the Ayo, we've no other choice than to go after the Poisoner!'

'You'll have your chance for vengeance soon enough,' I said to him. 'The droghul will come after *us*.'

I drew my sword and watched the play of sunlight on its blade.

'But why, Mirustral?' Yago said to me. 'We have five swords, and the droghul, as you call him, has only one.'

'No,' I told him, gazing into my sword's silustria. 'He will have all the swords of the Zuri, and those of the Red Priests, too.'

'No, they would never give him such aid. They would not dare ride in force into the Masud's lands! Then Rohaj would call for war, and the Zuri have lost the last three that we have fought.'

I tightened my fist around Alkaladur's hilt. I shook my head and said to Yago: 'The droghul will tell Tatuk and the Zuri that *we* are the well-poisoners. The Red Priests will encourage them to believe this. And the droghul will lead the Zuri back along his track to trap us. In such circumstances, would your chief still call for war?'

It was the law of the Ravirii, as Yago said, that a man must punish a well-poisoner even if his vengeance carried him into the lands of another tribe. And then Yago shouted: 'But it is the droghul who is the poisoner, not you!'

'How will we prove this once the Zuri have put us to the sword?'

'We Ravirii do not put well-poisoners to the sword,' he said. 'But never mind that. How do you know what you have said is true?'

'I . . . know,' I said, touching my sword to the scar cut into my forehead. 'It is what the droghul planned all along. I should have seen it.'

Yago looked along the line of tracks leading toward the falling sun. 'This droghul must be punished. Even if I die in punishing him.'

'Is it the droghul's death you wish or your own?'

'The law is the law,' he told me.

I pointed into the open spaces to the west and said, 'The droghul *will* lead the Zuri upon us. If we're caught out there, we'll have little hope of even getting close to the droghul.'

'But what other hope is there?'

I turned toward the northeast and pointed at the low mountains shining in the sun. 'If we can reach those highlands, we'll find better ground to stand against the Zuri. We'll be able to loose our arrows at our enemies as from a castle's battlements.'

Yago had little knowledge of bows and arrows, and less of castles, but he understood my strategy well enough. It didn't matter. As he told me: 'That is the country of the Avari, and when they discover us, they'll kill the Zuri and the droghul – *and* us.'

'Then you will have your vengeance after all,' I told him. 'And as you say, the dead are the dead.'

For a few moments Yago continued gazing at the mountains. Then he turned back to examine the droghul's tracks pointing into the west. 'If you are wrong in your surmise, we'll lose all chance of vengeance.'

'There is always a chance for vengeance,' I said, looking at the edge of my sword. 'And even if we do lose *this* chance, we might find water in the mountains, and so live to gain another.'

At this, Yago looked over at Turi, patting the neck of his sweating horse. The boy's lips were dusty and cracked. Something cracked inside Yago then. The law was the law, as he had said, but there was always a higher law. For all his talk about vengeance and death, the living were still the living, and Yago's heart beat quick and strong to keep his son among them.

'All right,' he finally told me. 'We'll go with you into the mountains.'

I turned to take council with my friends; their eyes all assented to the course I proposed. Without another word, I pointed Altaru toward the northeast and urged him to a quick walk. We made our way along the border between the Masud's lands and those of the Zuri. Our journey toward this new direction immediately brought relief, for the sun now fell upon our backs. The desert remained hot as a furnace, but at least the fiery orb above us no longer burned out our eyes.

Two hours later, we drank the last of our water. We spent the rest of the afternoon, it seemed, sweating all of it back out. I grew thirsty, for it seemed that I hadn't had a long, deep drink of water since the first well. I could feel the discomfort building inside Maram and the rest of my companions, especially the children. And Yago's dry, hot eyes seemed to assure me that as yet we knew nothing of real thirst.

In the last hour of the day, we came to a standing stone that marked the place where the lands of the Zuri, Masud and Avari touched upon each other. Yago and Turi were loath to go on another foot, for they dreaded entering the mysterious Avari's country. Then Kane caught sight of a dust plume in the west. This decided Yago; he smiled his doomful smile, and pressed his horse forward. But he kept looking backward over his shoulder, as did we all.

At first, with the great ball of fire of the setting sun nearly blinding me, I had a hard time making out the dust plume. But with each mile it grew larger. Our tired, parched horses could barely manage a brisk walk. I thought that the Zuri's horses – for I was sure that the droghul had led warriors of this tribe after us – must be well-watered. I tried to calculate rates and distances, but there was no need, for we had no choice but to continue on toward the mountains as quickly as we could.

These rocky prominences grew larger, too. Yago could tell us little of them. They seemed to be a spur running south off the White Mountains. Master Juwain pulled out one of his maps, but he could find nothing marked there that helped us. In the day's last light, I saw that the peaks ahead of us topped out much lower than any of the Yorgos range. Long canyons cut them northeast to southwest, and steep ravines ran down the sides of huge, triangular blades of rock into the canyons. Every square foot of these highlands seemed as dry as a bleached bone.

As the ground broke up into a hilly country, Maram took me aside and murmured to me, 'You care nothing for meting out vengeance upon the droghul, do you? You hope to lose him in the mountains, don't you?'

'If we can, Maram,' I murmured back to him. 'If we can.'

'If we *do*,' he said, licking his cracked lips, 'it will avail us nothing if we don't find water, and soon.'

He shooed away a few flies, then popped a barbark nut in his mouth. Sucking on them, he had told me, kept his tongue from drying out. I noticed that he had given up his habit of spitting upon the ground, electing to swallow the vile red juice instead.

Yago rode up to us and asked us, 'What is it you are discussing?'

'Ah . . . water,' Maram told him, gulping at the juice in his mouth. 'We were talking about water. Neither of us can see any likely places in those mountains to look for it.'

Yago stared at the mountains ahead of us. 'The Avari will know of water, for we are deep in their country. But they would not tell us of it.'

Maram lifted back his head to look up at the sky and said, 'It must rain upon those damn mountains sometime. Look at those clouds! Why do they drift to the north when the wind blows from the west?'

Yago studied the few, thin white clouds, moving north as Maram had observed. And he told us, 'There must be winds higher in the sky that blow them that way. But do not think that clouds will save you, thirsty pilgrims. It never rains here in the summer.'

I listened to the clopping of the horses' hooves against rocks. The flies were beginning to abate while the snakes and other desert creatures emerged from their holes to greet the coming of night. Everything seemed to stink of sweat and dust. With the dying of the sun, twilight darkened the desert and its stark landforms. We continued on at a slower pace, for the horses now had to take greater care where they placed their hooves on the stony ground.

It grew mercifully cooler. The air, however, for the first couple hours of night, remained warm enough to wring the sweat from us. Our thirst grew worse. No longer could we perceive a dust plume against the black, starry sky, but I sensed that the droghul and many others still pursued us. The dark would slow them, Yago said, but they would keep after us unless we could find mantles of bare, hard rock to ride across. And even then, when day came, a good tracker might be able to make out a faint chip in the rock, while the finest of Ravirii trackers might follow us even at night.

I kept my eyes fixed on the mountains. We finally came within a mile of them, and turned almost due north as we rode paralleling the ridgelines looking for a place of retreat. Any of the canyons, it seemed, might do as well as any other. But we might come across a veritable castle cut out of the stone above us, and still find ourselves doomed to die of thirst. And so I let Altaru fall back to where Estrella rode next to Atara. And I said to this tough, tired girl, 'If it comes to you that there might be water in any of these canyons, follow your heart and seek it out. And we'll follow you.'

Estrella nodded her head at this, and weakly clasped my hand. She tried to smile, but could not. For the thousandth time, I berated myself for taking children with me on such a dreadful journey.

It was past midnight when we came upon the mouth of a canyon little different from any of the others. But Estrella, after first looking at me for approval, led us straight into it. We began climbing up a wide notch between the masses of rock around us; I wondered if a river or stream had once worked its way through here. After about two miles of plodding over stony but mostly level ground, the canyon narrowed and dead-ended into a great rise of mountain. Three ravines cut its slopes and gave out into the canyon. Estrella drew up her horse before the centermost ravine. I could barely make out her face in the thin light as she stared up into it. It would be hard work to take our horses up this steep pitch in the dead of the night. Estrella seemed uncertain as to what we should do. She dismounted and walked a few dozen yards up into the ravine. She paused as if sniffing at the air. Then she walked back to me and held out her hands helplessly. I understood that she could not 'say' that there was water somewhere up this ravine; but neither could she say there was not.

'I doubt if there is water up there,' Yago said, dismounting and walking up to us. 'I doubt if there is water anywhere in these highlands.'

Everyone else dismounted then and came over to hold council. 'Perhaps another canyon,' Maram said.

'We can't go seeking out one canyon after the next all night,' Liljana said to us. 'We haven't the strength for that, or the water.'

Daj, standing next to Turi, started to say something then, but all that came out of his throat was a tortured croak. He was so tired he had to lean against Liljana to keep from falling over.

'We cannot go on like this,' Liljana said again. 'Let us stop for a few hours and see if there is any water about.'

'If we stop, we stay,' Yago said. 'I think the Zuri must be close.'

I thought this, too. I could almost feel the droghul's hand upon my face and hear him whispering in my mind, promising me cool water to drink if only I would lead him to the Maitreya.

Then Yago added, 'I think the Zuri will find this canyon. And then we will have no way out.'

Rock surrounded us on three sides; we would find no escape in any of those directions.

'I believe we should explore, as Liljana has said,' Master Juwain told us. 'At least let us see if we can make our way up the ravine and encamp up there, in those rocks.'

I peered up the ravine, where it gave out into a large, rocky shelf. It seemed that we had at least found our castle to defend.

The dry wind out of the west seemed to suck the thoughts from my mind so that I could not think clearly. And then Kane's voice, cutting through the night like a bright sword, laid bare our choices: 'So, men are only men, and we might defeat them no matter their numbers. But if we don't find water, we'll die.'

After that, we made our way up the ravine. We moved slowly, leading the horses along as best we could in the near-dark. More than once, we had to help the horses find places to plant their hooves as we practically pulled them up the slope. The ground rose steeply before us, and several boulders blocked our way. This chute of rock, I thought, would turn into a death trap for any of the Zuri who might try to storm their way up it toward us. Equally, it would turn into our tomb if thirst forced us back down it onto the Zuri's swords.

We finally came out upon the rock shelf, littered with more boulders. Maram collapsed, sitting down with his back pressed to one of these. Liljana looked for a level place to lay out our sleeping furs. Daj and Turi, who seemed to be forging a silent friendship, began wandering about the rocks on the slopes above the shelf in a desperate search for water. Estrella stood staring at this barren and cracked mountain slope. Not even a thorn bush or a sprig of bitterbroom grew here.

In the coolness of the deepest part of night, we made what we could of our 'camp'. Yago joined the children, searching for any scoop in the rocks or hidden hole that might once have held a few ounces of water or mud. Liljana squeezed a little slime out of the water skins; it moistened our throats but was not enough to drink. After setting out the bows and arrows on ground providing a clear line of sight down the ravine, Kane took off his cloak and went hunting. He managed to throw this garment over a rock owl, which he killed by snapping its neck. He used his knife to bleed it, filling up nearly two cups with a thick, blackish blood. Only Daj and Turi could bring themselves to drink this evil-looking liquid, and they each took a cup and drained it. Yago looked on approvingly. Then Kane dug out the owl's eyes, which he and Yago ate like grapes, sucking out the aqueous humors and then spitting out the hard lenses.

After the children and Yago returned to their search for water, Kane scowled at Maram and me – and the rest of us – and snarled out: 'So, you think you are thirsty, eh? Not thirsty enough, I say! Just wait until the sun rises tomorrow. Then you'll pray for a little blood, if you can find any, and you'll be grateful to lick the sweat from the horses' hides!'

He went over to grab up one of the bows and stand watch in the starlight, staring down the ravine into the canyon below.

And Maram sighed out, 'Well, what about the brandy? That's mostly water, isn't it?'

Master Juwain shook his head at this and said to him, 'I've told you before: spirits only dry out the body, worse than sea water. Please put this out of your mind.'

After another hour, when it grew bitterly cold, the children gave up their search in order to take a little rest, lying down with Maram, Master Juwain, Atara and Liljana. Yago continued prowling about the rocks above us. I tried to sleep but kept waking up in want of water to ease the burning in my throat. The stars shone down brightly through air that was too clear.

Then, near dawn, I heard Kane call out from where he stood watch above us: 'They come!'

I rose up stiffly from the rocky ground and climbed to where he stood on a prominence looking down through the canyon to the open desert in the west. Even two miles away, we could see the light of what must be torches, moving closer.

'So, so,' Kane said, stringing his longbow.

I tried to find some moisture in my mouth with which to wet my tongue. I said, 'I'm afraid I'm too parched to fight another battle.'

'Battle?' he growled out. 'Well, it might come to that yet. It all depends on whether our enemy has enough water to wait us out.'

When the torches began moving up through the mouth of the canyon, I woke up the others. The children, with Liljana, renewed what seemed a hopeless quest to find water. Maram and Yago joined Kane and me at the edge of the rocky shelf. So, a moment later, did Master Juwain and Atara, who used her unstrung bow to feel her way over the broken ground. She had hardly spoken ten words for all the last day. Now she came up to me and whispered in my ear. Her words burned with the rage of helplessness: 'I still can't *see*. I should break my bow and cast away the pieces!'

'It will return,' I whispered back to her. 'It will all return.'

She stood in the silence of the dark, shivering in the cold and shaking her head. She said to me, 'Tell me what *you* see.'

And so I did. As the night drew to an end, a faint light warmed the world. It slowly grew brighter. I tried to describe the way the sun's first rays touched the desert with a golden-red glow. It was all strangely beautiful, I said. This luminosity worked its way east until it filled the canyon's mouth and set its stark rocks on fire. Now, I told her, our enemy had no need of their torches. In the hard light of day, they tracked us more surely and swiftly. A mass of horsemen, perhaps sixty strong, worked their way up toward us. It seemed that they still hadn't seen us, half-hidden as we were behind the boulders on the rocky shelf. But I could easily see them. Most of the horsemen wore billowing white robes like unto Turi's and Yago's. Five of them, though, showed the bright carmine of tunics or surcoats: the color of the Red Priests. I could not guess what kind of garment covered the droghul of Morjin.

'The Poisoner comes!' Yago said from next to me as he pointed his saber down the ravine. 'Which one is he, Mirustral?'

'I can't quite tell,' I said to him. 'They are still too far away.'

'Not for long,' Maram muttered. 'We might as well jump up and announce ourselves so as to make things easier.'

He turned to stare at the slope of mountain looming large and dark behind us. I turned, too, looking for Liljana and the children. It seemed that Liljana must have pulled the children down into the cover of the rocks higher up.

'The sun will be up soon,' Maram muttered. He put down his

bow and took out his red crystal instead. He looked down at the horsemen moving slowly up the canyon. 'Well, let them come, then! They must be hungry after riding all night – I'll give them fire to eat!'

'No,' Master Juwain said, coming over to rest his hand on his arm. 'It's too dangerous.'

'The droghul comes,' I said to him. I blinked against the sick heat of my blood burning into my eyes. 'He surely comes, and he'll kill you with your own fire.'

'It might be our last chance,' Maram said as he pointed his crystal down into the canyon.

'No,' I told him. 'He'll turn your fire and kill us all.'

Yago turned to regard Maram, puzzled by the turn of our talk. It seemed that he knew nothing of the gelstei. There was no time to educate him, however, for just then a cry rang out through the canyon as one of the white-robed men below us pointed straight up the ravine toward our position.

'Maybe,' Maram said, 'I can at least burn that damn droghul before he burns me.'

The enemy moved still closer, and now I caught a gleam of yellow hair to match the yellow tunic of a man riding near the lead of the horsemen. The fire that whispered in my mind told me that this must be yet another incarnation of Morjin.

'So,' Kane's voice rumbled. 'So.'

'No fire,' I said to Maram. 'Not yet – let's see what they'll do.'

When the horsemen came to the ravine, they stopped and began dismounting. Some of them shouted up to us. I could not make out what they were saying. Kane nocked an arrow, and drew it back to his ear. Then he shook his head as he eased the tension on the bowstring. It was a long shot down to the men below us, about a hundred yards. Atara might possibly be able to pick off targets at such a distance, but Kane hated wasting arrows.

'You were right, Mirustal,' Yago said to me. 'This Poisoner and the Red Priests have their stingers sunk *very* deep into the Zuri. I didn't really think they would dare to cross the Avari's lands.'

A Zuri warrior, holding up a white banner of truce, began making his way up the ravine. One of the priests walked to his left. So narrow was this rocky chute that another man would have had difficulty fitting in beside them.

They came within thirty yards, close enough that I could see the priest's smooth, sunburnt face. He had red hair and blue eyes, like the men of Surrapam. Kane pulled back on his bowstring again, sighting his arrow upon him.

'No!' I called to him. 'They come under truce!'

'Truce?' Kane growled out. 'The bloody Red Priests would break it as readily as they'd squash a bug. Let me at least kill one of them and lighten our work.'

'No!' I said again. 'Let's hear what he has to say.'

'Lies, he'll say. How many must we listen to?'

The two men halted their climb twenty yards below us. The Zuri warrior had the look of Yago's people, with his black beard and dark, hard features. When I remarked that he looked much like the Masud I had seen at the well, Yago took insult, saying, 'Can you not see how his eyes are too close together, like a snake's? Look at his narrow forehead! And the cut of his robes, which are . . .'

As Yago began describing the different cut and stitching of the robes of the various tribes of the Ravirii, the much-fairer Red Priest called up to us: 'Well-poisoners! My name is Maslan, and I speak on behalf of Oalo, whom Tatuk has sent to bring you to justice! Lay down your weapons and surrender, and you shall be spared the punishment decreed for poisoners! Your children shall be taken into the Zuri tribe and well cared for.'

'Never!' Yago shouted back at him. 'Give my son to *you*? It is the yellow-hair you ride with who is the well-poisoner!'

Maslan turned to the warrior beside him as if to say: 'Do you see how they lie?'

Then he called up to us again: 'You are trapped here! I think you have no water. We can wait here until you drop of thirst.'

'Then wait!' Kane shouted down to him. 'Or send up as many as you please! We've arrows enough for you all!'

Maslan took from the Zuri warrior a waterskin, which he held up to his lips. He swished some water around in his mouth, then spat it out into the ravine. He called out: 'Any who surrender may have all the water they wish. Any who do not are welcome to lick these rocks.'

That was all he said to us. He turned his back to us, and led the Zuri warrior back down the ravine to the mass of our enemy gathered in the canyon below.

'Val,' Maram said to me. 'Put your sword through my throat! It will be better than dying of thirst or whatever torture the Red Priests have planned for us.'

'Be quiet,' I said to him, trying to think. 'There must be a way out.'

338

'What way?' Maram asked.

'To begin with, it might rain.'

Maram looked up at the sky, at the single cloud floating above the desert toward the north. He said, 'What other miracles do you hope for?'

'Estrella might yet find water.'

'And I,' Maram said, 'might sprout wings like a bird and simply fly out of here. But if I don't, and grow too weak and the worst befalls, please promise me you won't let the Red Priests have me?'

'I won't let them touch you,' I told him. 'Now be quiet. You waste water with every breath.'

There was nothing to do then but to wait. The Zuri and the Red Priests below us dismounted and made camp at the bottom of the ravine. I was sure that whoever Oalo might be, it was the droghul who really commanded Zuri and the priests, and took charge of this siege. I felt his presence like a burning quicksand sucking at my will to oppose him. I found myself wishing that it had been he who had showed himself in the ravine to offer his vile terms. Then Kane would have put an arrow through his heart, truce or no truce.

At last the sun rose over the rim of the mountains behind us, and rained down its killing rays. The cold of night bled from the air with startling quickness as it grew warmer and warmer. After a while the sun heated up the rocks around us like a natural oven. We began to sweat. Soon, I thought, we would all be ready to lick the rocks of the ravine, even as the priest had said.

For a few hours, we waited for our miracle. And then Kane, who had the eyes of an eagle if not the wings, caught sight of a dust plume moving quickly across the desert toward the mouth of the canyon. Soon, another mass of horsemen came into view. There must have been more than a hundred and fifty of them. Upon seeing them pounding up through the canyon, Maram gave up the last of his hope.

'Oh, my Lord!' Maram said. 'More Zuri!'

The arrival of these new warriors, however, did not seem to be welcomed by the Zuri encamped below us. They sprang up from beneath their flapping sun cloths and ran for their horses. I saw sixty sabers flashing in the sunlight. But they were outnumbered more than two to one. The new warriors thundered closer, drawing in more tightly as they rode up through the funnel of the canyon. They came to a halt almost shoulder to shoulder in a long line that completely blocked any exit into the desert. They waited on horseback with *their* sabers pointing at the Zuri fifty yards away.

'Can you not see?' Yago said to Maram, pointing out details in the garments of the newcomers, particularly the shawls drawn across their faces. 'Those are the Avari.'

He spoke this name as one might that of a werewolf or some other unnatural being.

'So,' Kane growled with a smile, '*now* who is trapped?'

As Maram stood with his strung bow, peering down the ravine into the canyon at these two groups of warriors, I felt him struggling to take a little cheer in this unexpected turn of events. But then Yago dashed his hopes, saying to Kane, 'Little good that it will do us. Likely the Avari will kill the Zuri, and then turn on us.'

I watched as two Zuri warriors rode out toward the Avari bearing a banner of truce. Two men in red robes rode with them, led by a man wearing a bright yellow tunic. His hair, I saw, shone golden. Now, at this distance, I could just barely make out the red dragon blazing from his tunic. From the Avari line, four men with swaddled faces urged their horses forward to meet them. They, too, bore a banner of truce. I wondered what lies Maslan and the droghul would tell the Avari as they sat holding council beneath the merciless sun.

I did not have to wait long to find out the answer to this question. The tallest of the four Avari, who all seemed to sit much higher on their horses than either the Zuri or the droghul, broke off council. He began riding slowly in the direction of the Zuri's line, which parted before him like a wave of water. He rode straight up into the ravine. Where the way grew too steep, he dismounted and walked beside his great, gray horse, leading it up toward the rocky shelf where Kane and Maram stood aiming arrows at him. Yago waited there, too, with his saber drawn. He had never met an Avari warrior, and was unsure how to greet him.

'May the sun warm your face,' Yago called out to him. 'May the rain fill your wells, Avari.'

'May the rain fill *your* wells, Masud.' He spoke with a strange accent, which changed the sounds of his words so that 'well' came out as 'weal', and 'rain' was rendered as 'reen'. From the tone of his voice and the deepness of his eyes, I guessed his age to be about thirty. 'From what I've been told, one of your wells has been poisoned by the very outlanders you ride with.'

The warrior climbed up and joined us on the rocky shelf. He

stood nearly as tall as I. Silver bracelets encrusted with blue stones flashed from his wrists. Beneath his head covering, his eyes shone bright as black onyx. He regarded Kane and me in astonishment.

'I am Sunji,' he informed us. 'Son of Jovayl, who is king of the Avari. My father sent me to discover who has invaded our realm, and why.'

I longed to tell him that I, too, was a prince of a realm far away. I wanted to give him my real name. But as I had relinquished all claim to honors and rank to live the life of a wanderer, I did not. Instead I told him much the same story that I had Yago. When I finished, Sunji stood staring at me as he might a viper.

'The one you call a droghol,' he said to me, pronouncing that name strangely, too, 'claims to be Morjin himself, king of the realm called Sakai. He claims that *you* are the poisoners of the Masud's well.'

'But why would we poison a well and so deny ourselves water?' I said to him. 'And why would one of the Masud ride with those who had poisoned his own people?'

'I do not know,' Sunji said to me. 'That is to be determined.'

'Determined *how*?' Maram asked him.

Sunji looked at Maram, with his fly-blown sores, as one might a leper. Then he said, 'There will be a trial. Either this Morjin or Mirustral is lying. And so Mirustral will come with me now, that he might stand face to face with Morjin.'

At the thought of this, my hand moved of its own to grip the hilt of my sword. And Kane pointed down into the canyon as he growled out to Sunji, 'I'll not let my friend go into that dragon's den alone!'

Sunji bowed his head to Kane. 'You may come as a second, then, Rowan Madeus, if that is really *your* name. And the Masud.'

He looked at Yago, who assented to Sunji's demand. And I said to Sunji, 'And what if we will not stand at trial?'

'Then you may stand here and let the sun determine your fate!'

It seemed that we had no choice. Sunji waited patiently while we made our preparations. Master Juwain came over to me and led me in a meditation, the same one as he had before I fought my duel with Salmelu. Atara, in silence, kissed me on the lips. As I moved to gather up Altaru's reins, Maram took me aside and said, 'I should come with you, too.'

'No, Maram,' I told him, looking down the ravine into the canyon. 'You must stay here and guard everyone, in case there is treachery. With your bow, if you can, and with your firestone, if you cannot.'

His eyes blurred with tears, and he nodded at me. 'But how will you stand against Morjin and all his lies?'

'I don't know,' I said. I clasped hands with him and smiled. 'But there will be a way – there is always a way.'

Kane and Yago, leading their horses, came up behind me. Then I pulled gently on Altaru's reins, and we followed Sunji down into the ravine.

21

We rode out onto the hardpack between the Avari and Zuri lines. The captain named Oalo waited there along with another Zuri warrior, still under the banner of truce. Next to them, on fine horses, sat Maslan and the droghul. In appearance, this double of Morjin seemed identical to the first droghul who had died so terribly in the forest of Acadu, except that he had two good arms and the sun had burned his fair face red. His hair shone all golden like the sun, as did his eyes. I could see nothing of his own will in these hideous orbs, and everything of Morjin. He radiated an overweening arrogance and the command of a king. The malevolence that poured out of him struck me like a hammer blow to the throat. I found myself bitterly wishing that I had not abandoned my steel mail. I wondered what armor I might find here against his sword, no less his inevitable lies and assault on my soul.

Three Avari warriors greeted Sunji, whom they treated as a prince. Although these three kept their faces covered, I could see from the webwork of creases around their black eyes that they were nearly old men. Sunji presented them as Laisar, Maidro and Avraym, and said that they were to be the judges of what was told here today.

With the fierce sun prompting all of us to speak concisely and quickly, we submitted to trial, all the while sitting on the backs of our horses. The droghul and I gave our respective accounts of what had occurred at the Masud well. We told of our journeys and our purposes, as much as we dared. The three judges listened closely. The warriors in the two lines behind us tried to listen, too. Twice, Oalo, an ugly, much-scarred man, interrupted in order to clarify matters or make important points, speaking self-importantly in

343

behalf of the Zuri's chief, Tatuk. Sunji silenced him both times. He, and he alone, as he told us, would conduct this trial.

After we had finished speaking, Sunji swept his saber from Kane to me and called out, 'You claim to be landless knights guarding pilgrims; the names you gave are Rowan Madeus and Mirustral. But King Morjin, if such he really is, tells that your true names are Kane and Valaysu Elahad. Do you claim that he has mistaken you for others?'

The three judges, I saw, leaned forward on their horses, waiting for me to answer. Maslan, as with the four other Red Priests in the Zuri line, regarded me as might a spider a fly trapped in a web. The droghul simply stared at me with unrelenting hatred.

'No, he has not mistaken us for others,' I said to Sunji. 'Those are our true names, though little else he has said about us or himself is true.'

Now the eyes of Laisar, Avraym and Maidro, who sat on their horses close to me, grew as stonelike as obsidian. I sensed doubt and disdain hardening the hearts of the Avari warriors who watched me.

'Do you think to convince us of what you put forth as true,' Sunji asked me, 'by readily admitting a lie?'

I gazed at the shawl wrapped around Sunji's face. I said to him, 'You and those of your tribe keep yourselves well-covered against the sun that would burn you. So it is with me and my companions. We have chosen these names to wear just so this droghul and his kind wouldn't discover us, as he has.'

It was a good answer, I thought, the best I could give, but none of the Ravirii approved of it, especially not Yago, who clearly didn't like it that I had kept secrets from him. He sat on his horse next to me gazing at me in anger.

'I do not know yet what to believe,' Sunji said, now pointing his saber at the droghul and then at me, 'but it is clear that the two of you are mortal enemies. The king of a realm called Sakai, or his sorcerous double, a droghul as you name him. And an outlawed prince of a faraway realm called Mesh.'

'I am no outlaw,' I said, wiping the sweat from my neck. 'I left my homeland of my own choice.'

'To seek this Well of Restoration that you have told of?'

I commanded my hand not to wipe at the sweat pouring from my face. It had come time to tell of things that *should* be kept a secret. I said, 'In a way. We seek the one who would use the Cup of Heaven to restore Ea. We call this one the Maitreya.'

344

As I told of the Lightstone, Sunji's eyes gleamed, and a great excitement filled the three Avari judges and rippled through their fellow warriors who sat watching us. Sunji allowed me to finish speaking and then said to me, 'Is this another of your truths clothed in the dirty robes of a lie? Do you ask us to believe that you would risk your lives journeying into the desert in search of this Maitreya?'

From the Avari line, which had moved in closer to us, a young man called out: 'What I cannot believe is his story of entering the Stone City. Burning holes through rock with sorcerous fire, and slaying dragons – dragons! And this man and a few companions slaying nearly a hundred men? He told that a blind woman fired arrows into their hearts! He lies, surely, and more, he must be mad to think that we should listen to such –'

'Be quiet, Daivayr!' Sunji suddenly barked out, cutting him off. He turned back to me and said, 'My brother is impulsive, as it is with the young. But he only voices questions we all have. You say that you risked your lives seeking the Cup of Heaven in the great Quest, as you do now in search of the one you call the Maitreya. Why?'

'Because it is the only hope for Ea – and for much more.' As Sunji and the three judges listened to every word I spoke, and the droghul's golden eyes never left mine, I tried to tell of my love for Ea's forests and mountains, her oceans and grass-covered plains. And it would all be burnt to ashes, I said, and washed in blood if Morjin and his Red Priests had their way. 'I . . . would see an end to war. The Maitreya might bring this abiding peace, if he can be found.'

'But how could you hope to find him,' Sunji asked me, 'if you do not even know his name or what tribe has given him birth?'

It was a good question, and I knew that my judges would find my answer weak as I said: 'There is one among us who is gifted in finding things.'

'Through the aid of sorceries?'

'We are not sorcerers!' I cried out.

Although the droghul's face remained implacable as he regarded me, his whole being lit up as with a triumphant smile. Then he opened his mouth to speak. His voice, ever golden and persuasive, swelled with a new power. His words fell like irresistible weapons that laid people open and left them utterly vulnerable to his command: 'This Elahad has impugned everything about me, going so far as to deny who I am. I *am* King of Sakai! I have risked much in coming into the desert, as I have. In the past, I have sent priests to your people – the bravest and freest of Ea's peoples! – to help them understand the nature of the menace that would undo us all. And to help them unite against sorcerers such as the Elahad and his kind. My priests have not always been well-received. I do not blame you Ravirii for this, as the world is hard and our enemies are not always as they seem. But we are *not* your enemies! I have come here, in my person, that you might hear the truth of things from my own lips.'

The droghul, I knew, almost had a mind of his own, although at the moment I could sense no particle or flame of his own self-ness. So compelling was the smoothness of his voice – the perfection of pitch and tone and utter certainty in itself – that he almost convinced *me* that he was the real Morjin.

'Lord Morjin,' Maslan said hoarsely, coughing at the dry air, 'is known in all lands as the most veracious of kings.'

No, I thought, the most *voracious*. If these desert tribes let him, he would swallow them up one by one as he had the great king-doms that surrounded them. Little sense of this peril, however, seemed to have made its mark on the Ravirii, at least not the Zuri gathered here. They seemed to regard Maslan and the other Red Priests as keepers of a great and mysterious power. They looked upon these five terrible men with something of the same awe that my people held for the masters of the Brotherhood. Only Oalo, I sensed, suspected how vile they really were. The tightness in his chest told me that he lived in great fear of them, even as the priests themselves dreaded the droghul and Morjin himself.

'I would enlist the aid of all the Ravirii tribes,' the droghul said, looking from Oalo to Yago and then at Sunji. 'The Lightstone has been taken back from the Elahad, who stole it and claimed it for himself. Even now, he seeks other stones of power that he might cast his ensorcellments over all peoples and all lands in hope of stealing back the golden cup yet again.'

'He lies!' I said, shaking my fist at him. 'He accuses me of his own evil dreams and deeds – even as he did the poisoning of the Masud well!'

'I do not lie,' the droghul said. 'And I am no poisoner.'

I tried to find the right words to gainsay this, but I could not. So excruciating was the burning of my blood, from the kirax within and the fiery sun pouring down on me, that I could hardly speak at all.

'The Cup of Heaven,' the droghul said, letting his golden voice carry out to the lines of Zuri and Avari warriors pressing in even closer, 'will remain safely in my hall in Argattha, where I invite any and all to come drink of its light.'

'The urna has been found!' Avraym marveled as he gazed at the droghul. Until now the judges of this trial had been as silent as stone.

'In my own lifetime, sought and found. All glory in the One!'

The droghul smiled at him, a bright, open smile all full of the promise of happiness and otherwordly riches, even love. And he said to Avraym and the other judges, and to all the Avari and Zuri: 'When the time comes and victory is ours, I shall bring the Lightstone into all lands. The Ravirii shall be its keepers, and here it will do its most wondrous work. A golden light will pour itself out onto the desert's sands. Trees will grow here again, soft grasses and flowers. Water will run in the dry river beds, and lakes will shine in the sun. The desert will be green again.'

'As it was, it shall be again,' Avraym intoned.

'All glory in the One,' Laisar said.

The droghul, I thought, through his master in Argattha, knew the Ravirii well, even as he knew all peoples. He gave them precisely what they wished to hear.

'This Elahad,' he said, 'claimed the Lightstone for himself. Even as he claimed to be the Maitreya.'

Sunji looked at me and asked, 'Is this true, Valashu Elahad?'

'I . . . yes, there was a moment,' I stammered out. 'Only a moment when I claimed this. But I was wrong.'

My admission did not make a good impression on those judging me. The droghul smiled at me. I could feel him using the raw power of Morjin's passions to pull at the heartstrings of everyone gathered here. He touched *their* passions. He played on their vanities and fears, and spoke to their deepest dreams. I vowed again that I would never use my gift this way to violate people's souls and work such evil.

'From his own lips, he admits another lie!' the droghul said. 'How many more must we hear before we judge him as what he is?'

How, I wondered, could I ever prevail here against this double of Morjin? The droghul sat up straight on his horse, disdainful of the sun and radiating all of Morjin's power and authority. Morjin was a king, even if an evil and false one, and people heeded what he said.

'The Elahad has no more respect for *you*,' the droghul said to the judges, 'than he does your laws. He and his fellow conspirators invaded your lands solely to flee a richly deserved justice. With his own hand, he poisoned the Masud well so that he could –'

'He lies!' I called out. 'Can't you hear how he lies?'

Sunji waved his sword at me. He said, 'You must keep your silence unless you have testimony to offer. Calling King Morjin a liar does not constitute such, nor will it serve you.'

The droghul bowed his head to Sunji, and then smiled at me. He drew in a breath of burning air in order to further defame me. His cleverness cut with all the precision of a surgeon's knife as he called out: 'When the Masud discovered the Elahad's true purpose, the Elahad poisoned their well to keep them from turning against him. And what is his purpose? He seeks *gelstei* and other stones of power. He found suchlike among the Masud, the very skystones that are sacred to the Avari.'

At this, Sunji touched the blue stones set into the silver of one of his bracelets. Avraym, I saw, wore a pendant fashioned of the same substance, as did Maidro and Laisar. I recalled seeing such jewelry among the gold bangles that Daj had gathered from the dead Masud.

Yago remembered this as well. He looked at me with suspicion eating at his hard face.

'The Elahad,' the droghul went on, 'would use the gelstei to take control of the Lightstone. Each of the conspirators has gained these gelstei and mastery over them.'

How, I wondered, could people ever mistake a lie for the truth? I knew from bitter experience that the truth always spoke with a clear and perfect voice, but too often it spoke too softly. People did not hear it, for they believed what they wanted to believe.

'Valashu Elahad – is this true?' Sunji asked me.

I turned to my right to see Kane's black eyes warning me to silence. But with the judges and everyone else looking at me, I could not keep silent. Neither could I lie.

'Yes,' I said, 'each of my companions and I keep one of the gelstei.'

'Show us these stones, then.'

I saw that Kane trembled to whip out his sword and cut off Sunji's head. Instead, he took out his baalstei and showed it to him and the three judges. At the sight of this black crystal, Avraym kissed his own hand and pressed it over his heart. So did Laisar and Maidro theirs. The droghul told that the black gelstei could be used to suck out the very fires of a man's soul, and Kane did not dispute this.

'So, it *can* be used this way,' Kane said, making a fist around his stone. He stared at the droghul with such hate that the droghul finally looked away. 'This *thing* of Morjin should know this, for Morjin himself has used a much greater baalstei to try to suck at the soul of the whole world and all her peoples.'

As he went on to tell of the Black Jade, the Avari warriors up and down their line kissed their hands and clasped them to their chests, as did the Zuri warriors in their line.

Then the droghul, for the first time seeming to struggle against Morjin's iron-fisted control of him, pointed at Kane and said, 'He, too, is a liar, like the Elahad. Can no one here feel him attacking you with this evil stone?'

With the sun sucking the life out of everyone gathered in this sweltering canyon, and Morjin perhaps wielding the Black Jade from afar, it was easy for Sunji and the judges to believe that Kane strove to lay an evil enchantment upon them. And so Sunji called to Kane: 'Put away your sorcerer's stone!'

Kane tucked away his gelstei, then said to Sunji, 'Ha – you know nothing of what you speak! All the gelstei were made out of the essence of the Lightstone itself. So, the baalstei were meant to control the fires of the tuaoi stones, for good, not ill.'

'The firestones,' the droghul explained. 'Even as we speak, the fat leper on that hill makes ready to wreak burning sorceries upon us.'

He pointed up the ravine where Maram, with Master Juwain and Liljana, stood watching us.

'The Elahad himself,' the droghul said, 'bears a sword wrought of the evilest of substances. He has used it to slay with all the deadliness of a scorpion.'

Sunji aimed his saber at me, then commanded Laisar, Avraym and Maidro to draw their sabers. He said to me, 'Let us see this sorcerous sword!'

I drew out Alkaladur then. The Ravirii of all three tribes gasped to behold its silvery brilliance. They drew back from it, too, for even as I held it up to the sun, red flames ran up and down its length. Only Kane, I thought, knew how badly I longed to stab its point into Morjin's heart – even into the droghul. But killing this dreadful creature would not kill Morjin. It would serve only to bring down the sabers of the Ravirii upon me and my friends.

'Break it!' the droghul cried out. 'Take this evil thing from the poisoner, and break it into pieces!'

'*You* take it!' I shouted back at him. I pointed my sword at him, and watched in horror as it blazed with even hotter flames. 'Let us cross swords, the two of us here and now, and let that be the test of things!'

Sunji turned to nod at the Avari warriors backing him up as if making sure they were ready to close in on me at a moment's notice. Then he said to me, 'This is no trial by combat; put away your sword.'

The Sword of Light, Alkaladur was called, the Sword of Truth. It caught me up in its fiery light. Then I sheathed it and sat gasping at the torrid air.

The sight of this burning blade seemed to stir something within the droghul. His jaws clamped shut as if he struggled to bite off the words forming in his throat. I sensed Morjin from afar, and too near, driving a heated iron into the droghul's spine to make him speak. And when the droghul finally did, he spoke too much – too much for me to bear: 'With that cursed sword, the Elahad murdered his own father and brothers when they discovered his sorceries and tried to drive him from Mesh!'

So bright did the sun blaze just then that I thought it would burn out my eyes.

'Father-killer!' one of the Red Priests called out. A Zuri warrior next to him repeated this accusation. And then, from both the Zuri and Avari lines came more cries: 'Father-killer! Well-poisoner! Sorcerer!'

The three judges stared at me in a silence even more terrible than these accusations.

He has won, I thought, looking at the droghul for the hidden hand of Morjin. *He will always win.*

'Father-killer! Father-killer! Father-killer!'

I had told of things as accurately as I knew how, and it seemed that I had only turned my judges against me. But had I really spoken *truly*? Inside me whispered a deep and beautiful voice that had never failed me; often, now, it called to me as loud and clear as a bell. I knew, though, that I was afraid to make this voice my own and shout it out so that others might hear it. I feared that they would *mis*hear it or misuse it – or use it against me. Even more, I feared wielding the truth as a sword that men could not resist, annihilating their wills so that mine might prevail. That was Morjin's way. As the golden eyes of the droghul fell upon me and I felt Morjin staring me down from far away, I knew that he wished me to fear this and to live in dread of my gift of valarda. In a hundred ways, perhaps even through the Black Jade, he had attacked my will toward all that was good and true. And so I spoke with what honesty I dared, but softly and weakly, in words that were often at least partial lies.

'Father-killer!' the warriors around me called out. 'Sorcerer! Well-poisoner!'

'What else is there to say?' the droghul shouted. It seemed that he had given up struggling against Morjin. 'These men and their kind are well-poisoners! Give them to us that *we* might give them justice!'

Morjin, I suddenly knew, wished to torture out of me and my friends our knowledge of the Maitreya even more than he wished our deaths. If the droghul and the Red Priests got their hands on us, I wondered how they would be able to crucify us in a land without wood? Perhaps they would settle on cutting apart Daj and Estrella piece by piece, knowing that I could never bear this.

'Well-poisoners! Well-poisoners! Kill the well-poisoners!'

What is truth? It is not merely faultlessness and honesty, the uncovering of facts, but rather the urge toward these things, and much more, the primeval drive to bring forth into the light of existence the deepest designs of the real. It is as clear and perfect as starlight, and it blazes with all the fierceness and power of the sun.

Well-poisoner! Sorcerer! Father-killer! Father-killer! Father-killer!

In the black centers of the droghul's eyes, Morjin sat on his Dragon Throne shouting these words at me. Then, at last, I drew in a deep breath of fiery air and shouted back at him: 'My father died defending our land from your armies! My brothers, too! My mother was nailed to wood by your bloody priests! They put my grandmother next to her! You, with your own fingers, tore out my beloved's eyes! I . . . could not stop this! I tried, with all my might, but I could not!'

I drew my sword, and red flames swirled about its shimmering silustria. With tears nearly blinding me, I told the assembled warriors more, things that I did not want to tell anyone, not even myself. I admitted that it was I who had led Atara and my other friends into Argattha, and so shook my fist at the stars. Although I hadn't slain my family I had brought about their deaths through hubris and hate. I loved the world, yes, and wanted to bring an end to war, but even more I hated Morjin and wanted with every breath to thrust my sword into his heart and make him die.

To the judges staring at me with their black, blurred eyes, to Sunji and Yago and all the warriors looking upon me in awe, even to the sky, I told of things simply as they were. There was no manipulation in this, no calculation to achieve a certain end. I wanted only that my judges, and the whole world, should know. Sorrow tore the truth from me. I held nothing back: all my anguish, guilt and grief came pouring out of me. All my love, and all my hate. The sun was a fierce thing in the sky, burning with a white-hot light, but this was more terrible, more beautiful, more real.

When I could speak no more, Sunji sat on his horse regarding me from beneath the shawl that covered most of his face. His bright, black eyes shone with a deep lucidity. After glancing at the droghul, he turned to the judges and told them, 'King Morjin is right – what more is there to say?'

He drew in a deep breath of air as he called out to everyone: 'The well-poisoner, and those who helped him, must be served justice. Laisar, what do *you* say?'

Laisar's old eyes grew hard with judgment as he pointed at the droghul and shouted, 'I say that this man, whether he is King Morjin or his mind-slave, is the poisoner!'

'I say this, too!' Maidro called out.

'And I,' Avraym said. 'Let the poisoner be served!'

All at once, the Avari warriors up and down their line began shouting out: 'Well-poisoner! Well-poisoner! Kill the well-poisoner!'

But the Zuri warriors, trapped between the Avari and the rocks where Maram and my other companions stood, kept their silence. It is one thing to hear the truth, and another to act upon it.

All eyes now fell upon the droghul, who held up his hand and cast his dreadful gaze to the right and left. He cried out: 'You must listen to me! The Elahad lies! It is he, not I, who is the –'

'Sorcerer! Well-poisoner! Well-poisoner! Kill the well-poisoner!'

Sunji, having heard from the judges, swept his sword from the droghul to Oalo, and then out to the Zuri warriors as he pronounced their doom: 'You have heeded too well the words of this sorcerer and poisoner, and those of his priests. But we have all heard the power of these words – the power of these lies. I cannot believe that you knew of the poisoner's deeds. Therefore you shall be spared his punishment. Lay down your swords, and you shall be free to go back to your home!'

'We *won't* lay down our swords!' Oalo shouted, drawing his saber. Its polished steel flashed in the sun. 'We won't make it easy for you to slaughter us here!'

'Truce-breaker!' Avraym called out to him. 'Drop your sword now, or die along with the Poisoner and his priests!'

'Throw down!' Laisar shouted at Oalo. He turned to the Zuri warriors and told them, 'All of you – throw down your swords!'

The sixty Zuri warriors hesitated for a moment. They looked from the droghul and Maslan at the center of the field to the four other Red Priests waiting with them in their line. It seemed that they feared these men more than they did Sunji and the Avari. And so they drew their swords and pointed them at the Avari rather than throwing them down.

'Damn you!' the droghul cried out to Sunji as he drew *his* sword. Torment ate at his eyes as he seemed for a moment to struggle against his distant master. But then his face hardened once again as he screamed out, 'Damn you, Avari! I'll poison *your* wells! I'll send armies to crucify your women and children, and make you drink their blood!'

As he screamed out even more vile threats, Laisar, Avraym and Maidro drew in closer to Sunji; with battle now imminent, ten Avari warriors galloped out from the line to join Sunji and the judges. They positioned themselves facing Oalo, Maslan and the droghul, forming a sort of wall protecting Kane, Yago and me.

'This is no trial by combat!' Sunji called out again to the Zuri. 'Throw down your swords!'

The droghul, however, pointed his sword straight at me. Only his hatred of Morjin's control of him, I thought, had so far kept him from trying to ride me down and hack me apart in full fury. But now he and Morjin were as one.

'Damn you, Elahad! You killed my *daughter*! My only girl! I executed your family, and so destroyed your past, but you have taken from me my hope for the future!'

'It was you who took this!' I called to him. 'You killed Jezi when you touched her with your foul hands!'

'Damn you!' he screamed at me. 'This time you die!'

And then, even as the Red Priests goaded the Zuri warriors to attack the advancing Avari line, the droghul spurred his horse straight at me.

22

Two of the ten Avari warriors that Sunji had called forward moved to stop him. But the droghul, with a thrust of his sword quicker than a striking snake, stabbed one of these warriors through the throat. His sword flashed out a moment later, cleaving the other warrior's skull. Then Sunji, the three judges and the other eight Avari closed in on him.

As the warriors of these two tribes came crashing together in a riot of gleaming sabers and darting horses, it seemed impossible that the Zuri could hold against the Avari. The Avari sat higher on larger horses, and their swords were longer, too. I had never seen warriors wield their swords with such prowess – no warriors except my own people, that is. In each of many individual duels, with saber clanging against saber, an Avari warrior slashed through his foe's defenses again and again. In truth, few of these duels remained individual, for the Avari were merciless and fell upon the outnumbered Zuri in twos and threes. Bright steel sliced through cotton garments, skin and bone. Men screamed in agony. The hardpacked earth of the desert ran red with blood.

I hoped to stay out of this battle, leaving matters to the Avari and Zuri. I sat on top of Altaru, holding back with Kane and Yago at my sides. I waited for Sunji to bring the droghul to justice: either slaying or capturing him. It should have been an easy thing for Sunji and the three judges, backed up by the eight Avari warriors, to cut him down. But two of the Red Priests and six Zuri warriors, with Oalo, rode forward to aid the frenzied, murderous droghul.

And then the droghul seemed to summon up some secret torment from within himself as he cried out in a voice ringing with a fell, new power: **VALARIIII!**

I felt a hundred daggers, like ice, pierce every part of me and seize hold of my limbs. So it was with Sunji and the Avari. Many of them lifted them lifted their swords with a dreadful slowness; many more simply froze altogether in terror.

VALARIIII!

Now Avraym dropped his saber and pressed his hands to his ears, even as Oalo plunged the point of his saber into his back. Sunji could hardly lift his saber to defend himself against the Red Priest attacking him. In the sea of screaming horses and men all around me, it seemed that the Avari were losing their will to slay the Zuri, while the Zuri warriors struck back at their executioners with a renewed fury. I did not know why the Zuri seemed immune to the droghul's terrible cry:

VALARIII!

All across the burning canyon, Avari warriors began dropping their swords or clinging to their horses. Now it was the Zuri who showed them no mercy. Their sabers slashed out like lightning as the Avari's screams became one with the droghul's.

'Damn you, Elahad! Damn the Valariii!'

The droghul cut down the last of the men drawn up in front of me. He ignored Kane, off to my right, who desperately battled two Zuri warriors. The droghul spurred his horse closer, then slashed his sword toward my face. I barely parried it, and its shiny steel clanged against Alkaladur's silustria and struck out flaming sparks. Again and again he tried to cleave me in two. My skin, with no armor protecting it, fairly twitched with a deep, sick fear. I moved slowly, so terribly slowly, as if trying to lift my sword through a raging stream of ice water. I knew that the droghul would kill me, and soon.

And then, from out of nowhere, it seemed, Yago came galloping forward in a whirl of dusty white robes and flashing steel. With perfect coordination, he swerved his horse and closed in just as the droghul raised back his sword to decapitate me. Yago leaned forward in his saddle, and quick as the wind sliced his saber through the droghul's throat. This vicious cut opened up the droghul's windpipe and the great artery there. Blood spurted, and a red froth flowed from the droghul's mouth. Although he could not speak to howl out his paralyzing cry, his eyes remained full of hate. They fixed on my eyes like red-hot nails. They told me that I had murdered *him*, Morjin's droghul, but that I could never touch the one who moved the droghul's limbs and mind. One day, and soon, Morjin would come to take a terrible vengeance. This the droghul promised me in his last moment of life. Then Yago's saber flashed out again, and this time cut clean through the droghul's neck and struck off his head.

After that, the battle did not last very long. The Avari warriors regained their wits and strength. Their terror at the droghul caused them to fall upon the remaining Zuri with great wrath. They killed them cruelly, down to the last man. Sunji himself put his saber through Oalo. Then he went about the field making sure that all the Zuri were dead.

I sat on top of Altaru, gasping for breath and staring down at the droghul's body. The bodies of warriors, Zuri and Avari, lay everywhere, baking in the hot sun. Already the flies had gone to work on their hideous, gaping wounds, and vultures came from afar to circle in the air.

Kane nudged his horse over to me. His black eyes flashed at me as if in joy that we had survived another battle, in one way the worst yet. He asked Yago how it was that the droghul's voice had left him untouched. Yago couldn't hear him. He moved closer to Kane, and threw his hands up to the sides of his head. His fingers dug free two sticky, red barbark nuts. It seemed that at the very beginning of the battle, he had used them to stop up his ears.

'The voice of that thing,' he said, pointing down at what was left of the droghul, 'could have frozen the sun itself. By what sorcery can a man stop another solely through his voice?'

I had no answer for him, and neither did Kane. The mystery of how the Zuri warriors had fought on beneath the droghul's piercing cry, however, was soon solved. Sunji rode back over to us, and opened his hand to show us a yellowish-white, greasy clot of matter.

'Beeswax,' he said to us, 'taken from the Zuri's ears. They came prepared to murder us.'

He told us that eighteen of his warriors had died in the battle, while another fifteen bore serious wounds. All the Zuri were dead. But one of the Red Priests who rode with them still lived.

'Come, Valashu Elahad, you must bear witness to this,' he said to me. 'You, as well, Kane. And you, Masud.'

We picked our way across the battlefield until we came to a large rock. The captured Red Priest had been bound with ropes and cast back against it. His long, gaunt face, like a living skull, was horrible to look upon. His eyes radiated both fear and hate. Three Avari warriors stood over him with their sabers drawn. Laisar and Maidro stood there, too. Laisar held in his hand a large, green bottle. He showed it to Yago and said, 'Poison – taken from the priest's saddlebags. It is proved beyond any doubt: the Morjin thing and his priests are all poisoners!'

And Maidro added, nodding at Yago, 'Surely they would have poisoned *our* wells, too.'

While the Avari went about preparing their dead for burial and tending their wounded, Master Juwain and Liljana came down from the rocky heights above – Maram and Atara, too. When Yago asked after Turi, Liljana coldly informed him that children had no place on a battlefield; Turi, she said, was safe in the company of Daj and Estrella.

'But the children need water,' she croaked out in a voice as dry as dust. 'We all do.'

Some of the Avari were surprised to learn that we had brought children with us, for Sunji had not yet had time to inform them of this. One old warrior, as tall as I, shook his head disapprovingly as he said, 'Children drink water even more quickly than a hot wind.'

Liljana, I thought, was ready to walk over and rip free the water-skin from the back of the warrior's horse. Then she espied the captured priest, and her whole body shuddered with revulsion. 'I *know* you – you were there that day in the throne room! *You* put the irons in the fire, the ones they used to burn Master Juwain! You were only a guard, then, filthy torturer!'

The priest looked up at her and said, 'Lord Morjin rewards those who serve him. Just as he does those who oppose him. I regret only that he didn't use the pincers to tear out *your* filthy tongue and that I won't live to see how he rewards you. But at least I had the pleasure of seeing him blind the scryer.'

Although Atara said nothing to this, I felt a cold rage building inside her. She stood orienting her blindfold toward the sound of his voice.

'If I had pincers, now,' he said, 'and my hands were free, I would gladly tear off her –'

Kane, stepping quickly over to him, delivered a vicious kick to his mouth, for a moment silencing him. The priest sat there almost choking on blood and broken teeth.

Sunji moved over to Kane and grabbed his arm to keep him from further assaulting the priest. He told him, 'This poisoner has helped kill my warriors, and his punishment is for the Avari to mete out.'

'So, we have grievances, too, as you have heard.'

'Would you kill him so easily then?'

'No, not *easily*,' Kane said. 'We have grievances, yes, but even more we have questions that must be answered.'

'You may ask all the questions you wish,' Maidro said to him, 'after we have given the poisoner to the sun.'

As Maidro explained, the Ravirii tribes, even the Avari, punished well-poisoners by staking them out naked beneath the blazing desert sun.

'It is a terrible death,' Maidro said to Kane.

'Terrible, yes,' Kane said. 'But the pain of it is spread out over too many hours. It would be better if this priest were made to take his own medicine. Hot irons would roast him just as well and loosen his tongue more readily!'

'Kane!' I said to him, hating the dark lights that filled up his eyes. I felt this darkness inside myself, and hated it even more.

'So, Val – what would you have us do then? The priest might be able to tell us if the droghul spoke of things. The droghul might have known what Morjin knows, eh? It would be folly, I say, to lead the *next* droghul straight to the Maitreya.'

'No,' I said to him, remembering my vow, 'no more torture.'

'But what if the third droghul,' he persisted, 'is waiting for us? What if this priest knows where?'

'And what if he doesn't? Would you have us do this evil thing to him only to achieve no good end?'

Kane stood staring at me, and gave no answer, which was answer enough. Then Master Juwain came forward. He, whose ear opening had been seared by one of Morjin's fire irons, said to Kane, 'If I can bear to see this man spared such torture, so can you.'

Liljana, whose mind Morjin had ravaged, reluctantly agreed with Master Juwain. Then Atara, gathering in all her memories of that terrible day in Argattha, tapped the end of her unstrung bow toward the priest and said, 'He is a torturer, and so it is fitting that he be repaid in kind. He is a crucifier – being staked out beneath the sun is like unto crucifixion, and only what he deserves. Justice is hard. But how are we to restore the world as it should be without justice?'

She spoke legalistically, with steel in her tongue and a cold heart. She seemed as opaque and impenetrable as a block of ice. At that moment, I felt that I could never really know her.

'Justice the poisoner shall have,' Sunji said to us. 'But we are in the desert now, and the desert ways shall prevail. Maidro, what do you say to this?'

'I say stake the poisoner to the sand!' Maidro called out.

'And you, Laisar – what do you say?'

'Stake him, and cut off his eyelids that he might meditate on the sun!'

The Avari, I thought, might be different in some ways from the other Ravirii tribes, but they were still a cruel, hard people.

I stood over the bound Red Priest, who tried to show brave but quaked inside with a terrible fear. If I let these people torture him, how would I be any different *from* him? This question enraged me, for I felt myself caught in an inescapable trap. I burned to put fire to the priest even more badly than did Kane; I wanted to know what he knew. Even more, I wanted that he should suffer as Master Juwain and Atara had suffered. I hated the One that had created a world of such evil need and vengeance – almost as much as I feared what might befall if we let the priest keep his silence.

'No,' I said again, drawing my sword, 'no torture!'

The three Avari warriors who guarded the priest angled their sabers toward me. I wondered if I could cut down all of them before one of them managed to put his sword into my armorless body.

'He is *our* captive!' Sunji called to me. 'He and his kind have killed my warriors! And foully killed the Masud at their well!'

I felt him grieving for his dead tribesmen; I had overheard one of the Avari say that he had lost a cousin and a nephew to the Zuri's swords. I gazed at Sunji, and at Yago. And I said to them, 'You have lost kinsmen and friends to the Red Dragon's poisoned claws, and the pain of such loss cannot be measured in numbers. But I have lost much, too. Four thousand of my countrymen died upon the Culhadosh Commons. All my brothers. Asaru, the greatest knight in our land, took a lance through his chest so that I might live. I have promised to join him in the stars rather than allow what he would have died a thousand times to prevent.'

I stood with my sword held back behind my head. Out of the side of my eye, I caught a gleam of glorre blazing as brightly as the sun. I felt as wild as a thousand suns. I was ready to stand against all the Avari warriors staring at me in awe, and if need be, all the armies of the Red Dragon.

Sunji finally could not bear looking at me. I knew that he did not want any more of his warriors to die; curiously, I sensed that he likewise did not want them to kill me. He turned to Yago and said, 'Masud – this stranger brings strange sentiments into our land. But it was your tribesmen, too, that the poisoner killed. And so I must ask you, too: what do you say?'

Shawls still covered the heads of the Avari, so it was difficult to guess what they looked like, but I thought it impossible that their faces could be any harder than Yago's face, with its harsh planes, knife-blade of a nose and thin lips set together like stone. I knew that he wanted to call for the Red Priest to die in the most painful way possible. And yet he hesitated before speaking. He looked at me. As I met his gaze, I couldn't help remembering how other Red Priests had staked my mother and grandmother to wood. I could still feel the agony of the nails burning through my own hands. I couldn't help wishing that no one would ever have to die this way again. Yago looked at me for a long time before he turned to answer Sunji's question.

'The punishment for well-poisoning is everywhere known,' he said. 'And yet there is another punishment, much older and less well-known. My great-grandfather told me of this: that in the old days well-poisoners were made to drink their own poison.'

'That is not told among the Avari,' Sunji said. He looked at the green bottle that Laisar still held, with great care, as he might a scorpion. Sunji continued, 'But it seems to me a just punishment. Fifteen of my warriors are wounded and must be taken back to my father's hadrah to be cared for. I do not care to linger here fighting off the vultures and hyenas until the poisoner manages to die.'

He took counsel with Laisar and Maidro, who agreed to Yago's proposition. Sunji bowed his head to me. Then he ordered the priest's bonds untied, and gave him the bottle of poison with his own hand. He stepped back quickly. Twenty Avari warriors stood around aiming stones at the priest's head in case he should attempt any treachery, such as throwing the poison at those who had condemned him to death.

The priest, however, was not that brave. Taking even the worst poison would be better than being staked out in the sun. With a trembling hand, the priest pulled open the bottle's cork stopper. He had to fight to bring the bottle up to his lips. And then, as I watched in horror, he threw back his head and drained the bottle in three huge gulps.

Compared to the other deaths planned for him, this one was merciful. And yet no death, I thought, was easy. Almost immediately, the priest's chest began working violently as he struggled for breath and his lips turned blue. He screamed like a dog crushed beneath a wagon's wheels. Tremors ripped through his whole body; as I watched, these intensified into such terrible convulsions that

I heard his bones begin to snap. Blood ran from his nose; he coughed and vomited bright red blood, and then stopped moving. He lay in the dirt whimpering in agony.

Before anyone could stop me, I raised up my sword and rushed forward. I stabbed the point of it into the back of the priest's neck, killing him instantly. I would never be sure whether I did this out of pity or hatred for a man who had helped torture Master Juwain and Atara.

None of the Avari objected to my hastening his end. The sight of the priest dying had sickened them, as it had me.

'I really must have some water,' Liljana called out. She stood almost faint by Atara's side, and it seemed the two women practically held each other up. 'I must take water to the children, *now.*'

She looked behind her at a warrior holding a waterskin. And the warrior barked at her: 'Avari water is for the Avari!'

Liljana dropped Atara's hand, and she began walking toward one of the riderless Zuri's horses to appropriate the waterskin slung on its back. But another warrior blocked her way, saying, 'The Zuri's water belongs to the Avari, too, as payment for the lives they took.'

Liljana, now furious, stalked straight up to Sunji and shouted, 'What is wrong with you? We've been without water a whole day! The children are suffering the worst of it! They'll *die* without water!'

Laisar, the old judge of the Avari, looked at Sunji a moment before turning back to Liljana. He shrugged his shoulders and said, 'They will die anyway. That is the law.'

'Law? What law?' Maram bellowed out. Until now, the priest's terrible death had driven him into silence. 'For mercy's sake, give us a little water!'

The Avari warriors, seeing Maram's oozing sores, drew back from him as from a leper. Then Sunji said to him, 'It is our way to kill those who enter our land uninvited, and it is a mercy that we haven't put you to the sword, for you have brought here only death.'

'Kill me then!' Maram said, pulling open his tunic in order to expose his hairy, much-bitten chest. 'Put your sword through my heart – it will be more merciful than making me die of thirst!'

At first, Sunji said nothing as to Maram's histrionics. Then he sighed out: 'The desert is hard, and so are our laws.'

Maram made no reply to this as he stood gripping his red crystal in his hand.

'The desert is hard,' Sunji repeated, 'and you are soft. You sweat more than a horse. You wear garments that invite the sun to steal your water.'

'Then let us have these robes of the Zuri,' Maram said. 'Give us water, and we'll leave your lands as quickly as we can.'

'To go where?' Sunji asked. 'If we gave you water, would you let the Masud guide you back the way you came, out of the desert?'

'No,' I said, hoping that I spoke for Maram. 'We must go on.'

'To find this Maitreya that you told of?'

'Yes, he,' I said. I stared toward the canyon's mouth, toward the west. 'He is out there, somewhere.'

'Foolish pilgrims,' Sunji said to me. 'I know nothing of this Maitreya, but much of the desert. You cannot cross the Zuri's lands, not now that you have helped kill the Zuri. Tatuk will be awaiting his warriors' return, and when he sees you instead, he'll stake *you* to the sand to make you tell what has happened here. The Red Priests, as you call them, have made a slave of Tatuk, I think. I think the Priests have also poisoned the minds of the Vuai in the south, and so you can't go that way either.'

'Then there must be another way,' I said to him. 'Help us.'

Sunji hesitated as he stared at me, but Laisar shook his head at this and said, 'All other ways, you'll find only death. And so helping you would only be a waste of water.'

'At least,' I said, looking at Liljana 'let us take a little water to the children. Whatever our foolishness, you shouldn't condemn them.'

But it wasn't to be that we took water to the children. It was they who brought it to us. As Sunji stood off a few paces conferring with Laisar and Maidro, I overheard one of them murmur, '. . . no water. The dead are the dead.' Just then, Liljana noticed Daj, Turi and Estrella hurrying down through the ravine toward us. She opened her mouth to scold them for disobeying her and not remaining in the rocks above. She closed her mouth a moment later. For she saw what we all saw: the children each bore water-skins, wet on the outside and sloshingly full of water.

The Avari warriors stood watching in puzzlement as the children made their way past the bodies of the dead straight toward us. The warriors' black, hard eyes told of their suspicion that we had lied to them about our need for water. And then Daj, in his high, piping boy's voice called out: 'Val! Liljana! Master Juwain! Estrella found water!'

The children came up to us, and the whole company of Avari warriors gathered around. The children, having already drunk their fill, gave waterskins first to Atara and Liljana, and then to Maram, Master Juwain, Kane and me. Turi seemed proud to slap one of these wet leather bags into his father's hands. So astonished were the Avari at this turn of events that none of them, not even Laisar or Maidro, thought to object that we were still drinking their water.

'They say she found water,' one of the Avari in the circle around us murmured. 'The girl did, in the rocks above.'

'Impossible,' another warrior said. 'There is no water in these hills.'

'There is water in those skins – where did it come from then?'

After we had all had a deep drink of water, we passed the water-skins to the thirsty Avari so that they might drink, too. Then Sunji asked Estrella to show him where she had found the water. She led us back up through the ravine. We passed over the shelf of rocks where our horses stood and then scrambled up the rocky slope behind it. With quick, lively gestures, Estrella pointed out a dark opening in the side of the hill. Daj explained that in their search for water, Estrella had found a crack in the rocks, which the children had excavated into this hole.

'It's a cave,' Daj said, pointing into the opening. 'It leads down to the water.'

The opening was just barely large enough to let a single man squeeze through it. Estrella led the way into the cave, and we followed. Maram declined this new adventure. As he said, 'In Argattha I went deep into the bowels of the earth, and never again.' Many of the Avari shared his sentiments, and waited outside with him. So did Atara. Whatever wonders the cave held, she would not be able to look upon them.

Estrella led us down through a tube of rock that opened out and up the deeper in we went. Master Juwain pointed out patches of goldish-red lichen growing on the walls and ceiling, and marveled that they seemed to give off a soft, glowing light. This radiance barely sufficed to illuminate the pendants of rock hanging down from the ceiling and the pinnacles rising up from the floor. Master Juwain identified the rock as limestone.

We felt the presence of water before we saw or heard it, for as we descended the air grew ever more humid. Estrella practically ran down and around a bend in the rock, and then drew up short where the cave dead-ended in what seemed a pool of water. But its rushing sound and the movement of the air above gave me to perceive that it was really an underground stream. I knelt down by its edge, and cupped my hands into it. I drank this water; it was cool and sweet, just like the water the children had brought to us.

'It is a *river* of water!' Laisar cried out. 'All glory in the One!'

He knelt down to drink of it, with Maidro and Sunji. Sunji had brought along a dry waterskin, which he now filled. He stood up and looked at Estrella in awe.

'The girl found water,' he said, 'and brought us to it.'

'Udra Mazda,' Laisar intoned, gazing at Estrella. 'All glory in the One.'

'Udra Mazda,' Maidro repeated, bowing to Estrella.

Sunji explained that this strange name meant Water Bringer or Water Maker; among the Avari, no one else was so revered, not even their king.

'You have brought much death with you,' Sunji said to me. 'But also much life.'

He smiled as he pointed down into the darkly gleaming river flowing past us. 'That is life for a thousand Avari.'

In order to drink, Sunji and his two judges had opened their shawls. I could now see their faces, and I marveled at what I beheld: their long noses, broad brows and the stark bones of their cheeks and chins seemed cut out of the same mold as the faces of the Valari. Their eyes were as my eyes. The signs had been there from the first, but I had been too thirsty and too full of dread of battle to see them. Their names recalled those of my dead countrymen: Avram, Laisu and Sunjay. And my brother, Mandru. Avari sounded nearly like Valari, and I suddenly knew that we had come across one of the lost tribes of my people.

As I stared at Sunji, he remarked upon this resemblance that he had noticed in Kane and me from the first, saying, 'When I saw you, Valashu, I wondered if one of my tribesmen might once have sired a child stolen away into another land. And so with Kane. There is a mystery here that I would like to understand. It is written that all men shall be as brothers. I would wish this of you and Kane. And Master Juwain and the boy, too – even the fat one. The women shall be our sisters. And the girl, Estrella, you call her, the Udra Mazda. For the time, at least, you shall all be of the Avari. And then we shall help you cross the desert.'

He did not confer with Maidro or Laisar in this decision, for their bright, black eyes gleamed with their consent. He dipped his hand into the river and used the water to wash the dust from my forehead. Then he clasped his wet hand against mine.

'You must tell me of your homeland,' he said to me. 'You must tell me of your people that you call Valari.'

Then, with a smile, gripping his newly-filled waterskin, he turned to walk up back through the cave and show *his* people the great treasure that Estrella had found.

23

Later that afternoon, with the day's heat finally escaping the earth's hold on it, we said goodbye to Yago and Turi. They would set out for the Masud's country and the hadrahs in the south where most of his tribe was encamped.

'I must tell Rodaj of what has happened here,' he said to me as he readied his horse for the journey. It turned out that he was one of the Masud chief's many nephews, and he knew Rodaj well. 'He will want to know that the Red Priests have poisoned the Zuri and Vuai – and I don't mean their wells.'

'Tell him also,' I said to him, 'to keep watch over the gap in the mountains by which we came into the desert. There you will find many stone statues. One day the Red Dragon will send soldiers through it.'

'Thank you, Valashu Elahad, for giving such consideration to the people of a tribe you hardly know.'

'I know you,' I told him.

'And I know you. It has been a pleasure fighting by your side.'

We clasped hands, and in his honest, brutal way, he added, 'I don't think you will live to return from out of the desert, but if you do, I shall ask my uncle to command that you'll be welcome in the Masud's lands.'

'Thank you,' I said.

'Thank *you* for helping me to avenge my tribesmen. It was the best thing I have ever done, cutting off that Morjin thing's head!'

With that he smiled grimly, and mounted his horse. He watched as Turi made his farewells to Daj and Estrella. Then they turned to ride back down through the canyon and out into the glowing red desert beyond.

We lingered a little longer. With the crisis of pursuit and battle behind us, Maram complained that his wounds hurt with particular acuteness. His sores, he said, burned as if someone had rubbed salt into them, and worse: 'Ah, it's as if something is eating into them – something is *moving* there, I can feel it!'

Master Juwain ordered him to remove his tunic, and this he did. He stood naked like a mountain of hairy white flesh. In the strong, clear light of the sun, we immediately saw what ailed him: it seemed that the flies had gotten to a dozen of his sores where his bandages had come loose, laying eggs there. The eggs must have recently hatched, for now his sores swarmed with little, squirming maggots.

'Oh, Lord!' Maram bellowed out, shaking his arms and legs and hopping about madly as if to shake loose the maggots. 'Get them off me!'

His shouts drew the attention of many Avari, who gathered around. Master Juwain laid his hand on Maram's shoulder to calm him, and said, 'We should let these creatures alone. They will eat the dead flesh and clean your wounds.'

'I don't care!' Maram bellowed again. 'I won't live like this! I can feel these worms eating me alive, and it's driving me mad!'

His frantic pleas finally persuaded Master Juwain to debride his sores with a scalpel and tweezers. One of the Avari took pity on Maram and produced a fresh bit of cloth that Master Juwain cut up into bandages. It wasn't enough to bind all of Maram's sores, but it would keep the flies out of the most serious of them.

'This is worse than the Vardaloon,' Maram said to me as he shooed away a couple of buzzing flies. 'We always knew that accursed wood would have an end, but it seems the desert goes on forever.'

Later that afternoon, when the Avari had finished burying their dead, they filled all their waterskins from the river that Estrella had discovered. They helped the wounded onto their horses and drew up in a loose formation. My friends and I, now swathed in the robes of the fallen Avari warriors, gathered near the front, for Sunji had invited us to ride with him. We set out into the dusk, with the first stars appearing in the heavens like countless glittering grains of sand.

It was Sunji's intention that we should journey to the Avari's greatest hadrah, which lay a day's ride toward the mountains to the north. There we would rest as long as we wished. There, too, Sunji would take counsel with King Jovayl and the Avari elders as to our best course.

'My father,' he said as we made our way over the darkening desert, 'will honor my pledge to help you. Though when he discovers that the girl is an udra mazda, he will not want to give her up to the desert.'

It was a mystery, he told me, whom the gift of finding water would touch.

'Such a gift is very rare,' he said, 'for an udra mazda is born only once every hundred years.'

He told me that he also wished to solve the mystery of our seeming kinship. As he put it: 'My tribe dwells *in* the desert, and so we are counted as being Ravirii. But we Avari are not like the peoples of the other tribes. The minstrels tell we are not *of* the desert; they sing that the Father of the Avari came here from the stars long, long ago.'

As the night deepened and the horses drove their hooves against the rocky ground, Sunji's account of the Avari's origins convinced me that they were indeed one the lost tribes of the Valari. Vast reaches of time and isolation here in the desert, though, had done their work upon the Avari's collective memory: the facts of history had degenerated into legend, and legend had become myth. According to the story that Sunji told me, the Father of the Avari had descended to earth riding upon the back of a fiery mare named Ea. It had been told that here on this barren world, called the Ar Ratham, or the Wrath of the One, the Father of the Avari would find the golden cup that would restore the desert to life and keep it from spreading to devour the whole of the world.

'After many years of searching over the dunes and across the burning sands,' Sunji told me, 'the Father of the Avari did indeed find the Kal Urna, which had been hidden in a cave. Upon drinking of its cool waters, the burning veils of mirage were lifted from his eyes, and he saw the world as it might be. He saw his mare, Ea, as she really was, and he gave her to drink of the waters of the Kal Urna. At once, the fires consuming her were put out, and Ea stood revealed as a beautiful woman. So happy was she to be restored to herself that she wept whole rivers of tears. These fell upon the desert's hadrahs, and there trees grew. But they were not enough to turn the desert green; only the Kal Urna held so much water. The Father of the Avari and Ea went forth to bring this sacred water everywhere. But then a man of one of the Ravirii tribes, in his cursed covetousness, cast his evil eyes upon the golden cup. His name was Ar Yun, which means the Cursed One. Ar Yun stole the golden cup from the Father of the Avari. It is said that a sandstorm sent by the One ate the flesh off his bones, and the Kal Urna was lost.'

As we rode past dark clumps of ursage and bitterbroom forcing their way up through the cracked earth, Maidro and Laisar pressed their horses in close to hear this telling of the Avari's ancient story. Daj and Estrella rode next to me, and they seemed eager to hear more. So did Kane. His eyes, beneath the cowl wrapped around his face, gleamed in the starlight.

'After that,' Sunji went on, 'the Father of the Avari took Ea as his wife, and she gave birth to our people. For generation after generation, the Avari have gone into the desert to search for the Kal Urna. It is said that one day, a great Udra Mazda born of the Avari will restore the sands to new life.'

I caught Sunji gazing at Estrella as if in hope that she might be this Udra Mazda. But he shook his head, for it was obvious that whatever people Estrella claimed as her own, she had not been born of the Avari.

I said to Sunji, 'What was the name of the Father of the Avari?'

'We call him Ar Raha, the Beloved of the One.'

I smiled and then told him of the history recorded by *my* people: of how Elahad had brought the Lightstone to Ea, only to be murdered by his brother, Aryu. Aryu, I said, had then stolen the golden cup and fled with it into the west. Elahad's son, Arahad, had led a vain search for Aryu and the Lightstone that had lasted a hundred years. When Arahad and his followers failed to find it, their descendants at last settled in the Morning Mountains under the leadership of Shavashar, Arahad's son and king of the Valari.

'It must be,' I told him, 'that your people were sons and daughters of Arahad, too, who remained in the desert. And so the Avari and the Valari are as one.'

From the back of his horse, Sunji regarded me as we rode across the starlit earth.

'Think of the names,' I told him. 'Ea. Ar Raha and Arahad; Ar Yun and Aryu – these are nearly the same, are they not?'

Sunji admitted that they were, then added, 'And your people's story is nearly the same as my people's. It is a pity, though, that many parts of it have been misremembered and come down to you as only myths.'

I smiled again, and was glad for the shawl that hid my face. I said to Sunji, 'Both our accounts, at least, tell that the Lightstone will restore the world to new life.'

'I do not know, Valaysu,' he said to me. 'Can the Lightstone really be the Kal Urna? I think perhaps this golden cup of yours is only one of your gelstei made after the image of the Kal Urna.'

'That is because you have not held it in your hands and beheld the stars shimmering inside it.'

'To see is to know,' he said to me as his eyes gleamed. 'And I would like to know the truth about this Lightstone of yours and the Maitreya. I will ponder what you have told me, and take counsel with my father and the elders when we reach Hadr Halona.'

This was the name of the Avari's greatest hadrah. After a long night's ride through rugged terrain that took us ever higher, with the Avari warriors and the confiscated Zuri horses strung out in a long line across the rocky desert, we came to this place of water just before dawn. The Avari had made a home for thousands of their people in a five-mile wide break between the mountains. The Hadr Halona proved to be more of a small city than an encampment. Although many woolen tents had been pitched around springs and the single lake, many houses had also been built of stone. As Sunji told me, these had walls ten feet thick and cellars dug thirty feet deep, down into the ground where it was always cool, even in the blazing heat of summer. But even the tent-dwellers found life within the hadrah more pleasant than in the open desert. It was higher here, and therefore cooler. The towering peaks above the hadrah held snow for at least part of the year, and gave this water to the Avari in streams that filled the lake. But most blessed of all were the hadrah's many trees: mostly the gnarled sakur trees that bloomed yearly with pretty pink flowers and gave a succulent fruit called a kammat. According to Laisar, it was a crime punishable by disembowelment to cut the sacred sakur trees for wood.

As we made our way down into the hadrah, sentinels standing on rocky prominences blew horns to announce our arrival. A thousand people, it seemed, roused themselves from their beds to come out and greet us. They stood in robes outside of their tents and houses, and lined the dusty lanes as we rode past. We created a great stir in the lives of the Avari, for they rarely welcomed strangers into the hadrah. Then, too, the news of the battle caused many to shout with excitement at the prospect of dividing up the Zuri's horses, swords, clothing and other spoils – and it set off rounds of wailing, too, in those who mourned sons, brothers or fathers killed in battle.

The house of Sunji's father, Jovayl, had been built near the valley's small, single lake. Compared to the houses around it, it rose up like a palace; but compared to the palaces of great kings that I had seen, it was little more than a hut. Its walls were of sandstone, plastered with dried mud and painted white. Slender sandstone pillars twelve feet high held up the tiled roof and fronted the house's porch. There, in the dawn's red light, Jovayl stood waiting to greet us. He was a tall man, like most of his people. Here, in the hadrah, where he had no worry about losing the moisture of his breath to the air, he wore no cowl to cover his face. The deep lines cut into his dark, ivory skin suggested that he had seen more than sixty years. His features were as aquiline as any eagle's, with a great, broken nose and black eyes that darted about in quick assessment as we rode up. He seemed more intelligent than cunning, and less cruel than hard. Sunji told me that the Avari's king was a simple man and a great warrior who had killed sixty-three men in battle.

He saw immediately that my companions and I were all exhausted. He ordered that baths be prepared for us, and food. We were to rest that day, he said, in his house's deepest rooms, set out with urns of cool water, bowls of fruit, flowers and fresh linens. Then, in a harsh, old voice like grinding stones, he told us, 'Tonight we will sit at feast and listen to the story of the Poisoner with the Voice of Ice and the Udra Mazda.'

We had no trouble heeding his command. The hospitality of King Jovayl's house afforded us the first real comfort we had known since leaving the Brotherhood's school many miles and many days before. In a steamy stone room in the back of King Jovayl's house, we washed the dust and grime from our bodies; then outside on the porch we filled ourselves with good food. We lay down to rest in dark, quiet rooms. When evening came, servants brought us robes woven of virgin lamb's wool. They were King Jovayl's gift to us, and we were to wear them to the feast.

This commenced at sunset, upstairs in the great room of King Jovayl's house. We joined King Jovayl's wife, Adri, and Sunji and young Daivayr in a sort of windowless hall hung with brightly-worked tapestries of cotton, which proved to be the Avari's most precious cloth. Other guests included Laisar and Maidro, and four other elders even more ancient. Three well-seasoned men – captains like Sunji – arrived, too, and their names were Arthayn, Noldayn and Ramji. We all sat on cushions arrayed in a great circle on top of a white woolen carpet. A small table, carved out of stone, was set in front of each of us. King Jovayl sat to the north, beneath a tapestry woven with silver swans and stars. I nearly wept to see this beautiful thing appearing as if by the magic of fate here in the middle of the desert.

We ate roasted lamb and kid, the fattest of King Jovayl's flocks. The Avari grew wheat on irrigated land, and so we had bread as well, stuffed with bits of garlic, onions and nuts, and hot from the ovens. With reverence, King Jovayl passed around a bowl of salt to sprinkle on these meats and breads. There were cheeses, too, and figs, oranges and the plump red fruit called a kammat. The Avari did not drink blood, as their enemies told, but they did celebrate with wine, and to Maram's delight, beer. His happiness in discovering these beverages being passed around the circle, however, lasted only as long as Master Juwain's murmured warning to him: 'Remember your vow!'

Maram sat next to me, and I heard him murmur back: 'In the desert, I nearly died of thirst, and now I'm dying of a different thirst, if you know what I mean. It would be *rude* of me to refuse King Jovayl's gracious hospitality, would it not?'

With a great smile he eagerly held up his silver wine cup.

But when Barsayr, a toothless old man, overheard this conversation, he passed the word to King Jovayl that Maram's vow of abstinence must be respected. And King Jovayl, sitting with his cup full and waiting to make a toast, raised his cup to Maram and called out, 'It takes a brave man to make and keep such a vow, and we all honor you. But you must toast with us, and so you shall have the most honorable of all drinks.'

He then asked one of his daughters, Saira, to fill Maram's cup with mare's milk. When this tall, pretty girl had carried out this request, Maram took a long look at the warm, greasy white liquid in his cup and muttered, 'Milk – it's barbaric to drink an animal's secretions. I might as well be made to drink a horse's saliva or sweat!'

'You didn't object to drinking the Ymanir's kalvaas,' I reminded him.

'That's because it was, ah, fermented. Besides, my sensibilities have grown more refined.'

He smiled politely, though, when King Jovayl lifted up his cup and spoke a requiem in remembrance of the Avari warriors who had fallen in the Battle of the Dragon Rocks, as they named it. After that, other Avari made other toasts: to King Jovayl's guests and to the nighttime sky, and most especially, to the new water that Estrella had found and to Estrella herself.

'It is strange that an udra mazda should come to us from beyond the desert,' King Jovayl said to us. He sat cross-legged on his cushions as he looked at me. 'And strange, too, that you propose to take this girl away from us so soon.'

During the feast, we had told the King as much as we had Sunji and his warriors. For hours, our talk had centered around the news that we brought and the seemingly miraculous things that we told to the Avari. Now it had come time to decide if King Jovayl would help us.

'Valaysu,' he said to me, 'you have told that you seek the one called the Maitreya in the lands across the desert, but you have not said where.'

'Nor can I, sir,' I said. 'It may be that your people will fight other battles with the Red Dragon's priests – if they are captured, the Kallimun know tortures that would make a stone talk.'

King Jovayl frowned at this. 'When I was a young man, these priests tried to establish an embassy here, but my father, Tavayr, had the good sense to send them away. Now, from the Zuri and Vuai, we see what happens when a tribe takes scorpions into its heart.'

He paused to look about, and continued, 'We see as well the wisdom of our elders' elders in turning strangers away from the Avari's country.'

I said nothing to this as I took a long drink of wine.

'Of course,' King Jovayl continued, looking from me to Estrella, 'our laws were made to serve us, and not the reverse, and so exceptions must be made. It is clear that in keeping strangers away we have also denied ourselves news of great and evil things occurring beyond our borders. I had not thought that any outsiders, not even the greatest of kings, could ever send an army into the desert. Now I am not so sure.'

He nodded at Arthayn, a square-faced man with eyes as cool as pools of water. A choker of bright skytones and silver encircled his neck. Arthayn had just returned from the north, where King Jovayl had sent him on a mission to avoid yet another war with the Sudi. Arthayn now gave a report of his journey, telling us: 'I saw none of these Red Priests in the Sudi's hadrah, but I heard talk that the new King of Yarkona wanted to send an embassy of *Kallimun* to the Sudi. I didn't know what that word meant, then. The Sudi believed that if they did not accept this embassy, King Ulanu would send an army down through the Nashthalan into the desert. There was a time when Yarkona was weak, but now it is strong.'

At the look of loathing that fell over Liljana's face at the mention of King Ulanu's name, King Jovayl turned to her and said, 'Do you know of this man?'

'We met him once,' Liljana told him. 'On our road to Argattha. I happened to hold out a sword just as Ulanu – he was only a count then – happened to slice off his nose on the tip of it.'

Although Liljana could not smile, her wry words caused nearly everyone else to smile. Then King Jovayl said to her, 'And you call yourself a pilgrim?'

'Then we *were* truly pilgrims,' she said, 'in quest of the Lightstone. Ulanu killed the best of us – the finest minstrel in the world! – and then nailed him to a cross of wood.'

'And what was this minstrel's name?'

'Alphanderry.'

For the thousandth time, I reflected on the miracle of Flick somehow taking on Alphanderry's face and form. I looked about the room for Flick's twinkling lights, but as always he winked in and out of existence according to a will beyond mine.

'A minstrel,' King Jovayl intoned, 'is the beloved of the One, for his heart sings with the words of the One.'

King Jovayl raised his cup in silent remembrance of our dead companion. Then he said to me, 'I have taken the counsel of our elders. We do not believe that this Lightstone that King Morjin claims can be the Kal Urna. Nor can the Maitreya you seek be the great Udra Mazda – not unless as a child he was once lost to the Avari and taken into the lands outside the desert. And yet we do not have claim upon all wisdom. If we are wrong, the Maitreya must be found and the Lightstone somehow must be taken back. And even if we are right that the Lightstone is only one of these gelstei of yours, King Morjin must be denied the use of it lest he send into the desert even worse things than droghuls. These are strange times, in which strangers can bring an udra mazda to us and new water be found. And so we have decided to help you. But help you *how*?'

'Help us to cross the desert,' I said simply.

'And how will you, strangers from wet lands, do this impossible thing even with our help?' King Jovayl sat on his cushions looking from Liljana to Maram to Daj. 'You cannot cross it to the far north – the way is too long, and the Sudi would kill you if thirst didn't first. Beyond the Sudi are the Idi, five hundred miles from here as the eagle flies, to the northwest. The southern way will take you through the Zuri's or Vuai's country, where the Red Priests will surely be waiting for you now.'

'Perhaps,' Maram said, 'we should then reconsider our plans. Perhaps we should go back through the Masud's country, and then turn far south, through Sunguru.'

'No,' Kane barked out. 'In Sunguru, we'll find hundreds of the bloody Red Priests – and even more acolytes under their command. As well, the armies of King Angand.'

I took a sip of wine, then said to King Jovayl, 'How would the Avari cross the desert then?'

'We wouldn't,' he told me. 'We don't.'

'But don't your minstrels sing that the Avari have gone everywhere in the desert, searching for the Kal Urna?'

'That is true, in ages past, we have gone almost everywhere.'

'Even, then, into the Tar Harath?'

At the mention of this immense hell at the heart of the Red Desert, King Jovayl's face grew hard and full of dread. So did the faces of every other Avari sitting down to dinner. King Jovayl said to me, 'I see the turn of your thoughts, Valaysu. But you cannot hope to cross the Tar Harath. That would be madness. Nothing lives there, not even scorpions or flies. There is no water – only rocks and sand, wind and sun. And then sun, and more sun.'

'Then the Avari never go into the Tar Harath?'

King Jovayl glanced at Sunji before turning back to me. 'We go *into* it, for we are Avari and the desert is ours.'

He told that men of his tribe often journeyed to the Golden Highlands to mine skystone out the rocks there. The deep blue skystone, as King Jovayl told us, was precious to the Avari, for it reminded them of the great vault of the heavens from which the Father of the Valari and Ea had once come. A few intrepid warriors had also ventured deeper into the Tar Harath in search of the fabled salt beds of a dried-up lake. As the Avari tell their children: 'Salt is life.' They usually do not say this of water, for that is too obvious. But in the desert, the salt dissolved in the blood and in the sweat pouring forth from the skin's pores was vital.

'In a thousand years, though, no Avari has ever found these salt beds,' King Jovayl told us. 'Just as no one has ever found water.'

Old Sarald pulled at the folds of flesh beneath his chin as he regarded King Jovayl with a bright, knowing look. King Jovayl took note of this and said to me, 'The eldest of the Avari's judges reminds me that I have not told all: it is said that there is water in the deep desert, though no Avari knows where. You must have heard word of this water yourselves, Valaysu.'

'No, we have not,' I said to him. 'Why would you think that?'

'Why, because when Sunji first questioned you, you admitted that you sought the Well of Restoration. That is the name of the water said to lie within the Tar Harath.'

I stared at King Jovayl in amazement. The inspiration for our story that we were pilgrims seeking the Well of Restoration had come from Maram one night on the Wendrush while he was deep into his third horn of beer. It seemed too incredible a coincidence that this name had just popped into his head, as he had claimed. When I turned to him now and caught his eye with a questioning look, he murmured to me: 'Ah, I must have been touched by the spirit of the One. Do you see *now* the value of brandy and beer? Why do you think they're called *spirits*?'

I tried not to smile at this as King Jovayl called out to him from the front of the room: 'What are saying, Prince Maram? Speak louder so that we all can hear you!'

'Ah, I was *saying* that you must be right, Wise King, that it would be madness for us to seek this Well of Restoration that even the hardiest of your warriors has not been able to find.'

Now I stared more intently at Maram, letting him feel my great desire to journey on.

'Ah, and that is *why*,' Maram continued, 'we must try to cross the Tar Harath after all – we're all mad, as you must have guessed, even to have come this far.'

Now I couldn't help smiling, nor could King Jovayl or Sunji or even Old Sarald and many others sitting at their little tables. King Jovayl nodded at Maram. 'It may be that only a madman could survive in the Tar Harath. And yet there is a chance for others to survive, one chance only. It may be that the udra mazda could lead you to this water.'

All eyes in the room now turned toward Estrella. This slight girl, with her dark curls and dreamy eyes, sat between Atara and Liljana, eating an orange. She seemed unused to people expecting such great and even miraculous things of her. And yet I knew that she expected great things of herself. What these might be, however, I thought that she could not say, not even to herself.

She put down her orange rind, and looked at me. Her eyes shone like dark, quiet pools. She seemed to have a rare sense of herself, and something more. She nodded her head to me. She smiled, then turned to bow to King Jovayl, too.

'It would be cruel to take this child, or any child, into the Tar Harath,' King Jovayl said to us. 'And yet your way has been nothing but cruel. That the udra mazda chooses this freely is a great thing.

376

We have drunk to her finding water; now let us drink to her finding such great courage.'

He commanded that everyone's cup be refilled again. Maram tried not to show his disgust at the prospect of have to swallow yet more warm milk. Estrella and Daj both seemed delighted to see their cups filled with wine – as far as I knew, their first taste of it.

'To Estrella!' King Jovayl said. 'May the One's light always point her way toward water!'

We all drank deeply then – all of us except the children, as Liljana permitted them a few sips of wine but no more. King Jovayl then called for an end to the feast and commanded that we should go to take our rest.

'Even with an udra mazda to guide you,' he said to me, 'a journey across the Tar Harath will be a desperate chance. I cannot supply you with men, horses and water until I have conferred with the Elders more. So go, rest – tonight and tomorrow. And then tomorrow night, I shall give you my answer.'

My companions and I went down to our rooms then, but I did not sleep very well because I shared a room with Maram, and he slept poorly. Despite his exhaustion, he kept moaning as he tossed and turned in his bed, struggling to find a position that did not put pressure on his sores. He grumbled and cursed and finally fell into oblivion vowing that he would never ogle another woman again.

But the next day, late in the morning, I found him outside leaning back against an orange tree near one of the hadrah's springs. He sat in the shade of this fragrant-smelling tree as he used a shard of a broken pot to scratch at his sores. He watched the children at play: with swords and dolls, and kicking a leather ball across the dusty square. He watched the Avari women, too. They came and went to draw water from the spring. They cast us looks of both curiosity and suspicion, and then hurried away.

'Ah, these Avari woman are as comely as those of the Morning Mountains,' Maram said to me as he fixed his gaze on a young matron bending over the walled-off spring. 'At least, I *think* they are – who can really tell with those ugly robes and shawls of theirs?'

'I thought that women no longer interested you,' I said to him.

'Did I say that? No, no, my friend, it is *I* who do not interest *them*. In truth, I think I repulse them. And who can blame them? I think they would rather take a leper into their arms.'

He scratched the edge of his potsherd across one of his bandages. After sniffing at this stained white wrapping, his face fell into a mask of disgust. He shooed away the buzzing flies then let loose a long, deep sigh.

'Master Juwain,' I said to him, 'worries because your wounds are not healing as they should. He believes it would be best for you to rest here.'

'A year would not be too long,' he said. 'That is, if I could just engage one of these women in a little, ah, conversation. And if not for these damn flies.'

His hand beat the air in front of his face as he tried to snatch up and crush one of the black flies bedeviling him. But he might as well have tried to grasp the wind.

'Master Juwain,' I said to him, 'believes that it might be best for you to *remain* here.'

'Remain here?' he said to me. 'And watch the rest of you go on without me?'

I said nothing as I watched him scratch at his bitten leg.

'Ah, do you think I haven't thought about it?' he said to me. 'I don't suppose these Avari would deny me wine, though they'll keep their women away from me as they would silk from a pig.'

He made a fist and punched out at a particularly large, loud fly. Then he said, 'The truth is, though, no matter how drunk I tried to remain, I couldn't get away from these damn bloody flies. Unless I go with you into the Tar Harath, where there are no flies, if King Jovayl is right. Then too . . .'

'Yes?'

'Then, too, I could never desert you.' He dropped his potsherd and clapped me on the shoulder. 'Haven't I told you that a hundred times?'

We traded smiles, then he said to me, 'In any case, King Jovayl might decide not to help us. Then we'll have the merry little choice between giving up our quest or going into the Tar Harath anyway where we'll die.'

I knew that he hoped for a good reason to give up our quest – and perhaps even longed for death to end his sufferings. But that evening, King Jovayl, according to his promise, sent us word of his decision. Sunji found me outside King Jovayl's house as I sat on a large rock and gazed out at the stars.

'You shall have my father's help in crossing the Tar Harath,' he told me. 'I, myself, am to lead three of our warriors and twenty horses to carry water across the sands.'

'Thank you,' I told him. 'The Avari are generous. And kind.'

'Sometimes we are. But some of the elders, I must tell you, spoke against this journey. They do not believe this Maitreya you hope to find really exists.'

'And you?'

'I have *seen* that Morjin thing you call a droghul. If such creatures of dark exist, why not a being of great light?'

Why not indeed? I wondered as I watched the bright stars.

'The elders,' he went on, 'believe that we Avari can live here as we have almost forever, keeping strangers away. But my father does not, and I do not. I believe that we will have to fight this new enemy, or die. Or worse: watch the world die.'

I clasped hands with him then and smiled sadly. Sunji, descended from Elahad and Arahad, was of Valari blood, even as I was. It seemed that it was the fate of our people ever to fight against the evil that Morjin and Angra Mainyu had made – that is, when we weren't busy fighting each other.

Sunji pointed at the dark line of hills against the glowing sky to the west. He said to me, 'I went into the deep desert once, and promised myself I never would again. But life is strange, is it not?'

Yes, life *was* strange and precious, I told myself as I watched the play of lights that pointed the way to the Tar Harath. We might yet come to death there, or anywhere, but for the time being at least our quest to find the Maitreya would go on.

24

For four days my companions and I rested at the Avari's hadrah. We ate good food and enjoyed good conversation, even as Maram bemoaned his wounds that wouldn't heal and beat away the biting black flies. King Jovayl sent out warriors and horses heavily laden with water into the west. The only well between the hadrah and the Tar Harath lay sixty miles toward the setting sun; no one knew whether or not at this time of year it would prove to be dry. As we learned when the warriors returned, the well *was* dry. And so the warriors had left a cache of water at the well. It wouldn't be enough to get us across the Tar Harath, but it would help us replenish the water that we brought with us.

Hours before dawn on the twenty-third of Soldru, a day that promised to be as hot as any that summer, all who would be journeying into the Tar Harath gathered by the springs. We filled our waterskins and slung them on the backs of our horses. The packhorses, of course, carried much more water than did our mounts and remounts – unless one considered that Altaru and Fire and our other old friends carried *us*, who were mostly water. I nearly wept when I learned of the Avari's plan for the horses, which was cruel: their packhorses would be given barely enough water to keep them alive. And then, if no additional water was found, as we and our mounts drank our precious water and lightened the packhorses' burdens waterskin by waterskin until nothing remained, the Avari would have to kill the now-useless horses to spare them from a worse death. As I had been told more than once: the ways of the desert were hard.

'If the worst befalls,' Sunji said to me, 'we'll have to reserve our water for ourselves and let our mounts go without. Not that this will save us for long, for if our mounts die, then *we* will die.'

In the quiet of the dark, with night's cold practically freezing us, I placed my hands over Altaru's ears so that my great stallion wouldn't have to hear such terrible words. I stroked his long neck and whispered to him: 'Don't worry, old friend, I won't let you be thirsty. You shall have water first before I drink, and if I must, I'll give you my own.'

He nickered in understanding, if not of my words, then of the bond of brotherhood that had taken us from land to land and battle to battle.

Sunji had chosen companions from his own tribe to go with us: Arthayn and a younger man named Nuradayn, whose black eyes burned with a desire to please his prince and do great things. Nuradayn seemed all whipcord muscle and quick, almost violent motions that blew out of the center of him like a whirlwind. I thought he might be impulsive or even wild, whereas I knew that Sunji's third companion was the opposite. This was Maidro. It surprised me that Sunji would choose an old man for such a difficult venture, but as Sunji told me: 'He is as hard as a rock and wiser in the ways of the desert than any man I know, even my father.'

When it came time for us to set out, King Jovayl rode up to the springs with his queen, Adri, and their two other children, Daivayr and Saira. They kept their farewell to Sunji brief. I overheard King Jovayl say to Sunji: 'Help Valaysu and his people to cross the desert, but do not go any farther than you must, and return as soon as you can. May the One always lead you to water.'

We assembled in a formation with Sunji and Maidro in the lead, followed by my companions and me, and then the packhorses, whom Arthayn and Nuradayn watched over. We made our way out of the hadrah as we had come, past the sentinels standing on high rocks. This time, in the deep of night before dawn, they did not blow their horns. I couldn't help wondering if Sunji and his warriors would ever return out of the Tar Harath to be heralded as the brave men they truly were.

Sunji led us on a course that wound through a series of low, rocky hills. In the near dark, we moved slowly lest one of the horses bruise a hoof and draw up lame. If a horse grew *too* lame, we would have kill it, and so come that much closer to killing our chances of success – as well as ourselves.

Just before dawn Flick made one of his mysterious appearances. Our four Avari companions marveled at his twinkling lights, and we explained as much as we knew of this luminous being. Maidro

381

took this as a good omen, saying, 'Look – Valaysu brings the very stars with him!'

An hour later the sun rose, and cast long shadows ahead of us against the gritty, hardpacked earth. Here, in the country near the hadrah, many things lived: ursage and bitterbroom, spike grass and soap grass, all glazed with a sticky, whitish alkali. Ostrakats ran across the desert on their two powerful legs chasing lizards and snakes, and even rabbits. We heard the roar of the distant lions who sometimes chased them. Other birds – the smaller sandrunners and rock sparrows – hunted beetles, grasshoppers and other insects. I was curious to lay eyes upon a strange creature that supposedly lived in these hills. Maidro called it a baboon, and said that the males protected their harems and young from the hyenas by the mere display of their hideous blue and red faces.

As we made our way west, the desert grew drier. The ursage and rockgrass thinned out, leaving the horses little forage. Soon they would have to subsist on the grain that the packhorses carried, along with the water. It was not good for the horses to go without grass, but there was no help for it. I prayed that in the Tar Harath, they wouldn't grow so hungry and maddened by thirst that they tried to eat sand.

After only a few hours into this leg of our journey, I noticed that Maram was having a very hard time of things. Every lurch and jolt against his saddle tormented him; he bit his own lip against the pain of his sores to keep from making complaint. Only the barbark nuts that he chewed, I thought, and some fierce inner fire kept him going.

He did not want to arise from our midday break; I felt him almost flogging himself to drive his great, afflicted body forward. That night, with the wind driving fine particles of grit into our mouths and eyes, he dismounted and collapsed down onto the warm ground. He ate the food that Liljana prepared for him with little enthusiasm. I knew that he was close to giving up hope.

Seeing this, I took Master Juwain aside and said to him, 'Maram is failing.'

'I'm afraid he is,' Master Juwain said to me. 'I don't know how to help him. All my ointments and medicines have availed not at all.'

'There is one medicine we might try.'

Master Juwain cast me a knowing and censorious look, and said, 'Do you mean the brandy? It would do nothing to heal him.'

'It wouldn't heal his body,' I admitted. 'But if we can strengthen his spirit, it might help him bear the grievances to his body.'

Master Juwain thought about this and smiled sadly. 'Why else would brandy be called "spirits"?'

'Just so,' I said, smiling too.

'I don't know,' Master Juwain said. 'If Maram had fallen into an icy river, and we had pulled him out and sat him by a fire, well, yes – then a tot of brandy might warm him. But I'm afraid that here in the desert it would serve only to parch him even more.'

'Only a tot, sir. And if that is too much, then just a taste. It can't parch him any more than this damn, dry wind.'

Master Juwain finally agreed to my proposal. He himself dug out one of the brandy bottles and measured a few drams of it into Maram's cup. When he approached Maram with it, Maram sat up and brightened like a boy on his birthday. As his hand closed around the cup, he cried out to Master Juwain, 'Oh, Lord! Oh, my Lord! Thank you, sir – may your breath be blessed for taking pity upon a poor pilgrim!'

In a blink of an eye, Maram tossed down the brandy. It instantly excited his thirst for more. When he understood that no more rations would be forthcoming that night, he seemed crestfallen. But only for a moment, for it occurred to him that if Master Juwain had consented to giving him this 'medicine' once, he might again.

'Tomorrow night, then?' Maram said to Master Juwain.

'I can't promise you that,' Master Juwain told him. 'It will depend on the need.'

'Oh, there'll be *need* enough,' Maram said, picking up his potsherd to scratch at his sores. 'I can promise you that.'

'We'll see. After another day's journey and thirty or forty miles of heat and dust, you might want only water to drink.'

But Maram appeared not to hear him. He gazed out into the dark distances to the west and murmured to himself: 'Ah, forty miles, then – forty miles equals one cup of brandy. Do you think I don't have the strength to journey forty *thousand* miles?'

That evening the wind blew even harder and beat against the walls of the three large tents that the Avari had brought with them and quickly erected. Maidro didn't like this wind any more than he had the heat of the day, for it stole too much moisture from us and made us even more thirsty. Heat and wind, sweat and water, miles behind us and miles still to come – these were the equations that concerned the Avari.

Neither Maidro nor Sunji, however, shared Kane's concern that we should stand watches in order to protect our encampment – at least not at first. As Sunji told us: 'The Zuri will not send more of their warriors into our land to be slaughtered so soon, and for the time, we are at peace with the Sudi. We have no other enemies, and even if we did, they would be unlikely to come across us here, so close to the Tar Harath.'

Kane, standing near one of the tents to survey the rocky terrain about us, squinted against the wind and said to Sunji: 'So, now that you've slaughtered four of Morjin's priests along with the Zuri, you've gained another enemy, and the worst one yet. Then, too, we've reason to suspect that Morjin will unleash another of his cursed droghuls upon us.'

At this, he glanced at Atara, who stood over by the horses brushing down her mare, Fire. I looked at her, too. According to her scryer's way, she said nothing about the third droghul that she had foretold, nor about any other vision. In truth, she had said nothing at all to me since our disagreement over the fate of the captured priest. Her coldness toward me cut as keenly as the chill of the desert night.

'Do you believe,' Sunji said to Kane, 'that this droghul is close?'

Kane glanced at me, and I shook my head. And Kane said to Sunji, 'We've no reason to think so. But then, we've no reason to think *not*.'

'Then perhaps you should remain awake to watch for him,' Sunji said with a yawn. 'But I would advise you to rest – in the desert, exhaustion can kill as surely as poison or swords.'

With that, he went inside his tent to take a few hours of sleep along with his three tribesmen. Atara, Liljana and Estrella shared the second tent, while I squeezed inside the third with Maram, Master Juwain and Daj. Kane, as stubborn as a stone, stood outside looking out at the darkened land around us and sniffing at the wind.

It blew incessantly all night, right through the tents' tightly woven wool, covering us with a fine powder. I found myself grateful for the shawl wrapped around my mouth and nose, though I hated feeling smothered by this mask of warm, moist wool almost as much as I did its itch and fusty stench. The Avari, I thought, might have inured themselves to the desert and all of its insults, but I never would.

We roused ourselves three hours before dawn. The four Avari breakfasted on some bread, dried antelope and a handful of figs, and we did the same. We fed the horses their rations of grain, then rode on into the coldest part of the night.

It was strange, I thought, how we all welcomed the rising of the sun almost as much as we dreaded it. The hellish sun could be death, but it was also life, even here in the desert. For a couple of hours, as the hills gave out and we rode across a gravel plain, the sun fell upon our dusty robes and warmed us. Then it grew *too* warm, and then hot. We sweated even more than did the horses, whose dusty coats turned into masses of muddy hair.

Later that morning we reached the last well before the Tar Harath. The Avari, hundreds of years ago, had dug a hole down through the bottom of an old lake-bed and built a stone wall around it. While Sunji and his people pulled up the waterskins that Jovayl's warriors had dropped down into the well, Maram sprawled out beneath our hastily erected sun cloth. He was so tired that he could hardly move. Flies buzzed around him trying to get through his stained robes to his raw, oozing wounds beneath. Master Juwain brought him a cup a water, which he gulped down in two swallows. Then he looked up at Master Juwain with the sorrowful eyes of a dog and begged for a bit of brandy.

'No – no more,' Master Juwain said. 'At least not until day's end.'

'This *is* the end,' Maram moaned. 'I don't know if I can get back on my horse.'

'You can,' I said to him. 'You must.'

'How many more miles, then, until we break for the day? Fifteen? Twenty?'

'It doesn't matter,' I said, smiling down at him. 'It doesn't matter if it's twenty thousand miles – we must keep on going.'

'Oh, Val, I don't know!' Maram said as he beat his fist at the flies attacking his eyes. 'I don't know, I don't know!'

I walked off near the well to confer with Master Juwain – and with Kane, Atara and Liljana. To Master Juwain, I said, 'It is too much for him. Perhaps you should use your gelstei to try to heal him.'

Master Juwain brought out his green stone, which gleamed like an emerald in the strong sunlight. He said, 'No – we've agreed that it's too dangerous to use, now.'

'And dangerous if you *don't* use it. Maram might die.'

Master Juwain rubbed the back of his head, now swaddled in dusty white wool. He stared at his sparkling crystal and said, 'I'm afraid that the Red Dragon can *feel* me contemplating using this, even across deserts and mountains.'

'Perhaps he can,' I said as I drew my sword. I nodded at Kane and then Liljana. 'Perhaps we can confuse him then. If Liljana were to put her mind to her gelstei at the same moment that Kane used his, then –'

'Then they both might die even before Maram does.'

These ominous words came from Atara. She stood beneath the blazing sun rolling her scryer's sphere between her hands. I bowed my head because I knew that she was right. And she said to me, 'If any of us should try to distract Morjin, it should be me.'

'No,' I told her, squinting against my sword's brilliant silustria. 'It should be *me*. Of all of us, Morjin has yet to find his way into my gelstei.'

'And that is precisely why your use of it won't distract him.'

As Sunji and the other Avari warriors looked on and Daj and Estrella watered the horses, I swung Alkaladur in a bright arc against the sky. 'If I could make Morjin feel the true power that I have sensed within this sword, then I might do more than distract him.'

'Yes, *you* might die,' Atara said to me coldly.

'And you?' I said to her, looking at her diamond-clear crystal. 'Would not using your gelstei be just as dangerous?'

'No, I don't think so. Morjin might try to show me the worst of torments, but what is that against what he has already taken from me?'

I remembered how Atara had once shared with me one of her terrible visions, and I said, 'He might trap you inside a world from which there would be no escape.'

Atara tapped her fingers against her blindfold. With the shawl wrapped over her nose and mouth, the whole of her face was now lost beneath coverings of cloth. 'The world is all darkness now, and what could be a worse trap than that?'

'No,' I said, resting my hand on her arm. 'I can't let you.'

She pulled away from me and gripped her sphere more tightly as she told me, 'You can't stop me. And you mustn't.'

We all finally agreed that Master Juwain should try to heal Maram, with Atara's help. When we put our proposal to him, he quickly consented, for he did not want to live another day scratching at his sores, or so he said. We helped him strip off his robes. I gritted my teeth against the sight of the bites marking nearly every part of his body. Some had grown scabs but many remained raw and open. Estrella and Daj came over and used cloths to shoo away the flies that buzzed around these ugly wounds. Master Juwain knelt next to Maram; he held his varistei over the cavities that Jezi Yaga had bitten out of Maram's chest. Atara stood ready with her clear crystal cupped in her hands. Sunji and the other Avari looked on in fascination and dread.

Master Juwain closed his eyes in meditation. Atara stood as still as a pinnacle of rock. After a while, Master Juwain looked down upon Maram with intense concentration. He gazed at his green gelstei, which he rotated slightly as if feeling for currents of life inside Maram that only he could perceive. We all remembered how the healing light from this crystal had made whole the arrow wound in Atara's lung and saved her from death.

'Hurry!' Maram said to Master Juwain. Despite the children's best efforts, the flies moved more quickly than their hands, and several flies had already found their way to wounds along Maram's legs and were busy sucking up the fluids that leaked out of him. 'Please, please – hurry!'

In a flash of light, soft green flames streaked out of both ends of Master Juwain's crystal. They bent downward and joined together in a glowing emerald ball. Then, like a fountain, this radiance fell down and filled the whole of one of Maram's wounds. I could almost feel the cool, healing light working its magic on Maram's tortured flesh.

'Oh, the pain!' Maram murmured out. 'The pain is going away!'

I looked over at Atara, all wrapped up in cloth like a mummy. She didn't move; it seemed that she didn't breathe.

'Good!' Maram murmured to Master Juwain. 'Ah, very good!'

I held my breath as the edges of the wound, touched with the fire's mysterious power, drew in and knitted together into a seamless expanse of hairy skin. I couldn't help smiling in triumph at this miracle.

Master Juwain repositioned his crystal above the wound torn out of the other half of Maram's chest. A fiery green light poured out of it. Maram smiled as this light fell upon him and suffused his flesh; then, without warning, his lips pulled back into a grimace. The light flared greener and brighter, deeper and hotter. And then, quickly, even hotter. It grew so hideous and hot that it seemed much more fire than light. Maram shouted to Master Juwain, 'Stop! Take it away! You're burning me, damn it!'

But Master Juwain, it seemed, could not take the crystal away. His fingers locked around it, and he stared down at Maram as a hideous light filled his gray eyes. And still the terrible fire poured out of his crystal and seared deeper into Maram's chest.

'Stop! Please! Stop, damn you! You're killing me!'

Maram, too, tried to move, but it seemed that some terrible thing had a hold of his nerves and muscles so that he could not roll out of the way. Kane and I closed in on Master Juwain then. We each grabbed one of his elbows and lifted him away from Maram. We carried him ten feet out into the desert. This availed Maram not at all, however, for the fire still erupted from the varistei and now snaked through the air in a streak of green to find its way into Maram's wound.

'Stop! Stop! Stop!'

Almost without thinking, I held out my hand to try to stop this strange fire that might soon kill Maram. It passed right through my flesh without the slightest burn, leaving me entirely untouched. It continued flaring and twisting through the air, and sizzling into Maram's chest.

'Val, your sword!' Kane cried out to me.

I remembered that the silustria, along with its other powers, could act as a shield against various energies: vital, mental or even physical. I let go of Master Juwain and drew my sword again. I sliced it down through the green fire, then held it still, letting the fire rain against it. Like a mirror, its brilliant surface reflected the varistei's light back into the varistei. Master Juwain's crystal grew quiescent then. It took only a moment for the spell to be broken.

Master Juwain's eyes suddenly cleared, and he dropped his crystal down into the dirt. He ran back over to Maram, knelt down and rested his hand on Maram's chest. I expected to see the wound all black and charred; instead, it gaped raw and red as freshly flayed meat. It seemed that the evil fire had drilled deep into Maram's muscle, almost down to the bone. Strangely, the terrible wound bled only a little.

'I'm sorry,' Master Juwain said, brushing back the hair out of Maram's eyes. 'I'm sorry, Brother Maram!'

For a few moments, Maram could do nothing more than grimace and groan. And then he clasped Master Juwain's hand and said, 'It's all right – I forgive you. But please remember that I'm still *Sar* Maram.'

Master Juwain walked off to retrieve his crystal, which he dropped into his deepest pocket as if he never wanted to see it again. He returned with a wad of cotton; he pressed it down into Maram's newly excavated wound and wrapped a long strip of cotton around Maram's chest and back to hold it in place. By way of explanation, he said to us, 'Never again. I nearly killed Maram, and the Lord of Lies nearly made *me* into a ghul.'

I stood near Atara, who remained motionless. I help up my sword toward the east as if to reflect back any illusions or evil visions that might emanate from that direction. I had no sense that my efforts aided Atara at all. But at last, the spell that had seized her, too, was broken.

Atara put away her scryer's crystal and called out, 'Is Maram all right?'

'Yes,' I told her, although this wasn't quite true. I grasped her arm, and wished that I could look into her eyes. 'Are *you* all right?'

She made no reply to this, directly. All she would say was: 'The world . . . is more than it seems. There *are* worse things than anything I ever imagined.'

Sunji and Maidro stepped closer then. Maidro looked from Master Juwain to Maram and said, 'If that wasn't sorcery, then I never hope to see such.'

Master Juwain explained more about the making and wielding of the gelstei crystals: what little had been passed down through the ages. Then he said, 'What once was called art is now wrongly called sorcery. Though if *you* wish to call the evil usage of these crystals sorcery, I won't dispute you.'

Liljana came over with a cloth soaked in an infusion made from kokun leaves, which was the only thing that eased the pain of Maram's flesh, at least for a time. She washed his body and tended his wounds with a gentleness that surprised me.

I expected that having suffered this new outrage that had nearly killed him, Maram might call for us to return to the Avari's hadrah. Instead he called for brandy.

'Ah, Master Juwain,' he said, tapping his hand lightly over his chest, 'it was you who drilled this hole in me, and so it is upon you to fill it in the only way that will truly help.'

So great was Master Juwain's guilt that he did not gainsay Maram's request. None of us did. Master Juwain poured much more than a few drams of brandy into Maram's cup, then watched as Maram drank it slowly.

'Thank you, sir,' Maram said. He sat up and ran his finger around the bowl of his cup, then licked it. 'You've made a new man of me.'

He held out his cup and gazed at the bottle of brandy that Master Juwain held in his gnarled hand.

389

'No, no more,' Master Juwain told him. 'At least not now. If you need a little at the end of the day, you shall have it.'

'Do you promise?'

'Yes, I suppose if I have to, I do promise.'

Maram's eyes gleamed, and a new strength flowed into him. I watched with amazement as he suddenly stood up to begin dressing. Our gelstei might hold undreamed-of powers – but so it seemed did a bottle of brandy.

We waited out the worst heat of the day there at the well, trying to sleep inside our stifling tents. When the killing sun had dropped much lower in the sky, we set out again to the west. We journeyed long past dusk and deep into a new series of hills, whose sharp ridgelines ran north and south. Maram counted out the miles like a miser adding coins to a vault. But we all knew that at the day's end, like a spendthrift, he would exchange them all in return for what had become his nightly libation.

Late that evening, we pitched our tents in a narrow valley between two of these lines of hills. Master Juwain noted that many of the stones in the valley seemed rounded, as of river stones. He worried that if a storm came up, the walls of rock around us might funnel the rain into a flashflood that could drown us.

'If it stormed, we *would* be swept away,' Maidro said to him. 'And if we had wings, we could simply fly out of here; indeed, we could fly clear across the desert.'

Arthayn and Nuradayn laughed at this as if they thought it was the funniest thing they had ever heard. Sunji looked up at the glittering sky, unmarred by even a single cloud. And Maidro, taking pity on Master Juwain, added, 'In Segadar and Yaradar it rains here, torrents and rivers. But never in Soldru for as long as the Avari have lived in the desert. So sleep in peace, Master Healer.'

That night, after Master Juwain had rewarded Maram as promised, we all slept in relative peace, if not in comfort. The rocks sticking out of the ground bruised us, even beneath our thick furs, and the air fell almost icy cold. Maram stirred in his sleep and awakened more than once, moaning at the new pain in his chest. In the hills around us, the hyenas let loose their eerie cries.

Maram, when it came time to ride again, surprised me by saddling his horse without grumbling. As he told me in the dark of the morning before true morning: 'Forty miles we'll cover today, if it's a good day, and the sooner they are behind us, the sooner I shall have my brandy.'

For a few hours, as we worked our way across the highlands,

we rode through near-darkness. Then the sun's first rays lit the hills with a golden-red fire. The rocks about us seemed to glow. Sunji, following an ancient route, led us up through a cleft between two hills as stark and barren as the moon. They were, he said, the last of this high country, and they marked the westernmost reaches of the Avari's realm.

'Now you will see,' he told me, turning on his horse toward me, 'what few men have seen.'

We came out on top of the cleft to behold the vast reaches of desert that opened out to the north, south and west. The wind, over the ages, had swept up the sand into mountains. Some of it shone white as the fine, shell-ground sand along a beach; some of it gleamed as red as the sandstone pinnacles and castle-like formations that stood even higher than the great dunes. In places, to the north, the sun fell upon swirls of red sand embedded in white and caused the dunes to glow with a lovely pink hue unlike anything I had ever seen. The sky framed this magnificent landscape with a blue so rich and deep it seemed almost like water. It was all so impossibly beautiful that I wanted to weep.

'The Tar Harath,' Sunji said to me. 'The womb of the desert.'

'It is . . . so lovely,' I said.

'It won't seem so in another three hours.' He pointed his finger out at the endless sweeps of sand. 'Not once we're out on the Hell's Anvil.'

'Ah, how far did you say it was across this?' Maram asked.

'No one really knows,' Sunji told him. 'It would be far, even if we were to ride as straight as an eagle flies. But if we must turn north or south in search of water, then . . .'

He did not finish his sentence. And so Maram could not calculate how many forty-mile segments he must complete in order to earn his rations of brandy. In any case, as Maidro explained, we couldn't always count on making forty miles in a day.

'There might be sandstorms that we'll have to wait out,' he said, 'and that will eat up the hours – and eat the flesh off our bones if we're impatient. There are quicksands, too, that we must avoid. The sand itself will tire the horses' legs, ours too when we walk, and so the journey will go more slowly.'

He said nothing about the sun, which made its way up the great arc of the sky like a white-hot iron cinder. But Master Juwain had already explained to us that in the desert the air held too little moisture to shield against the sun. And here, in the deep desert, the air was so thin and dry that the sun's fierce rays burned through it like starfire through the great nothingness of space.

For a while, as we worked down into the Tar Harath, the hills at our back blocked out the sun. But then we rode out onto the sand, and the sun rose higher. It streaked down upon us like a rain of flaming arrows. The sand threw it back into the air so that it seemed that we rode through a wall of flame. The air here was indeed thin – but not so thin that we couldn't feel it searing us through our coverings of wool. We rode past mid-morning, and it grew even hotter. And still the sun rose higher and brighter and hotter. It flared so hellishly hot that we stopped to pitch our tents. Climbing inside them provided protection from the sun, but did nothing to help us escape from the terrible heat.

'It is like breathing fire!' Maram gasped out a couple of hours past noon. He lay sweating on top of his furs, unable to sleep. 'It is like being cooked inside an oven!'

Master Juwain, Daj, Kane and I sprawled out on our furs near him. My robes were a sodden mass of wool smothering me.

'I can't stop sweating,' Maram complained. 'It seems I'm taking a bath with all my clothes on.'

'Do you see this?' Kane said, kneeling over him. He ran his finger through the sweat pooling on Maram's forehead. 'This is all that is keeping you from cooking. Your body is no different than other kinds of meat. Heat it up enough and it will roast like lamb.'

I did not want to think that the Tar Harath could grow so hot – or indeed, any hotter at all. But late in the afternoon, as we were readying ourselves for the second half of the day's journey, Maidro stood in his steaming woolen robe and shrugged his shoulders. 'This is still only Soldru – wait until Marud when grows *really* hot.'

How does one measure heat? An iron thrust into a bed of coals will glow red before white, but the searing agony of red-hot iron held against the flesh is scarcely any less terrible, as Master Juwain could attest. Some say that the dry heat of the desert is not so bad as the swelter of more humid climes such as the jungles of Uskudar, but I say that these wayfarers have never ventured into the Tar Harath. There is a heat on earth so hellishly hot that it drives burning nails into the lungs even as it nearly poaches the brain. Beyond this degree of anguish, it can grow no hotter, for if it did a man would die.

That evening, on our ride into the coolness of the descending dark, I knew that all of our thoughts were on death. Sunji and

Maidro fell into a deep silence, seeming to concentrate on finding the best route across the soft, shifting sand. I felt within them a deep longing, as for water, but I sensed that it was really a concentration on the need of life. They knew better than any of us how easily the desert could snuff it out. Both the children fought to master their suffering and fear, even as Master Juwain struggled not to play through his overactive mind multifarious scenarios of doom. It was Liljana's will, I thought, that if she could just manage to fill our bodies with good food and our spirits with good cheer, then no doom could touch us. Maram, of course, sought other means of dealing with the great, inescapable darkness. As for Kane, with his fathomless black eyes and great soul, it was his way to take death inside himself and laugh out to the stars his defiance and glee.

I worried most about Atara, not just because I loved her beyond all beauty and goodness, but because she revealed to me the least. She sat on top of her red mare swaddled in her robes and blindfold as beneath a tent of silence. Outside, the air still swirled up off the ground, dry and warm, but inside this brave woman welled a terrible coldness.

We made camp that night with one of the desert's sandstone castles at our back. Dunes had swept over part of this rock formation, but great mounds of rock two hundred feet high stuck up out of the sand. After our dinner of dried lamb and wheat cakes, Atara asked me to accompany her in a short climb up to the rocks behind us. Arm in arm, with Atara pushing her bow down into the sand with each step, we walked up along the crest of one of these dunes. We came upon some flat rocks and sat down facing the desert to the west. In the glittering black distances, Valura, the bright evening star, had almost set.

'I must speak to you,' Atara said to me, 'before it is too late.'

She had taken off her head covering so that only her blindfold remained. I gazed at the gleam of starlight on her face as I took her hand in mine. Her skin, like the rocks around us, was quickly losing its heat to the night.

'I was wrong,' she said, 'after the battle in that canyon. To call for the priest to be staked out to die in the sun – so horribly, horribly wrong. I called it justice. It *was* only justice, truly. But who of us desires that? Who would wish it upon herself?'

'Not I,' I said.

I thought of all the men I had slain – and of their widowed wives, vengeful brothers and children left with no one to protect or provide for them. I thought of *my* brothers, and my father and mother, and all my friends and countrymen who had died because I had told a single lie.

'It's kindness we need,' she said to me. 'And forgiveness.'

'But you've done nothing for which you need to be forgiven. Nothing more than anyone.'

'Haven't I? In the Skadarak –'

'Let's not speak of that place here,' I said to her. 'We've trials and torments enough ahead of us.'

'We do. You can't imagine . . .'

I looked at her and said, 'Tell me, then.'

'No, I'm sorry, I *can't* tell you. I can't even tell myself.'

I felt a coldness pulsing through her wrist, and I said, 'I've never seen you like this before.'

She fell quiet as she seemed to listen to the wind rattling sand against the rocks around us. Then she said, 'I'm so afraid. So horribly, horribly afraid.'

'You?'

She nodded her head. 'I think we will all die. And worse, before we die.'

I gripped her hand too tightly. It was one thing when Maram voiced such sentiments; it was another when Atara, greatest of scryers, spoke of such doom.

'You won't tell anyone I said that, will you? Especially not the children. I'm so afraid for the children.'

'As long as we're all right,' I reassured her, 'they will be all right.'

This, I thought, was something that Liljana might say. Too often, it seemed a little lie that I told myself.

'I'm so useless, now,' Atara said to me. 'I failed you again in the battle with the droghul. His voice! The Voice of Ice, the Avari call it. I should have fired an arrow through his throat!'

'It will all come back,' I said to her, squeezing her hand. 'Your sight, and more – I know it will.'

She shook her head at this, and fell again into silence. Her whole body seemed ready to shiver against the cold, driving wind.

'In the Skadarak,' she murmured, 'did you never think of leaving me behind?'

'No – I could never leave you!'

I would die, I told myself, a thousand times to keep her alive.

She sat shaking her head. The coldness spread out from her center into her limbs and hands. Her fingers pressed hard against mine as if feeling for something deep and indestructible.

'I think you *could* have,' she said to me.

'No – never!'

'I think that any of us could,' she said. 'There's always a choice, isn't there? These terrible, terrible choices of life. We're always so close to making the *wrong* choice. It's always there, the yes and the no, and I can't get away from it. It's like trying to flee from Morjin: the farther we go into the wilds of Ea, the more surely he finds us out and the nearer he seems. But I *must* escape it, don't you see? I can't live with the horror of it all.'

I listened to her breath push in and out of her chest. I said, 'But you *must* live. You can't give up – I won't allow it.'

Her voice softened as she said, 'You won't? Then help me, please.'

'How?'

She reached down to grab up a handful of sand. She sat letting the grains run through her fingers onto the rocks below us. 'What others feel inside them, you are able to feel, too. Sometimes, you can even touch *them* with your fire, your dreams. Can you not, then, take their nightmares away?'

I slowly shook my head. 'I'm not the Maitreya, Atara. And I'm not sure that even he could do as you say.'

'Please,' she said, leaning against me. She let her head rest against my shoulder. 'I'm so tired.'

She pressed her hand into mine, and I felt the cool, grittiness of sand as well as the stirring of a deeper and warmer thing.

'I'm so tired,' she murmured, 'of being tired.'

Her head pressed me like a great weight. The smell of her hair was musky and heavy.

'Take me away,' she said to me. 'Back to the Avari's hadrah – or even back to Mesh. Somewhere safe.'

I felt my heart beating hard up through my throat as I said, 'But nowhere in the world is safe for us now. We've spoken of this. Eventually –'

'I don't care what happens ten years from now, or even next month. I just want to be a safe for a single night. For an hour – why can't it all just go away?'

Why, indeed, I wondered as I sat listening to Atara's heavy breathing and looking out at the stars?

'Val, Val,' she said to me.

I was no scryer, but even so a vision came to me: of Atara and I going back to the Avari's hadrah to live in peace. We would wed, despite Atara's misgivings, and bear a child whom she could never behold. We might be happy, for a time, but sorrows would inevitably come for us. Atara would grow to hate rearing our son in blindness, and hate me for calling him into life. And most of all, she would hate life itself, especially when Morjin finally found us and our world became a nightmare.

Her fingers pulled at mine with a quiet, desperate urgency. I couldn't move; it seemed that I could hardly breathe. Only our thin coverings of skin kept the fire of my blood from burning into her, and hers into me.

'No,' I whispered.

It was as if I had slapped her face. The coldness suddenly flooded back into her, and she sat up straight.

'No,' she repeated, 'we always have a choice, don't we? You're so damn noble, you always choose what you do, even though someday, it will kill you.'

'Atara, I –'

'It will kill all of us, I'm afraid. It *might*. And I have to accept that, don't I? Because that's the beautiful, beautiful thing about you, that those of us who love you can't help choosing as *we* do, too.'

For a while, she sat there quietly weeping into the wind, and she would not let me touch her. I had a strange sense that she was almost glad that her eyes had been put out so that I couldn't see the pain and horror in them. Then she regathered her composure; in a clear, calm voice, she said to me, 'Tell me what you see then, in the deep desert to the west, where we must go.'

I described the sweeps of sand and rock in the dark distances before us. Then I stared out at the infinite black bowl of the sky and said, 'There are stars – so many stars. Never, not even on top of Mount Telshar, have I seen them so brilliant.'

Valura, I told her, gleamed like a bright diamond just at the edge of the horizon, while Icesse and Hyanne and the stars of the Mother hung higher in the sky. Although she could not see my finger, I pointed out Ahanu, the Eye of the Bull, and Helaku and Shinkun and a dozen other stars. Solaru and Aras, I said, shone more splendidly than any others; they were like blazing signposts lighting our way.

'And there,' I said as I moved my hand in an arc across the heavens, 'are the Seven Sisters. And beyond, the Golden Band, filling the blackness with glorre. I can almost see it. Sometimes, I do. It shimmers. It is strange, the way its light touches that of the stars and makes them seem even brighter. Now I know the *real* reason that the Avari go into the Tar Harath.'

I fell quiet as I looked into the black, brilliant deeps for Shavashar and Elianora, Ayasha and Yarashan and Asaru, and the other stars that called to me with the voices of my dead family. I called back to them, whispering their names: 'Karshur, Mandru, Ravar, Jonathay . . .'

My voice shook with longing. I heard it and hated it. I said to Atara: 'In all the sky, there isn't a single cloud. It's all so perfectly clear – clearer even than your crystal.'

'Is it? Tell me what you see in the sky, then.'

'Triumph. A great light unveiled. At the end of it all, the whole earth singing of what we have done. I see the one whom we seek. I see *you*, looking at me the way you once did. You *will* see again – I know you will.'

She laughed at this, not in joy, but only in sadness. Then she said softly, 'I think you lie. But I love you for trying to make me believe it.'

She kissed my hand, and stood up to walk back to our line of tents. I had to help her work her way down through the darkness, lest she stumble upon the rocks. Although she said nothing of the future, I knew that before we won any great triumph, if ever we did, we would suffer through many sweltering days of terror and pain.

25

Our sleep that night was as deep and cool as the air that fell down from the sky. We took comfort in the softness of the sand beneath our furs and the floors of our tents. Even Maram found ways to position his great body that did not unduly distress him. When it came time to journey again, his big voice boomed out into the darkness: 'There are five good things about this part of the desert. First, the sand makes a good bed. Second, there are no flies. And third, my nightly drink.'

'And the fourth and fifth good things?' I asked him.

If I expected him to extol the splendors of the heavens or the terrible beauty of the desert, then I would have been disappointed, for he said, 'The fourth and fifth good things are the same as the third.'

I smiled into the dark, glad that Maram had found at least a little good in this forsaken land. But he also suffered other things that were not good, as did we all. That day, as we pushed farther into the Tar Harath, it grew even hotter. The blazing sun reflected off the sand nearly burned out our eyes. Breathing itself became a torment, and we all coughed at the dust that the wind blew at our faces. This dust worked its way into the fibers of our clothing and the cracks in our skin. Movement, hour after hour sitting on horseback or walking through the sand, chafed our dirty, sweaty skin. Soon, as Master Juwain feared, the dust might work at us so that we all had sores in our flesh like Maram's.

So it went for the next four days. Our bodies grew thinner, for none of us wanted to eat very much in the unrelenting heat, not even at night when we fell exhausted into our beds. We sweated and drank from our waterskins, and drank and sweated some more. We wished for a good bath and clean clothing almost as much as oranges and kammats and other succulent fruits. We watched our water disappear, cup by cup and skin by skin. Once, after a long afternoon spent nearly dying on top of the burning sand, Maidro caught Maram washing the dust from his face and upbraided him: 'We've no water to spare for such extravagances,' he said to Maram in a raspy, dust-choked voice. 'Every drop of water you waste brings us all an inch closer to death.'

Maram bowed his head in shame, and he apologized for his thoughtlessness. But an hour later, I heard him mutter to himself: 'Every mile we cover brings me that much closer to my brandy. But what then, my friend? How many cups do you have left before our water runs out and brandy is *all* you have to drink? You can't bear the thirst, can you? No, no, you can't, and so I think that drowning yourself in brandy would be a better way to die.'

We made our way across the sun-seared Tar Harath mile by mile – but we did not cover as many miles each day as we hoped. The sand burned the horses' hooves and slowed them, as Maidro had said. We lost most of a day in circling around a miles-wide basin that Maidro feared contained quicksands. Maram objected to this detour, saying, 'This sand looks the same as any other – how do you know it's quicksand?'

And Maidro, who did not like to explain himself, told Maram, 'If you don't trust me, there is only one way to find out.'

He pointed his wrinkled old finger out toward the basin's sandy center. So despondent was Maram that he seemed to consider walking right out into it.

And then I heard him mutter: 'Ah, if there is no *Maram*, there is no purpose to the brandy that we've made our poor horses carry. And what will befall then? The brandy will be poured out into the sand. It would be a *crime* to waste it.'

He turned to Maidro and said more graciously, 'I'm sure you're right about the quicksand. Thank you for saving my miserable life.'

Just before dawn the next day, Arthayn killed the first of the packhorses by slicing his saber through its throat. The other horses had eaten all the grain that this unfortunate horse carried and had drunk its water, as well. For two days, the useless horse had plodded along relieved of its burden, but also denied food and drink. In truth, Arthayn should have killed the thirst-maddened beast the day before, but the Avari – and all of us – kept hoping that we might find water.

We never ceased scanning the rocks and sand and blue horizon for sign of this marvelous substance. We looked to Estrella in hope that she might lead us toward another hidden cave or perhaps some ancient, forgotten well. But she seemed to have no more sense of where we might find water than anyone else. Often she would gaze up at the sky with longing at the few small clouds, which here drifted toward the northwest.

'One cloud,' Maidro said, 'holds more water than a well. But the clouds go where *they* will, not where we wish. And they never shed their rain in the Tar Harath, not even, I think, at the command of an udra mazda.'

Later that day, at Maidro's command, Nuradayn killed the second packhorse. Maidro stood watching this slaughter and speaking with Sunji. Sunji then gathered everyone around him and announced, 'Our water has grown too little, and so we must forbear meat until new water is found.'

Here he looked at Estrella in utter confidence that she would somehow work another miracle. But Nuradayn, a young man given to wild surges of mood, looked out across the sun-baked dunes with doubt eating at his dark eyes.

The next morning, we came upon a single sandstone pinnacle so smooth and symmetrical that it might have been carved by the hand of man a million years ago. Here Estrella stopped her horse and looked up at the sky to watch a few puffy clouds drift past. Then she looked at me and pointed in the direction that the clouds were moving, toward the north.

'Estrella,' I said to Sunji and Maidro, 'wants us to turn that way.'

Estrella nodded her head at this and smiled.

Arthayn nudged his horse forward and squinted at the brilliance of the unbroken sweep of dunes. He said, 'There cannot be water there.'

Maidro's eyes filled with doubt, too, but he said, 'The girl is an udra mazda. She found water at the Dragon Rocks, in hills that were known to be dry.'

We held council then, and decided to turn toward the north, as Estrella had indicated. Maram, I thought, echoed all of our sentiments when he muttered: 'One direction in this damn desert seems as good as another. As they say, when you're going through Hell, keep on going.'

And so we set our course to the north, and slightly west. We journeyed for two more days without seeing any sign of water. During the day we relied on the sun and my sense of direction to hold a straight line across the sand; at night we navigated by the stars. With every mile farther into the heart of the Tar Harath, it seemed to grow only hotter and drier. The air in our faces burned us like the blast from a furnace. Our skin cracked, and the salt in our sweat worked its way into these raw wounds; it seared us as if we were being stabbed with fire-irons. Our noses grew so parched that they bled at the slightest touch. Things were simple in the deep desert, I thought, reduced to the most basic elements: sun and sky, sand and suffering.

Maram, upon grinding his teeth at the torture of his abrasive saddle, said to me, 'Don't you think it's strange that I, who have sought pleasures few men could bear, have instead found so much pain?'

I smiled beneath the cowl smothering me. I asked him, 'Do you still have the stone?'

Maram produced a roundish river stone with a hole burned through its middle. In the Vardaloon, he had used his gelstei to make this hole as a distraction against the mosquitoes. It was supposed to remind him that even the worst torments could be endured and would come to an end.

'I do have the stone,' Maram said to me. 'I only wish I were made of such substance – this damn sun is burning a hole in *me*!'

Later that day the third of our packhorses died, not from the slash of a sword, but from heatstroke: it simply collapsed onto the sand and coughed out its last breath from its frothy mouth. Nuradayn blamed himself for not dispatching it sooner, but as he put it: 'Each time we cut down one of the horses, it's like cutting off our own limbs.'

Travelling as we did by early morning and early night, we lost count of the days: one evening in our tent, Master Juwain sat rubbing his bald head as he told us that he thought it was the fourth of Marud. We lost track of distances, too. We measured our progress not by the mile, but by the hoof and the foot: it took all our strength to keep the horses moving forward, step by step, and when they grew too tired, we had to force ourselves to walk up one dune and down the next. Finally we reached a place where neither days nor miles nor even suffering mattered. In the middle of an expanse of sand nearly as featureless as a sheet of parchment, Maidro suddenly called for a halt. He called for a council, too.

'If we turn back now,' he said to us when we had all gathered around him, 'I believe that we might be able to return to the Hadr Halona.'

'No!' I cried out to him. I looked all around us at the blazing sand. Other than some dunes in the distance and a few low rocks sticking out of the ground, there was nothing to see. 'If we turn back now, we'll lose!'

'If we don't turn back and we don't find water,' Sunji said to me, 'we'll lose, too: our lives.'

'We'll find water,' I said. 'I know we will.'

I looked at Estrella, and so did the rest of us. This slender girl, sitting on top of her spent horse, looked up at the pretty clouds in the sky.

'She follows the clouds,' Sunji said, 'as she has for days. It will not avail us, but who can blame her?'

Estrella, he said, having been acclaimed as an udra mazda, must feel too keenly the desire to satisfy our expectations.

'But surely she must be stymied, as we are,' Sunji said. 'Surely she leads us on in false hope.'

Nuradayn, whose doubt had turned into despair, sucked in air through the bloody shawl wrapped over his nose and said, 'It may have been *false* for us to have named the girl an udra mazda. What if she found that cave by chance?'

For a while, beneath the day's dying sun, the four Avari debated the signs by which an udra mazda might be recognized. Maidro held that only the grace of the One could lead such a young girl to water, and that chance could have played no part in this miracle. Estrella, he told Nuradayn, was surely who they believed her to be. But then he added, 'Even an udra mazda, however, cannot find water where there *is* no water.'

We all gazed out at the burning sands where Estrella wanted us to go; almost none of us wanted to go there. The desert itself seemed to drive us back with a hellishly hot wind that seared our eyes. Nuradayn told of a sick heat that fell upon his brain whenever he contemplated taking another step along our course; he said that it must be the will of the One that we would surely die if we went on. We all, I thought, felt something like that. Even Kane regarded the barren terrain before us with a dread that was as powerful and deep as it was strange.

'It is a terrible chance you're asking us to take,' Sunji said to me.

I drew my sword and watched as the sun touched it with an impossible brightness. I shielded my eyes against its shimmering glorre, and I told him, 'We're well beyond chance now, as you have said. I believe our fate lies out there.'

I looked at Estrella and bowed my head to her. Either one had faith in people, or one did not.

'Fate,' Sunji said, looking out to the northwest.

'Fate,' Maidro repeated, shaking his head.

I saw in his old eyes what he saw: all of us lying dead on the sand without even the ants or the vultures to relieve us of our rotting flesh.

He gazed at Etrella, and then at me. I opened my heart to him then. I found within myself a fierce, fiery will to keep on going. For a moment, it burnt away my fear, and Maidro's as well.

'If we turned back now,' he said, 'we *might* still reach the Hadr Halona. But then, we might not.'

'One place,' Sunji said to him, 'is as good to die as another.'

Arthayn agreed with them, and so, reluctantly, did Nuradayn. I sat there beneath the merciless sun marveling at the courage of these warriors who did not have to make this journey nor fight this battle.

'One thing we must do, however,' Maidro said, 'if we are to go on.'

He told us that we must lighten the horses' burdens, and this meant jettisoning everything not vital to our survival. He was a harder man and more exacting than even Yago. And so we cast away many things that were dear to us. Liljana nearly wept at having to abandon the last of her galte cookware, as did Master Juwain when he removed his steel instruments and medicines from his polished wooden box and left the box to be buried by the sifting sands. Only with great difficulty could I bring myself to part with the chess set that Jonathay had given me at the outset of our first quest – and with Mandru's sharpening stone and Yarashan's copy of the Valkariad. Maram made a great show of surrendering up the heavy wool sweater that Behira had knitted for him. But this sacrifice proved insufficient to satisfy the implacable Maidro. When Maidro discovered that one of our horses carried seven bottles of brandy, he insisted that they, too, be left in the sand.

'But that is our whole reserve!' Maram cried out. 'It is madness to give up good medicine!'

'It is madness to make the horses carry it another mile!' Maidro snapped at him. 'Madness to bring it along in the first place, when this horse could have carried extra waterskins!'

They argued then, with a vehemence and heat like unto that of the desert all around us. For a moment, I thought Maram was ready to strike Maidro. But in the end, all of Maram's bluster could not prevail against this tough, old warrior. Maidro had his way, and we all watched as Nuradayn dropped the brandy bottles onto the sand.

'Damn you!' Maram shouted at Maidro. 'You'll kill me yet!'

He sat down near the bottles, and would not be moved. He shouted out to Sunji, 'You're right, Avari: One place is as good as another to die!'

Again, I worried that we would have to tie ropes around Maram and drag him across the desert. And then Master Juwain came over, and bent down to whisper in Maram's ear.

'Ah, all right – all right, then!' Maram pulled himself proudly back up. He stood glaring at Maidro. 'Let it not be said that Sar Maram Marshayk of the Five Horns abandoned his friends!'

As we made ready to resume our journey, I took Master Juwain aside and asked him, 'What did you say to him? Did you remind him how much we love him and couldn't go on without him?'

'No,' Master Juwain said with a smile. 'I reminded him that I'm still the keeper of the last bottle of brandy, and that he had better get back on his horse if he wants his ration tonight.'

We did not ride much farther that day. Just past dusk, we came upon some low rocks, and Maidro insisted that we should make camp in their lee. He did not say why. Apparently, his argument with Maram had driven him into a disagreeable silence.

We were all grateful for a chance to take a little extra sleep. Even Kane lay down inside the tent with us. I was not sure if he ever allowed himself to slip down into unconsciousness, but it seemed that he dwelt for hours in a realm of deep meditation and dreams.

Just after midnight, with a cold wind blowing against our tent, I felt his hand on my shoulder shaking me awake. I called out into the darkness: 'What is it?'

'Maram,' Kane said to me, 'has not returned.'

I rolled over to pat the empty sleeping fur where Maram should have been. I said to Kane, 'Return? Where did he go?'

'He said that he couldn't sleep. He said that he was going outside to look at the stars.'

Now I sat bolt upright; Maram, I thought, would no more give up his rest to look at the stars than he would to take a walk on the moon.

'How long ago, then?' I asked Kane.

'I'm not sure. An hour – maybe two.'

I grabbed for my sword, then worked my way out of our tent. Kane followed me. The brilliant starlight and half moon illuminated our encampment and the desert beyond. The Avari's tent and that of the women stood black and square in a line with ours, behind a rock formation twenty feet high. The horses stood there, too, as if frozen in the eerie stillness with which horses sleep. Maram's horse, I saw, remained with the others. I circled around the mound of rock, hoping to find Maram sitting on top of it or on one of its steps. I looked out into the desert, hoping to see his great shape looming above the starlit sands.

'Maram!' I whispered to the wind whipping out of the north-west. I turned to look off to the south and east, then shouted out, 'Maram! Maaa-ram! Where are you?'

My cries awakened everyone, who came out of their tents rubbing their eyes. I told them what had happened. It was Maidro, with his sharp old eyes, who discovered an additional set of tracks paralleling a mass of hoofprints pressed down into the sand in a long, churned-up groove leading from the direction by which we had come here, from the south. The tracks, Maidro told us, were surely Maram's, for they were deep and pointed back along our route.

'He has given up!' Nuradayn said, without thinking. 'But why didn't he take his horse?'

Nuradyan counted our waterskins, and determined that Maram had taken none of these, either.

'He has not given up,' I said to him, and everyone else. 'And he did not take his horse because he wished to steal out of here unheard.'

'But why?' Nuradayn asked.

I looked at Master Juwain, who looked back at me through the weak light. I said, 'Because he knew we would stop him from going back for the brandy.'

I moved to go saddle my horse, and Maram's, but then Maidro stopped me, laying his leathery old hand on my arm. 'No, Valaysu, do not go, not now. I fear that soon there will be a storm.'

I looked up at the glittering sky. Except for some clouds drifting toward the northwest, and strangely, up from the southwest, the sky was perfectly clear.

'Do you mean a *sandstorm*?' I said to him.

'I have seen signs of it all day,' he told me. 'It is why I wanted to make camp early, behind these rocks.'

'Then all the more reason that I must ride after Maram, before the storm comes.'

Maidro looked past the mound of rocks toward the northwest.

The wind from the darkened desert in that direction blew stronger and stronger even as we spoke.

'I think you do not have time,' Maidro told me. 'I think it will storm before another quarter of an hour has passed.'

'Then I must ride quickly,' I said.

Maidro's fingers closed around my arm like iron manacles. 'The storm will sweep away Maram's tracks. You will not find him. And then you both will die.'

'I must go after him!' I said, breaking away from his grip.

I turned again to saddle Altaru, but then Sunji, Arthayn and Nuradayn hurried up to me and grabbed my arms and waist. I surged against them, nearly pulling them up off the sand. But they were strong men, and they held me fast. And then Kane came up, too, and wrapped his mighty arm around my chest. He squeezed me tightly against him as his savage voice murmured in my ear: 'At least wait a few more minutes, as Maidro has said. If he is wrong about the storm, then ride, if you will. The delay will give Maram only that much longer to enjoy his drink. But if Maidro is right, then there is nothing you can do. So, Val, it is only fate!'

I did not want to listen to him. I twisted and stamped about, trying to shake Kane and the Avari off as a stag might hounds. None of my friends came to my aid. Master Juwain appreciated the terrible logic of Maidro's and Kane's argument, and so apparently did Liljana. They stood with the children watching the Avari restrain me. Atara, I sensed, no more wanted me to go galloping off into a sandstorm than she would want to see me plunge into a pool of lava. She waited in the starlight with her beautiful face all hard and cold.

And then there was no starlight – at least not in the northwest. There, the black glittering sky fell utterly black as if a shadow had devoured the stars. The shadow grew, obscuring even more of the sky, even as the wind built into a gale. It drove bits of sand against our garments and unprotected faces; it was like being burned by hundreds of heated iron cinders. In a moment, it seemed, the air about us turned into a gritty, blinding cloud.

'Inside the tents!' Maidro called out. 'Take the waterskins, and keep your shayals moistened!'

Shayal, I remembered as I coughed at the dust, was the Avari's word for shawl. I retreated back inside our tent as Maidro had commanded. So did everyone else. While Kane fastened the tent's opening, I poured water over my shawl and wrapped it around my face. I heard Master Juwain and Daj doing likewise. I could not see them, for our unlit tent had now fallen pitch black.

There was nothing to do then but wait. And wait we did inside our coverings of sheep and goat wool as the storm raged with the force of a whirlwind. Sand whipped in continuous streams against our tent; it was like a roaring thunder that would not cease. We prayed that the stakes holding down our tent would not pull out nor its fabric rip. We heard the horses whinnying in distress, as from far away, but we could do nothing for them. They would smother or not according to the protection that the rocks provided them and their animal wisdom and will to live. We, ourselves, breathed in and out through our moistened shawls, coughing at nearly every breath. We kept our eyes closed, lest the dust swirling inside the tent abrade them. In any case, there was nothing to see.

I tried not to think of Maram, trapped out on the wasteland in this terrible, blinding storm. I hoped that he, at least, had found the brandy before the dust swallowed him up. I missed his great presence beside me. It tormented me to lie there in utter darkness, counting the beats of my heart, minute after minute, hour after hour. I waited for the storm to abate, as did everyone else, but it seemed only to grow fiercer and stronger.

We waited all that night into the next day. The air inside the tent lightened slightly into a sort of dusty gloom. And then it grew black again as another night descended upon us and the wind continued to blow. It did not let up until early in the morning of the following day when it ceased abruptly – and strangely.

I came out of our tent to behold a landscape covered with sand, as it always was. In places – in front of our shield of rocks and out beyond – the wind had driven the sand into gleaming, new dunes. Otherwise, the desert looked the same as it always did. The sun blazed low over the eastern horizon, scattering bright light into a perfectly blue sky.

My first concern was for Altaru, and the rest of the horses. Miraculously, they had all survived the storm, though their hooves were buried in a powder-like sand and they were very thirsty. Nurdayn and Arthayn came out to begin watering them, and Sunji and Maidro walked up to me.

'Valaysu,' Maidro said to me, 'I do not think that Maram could have survived the storm. Two nights and a day, out on the sand.'

I stood staring off at the shimmering emptiness to the south, where we had abandoned the brandy.

'The horses survived,' I said to him simply.

'Yes, here behind these rocks. But out there, the wind –'

'Wind can't defeat Maram,' I half-shouted at him. 'Nor can sand, nor heat – nor even dragon fire. Only Maram can defeat Maram.'

As I moved to saddle my horse, Maidro said, 'Even before the storm, our position was perilous. And now –'

'Now my best friend is lost out there . . . somewhere! The storm obliterated our tracks, so he may not be able to find his way back here. He'll be waiting for me.'

'But how will you find him?'

'I don't know,' I told him. 'But I would have more hope if you would help me!'

Maidro looked at Sunji and Arthayn, who said, 'It is a waste of time, and therefore a waste of water. And therefore foolish beyond folly.'

I stood staring at him in the glare of the rising sun. Finally, he said to Maidro: 'I do not think anything will deter Valaysu. Therefore, we might as well help him, as he has asked.'

We spent all that day searching the desert for Maram. On our tired, parched horses, we rode south, east, west and north, scanning the dunes for any sign of Maram or his body. It was madness, as Maidro said, to go forth beneath the naked, noonday sun, but so we did. All of us nearly dropped from heatstroke. By the time that dusk approached, we had to return to our encampment to keep from falling off our horses.

'Two days now, alone and without water,' Maidro said to me over dinner that night. 'That is the limit of how long a man can live.'

'Four horns of Sarni beer is the limit of how much a man can drink,' I said to him. 'And yet Maram drank five horns and called for more.'

'It is not the same thing,' he told me.

'No, it is not, but I can't give up looking for Maram – not yet.'

That night, for a few hours, we rode out into the desert to search for Maram again. The starlight pouring down upon the pale sands showed not the slightest footprint that might have been made by him. We shouted out his name, but he did not answer us. The next morning, we resumed our quest, until the sun in the afternoon fell down upon us with a fire that we could not bear. When we quit for the day and met up back at our tents, I was forced to concede that the sun *could* defeat Maram – as it could anyone.

'Surely he is dead,' Maidro said to me. 'As we will be, too, if we do not leave this place and find water.'

I watched Estrella nibbling on a dried fig; Daj sat next to her moistening a battle biscuit with a little water so that he could chew it. In a voice as dry as the wind, I said, 'Surely Maram is dead – reason tells me this. Yet my heart tells me otherwise. If he died, I would know.'

I wondered if this were really true. Then Liljana, haggard and nearly dead of exhaustion herself, said to me: 'You always seem to know when Morjin or one of his kind is hunting you. Wouldn't you likewise know if Maram were still alive and seeking his way back here?'

'He is,' I said, trying to convince myself. 'He must be.'

I looked at Atara, who sat on a rock trying to get a comb through her dirty, matted hair. I said, 'I cannot give up hope yet, but neither can I ask everyone to remain here with me. If we don't find Maram soon, then it will be time to go on.'

At this, Sunji shot me a penetrating look and said, 'But what do you mean by "soon"?'

'Soon,' I said, echoing words that my father had once spoken, 'means soon. Now, why don't we rest before we go out looking for Maram again?'

Our search that night proved to be in vain. The moonlit dunes showed no footprint that Maram might have made nor any other sign of life. I returned to our tents with the others, and collapsed onto my furs. I could not sleep. I listened for the plaint of Maram calling to me; I did not hear him. I felt inside myself for the beating of his heart, however faint, but all that I could feel was the hard, painful hammering of my own. Then I called to him, in my mind, and from some deeper place inside me where a voice as real as the wind always whispered – and sometimes cracked out like a thunderbolt. This terrible sound seemed to tear through my heart and touch even the sands of the earth beneath me.

I was awakened just after first light when Nuradayn shouted out a warning. I came out of my tent, sword in hand, to see him watering the horses and pointing out into the desert. Everyone else left the tents, too, and joined us, looking east toward the rising sun.

The glare of this fiery orb nearly blinded us, so at first it was hard to make out the object of Nuradayn's excitement. But then I held my hand over my forehead and squinted, and this is what I saw: a creature more hideous than Jezi Yaga or Meliadus staggering toward us on two, bird-thin legs. The whole of his body seemed desiccated and shrunken, like a fruit left to bake in the sun. His ribs stood out like the frame of a wrecked ship; his belly had fallen in so that it practically clung to his spine. He was entirely naked, and his skin from head to foot had the look of sun-blackened leather. His lips seemed to have been peeled back from his teeth and gums, giving him the appearance of a flayed animal. Although many old wounds were eaten into his arms, chest, thighs and other parts of his body, none of them bled or oozed the slightest moisture. His eyes seemed as dry as bone, and fairly clicked about and rolled inside his skull as if he had no control over them. They appeared to see nothing – but to have *seen* much more than eyes should ever suffer or see.

'Is it a man?' Daj cried out, pointing at him.

'No,' I said, 'it is Maram.'

I took note of the long, ruby firestone tucked beneath Maram's armpit. His hands, I saw, looked to have been burned even worse than the rest of him so that they could not grasp this heavy crystal.

I rushed forward then, and so did everyone else. Maram fell into our arms. We carried him back to our tent; this proved no great feat as he must have weighed scarcely half what he had before the sun had stolen much of his water.

'Three and a half days!' Nuradayn marveled as he stood before our tent, looking inside. 'Who has ever heard of such a miracle?'

'All glory in the One,' Maidro said, staring at Maram. 'He should be dead.'

Sunji, looking on gravely, too, did not say what we were all thinking: that Maram *was* dead, and needed only a little more time before his heart stopped beating and his eyes closed forever.

'Vargh!' Maram said as I knelt beside him. 'Vargh!'

It took me a moment before I realized that he was trying to say my name.

Master Juwain and Liljana tried to get him to drink some water, but his tongue and throat were so parched that he could not swallow. And so Liljana moistened her fingers and touched them to his lips and tongue, which looked like a piece of blackened meat. She poured water directly over his body in the hope that his skin might absorb a little of it. Upon witnessing this waste, the four Avari who stood outside our tent shook their heads in silence.

'Vargh!' Maram said again. 'Sokki.'

Sokki, I thought, must mean, *sorry*.

These words came out like the croaking of a frog. His mouth and throat were too dry for him to speak intelligibly, but as Master Juwain and Liljana worked on him, he let loose a long series of

410

grunts, barks, hisses and moans that I tried to make sense of. I slowly pieced together what had happened, and shook my head in wonder at his story:

Maram had indeed gone after the brandy, but had never reached this trove. When the storm had fallen upon him, in the blinding sand, he couldn't follow our old tracks and so had drifted off his course. After an hour or so of believing that he might stumble upon the brandy, he instead came upon a low rock. This saved him. He took shelter behind the rock, where he could catch his breath and wait out the storm, much as we had, too. Since he had brought no water with him, however, he grew very thirsty. By the time the storm ended, he could think of nothing except water. He knew that he should try to find his way back to our encampment, but the desert seemed featureless, an endless expanse of sun-baked sand, and he did not know which way he should strike out. He tried to gauge direction by the sun; he walked north, hoping that he hadn't wandered too far. He saw no landmark that looked like the rocks near our tents. He walked on and on beneath the killing sun until it grew so hot that he had to stop. Then, like a desert rat, he dug down into the sand and buried himself to wait out the worst of the heat. Thus he did not see us searching for him, nor hear us calling to him.

When he emerged from his hole, thirst had maddened him. Now, all that he desired to drink was brandy. He wandered, in hope of finding the seven bottles that Nuradayn had dropped into the sand. The unceasing sun deranged both his wits and his senses. The wool of his robe and shawl tormented his wounds and seemed as heavy as a covering of burning iron, and so he cast them off. He continued wandering, certain that he would find an entire lake filled with brandy. Once – in a moment of terrible lucidity – he realized that we would be searching for him. And so he had tried to unleash the fire from his crystal in order to signal us. He could not control the powerful red gelstei, however, and had succeeded only in burning his hands.

After that, only his craving for brandy had kept him from dropping down into the sand and dying. He fancied that the earth itself would tell him where to search for it. Sometime during the previous night, in the darkness before dawn, he had heard me calling to him and telling him that I had found the brandy. If only he could make his way back to me, he could have all the brandy that he could drink.

'Vraddi!' he croaked out as he lay inside the tent. 'Vraddi!'

I knew that he was calling for brandy, and I implored Master Juwain to wet his mouth with a little brandy from the last remaining bottle. Master Juwain did as I asked. The few drops that he poured down Maram's throat were all that Maram could drink.

'We cannot remain here any longer,' Sunji said to me from outside the tent. 'I know that your friend is dying, but –'

'There is still hope,' I said to him. I came out of the tent to stand beside him. 'You are right, though, that we cannot remain. If Estrella can find water, perhaps another cave where it is moist and cool, then Maram might yet live.'

The dark look in Sunji's eyes told me that he no longer had much hope of Estrella finding water and none at all that it would help Maram if she did.

After that we fashioned a litter from the tent and its poles, and placed Maram upon it. We covered him against the rising sun. A little more work sufficed to secure the litter to one of the pack-horses, who would drag it atilt across the sand.

Then we set out again toward the northwest. We were all so tired that we had to fight to keep from falling off our horses. Maidro announced that we had so little water left, we must forbear eating altogether. None of us, I thought, except perhaps Kane, had any appetite left. I couldn't think of food; in truth, I could hardly think of water. As we made our way miles farther into the glaring sands of the Tar Harath, all my attention concentrated on Maram. Bound to his litter and wrapped up like a mummy that remained somehow alive, he moved up one dune and down the next; from time to time, he would call out to us a single word: 'Vraddi!'

And then there came a time when he called out no more. Master Juwain dismounted and determined that Maram had fallen into the deep sleep that sometimes precedes the even deeper sleep of death.

'Even if Estrella can find water,' Sunji said to me as we crested one of the endless dunes, 'I don't think it will help Maram now.'

'I don't think the udra mazda *will* find water,' Maidro said. He sat on his wasted horse staring out at the sun-seared distances. 'It is growing only hotter, and the glare more hellish by the mile.'

Estrella, almost as weak as a newborn, found the strength to urge her horse onward, across the blazing sands. I followed her; I tried to follow my dimly-remembered sense that there was a union of opposites: good and evil; brightness and dark; moisture and drought.

Then we came up on top of another dune, and my urge to turn

back from the fiery wasteland before us burned me like the kirax in my blood. I felt this urge to retreat flaring inside my companions and the four Avari, as well. I was so tired, fevered and thirsty that I could barely see. It seemed that we were riding on and on into a wavering emptiness. The air was sick with heat; it seemed to bend the hellish light and distort it in strange ways. Mirages swirled in the distance and then vanished into nothingness.

Something powerful seized hold of me, as of a great hand wrapped around my spine. I knew that I had experienced this strange sensation before, but I could not quite remember where. And then Estrella pointed into the heart of the terrible brilliance ahead of us. In the shimmering light there, I thought I could make out flashes of green that looked like trees.

'The sun has addled your wits,' Sunji said to me when I mentioned this. He squinted into the dazzling distances and shook his head. 'It is the madness that precedes sunstroke. We should pitch our tents and take shelter before it grows even hotter.'

I gazed down at Maram, bound to his litter, and I said, 'No, we must go on.'

It was Master Juwain who noticed the clouds above us: all puffy and white, and drifting in from the east, west and south toward a point just beyond the impossibly bright horizon.

'Strange,' Master Juwain murmured. 'How very strange!'

Liljana, who sat next to him on top of her exhausted horse, seemed to read his thoughts, and she said, 'Can it be that one of the Vilds lies here?'

At the look of puzzlement in Sunji's and Maidro's eyes, she told of the magic woods called Vilds that could be found at certain secret places in the world.

'You are all mad!' Sunji cried out. 'There cannot be such a hadrah at the heart of the Tar Harath!'

But then we forced ourselves to ride on another mile and crested yet another line of dunes. The air grew moist, as of a breeze off the sea. The shimmer out on the blinding sands suddenly fell from quicksilver to a bright and beautiful green.

'So,' Kane said. 'So.'

Now the veils of mirage finally parted to reveal an astonishing sight: great trees pushed their green crowns high above the desert's sands. And above this unbroken canopy hung thick layers of clouds rising up even higher into the sky. From the streaks of gray slanting downward toward the trees, it seemed that it must be raining.

'It cannot be!' Maidro murmured. 'It cannot be!'

413

He, and all of us, stared in wonder at the miles-wide forest in the middle of nowhere. His gaze fell upon Estrella, and he said, 'Bless the udra mazda!'

Sunji, Arthayn and Nuradayn all bowed their heads to Estrella, and so did I. Then Maidro nodded at me and added, 'Bless the Elahad, too. Without him, how would we have found the will to go on?'

The Avari seemed enraptured, even terrified, for although a few spindly trees grew in their hadrahs, they had never imagined anything like these lush, magnificent woods. Estrella smiled at them as if to say that the impossible was not only possible, but inevitable. Then she urged her horse forward, down toward the cool, abiding greenness of the Vild.

26

We rode straight from the desert into the shelter of giant trees rising almost two hundred feet above the forest floor. The air grew instantly cooler, and although the light dimmed, everything seemed strangely more clear. We all breathed more easily; the parched linings of our mouths and throats fairly drank in the moisture from the breeze wafting through the great oaks and maples. The sweet scent of flowers – anemone, trillium, honeysuckle and many others – nearly intoxicated us. Birds sang from all around us; I noticed Sunji's eyes grow wide with astonishment at the blue jays, yellow-breasted warblers and scarlet tangagers whose like he had never seen before, or even imagined. The four Avari, I thought, rode as if in a dream. Their terror at the mighty trees gradually bled away, to be replaced by awe and wonder.

'All glory in the One!' Maidro repeated like a mantra. 'And I have never seen such glory!'

'Out on the sand, I think we must have died,' Nuradayn said. 'And here, we've been reborn on earth a million years hence, after the desert has been restored.'

'Either that,' Arthayn said, 'or we all still *remain* out in the desert, hallucinating our final vision before death.'

Maidro shook his head at this as he unwrapped the shawl from his face. He breathed in deeply and said, 'No, this is real. In all my life, I have never felt anything *as* real, except perhaps the light of the stars. Behold those flowers, the white ones with the nine points! It's as if they hold starlight itself. Everything here – the grasses, the leaves, the bark on the trees – it all shines as from a light within!'

I smiled because I had rarely heard the taciturn Avari wax so poetic, or indeed speak so many words in one breath. Then Sunji, too, uncovered his face and smiled as he said simply: 'If this is death, give me more of it. I have never felt so alive.'

We dismounted and walked beside our horses over the soft, green grass. The power of the earth here was as palpable as the beating of my heart. Its fires did not burn, but seemed to stream into me like an elixir through my legs, mouth, eyes and the very pores of my skin. A new strength, vast and deep, touched my blood. I noticed Daj and Estrella stepping with a happier gait, while Liljana and Master Juwain got the best of their exhaustion and managed to drive the pains from their old bones. Atara, tapping her unstrung bow ahead of her to feel her way through the woods, trembled with a new hope. Even Kane seemed more alive here, if that were possible. He shook out the dust from his white hair and wiped the sweat from his savage eyes – and for a moment he stood revealed as an angel of bright and indestructible purpose.

It was Maram, however, who gave me the greatest joy. I nearly wept to see him open his eyes and croak out: 'Vraddi! Vraddi!'

I could not tell if he realized that we had once again entered one of Ea's magic woods. It didn't seem to matter. He was still alive, and even the bluebirds on the branches of the trees seemed to sing of this miracle.

After about a mile or so we came to a place where many crystals, like flowers in a garden, sprang up from the grass: rubies, amethyst, tourmaline and even diamonds. Master Juwain knelt down to examine a particularly lovely green crystal, and determined that it was an emerald. Then he turned to another nearby which looked just like it and added, 'And this is a varistei.'

Maidro shook his head in disbelief at this new wonder. I knew it must seem impossible to him that precious gems, much less magical gelstei, could simply grow out of the ground.

'But how can you tell it is a varistei?' I asked Master Juwain.

In answer, he drew out his green crystal – the one that had so nearly killed Maram.

'I can feel the life of *this* gelstei,' he said, holding his crystal down toward the rock garden, 'seeking out the life of *that* gelstei.'

Liljana, too, brought forth her crystal, and held the little whale figurine up to the side of her head. She told us, 'I can't hear Morjin breathing his filthy lies in my ears. I don't think he has power over our gelstei here.'

Her words prompted Atara to cup her scryer's sphere in her hand. She stood holding it in front of her blindfold. Then she

416

announced, 'He *can't* see us here! It's as if a dark cave has hidden us from him!'

She put away her kristei, and tucked her bow into the holster strapped to her horse. Then she walked straight over to where a starflower grew beneath a huge, old elm tree. She bent down to touch her finger precisely upon one of the filamentous stamens flowing out from the center of the starflower's white petals. She gathered up a bit of pollen on her fingertip and fairly ran back over to me, crying out, 'Oh, Val – you were right! I can *see* again!'

Her laughter filled the forest with a music sweeter than even the trilling of the birds.

'I am still afraid to try to heal Maram again,' Master Juwain said, gripping his gelstei in his hand. 'It may be that the Lord of Dragon Fire has only turned his sight away from us for a time.'

He said that it might be enough for us to find a pool or pond, and cover Maram's outraged skin with mud. Then, if we could use the brandy to moisten his mouth and throat enough for him to drink, we might slowly bring him back to life.

'That is good, good!' a high, piping voice called out to us as if from nowhere. I fairly jumped back five feet as a small, nut-brown man stepped out from behind an old oak tree. He wore a skirt of some silk-like fiber, and nothing else. It seemed that he had been eavesdropping on us. 'But it would be better, better for Anneli to tend to him.'

He presented himself as Kalevi, and said that he had been sent to take us to a place of healing deeper in the woods. There gathered many of his people, whom he called the Loikalii. He spoke with a strange accent so thick and lilting that I could barely make sense of his words. He gave us to understand that the Loikalii had been anticipating our arrival for many days.

'Those who come out of the desert,' he told us, 'are always burnt like unwatered plants, and always need healing.'

'Then have others come here before us?' Master Juwain asked him.

'Other giants, do you mean?' Kalevi said, looking up at Master Juwain, who was not a large man. 'No, no – *they* do not come. Never, never. But sometimes, we Loikalii go out into the desert. And *sometimes*, we even return. Now, come, yourselves, before it is too late for that one.'

So saying, he pointed at Maram, who lay on his litter savoring the dram of brandy that Liljana had slowly dripped into his mouth.

There was nothing to do then except to follow Kalevi through the forest. The four Avari all seemed amazed that our story of little people and giant trees had proved true. We walked in a line strung out beneath the leafy boughs above us. By the time we had gone another mile, the trees seemed to grow even higher. More flowers adorned the grass, and the lights of the Timpum appeared and twinkled brighter and brighter. These strange beings, with their swirls of ruby radiance, silver and many other colors, were everywhere. Sprays of gleaming amethyst filled the buttercups and tulips; splendid teardrops, like sapphire necklaces glittering in the sun, encircled the trunk of a maple sapling and a much larger birch. Some of the Timpum were as tiny as particles of diamond dust, while others encompassed whole trees like a raiment woven of pure light. No two of the Timpum seemed exactly the same, any more than the face of one man exactly resembled that of another, even though they be twin brothers. All of the Timpum, however, blazed with a deep and beautiful life. They spun and danced all around us, in all their fiery millions, in sheer delight.

Master Juwain, never one to offer up simple explanations where an arcane verse would serve as well, looked from the mystified Sunji to Maidro and then at Nuradayn as he recited an old, old rhyme that my companions and I had heard more than once:

> There is a place 'tween earth and time,
> In some forsaken desert clime
> Of woods and brooks and vernal glades,
> Whose healing magic never fades.
>
> An island in a sandy sea,
> Abode of secret greenery
> Where giant trees and emeralds grow,
> Where leaves and grass and flowers glow.
>
> And there no bitter bloom of spite
> To blight the forest's living light,
> No sword, no spear, no axe, no knife
> To tear the sweetest sprigs of life.
>
> The deeper life for which we yearn,
> Immortal flame that doesn't burn,
> The sacred sparks, ablaze, unseen –
> The children of the Galadin.

> *Beneath the trees they gloze and gleam,*
> *And whirl and play and dance and dream*
> *Of wider woods beyond the sea*
> *Where they shall dwell eternally.*

'I have changed a few of the words,' Master Juwain told Maidro and Sunji, 'to suit the circumstances of *this* Vild. As for the Timpum, they are all around you, though you cannot see them. But they are of the same substance, I believe, as Flick.'

At this, Flick suddenly flared into sight. The Avari gazed at him once more in wonder. So did Kalevi – but for different reasons. He cried out, 'One of the Bright Ones walks with you! How is it that you can see him?'

I told him of how Master Juwain, Maram, Atara and I had found one of the Lokilani's Vilds in faroff Alonia and had eaten the sacred timana, which had gifted us with vision of the Timpum.

'Good, good!' Kalevi said. Then he swept his hand toward Sunji and the other Avari and added, 'But these men did not eat the timana, yes? And they behold the Bright One, even so. Why? Why? It must be because he is so bright – the brightest I have ever seen!'

As he spoke, the bits of light making up Flick's form blazed like tiny suns. Glorre radiated out from his center and filled the woods.

'This color!' Kalevi cried out. 'We have seen it before, but never here – never, never! The Loikalii must look upon this one! Come, come!'

He urged us onward, beneath the giant trees. With every furlong that we walked deeper into the woods, they seemed to grow even higher. We came upon the first astors, much smaller, but more beautiful than even the white birches, for their leaves shone golden and their bark gleamed with the soft shimmer of silver. Some bore clusters of timanas: small, round, golden fruits, sweet to the tongue and even sweeter to the spirit. Their flesh could open doors to another world, but could also kill.

At last we entered a glade ringed with silver maples and filled with lovely astor trees. The Loikalii had all gathered there – all who lived in this Vild, or so Kalevi said. Three hundred men, women and children dressed much as Kalevi spread out in a great circle to welcome us. In our entrance to the Alonian Vild, their kinsmen had aimed arrows at us; these people, instead, held out to us their small, brown hands cupping gourds filled with water.

'We have been waiting for you,' a regal-looking woman called

419

out to us. She stood in front of the ring of her people. She seemed of an age with Liljana, with graying hair and wrinkles creasing her wise face, but her eyes were as green and as full of life as spring leaves. She presented herself as Maira, and told us: 'Our water is yours.'

These words made a good impression on the Avari, who bowed their heads to honor Maira and her people. The Loikalii closed in upon us then, and we spent some time accepting the gourds from them and drinking water as sweet and cool as the sap running through a tree. Then Maira presented to us a beautiful young woman named Anneli, who was taller than most of the other Loikalii. Her hair flowed in black waves over her shoulders and back, and she wore a great green stone around her neck. I sensed that this crystal must be a varistei; so did Master Juwain. When Maira announced that Anneli was a great healer, Master Juwain inclined his head toward her in respect.

'Anneli,' Maira said to us, pointing at Maram, 'will take the burnt one inside her house to be made whole again – if it is not too late.'

'Vraddi,' Maram croaked out from his litter as he looked up at Maira. Then his gaze fell upon the lovely Anneli, and his voice grew louder: 'Vraddi!'

Anneli misunderstood what Maram was asking for. She came over to him and held out her slender hand to keep back one of the Loikalii women trying to get Maram to drink from her gourd. Then Anneli tenderly brushed back the filthy hair plastered to Maram's forehead. In a voice like a song, she piped out: 'This flower needs much water, but too much too soon will drown him.'

Maira nodded her head at Anneli, and then looked at my companions and me. She told us, 'Houses have been made ready for the rest of you. You must sleep now, and eat and drink, and then sleep some more. And then we will speak: of the Burning Lands and the Bright One you call Flick – and of the Dark One we call Asangal and others name as Ang Ar Mai Nyu. And of *his* disciple, the Morajin. Until then – and after, after! – the Forest shall be your home.'

While the Loikalii men and women melted off into the woods to gather nuts and fruits, which was most of their work, Kalevi escorted us to a little lake, where we stripped ourselves naked and used fragrant leaves to wash the grime from our bodies. He gave us garments – tunics woven of silk – to wear. Then he led us a short distance to our 'houses'. These proved to be nothing more, and nothing less, than the hollowed-out trunks of huge, living trees called olindas. As Kalevi told us, his people had little need of shelter, for the Forest never grew very hot or very cold. Even when it rained, the canopies of the oaks and other great trees protected them. A few of the Loikalii therefore lived their entire lives outside of their houses, but most of them liked to sleep inside the wooden walls of the olinda tree.

'The trees give us their strength,' Kalevi said to us as he stopped near one of the towering olindas. 'As they will to you.'

A sort of doorway almost wide enough to ride a horse through opened through the trunk of one of the olindas, which must have been a hundred feet around. Its dark interior seemed to have been scooped out, though Kalevi gave me to understand that these trees grew this way mostly of their own accord, with very little help from the Loikalii.

'We do not shape *these* trees,' he told us, 'but deeper in the wood, you might see the bonsails, which are almost as beautiful as the astors. Now, come, come! – rest, as Maira has said!'

He left us to make ourselves comfortable inside our three houses. After seeing to the horses, the Avari went inside a great olinda. Atara, Liljana and Estrella shared the shelter of a second tree, while Kane, Daj, Master Juwain and I set up inside the third. There was little work for us to do. We had no need even to roll out our dusty, stinking sleeping furs, for the interior of the olinda had been lined with a thick carpet of leaves, and mats of woven silk laid out on top of them. Someone had stocked our new home with gourds of water and others full of fresh fruits and nuts. We had to share our simple living quarters with the spiders and insects who also dwelled there, but we were all so tired that we didn't mind this web-spinning and buzzing company.

And so we all lay down to take our rest – all of us except Master Juwain. He bore a heavy burden of guilt at having so nearly killed Maram with his crystal, and he would not suffer Anneli to try to heal Maram alone with her varistei. Anneli, a woman of generous heart, gladly invited Master Juwain into her house. While we slept, the two of them spent many long hours tending to Maram.

For the next three days, we did little more than eat, sleep and walk through the Loikalii's woods. Liljana could not even manage to wash our sweat-stained clothing, for the Loikalii insisted on soaking our woolens in water full of the same leaves with which we had washed ourselves. They brought us water to drink and a never-ending supply of delicious things to eat. After they overcame their fear of our horses, they even took on the task of watering them with their own hands.

We saw Master Juwain only twice during this time, and Maram not at all. One evening, Daj stole close to Anneli's house, but was not allowed inside. He later told us of flashes of emerald lighting up the tree's interior, and of Maram calling out softly for water. On the fourth day after our entrance into the Vild, Anneli and Master Juwain emerged to tell us that Maram would be all right. On the fifth day, Maram himself walked out of Anneli's house under the power of his own two legs. He was nearly naked; like the Loikalii, he wore only a narrow band of a skirt that barely covered his loins. His flesh, no less his eyes, gleamed. I could hardly believe the wonders that Anneli and Master Juwain had worked upon him.

He stood boldly without shame so that we could regard him. Although he was much thinner than when we had set out from Mesh, he was still Maram: thick of bone and thew, and radiating a raw, rude vitality. All the sores were gone from his flesh – all save one. Neither Anneli nor Master Juwain had been able to heal the terrible burn that Master Juwain's gelstei had seared into his chest. A large leaf covered this wound. But the rest of Maram's skin, even his hands, had taken on their usual ruddy color and showed little of the more angry red of a sunscalding or other burn.

Maram gazed at Anneli as if utterly enchanted by this lovely woman who had healed him. His desires had obviously moved on from brandy to more fiery things.

Maira ordered a feast to celebrate Maram's recovery and to honor us. That evening, we gathered beneath the astor trees, whose leaves gave off a soft, golden light. The whole tribe of Loikalii sat themselves down around many large mats placed throughout the grove. As at our other feasts in the other Vilds, these mats would serve as tables on which the Loikalii set bowls full of their simple yet sustaining food.

'In many ways,' Master Juwain remarked as we and the Avari joined Maira, Anneli, Kalevi and several other Loikalii around a particularly large mat, 'these people are quite similar to their kinsmen. But in other ways . . . .'

His voice trailed off as Maira shot him a sharp, penetrating look. She seemed much more knowledgeable about us, and the world outside, than the other Lokilani whom we had met. Although she exuded congeniality and sweetness, I sensed that she could also be as forceful and determined as any of Ea's queens.

When we had finished filling ourselves with nutbread and honey and other delicious things, she passed me a gourd full of elderberry wine with a graceful motion of her hand and the most radiant of smiles. She would not abide Master Juwain's protestations that Maram should be denied strong drink; she passed Maram wine too: more than one gourd's worth, and then more than three. She seemed not to mind the way that Maram gazed at Anneli, though a couple of the other Loikalii present could not countenance his obvious infatuation. She smiled at him in amusement, and then directed our conversation toward matters that we had put off discussing for five days.

'Tell us, Val'Alahad,' she said to me, 'of yourselves and your journey.'

And so I did. While the Loikalii at our table and the others nearby turned toward me, I told of our quest, as much as I thought wise. The hours flowed into evening, and evening turned toward night. The radiance of the astor leaves lit the grove, and it fell cool. No mosquitoes, however, came out to bite the Loikalii's nearly naked bodies. It seemed that they allowed into their woods only those living things that pleased them. Other things, however, darker things, they could not keep out.

'We have *seen* the Morajin,' she told us. 'The Earthkiller, our cousins call him. The Burning One that *you* call the Red Dragon: he burns, inside, as if his blood is on fire. It is worse than the scorching of the sun, for that can destroy only flesh. But the Morajin's soul! It is all black and twisted, like a worm dropped onto hot coals. We have seen this! He would kill all that displeases him, even the best of himself. He sends his armies throughout all lands, killing and killing until the earth cannot bear it. Soon, soon, we fear, all of the earth's trees will be cut down and her soil burnt barren. It will be as it is in the Burning Lands outside of the Forest.'

She seemed to blame the desolation of the desert on Morjin, and on his master, whom she called Ang Ar Mai Nyu. How she knew of either of them – or of anything outside of her woods – was not clear. I could not imagine any of her delicate, gentle people crossing the desert to lands so faraway and forbidding as Sakai in the heart of the White Mountains.

Her words disturbed all of us, and Master Juwain especially. He rubbed at his smooth scalp as he looked at Maira and said, 'Surely the desert has causes other than the hand of the Red Dragon. Why, the Crescent Mountains, to the west, which block the moisture from the ocean. The pattern of the winds, which blow –'

'The winds blow enough moisture our way,' Maira said, cutting him off. She smiled at him nicely, but I could tell that she had little patience for his perpetual questioning and turning things over and over in his mind. 'Grass could grow where now there is only the sand. And more moisture could be summoned – enough to make the Forest grow across the whole of the Burning Lands.'

Here she glanced to her right at an old woman named Oni. Oni had white hair and withered breasts, but her eyes still held much life. She cupped between her hands a small, bluish bowl that looked something like frozen water. I wondered immediately if it were made of some kind of gelstei that I had never seen before.

'If you can truly summon the clouds,' Master Juwain said, addressing both Maira and Oni, 'as it seems you can, then why hasn't the desert been made green again?'

'The Loikalii,' Maira said to us, 'long, long ago were sent to this place to re-enchant the earth. A great evil occurred here, long past long ago. It opened up the earth to the deep fires, the black fires which scorched the soil, out and out across the Burning Lands.'

Master Juwain nodded his head in deep contemplation; I could almost hear him wondering what kind of evil event or sorcery could have channelled the telluric currents so as to create a wasteland hundreds of miles wide.

'But you have succeeded *here*,' he said, looking at the astor trees above us. 'I have never known a more enchanting place.'

'We have *not* succeeded here,' Maira said. 'We have sent our people out on the sands to plant seeds so that the Forest might widen. All have failed. Even in this place, if we did not fight to make the Forest grow, the trees would wither and die and be lost into the sand.'

She went on to tell of an ancient dark thing, perhaps a crystal, buried beneath the soil somewhere on earth. She said that it had the power to draw life from the earth and allow its inner fires to burn unchecked and wreak destruction upon all things. Kane scowled at this, and his eyes found mine; it was obvious that Maira must be speaking of the Black Jade. I recounted then of our crossing of the Skadarak and what we knew of this powerful gelstei.

'The Black Jade,' Maira said as she looked from Oni to Anneli and then back at me. 'You have named it well. We have felt how the Morajin seeks his way deeper and deeper into its heart. We know that Ang Ar Mai Nyu aids him. Why, why, we have asked ourselves? Soon, we fear, the Morajin will loose the earth's fires and burn open the very sky. Then the evil that created the Burning

Lands will blight the stars. Their earths – so many, many! – will be burnt, too. The Forest that covers them will die. It will be as you said it was at the heart of the Skadarak: everything blackened and covered with bones. And then it will be as it is here, beyond our trees: nothing but burning sands, everywhere and forever.'

I gazed at her in wonder of how her dread of the future so nearly matched my own. Then she took a sip of her wine and shook her head furiously. 'But we must not let this *be*! If the Morajin gains power, utterly, over the Black Jade, he will invade the Forest. First, with his eyes and with dark dreams. And soon after, with steel and fire.'

Here she glanced at the hilt of Kane's sword and shook her head in loathing. A similar look on Oni's face told me that, in some ways at least, the Loikalii did not welcome our presence in their woods.

I took a sip of wine, too, and then said to Maira, 'You know a great deal about matters of which we have learned only with difficulty. And that few others even suspect. How, then? Are there scryers among you?'

Maira looked quickly at Oni, who spoke in a cranky, quavering voice, saying, 'Do you see, Maira? I told you they would want to know.'

Oni's angry, relentless stare seemed to disconcert Maira, who glanced at Atara and said, 'No, none of us can see the future, not as you can. But sometimes, we can see things far, far away.'

'How, then?' I asked again.

Now Oni stared at me as she shook her head. She said to Maira, 'No, no – they mustn't see!'

Her hands gripped her crystal bowl, and I suddenly knew that it had been Oni who had sent the sandstorm that had so nearly killed us. There was something wild about this old woman, I thought, like the wind. I sensed that she acted by the force of her own will and no one else's, not even Maira's.

'I believe that they *must* see,' Maira said to her. 'How else are they to find the Shining One they seek? And how else to keep the Morajin from using the gelstei they call the Lightstone?'

'No,' Oni said, as stubborn as a stone. 'The giants are clumsy and stupid, and bring an evil of their own into the Forest.'

She stared at the hilt of my sword; after a while, she raised up her angry old eyes and stared at me.

'They are *not* stupid,' Maira said to her. 'And whose heart is wholly pure?'

'No, no – they must not see!'

'*I* have seen this,' Maira said to her. 'And you have, too: that the time is coming when either the Forest will grow across the Burning Lands, or the Burning Lands will devour the Forest – and soon, soon. Which will it be?'

While the evening deepened, they argued back and forth, but no word or reason from Maira could prevail against Oni's obduracy. And then there occurred a miracle beyond reason or resistance: Flick fell out of the night like a comet. He hovered in the air radiating an intense glorre. This light seemed to draw many other Timpum from out of the trees around us. It touched them so that they glowed with glorre, too. Then these thousands of splendid beings passed the fire back to Flick so that he blazed ever brighter. Back and forth it passed, many, many times, Flick feeding the Timpum and they feeding him until the whole host of little lights shimmered with great brilliance.

'Do you see?' Kalevi cried out, pointing at Flick. 'The angel fire – I did not imagine it! The giants call it glorre!'

'Glorre! Glorre! Glorre!' the many Loikalii at their tables chanted.

'It is a sign!' Kalevi cried out again, turning to Oni. 'You must take them to the Water!'

'Take them! Take them! Take them!' his tribesmates chanted.

I drew my sword and held it up toward Flick. Its mirrored surface seemed perfectly to reflect his fiery form. Whether it picked up the glorre pouring out of him or shone from within with this singular color was hard to tell.

'All right,' Oni said at last as she gazed at my sword. I saw for the first time how lovely her eyes really were. The ice inside her seemed utterly to have melted. 'In the morning, I will take them to the Water. But now, we should eat the flesh of the angels – and dance and sing!'

She smiled, and years fell away from her. Then bowls full of golden, ripe timanas were brought forth so that we might eat the sacred fruit and deepen our visions of the Timpum, and all living things. Daj and Estrella, to their disappointment, were not allowed to touch the timanas, for the Loikalii counted them as children even though they stood as high as many of the Loikalii women and men. Sunji, Maidro, Arthayn and Nuradayn, however, each picked up a fat, gleaming timana. Maira warned them that the very taste of it sometimes killed. Sunji, speaking for all the Avari, said that they would risk it. As he put it: 'We have borne heat, wind, sand and sun to come this far. It is said that if a man dies

426

in the desert seeking visions, he doesn't really die when he dies. And so we will gladly eat these fruits that you have given us.'

And so he did, along with the other Avari. That night, none of them died, nor did anyone else in the grove partaking in this part of the feast. The Avari finally beheld what we had looked upon for several days but could never take for granted: the millions of Timpum in their glory, gleaming as brightly as the stars and whirling ecstatically in and out of the astor trees. Old Maidro, upon standing up to dance with us and the hundreds of Loikalii forming up into circles, laughed like a young man and called out: 'I'm still alive, but I'm finally *ready* to die!'

Later that night, after it came time for rest, we returned to our olinda trees. Maram, though, did not come with us. He claimed that Anneli had yet to heal him wholly, and so he would sleep inside her house so that she might bestow upon him her gifts.

Just before going off with her, he took me aside and draped his arm across my shoulders. His breath, heavy with the vapors of elderberry wine, blasted into my face as he said, 'Ah, Val, there is healing and then there is *healing*, do you understand? Maidro might be ready to die, but I'm not. No, no – it's time I truly *lived* again.'

And with that, this irrepressible man who had come so close to breathing his last breath, walked off into the woods happily singing his favorite song.

27

In the morning, we all gathered in the grove, where Maira and Oni met us – along with all the other Loikalii. They thought nothing, it seemed, of giving up their work in favor of witnessing whatever event was about to occur. Oni led us through the trees in a winding way that followed no path. In the strong light raining down through the emerald leaves, the Timpum seemed to shine even more brightly than they had the previous night. So did the flowers and the birds and every other living thing in these mysterious woods.

At last we came into a clearing. A pool of water, fifty feet wide, gleamed in its center. The Loikalii sat around it on low banks of grass. Oni stood beside the pool's rippling waters with Maira and me – and with Kane. Although no one had invited him in so close, no one seemed to find the courage to warn him away. The Loikalii allowed no large predators into their woods, but Kane was like a tiger, pacing back and forth with a barely contained fire tormenting his great body as his fathomless eyes fixed on the pool.

Oni cupped her pale blue bowl in her hands, and shut her eyes. Almost immediately, the breeze died. A stillness fell upon the air over the pool. The only sounds were the songs of the birds deeper in the trees and Kane's restless footfalls.

'Be quiet!' Oni finally hissed at Kane. She opened her eyes and glared at him. 'Or else leave this place!'

Kane stared right back at her with a fiery gaze that might have wilted a tree. But he finally did as she had commanded, freezing into motionlessness like a great cat ready to spring. His bright, black eyes took in the glimmer of the pool.

As my heart drummed inside me, the waters of the pool grew stiller and clearer. I noticed that it sat within a bed of crystal that

428

might have been diamond. No lily pad nor lake skimmer nor even a twig or a speck of dust floated upon this water. It came to me that I had never seen water so pure and deep.

'The waters of all worlds flow into each other,' Oni's voice intoned – a million miles away, it seemed. 'The waters of all things are one; in the end, there is only one Water.'

Now the pool's waters stilled with an utter clarity. In its depths – it was like looking through air – I beheld mountains and waterfalls and a great, shimmering city. Crystalline towers half a mile high stood on rocky prominences above a broad valley. It must have been autumn there, for the valley's contours showed the yellows of aspens and maples' blazing reds – as well groves of astor trees whose golden foliage blanketed the earth. Throughout the valley and above it, upon rocky hills, stood many graceful buildings and houses agleam with the colors of living stone: azure and cinnabar, magenta, saffron and aquamarine. I knew that all these structures had been built by the hand of man, but so perfect were they in design and in harmony with the landforms of the valley that it seemed here art and nature were as one. I couldn't help recalling the wondrous city that Ymanir had built high in the White Mountains: Alundil, the City of the Stars.

The valley's beauty called to something ancient within me. Without quite knowing what I was doing, I reached out my hand toward it. This simple motion unsettled my balance. Even as Kane's hand struck out to try to catch me, I found myself teetering at the edge of the pool, and then stumbling forward. I hit the water with a great splash. Its coldness stabbed into me like a thousand icy needles. The weight of my sword, strapped to my back, helped to pull me under, down and down into a deepening gloom for what seemed forever. I pulled hard with my hands against cold currents and kicked my feet. I swam up and up toward the light streaming through the water. Finally, with a gasp of air I broke from the surface of the pool into a burst of brilliant sunshine. I shook back my wet hair. I blinked my eyes because I could not believe what they beheld. Kane and Oni and everyone else who had gathered by the pool – the Loikalii, the Avari, too – were gone. The city that I had descried within the pool now spread out all around me, amethyst towers rising up from the mountainsides to my right and left. Upon the pool's grassy banks stood tall men and women with jet black hair and eyes as bright and black as my deepest dreams.

One of them, a man wearing a blue tunic trimmed in gold and

a fillet of silver binding back his long hair, held out his hand to me and pulled me dripping and shivering from the pool. A woman – I had never seen a queen so striking, not even my mother – covered me with a long, thick robe of new lamb's wool. A man who might have been her brother stood smiling at me in welcome; the diamonds encrusting his tunic shone more brilliantly than a knight's armor. All these people, I thought, were like unto the Valari of my home, only more beautiful and even nobler in aspect. It came to me then that they *were* Valari, the true and ancient Valari, for I knew somehow that I had stepped out upon another world and looked upon twelve of the Star People.

'*Talinna ira vos,*' the queenlike woman said to me. '*Lila satna garad.*'

She spoke more words to me, and so did the others. As with veils pulled back to reveal a familiar face, their meaning became clearer and clearer. I realized that they were speaking in a language similar to ancient Ardik, which is to the language of the angels as the common tongue is to Ardik.

They gave me their names: Asha, Eva, Varjan, Jessur, Eldru and Shivaj. And Kavalad, Aja, Saya, Jerusha, Varda and Ramadar. They gave me to understand that they had come here to greet me; that seemed almost impossible, but I sensed that they were not lying. Something about the structure of their language made it unnatural to utter anything false or guileful. In the clear consonants and liquid vowels that poured from their beautiful lips, no less the light sparking in their eyes, I sensed only a strong intent toward goodness and truth. They each embodied these qualities, along with a nobility that I had seen in my father and mother, but few others. They were men and women, I thought, as I had always imagined men and women to be.

So awestruck was I that I could hardly speak. But I finally remembered my manners, and bowed my head to Ramadar, the man who had pulled me from the pool. I found my voice and stammered out: '*Satnamon Valashu – Valashu Elahad.*'

'*Valashu,*' he repeated, bowing to me. Then he pointed up at the deep blue sky, where a blue sun shone with a dazzling light. '*Val al'Ashu ni al'Elahad – vos ari arda valas.*'

My heart beat like a soaring swan within me as the meaning of what Ramadar had said became clear and confirmed what I knew to be true: 'Star-of-the-Morning of the line of Elahad, you have journeyed deep into the stars.'

Only the dead, I thought, made such journeys. For several hours,

I struggled to speak to them in their beautiful language. The sun dried my tunic, then began to drop toward the blazing hills in the west. There, the light off the houses ran through a riot of shifting colors: violet and carnelian; ocher, turquoise and red. A few of the Star People – Eva, Saya and Jessur – walked off to their houses and returned with delicious foods whose like I had never seen nor tasted. It grew darker, and the stars came out, and then I *knew* that I had left Ea, for the constellations here were all strange and lit up the sky with a brilliance beyond that of any sky I had ever beheld, even the infinite black and silver dome above the Tar Harath.

As the Star People's words became ever clearer to me, so did mine to them. I gained a clearer understanding of their purpose and how they had come to be waiting here to greet me. They had their scryers, too, it seemed. One of them had foretold my journey, and had warned that once I beheld the beauty of their city, Iveram, I would never want to leave. This was so. In gazing out at the mountains and waterfalls above the city's twinkling lights, it seemed that I had finally come home.

'You, Valashu, are welcome to remain with us,' Ramadar said to me. Although his long, grave face and bold eyes reminded me of my father, it seemed that he bore no higher rank than any other of his eleven companions. 'But we have been sent here to persuade you that you must go back.'

Was I not dead, then, after all? But go back to what, I thought? To a woman whom I could never marry? To friends whom I led on and on in a quest likely to find only their deaths? To a doomed world?

Although I had spoken around these doubts for many hours with Ramadar and the other Star People, I had not made them explicit. It didn't matter. They sensed the volcano of fury and anguish that fumed inside me. They, too, perhaps in greater measure than I, bore the gift of valarda.

'Our lives present us with many choices,' Ramadar told me. 'But in the end, only one path will have been walked. We believe that yours lies back, toward the world you call Ea.'

'Perhaps it does,' I said. I turned to looked at Asha, and then at Eva, whose long black hair showed strands of silver and whose eyes shone with kindness and concern for me. 'Why don't you then come with me? All of you – and any of you who live here?'

I went on to say that many thousands of men and women willing to make this journey could surely be found in Iveram and

431

other cities of their world, which they named as Givene. Under a brilliant banner emblazoned with Givene's most brilliant stars, we could assemble a great host of warriors who would throw down Morjin and bring peace to Ea.

'No, Valashu, that we may not do,' Eva said to me. Her voice fell over me as cool and gentle as the wind blowing off the mountains. 'You know that we may not go to Ea, and you know why.'

'Because you are too pure to go down into Hell?'

Although I had eaten here the sweetest of fruits, there remained in my mouth a terrible bitterness.

'No, that we are not,' she said with a sad smile. 'Neither are the Elijin nor the Galadin. And it is *because* we are not that we may not go to Ea.'

Shivaj, a man with quick, hot eyes and a proud cast of chin, was more brusque than Eva. He said simply, 'The Galadin forbid it.'

'But what if this forbiddance were lifted?' I said.

'Long ago the forbiddance was lifted,' Shivaj said in a voice like a hammered gong, 'and a great Elijin became the Red Dragon. And Kalkin became the one you call Kane.'

'But one last time,' I said. 'One last battle – Morjin could not stand against a million Valari of Givene armed with spears and swords!'

'You do not know that,' Eva said to me. 'Not even our scryers can foresee what Morjin might do, armed with the Lightstone and the wrath of the Dark One filling his heart.'

'But we could win!' I cried out.

'Yes, we could win,' Ramadar said to me. His black eyes and noble bearing fell upon me with a heavy weight. 'The Valari could stand triumphant on Ea's soil beneath a star-silvered banner, holding high the Cup of Heaven that we had claimed. As we did once before. We remember too well how Elahad's brother fell mad and slew Elahad over the Lightstone. How Valari slew Valari in a bloodbath that has grown only deeper and redder with the passing of the ages. How will it end? *Not* with more Valari going to Ea. You are Valashu ni al'Elahad, the last and only heir of the Elahad. The stain of his murder lies upon all the Valari, on Ea and elsewhere, but it is upon *you* to put things right and end what was begun on Ea so long ago.'

He added that I was also Valashu ni al'Adar, the last of the great Adar's descendents and therefore the rightful guardian of the Lightstone. My task, he said, was to reclaim the Cup of Heaven for the Maitreya.

I stared hard into Ramadar's bright eyes and asked, 'While you and your people remain safe here on Givene and watch events unfold through the waters of your pool? Are you afraid to fight, then?'

He pointed at my sword and said, 'There are different ways of fighting. The one who sits on the Dragon throne *might* be brought down by the edge of your sword, but the Dark One will never be. That will require a different kind of sword, finer than silustria, as pure in essence as light. It is upon us, and even more the Elijin and Galadin, to help forge it.'

I remembered lines of a verse graven in my heart:

> *Valarda, like molten steel,*
> *Like tears, like waves of singing light,*
> *Which angel fire has set its seal*
> *And breath of angels polished bright.*

'The true Alkaladur,' I said bitterly. 'This truly impossible thing.'

At this Eva smiled at me and said, 'The Valari were meant to be warriors of the spirit. In the end, Valashu, you were, too.'

I said nothing as I looked into the impossibly deep pools of Eva's eyes.

'The War of the Stone,' she said, 'goes on across the stars as it has for a million years. We fight it as we must, for it *must* be won, and the Valkariad must come. If not in our time, then in our children's, or our children's children.'

'All right,' I finally said, 'fight as you must, then. But must *all* your people, in all their millions, fight your way? Can you not spare a few thousands to come to Ea and fight *our* way?'

'No,' she said sadly, 'the Galadin forbid it.'

'Then damn the Galadin!' I snarled out. The rage in my voice stunned me; it seemed to shock Eva and Ramadar and the others standing about the dark pool. 'If they won't help, then damn them!'

'Valashu – you know not what you say!'

Eva and Varjan – Asha and Shivaj, too – stared at me in horror. And I stared right back at them as I called out, 'I may not know what *I* say. But how is it that *you* know what the Galadin say?'

'From time to time,' Eva told me, 'one of the mighty Elijin walks our world and brings us their words.'

'Then you bow to their will?'

'Even as a warrior of your world does to his king,' Ramadar told me. 'And even as the Galadin themselves follow the light of the Ieldra, and the Ieldra work the will of the One.'

433

I shook my head at this even as my hand closed hard and hurtful around the hilt of my sword.

'If you doubt, then look!' Eva said to me as she pointed at the pool. 'Look – and listen!'

For a while, in the quiet of the cool night, as Eva and the others moved in closer around me, I gazed into the pool. It had fallen so dark that only the faintest shimmer of starlight played upon its black waters. Then a radiance began welling up from deep inside it. Words, perfectly pitched like ringing bells, poured forth in a beautiful song. They reminded me of the immortal words that Alphanderry had sung out in the pass of the Kul Moroth: *La valaha eshama halla, lais arda alhalla raj erathe . . .*' As in the moments before Alphanderry had died, the words blended so harmoniously into the music and the music into the words that it seemed they were one.

I sensed that those around me understood more of this song than I did. I watched as the pool grew brighter and ever clearer. Just below its perfectly still surface I caught sight of another body of water, much larger: a silver lake, very lovely, and beside it on a hilly bank grew a great and glorious astor tree. Framing it, in the distance, were two white-capped mountains. This could only be Irdrasil, the world-tree of legend and dreams, and the mountains Vayu and Telshar – the ageless and true Telshar, after which the sacred peak rising above my father's castle had been named. Just as I had beheld Givene through the waters of the pool in one of Ea's Vilds, I knew that now I looked upon the Galadin's world of Agathad.

'Ashtoreth,' I said, murmuring out the name of one of the greatest of the Galadin. 'Valoreth.'

It was hard to tell, but in the music sounding from deep inside the pool, I thought I heard the breath and heartbeat of my own name.

'The blessed tree!' Eva whispered from beside me.

The whole world shimmered with the numinous color of Irdrasil's perfect leaves. In the shadings and tones pulsing out of the great tree, I sensed unfathomed layers of the angels' language and deeper unities: the melodies of all music and all the words ever spoken. The Galadin, I thought, must understand this, just as they surely understood the language of light that fell upon Agathad. Thus did the Ieldra speak to them and bring them the word of the One.

Lais arda alhalla raja Valashu ni al'Elahad ni al'Adar . . .

I thought it a miracle that I, too, should grasp this eternal language. Who was I to speak to the Ieldra or to stand before their fiery tree as they spoke to me? It came to me that I understood only the tiniest part of what these luminous beings had to tell me, and yet that part contained its entirety and essence: that I must vanquish my fear of death, both in dealing it out to others and in dying myself. And I must return to Ea to fulfill my fate.

'No!' I cried out from within the deep, dark pools of my heart. I wondered if the Ieldra – or the Galadin – could understand the flashes of fire lighting up my eyes. 'What can *you* really know of Ea? To feel your flesh burning up or to scream as a length of steel is driven through your insides? *You* do not die nailed to crosses! You do not even die!'

I expected no answer to the fury that raged through me. And then, through the Star People's pool, I watched with awe as the glorre of the great astor tree faraway blazed with a terrible and beautiful light.

Valashu Elahad.

In the end, I knew, we each opened ourselves to this light, or not.

Valashu.

Or perhaps this eternal light opened itself to us and drew us within. For a moment that seemed to last forever, I stood in a place that could not be: the pristine fields of Culhadosh Commons on another world across the universe. Its green acres were undefiled by the terror of Morjin's armies. None of the slain lay in bloody heaps upon the grass, not my father nor my brothers. In truth, it seemed that those closest to me hadn't died at all, for out of the stream of sunlight spilling down upon the pasture coalesced the faces and forms of Karshur, Mandru, Jonathay, Ravar and Yarashan. My brother, Asaru, dressed in a suit of brilliant diamonds, stood with my father at the center of the field. So did my mother and my grandmother, whom I called Nona.

No wounds marred their flesh as they smiled at me, warm smiles that filled the whole of my being. My father told me that I must return to Mesh to become king, while my mother, in the soft light of her eyes, conveyed to me the simplest of truths: that men and women could die but love never could. The force pouring from her heart into mine made me weep. I did not want to leave her. They spoke to me for a long time; there was a sense in which I was speaking with myself. But my father reminded me that I was still of the living and could not remain with the dead. He promised me, however, that he would never leave my side. He told me, too, that help would be sent to me. Then he smiled one last time, and dissolved back into light, along with my mother, grandmother and brothers.

I found myself still standing by the edge of the pool on Givene with the Star People. They asked me what I had experienced, and I told them. Then I said, 'I do not know if I saw things outside and beyond myself, or was only dreaming.'

Eva nodded her head at this, and told me mysteriously, 'Sometimes, there is no difference.'

I noticed that the sun had risen over the mountains in the east and its light painted the houses and towers in the hills around us a softly blazing blue. It came to me that my friends on Ea might have given me up as dead.

And when I stared back into the pool, I no longer saw Vayu and Telshar and the great astor tree of Agathad, but only the smaller pool in the Loikalii's Vild into which I had fallen. Oni and Kane stood above it looking down into its black waters with wonder and dread; so did Maram and my other companions, and all the Loikalii.

'You must go back,' Ramadar said to me. He told me of the understanding that he had gleaned from his own gazing at Irdrasil: 'Help will be sent with you.'

I nodded my head as he clasped my hand; Eva embraced me, and so did the others. Then Ramadar pressed into my hand a perfectly-cut diamond the size of a walnut. He told me, 'This was taken from the crown that Adar once wore. Elahad should have brought the crown with him to Ea, but he would not wear it until Ea was made one with the worlds of the stars and the great Maitreya came forth. The crown has been lost, but we have kept this last stone all these ages. Take it back with you that you might remember what you have seen and who you really are.'

I gripped my hand around the huge diamond. I bowed my head to Ramadar. Then, with a final look at the waterfalls spilling down toward the shimmering city around me, I dived back into the pool.

The moment I broke from its cold waters, Kane's hand snapped out and locked onto mine. With a single heave that nearly dislocated my shoulder, he pulled me up onto the pool's banks. Water fell off my sodden hair and clothing onto the grass. Master Juwain and Maram hurried over to me, and so did Liljana, Atara, Daj and Estrella. Even Flick spun in a whirl of sparks as if astonished at my reappearance. Maira and Anneli and the Loikalii gathered in as close as they could. The great trees of the vild towered high above us.

'Val!' Maram shouted at me. He squeezed the back of my neck as if to reassure himself that I had really returned to him. 'We thought you were gone – sucked down into the bowels of the earth!'

I saw that Maram's loin covering was soaking wet, as was Kane's tunic. It seemed they had dived into the pool after me.

Master Juwain stepped forward to look into my eyes. 'You should not be conscious – not even alive! You were under for too long!'

'For most of a day,' I said, shaking the water from my hair.

'Not *that* long,' Master Juwain said. 'But ten minutes is long enough to kill – I suppose that we should be glad that the lack of air has served only to confuse you.'

I told him, 'But, sir, I am *not* confused. I stood on the banks of another pool on another world and watched the sun set and then rise again.'

He and all the others listened intently as I described what had happened to me since I fell into the pool. Finally, Oni fixed me with one of her withering gazes and said, 'The Water only gives visions of places faraway. It must be that one of these visions captured you and convinced you that it was real.'

I shook my head at this, wondering if it could be true. Then I felt in my hand the great diamond that I still held. Sunlight reflected off its many facets in a brilliance of colors. This convinced almost everyone of the veracity of my story, but Oni only squinted her old eyes and said, 'Perhaps such diamonds grow at the bottom of the Water.'

As she pointed at the pool and stared into it, its waters grew ever calmer and clearer. After a while, they stilled so that its surface fell as smooth as glass. In the silver of this liquid mirror, I caught flashes of great purple towers gleaming beneath a blue sun, and a great golden-leaved tree whose light never failed, not even in the darkest of nights. And then a brilliant light filled the pool, dissolving all that I beheld into a blaze of glorre. Without warning, it poured forth in a stream of fire that shot up and fell upon Flick. A song like the ringing of perfectly tuned crystals poured forth, too, and the music and the fire were as one. Everyone stood back as Flick's whirling lights flared brighter and brighter. I watched awestruck as this radiance gathered itself into the form of Alphanderry. He was like unto the strange being that had appeared before us several times on our journeys, and yet different, too. Although I knew well enough that our old friend had died in the

Kul Moroth, the man who stood suddenly shaped and whole before us seemed almost alive.

'Val!' he cried out to me. He turned his head toward my other companions and smiled. 'Maram, Liljana, Master Juwain . . . Kane.'

Kane stared at this instantiation of Alphanderry with both sadness and joy filling up his eyes. He cried out: 'My little friend!' But he made no move to embrace him.

Daj, however, suffered from no such restraint. He stepped up to Alphanderry as if intending to touch his arm. His hand passed right through him – not, however, as before, as through a beam of light, but more like a hand dipped into water. It left ripples and a wake in whatever shimmering substance Alphanderry was made of.

Alphanderry smiled at Daj, and at Estrella who stood next to him. He looked at her deeply and for a long time. Then his gaze fell upon Atara and the blindfold binding her face, and he said, 'It is good to see you again after all this time, though it pains me that you cannot see me. What happened to you, Atara?'

'You do not know?'

He shook his head. 'I *almost* know. The memory is there, somewhere, but I cannot find it.'

For a while we stood there recounting the many events that had occurred after Alphanderry's death in the Kul Moroth: our entrance into Khaisham and the great library; our journey across the White Mountains and the battle inside Argattha in which we had claimed the Lightstone. Although Atara would not speak of her blinding, Alphanderry must have guessed that she had left her eyes behind in Morjin's throne room. When our story moved on to the tragedy of Morjin invading Mesh and stealing back the Lightstone, and all that had happened since, Alphanderry rubbed at his curly black hair and told us: 'It is as if I was *there*, somehow, at the heart of all these things you say have happened.'

'But you *were* there!' I said to him.

'As the one you call Flick?'

At this, he held out his hand as if beckoning one of the nearby Timpum floating above a patch of lilies. The Timpum – it was all blue and golden like a ball of light – drifted over and settled in the center of Alphanderry's palm. I watched amazed as Alphanderry's hand broke apart into a shimmer of silver and crimson and then reassembled itself a moment later. And Alphanderry told me, 'I am *not* Flick. And yet, I am not *other* than Flick, too. It is hard to explain.'

Explanations, I thought, had never been Alphanderry's gift. He was a poet and a minstrel. His triangular face was full of all the wildness and spontaneity that we had all loved, and with wit and imagination, too. His wide, sensual lips pulled up in a dazzling smile that lit up his whole face and caused the deep creases around his eyes to flare out like the rays of the sun. His innate playfulness caught others up like fire. He had always been a dreamy man, living in some intensely beautiful inner world that he delighted in sharing with others. His large brown eyes told of his longing for places even more splendid than Givene or Agathad. And yet something new warmed his soul – or perhaps it was only a change in direction of his oldest and deepest impulse, as natural as breathing out once one has fully breathed in. As he gazed at the Timpum shining in his hand – and then at Estrella and the lilies around the pool and the astor trees and the rocks and grasses in the Loikalii's woods – I sensed within him an overwhelming desire to sing not just *of* the wonder of the world, but to sing *to* the world, to fill the flowers with music and make everything come alive in a way it never had before.

He seemed as puzzled at his own existence as I was. I looked to Oni and Maira to see if they might offer some understanding of this miracle, but they and the other Loikalii had never witnessed one of the Timpum transformed this way. Oni stood watching Alphanderry with worship lighting up her old face. Even Kane seemed mystified, for I heard him mutter, 'My little, dear little friend – how, how?'

Oni now had little left to show us in her magic pool, and there was little that we still wished to see. She suggested returning to the astor grove in order to make another feast in honor of Alphanderry's return to us. No one objected. I kept waiting for Alphanderry to vanish back into a whirl of lights, but he remained as solid and real as he could be. With Daj and Estrella close by him and many of the Loikalii children gathering in close, he walked through the woods singing a sweet, silly song that delighted them.

That evening, though, when the Loikalii spread out their fruits and nuts and delicious forest foods on their leaf-woven mats, Alphanderry sang other songs. With Kane playing the mandolet that Alphanderry still could not quite grasp, Alphanderry gave voice to a melody so lovely and compelling that all of us joined him, though we did not know what the words we intoned meant. I marveled that many of the Timpum came shimmering and streaking from out of the woods to add their strange chiming sounds to the chorus. Even the great trees above us sang, in silence, as the stars far beyond the world sang out with light.

28

We remained in the Loikalii's woods for two more days. I kept waiting for Alphanderry to fade back into the lesser splendor of Flick, but he seemed to grow only more and more real. Although he ate no food nor drank any drop of water, he walked through the woods like any other man, and he laughed and joked with us as we gathered stores for the remaining part of our journey.

We could not put this off any longer. We all dreaded leaving the shelter of the lovely trees to go out into the blazing hell of the Tar Harath. Maram especially moved with a sloth and sullenness hard to bear, cursing under his breath as he helped fill up the waterskins from one of the Loikalii's pools. He cast numerous, longing looks at Anneli, who seemed loath to leave his side. His resentment weighed heavily upon me, as did the need to say farewell to Sunji and the Avari. There was no help for this. When we had stowed the last waterskin and bag of fresh cherries on the packhorses, in the coolness of a mid-Marud morning with the birds singing all around us, we held council with Sunji and his fellow warriors beneath an old, spreading astor tree.

'Your father,' I said to Sunji, 'enjoined you to help us cross the desert, but to go only as far as you must. You have come that far, perhaps even farther. Now you must return to tell King Jovayl of the great thing that you have done.'

While Maidro, Nurathayn and Arthayn regarded me with questioning looks, Sunji said, 'But you still have the rest of the Tar Harath to cross! And beyond that, the lands of the Yieshi!'

And Maidro added, 'Who will warn you of sandstorms? Who will keep you from drowning in quicksands? Who will help you find water?'

This last question needed no answer, for everyone's gaze fell upon Estrella, who sat near Alphanderry's brilliant form playing some sort of game with him in the graceful movements of their fingers and hands. And I said to the Avari: 'We would never have reached this place without your help. But once we leave here, we journey to the mountains in the west, and beyond. If you were to go with us as far as the mountains, and then try to return by yourselves to your hadrah across the whole breadth of the Tar Harath, then you must take water again here, or die. Without Estrella to lead you, you would be unlikely to find these woods. This is too great a risk, and I cannot ask you to bear it.'

Sunji and his fellow warriors were brave men, but they were practical, too, as were all the peoples of the Red Desert. They saw the logic of what I said. Nuradyan, however, upon watching Estrella and Alphanderry with wonder, said, 'But we could go with you to the *end* of your quest!'

This, though, Sunji was unwilling to do. He said to Nuradayn, and to all of us: 'My father's wishes must be obeyed, and we must return home as soon as we can. In autumn, I think, there will be war with the Zuri. Valaysu is right, I think, that the Dragon will not leave the killing of his Red Priests unavenged. Valaysu has his battles, and we have ours.'

He stood up to embrace me then, and it surprised me to see tears flowing freely from his eyes.

'All right,' Maidro said, embracing me, too, 'then we must say farewell, and I will wish you well: May the One always lead you to water.'

Just then Oni surprised us by marching into the grove at the head of a contingent of the Loikalii, including Maira, Kalevi and three elders. Oni walked straight up to Estrella, and held out to her the blue, crystal bowl that was so dear to her. And she told her: 'Take this, that the One might always lead water to *you*.'

Estrella's hands closed around the little bowl, and she looked up at Oni with deep gratitude. Then Oni bent to kiss the top of her curly head. Since Estrella remained as mute as the trees around us, I spoke for her, saying to Oni, 'You have given us a great gift, perhaps even the gift of life itself. But how will you summon the rain without your gelstei?'

At this, Oni cast me one of her mysterious looks and said, 'Don't worry, giant man, we have our ways.'

Liljana, who was more practical than I, studied the gleaming

441

blue bowl that Estrella held and said, 'But how will she know how to use it?'

Her question really needed no answer, for we had all found our way into our gelstei largely unaided. I thought Oni's response interesting, however, for she looked at the radiance streaming down through the golden astor leaves and said, 'How do the trees know how to use the light of the sun?'

When it came time to saddle the horses and leave the woods, another surprise awaited me, but this one was heartbreaking. Maram, holding Anneli's hand, strolled into the assembly place near our olinda trees and announced that he would not be coming with us.

'I'm sorry, Val, but I've come too far already, and it is too much – too, too much.'

We stood near the stamping horses. My heart beat with a sick thudding in my chest as I stared at Maram in disbelief. I could find no words to say.

'I'm sorry, my friends,' he said to all of us, 'but I just can't go on.'

He wiped at the corner of his eye, and would not look at me. It came to me that this was just another of his vastations, when doubt and fear worked at his insides and made jelly of his muscles and bones and his will to move himself in the right direction. As always, I believed, a brilliant fire would soon burn away his deepest affliction and leave a noble being standing straight and unvanquishable. As always, I had only to light the torch.

'Maram,' I said, stepping up close to him to grasp his shoulder.

'No, no – do not look at me that way!'

How could I not look at this vain, vexatious yet great man whom I loved as much as I did anyone?

'Please, Val – this is too hard!'

As I searched for the right thing to say to him, Kane barked out at him: 'Watch that your courage doesn't fail you now!'

Atara stepped up to him and said, 'The worst of our journey is behind us.'

Liljana came over to touch her hand to his cheek. 'We know how you've suffered – who knows better than your friends? But it's almost over. I have to believe that.'

'No, no, it will never be over,' Maram said. 'I do not think you will ever find the Maitreya.'

He stood squeezing Anneli's hand and still would not look at me.

'We need you, Maram,' I said at last.

Estrella came over and pulled gently at his hand to indicate her intense desire that he should change his mind and journey on with us. Alphanderry told him of the great wonders of the world that he might experience if only he found the will to ride a few hundred more miles. Kane turned to me with a helpless look softening his savage face.

'Maram,' I said, again touching his shoulder.

He still ignored me, turning to unwrap his old traveling cloak from around his firestone. He lifted up this great, ruby crystal and said, 'I never really believed that this would be made whole again. I never believed that *I* would be made whole again. Can I hold love's bright flame? For a day or a year? That's all that *really* matters. In the end, it all comes down to love.'

His gaze fell in adoration upon Anneli for a moment and then finally met mine. All of his anguish came flooding into me. All of his dreams and desires filled me with a pain that I could not bear. I blinked my eyes against the burning there, and said to him, 'All right, Maram, stay if you must, and peace be with you.'

If I searched inside myself for the truth of things, hadn't I always known it would come to this?

'Don't look at me like that!' Maram called out to me again.

I could no longer bear for him to suffer, not another arrow wound to his flesh or a sunburn or a day of fruitless fighting an enemy that could not be defeated. I could not bear that his great heart should remain empty of that for which he most yearned. I said to him, 'Stay – take Anneli for your bride. Have children. Be happy, my friend.'

I looked at him as he looked at me, and I could not hold inside the bright, warm thing that made my heart hurt.

'Damn you, Val!' he said to me. 'You're cruel! You make it easy for me – and so make it hard. So damn, damn hard!'

We embraced each other then, and wept like boys. Then it came time to saddle the horses for rest of our journey. Maram watched me fasten the straps beneath Altaru's great body, and he said to me, 'Ah, surely I was wrong in what I said about the Maitreya. You *will* find him! And on your return, you'll pass back through these woods again – I know you will!'

He forced himself to smile, huge and deep, but I could tell that he did not believe what he had said. I, however, had to act *as if* I believed it. And so with great gratitude we said farewell to the people of the forest. We mounted our horses and rode through the silent trees.

When we came out upon the sands of the Tar Harath, a blast of terrible heat instantly burned the moisture from my eyes. There came another parting, as Sunji and the Avari turned south and east while we forced ourselves to point our mounts toward the great dunes gleaming in the west. Soon, the Avari were lost to our sight among the sweeps and swells of this vast country. Then the Loikalii's Vild vanished into the glare of the deepening distances. Never, not even after my family's death, had I felt so alone.

Over the next few days of our journey, my friends said little to me, for I could not bear the sound of their voices. Our lives settled into a harsh routine: strike our goat-hair tents hours before dawn and ride into the growing heat of the morning. When the air became a blazing furnace searing our eyes and sucking our bodies' moisture clean out of the fibers of the robes that the Avari had given us, we pitched our tents again and lay sweating and suffering until it came time to set out into the cooling air of the late after-noon. We plodded on across the evening's starlit sands; when exhaustion finally weakened us and the icy cold of deep night drove through our garments like knives, we crawled inside our tents yet again to take a few hours of sleep.

I led us on a straight course southwest toward the Crescent Mountains. No lesser mountains or rocky hills rose up out of the desert to impede us or to cause us to make a detour. The heat of the Tar Harath, after the cool greenery of the Loikalii's woods, seemed even more hellish than the baking misery that had so nearly killed us in the desert's easternmost reaches.

There seemed no end to it. Although I knew from the maps that we would eventually reach the great Crescent Mountains, and the Tar Harath give out many miles before that, my ears, eyes and heart told me differently. There was only desert in all directions, day after day. The wind blew particles of stinging sand across a sun-seared emptiness that seemed to go on forever. I turned often toward the direction that I imagined the Vild to lie, hoping that Maram might have changed his mind and that I might see him riding after us. I felt him close to me, his great heart booming out his remorse at deserting me and his desire to reunite in our quest. But I searched the wavering sand behind us in vain.

We all, I thought, grieved Maram's absence; it was as if there was a hole in the earth where a great mountain had stood. One night, over dinner, Liljana admitted that she missed Maram's grum-bling and drinking almost as much as she did his bawdy songs and unchainable zest for life. She had little appetite for the last of the cherries and other fresh fruit that we had taken from the Loikalii's woods. I had none. I sat staring at my untouched food; I sipped the few drams of brandy that I poured into my cup in remembrance of happier times.

If we had lost one companion, however, we had gained another – almost – in Alphanderry. His presence did not fade with our passing from the Vild, nor did he often dissolve back into his old radiance as Flick. He 'rode' along with us on top of one of the packhorses, if that was the right word to describe the actions of a being who possessed neither solidity nor weight. I wondered if he could simply soar through the air like a brilliant bird or streak onward like the rays of the sun. It seemed, though, that such means of movement were impossible for him when he remained in his human form. As we neared the end of the Tar Harath, or so we hoped, Alphanderry rode or walked, even as we did.

He did not, however, eat or drink or sleep or sweat. If he suffered along with us, it was not from the world's hardships, at least not in their physical aspects. I sensed that he anguished over our anguish, as any good friend would. He, too, I thought, missed Maram. From his own memory of Maram and our descriptions of Maram's valor at the Siege of Khaisham and many times since, he composed lines that he called 'An Ode To A Five-Horned Man'. His voice, cool and flowing, refreshed us even more than water, and the song reminded us that Maram remained close to us, at least in spirit.

On the fourth night since our leaving the Loikalii's forest, we gathered around a single candle that Liljana had lit. Kane sat plucking the mandolet's strings while Alphanderry sang of the time when Maram had mistaken a bear licking honey from his face for one of his lovers. When Alphanderry had finished and the wind came whooshing out of the west, we spoke yet again of the mystery of Alphanderry's existence. Daj wondered how it was possible for this almost-real being woven of light to possess Alphanderry's very real memories.

It was Liljana who tried to answer him. In the words that poured out of her, I heard her fervor for the wisdom and teachings of her ancient order: 'All men and women die, for they are born from the world and must return to it. But the world itself never dies – not unless one such as Angra Mainyu comes with fire to destroy it. We are all *of* this immortal world. *Not* just in the water of our blood or in the minerals of our bones, but in our thoughts, our passions and our dreams. And in our memories. My Sisters of old believed that all we ever experience, the world experiences, too. As we remember, so does the world remember. Should it not be, then, that as the world remembers, *we* remember? Ea is Alphanderry's mother, and it must be that She, herself, whispers these memories in his mind. It must be that she has the power to remake him in greater glory, even as She once gave him birth.'

Master Juwain, twirling his cursed varistei between his fingers, said, 'I believe that Liljana is right. In spirit, she is right. But I think there is much more to this matter than she has told. Alphanderry *is* of this world, as is water or light or the crystal of the gelstei, whose deepest structure we may never understand. But surely he is something more, too. Something from *beyond* the world. It is said that once the Galadin walked upon Ea, and left some part of their shining substance behind in the Lokalani's Vilds – what else can the Timpum really be? Unless the Timpum are even *more* than this: some part or impulse of the Ieldra themselves. My Brotherhood teaches that the Ieldra dwell in the bright, black emptiness of Ninsun, at the center of all things. *Everything* dwells there: all time, all space, all matter, all memory. The universe itself, not just the world, remembers all that is and has ever occurred, down to the tumbling points on the tiniest grain of sand driven by a whirlwind. The Akashic Memory, my order has named this record. Over the ages, a few masters of my Brotherhood have been able to call upon a wisdom and memories far beyond themselves. It must be these memories, some special part, that Alphanderry calls upon to make his verses. It must be from these memories that the Shining Ones somehow make *him*.'

Alphanderry, sitting across from me, listened respectfully to what Master Juwain said, though without particular concentration. He seemed not to care *how* he came to be, only *that* he somehow existed again. He took delight in this. His smile nearly lit up the night. He turned toward Daj and Estrella, who had not known him of old, and said, 'Master Juwain is wise in the ways of philosophy, and many other things, and we have much to learn from him. But creation might not be as much of a mystery as he makes it. Even the creation of a man. Daj, will you help me with this? Estrella?'

As Estrella looked at Alphanderry in puzzlement, Daj asked him, 'What do you mean, sir?'

'Please,' Alphanderry said to him, 'save the "sir" for masters of the Brotherhood and other illuminaries. I'm just a maker of songs – and of men, as you will see and aid in the making. Now, this

446

man who doesn't quite yet exist but somehow always exists, whom *we'll* call into being – what is the first thing that we should know about him?'

Daj's eyes brightened at being drawn into this diversion, and he said, 'I don't know – his name?'

'Yes, good, good – his name. Well, what is it?'

'But how should I know?'

'Think, then!'

As Daj closed his eyes as if running through a list of names of all the people he had ever known, Alphanderry reached out to tap him on his head. But since Daj could not feel the substance of his hand, Alphanderry called out to him instead: 'Do not think with *this*! Not in this matter. Think with *that.*'

So saying, he laid his shimmering hand over Daj's heart and smiled at him. And he added, 'Come on, quickly now, the name is there, and you know it!'

And Daj blurted out: 'Might it be Aldarian?'

'Good – a good name, noble and strong. A little dull, perhaps. Is our man dull?'

'No, just the opposite. He is clever and cunning.'

'Then we don't have his true name yet, do we?'

A fire flared deep within Daj, and he called out with more certainty: 'His name is Eleikar!'

'Hoy! Eleikar – so it is. Well, what does our Eleikar desire more than anything else?'

And Daj told him: 'Vengeance! Eleikar's father was a great knight. A wicked king coveted his mother for a concubine, and when he could not have her, he killed Eleikar's father and took his mother anyway. To save her honor, Eleikar's mother poisoned herself.'

'And what became of Eleikar?'

'He fled with his brothers and sisters into the wilderness. The king's men hunted them down like pigs, sticking them with spears. They killed everyone except Eleikar.'

'And how did Eleikar survive?'

'By playing dead – even when the king's men stuck his face and legs for sport. The wolves of the forest rescued him. They licked his wounds and brought him fresh meat to eat. He lived with them, in a cave, until he grew into a man.'

'Hoy,' Alphanderry said, nodding sadly, 'then Eleikar must have many scars.'

'Many,' Daj said. He tapped his cheekbone and added, 'He bears

447

one here, shaped like a crescent moon. He bears his father's scimitar, of the same shape. His only desire is to get close enough to the king to use it.'

Alphanderry nodded his head again and asked, 'Is this his *only* desire?'

As Daj fell into a puzzled silence, Alphanderry turned to Estrella and put the same question to her. She could not, of course, give voice to her answer. But her quicksilver eyes flowed with all her deep passion for life, and her fingers danced in that secret language of play and dreams that only Daj seemed to understand.

At the frown that knitted Daj's eyebrows together, Alphanderry said to him: 'Well? *Is* vengeance all that he desires?'

Daj scowled at Estrella and said, 'No, there is something else. It seems that Eleikar has fallen in love with the wicked king's daughter.'

For another couple of hours, as the night deepened and the air fell bitterly cold, Alphanderry continued this game of quizzing the children and summoning out of near-nothingness a wild, star-crossed man named Eleikar. As their story built in elaboration and complexity, so did Eleikar gain his essential characteristics: bright, burning, sorrowful, adoring, doomed. He was a man who howled his wrath at the moon, and whispered to his beloved all of his overflowing joy of life. I winced to hear Daj declaim that Eleikar was immortal, not because Eleikar could not be slain, but because he would love as no man ever had before, and minstrels for many ages would sing of him. I marveled at how Eleikar came alive out of a few words spoken by a whip-scarred boy and the gestures of a mute slave girl, and seemed more real than many men I had known.

It was a strange magic that Alphanderry wove, and while Kane smiled strangely at Alphanderry's unusual exercise, neither Master Juwain nor Liljana quite approved of it. Minstrels, to their way of thinking, sang of love or the beauty of the sea, or recounted the feats of ancient heroes who had really lived. Liljana scolded Alphanderry for trying to usurp the prerogatives of the Ieldra or even the One, saying to him: 'Your Eleikar moves according to your whims and designs, but it is not so with real men. With *women*, shaped after the image of Ea herself. *We* are all imbued with free will. Isn't this is the essence of what it means to be alive?'

We all carried this question off to bed; I thought of little else over the hot, dusty miles of our journey the next day. Alphanderry's very existence seemed a window into the great mystery of life and death. I came to see him not as a challenger of the power of the Ieldra but as their fulfillment and gift. He, merely in being, was a promise that our lives were not lived in vain.

Nothing is lost, I thought as I gazed at Alphanderry sitting happily on top of his swaying packhorse. *The world must remember*.

I recalled the faces and voices of my family whom I had left behind in a place impossibly far away. A great hope came to me then. Truly, we each blazed with the bright flame of free will, and if we worked this will truly, then we might suffer or die but we would never fall to evil and be enslaved. And so we would somehow live, in honor and beauty, throughout eternity.

Nothing is lost, for the whole universe remembers.

With this thought, however, as with ravening lions chasing a gazelle, came a terrible fear. I recalled what Kane had once told me: that two paths only wound their way into the mists of the future. Either men would become as angels, and the brightest of the Galadin would advance to the order of the Ieldra in a Great Progression known as the Valkariad, or Angra Mainyu and his kind would be freed from Damoom, and a darkness without end would befall the stars. But the Ieldra would not abide such total and final evil, and so they would destroy the stars and the whole universe of Eluru that contained them. Nothing of the universe would be left, and so nothing would remain to remember anything.

All will be lost. It is not enough to choose freely and fight nobly. We must win.

Triumph, however, seemed impossible without Maram at my side. As I gazed into the blood-red dunes where the sun died into the west, it took all my will to keep riding on as if any real hope still remained.

That evening, as Liljana rationed out our water and Master Juwain morosely read from the *Saganom Elu*, I knew that I could not let them drown in the darkness of despair, much less the children. They needed to believe in a story where things came out right. So did I. Someday, perhaps, the minstrels would sing of my companions and me, and I would have them tell that we fought like the heroes of old to vanquish our enemies, down to our last breaths.

And so I stood before the glowing candle, and I added my voice to the game that Alphanderry had begun, saying to Daj and Estrella: 'Eleikar must have his revenge upon the king, and he must love the princess, too, as the sun does the earth, for that is his fate. So it seems that it is his fate to live and die tragically. But perhaps there is more to Eleikar than we see.'

'What, then?' Daj asked me.

'That remains unknown. Perhaps it can't *be* known, by us. But Eleikar, if he is truly to come alive, might see what we cannot.'

'But what could that be?'

'A way out of his dilemma.'

'But what if there *is* no way out?'

'There is always a way,' I told him. 'A king once said this to me: "How is it possible that the impossible is not only possible but inevitable?"'

As the candle flicked and glozed, Daj pondered this, then said, 'I can't see the answer to *that* riddle, either. Perhaps I will by the time we reach Hesperu – if we ever do.'

'We will, Daj.'

'Without Maram?'

'Yes, if we have to, without Maram.'

'Then you really believe that there is a chance we might find the Maitreya before Morjin does?'

As I gazed up at the millions of lights above us, more splendid at the center of the Tar Harath than any place else on earth, something blazed inside me, and I said, 'We *will* find the Maitreya. And on our journey back to the Brotherhood School, we'll return to the Loikalii's woods. We'll sit with Maram again and eat raspberries together. We'll bring him a bottle of the finest Hesperuk brandy and make a toast to love – I swear we will!'

All of my friends looked up at me and smiled – everyone except Atara, who could not look at anything, and Liljana, who could not smile. But Atara's hand found mine and squeezed me tightly as she said, 'Val – I can *see* the Yieshi well! We *will* reach it! And beyond the desert, the mountains leading to Hesperu!'

Although Liljana's face remained as stern as stone, her eyes warmed even so. 'We still have a long way to go before we find this brandy you speak of, much less the Maitreya. Now, why don't we get some sleep, while we can?'

The next day, our journey proved no less arduous than any other but we bore the pain of it in better spirits. Not until the day following did we finally came out of the Tar Harath into the western reaches of the Red Desert.

We celebrated surviving the worst hell on earth by drinking the last of our water and gazing out optimistically into the country that opened before us. Here the dunes gave way to the harder sands of a plain nearly as flat as one of the skillets that Liljana had been forced to abandon. Here the air was cooler, slightly. Ursage and spiny sage grew in ragged clumps, and a few strands of rock-grass forced their way out of cracks in the ground. I watched a scorpion dragging a dead lizard through this grass, while farther to the west, in the air, a hawk soared over the desert. The sun remained a white-hot iron searing our eyes, but in its fierce light I found not the foreburn of death but rather the brightness of hope.

'How far is it,' I asked Atara, riding over to her, 'to the Yieshi well?'

'I'm not sure,' she told me from beneath the sweat-stained shawl that covered her face. 'I cannot *see* distances with my sight as you can with your eyes. But perhaps twenty miles.'

From here, I guessed that it couldn't be more than a hundred and twenty miles to the mountains and the streams that we presumed we would find there. But without any water at all, it might as well have been a hundred and twenty *thousand* miles.

By late morning, my mouth and throat had grown so dry, I could speak only in croaks, like a toad. By midafternoon, with the sweat soaking my robes, I could think of nothing but water. I was ready to try to chew the juices out of the bitter soap grass or even to bite open my horse's neck to drink down a little blood. The burning thirst of my friends made mine a hundred times worse.

Then, near the day's end, we crested a swell of ground and found ourselves looking down into a depression that might have been made by the drying-up of a lake. Two black tents poked up against the brown, sun-baked earth. At the center of the depression stood the circular wall of rocks: the Yieshi's well. A half dozen of the Yieshi stood there, too, or so we presumed the dun-robed figures near the well to be.

At the sight of us, just after Alphanderry had vanished into nothingness, one of them drew a saber that flashed in the late afternoon light. We rode closer, and I saw that he was about ten years older than I, with a face as sharp as obsidian and a scowl showing rows of white teeth. A young woman called to a boy tending some nearby goats, and then gathered two other children behind the meager protection of the well. An older woman with skin like dark, wrinkled leather hurried over to the well, too. I guessed that she must be the man's mother.

We rode even closer, and the eyes of all the Yieshi grew wide with astonishment. The man shouted out to us: 'Who are you? From where do you come?'

Ten yards from the well, we all climbed down off our horses. I moistened my lips with some of the sweat pouring from Altaru's neck, and I croaked out to him: 'I am Mirustral, and we are pilgrims seeking the Well of Restoration. And we have come from the east, across the Tar Harath.'

As I pointed behind us at the glowing duneland, the man's astonishment turned to disbelief. He shouted at me: 'No one crosses the Tar Harath! You are a liar – either that or the sun has made you mad!'

'The sun has made me thirsty,' I said to him. 'And my friends, too. Have you any water to spare?'

The man looked at the old woman standing behind the well, and then looked back at me. He shook his sword at me and said, 'For madmen we have none, for that would be a waste. And for liars, we have only steel!'

Kane, perhaps even thirstier than I (and perhaps a little mad), whipped free his long kalama and advanced on the man. He growled out, 'So, we have steel for you, too! Let's see whose is quicker and sharper!'

'Kane!' I called out. I moved to grab him, but he was too quick for me. And so I shouted, with greater force: 'Kane! Let us give them gold for their water, not steel!'

Although the old woman's face brightened at this, it seemed that Kane hadn't heard me. He might have succeeded in quickly cutting down this bellicose man if Estrella hadn't sprinted forward, throwing her arms around Kane's waist and looking up with her dark, warm eyes as if pleading with Kane to put away his sword.

Kane came to a halt and rested his hand on top of Estrella's head. He glared at the man with black eyes full of fire.

Now Liljana came forward and walked past the swords of both Kane and the startled Yieshi man, straight up to the well. She held out a gold coin to the old woman and said, 'We are neither mad nor liars – nor are we thieves. Why don't we sit together and tell our stories? At least let our children have a little water, if you've none for us.'

As quick as an ostrakat pecking up a lizard, the old woman's hand darted out and snatched up the coin. Then her face softened, and she said to the younger woman: 'Let them have water, Rani.'

The younger woman heaved a leather skin into the well. It made

452

no splash but only sent up a sound like that of wet clothes beaten against a rock. Moments later Rani drew up a bucketful of muddy water that seemed more mud than water.

'You shall all of you drink, not just your children,' the old woman said to me. 'But we've no water to spare for your horses.'

After that Kane and the Yieshi man sheathed their swords. His name proved to be Manoj, and he presented to us his mother, Zarita, his wife and their children: Tareesh, Lia and Yiera. While Rani went to work filtering the well water through a filthy cloth, we sat on goatskins to tell our stories, even as Liljana had suggested.

It took some time to get Manoj to speak, but when he finally did, he was cordial enough, if not friendly. He eyed Kane suspiciously as he told us that he had quarrelled with the cousins of his clan, who had gone on to the wells in the north to wait out the heat of the summer. Manoj, though, had chosen to remain alone with the rest of his family at this well, where they eked out a living from a few goats and sheep, and a little dirty water.

When Rani had finished her work, she hefted up a waterskin and went around filling our cups. I didn't mind the earthy, slightly brackish taste of the water. In truth, I had to restrain myself from gulping down the precious liquid like a dog lest I spill a single drop on the dry ground.

'Very well, Mirustral,' Manoj said to me when I had drunk my fill. 'Now tell me how it is possible for pilgrims to cross the Tar Harath.'

In the last heat of the day, I told him about the much greater heat of the deep desert and how the four Avari warriors had helped us survive it. Although I could not give away the secret of the Vild, I admitted that we had found water in a place where none believed water to be.

'I've heard it said that there is water hidden by the dunes,' Manoj told us, 'but I never believed it. If this girl led you to it, then she is a treasure greater than gold.'

He nodded his head at Estrella, who sat cupping Oni's blue bowl between her hands. Ever since we had left the Loikalii's woods, she had tried to unleash the gelstei's power.

'Perhaps,' Manoj said, 'she will lead you to water in the miles between here and the mountains.'

'Is there no other well in all that distance?'

Manoj shook his head. 'There *is* a well, but it is dry, stone dry, as it will remain until Ashavar, when the rains come.'

453

I looked off into the west, at the dusty, dry folds of ground where bits of thornbush and spike grass grew. I said, 'We cannot go on to look for more water without water *now*, for our horses.'

I turned to watch Altaru sweating in the sun. It pained me that I had broken my promise to him by drinking before he did, but there was no help for it. I could not give him, or any of the horses, water that the Yieshi denied us.

Manoj regarded him, too, and then looked at Atara's roan mare, Fire. He said, 'Those are fine horses, the best I have seen, even if too thin. We *might* find water for them, but we haven't enough for your other horses – we've barely enough to get us through the summer.'

This, I thought, looking at Manoj's skinny goats grazing about, must be true. If his well ran dry, he and his family would perish. We could not buy or play upon his sympathies to yield up what he could not give us. But neither could we water Altaru and Fire and simply let our other horses die.

'I'm sorry, Mirustral,' Manoj told me.

As it became clear that we remained in a desperate plight, Estrella squeezed her blue crystal with a surprising fierceness. Something inside her seemed suddenly to click, like an iron key fitting into a lock. She rose up and looked about her. She began walking, out into the desert where she came upon a low, flat rock near a thorn-bush. There she stood, facing west and holding up her blue bowl to the sky.

'Father, what is she doing?'

This question came from Lia, a girl about Estrella's age.

It was Daj who answered Lia, saying: 'She is summoning rain.'

Manoj and his family must have thought Daj mad after all, and Estrella more so, for she stood gazing in the direction of the setting sun and did not move. Almost immediately, however, the wind began blowing out of the west. It built quickly and unrelentingly to nearly the force of a gale, and drove sand in a stinging brown blanket across the Yiehsi's encampment.

I shielded my eyes and watched awed as the first dark clouds appeared on the horizon; the wind drove them straight toward us at an astonishing speed. The air fell colder and moister, and ran with electric currents. Whips of lightning cracked down from the clouds, splitting the ground with flashes of brilliant white-orange fire. Then the sky above us grew nearly as black as night. Manoj's children fled into the comfort of their mother's and grandmother's robes, but they could give them no protection from this wild storm.

A great thunderbolt shook the earth beneath us, and a strange burning smell charged the air.

And then the clouds opened, unleashing rain in sheets and streams. It rained so hard that we could scarcely breathe. Our robes quickly soaked through as if plunged into a lake. We cringed and shivered against the icy torrents raging down from above us.

Then Kane let loose a great laugh that tore from his lungs like a thunder of his own. He stood and stripped off his useless clothing, standing naked beneath the black sky. He raised back his head as he opened his mouth and let the rain pour down his throat. He raised his hands straight up as if summoning the heaven's lightning himself. To Manoj, he must have seemed as mad as the world about us. But Kane was the first of us to seize the moment, grabbing up waterskins from the terrified horses and opening them to the deluge. It alarmed me how quickly the skins swelled with water.

The ground beneath us, too, began overflowing like a suddenly rising lake. If this storm had caught us in a ravine, raging rivers of water would surely have drowned us; as it was, I feared that this ancient basin might prove a deathtrap if it rained much longer, for there was no drainage here and the sky seemed to hold entire oceans of water. I shouted at Estrella to put down her bowl; she did not hear me. She remained standing against the storm's ferocity with her eyes closed and her arms frozen out, holding up the blue bowl. The rain had now filled it many times over, and water poured from it as from an infinite source. I ran over to her then. I eased the bowl out of her cold fingers, and tried to cover her with my robe. She finally opened her eyes. Her smile drove through the storm like the sun.

Soon after that, it stopped raining. The clouds broke apart, blew away and vanished into the blueness of the twilight sky. The desert about the well had been changed into a wetlands of pools, puddles and water holes drilled down into acres of mud. Rani, with bucket in hand, discovered that the well was full – fuller than it had ever been before, even in the months of winter.

'Rain in Marud!' she marveled, looking about the well. 'You are not pilgrims, but sorcerers!'

Then she gazed at Estrella in awe. 'No, I should call you instead a water witch as lived in the ancient ages – a worker of miracles!'

That night, in honor of miracles, Manoj slaughtered his fattest goat and roasted it beneath the light of the moon. The fire, made from moist, woody thornbush dried our garments even as the

455

greasy smoke worked its way into our skin and hair. We ate succulent meat and goat cheese. Manoj fed Estrella choice tidbits from his own hand and wanted to know how she had called up the storm. So did Master Juwain.

But their words only amused Estrella. She suddenly hooked together her thumbs, shiny with goat grease, and moved her fingers up and down around them as of the flapping of wings. Her face came alive with a succession of delightful expressions, and she made other signs, with her fingers and hands. Daj interpreted this mysterious language as best he could, telling Master Juwain: 'It is like this, sir: everything touches upon everything else. And so even the tiniest act can ripple out into the world with great effects. The beating of a butterfly's wings can cause a whirlwind a thousand miles away. I think Estrella has found a way to be that butterfly.'

Manoj considered this as he called for Rani to pour some fermented goat's milk for us to drink. He looked at Estrella and said, 'Well, then, little butterfly – where will you fly to next?'

I sensed that he wished to follow us on our quest, to see what other miracles Estrella might bring forth. For his sake, and ours, I told him only that we sought a wondrous source of healing deep in the mountains.

'In Sandar?' he asked us.

Sandar, I thought, letting that name's sounds play out inside me. Could he mean Senta? For nearly a thousand miles we had debated our route into Hesperu. Once we had decided on crossing the Red Desert and the Crescent Mountains, it seemed wisest to go down into the north of Hesperu through Senta in the mountains' southern part. A good road, we knew, led from Senta through that difficult terrain. But how we were to negotiate the even more difficult terrain between the edge of the desert and Senta had remained a mystery.

'You *must* be bound for Sandar,' Manoj said to us. 'Like the pilgrims of old.'

Senta, of course, had drawn pilgrims from across Ea for ages: all from roads leading from Surrapam, Sunguru or Hesperu itself. We knew of no ancient route from the Yieshi's lands to this fabled city.

Master Juwain regarded Manoj with his clear, old eyes as he rubbed the back of his head and asked, 'And how did the ancient pilgrims find their way to Sandar?'

'From the Dead City.'

The puzzled look that Master Juwain traded with Kane caused

Manoj to add: 'It was once called Souzam. It is said that there is a road leading out of there to the west – at least there was once. No Yieshi would ever go into the mountains to find out if this is true.'

Further questioning prompted Manoj to tell Master Juwain that the Dead City, or Souzam, lay only a hundred miles from his well at the foot of the Crescent Mountains.

'But if you are considering journeying that way,' Manoj told us, 'do not. Do not go into the mountains at all, I beg you.'

'Why not?' I asked him.

'Because the mountains are cursed,' he told me. 'The Dead People dwell there.'

Fate, it seemed, after slinging fire and arrows at us for too long, had at last opened a door to better fortune. The gleam in Master Juwain's and Kane's eyes, no less my own, told me that we would indeed journey at least as far as the Dead City to see what we might see.

We stayed up late that night, for the ground was too wet for easy sleeping. Manoj had many old tales that he wished to share with us – and many that he wished to hear. After his third cup of fermented milk, we finally got him to tell us exactly how we might find the Dead City. Just before dawn, we arose to say goodbye to him and his family. And he told us: 'I would ride with you, as far as the mountains, to see that you are safe. But I must remain here to make sure that my wife and children are safe. The Zuri have raided into our lands, and although I do not think they would come this far in Marud, it is said that sorcerers have poisoned the mind of Tatuk and now direct his decisions. I would make war upon the Zuri before they grow too bold, but my cousins have disputed the need.'

As I stood by Altaru, who was happy at having drunk gallons of fresh water, I clapped Manoj on the arm and told him: 'Remain here then, and keep your family safe. And keep your sword sharp, Yieshi.'

We rode off into the desert to the west. Estrella's rain had made the desiccated rock grass and bitterbroom magically green. Brilliant pink flowers bloomed from the thornbush. The sandrunners, rabbits, lizards and other desert creatures all seemed restored to new life.

All that day and the next we travelled toward the mountains, following the landmarks that Manoj had described to us. We found the second Yieshi well, too. It was not dry but full. We drank from

457

it and topped up our waterskins, and continued on our way. The mountains came into view and built before us, ever higher, ever clearer, shadowed in purple and capped in white. On our third day out from Manoj's well, we came upon Souzam, which he had called the Dead City. It seemed nothing more than a few acres of ancient stone buildings and mud-brick houses half-buried in sand. Most of the streets were broken, and the stones of a great aqueduct's arch had long since cracked and fallen apart. It seemed that no one had lived here for ten thousand years. A quick search turned up some hyenas making a den in one of the buildings, but we came across no other inhabitants.

We found the road that Manoj had told of easily enough, although it, too, was nearly buried in sand and its paving stones cracked in a thousand places. We followed it out of the city, up into the bone dry foothills. It wound up through a canyon. On its rugged slopes grew thornbush and other plants that we had seen for too many miles. From the rounded stones strung out in a snaking curve along the bottom of the canyon, we saw that once a stream or river had flowed here.

As we worked our way higher, the sands of the stream bed darkened with moisture. The tough desert vegetation gave way to juniper, cottonwoods and the first pine trees. Master Juwain remarked upon the extremes of the Crescent Mountains: in the range's western slopes, running from Surrapam down into Hesperu, the mountains caught the wet winds of the ocean and wrung out the rain. And there grew the lushest, greenest forests in the world. Its eastern slopes, as we now saw, were nearly as dry as the desert beyond. But they became moister and cooler with every mile higher that we climbed into the mountains.

We camped that night in sight of a great, white-capped peak. We ate some goat cheese and drank our water in good confidence that we would soon find more. That morning, a few miles higher, the stream bed filled with mud; a few miles higher still, a trickle of water flowed down to the desert that it would never quite reach. By midafternoon the trickle had become a good-sized stream. And then, almost without warning, we came up around the curve of a mountain into a beautiful valley full of aspen trees, wildflowers, miles of thick green grass and herds of antelope that grazed upon it – into heaven.

29

Maram would have enjoyed our feast that night, made from a roasted antelope that I had killed with a quick arrow. Most of all, he would have delighted in the honey that Kane took from a beehive in a fallen tree.

None of us, not even Kane, knew anything about the mountainous terrain ahead of us. Surely, we all thought, we would find cities or at least villages in such a rich land.

Liljana, still chafing at having to abandon her beloved cookware, announced, 'Perhaps we will find a village and a smith who might sell us a few pots?'

'And find as well Kallimun spies?' Kane growled at her. 'We're too close to Hesperu now, and it won't do to expose ourselves for no good need. It will be chance enough to pass through Senta, but I see no other way.' He walked over to the low fence of brush and logs that we had built up encircling our fire. It was the first fortified camp we had made since the mountains beyond Acadu. 'Manoj called this the land of the Dead People. Let's not join them.'

The next morning, as we wound our way southwest, we saw no sign of the road's makers nor indeed of anyone. The valley, and others through the mountains that lay beyond it, proved densely inhabited but not by man. Elk and wild horses kept company with the antelope, as did badgers, bears, boars, rabbits and other furry creatures we saw chewing the browse from bushes or darting through the trees of the mountains' forests. Flowers grew everywhere, but especially brightened the acres of thick grass in the valleys' lower reaches. We moved slowly, pausing often to let our horses fatten on this grass. The land seemed as wild as any we had ever crossed.

And then the next day the road led straight into a small town, dead and deserted like Souzam. Ten miles farther up the road we came to a city thrice Souzam's size, though it was hard to tell for here field and forest overgrew what must have once been wooden houses and lanes passing between them, just as the desert had swallowed parts of Souzam. Death indeed haunted this place. I found myself wishing for the familiar sound of Maram's voice, moaning out his dread of ghosts. Here, among the ruins of ancient temples and what looked to be a large palace, Maram himself seemed almost a ghost, and I could not shake the sense that he rode at my side or just behind us.

'What happened,' I called out into the cool air, giving voice to a sentiment that Maram would have shared, 'to the poor people of this city? And of Souzam – all those who once dwelled in these mountains?'

I looked to Kane for an answer, but he sat on top of his horse using his strong, white teeth to tweezer out a bee's stinger still embedded in his skin. He shrugged his shoulders. And Master Juwain said, 'It might have been the Great Death. In 1047 of the Age of the Dragon, the plague spread out of Argattha into all lands, in some places killing nine people out of ten. It might be that there were lands where *all* died – or at least, no one remained to make accounts.'

He wanted to search through the ruins for a library but Kane gainsaid such a quest, growling out, '1047 – has it really been almost two thousand years since Morjin bred that filthy plague? So, any books here that told of it would long since have rotted apart.'

He went on to curse Morjin for using a green gelstei to create the hideous, hemorrhagic disease meant to afflict the blood of all the Valari – and the Valari only.

'So, he failed – the green gelstei are *hard* to use, eh?' he said, looking at Master Juwain. 'The Lord of Pestilence killed more of his own people than he did Valari.'

He didn't add what we all feared: that with the Lightstone in his grasp, he would be soon breed even worse plagues than the Great Death.

After that, we continued our journey up the road. This band of bricks and stones wound still higher and gradually turned past snowy peaks toward the south. Our dread of the Great Death, if not ghosts, impelled us to hurry from this rich country, but over the next days we continued moving slowly, pausing often to let the horses graze upon all the grass they wished to eat. In truth, we all still suffered from the ravages of the desert. We needed time to heal. And our suspicion that a droghul awaited us farther up the road checked our enthusiasm for swift travel. We hunted and filled our bellies with meat, even as Liljana found wild potatoes growing along our way, and much fruit: raspberries and black-berries, cherries, peaches and plums. We made feast of all these foods, and of the trout and rockfish that we pulled out of mountain streams. Kane called this land a hunter's paradise, and that it was. Liljana simply called it paradise. Rain fell upon us in perfect intervals and amounts, and so it was with the sunshine. It seemed strange that after fighting so hard for so long, against both man and nature, we should find a place where the world welcomed us and fed both our bodies and souls.

Daj and Estrella especially seemed to thrive here. Their small frames filled out, and their faces lost the haggard, haunted look that hundreds of miles of desert travel – to say nothing of the Skadarak – had worn into them. The sharp edge of guilt I felt at taking them on this quest dulled, slightly. It made me happy to see them happy, taking all the sustenance and sleep they needed, and more, playing games once again. They made fast friends with Alphanderry. His materializations and vanishings remained a mystery. The children, though, accepted the presence of this strange being in a way that we, his old friends, could not. They sat often with Alphanderry, continuing their elaboration of Eleikar's story and bringing this figmental character more and more to life. One night, with the fire crackling and the owls hooing deep in the forest, I heard Alphanderry say to Daj: 'Hoy, our Eleikar is *still* in an impossible fix, loving the wicked king's daughter, all the while knowing he must kill the king, whom the princess still loves, wickedness or no. Eleikar's dilemma reminds me of a riddle I once heard: "How do you capture a beautiful bird without killing its spirit?"'

Daj considered this a moment, and then turned to Estrella, who suddenly smiled and looked up at the sparkling heavens. And Daj blurted out: 'By becoming the sky!'

'Hoy, good, good – indeed, by becoming the sky!' Alphanderry said to Daj. 'What is it, then, that Eleikar must become to keep his head on his shoulders and keep the princess from hating him?'

Neither Daj nor Estrella, however, had an answer for him, and neither did I. I watched Alphanderry's face sparkling even in the thick of night as he said, 'We might think that we need to solve

461

Eleikar's conundrum for him. But give it time, and *he* will solve it, himself – you'll see!'

We slept well that night, and journeyed on the next day, and the following days, in high spirits. The peaks of the Crescent Mountains cut the sky above us like rows of ice-sharp white teeth. In places, along rivers where the road held good, we clopped along over ancient stones. In other places thick forests obliterated the road, and there we had to pick our way more carefully, sometimes guessing from the lay of the land where we might find the road again. In ten days of such travel, we put many miles behind us. It couldn't be many more, I thought, until we came upon the tiny kingdom of Senta, and the much greater realm of Hesperu beyond that. I sensed with a rising heat of my blood that *our* story – at least our quest to find the Maitreya or not – was quickly coming to an end.

On the fourth of Soal, late in the afternoon, we came to a place where a wall of mountains blocked our way. We had lost the thread of the road a good five miles back and could not tell if a pass might cut this escarpment to our left, up and around the rocky slopes of a pyramid mountain, or to our right, to the west, through a dense forest of oak, cedar and silver fir.

'Here we have need of one of your Way Rhymes,' I said to Master Juwain. 'Or failing that, a guess.'

Master Juwain peered at the stark terrain ahead of us and said, 'Left, I think. I can almost see where a road once wound up around that mountain.'

So, I thought, shielding my eyes against the glare of the mountains' snowy slopes, could I.

Kane swept his hand at the escarpment and said, 'Senta lies within a great bowl. These might be the mountains forming the bowl's northern part – their backside. I have a memory of that peak, I think, though I beheld it long ago and from a different vantage. If it *is* that mountain, then I would say our way lies to the left.'

'Then let us make camp here for the night,' I said, 'and in the morning we'll see if you are right.'

'If I *am* right,' Kane said, 'if the way is not blocked, we'll reach Senta tomorrow. So, we must decide if we will go into the caverns.'

All my life I had heard of the Singing Caves of Senta, and for much of that time I had wondered if they could possibly be real.

'If we are to put ourselves forward as pilgrims,' Master Juwain said, 'as it seems we must, then the Sentans would think it strange if we *didn't* go into the caverns.'

His gray eyes gleamed with the light off the glacier high above us. I knew that he wasn't about to cross half the earth only to surrender up the chance to behold one of Ea's greatest wonders.

'I would like to hear the caverns' songs,' Liljana said.

'I would, too,' Atara added. 'There might be a *chance* that one of the voices in the caverns will tell of the Maitreya.'

'Ha – do you think you'll understand anything?' Kane asked. 'There are thousands of voices, millions, and if you go into the caverns, you'll hear gobbledygook. You will see – it will drive you mad.'

I thought about this for a moment, then looked at Kane. 'Mad, as it was for us with the Skadarak?'

Kane's eyes darkened and he said softly, 'No, not like that. The voices all *do* speak truly, I think. But in the presence of the truth, people are like stones in water. They can sit there forever, thirsting, and remain as dry as chalk.'

I glanced at Estrella, then clapped him on the arm and said, 'Let us hope that some people are rather like sponges. Let us go into the caverns and hope for the best.'

Kane slowly nodded his head at this, and my smile made him smile. 'All right, Valashu. But I tell you that you will hear things in those damn caverns that will be hard for you to hear.'

I thought about this for half the night, and all the next morning as we set out again and worked our way up to the left, over the humps and folds of the pyramid mountain. Its eastern slopes, at this great height, with the air cool and thin, were covered mostly with silver fir and little undergrowth, and so we had little difficulty passing through the open spaces between the tall trees. Our luck held good, for we espied the white ridgeline of a low pass ahead of us and encountered no very steep grades or rockfalls to block our way. And then we came upon the road again. Here it was nothing more than a rubble of old, shattered stones, but it held true for a few more miles, taking us up almost all the way to the lip of the pass. We breathed hard at the cutting air, hurrying up this last leg of the ascent to see if Kane was right. Then we stood on a snowy shelf of ground as we looked down into a bowl of land twelve miles wide that was the ancient and entire kingdom of Senta.

The city of Senta stood near the bowl's midpoint. From this distance I could make out the cuts of the winding streets and the larger buildings, some of them domed and gleaming with veneers of gold. Kane pointed out King Yulmar's palace, on the wooded heights to the west of the city. More gold flashed from the towers and domes there, and I caught a brilliant sparkle, as of encrusted diamonds. Senta, which had extracted tolls and bribes from pilgrims for thousands of years, was famous for its wealth. According to Kane, it enjoyed a natural bounty, as well. Through the forest rising between the king's palace and the sheltering wall of mountains ran deer, foxes and boar, and other game that the king and Senta's nobles hunted. To the north of the city, and sweeping in a wide swath around it to the east and south, the Sentans cultivated some of the richest-looking farmland I had ever seen. The greenness of these acres colored the entire kingdom. And it was all crowned by huge, sharp, white peaks in a vast and gleaming circle, and higher still, by the brilliant blue sky.

Kane pointed past the city perhaps a mile to the south where a rocky prominence rose up, too large to be called a hill and yet not quite high enough to challenge the mountains that framed it.

'There are the Singing Caves,' Kane said. 'They go down through the side of that rock.'

We could see the road to it as a narrow streak of bluish-gray against the greenness of fields. Three other roads led into (or out of) Senta: to the west, the road to Surrapam, which cut through a high pass before curving back north on its winding way through the Crescent Mountains. To our left, built on a line toward the southeast, ran the Sunguru road. And nearly straight ahead, passing around the rocky prominence and then into the city, gleamed the ancient road that we would take into Hesperu.

No road, unfortunately, led from the pass upon which we stood down into the city. We had a hard time picking our way slowly down through the rattling scree, and were grateful to enter the line of trees where the grade eased and the ground smoothed out. Soon we came out of the forest into a wheatfield, to the surprise of the farmer at work there: a stout, red-haired man with pale blue eyes who directed us toward the city. We planned to stay at one of the inns built on the hill at the very foot of the Singing Caves. Though it would no doubt be costly, Kane insisted we should remain close to the Hesperu Road and the pass to the south out of Senta in case we encountered troubles and needed to make a hasty escape.

Soon we found ourselves riding through the streets of Senta's northern district, past shops and steeply gabled houses that were like those of my home. They were built flush with one another of good granite that might have endured here for thousands of years. We found the Hesperu Road near the center of the city, where, in a great square, it intersected the Sunguru Road coming in from the east. Along the storefronts, we saw many more people plying their trades and going about their business – though not nearly as many, we were given to understand, as in years past. Most of them, I thought, were Sentans. Red hair and blue eyes predominated among them, and I wondered if some wandering tribe from Surrapam had made its way south through the mountains to settle this kingdom during the Age of the Mother long, long ago. Some showed darker, almost mahogany-colored skins and black rings of hair, and these I took to be Hesperuks, in origin if not allegiance to King Arsu. Some were a blending of kinds and colors, and it amazed me to come across a young man as brown as coffee, with sparking green eyes and a curly red mane falling to his shoulders. The few pilgrims we saw seemed to be Hesperuk or Sung, with their almond eyes and straight black hair. But I bowed my head to a band of Galdans, to three blond Thalunes and to a lone Saryak warrior from Uskudar, whose face seemed carved of jet and who stood as high as the ceilings of most houses. In such company, my friends and I did not attract undue attention.

As we moved into Senta's southern districts, closer to the caverns, we came upon inns and the shops of craftsmen who had long serviced pilgrims: armorers, barbers, seamstresses, saddlers, cobblers and wheelwrights – and many others. We stopped at a tinker's so that Liljana could finally buy her pots and pans, and we visited a miller and a butcher in order to lay in stores. It was from the butcher, all sweaty and bloody from cutting up a lamb, that we heard news out of Hesperu and other lands.

'They say there was a rising in Surrapam,' he told us as he weighed out some slabs of salt pork. 'And a new rebellion in Hesperu, in the Haraland – that lies in Hesperu's north, brave pilgrims, just over the mountains. You didn't come here by way of Hesperu, did you? Few now do. Anyway, it's said that King Arsu has marched north with his army out of Khevaju to put down the rebellion. There are those who fear that he will march right into Senta, but he can't even hold onto his conquests and keep his evil empire together. And if he *did* try to force his way through the Khal Arrak, we would stop him in the narrows of the pass.'

To emphasize his point – and his own bravery – he picked up a bloody cleaver and waved it about. And he added, 'Senta will never fall; you can take *that* as a prophecy – and take it back to your homelands, wherever they are.'

Others, however, were not so confident of Senta's ability to withstand King Arsu, and his master, the Red Dragon. After we had finished with the butcher, we came across an old, blind woman begging alms beneath the eves of the adjacent fletcher's shop. She had the straight hair and wheat-colored skin of the Sung, and her eyes might once have been like large almonds before being gouged out. Atara took pity on her, and pressed a gold coin into the woman's trembling hand. And the woman, whose name was Zhenna, murmured to her: 'Bless you, my lady. But you should be careful with whom you speak. Alfar, the butcher, is a good man, but he talks too freely. The Red Dragon's ears are very keen, if you understand me, and they are everywhere.'

'If we were to take your advice,' Liljana said, stepping up close to her, 'we should not speak to *you*. How is it that you are willing to speak to *us*?'

'Because I like your smell,' Zhenna said, turning from Atara to smile towards Daj and Estrella. She reached out and fumbled to grasp Liljana's hand. 'And because I, too, was once a pilgrim like you.'

She told us that years ago, when King Angand had come to Sunguru's throne and had made the first moves toward an alliance with Morjin, she had been the wife of the Duke of Nazca. The Duke, in secret, had rallied nobles to oppose the alliance – and, if need be, to oppose King Angand himself. But sometimes there are secrets within secrets. By ill fate, one of the nobles had proved to be of the Order of the Dragon and had betrayed the Duke to King Angand and the Kallimun priests who sat at his court. As an example, King Angand had ordered the Duke crucified and had Zhenna cruelly blinded. She had then fled Sunguru, making the pilgrimage to Senta, and had remained here ever since.

'I've lived off the kindness of the Sentans and strangers such as yourselves,' she told us. 'But everyone looks to the south now, and they hoard their coins. Who has the strength to resist King Arsu? Once, Senta made alliance with Sunguru and Surrapam to keep the Hesperuks at bay, but I'm afraid that time is past.'

'I should think that even King Yulmar's few warriors,' I said to her, 'could wreak harm on King Arsu's army, if they tried to force the pass.'

'Alfar, too,' she said to me, 'speaks always of the Hesperuk army. But why should King Arsu waste his soldiers in an invasion when those who look to the Red Dragon will do his work for him? It's said that Galda fell from within, and so, I fear, it will be here.'

'Why don't you leave here, then?' I asked her.

'Where would I go?' Zhenna said to me. 'At least here, for ten days at the New Year, King Yulmar opens the caverns to such as I. The songs! Not even the larks make such music! As you will hear – you will hear!'

Atara gave her another coin and said to her, 'We should go on. Perhaps it would be best if you weren't seen talking with us.'

Zhenna straightened her shoulders and held her head up high. She said, 'What more can they take from me? I've only one wish, and that is to go into the caverns one more time. Somewhere, in the lower caverns, I think, where the opals grow, they sing of a land without tyrants, without evil or war. A land that the Red Dragon cannot touch.'

I shook my head against the throbbing there, and told her: 'I think there is no place on earth like that.'

'No, young man,' she said, grasping my hand, 'there *must* be. Someday I will go there. It will be my last pilgrimage.'

She smiled at me and squeezed my hand. I thought to take her with us and pay her admittance to the caverns, but she said that King Yulmar's stewards, who guarded them, would not allow that. She shooed me toward my horse, and said, 'Go, and listen well, brave knight. The land that I told of – it is called Ansunna.'

Past a district where the air reeked of tannin, roasting meats and perfume wafting from the open windows of the brothels, we came out into farmland, and smelled instead freshly turned earth and the dung used to fertilize the fields. It did not take us very long to wind our way up the wooded hill at the base of Mount Miru, as the Sentans called the huge rock that contained the caverns. Two inns stood upon the top of the hill: The Inn of the Caves and the larger, rambling Inn of the Clouds, painted white. Kane liked the size and look of this inn, and so we rented rooms there. We gave our horses into the keeping of the stableboys. The innkeeper insisted that we should have a hot bath and a change of clothes before going into the caverns. And so it was late in the afternoon when we walked along a flagstoned path at the top of the hill with the shadowed, granite face of Mount Miru above us.

We were the last pilgrims that day to seek admittance at the entrance to the caverns, a house-sized scoop in the rock of the face of Mount Miru. The Sentans called it the First Cavern, but it did not seem natural: most of its surface gleamed with an obsidian-like glaze. I wondered if men had once melted out this hollow from solid rock with the aid of a firestone.

At a long, gilded table set on a carpet in the recesses of the cavern sat a lean, dark-haired man decked out in gilded armor. Two other men similarly dressed but with spears in their hands and short swords on their ruby-studded belts stood leaning against it. These I took to be Stewards of the Caves. As we drew up in front of the table, the seated man said, 'My name is Sylar, good pilgrims, and I am Lord of the Caves. We ask only three things of you: a small donation to help pay for the upkeep of the Caves and that you take from them all the wonder that you are about to see and hear.'

I studied Sylar's sharp eyes and nose, and the tiny round scars pocking his dark, sallow skin. Long ringlets of black hair, scented with sandalwood oil, hung down over the plate armor encasing his chest. He had a kindly, helpful manner about him, but his smile, somewhat forced, hinted at deep resentments and suspicions.

'And what is the third thing?' I asked him.

He directed my attention to a rock the size of a wagon rising up from the cavern's floor behind us. I saw that this rock, too, did not seem a natural part of the mountain, for it was of basalt, as black as night and all greasy looking. A face, hideous as a demon's, had been carved into the rock's smooth surface. Two blue stones resembling lapis had been set below the demon's bulging brows as eyes. The demon's mouth turned up in a tormented smile, and a large black hole at its center opened like a throat drilled deep into the rock.

'The third thing we ask,' Sylar said to us, 'is that you *not* take any stone or crystal from the caverns. There is a demon of desire inside all of us, but if you give in to its lusts, you will not gain new treasure but only lose that which is even more precious.'

He explained that each pilgrim, upon exiting the cavern, would be required to put his hand inside the demon's mouth. He would then be asked if he had removed anything from the caverns. If the pilgrim told the truth, all would be well. If the pilgrim lied, however, he would forfeit his hand. It seemed that the ancients had connected a mechanism to the demon's eyes, which were truth stones. Upon being activated, the mechanism would bring down a massive, razor-sharp blade upon the wrist of any palterer or prevaricator.

'But that is horrible!' Atara cried out. 'To lose a hand so! How long has it been, then, since a pilgrim perjured himself?'

'Never in my lifetime,' Sylar told her. He seemed almost disappointed that he had never had the opportunity to see the demon do its work. 'But two hundred years ago, it is said that a prince of Karabuk boasted that no gelstei could look through his mind into his heart. What is left of his hand adorns that wall.'

He pointed toward the back of the hollow where two more stewards stood guarding iron doors that led into the caverns. On the wall to the left and right of the doors, seemingly cemented into the rock, gleamed the yellow-white bones of many human hands. Kane, I thought, should have warned us against such a bizarre and gruesome display, but he had retreated inside one of his depthless silences.

The 'Lord of the Caves' turned to look at me in a way that I did not like. And I told him, 'We are no thieves.'

'No, of course not – anyone could see that.' Sylar's dark, inquisitive eyes studied my face, and then fell upon my sword, strapped to my back. I had wrapped a strip of plain leather around its hilt to conceal the diamond pommel and the seven diamonds set into the black jade. 'You are no doubt a hired sword engaged to protect these good pilgrims, and perhaps even a pilgrim yourself?'

The scorn in his voice made my ears burn, and I wanted to shout out that I was no mercenary but a knight and a prince of Mesh. Instead, I kept my silence.

'A hired sword . . . from where?' he asked me. 'You have the look of the Valari, I think. A couple of Valari visited the caverns not two years ago, during the great Quest. I think they said they were Waashians.'

'I call no land my home,' I told him.

'I see.' Then Sylar's eyes turned to Atara's unstrung bow, which she tapped against the ground, seeming to feel her way. I was glad that Liljana had sewn the three arrows that Atara had brought with her within the lining of her cloak.

'A woman, bearing a bow without arrows,' Sylar said, 'and a blind one at that. I am not sure if I've ever seen a stranger sight.'

'I was a warrior before being blinded in battle,' Atara told him. 'My bow is sacred to me, and makes a good enough staff.'

'A warrior woman,' Sylar mused. 'I think I have heard of such, in Thalu – you must be Thalune, then? Well, many of the blind come here hoping to ease their suffering. It's said that the blind gain keener hearing to make up for what was lost. If that is true, then very soon, when you hear the songs of the angels, you will not regret your misfortune.'

469

He went on to explain to us that the deepest caverns held the most beautiful songs as well as the loveliest crystals, adding, 'Now, it is the way of things here for honored pilgrims such as yourselves to show their devotion, as the sun does its gold. The more gold, the greater the honor, do you understand? And the deeper the devotion, the deeper the songs that the good pilgrim will hear.'

Kane growled out, 'Are you telling us that the lower caverns are open only to those who'll pay to see them?'

The look in Kane's black eyes just then alarmed the two guards leaning against the table, for they stood up straight and ground the iron-shod butts of their spears against the cavern's rocky floor. And Sylar, in a voice as smooth as silk, said, 'No, good pilgrim – of course not! That would go against the King's decree. All the caverns are open to all who come here. But so many come, and so many wish to linger in the lower caverns that unfortunately we must limit the time of their visits. Of course, we like to reserve the greatest spans of time for those who are most deeply devoted.'

Liljana, who could haggle the scales off a dragon, bowed her head to him and asked, 'And how much devotion do you think a pilgrim should show in order to spend as long inside the caverns as she pleases?'

So sweetly and yet compellingly did her voice sound out that Sylar forget the first rule of negotiating, and he was the first to name a price, saying, 'Surely six ounces would not be too much.'

'All right – six silver ounces,' Liljana said, reaching for the coins bulging out her purse.

'No, madam – six *gold* ounces.' Sylar smiled at her and added, 'Alonian archers would be good – that is one currency, at least, that hasn't been debased. You *are* Alonian, aren't you? A poor knight's widow, I heard you say, though I think you have the look of a queen.'

His smile, as fluid as heated oil, produced no like response in her. Her gaze fixed on him as she said, 'Three gold archers seems to me a very great devotion.'

Sylar's smile widened as he snapped at her offer and said, 'Very well, then – three archers for each of the seven of you. Twenty-one altogether.'

'Three archers apiece!' Liljana cried out. 'Why didn't you say so from the first? We're only poor pilgrims – and even poorer for having come so far.'

'Two archers apiece, then. Let it not be said that Sylar of the Caves takes advantage of blind women and grandmothers.'

470

Liljana appeared to consider this. She gathered Estrella and Daj close to her, then asked, 'Have you children, Lord Steward? You wouldn't wish to impoverish ours, would you?'

And so the haggling continued until in the end Sylar raised his hands in a gesture of helplessness and agreed to accept five gold ounces, total, for our admission to the caverns: one for each adult, and none at all for the children. I watched Liljana count the coins out of her purse. They were full-weight, Alonian ounces, with the face of the deceased King Kiritan stamped into one side and the image of an archer drawing a longbow on the other.

'Very well, *grandmother*,' Sylar said to Liljana after he had put away the coins. He glared at her as if he had lost the ability to smile then waved us toward the opened iron doors.

'You played him like a hooked fish,' I whispered to her as I walked beside her.

I heard my words less as a compliment than an accusation. Not often did Liljana allow anyone to see the skills in manipulating men that had made her Materix of the Maitriche Telu.

'The signs were written on his face for anyone to read,' she whispered back to me. 'Still, that is one fish who is more slippery than I would like. Let us not be any longer about our business than we must.'

I nodded my head, and looked over at the blue-eyed demon behind us. Then I turned to lead the way into the Singing Caves.

30

The first thing I noted upon entering the next cavern was not sound but light. A soft, variously-hued radiance seemed to pour forth from the curving cavern walls and ceilings from no single source. A closer inspection revealed that the crystals studding the cavern's smooth rock each glowed from within. There were millions of them. Some were nearly as tiny as grains of sand; the largest were the size of Master Juwain's varistei, which nearly fit into his opened palm. They glittered through the whole of the cavern in a rainbow of colors: carmine; orange; citron; emerald; azure; indigo and violet. Most of the crystals were clear, like precious jewels, though many swirled with piebald or iridescent patterns, more like opals or pearls. Among these, Master Juwain identified many music marbles, touch stones and thought stones, all of the same family of gelstei. He guessed that the other crystals in this chamber were of some sort of related gelstei, but he did not really know.

The cavern had been shaped like a bubble of blown glass, only pinched-in and elongated as it opened down into the earth. We made our way slowly toward its center. This required us to move down steps that had been cut into the floor of the cavern long ago, a rather difficult feat since the cavern's splendor drew the eye not downward but out and up. A few crystals did sprout up from the floor like glowing mushrooms, but we guessed that most there had long since been broken off or chiseled out to make room for the pathways and open spaces upon which pilgrims might stand. There was nothing to do here, I thought, but to stand and stare in awe – and to listen.

As Kane had promised, thousands, perhaps millions, of voices filled the air. Not all of them, or even most of them, sang. I heard wails and laments, chants, thanksgivings, cries of joy and invocations. The bray of an old warrior telling of his victories vied with the shrillness of a bereft woman wondering why plague and war had taken the lives of her nine children. At first this cacophony nearly drowned me like an ocean's wave slamming my body underwater against hard sand. The raw emotion in the multitude of voices, all speaking with passion and truth, nearly crushed the blood from my chest. I threw my hands over my ears to block out this immense sound. It helped only a little, for I could feel my flesh and my very hand bones vibrating in harmony with the voices filling up the cavern, and pushing the sound only deeper into me. I saw Master Juwain put his finger to one of the wall's vibrating crystals, which he had named as a touch stone. I remembered that the lovely, variegated touch stones recorded and played people's sentiments, instead of music, for others to feel.

'This *is* madness!' I cried out, looking at Kane. 'I cannot even hear myself think!'

Kane's jaws ground together as he glared back at me and slowly nodded his head.

'How do you bear it?' I asked him.

My words seemed lost into the great noise about us. My other companions, however, did not seem as troubled by it as I was. Master Juwain told me that he could make out a voice reciting in ancient Ardik the long lost epic of Azariel – as well as another speaking in Marouan of the forging of the first of the blue gelstei. He did not pause to await my response, for two streams of sound sufficed to fill him to overflowing. I marveled that he seemed able to concentrate his awareness on only two, to the exclusion of the many others. So it seemed with Daj, who would not tell of what sounds enchanted him. He only stared at a cluster of aquamarine crystals as if soaring through a dream. Liljana asked if I could hear the voice of Seki the First telling of the building of the Temple of Life in the Age of the Mother. And of a boy asking after his missing father and a young woman singing of her love for a man named Seasar – and a dozen other threads of utterances that she somehow sorted out within herself and wove into a pattern making sense to her. Atara likewise shared this gift, and so, perhaps did Estrella. This slender girl seemed to open herself to the thousands of voices echoing through the cavern as if she somehow could hold each of them inside her.

'If I remember aright,' Kane shouted at me, 'it gets better in the lower caverns. So, let's get on with things, then.'

He turned to walk down the steps where they cut through a particularly steep stretch of the cavern's floor. I followed him gladly, and so, less gladly, did the others. The deepest part of the cavern narrowed into a tube, as of a corridor connecting two parts of a castle. Here, no crystals arose from the smooth rock encasing us, and the voices died almost to a murmur. I breathed out a sigh of relief. I felt myself building stony walls inside my heart against the surge of sound and people's passions that would surely assault me upon our entrance to the next cavern.

The third cavern proved much smaller than the second: barely the size of a servingwoman's chambers, with great, inward bulges in its crystal-lined walls that made it feel even smaller. The seven of us crowded in together only with difficulty, and we did not long remain. I noted, though, that the crystals in this cavern grew larger, some reaching nearly a foot in length. Strangely, the voices grew fewer in number and less strident, though perhaps I was learning to block out the sounds and words that most vexed me.

In the fourth cavern, deeper still, pink and silvery crystals grew out of the walls and floor like swords. The path through them cut steep and narrow, and we had to move with care lest we impale ourselves on their glittering points. Atara took my hand, and asked me if I could make out the voice of a minstrel singing in Old High Lorranda the *Gest of Nodin and Yurieth*. I could not. I wondered that we each seemed to apprehend different voices. I had a strange sense that the crystals here possessed desires of their own. Somehow the crystals, I thought, as of a gosharp's strings resonating with each other, attuned themselves to something deep and individual inside each of us and directed the sounds that pleased them into our ears and hearts.

Daj hadn't yet learned Lorranda, which Maram had called the language of love. He lifted his face toward the ceiling, hung with long, amethyst-like pendants and pulsing golden crystals. And in his high, piping boy's voice, he called out: 'I have a song for you! It's called the *Gest of Eleikar and Ayeshtan*, Princess of Khalind. It tells of how Eleikar slew the wicked King Ivar and gained Khalind's throne.'

Upon the sound of his bold words, Alphanderry appeared out of the cavern's close air. He stood in the radiance pouring down from the thousands of gelstei gleaming upon the cavern's ceiling and walls. He smiled at Daj, and said, 'Hoy, the song – let's hear the song!'

Master Juwain, however, was not so pleased by Daj's enthusiasm, nor did he appear eager to listen to the story that Daj,

Estrella and Alphanderry had nearly finished making. He turned his lumpy face toward the boy, and chastened him, saying, 'Your story is still incomplete.'

Daj shrugged his shoulders as he cocked his ear toward a particularly large ruby crystal pointing down from the ceiling thirty feet above our heads. He said, 'Other stories are incomplete, too. Other songs are. The story of the whole world . . . has yet to be finished.'

'There is a time for singing, and a time for listening.'

'But I just want to sing of Eleikar, and listen to these stones sing back! Maybe the next people passing through will hear it and know how to complete the story if we don't – and if Eleikar himself doesn't, or even dies before he has the chance.'

'Dajarian,' Master Juwain said to him, 'Eleikar *cannot* really die.'

'That's just it, sir – we can't *let* him die.'

'He cannot die because he is not real.'

'He's real to me, sir.'

Master Juwain sighed as he rubbed the back of his shiny head and regarded Daj. Not two years ago, when we had rescued Daj from the Dragon's clutches, the horrors of Argattha had killed something precious and innocent in him, and he had been more callous of countenance and soul than a battle-hardened warrior. Now, the boy lived within him again, and a world of beauty and hope, and it gladdened my heart to see that.

'It is said,' Master Juwain explained to him, 'that only words spoken truly and with deep conviction can be recorded here.'

'I will speak the truth,' Daj assured him.

'But your story is an invention.'

'But what of Nodin and Yurieth, then?'

'Well, *they* are real. It is almost certain that they lived in the vanished kingdom of Osh, during the Age of Swords.'

'But Eleikar and Ayeshtan live inside me! A story doesn't have to be *really* real to be true.'

Master Juwain sighed as he rested his gnarled hand on a small purple crystal sprouting out of a rocky rise in the floor. It would have been an easy thing, I saw, for him to snap it off and put it in his pocket.

'All right,' he said to Daj. 'Speak as you will, and let us hear if these stones speak back.'

Daj stood up straight, and without hesitation, in a voice as steady and full of fire as the desert sun, recited the first verses into which he and Alphanderry, with Estrella's assent, had rendered their story:

In Khalind, once upon a time,
A boy's revenge, upon a crime . . .

We all stood listening as Daj sang out his story. After he had
completed the first three stanzas, he fell into a silence. He stared
at the lacy, white crystals adorning the wall before him. He waited
for them to begin sparkling like diamonds.

An echo, reflected back from a mountain's rock, reaches the ear
faster than any bird can fly. We waited for a good ten count, and
then thrice that long, and the only voices that any of us heard
belonged to departed wanderers, minstrels, merchants and queens,
but not to boys barely ten years old. And then, with a suddenness
that froze the breath in my throat, the space about us fell dead
quiet. The cavern itself seemed to be listening. And then Daj's
words, in Daj's earnest voice, fell out of the air like perfectly formed
jewels:

In Khalind, once upon a time,
A boy's revenge, upon a crime
So dark the demons shriek and sing
The torment of a wicked king . . .

When the song stones had finished speaking back Daj's verses,
Master Juwain rested his hand on top of Daj's tousled hair and
smiled at him. 'Well, lad, I must admit that I was wrong. Very
wrong. There is truth, and then there is *truth.*'

'I *told* you,' Daj said, beaming at him.

'And then there is that which we came here to find,' Master
Juwain said. He looked from Daj to Liljana, and then at Atara and
me. 'Well-made verses, whether old or new, are always a delight
to hear. But has anyone heard tell of the Shining One?'

We all had. Over the centuries, many had come into the caverns
to sing of Ea's Maitreyas. Most of their songs were ancient and
told of miracles of healing: In the third cavern, I had listened
intently as a nameless woman gave praise to Godavanni the
Glorious, relating how he had laid his hands upon her son's withered leg and made it whole again. A master of the Brotherhood –
a man who called himself Navarran – told of his reverence for
Alesar Tal's powers of soul and uplifting others' spirits. He had
wondered if Alesar might be the Maitreya foretold for the end of
the Age of the Mother, but he had never determined this, for
Alesar had never caught sight of the lost Lightstone and had died

in obscurity, just another healer who lived out his life in one of the Brotherhood's schools. Liljana, as she informed us, had heard a song praising a Maitreya known simply as the Erikur. As the Maitreyas born near the endings of the known ages were accounted for, Liljana concluded that the Erikur had worked his wonders during one of the Lost Ages, after Aryu had slain Elahad and men and women lived nearly wild in lands whose names were lost to time.

And then there was Issayu. Born in the year 2261 of the Age of the Swords on the island of Maroua, he had grown into manhood talking to the dolphins and healing the blind. Of him it was sung that 'his hands were like the ocean's waters and his eyes like the sun'. Thaddariam, the Grandmaster of the Brotherhood, upon testing Issayu, had proclaimed him as the Shining One. Many looked to Issayu to end the terror of that age and bring a time of peace and healing. But after Morjin had conquered the Elyssu in 2284, he had captured and seduced Issayu, promising to bestow upon him the Lightstone and the gift of immortality. Of course Morjin had never actually allowed Issayu to hold the Cup of Heaven in his hands. The Lord of Lies had slowly perverted Issayu by requiring him to do darker and darker deeds in hope someday of becoming a great Wielder of Light. In the end, when Issayu had discovered how Morjin had twisted his heart and poisoned his soul, he had despaired and had killed himself by throwing himself out of a tower upon the rocks overlooking the sea.

All these accounts, and there were thousands of them, were ancient. But others seemed less old. Many people had come into the caverns to sing of their hope for the *coming* Maitreya, the Cosmic Maitreya – the last of the Shining Ones who would bring an end to the dark ages of Ea and herald in the Age of Light. Their many prayers and chants were variations of these words:

> *Hail Maitreya, Lord of Light,*
> *Open up our deepest sight,*
> *Shine like sun, forever bright,*
> *Bring an end to darkest night.*

At least fifty voices were new, for they told of King Kiritan's calling of the great Quest and how the Lightstone had been found. Soon, it was sung, the Cup of Heaven would find its way into the hands of the Maitreya. Indeed, this great-souled being might already have come forth: in the person of a blacksmith's son in

Alonia or a fisherman on one of the islands off Thalu or a Galdan healer – or even in the unlikely form of a prince of Mesh named Valashu Elahad. As I stood beneath purple and white crystals vibrating like a mandolet's strings, I tried to take in the dozens of hints as to where the Maitreya might have been born and who he might be. So, I thought, did Master Juwain and Liljana and my other friends. We listened most intently for accounts of healings and other miracles out of the lands in the north of Hesperu.

'Let us go deeper,' Kane finally said as he looked toward the passage to the next cavern. 'Let us hope that as the songs grow deeper, we will hear what we came to hear.'

We followed his lead. The fifth cavern twisted off sharply to the right, and down, many more feet into the earth. Virescent crystals the length of spears stuck up from the floor and hung down from the ceiling above our heads. A few of these flowed from the ceiling *to* the floor like delicate, translucent pillars. As I made my way through this narrow chamber, I seemed able to pick out single songs and concentrate my awareness upon them. In the sixth cavern, full of pendants, plumes and other lovely rock formations glistering with the fire of opals, individual verses and words became ever clearer even as the thousands of distracting voices faded to a murmur. It seemed that I had the power to let live within myself only those songs that touched me most deeply.

'I wonder,' Alphanderry said, 'if this is where Venkatil heard the voice telling him to seek for the Lightstone in the Tower of the Sun. I wonder if he also knew where the Maitreya might have been born.'

At last we came into the seventh cavern, nearly as round and vast as King Kiritan's hall in faraway Tria. The air fell quiet as over a field just before a battle. A hundred feet above our heads, amethyst, turquoise and rose crystals hung silent and still. Great pinnacles, jacketed in some pearly white substance, pointed up from the floor. They caught the glittering greens, reds and blues pouring off the cavern's curving walls; they caught the light of our eyes and seemed to drink in our breath and the sound our beating hearts.

'Why can't I *hear* anything here?' Daj whispered to Master Juwain.

Master Juwain, however, stood staring up at the brilliant dome above us and rubbing at his jaw in deep concentration, and so it was Alphanderry who answered Daj's question.

'What do you *want* to hear?' he asked Daj. 'This is the seventh cavern, and it's said that here a man may apprehend anything he wishes, as long he truly *wishes* it.'

'I don't know what I want to hear,' Daj told him. He watched, as did I, as Alphanderry's form glittered with scarlet and silver lights. 'Something about the Maitreya?'

'You don't sound very certain.'

'Well, that's what I *should* want to hear, shouldn't I?'

'Only you know that,' Alphanderry told him. His luminous eyes seemed to look right through Daj's hard-set face. 'Is there someone you'd rather hear about?'

Daj stared off at one of the opalescent pillars connecting the floor to the domed ceiling high above us, and he nodded his head.

'Who, then?'

And Daj whispered, 'My mother.'

Alphanderry thought about this and told him, 'Then you must listen deeply, and you will hear of her.'

'But how is that possible? No one who knew her . . . could have come here to sing of her.'

'No, Daj, many have come: minstrels from across Ea for thousands of years. This chamber is known as the Minstrels' Cavern. Here they have sung of everything that can be sung.'

'But my mother –'

'She still lives, in the songs the minstrels have sung of *their* mothers. Listen, and you will hear.'

As Daj fell silent, casting his eyes down upon the marbled stones about us, Alphanderry turned to Liljana and asked, 'What song would most brighten your spirits?'

Without hesitation Liljana told him, 'A song of *the* Mother.'

Alphanderry slowly nodded his head, then looked at Master Juwain.

'What do *you* wish to hear?'

And Master Juwain told him, 'That which cannot be heard.'

'And you, Kane?' Alphanderry asked, peering over at our grim-faced friend.

But Kane stared at him in silence, answering him only in the fury of his blazing eyes.

'Atara?' Alphanderry asked, looking away from him.

Atara smiled as she said, 'Why, a love song, of course.'

Alphanderry paused to regard Estrella, who gazed right back at him with a soft radiance lighting up her face. I thought she might be happy listening to any song, or to all of them. And then Alphanderry turned toward me.

'Val – what do you most want to hear?'

What *did* I wish to hear, I wondered? The location and identity of the Maitreya? The secret of life and death? Words assuring me that Daj and Estrella would somehow grow up in safety and that Atara would have all the love that she could bear? Or did I wish even more to learn of a cure for the poison burning up my soul?

I drew in a deep breath of the cavern's cool air, and I said, 'I want to hear how Morjin might be defeated.'

At this, Kane smiled savagely, baring his glittering white teeth. Atara's hand reached out to grip mine. Liljana and my other companions looked at me quietly. Finally, Alphanderry said to me, 'I do not know what minstrel would have sung of that, but why don't we all listen, even so?'

And so we did. We found a clear place on the cavern's floor near its center, and positioned ourselves facing whatever part of the cavern called to us. And then we waited.

At first, there was nothing to hear – nothing more than the susurrus of our breaths and a faint drumming that sounded almost like the heartbeat of the earth. I set my hand upon the leather wrapped around the hilt of my sword; I could smell the sweat and oils worked into it, as I could the moistness of stone. There was a strange taste to the air. Across the cavern from me, where its walls gleamed with silver swirls, the light pouring out of the crystals grew suddenly stronger. The crystals themselves rang out like chimes, and voices fell out all around us.

As before, there were many of them. But here, in the seventh cavern deep in the earth, they did not resound as a multitudinous noise or even as chords, but rather progressed like the notes of a melody, one by one. I listened as the rich baritone of one minstrel gave way to the booming bass of another, only to be followed by an even deeper voice trolling out in verse or song, and then yet another. Many of the minstrels had not put their names to their compositions or the ancient ballads and epics they recited; others had: Agasha, Mingan, Kamilah, Hauk Eskil, Mahamanu and Azureus. In the Minstrels' Cavern, I thought, names mattered less than the virtue of the voices that spoke them. I sensed that minstrels from across Ea had come to this place, century after century, age after age, to vie with one another in singing the most beautiful song. No gold medallion would be given to the winner of this age-old competition, for it remained ongoing, and living minstrels might always hope to outsing even the greatest of the ancients. It was enough, I thought, that their words would live on long after they themselves had died, perhaps to the very ending of the world.

For an hour, it seemed, I stood nearly as still as one of the cavern's stone pillars, listening. I thought it would be impossible ever to single out any one minstrel's song as being the most beautiful or true. Some of their voices trilled out high and sweet, like the piping of birds, and soared up to the sky; other voices rang out low and long like gongs or bells that resonated with something deep inside my heart. Once or twice the minstrels attained to the truly angelic, and in the rhymes they intoned and the rhythms of their strange words, I caught hint of the grace of the language of the Galadin.

It was the singing of one of these ancient minstrels that most drew me. I couldn't help listening, for his voice was clear and strong, and rang out with the brightness of struck silver. In his heart-piercing song, I heard much that seemed lovely, but even more that was plaintive and pained. The immense suffering of this nameless minstrel made my throat hurt. His words cut open my soul, and burned with a terrible beauty that drove deep into me and filled my blood with fire.

At first, I took little sense from these blazing words, for the minstrel sang them in ancient Ardik, a language that I never translated easily. But the more he chanted out his verses, the more I could apprehend. I found myself drawing my sword nearly a foot out of its sheath. Alkaladur's shimmering silver gelstei seemed to resonate with something in the minstrel's music, and within the minstrel himself. A strange thing happened then: the meaning of the minstrel's words suddenly became utterly clear to me, as though light shone through a diamond. And the mystery of the minstrel's identity stood revealed.

His name was Morjin. But he was not the Morjin that I had battled in Argattha and had hated ever since, nor did his voice sound the same as that of the man who had taken on the mantle of the Red Dragon. No, I thought, this was a different Morjin, a younger Morjin not yet completely corrupted by the evils he had wrought upon the world. His voice was sweeter, gentler and less sure of itself. It reverberated with a different pitch and tone. In its plangent insistence on trying to uncover the truth, I heard almost as much love as I did hate.

This Morjin of old had a story to tell, and he had come here to tell it. He had come to open his heart, and perhaps something more, too. In the most exquisitely sad music that I had ever heard, these words of an immortal who had once belonged to the Elijik order sounded out deep inside the earth:

*Let none hear my voice except my brothers in spirit, for only they will understand: I have slain a man. I, of those who are not permitted to slay, have done this thing which cannot be undone. In the dark of the moon, on a black night in winter with the wolves howling in the hills, I bade a man to look out the window upon the stars, and I put a knife into his back. Into his heart – how else to slay this man who was more than a man? To slay? Why do I bite my tongue to keep from saying the true word for what I have done? And that is murder. Let me shout that, here, in the hollow of the earth to these pretty stones, as I soon must shout it to the stars: **That is murder!** And I am therefore a murderer – at last.*

*Iojin. You were my brother, in spirit, and my brother in a great quest. You always knew my heart. How could I hide from you that which had begun to live inside me, with a ferocity like unto starfire feeding upon an infinite source? I burned, and so you burned, in touching my heart. You knew what golden source of light blazed in all my thoughts so that I could not sleep. You knew that I must someday try to claim **IT** – I think you knew this before I knew it myself. I burned, and so you burned, with compassion for me. I wept to know that you did not hate me for this dragon fire that consumed me, but only loved me. But you feared me, too, even as I feared myself.*

*How could you, Iojin of the Waters, not have wanted to go to the others in fear of me, in fear for me, and in fear for what we had come here to do? In fear for the world? Did you count this as betrayal? No, I do not think you would have, for you loved me as a brother, and would never have suffered anyone or anything to have grieved me. And yet, Garain, I think, would have betrayed me to the Bright Ones who sent us here. And Kalkin even worse: you, so gentle of heart, could never look into his heart, as fiery as a star, as black as death. He, the mighty Kalkin, might have murdered me. He would have – I feel this in my heart. When I claimed **IT**, he proved his baseness by murdering men, lesser men, before I slew him and cast his body into the sea.*

Upon these words, I couldn't help looking over at Kane, who stood grinding his jaws together as he wept silently, perhaps to the sound of some song that I could not hear. And then Morjin's beautiful voice captured me again:

And so, by evil fate, I had to murder my brother. When I stabbed you, you screamed and screamed – I didn't know it would hurt so badly or take you so long to die. I watched the light go out of your eyes. Your beautiful eyes, like bright pools, beloved by all, and not just me. But the last light was for me. I see it still, like the setting of the moon, and cannot forget. Just as I cannot forget the burn of blood that stained my hands, for it was so warm and bright. I cannot wash it away, nor do I wish to. For your blood became my blood, my very life. It fed me, and feeds me still. Out of your death, the Dragon was born, and that is a very great thing.

If your eyes could look into mine now, would I see forgiveness there? Would you understand? I think you would. You, who loved me and would have died for me, and did die, without my asking you. You always wanted me to shine like the Bright Ones themselves; now I do. But I think I would see tears in your eyes, too. You would weep for yourself, as I weep. You would weep for me, your friend, your brother, who screamed himself at the agony of the knife and died even as you died.

I think always of both these men: their beauty, their goodness, their grace. Their . . . innocence. I cannot bear that they should be cast into a black pit, never again to smell the honeysuckle in high summer or to gaze upon the brilliance of the winter stars. Never again to sing. I cannot bear that the One made the world so. Now that I am who I am, I will not bear it. I will breathe all my fire into this hateful creation, and out of its immolation, as the silver swan is reborn out of the ashes of its death pyre, I will make things anew.

This, though it will be no consolation to you now, I promise: that I will use the stone of light to bring only good things into the world – as good and beautiful as you. I will bring peace to Ea. And peace to the stars and every part of Eluru. When my work is done, I will turn all my thoughts and memories upon you. All my will. For nine score days and nights, I have asked myself if I have done the right thing. I have kept the knife always close to me. How shall I use it? Only you can tell me. And so I have come here to sing, that you might live again. If my heart is true, there will be an opening. I will enter into a cavern, not icy and dark, but gleaming with great crystals and full of light. And I will sing. If my words are perfect, if the music is as beautifully made as were you, I will breathe my breath into you. And you will live again. I will clasp your hand in mine; I will touch my hand to your wound and make it whole. I will look once more into your eyes, full of wonder, full of forgiveness, full of light. And I will live again, too, and all will be well.

Music poured forth from Morjin's throat then, and its lovely notes seemed to rise and seek form in the music of the Galadin. I heard in Morjin's voice a terrible striving for pure tones and all that was beautiful and good. But something deep in the sounding of his soul hissed with self-deception and untruth. I grit my teeth against the poisonous lie built into the very heart of his song.

A faint sound from somewhere in the caverns above us caused me to break my concentration on this eulogy – or perhaps it was a prayer. I stood breathing hard against the sharp pain stabbing through my chest. I turned my head, and Morjin's anguished words died to a whisper. Kane still stood beside me, weeping freely now, as did Daj and Estrella behind him. Master Juwain stared up at the cavern's crystalline ceiling as if listening to some impossibly brilliant song. Atara leaned back against the opalescent pillar to my right. The smile that broke upon her face warmed my heart; I sensed that one of the immortal minstrels had given her a love song as beautiful as her dreams. Liljana, however, seemed also to have been startled out of her rapture. She cocked her ear toward the opening to the sixth cavern above us, and said to me, 'Did you hear anything?'

Her voice broke the spell woven by the minstrels' songs. Kane, through blurry eyes, peered at the stairs leading up to the sixth cavern, and his hand fell upon the hilt of his sword.

The sound of boots slapping against stone now clearly echoed out into our cavern. As we waited, this noise grew louder. Then, from out of the corridor at the top of the stairs, one of the Stewards of the Caves appeared. He grunted as he made his way down the stairs, followed by another guard, as dark and thin as he was fair and fat. Between grunts and the banging of his spear butt against the stone steps, he called out to us, 'Good pilgrims! Good pilgrims!'

When they had come closer, winding their way between the sharp crystals projecting up from the floor, an annoyed Liljana called back to him, 'You disturb us, good steward! Did we not agree that we were to be left here, alone, for as long as we wished?'

'But Madam Maida!' he said, fairly shouting out the name Liljana had given the stewards, 'that is just why we have come: we *have* been left alone. I fear treachery!'

The steward, whose name was Babul, came panting up to us. He stood next to the second steward, Pirro, and explained what had happened:

'After you went into the caverns,' he said, 'Lord Sylar posted Pirro and me by the doors while he held conference with Tarran,

Elkar and Hakun. I tried to hear what he said to them, but I couldn't. I didn't like the sound of his voice. I never liked *him* – King Yulmar made him Lord of the Caves only because he married the King's niece. There was always something *wrong* about him. He spoke of the Red Dragon too often, if you know what I mean. He never trusted me, either, nor Pirro here. I didn't want to do as he bade us, but he *is* my lord, and I had no choice.'

Liljana quietly listened to his story, inviting him to say more in the openness of her manner. But Kane finally lost patience, and grabbed hold of Babul's arm: 'So – out with, man: what did Lord Sylar bid you to do?'

Babul swallowed, and I saw the apple of his throat pushing up and down beneath the folds of fat there. He could not look at Kane as he said, 'After the sun had set and it was dark, Lord Sylar sent Taran riding off – where, I don't know. He came up to me and Pirro, and told us that you were a band of thieves – as clever as rats, he said. He had sworn an oath, he said, to protect the caverns' treasures, and wasn't about to let you defile them. He sent Pirro and me to find you. We were to tell you that Lord Sylar had discovered one of Madam Maida's coins to be counterfeit: of gold-plated lead. You were to pay us another, or to leave the caverns for good. We were to escort you back to the first cavern, and there you would be arrested. Lord Sylar had Elkar and Harun make ready the chains.'

'So,' Kane growled, squeezing Babul's arm more tightly. 'You were to capture us with this ploy of Sylar! So much for speaking the truth!'

'He told us you were *thieves*!' Babul said, his face reddening. 'What could we do?'

'What *did* you do, then? What happened, that you decided to betray your lord to us?'

Babul looked over at Pirro, who seemed to be trying to restrain his hand from grasping the hilt of his sword. And Babul told Kane: 'As soon as we had gone a dozen yards into the second cavern, Lord Sylar had Elkar and Harun close the doors behind us. He locked us in! I heard them laughing outside. I don't know why they imprisoned us, along with you.'

'No, you don't *know*,' Kane muttered as his knuckles grew white against Babul's arm. 'But you suspect, don't you? You said there was something *wrong* about this Sylar, eh?'

Babul nodded his head. He licked at his lips and told us, 'This is a bad time in Senta – a bad time everywhere, I think. It's said

485

that the Dragon's Red Priests have many friends in Senta, secret friends they call themselves. *Spies*, I call them. Traitors and snakes. It's said that they are everywhere. I am afraid that Lord Sylar is one of these.'

Kane suddenly released Babul, who stood rubbing his arm. Kane looked straight at Liljana, who returned his stare. I could see the question in Kane's eyes: was Babul's story to be believed or was it only a ploy within a ploy?

Liljana nodded almost imperceptibly to signal her belief that Babul was telling the truth. And then Kane snarled out, 'Back, then! Back up to the doors!'

Without waiting a moment longer, he bounded like a great cat for the stairs leading up to the sixth cavern. The rest of us followed him. Master Juwain could not move as quickly, and he managed to cut his leg on one of the crystals lining our path. Babul, practically dragging his spear behind him, fell far back as he puffed and panted for air. Although he was as fat as Maram, he seemed to possess none of Maram's stamina and strength. I held back near him, and Pirro, to make sure they didn't decide to put their spears into our backs.

But it seemed that they intended no treachery toward us. It seemed as well that we must hurry to escape from the caverns, or be trapped here to await whatever priest or assassin Sylar might have summoned.

31

We raced up and back through the caverns, one by one. When we came into the second cavern, I saw that we had been shut in by the massive iron doors. Kane waited for us in front of them; his eyes picked apart the doors' joints and the surrounding rock as if looking for any weakness. With his sword in hand, he suddenly leaped toward the doors, slamming his shoulder against the crack where they came together. There came a great bang and a groaning of iron, and I was afraid that Kane had broken his bones. But his savage effort failed to budge the doors even an inch.

'Damn them!' Kane muttered. He slapped his open hand against hard iron with such force that bits of rust flew out into the air. 'Damn them!'

Muffled voices sounded from beyond the door, and I sensed that Sylar and the two other stewards stood guard there. Without warning, Kane grabbed Babul's spear and used the iron-shod butt to hammer at the doors as he cried out, 'Open up! Open, I say!'

From the first cavern past the doors came the sound of laughter.

'Sylar – open the damn doors!'

The laughter grew louder, and I could plainly hear Sylar's voice as he called out to us: 'Soon enough we'll open the doors, cursed pilgrims. But you'll not be happy when we do.'

Liljana came up to the door and shouted out: 'We've more gold – diamonds, too! Open the door, and we'll give you all you wish!'

'Can you give me what I *really* wish? No, not with gold, or even diamonds.'

There resounded a smug laughter that made me want to tear off Sylar's head. Then he added, 'In the end, you *will* give me what I wish, though. And I'll have your treasure out of you, too.'

It came to me in a flash that what he wished was to be made a Red Priest of the Kallimun. These hated executors of Morjin recruited from devoted members of the Order of the Dragon, to which Sylar and the other stewards must belong. Thus had Morjin's priests suborned even princes. I remembered the red dragon tattooed on Salmelu Aradar's forehead, to the shame of Ishka and all the Valari kingdoms.

Kane must have shared my thinking, for he raised back his head and howled out: 'Trapped! Cursed acolytes with their cursed secret marks! Damn them!'

He motioned for Alphanderry to come closer to him, and asked him, 'Is there anything you can do?'

A glimmer of light played beneath Alphanderry's skin as his hand felt along the crack between the door. Then Alphanderry looked off at Kane, and shook his head. Whatever wondrous substance he was made of, it could not pass through solid iron.

We moved off deeper into the cavern, and we held council as we decided what to do. Kane believed that Sylar must have sent the steward Tarran for reinforcements; clearly Sylar was waiting for them before opening the doors.

'There must be a way out,' I murmured. 'There is always a way.'

It seemed that an answer must be whispering in my mind, but the roar of voices deafened me so that I could not hear it.

'I should have *seen* it,' Kane growled to me, staring at the doors. It was his way of apologizing. 'To be captured so – so damn *easily*, after following our star so long and so far.'

But even as he uttered the word 'star', Master Juwain's eyes lit up, and he thumped the side of his head with his hand. Then he called out:

The road toward heavens' starry crown
Goes ever up but always down.

At this, Liljana's face soured, and she said to him, 'This is no time for one of your Way Rhymes.'

'It is *precisely* the time,' Master Juwain told her, 'since things have grown dark and we desperately need a way out of here. I should have seen it! *I* should have, from the first.'

'Seen what, sir?' I asked him.

He pointed back toward the corridor leading into the next cavern. He said, 'If we would see the stars again, we must go down. Down to the seventh cavern.'

'But there is no way out of it except up to the sixth cavern.'

'Are you sure?'

I shrugged my shoulders. 'Not even with the songs of the angels could we sing our way through solid rock.'

'No, perhaps not. But we might find a way out of it into the *succeeding* cavern – the true seventh cavern.'

I looked at him in confusion, and so did Liljana and everyone else. And Master Juwain nodded his head toward the iron doors and explained: 'That hollow outside was clearly made by a firestone long ago; I don't count it as a true cavern. Therefore, this chamber where we stand is the true first cavern, and the Minstrels' Cavern is only the sixth.'

My confusion only deepened as I stared at him. The cavern's crystals cast a rainbow radiance upon his shining head.

Kane scowled at him and said, 'So – so what? Then there are only six of what you call true caverns here.'

'No, there are *seven* caverns to the Singing Caves of Senta – this is known. Therefore there must be an opening out of the Minstrels' Cavern into an even deeper one.'

'What makes you so sure of that, eh?'

'Because there are seven musical notes, and seven colors to the spectrum – seven chakras along the spine, as well. And many, many other sevens. It is the Law of the Seven, and I feel certain that it applies here.'

While Kane stood considering this, Babul looked at Master Juwain and said, 'But Master Javas, I have been a steward here for fifteen years, and my father and grandfather served here before me. No one has ever heard any mention of a secret cavern.'

'And that,' Pirro added in a high, whiny voice, 'is because there *is* no secret cavern.'

'And even if there was,' Babul said, 'how would that help us? We would only be trapped that much deeper in the earth.'

'No, we might escape,' Master Juwain said. 'Sometimes underground rivers flow through caves. And there might be cracks off the seventh cavern, corridors leading out of it and up into the mountain – or even out its back side. Who knows? This mountain might even be riddled with tunnels as is Skartaru.'

At the mention of the Black Mountain beneath which the city of Argattha was buried, and where Morjin dwelled, I made a fist around the hilt of my sword. Then I heard Morjin's voice singing from deep in the earth, and I told Master Juwain and the rest of my friends what I had learned of Morjin in the seventh – or sixth – cavern.

'I believe that he was seeking something there,' I said. 'Something beyond listening to the minstrels and leaving his song. It *might* have been a secret cavern.'

Atara turned toward the dark opening leading down into the mountain. A slight shaking of her head gave me to understand that if any secret, seventh cavern was hidden beyond the sixth, she had seen no vision of it. But then she said, 'Why don't we go back, even so? Can anyone think of a better plan?'

Again, I led the way into the earth. We strung out in a line, like ants, with my friends behind me and the two stewards directly in front of Kane, who took the rear. When we came out into the Minstrels' Cavern, Kane posted himself at the top of the stairs to warn us in case Sylar and his men came for us. The rest of us spread out to examine the cavern's walls. A secret door to a secret cavern, as Master Juwain reasoned, would certainly be outlined by cracks in the walls' gleaming crystals. But there were thousands of cracks, many of which cleaved along the crystals' bases in clean planes. And some of these cracks, I thought, would be invisible to the eye, rather like the seam in a broken crust of bread after the two halves had been fitted back together.

When we were ready to abandon our search as a long and probably hopeless work, I noticed Estrella standing motionless before a particularly lovely part of the cavern. Her eyes caught the colors of the crystals there, and I could not tell whether their radiance came from without or within.

'Estrella?' I said, moving over to her. 'What do you see?'

I traced my finger along the edges and facets of azure crystals. I could find no cracks that might have been the outline of a doorway. 'Estrella?' I said again.

This bright-eyed girl remained frozen, gazing at the crystalline wall. I remembered that the Avarii had called her an *udra mazda*, who had found water in a nearly waterless desert. And more, Master Juwain had identified her as a *seard*, who could make her heart one with hidden things.

'Estrella – do you think there is a door here? How can there be?'

Daj came over to me and touched me on the arm. He said, 'Don't you remember the door to the secret passage off Lord Morjin's chambers?'

In fact, at that very moment, I was thinking of exactly that door in the black depths of Argattha. And of how a password spoken in ancient Ardik had opened it.

Master Juwain examined the wall in front of Estrella, and said, 'I don't think there is a door here. And if there is, how would we ever discover the word that might open it?'

I drew my sword and pointed it toward the wall. The two stewards gasped to see its silustria flare with a soft light. Something bright flared within me, too. From bits and pieces out of my memory – the poignancy of Morjin's words, the yearning of his song and the beauty of other songs that I had heard in darker places – a sparkling pattern took shape. And I said to Master Juwain, 'Perhaps not a word, then, but a language. Perhaps we *can* sing our way through solid rock.'

I turned to Alphanderry and said, 'Do you remember the Kul Moroth?'

Alphanderry nodded his head. 'Yes, I remember.'

'The way you sang there, and other times since – can you sing that way now?'

'I can try,' he said. He looked across the cavern at Kane standing at the top of the stairs. 'It might help if I had accompaniment.'

Kane nodded his assent and came down to us. He unslung the mandolet that he had brought with him into the caverns. After quickly tuning it, he looked at Alphanderry and said, 'So.'

And so as Kane began plucking the mandolet's strings, Alphanderry sang. He directed his strong, clear voice at the wall before him. His words, pouring forth in ever more perfect form, with exquisite grace, seemed to melt into a music so beautiful that I found myself weeping and laughing, all at once. And all at once, the crystals on the wall seemed to lose their solidity and run with a sparkle and fluidness like unto water. With great care, I pushed the point of my sword toward these crystals. The silustria sliced deep into them; the substance of the crystals seemed to flow around my sword like an azure waterfall, and yet strangely did not move or lose its shape. And still Kane played, and still Alphanderry sang, and my heart surged with great joy to hear once more the language of the Galadin. Of all the minstrels who had ever given their voices to this cavern, I thought that none could compare with Alphanderry. I watched as the jewel-like crystals began changing once again. Their liquidity gave way to an even less solid substance, more like air, and then finally shimmered before me like a curtain of light.

Alphanderry stopped singing, and gazed in wonder at what his music had accomplished. As I pulled back my sword, now gleaming like a mirror, Master Juwain stared at the cavern's wall. A great oval, like a door, stood limned against that part of the wall that remained hard crystal. I could not see through it to determine if another cavern lay beyond. It was like trying to look through the sky's brilliant blueness to apprehend the stars.

Master Juwain brought forth a copper coin and tossed it at the wall. It passed straight through the light-wrought crystals and disappeared. I heard the tinkling of metal as it seemed that the coin struck rock on the other side.

'The Law of the Seven, indeed,' I said, smiling at Master Juwain.

Pirro, trembling with his hand held palm outward as if to ward away a blow, shook his thin head at the wall and cried out, 'Sorcery! You are not thieves, but sorcerers!'

Babul, however, seemed made of more courageous stuff. He gazed at the seeming doorway into the crystalline wall and said, 'If they are sorcerers, then let us give thanks for their magic. Could there *really* be a seventh cavern through there?'

'Who would want to walk through *that*,' Pirro said, pointing at the frozen cascades of light, 'to find out?'

My companions and I, of course, would. When Pirro saw this, he declared that he would not follow us, not even for a cartful of diamonds.

'Then go back,' Kane growled at him, pointing up the steps to the higher caverns. 'At least stand guard, and give warning if Sylar comes.'

Without waiting for Pirro's assent, Kane turned toward me. 'Val?'

'I will go first,' I told him.

'But what if the opening closes behind you, and we cannot reopen it?'

'I'll have to take that chance.'

'No – let this Babul take it! He was ready enough to trick us into Sylar's chains. Let him redeem himself by doing us this service.'

As Babul stared straight ahead at the wall, his red face blanched. Kane seemed ready to propel his large form through the even larger opening. And I said to Kane, 'No, it is upon me.'

And then without another word, I turned and stepped through the curtain of light into the seventh cavern. I wanted to cry out to my friends that this passage had been no more difficult than walking through the doorway of my father's library in the Elahad castle. I could not, however, speak. For the chamber that opened before me was no mere cavern, but seemed almost another world.

492

It was spherical in shape, and vast, as if the entire inside of the mountain had been hollowed out. The crystals here rose out the floor, wall or ceiling as long and thick as the trunks of trees. They pointed inward, toward the chamber's center, and most showed six facets, like the sides of a honeycomb's cell. The crystals gleamed with bright blues and scintillating reds – and with flaming oranges, yellows and the other hues of the spectrum.

'Oh, my Lord!' I whispered, wishing that Maram had come this far. 'Oh, my Lord!'

From somewhere behind me, I heard Kane shout out: 'Val, do you hear me? Are you all right?'

And I called back to him: 'Yes . . . I am. Truly I am.'

'Should we come, then?'

'Yes, come – come now!'

A moment later Kane passed through the light curtain, followed by Liljana, Atara, Estrella, Daj and Master Juwain. Then Babul dared to enter this seventh cavern as well. He joined us and stood staring out into the cavern's center, which wavered in the distance as of an infinite depth.

'Ten of King Yulmar's palaces,' Babul exclaimed, 'would fit into this space! Twenty or thirty – I do not know!'

We stood together on a shelf of plain rock jutting out from the cavern's wall perhaps halfway up the sphere's circumference. A long, wide stairway carved into the rock led down the cavern's curving slope below us to a larger clearing, circular in shape, at the very bottom of the cavern. There seemed nothing else to do but to walk down to it.

'You,' Kane said to Babul, 'are a Steward of Caves, eh? Guardians, you call yourselves. So, you will stay here and guard this doorway. If Pirro calls out a warning to you or if the door begins to close, you will call out a warning to us, do you understand?'

Few men were willing to argue with Kane. As Babul nodded his head and his chin disappeared into his neck, I turned to go down the stairs. My friends walked behind me. Our way led between the great crystals, like a straight path through a forest. I saw almost immediately that we would not find an exit from this cavern as Master Juwain had wished. The substance of the walls and floor out of which the crystals grew gleamed like black glass, without the slightest flaw or crack that we could detect. The perfection of this chamber, in substance and shape, both awed and mystified me.

At last we worked down the curve of the cavern to the bare circle at its bottom. I could see Babul perched on the rocky shelf to our right, high above us. Crystals, like great, ruby obelisks, rose up around us out of what seemed to be pure obsidian. High above us, straight across the cavern, other crystals hung suspended over our heads like impossibly huge swords.

'Oh, my Lord!' I whispered again. I thought that Maram would perhaps not like standing here after all.

'What *is* this place?' Daj said, looking up at Master Juwain. 'Can these crystals really be gelstei?'

'*Can* they be?' Master Juwain said. He stepped over to one of the great crystals and laid his hand upon it. 'Can they truly be?'

'Men,' Liljana said, running her hand along the face of a ruby monolith, 'could not have made such things.'

'Men, no – perhaps not the Ardun. But might have the angels?'

Liljana stared off in wonder as she shook her head.

'But if not the Galadin,' Master Juwain said, 'then who? All the gelstei of which we have record were forged by the hand of man.'

'But what of the gelstei that grew out of the earth in the vilds?'

Master Juwain thought about this and said, 'If not forged, then cultivated. The Lokilani tend their crystals as farmers do their crops.'

'But it is the earth that *grows* the crystals.'

'What are you thinking?'

Liljana swept her hand out at the rainbow of colors pouring out of the huge crystals. 'I feel certain that the Mother gave birth to this place. Perhaps man and the earth created it together.'

'How, then?'

'You always concern yourself with the *how* of things. But what I wonder is *why*?'

All this time Kane had remained silent. But then he raised up his eyes and spoke in a sad, deep voice that rang out as if from another land far away.

'I have a memory,' he told us. 'A memory of a memory. I think I heard of such a place long, long ago. It was called Ansunna.'

He looked at me, and then at Liljana. His black eyes seemed to grow ever brighter and clearer as he stood there remembering. 'These caverns *are* a creation of the living earth and the Galadin of old. The Bright Ones once walked the earth, eh? In the Elder Ages, I think they came here and planted in the ground the seeds of the gelstei – the great gelstei that grew into these great crystals.'

494

Here he smacked his hand against one of the ruby pillars so hard that it seemed the whole earth shook. And Master Juwain said to him, 'But you cannot mean the *great* gelstei!'

I thought of the seven clear crystals, colored red through violet, that Abrasax and the masters of the Brotherhood kept safe about their persons high in the White Mountains. They called them the Seven Openers, and although small in size, Abrasax had believed them to be made of the same substance as the great gelstei used in the creation of the universe.

'I mean just that,' Kane said to Master Juwain. He turned to Liljana, and his voice softened as he said, 'So, this is the *why* of things, eh? The great gelstei, in their highest purpose, are to be used in creation.'

Master Juwain stepped over to the crystal rising up near Kane. 'You can't mean that these are the great gelstei used in Eluru's creation!'

'No, surely not,' Kane told him. 'The gelstei of which you speak are surely almost infinitely vaster – as far beyond these little rocks as the Ieldra are the Galadin.'

Master Juwain gazed up as if looking for the point of the great crystal a hundred feet above us. 'Then what are these gelstei *for*?'

Kane began pacing around the circle, casting quick glances to his right or left across the cavern, at Babul standing far away on his rocky shelf and the dangling green and yellow crystals of the cavern's ceiling. I could scarcely bear the flood of feelings pouring out of him: curiosity, remorse, anticipation, sorrow and all his wild joy of life.

'So,' he finally said, 'a day must come when the Galadin will become Ieldra and use the gelstei to sing into creation a new universe. I believe that Ashtoreth and Valoreth – even Asangal and many other Galadin – once came here to sing.'

He went on say that just as boys practiced with wooden swords before becoming warriors who wielded razor-sharp steel, so the Galadin must prepare themselves for the great task that lay ahead of them.

'But of what did they sing, then?' Daj asked Kane.

'Who knows?' Kane told him. 'But *this* was said about the place called Ansunna: that it held a great magic. Whatever one spoke truly, with the voice of the soul, would be made real.'

'That would be magic, indeed,' Master Juwain said, 'for wishes to come true.'

'I didn't say *wishes*,' Kane snapped at him. 'We *wish* that our

desires be fulfilled, and we desire that which most pleases or bene-
fits us. But the soul has other desires, eh? And its deepest desire
is always in accord with that of the One. What does the One *will*?
Discover *that* within yourself and speak it truly, without wish or
regard for yourself, and it will be.'

Master Juwain rubbed his gleaming head as he thought about
this. And then Atara said, 'But only, it would seem for the Galadin,
for who of us can ever hope to sing as they sing?'

Kane gazed at Alphanderry a moment before saying, 'Who,
indeed?'

Estrella, who could not sing or even speak, caught Kane's attention with a flutter of her fingers and a smile. Their eyes met, and
something seemed to snap inside him like an overstretched
bowstring. He said, 'There is singing, and there is *singing*. The Ieldra
do not have voices as men do, and yet from them pours forth the
music of creation.'

In the Loikalii's vild, I had stood staring at the great astor tree,
Irdrasil, as a glorre-infused radiance poured out of it. I could almost
hear the Ieldra whispering to me still; I knew that the deepest
voice of all spoke not in impossible-to-learn tones but in the
language of light.

'This, too, I believe, was said,' Kane told us. His fathomless eyes
drank in the cavern's colors. 'That one should not speak of abstrac-
tions such as peace, compassion or love. That which *is*, always is,
eh? It partakes of the eternal realm. But that which would be, in
creation, comes forth within *this* realm. Like the world itself, it
must be a physical thing.'

A question seemed to divide him, like a chasm through solid
rock. It divided me, as well. How, I wondered, could I distinguish
what *I* wanted from the will of the One? Did I long for Atara to
see with new eyes for her sake or my own? And what of my hope
that someday I would hear sweet song pouring from Estrella's
throat, no less my darker desire to plunge my sword through
Morjin's heart? A hundred wants and needs formed up inside me
with an almost palpable presence. I tried to listen for the whispering of my soul and to sing out with all my heart my deepest
desire. But I felt lost inside this vast cavern, like a sleeper within
a dream. There came a moment when I wished for nothing more
than to stand outside beneath the stars again, to feel the wind on
my face and for Maram to press a cup of brandy into my hand as
his great voice boomed out that it was good to be alive.

As we all stood there in the womb of the earth, staring off in silence, the great gelstei crystals came alive with a deep light. It passed from one crystal to the next, red to yellow, violet to blue, so that each crystal seemed to partake of the radiance of all the thousands of others. The splendor they cast out into the cavern colored the very air so that it shimmered a brilliant glorre.

And yet, I thought, the crystals shone less brilliantly than they should have. A too-familiar dread crept up my bones into my spine. My sword smoldered with hidden flames, as did my heart, and I felt Morjin's presence here. Surely he knew of this place, even if he had never found the purity of voice to sing his way into it. But now, I sensed, from a thousand miles away he used the power of the Lightstone to sing a different and darker kind of song. The Galadin once might have spoken their desires to these beautiful crystals, as did we; the Red Dragon would speak his demands. And the great gelstei spoke back. When I emptied myself of all wishes and listened hard enough, I heard the saddest song of all. For here the earth herself sang: long, lovely, low and deep. She sang of the Black Jade buried within her flesh like a poisoned arrowhead; she told of Morjin delving down through the rock beneath Skartaru and doing terrible things. She lamented her own darkening, and sang of her dread of the day when Morjin would free the Dark One and the earth would finally sicken and die.

It came to me that we would never find our way out of the Singing Caves if we stood frozen listening to such tormented songs. I wondered how we would find our way at all. And then I heard another song, or rather a voice, that dashed our hopes of escape. For Babul, high on his slab of rock above us, suddenly called out to us: 'Mirustral! Rowan! Pirro has given the warning! He heard shouts beyond the doors, and says that Sylar comes for us! What shall we do?'

What indeed, I wondered, as I looked at Kane?

And then a moment later, Babul shouted out again: 'The doorway! It is closing!'

We all turned to face the gleaming azure crystals on the curving wall above us. Master Juwain said, 'If we let ourselves be closed in, we'll be safe from Sylar and his men.'

And Kane snarled at him, 'You mean, entombed!'

'No – when Sylar finds us vanished, he'll attribute it to sorcery. We can reopen the door another time, and make our escape.'

'So you say. But what if Sylar does *not* attribute our vanishing to sorcery? What if that damn Pirro betrays us, and Sylar sets miners to chiselling away here and discovers this cavern?'

He did not have to add that if Sylar really belonged to the Order of the Dragon, then Morjin would be told of anything he discovered.

'Good pilgrims!' Babul cried out, 'the doorway!'

'So, I'd rather die trying to fight our way out,' Kane said.

'So would I,' I told him. Then I turned toward the stairs. 'Hurry, then, before we *are* trapped in here.'

We ran up the stairs to the shimmering doorway. The opening appeared to be gelling into something more solid. I urged everyone through and then jumped after them through the wall into the sixth or Minstrels' Cavern; it was like passing through freezing water.

'The doors!' Pirro's voice rang out from above us. He stood at the mouth of the fifth cavern shouting down to us. 'They're going to open the doors!'

I led the way running toward him. I had to pace myself up the stairs, and all the way back up through the other sloping chambers, lest the climb burn up my limbs and wind me. Then I came into the first cavern. There, in that hollow of gleaming crystals, I stood gasping for air. My friends joined me, one by one. At the front of the cavern, the iron doors remained shut, and I could hear no sound from beyond them.

'What shall we do?' Babul said again, whispering to me. 'We are few, and they will surely be many.'

Just then something banged the door outside, and there came the jangle of what sounded like keys.

'Form up!' I whispered, stepping closer to the door.

Kane, sword in hand, stood by my right side, while to my left, Babul and Pirro pressed close to each other and pointed their spears at the doors. Liljana, Master Juwain, Estrella and Daj gathered behind us. Liljana had drawn the long knife that she wore concealed beneath her robes, while Daj gripped his short sword. Farther to my right and behind me, Atara had stationed herself at an angle to the door. She had cut free from her cloak the three arrows sewn into it, and had nocked one of them to the string of her bow. She pulled back the arrow to her ear, somehow aiming its steel point in the direction of the crack between the doors. I wondered how long she could hold her great bow at full draw.

The sound of a key grating inside the iron lock of the doors sent a thrill of fear shooting through me. And Pirro whispered out into the dank, close air: 'I could not tell how many they are.'

I heard Kane whisper back to him, 'We'll kill them all, few or many. We must be prepared for anything.'

But I was not, despite Kane's fierce words, prepared for what awaited us on the other side of the doors. Finally, with much creaking, these great slabs of iron began to swing open. Torchlight spilled into the cavern, and limned against its red glow stood a single man. I blinked my eyes in wonder. I could not believe what I saw, although I was overjoyed at the sight that greeted me.

'My Lord!' a familiar voice called out to me. 'Oh, my Lord!'

It was Maram.

32

We hurried out into the scoop of rock called the first cavern. The bodies of Elkar and Harun lay sprawled near the table where Sylar had collected our gold. Elkar's slashed throat oozed blood, while Harun fairly floated in a dark pool building out from a terrible wound in his chest. Just in front of the demon rock slumped another form: Sylar's, I guessed from the gilded armor. His body had been decapitated. Although I looked about the bloodstained cavern floor, I could not see his head.

'But how did you come to be here?' I asked Maram. We stood over Sylar's corpse gazing at each other in amazement. I noted the blood dripping off Maram's drawn sword. 'What happened?'

'Ah, Val!' Maram said as he embraced me with his free arm, '*I* happened along just in time, I think, else you would have been dead, or worse.'

He explained that after arriving at the Inn of the Clouds in the dead of night, he had asked after us and learned that we had not returned from the Singing Caves. Thinking to surprise us, he had hurried after us, up the flagstone path leading from the inn beneath the face of Mount Miru. As he had approached the caverns' entrance, however, a cruel laughter had given him warning. And so, like a bear sniffing out a new lair, he had stalked up to the caverns in near silence.

'As I drew closer,' he told us, 'I hid behind that rock.'

He pointed at a large boulder ten yards away just outside the cavern.

Then he pointed at the bodies of Elkar, Harun and Sylar.

'I heard them boasting that they had locked you inside the caverns,' he went on. He pointed his sword toward Sylar's head-less torso. 'That one was their captain, wasn't he? He said that they would be given a great reward for capturing you. I gathered that he had sent another of these guards for reinforcements.'

Kane sprang up to Maram and grasped his arm. 'Did you hear Sylar say where he sent him?'

Maram nodded. 'To Hesperu, to return this very night with one of the Red Priests and a cadre of Crucifiers . . .'

'Did Sylar,' Kane asked Maram with a tightening of his fist, 'say the name of the Red Priest?'

Maram pried Kane's fingers from his arm and took a step back. He looked down at Sylar's remains beneath the demon's stony, grinning face. 'I *waited* for him to say it. Or for one of his men. But all they seemed to want to talk about was Mouth of Truth, as they called it. Sylar lamented that they couldn't test it on you. I couldn't listen to that, do you understand? I couldn't wait forever, and so I did what I did.'

And what Maram had done, as Maram now told us, was to charge from out behind his rock with his sword in his hand. Before the hapless guards realized that a fierce warrior was upon them, he had slashed open the astonished Elkar's throat with a lightning cut of his sword and then thrust its point through Harun's armor at the shoulder joint, deep into Harun's chest. He had then turned upon Sylar.

'For *him*,' Maram said, nudging Sylar's body with his boot, 'I didn't have to use my sword.'

'Then what happened to him?' Daj asked.

'I grabbed him,' Maram said, 'before he could draw *his* sword. He fought like a fish, but I, ah, subdued him. I asked him the name of the Red Priest, but he wouldn't tell me. And so I hammer-locked him, and pushed his head inside this.'

Maram slapped his hand against the smooth rock carved with the demon's face. I noticed the fresh blood staining the lips of the Mouth of Truth.

'You put Lord Sylar inside of Old Ugly?' Babul called out.

'Just his head and neck,' Maram replied. 'I told him that I'd let him go free if he gave me the Red Priest's name and told me where Tarran was bound; if he didn't, I told him I'd break his filthy neck. I *did* almost have to break it, too. Finally, though, Sylar gave me a name: Ra Jaumal. I knew he was lying the moment he spoke it.'

According to Maram, as soon as Sylar had spoken the name of Ra Jaumal, the demon's eyes had flared bright blue and from within the rock had come the sound of whirring gears and metal

501

whooshing through the air. Maram never laid eyes on the falling blade that had severed Sylar's head. But he had felt the impact of steel against flesh and bone through Sylar's shocked body.

'Lord Sylar,' Babul said, staring down at the bloody stone, 'always wanted to test Old Ugly. But I don't think he really believed it would do its work.'

'So,' Kane said, gazing at the reddened Mouth of Truth.

He drew forth a round, reddish rock called a bloodstone, and moved over to Elkar's body. He held the little gelstei over Elkar's forehead; a crimson light pouring out of the bloodstone illumined the secret mark of the Red Dragon tattooed there. It remained a burning crimson in Elkar's flesh even after Kane closed his fist around his bloodstone.

'I should have used *this* on him and that damn Sylar before we went into the caverns,' Kane sighed as he rose up again. 'But it's hard to expose our enemies without exposing *us*.'

He turned to Maram and asked, 'Do you think Sylar knew who we are?'

Maram shook his head. 'No, I got no sense of that. He spoke only of having been alerted to look for a band of pilgrims such as us. I believe that it was his own idea to lock you inside and send for the Red Priest. He seemed proud of his initiative.'

'It may be,' Liljana said, stepping closer, 'that the Lord of Lies deduced that we would come to Senta. And warned whoever Sylar reported to that he should watch for us.'

'Whoever that is,' Kane said, 'will be warned soon enough if we're not quick. And every other Red Priest in Senta and down into Hesperu.'

I noticed Babul and Pirro standing in a little too closely and fairly hanging on Kane's every word. I didn't like it that he spoke so freely in front of them.

'But who *are* you, then,' Babul asked me, 'that the Lord of Lies would hunt you?'

I felt a darkness building inside Kane, who said, 'Go ahead and tell them. They might as well know before they join the others.'

And with that, he drew his sword and turned toward Babul.

'No!' I cried out. I took a step closer to Kane. 'No . . . Rowan!'

Babul tried to use his spear to defend himself and perhaps thrust its long, gleaming point into Kane before Kane could kill him. But Kane knocked away Babul's spear as easily as he might have parried the thrust of a child. I grabbed onto Kane's arm then before his wrath drove him to do something that he didn't really wish to do. I pulled him back, out the range of Babul's and Pirro's spears.

'No!' I said to him again.

He whirled to face me, and his eyes burned into mine. 'They know too much! We can't just leave them behind us!'

'Perhaps they do,' I told him. 'But we can't just slay innocent men!'

'Innocent,' Kane spat out, glancing at the badly frightened Babul. 'Who is truly innocent?'

'We cannot slay them!' I shouted.

'Would you have us risk everything to preserve the lives of *these*?'

In answer, I tightened my grip around his arm. Behind me and to my right, I saw Estrella step in front of Babul as she fearlessly looked up at Kane.

'So,' Kane said as he gazed at her. I watched as the fire in his eyes died into a smoldering rage. He seemed to command his arm to sheathe his sword, and I let go of him so that he could.

'Good pilgrim,' Babul said to Kane as he wiped the sweat from his neck, 'I will guard your secrets as I do the caverns themselves, with my life!'

'Ha – that you will!' Kane snarled at him.

He took a step closer to Babul even as Babul took a step back. Then Kane sprang forward past Estrella, brushing aside Babul's spear with a savage motion. He opened his fist to let the blood-stone's light shine on Babul's forehead. But the gelstei's radiance failed to bring forth any secret tattoo. A similar test of Pirro proved him also to be free of the Dragon's mark.

'All right, then, we shall give you our trust,' Kane told them. 'Do not betray it. You know that the Red Dragon hunts us; you do not want *me* to hunt *you*. I must leave now, but I will return. If I learn you've spoken of us or what lies beyond what you call the seventh cavern, then I *shall* slay you – you and your families: your wives, your fathers, sisters and children!'

It was a terrible thing for him to say, and the force of his breath breaking from his lips made both Babul and Pirro quail. Then Kane turned toward the flagstone path gleaming gray-white in the glister of the torches. He caught my eye, and said, 'If I ride fast enough, I may be able to overtake Sylar's messenger before he reaches the Red Priest he's been sent to.'

'Alone?' I said to him.

'Yes – I'll do *this* work better alone.'

'But how will we find you, then?'

'Follow me tonight, as soon as you can,' he told me. 'Ride quickly, but don't ruin the horses. And tomorrow, I'll find *you*.'

So saying, he sprang forward and began running down the path back toward the Inn of the Clouds. He vanished like a great cat into the dark folds of night.

Babul, as if all his strength had bled away, staggered over to the chair behind the table and slumped down into it. He gazed at Sylar's headless body as he used a scarf to mop the sweat from his forehead. He said to me, 'The King will have to be informed of what occurred here. If we're to guard your secrets, what story shall we give him?'

'What sort of man is King Yulmar?' I asked him.

'A man of honor, it's said. And a courageous one. When the Red Priests sent assassins to kill Prince Paomar, the King came out of his chambers where he was safely guarded to fight the assassins sword to sword. He took a wound to his arm before the assassins were killed. He has no cause to love the Red Priests or their master, if that is what you were wondering.'

I nodded my head as I told Babul: 'Then give your king the truth. Tell him that Sylar had joined the Order of the Dragon – Elkar, Harun and Tarran, too. Tell him that they locked you inside the caverns, along with the Red Dragon's enemies. Do not give him our names or say where we are bound. And do not tell him of the true seventh cavern.'

I could see from the flickers of light in Babul's and Pirro's eyes that this last would be a hard secret to keep and take with them to their graves. Pirro, I thought, would have a harder time keeping any secrets at all, for he looked at me and said, 'But what if the King *demands* that we tell him all that we know?'

'Then tell him that you've vowed to protect our identities. If he is a man of honor, he'll respect that.'

'But we've vowed nothing,' Pirro said.

'Then do so now,' I told him.

Pirro looked over at Babul and nodded his head at him. And Babul said to me, 'All right, then, we do.'

But this, I thought, was not quite good enough, for I sensed a gnawing doubt in both Babul and Pirro. I told them, 'Do not vow to do that which you cannot do. You must be certain of yourselves, and before we leave, we must be certain of you.'

'But we've given you our vows – what more do you want?'

In answer, I looked over at the demon rock and said, 'Give your vows to it.'

Babul's face blanched as he stared at the demon's mouth, but he slowly nodded his head. He stood up and walked over to where Sylar lay beneath it. Again, he used his crumpled scarf to mop his forehead. He swallowed, hard, and cleared his throat. I felt him fighting to find within himself all his will to be brave and true. Finally, he pushed his hand inside the demon's mouth and declared: 'I vow to keep your secrets, as you have asked.'

Babul closed his eyes and waited, as did we. When the demon failed to take his hand, he quickly removed it and stood staring at his open palm and five fingers in wonder. It was as if he were seeing himself for the first time and beholding long-desired possibilities.

Pirro likewise endured this trial that I urged upon him; afterwards, strangely, he seemed not to hate me but only to be glad to have found new resolve and a courage to match Babul's. He said to me, 'Senta will never fall, at least not from within as Galda did. If you pass back this way and I am still a guard here, you will be welcome. Perhaps next time, I'll even dare to go into the cavern that I will not speak of and does not really exist.'

He smiled as he bowed his head to me, and I bowed back. Then Babul assured me that he and Pirro would wait a few more hours before making their report in order to give us time to ride away from here. I felt certain that they would do as they promised.

We said farewell, and turned to make our way back down the path. When we reached the Inn of the Clouds, we had no need to awaken the innkeeper, for Kane already had. As the innkeeper told us, Kane had galloped off into the night less than half an hour before.

'It's unheard of,' the small, pot-bellied man told us, 'for our guests to flee like thieves in the night before they've even slept in their beds. I hope your accommodations didn't disappoint you?'

I assured him that his inn was the most splendid we had ever seen, but said that urgent business called us elsewhere. According to Kane's instructions, the innkeeper had our horses saddled and ready outside the white colonnades fronting the portico of this rather grandiose inn. Without further explanation, we mounted and trotted off down the road. In the light of the stars, we followed this well-paved track that led down from Mount Miru and wound around its rocky mass to the east, where it joined the road to Hesperu.

It was now well past midnight, and no other travelers ventured forth, neither southward towards Hesperu nor from it. We clopped along over smooth, star-washed stones. Fields of rippling wheat opened out on either side of us. The crickets there chirped with a million tiny voices. As we passed by farmhouses standing alone beneath the black and silver sky, dogs barked out their warnings into the night.

When I was sure that no one had followed us, I called for a halt and turned toward Maram. I said to him, 'Well?'

'Well, *what*?' he called back.

Master Juwain, Atara and everyone else reined in their horses around us in the center of the deserted road. And I said to Maram: 'How did you find us? And why did you leave the Vild? And what did you –'

'Ah, Val, Val!' he said, holding up his hand and smiling. 'I'll tell you everything, though there's really very little to tell. I left the Vild because I could not remain. You see, I knew you would need me.'

The story he now related was indeed neither long nor complicated. It seemed that two days after the rest of us had ridden out of the Vild into the desert, a great disquiet had come over Maram. He realized that even though he cherished Anneli and loved the quiet peace of the Vild, other things remained even dearer to him. And so upon steeling himself for a long and solitary journey, he had said goodbye to the weeping Anneli and the other Loikalii, and went out into the desert. He found the Tar Harath to be just as hot and hellish as he had remembered. He followed our tracks west and then came upon the well of Manoj and his family. Manoj, when he learned that Maram was our companion, was only too happy to give him stores and water from his well, still full from the storm that Estrella had summoned. He told him, too, of the Dead City and the road leading up into the mountains. Maram had followed this road, even as we had, up through the lovely green valleys of the Crescent Mountains. He had searched out our old camps, one by one. He travelled as quickly as he could, trying to eat up our lead, for an unusual urgency drove him on. At last, he had found his way into Senta. Since Kane had spoken of the Inn of the Clouds, Maram had first looked for us there.

'It was strange,' he told me. 'There I was in the Loikalii's wood one fine morning eating cherries with Anneli, and I heard you calling to me. And on the road, all those days, I felt you wishing that I hadn't stayed behind. You *did* wish this, didn't you? You did call me?'

'Yes, Maram, I did,' I told him. But I didn't quite know how to explain that I had wished this most intently and called out the loudest scarcely an hour before in the cavern called Ansunna, where one's dreams and deepest desires might be made real.

Master Juwain, I noticed, was looking at me with great curiosity, as was Liljana. Then Maram insisted that we climb down off our horses, and so we did. He brought out two cups and the very last of his brandy. After filling them, he gave one into my hand and raised up the other. Starlight illumined the wide smile breaking upon his face, and the wind whipped at his hair. Then he clinked cups with me, and drank down his brandy, as did I. He embraced me as he thumped my back and cried out, 'Val, Val – it's good to see you again! It's good to be alive!'

Was it possible, I wondered? Could it be that what I had wished for most fervently in the seventh cavern had somehow come to pass?

When I remarked upon the mystery of how Maram could have acted upon my wish many days before I even wished it, Atara turned toward me and said, 'Time is strange. In the eternal realm, that of the One, there is no time. But even in *this* realm, all things of the world take their being from the One, and there are moments when past, future and present are as one. If I can cast my second sight into time that is yet to be, why shouldn't you be able to sing your wishes into the past?'

Why not, indeed? I wondered as I watched Maram licking drops of brandy from his moustache.

Our talk of wishes and singing impelled a recounting of what we had found inside the Singing Caves. I almost couldn't bear to tell Maram of the marvels he had missed. He was a man who loved music and beauty almost as much as he did women and wine. If he had stood in the great cavern of the Galadin by my side and had sung out with his great heart, I wondered what he would have wished for?

'Ah, but it's too bad I *didn't* hear all those songs,' he said to us. 'Maybe we should consider going back, then. We still have some hours before daybreak. Wasn't the whole idea of passing through Senta to gain some sort of idea as to where we might find the Maitreya?'

I was about to tell him that we had heard thousands of mentions of the Maitreya, all to no avail, when Daj straightened up on top of his horse, and called out in his high voice, 'But we do know! At least, we know where we might look for him.'

We turned to stare at Daj. I said to him, '*What* do you know? And why didn't you tell us before?'

'I'm sorry,' he said to me, 'but I heard someone singing of this in the Minstrels' Cavern just as we were passing back through it. I thought that there would soon be a battle, and when there wasn't, when the doors opened and we found everyone dead and Kane hurried off, and then we did, too – well, there hasn't been *time* to tell you.'

'We've time now,' I said, looking up at the stars.

And Daj told us, 'It was a woman's voice – I never heard her name. She came to Senta to sing praises of a man, a healer who had saved her daughter. Some incurable disease it was, and the daughter was wasting away. Just a year ago! She never spoke the healer's name, either. But she said that he had brought a bright light back into her life, and she called this man her "Shining One".'

'Oh, excellent!' Maram said. 'A nameless women praising a nameless man for a miracle that occurred we know not where.'

'But we *do* know where!' Daj said to Maram. 'The woman said that her husband had crossed the whole north of Hesperu to bring her daughter to this healer. In a place called Jhamrul.'

Daj, though he had been born in Hesperu's Haraland, could not tell me if Jhamrul might be a district, city or village, nor did he have any idea where we might find this place. Master Juwain got out his maps then, but the light of the stars proved too little to read by. But Master Juwain had an excellent memory, and he could not recall any marking on his maps of that name.

'We'll have to ask after this Jhamrul, then,' he said. 'When we reach Hesperu, surely someone will have heard of it.'

According to his maps and what he had learned through making inquiries, it was nine miles from the Singing Caves to Hesperu's frontier, and then another nine miles down from the mountains into the populated parts of the Haraland. Without wasting any more words, we resumed our journey. We all hoped, I thought, that we were nearing its culmination, if not its end.

Only one road led from Senta into Hesperu. We followed it through the rocky bowl in which this tiny kingdom was sited to the southern wall of sheltering mountains. Weariness worked deep into me so that I felt every jolt of my horse down into my bones. It was even worse for the others, and I feared that we were all too tired to ride through the night. We could not, however, remain within the reach of King Yulmar should Babul and Pirro break their vows and King Yulmar prove to be neither as honorable nor courageous as they had promised. And so we drove ourselves and our horses over the rocky, rising ground with as much speed as we could summon.

Soon we worked our way up to a high pass between rows of ice-capped peaks gleaming in the starlight to either side of us. The air fell cooler and shimmered with the brilliance of the stars. Which one, I wondered, might point our way to the Maitreya? Was he sleeping somewhere down in the land beyond the mountains? Or did he stand awake on some hilltop or in a window gazing up at the same bright stellar vista as did I?

Time is strange, Atara had said to me. That night, on our push into Hesperu, the hours seemed to draw out almost endlessly long as if the world itself hung perfectly balanced in black space and could never move. And yet taken as a whole, the night fairly flew by, and I could no more hold onto the fleeting moments than I could a streaking arrow. I felt myself rushing toward my fate. Whatever star called *me* onward pulled with a force I could not resist and filled my blood with an unquenchable fire.

At last we found ourselves braving the narrows of the pass called the Khal Arrak. Here, in a cut through the earth scarcely a quarter mile wide, walls of rock rose up to our left and right. Long ago Senta and Hesperu had agreed that this place should mark the frontier between their two kingdoms. I thought it curious that neither had built any sort of fortress here to guard their side of the pass. But then I had grown to manhood in Mesh, where twenty-two kel keeps guarded the passes into Ishka, Waas and the plains of the Wendrush where the warriors of the Urtuk and Mansurii tribes cast hateful and envious eyes upon my homeland. Enemies surrounded Mesh on all sides, but for thousands of years Senta and Hesperu had dwelt with each other in peace. Although King Arsu might have thrown in with the Red Dragon and made noises of war that disturbed the Sentans, it seemed that both he and King Yulmar wanted to believe the fiction that Senta had nothing to fear from Hesperu, or the reverse. Or perhaps it was a point of pride. In either case, it worked to our advantage that no soldiers stopped us to question us and make sure that we weren't revolutionists sent to subvert King Arsu's realm.

'It's too quiet,' Maram said to me in a low voice as we moved along the narrow road. The sharp tattoo of our horses' hooves striking stone echoed off the rocky walls around us. 'I can hear my belly grumbling – I missed dinner, you know. Ah, I can hear *myself* grumbling, and I should tell you I'm sick of it. And sick of forsaken

509

places like this. Have you noticed that the nastiest of surprises have invariably awaited us in mountain passes?'

I thought of the stormy pass high in the White Mountains where Ymiru and the 'Frost Giants' had sprung up out of banks of snow and had nearly clubbed us to death with their fearsome borkors. I remembered, too, the great white ghul of a bear sent by Morjin to slay us beneath the slopes of Mount Korukel, and of course the first droghul who had come upon us in the cleft of ground between the Asses' Ears. And later, Jezi Yaga. Most of all, I couldn't shake loose from my mind the images of Atara nearly dying from a dreadful arrow wound in the Kul Moroth, where Morjin's soldiers under Count Ulanu *had* in fact sent Alphanderry on to death.

'It will be all right,' I murmured to Maram. The wind whooshing through the Khal Arrak carried scents of wildflowers and wet rock. 'Nothing will happen to us here.'

I was filled with great hope. The glimmer off the glaciers above us cast a faint light upon Maram's face. It was a magnificent thing that he had done, journeying across hundreds of miles of Ea's wilds by himself.

'Maram, have I thanked you for saving my life . . . again?'

'Ah, I *did* save you, didn't I? There was no way out of those damn caverns, was there?'

'I can't think that we escaped them,' I said, looking at the rocks pressing in upon us, 'only to be trapped here. Surely our fate lies farther on.'

'Surely it does,' he said. 'But how *far* on? A mile? Two? If Kane fails to stop that rider, we'll likely meet a Red Priest and a cadre of Crucifiers coming our way.'

'Kane won't fail,' I told him. 'And if he does, once we're out of this gorge, we'll hide far from the road.'

For another mile, however, I listened to every hoofbeat and breath as we wound our way through the pass's narrows. Then, in terrain that must have been claimed by Hesperu, the narrows gave out into a gap several miles wide. A razor-backed ridge marbled with snow rose up to our left while humps of broken ground gleamed in the starlight to our right. I espied many large boulders, behind which we might hide at need. But the earth remained quiet, and so we followed the road as it twisted sharply right and left on its descent into Hesperu.

Dawn's light revealed that we were passing through a valley full of trees lower down and ragged snowfields higher along steel-gray slopes. To the sides of the road, the slanting fields glowed orange with the lichens growing on rocks, and showed the greens, purples and whites of mosses, sky pilots and saxifrage. With every mile that we rode further into this new realm, we lost elevation and the snow quickly gave way to swaths of emerald forest. The valley broke up into a hilly country that opened out to the east, west and south. Behind us, limned against a blue sky, the white peaks of the Crescent Mountains guarded the tiny kingdom of Senta. And then the road led us into a thick forest of dogwoods and oak, and the sky vanished from sight.

Two hours later, as we were rounding a bend in the road, I stopped suddenly and drew my sword. My eyes fixed on a large oak, covered with moss and hung with vines. And then a familiar voice called out to us, 'It's good I'm no Red Priest with a gang of Crucifiers at my call, for I heard you coming a half mile away.' And Kane stepped from behind the tree's cover.

He gave no welcoming smile as he began pacing toward us with a heavy step. Over his back he slung his heavy leather saddle.

'Where is your horse?' I asked him, looking for the Hell Witch.

'Dead,' he sighed out. 'I had to ride her into the ground trying to catch up with that damned traitor.'

'And did you?'

We all waited for the answer to this question.

'Yes,' he finally said. Although speech seemed to distress him, he added, 'We needn't worry about the Kallimun being warned of us, at least not here and not yet. Now, why don't we take a little breakfast? There's a stream down the road not far from here.'

When we came to the stream, we moved off into the woods, and Liljana cooked us a breakfast of ham, fried eggs and toasted wheat bread. I had never seen Kane eat with so little appetite. He sat on a downed tree poking at a piece of ham with his dagger, and then staring at the blade's shiny steel. Even the news that we hoped to find the Maitreya in a place called Jhamrul failed to enliven him.

After that we took a few hours of rest while Kane stood guard over us. Before I drifted off, I saw Kane staring at his hand as if he had to will himself to keep his eyes open. But I sensed a terrible and ancient torment that ate at his heart and kept him from joining us in sleep.

When it came time to set out, Kane threw his saddle on top of one of the remounts. If riding this big gelding in place of the Hell Witch vexed Kane, he gave no sign of it. In truth, he did not speak at all, and he hardly moved his dark eyes, not even to scan the woods for enemies.

Later that day, we came down into a flatter country of low, wooded hills and rolling farmland. The air grew sweltering, and seemed to soak the earth like boiling water. We all sweated beneath our thin robes, and swatted at the tiny gnats that came to bite us. The road led us over streams on rotting wooden bridges, and then over a much larger stone construction joining the muddy banks of one of the Haraland's numerous rivers. Not far from it we encountered a woodcutter who had bound some faggots of oak across the back of his dog, a giant mastiff. The flesh of the dog's hindquarters had been ripped open: it looked as if the woodcutter had whipped him. I wanted to give this cruel-looking man a wide berth, but Master Juwain insisted that we should ask him for directions.

'Jhamrul?' the man said to us, scratching at his greasy beard. 'I never heard of it. Why would pilgrims such as yourselves want to go there?'

'We seek the Well of Restoration,' Master Juwain told him, 'said to lie near there.'

'The Well of Restoration? I never heard of that, either. And I don't want to.'

The gaze of his bleary eyes took in Daj and Estrella sitting on their horses and finally came to rest on Kane. Something tightened inside the woodcutter then, and he gripped his axe and said, 'You pilgrims should keep to this road, and not go wandering about where you don't belong. Now, let me be on my way – I've work to do.'

A farmer whom we came across an hour later proved no friendlier and no more helpful. And so we continued down the road, asking after Jhamrul, although I dreaded what we might find around the next bend or awaiting us in the Haraland's towns. I hated nearly everything about this country: the steamy, stifling air overlaying field and forest, its sullen people, and even its strange flowers, all waxy with bizarre colors and exuding a sickening, too-sweet fragrance. The very smell of the Haraland tormented me, for it was of sweat and dung running off sun-baked fields into muddy rivers – and of blood, fear, decay and death.

I had thought Kane inured to such things – indeed, to anything and everything that might distress a man. But I sensed a great pain gnawing at his insides like a rabid rat. That night we made camp in a wood by a wheatfield, and after dinner I stood with him at the edge of the trees looking out at the stalks of wheat glimmering in the starlight. And I said to him, 'I've never seen you like this.'

He stood like a statue frozen by Jezi Yaga. Finally, a little light came into his face, and he said, 'How much of me have you really seen, eh?'

'Was it Tarran, then? What happened with him?'

'So, death happened, as it does to us all,' he growled. 'And before the end, just as I put my knife into him, despair. I saw it in his eyes, Valashu. I smelled it fouling his soul. This black, black, cursed thing.'

I rested my hand on his shoulder and said, 'But you did what you had to do. How many times have you killed at need?'

'So, how *many* times, eh?' He stared out into the wavering silver and black wheat. 'I tell you, if every blade of grass here were a man, then I've mowed down a thousand fields, ten thousand. And all unripened, don't you see?'

I thought I *did* see, and I rested my other hand on the hilt of the sword that Kane himself had forged so long ago. And I said to him, 'It must all come to an end – the killing must.'

'Yes, it *must*. And soon, Valashu, soon.'

The black centers of his black eyes seemed to drink up what little light the stars cast down to earth here. And he said, 'The one we seek is close – I know he is. He is waiting for us. We must find him. *I* must. Morjin slaughtered Godavanni in front of my eyes, but this time, if I must, I'll send all his armies to hell to keep the Maitreya safe.'

I gazed south and west at the other farms and woods stretching out to the horizon. 'The man told of in Jhamrul might or might not be the one we seek. It might be harder than we hope to find him.'

'Hard, yes – but we *will* find him.'

Behind us, Estrella sat around the fire with our other friends drinking tea. I inclined my head toward her, and asked Kane, 'Do you believe that she will show us the Shining One?'

'I do. And in the end, the Shining One will show himself. Do you remember the three signs by which the Maitreya will be known?'

I nodded my head. 'In his looking upon all with an equal eye, and his unshakeable courage at all times. And in his steady abidance in the One.'

'So. So it must be. The Maitreya dwells, always, in the realm of the One.'

I said to Kane, 'I know what you say must be true, but I don't really understand it. In Tria, I was told that the Maitreya was of *this* realm. He is always one of the Ardun, born of the earth.'

Kane smiled at this and said, 'That ghost told you this, eh? The Urudjin whom the Galadin sent to deliver that verse. Do you remember it? Can you recite it for me, now?'

I nodded my head again. Then I drew in a deep breath and called out:

> *The Ardun, born of earth, delight*
> *In flowers, butterflies, bright*
> *New snow beneath the bluest sky,*
> *All things of earth that live and die.*
>
> *Valari sail beyond the sky*
> *Where heaven's splendors terrify;*
> *In ancient longing to unite,*
> *They seek a deeper, deathless light.*
>
> *The angels, too, with searing sight*
> *Behold the blazing, starry height;*
> *Reborn from fire, in flame they fly*
> *Like silver swans: to live, they die.*
>
> *The Shining Ones who live and die*
> *Between the whirling earth and sky*
> *Make still the sun, all things ignite –*
> *And earth and heaven reunite.*
>
> *The Fearless Ones find day in night*
> *And in themselves the deathless light,*
> *In flower, bird and butterfly,*
> *In love: thus dying, do not die.*
>
> *They see all things with equal eye:*
> *The stones and stars, the earth and sky,*
> *The Galadin, blazing bright,*
> *The Elijin, Valari knight.*
>
> *They bring to them the deathless light,*
> *Their fearlessness and sacred sight;*
> *To slay the doubts that terrify:*
> *Their gift to them to gladly die.*

514

And so on wings the angels fly,
Valari sail beyond the sky,
But they are never Lords of Light,
And not for them the Stone of Light.

'So,' Kane said, his eyes agleam, 'the Maitreya dwells, always, in *this* world, as well. Ultimately, as Abrasax told us, the realm of the One and the realm of the earth are not two.'

I thought about this for a while, then said, 'But I still don't understand why the Maitreya is never a Valari or even one of the higher orders, but always born of the Ardun.'

'Do you remember what I told you in the Skadarak, that the Galadin must overcome their fear of death?'

I nodded my head as I listened to the crickets chirping fast and loud in the fields. Behind us, I heard Atara laughing at some lewd joke that Maram had made. Liljana busied herself roasting up some honey-lemon tarts for our dessert, and their pungent fragrance wafted out into the air. For a single moment, the whole world seemed infinitely sweet.

'So,' Kane said, 'this overcoming is *hard*. The path toward becoming an Elijin and Galadin is itself almost impossibly hard and long beyond measure. For everyone, that is, except the Shining One.'

'But the Maitreyas are never of the Galadin!' I said.

'No, they are not. But they *could* be, eh? That is the beauty of Shining Ones, their sweet, sweet, terrible beauty. A long lifetime it takes for a man to advance to the Elijin, and sometimes ages for an Elijin to progress to the Galidik order. But for the Shining Ones, this becoming could occur in the flash of a moment.'

An old verse came unbidden into my mind:

And down into the dark,
No eyes, no lips, no spark.
The dying of the light,
The neverness of night.

I told these words to Kane, then said, 'The Maitreya chooses death, then. Death over infinitely long life.'

'No – he chooses one path over the other. He chooses infinite life.'

'But he *dies*!'

'No, he *lives*, truly lives, such as few ever do. Every moment in

515

this realm, everything he touches: a rock, a tree, a child's face, blazing with the light of the One.'

'But he still must die. Why, then?'

Kane looked off into the star-silvered fields around us, and his face fell sad and strange with an ancient yearning. And he said to me, 'It is his gift to us. The Maitreya lives with a wild joy of life; he dies with equal delight. "To gladly die", Valashu. It is this *gladness* that pours out through the Maitreya and the Lightstone in his hands, long before his end actually comes. It has great power. It fills the world, and all worlds, and joins the earth to the heavens. Of men it makes angels. It . . . heals.'

I could feel his heart beating quick and strong deep inside him with a rhythm that matched my own. And then he said to me, 'In such gladness, how can fear ever dwell?'

'His gift,' I whispered, looking up at the stars.

'And that is why,' Kane said, 'the Maitreya is always chosen of the Ardun. The higher orders have already set out on the path toward immortality. For the Elijin, theirs is not to die until their ending as Galadin in a new creation – not unless they are done in by accident or treachery first. As for the Valari, who have beheld the beauty of Star-Home, with their eyes or in their dreams – they have already taken one step through the doorway of everlasting life into another world. Is it not so with you?'

'Yes, it is so,' I said to him. 'I have stood with the true Valari, in a place where life was honored instead of death.'

'So – so have I, long ago.' Kane's jaws closed with a snap like that of a wolf, then ground together as the muscles beneath his cheeks popped out. Then he said, 'But the Maitreya's whole purpose in being is to show that there is no true death.'

'"To live, I die,"' I said, quoting from one of my father's favourite passages of the *Saganom Elu*. 'The faith of the Valari.'

Kane smiled at this as he looked at me. 'This, too, is said: "They who die before they die – they do not die when they die."'

'I wish that I could believe that,' I said, swallowing against the hot acids burning the back of my throat.

'So, *beliefs* are useless,' Kane snarled at me. 'You must *know* it – or know it not.'

'I know *this* realm,' I said, looking out at the wheatfields of the Haraland. Somewhere down the road or across wide rivers, I knew that we would come upon other traitors or enemies such as Tarran. We would see soldiers hacked to pieces and grandmothers torn and bloodied, and men nailed to crosses of wood. 'If this is truly the same as the realm of the One, then why grieve death or the need to kill?'

Kane's jaws clenched, and so did his fists. His eyes seemed to grow darker, like two black holes drilled into his savage face. For a moment, I thought he wanted to draw his sword and run me through with cold steel. And then something within him softened, and he said to me, 'That is Morjin's mistake – and Asangal's. I did not say that the two realms are identical, only not two. All that is, here on earth, the flowers and the butterflies, no less Morjin himself, are *precious*. Life is, Valashu – so infinitely precious. But so many live almost wholly within this realm. They do not *see* the other realm. They do not know. Thus they do not really *live*. When they die, they truly die and lose everything. And when such as *I*, and you, send them on before their time, before they ever open their eyes, we cut them off . . . from everything. And that's the hell of it. The bloody, bloody hell of this cursed world we've made for ourselves.'

He drew in a long breath as he looked at me. Then he said, 'And that is why we must find the Maitreya. Keeping Morjin from using the Lightstone is one thing. But it is another to keep the world from losing its soul.'

Without another word, he whirled about and left me there at the edge of the wheatfield. *Would* we ever find the Maitreya, I wondered? Tomorrow we would continue our journey into this stifling realm of our enemies that I had hated nearly upon first sight. Somewhere on the road ahead of us, I sensed, we would find torment, blood and death, for that was the world. But the world must be more than that, too, or so I told myself. And with that small comfort, I turned back toward our campfire to listen to Alphanderry sing and to eat some of the honey tarts that Liljana had made for us.

33

In the morning we continued down the road, the Senta Road as the Hesperuks called it, and according to the Sentans, the Iskull Road, for it led almost straight south through the whole length of Hesperu, paralleling the Rhul River and passing through the great city of Khevaju on its way to Iskull, where the Rhul emptied into the Southern Ocean. The country flattened out even more, with the low hills shrinking down into a steaming green plain. The first good-sized town we came to was named Nubur, and there we asked after Jhamrul. No one seemed to have heard of it. In the town square, built around a widened portion of the Senta Road, we went from shop to shop querying blacksmiths, barbers and the like, and attracting too much attention. A wheelwright wondered a little too loudly why pilgrims would seek a place called Jhamrul instead of Iskull, where pilgrims for ages had embarked from or landed in Hesperu. Finally, to a cooper named Goro, we admitted that we sought a place called the Well of Restoration.

'The Well of Restoration, you say!' Goro barked out as he eyed us. We had dismounted, and stood outside his shop near the huge barrel that signified his trade. 'Tell me about this Well of Restoration!'

Goro was a big man, with a big voice that carried out into the square, where many Hesperuks went about their business or took a little rest beneath one of the spreading almond trees. In shape, with his huge chest and deep belly, he resembled one of the barrels that he made out of wooden staves and hoops of iron. His black, curly hair had been trimmed close to his roundish head, as had his beard. His dark eyes seemed a little too small for his face, which had fallen suddenly suspicious.

I explained that we were returning from Senta, where we had learned of a fount of healing that might make Atara whole.

'Too many have been blinded these days,' Goro said as he looked at Atara. For a moment, I felt a tenderness trying to fight its way up from inside him. But then his heart hardened, and so did his face as he said, 'But then, many have made errors and suffered their correction.'

'I don't know what you mean by error,' Atara said, 'or its correction. I was blinded in battle, where an evil man took my eyes.'

'That, in itself, is an error,' Goro told her. He looked from me to Master Juwain, and then at Liljana and the children. 'Not to know error is counted by some as an Error Major, and if the ignorance is willful or defiant, even as an Error Mortal. You should have been told this when you got off your ship in Iskull.'

'We did not come to Senta by way of Iskull,' Liljana told him, 'and so we are new to Hesperu.'

Our encounter had attracted the interest of a bookseller, who had come out of the adjacent shop. He was a small, neat man wearing an impeccably clean tunic of white cotton trimmed at the cuffs and hem with blue silk. His black ringlets of hair gleamed with a fragrant-smelling oil, and he wore gold rings around four of his ten fingers. He presented himself as Vasul, and he said to Goro: 'What is this talk about Errors Major and Errors Mortal?'

A dozen yards out in the square, whose shiny cobblestones seemed to have been scrubbed of the stain of horse dung and swept clean of the tiniest particle of dirt, a few of the other townsfolk passing along had turned their curious faces toward us. I decided that this would be an excellent time to make our farewell and be on our way.

But just as I took a step toward my horse, Goro called out to me: 'Just a moment, pilgrim! We were discussing *errors*, and yours at that.'

In looking at the stubbornness of censure that befell Goro's face, I had a keen sense that things would go worse for us if we fled instead of remaining. And so I, and my friends, waited to hear what Goro would say.

'Let us,' Goro told, 'read the relevant passages in the Black Book. Will you oblige me, pilgrim?'

He stared straight at me, and it took me some moments before I realized that he was referring to that compendium of evil and lies called the *Darakul Elu*. Morjin had written it himself in mockery of the *Saganom Elu*. Most editions of it were bound in leather dyed a dark black, hence its more common name.

'We are traveling light,' I told him, 'and it seemed wise not to burden ourselves with books.'

I glanced at Master Juwain; this was one time where his copy of the *Saganom Elu* was nowhere to be seen, and I silently gave thanks for that.

'A *burden*!' Goro cried out. He turned to Vasul and said, 'Do you see? They willfully keep themselves in ignorance. Is that not an Error Mortal?'

'It might be,' Vasul said, 'if they were of Hesperu. But other lands have other ways.'

His words, however, which were meant to placate Goro, seemed only to anger him. Goro's dark face grew darker as he barked out: 'My son, Ugo, was killed last year, in Surrapam, fighting the errants so that our priests might bring the Way of the Dragon to the north. His blood washes clean the ground where he lies. After the campaign is finished, all the errants there who haven't been cruci-fied will turn to the Way. And so it will be, soon, in all lands. And so these pilgrims would do well to learn *our* ways, since their journey has afforded them so great a chance.'

Now a man whose clay-stained hands proclaimed him as a potter stepped closer, and so did a middling old woman and a much younger one with a baby girl in her arms: a mother, daughter, and granddaughter, or so I guessed. I wanted badly to jump on Altaru's back and gallop out of this trap of a town, but it was too late for that.

'All families,' Goro instructed me, 'must keep at least one copy of the Black Book. If you are pilgrims bound by blood or oaths, you count as a family.'

'Then we should treat them as a family,' Vasul said to him. 'Where is our kindness to these strangers? Where is our hospi-tality?'

'The best kindness we could offer them is to correct their errors.'

'Then let us help them,' Vasul said to Goro. 'Wait here with them, won't you?'

With that, he disappeared into his shop, and then came out a few moments later bearing a large, thick book. Gold leaf had been worked into the edges of its pages; a large dragon – of a red so dark it gleamed almost black – had been embossed upon the book's leather cover. More leaf, I saw, had been used to render the dragon's eyes a brilliant gold.

'One of my scribes,' Vasul said to us, 'finished lettering this only last week. As you can see, it is beautifully illuminated.'

He opened the book to show us golden characters through which sunlight streamed as through glowing windows. He came to a page worked with the brilliant figure of the angel, Asangal, giving the Lightstone into Morjin's outstretched hands. Another page depicted the crucifixion of Kalkamesh. The scene's vividness nearly made me weep: a great being nailed to stone on the side of a black mountain, as above him a dragon beat the air with his leathery wings and used his talons to tear out Kalkamesh's liver.

'Here,' Vasul said to me, coming to a page near the middle of the book. 'This passage is from the *Healings*, under *Miracles*. Read it to us, won't you?'

He gave the book to me, and tapped a gold-ringed finger against the top of the page. The finely-wrought letters inked into the paper burned my eyes like fire. I could not bring myself to give voice to the words; it was like holding in my mouth pure poison.

'Read!' Goro told me. 'It's nearly noon, and I've a barrel to finish.'

More people had now gathered around. I began mumbling out the words of the passage.

'Louder!' Goro barked out. 'I can't hear you!'

I drew in a deep breath, and with greater force, if not enthusiasm, I recited:

'"*If a man should lose limb or eye, let him not despair or drink the potions of conjurors or witches. Let him turn the eye of his soul toward the One's light and he who brings it to earth, for the only true restoration lies in the hands of the Maitreya.*"'

I finished reading, and Goro suddenly shouted at me: 'The only true restoration is in the hands of the Maitreya! Remember this, pilgrim! This Well of Restoration you seek is a figment. And your desire to seek it must be corrected.'

I told Goro that I would surely remember the passage. But this wasn't good enough for him.

'Read it again!' he commanded me.

'What?' I said.

'Read it again, nine times more, and louder.' He turned to look at Master Juwain. 'And the rest of you shall recite it, ten times each!'

'By what authority,' I asked him, 'do you demand this of us?'

By now, Goro had so swollen up with righteous anger and pride that it seemed his head might burst. And so it was Vasul who answered for him, saying, 'It is upon everyone to correct the errors of each other, and especially their own. That is the Way of the Dragon.'

Vasul, and others crowding in close, waited to see what I would do. But Goro lost patience, and called out: 'Read the passage!'

And so I did. Nine more times I read out loud these duplicitous words of Morjin. I gave the book to Master Juwain, and he reluctantly recited to Goro and Vasul, and to the crowd, as well. So did Maram, Liljana and Daj; so, in a quavering voice that nearly broke my heart, did Atara. When she failed to pass the book to Estrella, Goro berated her.

'*All* of you shall recite the verse,' Goro commanded.

If Atara had still possessed eyes, she would have fired off arrows of hate with them. She snapped at Goro: 'But the girl is mute!'

At the sharpness of her voice, Goro's fingers clenched as if he longed to correct her contempt with his fist. But then he asked Atara, 'Can she see still read?'

'No, she never learned the art.'

'Can she still hear?'

Atara looked at Estrella and nodded her head.

'Good,' Goro said. 'Then she will have heard the passage enough that she might recite it within her heart. Ten times.'

He turned his gaze on Estrella, who stood there on smooth cobblestones staring back at him. In the silence that fell over the square, everyone waited as they watched Estrella. She remained almost motionless as the leaves of the nearby almond trees fluttered in the breeze. Whether or not she recited Morjin's words within herself, not even the wind could know.

Finally, Goro grabbed up the book and extended it toward Kane. 'Read!' he told him.

Kane did not move. His eyes looked past the big black book and fixed on Goro's eyes. I thought he might be ready to tear them out of his head.

'Read, now, pilgrim! We haven't got all day!'

I felt Kane's fingers burning to grip the hilt of his sword. I knew that he could whip it out of its sheath and strike off Goro's head before Goro had time to change the expression of his belligerent face.

At last, with a furious motion, Kane took hold of the book. By bad chance, it seemed, it fell open to the illumination of Kalkamesh's crucifixion. Kane stared for a long few moments at the dragon's bloody talon ripping open Kalkamesh's side. I knew he trembled to cut off Goro's life years before its time, and Vasul's life, too – and the lives of a nearby baker and barber and all the other townspeople gathering in the square. The fire in Kane's eyes told me that he had returned to his savage self, and I hated *my*self for liking him better that way.

'So,' Kane growled. 'So.'

His blunt fingers fairly tore through the book's pages. When he came to the passage that we had all read, he snarled out:

'"*If a man should lose limb or eye, let him not despair or drink the potions of conjurors or witches. Let him turn the eye of his soul toward the One's light and he who brings it to earth, for the only true restoration lies in the hands of the Maitreya.*"'

'There!' he shouted at Goro.

'Good!' Goro said to him. He shot Kane a dark smile. 'Now complete the passage for us.'

'What!'

'The passage is incomplete. You'll find the words that should come next, if you search in your heart for them.'

If Kane searched in his heart just then, I thought, he would find a ravening beast that would tear both Goro and himself apart.

'I don't know what you're talking about!' Kane said.

'Then I shall help you.' Goro seemed very satisfied with himself as he smiled and drew in a breath of air. Then he recited the self-same passage, ending with:

'"*For the only true restoration lies in the hands of the Maitreya . . . and his name is Morjin!*"'

'But that is not written!' Kane said, smacking his knuckles into the book.

Vasul pulled at his rings of oiled hair, and said to him, 'It *is* written, surely. The *Darakul Elu* is a living text, dwelling within the heart of the One, and therefore within the hearts of men. It always grows, even as a child grows to a man and then to an angel. And surely, Lord Morjin is the Shining One.'

A gray-haired woman standing in close called out in an awed voice, 'The heralds came with the news just last month, on the thirteenth of Marud: Lord Morjin has claimed the Lightstone and has been revealed as the Maitreya. And so his dominion is not just all of Ea, but over men's minds and hearts, as well.'

'And over our destinies!' another woman shouted.

'"*He is the coming of the sun after night,*" someone else quoted. '"*He is the bringer of the new age.*"'

'He is *coming*, himself!' the potter called out. 'It is said that Lord

Morjin will soon visit Hesperu, and honor King Arsu for his conquest of Surrapam. He brings blessings for all those who have battled the errants.'

This news, if news it really was, caused many crowding the square to let out a great cheer of anticipation. But not everyone seemed to shout with equal enthusiasm. I felt sure that the cobbler standing behind the potter loudly praised Morjin only so that he could be *heard* praising Morjin. So it was with the woman holding the baby, and the barber, and others. A few failed to join the chorus altogether. One of these, a large man bearing an iron-shod staff, rubbed at the scar of a dragon that had been branded into his cheek. As it had been in Sakai, too many of the people here bore signs of torture: brandings, amputations, tongue clippings and eyes put out. I prayed that none of these mutilations were the correctives for Errors Minor.

Goro still waited for Kane to recite the passage – and the noxious amendment that he had added to it. I thought that Kane would rather die than say these words, but he surprised me, spitting them out nine more times to Goro's and Vasul's satisfaction. Then he turned to climb on top of his horse.

'Where are you going, pilgrim?' Goro said to him. 'We're not finished here.'

'No? Are we not?'

Kane's hand crept closer to his sword's hilt. I felt sure that he was about to commit an Error Mortal.

'What would you have of us?' I asked Goro as I grabbed Kane's arm.

'It's not what *I* would have,' Goro said. He looked at Vasul. 'I believe their errors call for, at the very least, a payment to the Dragon.'

'I agree,' Vasul said, smiling at me. 'I should think a dragongild of at least twenty ounces. Gold ounces, of course.'

'Twenty gold pieces!' Maram cried out. 'That is robbery!'

'No,' Vasul told him, 'it is only correction. As it is said in the Black Book, gold washes clean the stain of error.'

Various mumblings and protests from the crowd gave me to understand that this was also said of pain and blood.

'How can *our* gold filling *your* pockets,' Maram asked him, 'wash anything clean?'

Where his question angered Goro, it seemed only to wound Vasul. He held out his hands as if to ask why fate had driven him to deal with unreasoning errants. Then he explained, 'The book I have given you would sell for five gold ounces itself, and is in any case priceless. The dragongild that we ask of you will be given to the Kallimun school up on Crow's Hill, that the children of Nubur shall be educated to avoid errors in all their forms. In the end, all belongs to the Dragon, anyway.'

'So,' Kane said to Vasul, 'since you *ask* this dragongild of us, we are free not to pay it, eh?'

Goro stood eyeing Kane as if wondering if he had the strength to crush the breath out of him. But it was one thing, I thought, to heft barrels all day and another to grapple with Kane.

'You're free to commit any errors you wish,' Goro snapped at him. 'We've only suggested these correctives to help you. If you disagree with our assessments, we can always go up to the Kallimun castle. It's said that Ra Parvu is the one of the wisest of the Red Priests. He is far more skilled than we in distinguishing Errors Minor from Errors Major.'

Out in the crowd to my left, I took note of a pot-bellied man I recognized as a carpenter. I overheard him proudly telling someone that he had kept the Red Priests well supplied with crosses as correctives to Errors Mortal.

Liljana stepped up closer to Goro and told him, 'We don't *have* twenty gold pieces. We're only poor pilgrims trying make our way to Iskull.'

'Iskull?' Goro said. 'But you told that you were trying to find a Well of Restoration.'

'We,' Liljana said, looking from Kane to me, 'have realized that it cannot exist, after all. And we thank you for helping us see our error.'

Goro's beady eyes bored into Liljana to determine if she was mocking him. Although Liljana no longer possessed the means to smile at him in reassurance, her kindly, round face filled with sincerity and a great calm. She seemed genuinely grateful to Goro and Vasul. All her skills as the Materix of the Maitriche Telu, I thought, went into this persuasion. I marveled at how the pitch of her voice seemed perfectly calibrated to pump up Goro's vanity even while soothing his belligerence and urge toward cruelty. I sensed that she waited for me to help things along. I needed only to smile at him and bow my head in acquiescence, and most of all, to nudge his heart with the slightest touch of the valarda. But I could not. And so, for a moment, our fate hung in the balance.

'If you determine that we should give *all* our money to the Dragon,' Liljana said to Goro, 'then we won't be able to make the journey to Iskull. And so we won't be able to greet Lord Morjin as he comes up the Senta Road, as we would like to do. And so what chance would we have of seeing sight restored to our poor companion?'

At this, Liljana gazed at Atara. Her words pleased the crowd and softened the hearts of both Vasul and Goro. In the end, Liljana was able to bargain down our 'dragongild' to ten gold pieces: a true miracle, considering that we were in no position to bargain.

'Ten gold ounces, then,' Goro finally said to Liljana. 'Alonian archers, is that right?'

Although Goro and Vasul might not like strangers bringing dangerous sentiments into their realm, they had no objection to good Alonian gold. As we would learn, the Hesperuk currency had been debased to near worthlessness to pay for the Surrapam war.

'Good!' Goro called out as Liljana counted the coins into his hand. 'Then I would like to wish you well on your pilgrimage. May the mercy of the Dragon be upon you!'

Vasul and others in the crowd repeated this blessing, then bade us farewell. As quickly as we could without appearing overhasty, we mounted our horses and made our way out of the square. We said nothing as we rode through Nubur's streets to the edge of the town. Even through the wheatfields and farmland stretching on for five miles to the south, we kept our mouths shut and our eyes upon the road. The iron shoes nailed to our horses' hooves beat against worn stone, again and again. Then, at last, as we entered a forest full of chittering blue and yellow birds, Maram sighed out: 'That was close.'

'The mercy of the Dragon, indeed!' Kane snarled as he looked at Atara riding on in silence. He turned in his saddle to gaze back toward Nubur. 'I'd like to steal back there tonight and rouse those two thieves from their beds with a little of *my* mercy. How many other travelers do you think they've squeezed gold from with their little game, eh?'

'Their little game might have gotten us killed,' Maram said, 'but for Liljana's cleverness. And deceit.'

Maram's words both pleased and wounded Liljana. She looked at him and huffed out, 'I said nothing to that greedy cooper that wasn't true.'

'Ah, is *that* true? Would you really like to greet Morjin upon this road?'

The harsh lines that seamed Liljana's face hinted at how badly she *would* like to greet Morjin: with the full fury of her mind pouring itself out through the lens of her blue gelstei. Even as Atara would like to greet him with arrows and I would like to give him the blessings of my sword.

'One thing seems clear,' Liljana said. 'We can't go about this land telling everyone we're seeking the Well of Restoration. That surely *is* an error.'

'I'm afraid that we can't tell everyone, either, that we're seeking the Red Dragon,' Master Juwain said. 'I would not want the Kallimun to hear that we eight pilgrims were asking after him.'

'Perhaps,' Maram said, scratching his beard, 'it's too dangerous for us to pose as pilgrims at all. I think we need a new guise.'

'What, then?'

As we clopped along down the road into a wall of moist, hot air, Maram looked up at a lark perched on the branch of a teak tree and singing out its sweet song. And Maram smiled as he said, 'I have an idea.'

Later that day we came to a town called Sumru, where we spent the night camping out in the surrounding woods. Before dawn, with the air still nearly black and whining with mosquitoes, we roused ourselves and turned west onto a narrow road leading out of Sumru through the forest. The great teak trees and thick under-growth, we hoped, would hide us from the eyes of our enemies, if any had been sent to spy upon us. After a few hours of swift riding, we came into a more populous region, and turned north-west onto a muddy little road that took us into a town named Ramlan. There, with the last of our money, we went about the various shops making purchases: bright bolts of cloth and colored swatches of leather; herbs and paper and ink; paints of various colors, and brushes, large and small; a great cart that it would take two horses to pull, and a load of planks of cured wood to fill it. And other things. Kane went to a swordsmith and ordered knives made according to precise specifications. From one of Ramlan's blacksmiths, Hartu the Hammer, as he was called, he also ordered chains and a cask of nails. We had to wait all the rest of that day and half the next for Hartu to pound out the nails from long strips of glowing red iron. When he had finished this hot, sweaty work, he gave the cask to Kane, and tried to dispel his uneasiness toward him, and us, by saying, 'I haven't made so many nails since Lord Mansarian came through here five years ago to punish the errants up toward Yor. You haven't said what you want all this iron for; I should think the nails are too small for putting anyone up on wood, even children – ha, ha!'

527

I didn't like his nervous laughter, or the way he looked at Daj and Estrella. I didn't like the way the people of Ramlan looked at *us*, as if wondering why pilgrims had left the Senta Road to go wandering about the countryside. I was glad to help hitch two of our packhorses to the cart, and then lead the way out of Ramlan even deeper into the Haraland.

We spent the rest of the day working along muddy farm roads, turning left or right, north or south, so as to confound any who might witness our passage and want to report us. Toward dusk we entered a large wood and found what seemed an old track leading into the heart of the trees. It seemed perfect for our needs. While Kane guarded our rear, I rode on ahead to look for footprints or other sign of habitation, but it seemed that no one had used this track for a long time. We finally came into a clearing. The heap of stones at its center looked to be a cottage that had fallen in upon itself ages ago. Kane wanted to set to work immediately, but we had to use the last light of day to make our camp.

In the morning, though, Kane rose at dawn, and began banging nails into the wooden planks with a great noise that awoke everyone. I helped him build a sort of small chalet onto the bed of the cart, and so did Daj and Maram. While we sweated in the humid morning air, Liljana took out scissors, needle and thread to shape and sew the bolts of cloth together. Atara helped her. This surprised me, for I had not known she possessed such skills. As she put it, 'I *was* once a princess, and my father expected me to learn the womanly arts – so that I could marry well and provide him with grandchildren.'

Estrella, however, had little talent for sewing, and so she played the flute for us to provide music while we worked. Alphanderry came forth and accompanied her, singing out a rather bawdy ballad whose rhythms seemed timed to reinforce the hammering of Kane's nails. Later that day, when it came time to paint the little traveling house that our cart had become, Estrella picked up a small brush while Alphanderry continued entertaining us. As it happened, she had a rare gift for using brightly colored paints to render birds and flowers and the like, though she could not tell us where she had come by it. Alphanderry, of course, could grasp no brush in his hand, nor anything else. But day by day, he seemed to appear ever more substantial, as if he was somehow growing used to the world again. He called out ideas for figures to Estrella, and to Kane and Maram, who also helped with the painting. I took great delight in the delight with which Estrella brought to

528

life a golden astor tree and a rising sun and a dark blue panel full of stars. I had to stop her, though, from depicting a great silver swan. When she discovered that her enthusiasm had carried her away into an error that might have betrayed us, she wasted no time in self-recrimination, but only used her brush to quickly transform the swan into a winged horse. It joined other animal figures, some fantastical and some not: diving dolphins and a chimera; an eagle in flight and a two-headed serpent and a great blue bear. Liljana suggested we paint a dragon against one of the red panels, but it was thought that the Hesperuks might take offence at a golden or green one. None of us could bear to see a red dragon defiling our wildly and beautifully decorated house, though Kane wryly remarked that it would do no harm to paint a red one against red. That way, we could always tell the curious that the great Red Dragon always dwelled within our house, unseen, as it did within the hearts of men.

It took us four days to complete our preparations. When we were ready to set out again, I stood staring at the cart and admiring the fine detail with which Estrella had embellished a mandolet, a tarot card and the figure of a costumed man juggling seven brightly colored balls. I smiled to see how closely this man resembled Kane. The likeness became even more striking when Liljana brought forth one of the costumes that she had been sewing and bade Kane to put it on. This, with much grumbling and cursing, he did. She then gave him seven leather balls which she had filled with dried rice and stitched shut. Their colors ranged from blood red to a brilliant violet, as of a rainbow.

As we all stood around watching, Kane tossed the balls into the air, one after the other, and with lightning-quick motions of his hands, kept them streaming in an arc that seemed a rainbow of its own. I knew then that Maram's idea might possibly work: Kane would certainly be our juggler. (And, at need, our strongman, magician and mandolet player.) Atara, who brought forth a clear, gleaming sphere that we had purchased from a glassblower in Ramlan, would tell people's fortunes. Master Juwain would act as a reader of horoscopes and tarot cards, while Liljana would pose as a potionist and Daj as her assistant. I began practicing on a long flute also acquired in Ramlan, intending to accompany Estrella, who held dear the flute that I had given her more than a year ago in Ishka. We both would provide music for Alphanderry, our minstrel. As Estrella also evinced great expressiveness with her eyes, hands and movements, she might also act as a mime. And Maram, of course, would be our fool.

'We needn't actually *perform*,' he told us after Liljana had helped him try on his silly clown's costume. 'In fact, I'm sure it will go better for us if we don't. But at least we should be able to move about freely – doesn't everyone welcome a traveling troupe?'

Such troupes of players, of course, had journeyed from land to land for thousands of years. They called no kingdom their own, and no kingdom made claim on their loyalties and rarely dared even to tax them.

'These Hesperuks are a grim people,' Maram said, 'but at least they haven't yet outlawed entertainment.'

Daj, however, having been born in the Haraland, took objection to this, saying, 'My people are *not* grim. In my father's house, there was always wine and song. No one was afraid to laugh. My father, once when I was very young, took us to see one of the troupes that came up from the south. There was a tightrope walker and a man who ate fire. I can't remember their names.'

Maram reached up to jingle one of the bells hanging down from his yellow and blue cap. He said, 'Well, I hope people will forget *our* names as readily. But *we* mustn't, and so let's go over them one more time.'

Mirustral I was to be no longer, and certainly not Valashu Elahad. Maram now nodded at me and addressed me as Arajun, and Atara as Kalinda. Liljana had chosen the new name of Mother Magda, while Master Juwain was to go by Tedorik and Daj as Jaiyu. Kane had transformed into Taras, and Estrella into Mira. Alphanderry would sing under the name of Thierraval. And Maram had become Garath the Fool.

We left the woods as we had come, and turned onto one of the Haraland's back roads. Although we journeyed toward no particular destination, we felt the need to complete our quest with all possible speed. Our pace, however, limited by the speed of the heavy cart, proved slow. Its huge, iron-shod wheels left long grooves in the soft roads and from time to time became stuck in mud. Finally, I decided to hitch Altaru to the cart. He hated this new, grinding work, and looked at me as if I had betrayed him. But he was as strong as any draft horse, and had something of a draft horse's look. And this, I thought, might work to our advantage in case anyone questioned us too closely.

For the next five days, we wandered from town to town asking people if they had ever heard of a place called Jhamrul. No one had. We listened for talk of healers and unusual healings, too. We worked our way into the heart of the Haraland, east and south. As we drew closer to the Iona River, which flowed down from the mountains into the great Ayo, the land grew almost perfectly flat. The Haralanders here cultivated little wheat, but much millet, maize, beans and a sickly-sweet orange root called a yam. The various towns and villages – Urun, Skah, Malku and Nirrun – smelled of cinnamon and chocolate, which the Haralanders ground up with other spices and made into a sort of sauce for chicken, lamb and pork and strange meats such as squaj and kresh, taken from the giant lizards that infested Hesperu's watercourses. At first we encountered no troubles more vexatious than roads flooded from torrential rains and repeated requests that we encamp and give a show. And then, five miles outside of Nirrun, we ran straight into a company of soldiers coming up the road from the south.

There were fourteen of them, accoutred in heavy, fish-scale armor and riding worn horses. Their captain, a long-faced man named Riquis, waited impatiently while we maneuvered the cart onto a beanfield off the side of the road. The ground was mushy from the recent rains, and instantly mired the cart's great wheels. The soldiers, of course, might have ridden around us with greater ease, but that was not the way of things in Hesperu.

Riquis' sergeant, a stout man with a thick, black beard that spilled down over the collar of his armor, watched us with a growing interest. His covetous eyes fastened like fishhooks on Altaru and Fire. He said to Riquis: 'My lord – look at those horses! I've never seen finer ones!'

'They are fine indeed,' Riquis said as his calculating gaze fell upon Altaru. 'How does a band of players come by such horses?'

I stood in the mud by Altaru with my hand stroking his neck. To Riquis, I said, 'A gift, my lord, from a lord of a land far away.'

I did not tell him that the lord was named Duke Gorador of Daksh.

'He must have liked your performance marvelously well to have given you such a gift,' Riquis said to me.

I tried not to look Riquis eye to eye as I said, 'We're but poor players who do as we can.'

Riquis nodded his head at what he took to be modesty. Then his sergeant said to him, 'Why don't we see how well they *can* do? It's been half a year since I saw a show.'

'I would like that,' Riquis said. 'Unfortunately, though, we haven't the time.'

Although he did not reveal his business, I gathered that his company had been summoned to Avrian, some forty miles to the north on the Iona River. As we had been told in Senta, King Asru had laid siege to Avrian for two bitter months before he had finally taken the city.

'It's said they've crucified a thousand men,' Riquis told us. 'King Angand has arrived from Sunguru, and has joined King Arsu to witness Avrian's destruction. If you truly wish for an appreciative audience, then you should perform for the King. He is a lover of all arts and entertainments, or so it's said.'

'Perhaps one day,' I told him, 'we'll be so fortunate.'

The sergeant returned to the matter that had originally caught his attention. He said, 'If we don't have time for a show, then let's requisition these horses and be done with it, my lord.'

My hand froze fast against Altaru's warm, sweating neck. I calculated the distance, in inches, to the wagon where I had hidden my sword. I calculated the thickness of the soldiers' armor and the length of their spears, as well, and the slight art they seemed to have with such weaponry. I thought that Kane, Maram and I might possibly kill most of them before the survivors lost heart and fled.

'Lord Riquis,' I said to this grim captain, 'this horse was a gift, and so it would be bad manners if we ourselves were to give him away.'

'This horse,' Master Juwain said, nodding at Altaru, 'is our strongest. We would be hard put to find another to draw so heavy a cart.'

'And where, diviner,' Riquis asked, 'were you given this beast?'

Master Juwain, who hated lying even more than I did, said, 'The horse comes from Anjo.'

'And where is that?'

'It lies in the Morning Mountains.'

'And where is *that*?'

'Far away, northeast, past the White Mountains and across the plains of the Wendrush.'

'Oh,' Riquis spat out, 'the Dark Lands. Where, it's said, dwell the Valari.'

This word seemed to hang in the air like a ringing bell. I wrapped my fingers around Altaru's mane as I tried not to look at Riquis.

'Have you performed for the Valari, then?' Riquis asked. 'Horse or no, you are well away from those demons.'

Then he quoted a passage from the Black Book.

'"All who follow the Way of the Dragon, and follow it truly, are of the Light and shall walk the path of the angels. All who do not are of the Dark, and shall be destroyed."'

Liljana, who had a mind as sharp as Godhran steel and could use it to rip apart others' arguments, said to Riquis: 'But surely, the Way of the Dragon is open to everyone, even the Valari.'

'Surely it is,' Riquis said. 'But the Valari, long ago, at the beginning of time, turned away from the Light. Willfully. They poisoned their spirits, and so became demons.'

'Not all of them seemed so evil when we passed through their realm.'

'But is it not so with the cleverest of demons? That which is foul often appears as fair, and the darkest of the Dark as Light.'

Liljana threw her arm around Daj, who stood by her side. And she said, 'But what child is born in darkness? And is it not upon all of us to bring to the errants the –'

'Do not weep for the demonspawn,' Riquis told her. 'In darkness they *are* born, and to darkness they shall return. It is coming, Mother – the Great Crusade is coming. The Kariad, when whole forests shall be felled in order to make crosses for the Valari people. Soon, King Arsu will lead our armies into the Dark Lands, into Eanna and the far north. Any day now, it's said, the King will march with King Angand back down to Khevaju, and then we shall need all the good men and good horses to bear them that we can find.'

This news gave us good reason to reconsider our course, for we had been drifting closer and closer to the Iona River, which it now seemed we must avoid at any cost.

Riquis drew in a great gulp of the muggy air, and stared at Liljana. And then he surprised me, saying, 'But we also need fine players to keep our soldiers' spirits bright. And so keep your horses, Mother. Perhaps one day you'll return to the Dark Lands to perform for our company when we have raised high the standard of the Dragon over the Valari's graves.'

As Maram had said, doesn't everyone welcome a traveling troupe?

Liljana thanked Riquis for his mercy, and presented him and his sergeant with a love potion, which might help them open their hearts and hold their spears up high when they reached Avrian, or so she told them. Riquis and his soldiers rode off quickly after that. And so did we. We turned east and south through the steaming countryside, away from Avrian and the road that King Arsu's army would soon march down along the Iona river. In villages and small farms, we continued inquiring after Jhamrul. As we thought it might arouse too much suspicion to ask directly if anyone knew of any miracles of healing, we spoke of our desire to see Atara made whole again, in hope that somebody might volunteer information that would help us. But when we broached this matter, more than one Haralander stared at us in cold silence. And one woman, a silver-haired grandmother, admitted that she knew of a fine healer up near Sagarun, a young man who had been taken by the Kallimun and never seen again. Even this man, however, she told us, had never been known to heal the blind.

With every day and hour that we remained within this hateful realm, it seemed less and less likely that we would ever come across Jhamrul, and more and more likely that we would be found out, taken and tortured. Torture seemed the fate of everyone who dwelt here, for the Way of the Dragon not only made cruel use of people's bodies and possessions, but twisted their spirits and seared them with fire.

As we drove our painted cart down muddy roads and through poor towns whose houses were built of dried mud and straw, we saw men and women wearing placards that proclaimed their errors. We learned to 'read' the various symbols branded into their cheeks or foreheads: a star usually signified minor defiance of some lord or master whereas an eye within a triangle told of the errant's hubris, in aspiring to a station for which he had no claim. Theft, of course, was usually punished by amputation, though minor pilferings or greed might call for nothing more than the searing of a grasping hand into one's flesh. And so with other symbols for other crimes.

I might have thought that the Haralanders would try to cover these mutilations in shame. But so disfigured were they in their souls that many bore their scars openly and even blatantly: in the village of Dakai, I saw a streetsweeper going about naked but for a loincloth, and proudly displaying a star, triangle, bell, hand, circle, butterfly and other signs branded all across his shiny brown torso, arms and legs. It was as if he used these scars to cry out to everyone: 'Do you see how much I've suffered to try to walk the Way of the Dragon? Do you see how much I've sacrificed in pain that others might learn from my errors?' It astonished me to learn that errants, when facing a branding, were expected to perform this atrocity upon themselves, and that many actually did. It seemed they were burning into their very nerve fibers the imperative that they existed only to execute the will of the Red Dragon.

We had tramped through the Haraland many days, however, before we came across the first crucifixion. In the town square of Yosun, a slender man had been put up on wood for all to see. I was driving the cart that day, and stopped it on hardpacked earth stained with blood. I climbed down and joined the crowd gathered around the cross. Four soldiers covered in iron scales and bearing spears would not let any of the townsfolk too near the crucified man. I saw that great iron spikes split his hands and feet, and his trembling legs seemed no longer able to push against the footpiece to which he was nailed. He gasped for breath. Two days in the hot Haraland sun had nearly blackened his naked body. His dark eyes stared out as at nothing, and I knew he was close to death.

Although it was hard to tell because desiccation and anguish had contorted his face, I thought he was of an age with me. To a woman standing near me, I asked, 'What was his error?'

'He killed his brother,' she told me.

'Killed his brother!' I cried out. I could think of few worse crimes.

But there was more to the story than that. From a wheelwright who had known the young man, whose name was Tristan, I learned that Tristan's brother, Alok, had flown into a rage and had struck the local Red Priest. It seemed that the priest, Ra Sadun, upon learning of the defiant ways of a third brother only six years old, had come to take the boy from Tristan's and Alok's house to be raised in the Kallimun school. As the Kallimun say, 'Give us the child, and we shall give you the man.'

But Alok had not wanted to give away his youngest brother. Perhaps he feared that the Red Priests would castrate him, as they often did with boys so that they might more beautifully sing the praises of Angra Mainyu and Morjin. Perhaps he dreaded even darker things. Clearly, though, he had not believed Ra Sadun's assertion that the abduction of his youngest brother was a mercy, the only way to save the boy. And so he had hammered his fist into Ra Sadun's nose, drawing blood. After Ra Sadun had gone away to summon the soldiers, Tristan took up a carving knife and killed Alok. The dishonor that Alok had brought upon their family, Tristan claimed, was too great for him to bear. Alok's blood, he told everyone, would wash it clean. But many of the townfolk of Yosun believed that Tristan had stabbed Alok to *save* him from the terrible punishment of crucifixion. Ra Sadun must have believed this, too, for he had ordered the soldiers to seize Tristan and crucify him in his brother's place.

'The Dragon is not to be cheated,' the wheelwright told me. He was an old whitebeard whose hands seemed as hard as the wooden spokes he worked. He waved one of them at Tristan, fastened to the cross above the square. 'If you ask me, though, Tristan *did* kill Alok out of honor. He loved his brother, yes, but I say he loved his family's honor even more. And who could suffer anyone to live who had struck a priest?'

Slayings of honor, of course, had a long tradition in the Haraland. Nobles fought duels over real or imagined insults; men murdered the prurient for staring too boldly at their wives; brothers put to death their own sisters for adultery and other lasciviousness that mocked marriage and brought shame upon their families.

The wheelwright gazed up at the dying man with a whitish rheum filling his eyes. He said to me, 'There was a time when the Red Priests would have praised Tristan for what he did. Now they put him on a cross.'

The whole spirit of the Way of the Dragon, as I understood it, was that people were supposed to divine Morjin's will, make it their own and carry it out in their hearts and deeds. But this will could prove difficult to perceive, for it always changed.

'I think it's Arch Uttam,' the wheelwright said to me. This was not the first time I had heard the name of Hesperu's High Priest. 'They say the Kallimun will no longer tolerate honor killings of any sort. All right, I say, all honor to Lord Morjin, and who is anyone to assert his own honor against what's best for the realm? But sometimes it's hard to *know* what's best. I don't understand why the priests don't make things more clear. I don't understand why King Arsu doesn't *make* them make things more clear. It's enough to drive a man mad. I'm not complaining, of course, but I just wish I could get through one day without worrying I've made some error I didn't even know *was* an error. I suppose Arch Uttam just wants to bring order to the Haraland, as does everyone. They say Lord Morjin will visit here soon, and so it won't do for him to have to see men going around murdering their own brothers.'

It astonished me that the wheelwright bore no mark of brandings anywhere that I could see, for it seemed that the looseness of his lips would long since have tripped him up into making an Error Major. I took advantage of his loquaciousness to ask if he had ever heard of a place called Jhamrul; he hadn't. When I brought up the matter of miraculous healings, as slyly as I could, he seemed to remember that he was talking to a strange player in a public square at a crucifixion, and not holding forth over a mug of beer in his home. And so he gave me a response that I had grown well-tired of: 'They say the only true restoration lies in the hands of the Maitreya. Of course, I don't know if even Lord Morjin could restore poor Tristan now.'

In truth, no one or nothing could, for Tristan's head suddenly dropped down upon his chest as his strength gave out and he died. I felt it, like a hole opening inside myself through which an icy black wind blew. A terrible thought came to me then: what if we had come here too late and Tristan had been the one whom we sought? But how could that be, I wondered? Tristan was a murderer of men, even as I was myself.

After that they cut down the body for burial, and we prepared to leave. But the wheelwright, who knew Tristan's mother, implored me to give a show so that we might cheer the poor woman. I did not think that anything in the world could help her just then, for she bent over weeping uncontrollably as she wrapped Tristan's body in a white linen. She reminded me of my own mother, not in appearance, for she was short and stout, but in the depth of love that poured out of her.

In the end, I agreed to the wheelwright's request, although I doubted if any of the townsfolk would want to see a show that day. But the people of Yosun surprised me. Later that afternoon, after the burial, my friends and I donned our costumes and set up in the town square. More people packed into it than had been present at the crucifixion. It was as if they desired any song, story or spectacle that might drive the sight of Tristan from their minds. Tristan's mother, whose name was Uja, stood closest to the circle that we had marked off with a painted rope. It seemed almost profane to perform on ground still stained with Tristan's blood.

But perform we did. Kane brought out his colored balls, and hurled them high into the air. When he had finished juggling, he took off his shirt and stood half naked before the crowd. So perfect was he in the proportions of his limbs and body that it wasn't readily obvious what a large man he really was. But now he displayed his great strength for all to behold. He brought out an iron chain, and invited the wheelwright and several other men from the audience to test it and wrap it around his mighty chest, locking it tightly. Then, with a huge and quick inbreath of air, his chest swelled out like a bellows, snapping the chain with a sharp crack of iron, to the delight of the crowd.

After that Maram came out and clowned around, pretending to try to break this selfsame chain with heavings of his belly. Failing this feat, he gave up in order to ogle Yosun's most beautiful women. When Yosun's fathers and brothers grew uneasy with his attentions, Maram seemed to remember his restraint, and used the chain as a reminder, wrapping it around his loins. A moment later, however, he fell back into lust, and thrust out his hips toward the crowd as he stepped forward with a leer lighting up his face, only to be jerked up short by his pulling on the chain. I thought his act too lewd for the severe Haralanders, and I feared that one of the men might draw a sword and decapitate him, or worse. But again the townsfolk surprised me. They laughed heartily at Maram's antics. There was something curious, I thought, in the way that a fool could play to the heart of people's foibles and fears, and get away with things that no one else could.

Toward the end of our show, Estrella and I took up our flutes and Kane his mandolet, even as Liljana opened the painted door of our cart for Alphanderry to make a mysterious appearance. Maram announced that Thierraval was too shy to mingle with the crowd, but had consented to sing for everyone. The single song that Alphanderry gave to the people was sorrowful and yet full of brilliant hope, and made many of the men, women and children weep. After Alphanderry had finished and gone back inside the cart – and Atara began telling fortunes while Liljana sold potions – Tristan's mother came forward to thank us. She tried to give us a few coins for our efforts, but I told her that she should save them to buy candles to burn for her sons. Others, however, dropped into Maram's fool's cap many copper coins and even a few pieces of silver. They wished us well on our journey, and asked when we might return.

When Maram hefted the jingling silver in his cap, he looked at me and said, 'Well, we failed at being princes, but it seems we might have a future as players.'

In the days following that, after we had left Yosun miles behind us, we gave other performances in other towns. Liljana insisted that we needed the money to replenish our dwindling stores, if not our purse that we had emptied of gold in Nubur and Ramlan. But we had even deeper desires. We played, I thought, to encourage the nearly-enslaved Haralanders, and more, to inspirit ourselves. It was as if we needed to know there remained one small part of the world that we could still command and make beautiful.

The cross holding up Tristan was only the first of many that we passed by. We never became inured to their sight. The cruel wasting of so many lives cut at something sacred inside all of us, but seemed to wound Estrella the most deeply. Although she had borne the torments of the Red Desert, and much else, without complaint, I thought she might not be able to go on much longer. And then one day, on a rainy forest road outside of Lachun, we came upon a solitary cross. The very small body it bore was that of a child. We could not tell its sex, for the sun had baked its bloated flesh black, and the crows had long since gone to work on it, pecking the corpse nearly to the bone. We could find no one about to tell us what this child's error could possibly have been. After we had cut down the remains and buried them, Estrella stood weeping over the grave in her strange, silent way that was so much worse than another person's sobbing. Crucifixion, the Hesperuks say, is a mercy, for it gives the crucified nearly infinite time to go down into the soul and correct one's errors. It might truly have been a mercy, I thought, if Estrella had died at so young an age in Argattha so as to spare her the anguish that now tore through her like a torturer's skive opening up her insides. I felt her fighting this terrible pain with all her will and every breath; and more, she seemed to beat back in fury the black, bitter thing that had been working at her heart since our passage of the Skadarak. I wept with her because it seemed that in the end, evil must always win.

The following morning, however, the rain stopped and rays of brilliant sunshine drove down through the spaces between the clouds. Estrella insisted on leading us west, toward the Iona River. Whether the previous day's suffering had opened up some secret part of her or whether she merely followed her instinct, she could not tell us. But she led us straight to a town full of swordmakers and armorers. It was from a blacksmith there, in a seemingly chance conversation, that we learned of a village not very far away whose name was Jhamrul.

34

The place that we had been seeking for so many days lay fifty miles to the northwest, across the Iona River – and somewhere below the mountains, to the east of Ghurlan but west of the Rhul River. Although this fit Master Matai's prediction, Maram objected to our new course, saying, 'But what if we find nothing there? We can't just go tramping from town to town forever on the basis of some horoscope that *might*, or might not be, the Maitreya's! Every time I see a carpenter sawing out a beam of wood, I wonder if he's making it just for me.'

He complained further that first we would have to cross the Iona and the road that King Arsu and his army were coming down.

'That's true,' I told him. 'And so the sooner we set out, the better our chance of avoiding them.'

We turned our cart onto a dirt track leading to the city of Assul. There, if the blacksmith was right, we would find a road running east to west, over the Black Bridge spanning the Iona and then on to Ghurlan. Jhamrul lay just to the north of this road, in the hills some forty miles before Ghurlan – or so we hoped.

We all, I thought, chafed at the slowness of our pace, set by our cart's grinding wheels. We considered unhitching Altaru from the cart for a wild dash to Jhamrul, and then out of Hesperu altogether, but this seemed too great a risk. And so we worked our way to Assul, a neat, quiet, little city. The road that the blacksmith had told of proved to be a ribbon of broken paving stones and patches of mud. My father never would have tolerated such dilapidation of a major road, but then he had never imagined that rebellion might tear his kingdom apart. As we moved across the rich bottomland closer to the Iona River, we encountered gangs of corvée laborers hard at work repairing the road. They swung their

540

picks and lifted their shovels with a rare enthusiasm, as if taking great pride that they had been chosen to restore King Arsu's realm to greatness. One of these gangs struggled mightily, with ropes and teams of snorting mules, to erect a giant marble carving of Morjin off to the side of the road. I heard someone say that this statue would stand for ten thousand years; I prayed that it would sink into the soft, black loam as into quicksand, and vanish overnight into the bowels of the earth.

Other laborers, however, did not seem so happy. Close to the river, the Haralanders cultivated cotton and rice, and we passed swarms of men stripped nearly naked as sweat poured off their bodies and they bent down in the bog-like fields hoeing and pulling up weeds. Many were slaves, and quite a few of these had been brought down from Surrapam, branded and bound in chains. The hot Hesperu sun burnt their fair skins raw and bloody. More than a few serfs worked spreading dung in these fields, too. Their masters seemed to whip them as ferociously as they did their slaves.

It seemed to me that nearly everyone in Hesperu, from the lowliest gong farmer to the King, was a slave of some sort, for they all made obeisance to Morjin – and to each other. In Ramlan, I had heard a saying: 'Every man has a master.' It seemed a perfect expression of the degradation of people all through the Dragon Kingdoms. In this land of crosses and carvings of monsters, everyone in principle was bound to someone else. And now, according to King Arsu's edicts, many of them had to bow to a new class of masters. The Haralanders called them 'New Lords', and these were mostly common men such as the bookseller and cooper in Nubur who had enriched themselves on the dragongild, and with the Kallimun's blessing, purchased their titles from the King. It was one of these New Lords, a Lord Rodas, who stopped us on the rundown Ghurlan road just as we were about to cross the Black Bridge over the turbid waters of the Iona River.

Lord Rodas was a small, thin-faced man whose scraggly beard did not make up for his lack of chin. He wore silk pantaloons and a blue silk doublet embroidered with gold. The six hirelings accompanying him were richly attired in a purple and yellow livery, and they bore lances and swords but no armor. They waited on horseback as Lord Rodas positioned his gray gelding in the middle of the road, blocking our cart.

'Greetings, *my* good players,' he said to us.

As he informed us in a voice as smooth as safflower oil, all traveling troupes in the Haraland between the Iona River and the Rhul had come under his command.

'And it is my command,' he informed us, 'that you are *not* to cross this bridge until you've paid me a levy of forty silver ounces.'

I glanced at Kane, on top of the packhorse we had converted to a mount. His eyes were pools of fire. I did not think that either Lord Rodas or his six hirelings had any idea how close they were to death.

Despite Lord Rodas' weak appearance, he had a great strength of stubbornness, and Liljana was able to bargain him down only a little, to a squeeze of thirty silver pieces – the last of our money.

'I can only think,' he told us, 'that it will go harder for you in the west. There, Lord Olum has taken charge of all troupes. You'll only have to pay him another levy, and a stiffer one at that. Well, be on your way then, before I change my mind – the mercy of the Dragon be with you!'

He moved his horse aside and rudely waved us by. As we rolled past him, I overheard him complaining to one of his hirelings about this Lord Olum; it seemed that Lord Rodas and his men planned to intercept King Arsu and his army when they came down the Iona road so as to denounce Lord Olum for making the grave error of holding back the levies that he collected, and thus cheating the King.

On the other side of the river, on the road that led down from Avrian through Orun, we saw no sign of the King's vanguard, and we gave thanks for that. Neither Lord Olum nor anyone claiming to act in his stead stopped us to demand money, and we were grateful for that as well. Quickly, we made our way through rice bogs and cotton patches, which soon gave way to fields of millet and maize. The weather held clear, and we made a good distance that day, despite the potholes in the crumbling road.

For two days after that, we followed this road west toward Ghurlan. It climbed gradually up into a country of low hills covered with ginseng, chicory and poppies – and groves of almond trees and pecans. The air grew less close and humid, and slightly cooler. About thirty-five miles from the Iona, a farmer pointed us toward a dirt road cutting off north through these hills. He told us that if we drove our cart up the road for another five miles past Hagberry Hill, we would come to Jhamrul. His directions proved true, and we found the long-sought village nestled in a wooded notch.

There was little to it: some forty houses and other buildings surrounded by almond and pecan groves, and fields of red wheat growing on the hills' terraces. It seemed impossible that we could simply go down into this pretty place and ask after the Maitreya, but this is what we did. Or rather, we made our way into the village square, where we asked the blacksmith if Jhamrul had any healers who might be able to help us. The blacksmith directed us to the house of Jhamrul's only healer – indeed, the only healer for miles about, for apparently the nearby villages of Sojun, Eslu and Nur also sent their sick and injured to this renowned man. His name was Mangus, but it seemed that the village folk referred to him more reverentially as the Master.

We found his house to the north of the village on the side of a hill; it was built of good, gray granite instead of the mud bricks more common in Hesperuk constructions. As we rolled up the lane fronting the house, we saw an old woman, a slave, working in the herb garden to its side. On the other side, fig trees grew, while behind it, a dark-haired man stood in a pasture tending some goats. The house itself was a good size, with sweeping, red-tiled roofs covering its four sections. The front doors – wide enough to drive our cart through – stood open to reveal a courtyard with roses growing on white trellises and a mossy fountain at its center. Another old woman waited by these doors to greet us. She, however, could not be mistaken for a slave, for she wore a fine silk robe embroidered with flowers and a necklace of opals and black onyx. She gave her name as Zhor, and she told us that she was Mangus's wife.

I glanced at Master Juwain as I tried to hide my chagrin; unless Mangus had married forty years beyond his age, he could not be the one we sought. If Master Matai's astrological calculations proved true, the Maitreya would have been born, as I was, on the ninth of Triolet in the year 2792, and would therefore be only twenty-two years old.

Zhor invited us inside the atrium while a servant went to summon Mangus. With her own hand, she picked up a large urn and poured us glasses of lemon squash, sweetened with mint and honey. As we waited by the burbling water of the fountain, I noted a pedestal holding up a marble bust of Morjin. Its eyes stared upward; following their blind gaze I saw above the arch of the doorway behind us, almost too high to read, a gold-trimmed scroll listing in an elegant, red-inked script the steps that one must take to walk the Way of the Dragon:

RIGHT UNDERSTANDING
RIGHT THOUGHT
RIGHT SPEECH
RIGHT DEED
RIGHT REVERENCE
RIGHT SUBMISSION

As I was brooding over all the ways that Morjin had perverted what should have been noble virtues, in his *Darakul Elu* – and in pain and blood – the 'Master' came into the atrium. He glided toward us as if buoyed within an air of great dignity. His white hair hung in perfectly oiled curls about his shoulders. He wore a tunic of red silk and red pantaloons, and a longer outer robe of white cotton that draped down to his silver slippers. I noticed a few, faint pinkish stains that it seemed his servants had been unable to wash out of it. His cleanly shaved, stern face, which shone with kindness and concern, reminded me of my grandfather's. As well, I liked his eyes, which shone with kindness and concern. But his eyes held the same cloud of suspicion that I had seen too often since we had come into Hesperu.

We made our presentations, and told him of our concern for Atara's blindness and the wound on Maram's chest that would not be healed; we paid him what little silver we had gained in a performance on the road. Then he led Atara, Maram and me into a small room off the atrium. White tiles covered this chamber's floor and walls, and it smelled of mint and old herbs, as well as blood. Old blood stains, I saw, marred the grain of the wooden chair at the center of the room, as well as a table near one of the walls. Mangus invited Atara to sit down in the chair, while Maram pulled off his tunic and stretched out on the table.

When Mangus unwrapped the bandage from around Atara's face, I felt my heart beating more quickly to the rhythm of Mangus's pounding pulse. My throat burned as Mangus drew in a deep breath of air. For a moment, a surging hope built inside me. I wondered if Master Matai might have been wrong, and the one we sought was really an old man after all.

But Mangus only stared sadly at Atara and said to her, 'I'm sorry, Kalinda, but *I* cannot help you. I know of no one who can. Except, of course, the Maitreya. I have heard that Lord Morjin might be coming to Hesperu. Perhaps you should seek him out. If he were to lay his hands upon your face, to touch his fingers beneath your brows, then –'

'Thank you,' Atara said to Mangus as her whole body stiffened. The coldness that came into her nearly froze the blood in my heart. 'I had hoped that you might be able to heal me, but I thank you for your suggestion. If it is my fate, I shall certainly seek out the Red Dragon.'

Mangus sighed at Atara's obvious distress, and bowed his head to her. Then he sighed again before stepping over to Maram. It did not take him long to get Maram's bandage off and unpack the layers of cotton stuffed down into the single remaining wound in Maram's chest. Although he kept his face hard and expressionless, I felt his churning disgust at the sight of this raw, oozing opening that Jezi Yaga had torn into Maram. The bloody, stinking bandages he cast into a bronze basin. He rested his old hand on the other half of Maram's thickly-haired chest, and asked him, 'You say your horse bit you here nearly three months ago? Have you tried setting maggots to the wound?'

Maram's eyes rolled upward. He said, 'On the road some miles back we met, ah, a healer who advised me that maggots would clean the wound. The damn worms burned me sorely, but didn't help.'

Mangus smiled at Maram, then told him, 'Once, a soldier was brought to me – Sefu was his name. He had carried an arrowpoint in his lung for nearly three *years*. It was said that sixty-seven pots of pus had been drained from him. Although I was unable to draw the arrowpoint, I made a plaster for the wound. After a month, it began to close, and after two more, it healed successfully, though Sefu complained that he could still feel the arrow's steel when he breathed too deeply.'

At that point, I slipped these words out: 'We had heard that you cured a girl of an incurable wasting disease.'

Something moved inside of Mangus as if he had swallowed a live worm. His sad smile, I thought, hid a great deal. He gazed out the window at the pasture; he seemed deep in contemplation. Then he walked over to the open window, cupped his hands around his mouth and cried out, 'Bemossed! I have need of you!'

He turned back toward us. He glanced at Maram and said, 'I must be alone with Garath now.'

A few moments later, as Atara and I were making our way toward the door, a young man rushed into the room. The looseness of his rough wool tunic did little to conceal his slender, sun-browned limbs and what appeared to be whip scars seaming the flesh of his upper back around his neck. He was tall, for a Hesperuk, and comely, with rather soft features and a gentle-looking face. A black cross had been tattooed into his forehead above the space between his eyes. His eyes, I noticed, were of a deep umber color and as large and luminous as any eyes I had ever seen.

'Bemossed,' Mangus commanded his slave. He pointed at the foul bandages in the basin. 'Dispose of these. Then go out to the pasture and kill me a goat, that we might make sacrifice.'

Bemossed bowed to Mangus, and picked up the basin. He exited the chamber without a glance at anyone. We left Maram to Mangus's dubious ministrations, then followed Bemossed into the atrium, where we waited as he left the house by way of the rear door. A short while later, the scream of a goat broke the atrium's peace. Not even the tinkling fountain could drown out this terrible sound.

Mangus's wife poured us more of our lemony refreshment, but I could not bring myself to drink it. She told us that she had other duties to attend to, and excused herself, leaving us to ourselves. I waited, staring at the bust of Morjin as I wondered why Mangus had needed to be alone with Maram. Soon Bemossed returned, bearing a large bronze urn. Its contents sloshed against its sides as he moved through the atrium, and I smelled fresh blood. Then he went into his master's healing chamber, and shut the door behind him.

The tang of the lemons wafting into the air nearly sickened me. I looked over the rim of my glass at Liljana and Master Juwain, who were staring at Estrella. She sat on a stone bench near the fountain gazing with great intensity at the chamber's closed door. Her dark, liquid eyes rippled with little lights like quicksilver. Then her face came alive with a burning radiance as if a bolt of lightning had split the air above her. She jumped up from her bench. She looked at Daj as her fingers began fluttering as quickly as a hummingbird's wings. She looked at me. She fairly danced over to me, and took hold of my hand, gently pulling at me. Again, she stared at the closed door to the chamber into which Bemossed had disappeared. I almost couldn't bear the bright bursts of blood I felt pulsing out of her racing heart. I couldn't bear the brightness of her eyes, for in these twin pools of delight, I saw all her wonder and burning hope for the slave called Bemossed.

'He?' I said to Estrella. 'This one – are you sure?'

Estrella smiled, all warm and brilliant like the sun, and she quickly nodded her head. A dying scryer had once told me that she would show me the Maitreya; now that the moment had finally come, I almost couldn't believe it.

'So,' Kane said, coming over to lay his hand on Estrella's head. 'So.'

Master Juwain muttered something about wanting to know the day and hour of Bemossed's birth, while Atara stood icily still within a strange silence. Daj said, 'But he *looks* just like everyone else! What should we do now?'

His question, I thought, was very much to the point. There seemed nothing to do but wait, and so wait we did. I listened to the water splashing in the fountain drop by drop, and felt Estrella's hand gripping mine excitedly as a new life coursed through her veins. Kane's unfathomable eyes fixed on the door. If a dragon had burst into the atrium just then, Kane would have tried to fight it back with his bare hands. And yet I felt a deep doubt eating at him, too.

At last the door opened, and Mangus came out, followed by Maram and Bemossed. My eyes quickly took in Bemossed's curly black hair and neatly trimmed beard. He bore the same bronze basin, now full of more wads of stained cotton and blood. His motions were light and quick, yet sure, and he hastened out of the atrium as he had before. I wanted to stop and question him, but there seemed no way to do this gracefully.

Mangus cast no more light on the mystery of this man. All he said to us was: 'Garath's plaster will need to be changed tomorrow. And on the day following. After that, you may be on your way, wherever you are bound.'

He bowed to us, and then showed us to the front door. We left his house as we had come, driving the cart down the lane that led back to the village. When we had gone half a mile, I stopped the cart by a pasture full of sheep and looked at Maram. He sat on his horse, with his hand lightly pressed to his chest.

'Tell me what happened to you!' I said to him.

'Tell *you*?' he said. His gaze fell upon Estrella, who sat with me on the seat of the cart. 'Tell *me*! You all look as if you ate morning glory seeds and stared too long at the sun.'

I explained to him that our quest might very well have come to an end. And then he recounted what had happened in the closed chamber with Mangus and Bemossed: 'I couldn't see very much because Mangus covered my face with a cloth: it was of silk, thick and yellow and emblazoned with a Red Dragon. And fairly soaked in some perfume. Strange, I thought, very strange. But Mangus told me that I should meditate beneath the Dragon's protection. Meditate! He told me that he must wash my wound

547

with medicines. The cloth, he said, would protect me from their stench. It helped, I suppose, but only a little. I don't know *what* that damned quack packed the poultice with. But I smelled spirits and peppermint oil, and sandalwood, too, I think. And something *really* foul. And – I'm loathe to believe this, Val – that stinking goat's blood.'

Maram pushed his hand down beneath the collar of his tunic as if intending to rip off the bandages bound to his chest. But Master Juwain nudged his horse up close to Maram and said, 'No, leave it be. Let us wait a few days to see if the poultice actually helps. Perhaps Mangus is not as much of a quack as you fear.'

'But what would he want with an animal's *blood*?'

I turned to open the cart's front door, behind my seat. After looking about at the nearby houses and pasture to see if anyone might be watching us, I pulled out my scabbarded sword. I drew Alkaladur, then pointed it back up the hill toward Mangus's house. The blade flared a soft glorre.

'The blood was used to purify,' I said with a sudden sureness.

'To purify *me*?' Maram said, shuddering.

'No,' I told him. 'Don't you remember Argattha? I heard one of the priests there speak of sacrificing virgins . . . for their blood. Blood washes clean, as the Kallimun says, yes? But I don't suppose Mangus finds virgins so easy to come by, and so he has to slay innocent goats instead.'

Maram's hand worked beneath his tunic as the light of understanding filled his eyes. 'That slave, then? The one Estrella believes to be the –'

'He *is* the Maitreya,' I said softly. 'He must be.'

'But, Val, the mark – the black cross! How could fate be so cruel as to make the Maitreya a damned Hajarim?'

I smiled grimly as I sheathed my sword. The Hajarim of Hesperu and the other Dragon Kingdoms, I thought, *were* truly damned, for no other orders of humanity – not even murderers or slaves taken in war – were treated so vilely. Most people loathed them as they did blowflies. Hajarim were born of Hajarim, and so it had been for ages, far back into the mists of time. No one knew their origins. But too many agreed that the Hajarim must perform the lowliest and most hated of tasks: gong farming and cleaning stables and streets; slaughtering animals, butchering their meat and tanning their hides. The Hajarim handled the dead. Not all the Hajarim were slaves, and not all slaves were Hajarim, particularly in Hesperu, with so many ships packed with men arriving from

Surrapam. Slave or free, however, whatever 'free' still meant, the Hajarim were forbidden even to brush against the garments of others or let their exhalations fall too near their faces. Above all, they must never touch their hands to another's person.

'That slave *did* touch me,' Maram said. 'At least, I think he did. Someone laid a hand upon my wound – it didn't *feel* like an old man's hand.'

His great body shuddered, and he turned to look back up at Mangus's house.

'You, too, then?' I asked him. 'Everyone here hates the Hajarim.'

Maram's face soured as he said, 'It doesn't bother me that Bemossed is Hajarim. But that he washed his hands in blood before laying them upon me – *that* vexes me sorely.'

'But how else to clean,' Atara asked him, 'the uncleanable?'

I thought of the black cross that blighted Bemossed's forehead; all Hajarim babies were marked thus at birth, an ineradicable sign of their error in even being born.

'I don't think we should concern ourselves with the rites of these Hesperuks,' Master Juwain said. 'No blood, a goat's or a virgin's, is going to do very much toward healing Maram's wound. But the Maitreya might. Let us see if we can find out more about this Bemossed.'

Toward this end, we returned to the village and set up in the square for a show. We waited some hours for the word of our performance to spread to the outlying farms, and even to the nearby village of Nur. At dusk, with many curious people packing the square, we donned our costumes as we had a dozen times before. Kane broke his chain, and Alphanderry sang. Atara told several young women that they would find love and happiness. And Maram made the women, men and children laugh. Afterwards, a fletcher and a barber vied for the dubious honor of sharing conversation and spirits with Garath the Fool. Maram matched these men in a drinkfest, one cup of brandy following another until tongues loosened and words began to flow. But Maram, being Maram, kept his wits about him while the two men spoke much more freely than they should have. It was nearly midnight when Maram staggered back to where we had made camp in a fallow wheatfield at the edge of the village. Despite the late hour, we gathered around a little fire to sip some tea and compare stories.

'Ah, perhaps Bemossed *is* the one we've been seeking,' Maram said to us. He belched up a burble of brandy. 'The very, very one.'

From what Maram had learned from his inebriated new friends, and Atara during her fortune telling – and the rest of us in various conversations with seamstresses, cobblers and the like – we pieced together a little about Bemossed: He had been born in the north near Avrian, and separated from his parents at an early age. After being sold and resold numerous times, he had finally run away from a cruel master, a leather-seller named Chadu. But Chadu had recaptured him, and despite custom, had whipped him, nearly stripping the meat from his bones. After that, Bemossed would not do any work for Chadu, refusing even to lift a broom to sweep the floors of Chadu's house. Chadu threatened to strangle him, but Bemossed told him that he would not carry out any more of Chadu's commands. And so in disgust, Chadu had journeyed to Jhamrul, where he had heard that a healer had need of a Hajarim to dispose of bandages, amputated limbs and perform other filthy tasks. And so, seven years previously, Mangus had bought Bemossed and put him to work.

'I heard,' Atara said, 'that a great lord brought his dying daughter here. That the girl was coughing out her lungs with consumption. I don't think Mangus could have cured that with his medicines. Perhaps Bemossed –'

'The barber also told me of that lord and his child,' Maram said, interrupting her. 'Apparently, the lord wouldn't leave her alone with an old man and a Hajarim. So he must have *seen* Bemossed laying his hands upon her. But no one speaks of it openly.'

Bemossed's talent for healing, it seemed, was a secret that was no real secret.

'But they *do* speak of it,' Maram said. 'They call *Mangus* "The Master", but they know the truth. And it can't be long, I think, before others outside the village will know, too. The barber told me that only a few months ago, the Kallimun sent a man down from Kharun to question Mangus. I'm sure that damn priest went away with his purse full of gold – they say that no one is more faithful in paying the weregild than Mangus.'

I laid my hand on Maram's shoulder. 'I can only hope that the villagers will come to speak of how Mangus healed Garath the Fool. Is your wound any better?'

'*All* of my wounds, inside and out, are better when I've had a little drink,' Maram said, rubbing his chest. 'Who needs the Maitreya when you have brandy, eh? But no, it's not *really* better – not as when Master Juwain healed Atara with his crystal.'

Master Juwain sat holding his mug of tea in both hands; he had long since put away his emerald varistei – I hoped not forever.

'I can only pray your wound will heal now, too,' Master Juwain said to Maram. 'But if it doesn't, that is no proof that Bemossed is not the Maitreya. As we say: "Absence of evidence is not evidence of absence."'

I thought about all that had befallen since I had mistakenly claimed to be who I could never be. Then I said, 'Proof that he is not the Maitreya might be neither pleasant nor easy to come by.'

'I'm more interested in proof that he *is* the Maitreya,' Master Juwain said. 'Or at least good evidence.'

At this, I looked at Estrella, and so did Kane and Maram. She sat gazing at the fire as if she hadn't heard a word we had spoken. Her face fairly gleamed with a deep and splendid light.

'What better evidence than *that*?' I asked Master Juwain.

'Perhaps no *better* evidence,' Master Juwain admitted as he looked at her. 'But I should like some *objective* evidence.'

I nodded my head at this. Once, I had been wrong in this matter, and must never be again.

'If only,' Master Juwain said, 'we could discover exactly where Bemossed was born, and when.'

I thought about this too, and then I said, 'I doubt if any of the villagers can tell us that. But Bemossed himself might know. Why don't I try to talk to him tomorrow?'

'Ah, and what then?' Maram asked. 'Suppose that he confirms Master Matai's calculations, down to the minute of his birth? What shall we do then?'

I gazed at the orange flames of the fire, and I said, 'Everyone wants to join a traveling troupe, yes? Why don't we invite Bemossed to run off with us?'

We went to bed after that, but I couldn't sleep. I kept going over in my mind all that I wanted to ask Bemossed, and more, all that my heart most deeply desired from him. Could he *truly* be the one we sought, I wondered? For more than a year, I had schemed and fought to reach this place, but never with a very good idea of what might happen next. My last thought before trying to meditate was that we had met the Maitreya – perhaps – and now we must keep him from the Kallimun and Morjin.

35

In the morning, I took up my flute and went for a hike in the hills above the village. As I had hoped, I found Bemossed tending his goats in the meadow not very far from Mangus's house. He sat on a large rock, and appeared to be watching the sun pouring off the petals of some pink and white wildflowers – I did not know their names. The grass here grew a lighter green than that of Mesh, and seemed strange to me, too, as did Bemossed himself. When I drew within a few yards of him, he leaped up from his rock and turned toward me. He called out, 'Master Musician! I did not hear you approaching me.'

I sat down on the grass across from the rock, and invited him to sit back down, too. I smiled and said, 'Why don't you call me Arajun?'

'All right – Master Arajun, then. Where is Garath? Is it time to change his dressing?'

I looked down the hill toward the field where we had stopped our cart. I said, 'He'll be along in a while. I wanted to take a walk before the sun grew too high.'

Bemossed nodded his head at this. He pointed at my flute and said, 'To walk and play to the birds? I heard you last night in the square, playing to the people.'

'You did? I didn't see you there.'

'I stood near the almond trees.'

'So far away? But you couldn't have heard very much.'

'I couldn't come any closer.' He shrugged his shoulders and said simply, 'I am Hajarim.'

I sat looking at his finely-made head, his deep eyes and long eyelashes. His hands, long and expressive, moved while he spoke as if to music. In manner, he seemed thoughtful and polite. I felt that he had a keen sense of himself that he tried to keep hidden from others. But a certain grace and natural nobility shone out from within him, even so. Except for the black cross tattooed into his skin, it would have been impossible to guess at his lowly birth.

'My companions and I,' I told him, 'have journeyed to many kingdoms. In other places, there are no Hajarim, nor slaves either.'

'No Hajarim?' he said, touching the mark on his forehead. 'No slaves? But what lands are these?'

'The Free Kingdoms, in the north.'

'Do you mean, the Dark Lands? It is said that men mate with animals there, and eat their own dead.'

'Do you believe that?'

Bemossed hesitated as he dared a deep look at me. I felt within him a bright, burning awareness and an incredibly strong will toward the truth. But other things dwelled there, too, and he quickly broke off the meeting of our eyes. And he stammered out, 'It . . . is said.'

He gazed at the dozen goats spread out below us tearing up the grass. I could sense him choosing his words with great care. In Hesperu, speaking bluntly could earn a visit from the Crucifiers and a tearing out of the tongue with hot pincers so that one would never speak the wrong words again.

'It is a lovely day,' he finally said. He looked farther up the pasture at a grove of cherry trees where a pair of bluebirds sat on a branch singing. 'It will rain this afternoon, though, I think.'

'Bemossed,' I murmured into the soft breeze.

This young man who seemed of an age with me forced himself to look at me again, and this time he held the gaze. His eyes shone warm and sweet, and seemed inextinguishable. Something incredibly bright there burned into me like lightning. I felt him trying to turn away from this thing, but one might as well try to keep the earth from turning and stop the rising of the sun. I had a strange sense that he knew exactly what I was about, and wanted to trust me, as I did him.

'Yes, Master Musician?' he said to me.

I held my flute up to the sun's onstreaming rays. I said, 'I can play a few melodies, but I'm hardly a master.'

'All free men are masters to such as I.'

'I'm hardly free,' I told him. The memory of my family's slaughter, I knew, bound me in a dark prison as surely as any chain. 'Who is free any more? It is said that a Lord Olum is now master of all traveling troupes, and others as well.'

Bemossed looked at a hawk soaring high on the wind above us. He said, 'The birds are free. People's hearts are free.'

This, I thought, was a dangerous half-quote from the *Darakul Elu*: there, it was written that people's hearts were free when they beat in time to the heart of the Red Dragon.

'A man should always follow his own heart,' I said to him.

'I heard you following yours last night. In your music. The way you played. I heard such a longing for freedom.'

Bemossed dared a great deal in what he said to me and the way that he said it. He didn't appear to mind. There was steel inside him, and more, something as brilliant and adamantine as diamond. It was as if he had long since willed himself to act with little concern for what might befall himself. His courage shone out like that of my brothers.

'You must know what it is like to long for freedom,' I told him. 'They say you ran away from your master when you were younger.'

'Chedu,' he said, rubbing at the scars on the back of his neck. A darkness fell over his face like a dust-cloud covering the sun. 'He made me do . . . evil things.'

'But you do not complain that he did evil things to you?'

He shrugged his shoulders again. His gaze took in the white flowers nearby, Mangus's house and the village below us, and the hills and sky beyond that. Something inside him flowed all golden like melting honey. Life, I thought, had treated him cruelly, and yet he seemed to have great affection for every part of the world that he beheld or contemplated – almost every part.

'Chedu,' he said again, 'wanted me to flay a piglet alive. So that he could sell a living skin to rejuvenate the flesh of a great lord, he told me. But I knew he really wanted to grieve me by making me torture a helpless animal, and so I couldn't. After that, I kept thinking about flaying *Chedu*. So I ran away.'

'And when he recaptured you, it's said, you refused to obey him.'

'I would rather have died.'

'And so he whipped you – nearly to death?'

Bemossed smiled sadly as he said, 'With a Dragon's Scourge. Have you seen one at work? The Crucifiers tie bits of steel to thongs, and call them the Dragon's Teeth. Chedu wanted to use it to strip the skin off me.'

'What stopped him, then?'

'The Crucifiers did. A priest, Ra Amru, came along in time to save me.' Now Bemossed's smile grew bright with irony. 'You see, he reminded Chedu that I was Hajarim.'

The blood of the Hajarim, I remembered, was thought to be so unclean that even the priests of the Kallimun were forbidden to spill it. And so Hajarim were usually burnt or racked in correction for their errors, or if condemned to death, strangled. The black cross signified that, like animals, the Hajarim weren't even worthy of being crucified.

I said to Bemossed, 'You had other masters before Chedu, yes?'

He nodded his head. 'Chedu was the worst of them, but not the first.'

'And who would that be?'

'Lord Kullian. My father served him, and I was born on his estate.'

The story that Bemossed now told me made me grit my teeth against all the madness and hurts of the world. It seemed that for the first years of his childhood, Bemossed had lived quietly with both his father and mother, in the expectation that he would learn his father's trade of butchering. But then, in one of the wars of the north, Lord Kullian had joined a rebellion against the young King Arsu. King Arsu's soldiers finally came to kill Lord Kullian and confiscate his lands. Bemossed's father died trying to protect Lord Kullian, and Bemossed's mother suffered a broken mouth trying to protect Bemossed. The blood from this wound had defiled the cut fist of one of the soldiers, and his captain immediately ordered Bemossed's mother to be buried alive. Bemossed himself they made to help dig the grave. After that, he was sold as a gong farmer cleaning out the latrines of local notables. And then resold to a succession of masters, ending with Chedu and Mangus.

I did not know what to say upon hearing of these terrible things. And so I forced out, 'That is war.'

Bemossed shrugged his shoulders. 'Others have suffered much worse than I.'

I thought of King Arsu's present campaign, and the thousand men he had mounted on crosses. I looked at Bemossed. 'You say you were born near Avrian?'

'I think so. I think I was three or four when they killed my parents.'

'And how old are you now?'

'Twenty-two, I think. Perhaps twenty-three.'

'You don't know? Didn't anyone ever tell you the date of your birth?'

'No – why should they have?'

The sun falling on his face seemed to bring out much of his

essence, and I saw him as many things at once: sad, compassionate, strong, innocent and wise. I thought he lived too close to the dark, turbid currents of the unknown self that flowed inside of everyone. And yet I felt a wild joy of life surging there, too. And so I said to him, 'Most people celebrate the day they were born.'

'Most free people, perhaps.'

I watched as he rose up off his rock and went over to scratch beneath the jaw of one of the goats. I could not imagine him ever using a sharp knife to slit this gentle animal's throat, and I said to him, 'Do you ever think about being free?'

He looked up at the hawk still circling on the morning's rising wind. I felt him building inside himself a wall of stone to keep his storming passions within – even as I tried to keep those of others without. Then he said a strange thing: 'Does a bird think of flying beyond the sky?'

I caught his gaze and said, 'You hate your service with Mangus, don't you?'

'But why would you think that?'

'Because I know about hate,' I told him.

A gentleness came into him as he looked at me. 'I think you do, Master Arajun. And I think you speak about things that it is best not to speak about.'

'Then let us not speak but act,' I said to him. 'Tomorrow, after Mangus changes Garath's dressing, we shall leave Jhamrul. We have need of a healer – why don't you come with us?'

His eyes grew restless and bright. He called out softly, 'A healer, you say? But I am Hajarim!'

'Truly, you are. But you must know what the people of your village say about you.'

'They do not understand.'

'With some power you were born with,' I said to him, 'with some virtue that runs like fire along your blood, you lay your hands on others, and they are healed.'

He lifted his hand away from the goat's throat and looked at it. 'You . . . do not understand. I can do nothing to heal anyone. I'm only a slave.'

I wanted to tell him that he might heal the whole world. But old doubts tore into me, and terrible memories, too, and because I wasn't wholly open with him, he couldn't quite bring himself to trust me.

'Bemossed,' I said again, rising up off the grass.

Then I crossed over to him and took hold of his hand.

At the touching of my palm to his, he gasped in astonishment. His eyes went wide with horror, exaltation, delight and dread. I stared at him deeply, as he did me; it was like staring at the sun.

'You . . . do not know what you do,' he told me. He seemed to be searching for something in me as his hand gripped mine. I felt in him a vast, cold loneliness and a wild hope, too. 'What do you do?'

There was a moment. Something inside him seemed to pull me into a place of deep brilliance. I felt time slowing down as the whole world suddenly stopped. The trilled-out notes of the blue-birds hung like drops of silver in the air. The birds themselves brightened with an impossible blue, as if their feathers flamed with a lovely fire that didn't burn. Along the hills, the grasses and flowers shimmered green and pink and white. Everything – the meadow and the goats grazing upon it, the sun above and the earth beneath my feet and Bemossed's hand within mine – seemed to be made of a single substance that kept pouring itself out in a blaze of light. In this splendid land we dwelled nearly forever. But then some fearful thing buried in Bemossed's heart, or perhaps within mine, darkened the meadow and drove us back into the world. I saw that the goats were just goats, the grass was only grass, and the sky shone no bluer than it ever did. And Bemossed was only a man, even as I was.

He looked at our clasped hands, and I thought that in his whole life since his parents' deaths, no one had ever willingly touched him. He said to me, 'What do you want?'

'You don't have to remain a slave,' I told him. 'Come away with us, and we'll leave Hesperu.'

'To go to the Dark Lands?'

'The only darkness in any land,' I said, 'is what men have brought into it.'

'And what have you brought into the world . . . Arajun?'

I knew that I could lie to him, in my words, but not in the light of my eyes. His hold on my hand suddenly tightened. I had spent too many hours of my life gripping a sword, and so I was stronger than he in my sinews and bones. But his will beat at mine with all the fire of the desert sun. I could keep no secret from him. He must have sensed the hatred poisoning me, and more, that I was a slayer of men, for he let go of my hand as he might a heated iron. I stood staring at him in shame. The day before he had washed in the gore of a goat, and yet it was I who had blood upon my hands.

'Come with us,' I said again. 'My friends all agree that you would be a welcome addition to our troupe.'

I felt him wanting to leap toward this offer as a starving wolf toward meat. But something stopped him up short.

'No,' he said, 'I would only be caught, and this time I *would* be strangled.'

I did not, at that moment, sense in him any fear of death. But something else grieved him terribly, some dark thing that I could not see.

'You *won't* be caught,' I told him. 'We'll protect you.'

'But how can anyone protect me?'

'We won't let anyone take you.'

He looked down the hill at where the bright colors of our cart blazed in the distance. 'You have *weapons* hidden away, don't you? You, and the strongman, Taras?'

I remained silent as I gazed into the luminous centers of his eyes.

'You would kill, wouldn't you? Kill to keep your freedom?'

I said nothing to this accusation, and so said everything.

He looked at me with a terrible longing, as if that which he had sought his entire life lay just beyond his grasp. His voice grew sad almost beyond bearing as he told me, 'I'm sorry, but I can't go with you.'

'But don't you want to be *free*!' I cried out to him.

His eyes pulled away from mine, and seemed to drink in the cherries all red and ripe along the branches of the tree. The sky opened out into an infinite blueness beyond it. I felt him return to that shining place that was his secret home. This time, however, he could not take me with him.

'I am free right now,' he finally said to me. He looked back at me, and the burning in his eyes brought tears into mine. 'All men are free. They just don't know it.'

After that, he asked me to play a song on my flute, and this I did. There seemed nothing more to say. When I finished, I bade him farewell and walked back through the meadow's swishing grasses to the field where our cart stood. My friends immediately gathered around me.

'Well, what did you find out?' Maram asked me.

'Not as much as we hoped,' I admitted. I turned to Master Juwain and recounted much of what Bemossed had told me. Then I said, 'It would be nearly impossible to trace back Bemossed's owners to anyone who might have known about his birth. Probably anyone who *did* know was killed or sold off at the pillaging of Lord Kullian's estate.'

'But we can't be certain of that,' Master Juwain said to me.

'No, we can't. But we can't either go up around Avrian asking where Lord Kullian's old estate might lie and if anyone thereabouts remembers a slave boy named Bemossed.'

Master Juwain rubbed at this bald head, gleaming in the morning sunlight. His disappointment seemed as thick as the porridge that Liljana had prepared for breakfast.

'I'm sorry, sir,' I said to him. 'But likely we will never know the day of Bemossed's birth.'

'But Master Matai's horoscope –'

'Has led us this far,' I said. 'And we should be glad for that. For I'm nearly certain that Bemossed is the Maitreya.'

Kane held a jangling chain in his hands as he inspected its black iron for weak links. Then his black eyes fixed on me, and he said, 'But what of the signs, then, eh? Do you think you are able to tell? Does this goatherd look upon all with an equal eye?'

I thought of Chedu who had nearly skinned Bemossed alive, and I said, 'Nearly all.'

'Is his courage unshakeable?'

'He has little fear of death, I think.'

'But does he abide steadily in the One?'

I drew in a long breath as I looked up the green hills above us. I said, 'He *could* abide there – I'm certain he could.'

At this, Master Juwain's lips tightened as if he had sucked on a sour cherry. 'But did he give any other sign, in his words or manner, that he might be the Maitreya?'

I smiled sadly as I said, 'He wouldn't even admit to being a healer.'

Master Juwain sighed at this and said, 'I was afraid it might be thus. Do you remember the verse, Val?'

I nodded my head, then recited lines from an ancient verse that had once perplexed me and led me to make the greatest error of my life:

> *The Shining One*
> *In innocence sleeps*
> *Inside his heart*
> *Angel fire sleeps*
> *And when he wakes*
> *The fire leaps.*

About the Maitreya
One thing is known:
That to himself
He always is known
When the moment comes
To claim the Lightstone.

'As it was thought with you,' Master Juwain said to me, 'Bemossed is young, and it may be that his time has not yet come to awaken. And so he may not know that he is the Maitreya. Unfortunately, we don't either.'

I stepped over the cart and drew forth my sword. When I pointed it up the hill toward Bemossed and his goats, its fiery light still ran with glorre. And I said to Master Juwain, 'But we *do* know . . . that he might be the Maitreya.'

'So might others be. Others with whom we could confirm their hour of birth. Perhaps we should still search for them.'

'Perhaps we should,' I said, 'but we must take Bemossed with us.'

'But how, Val?' Maram asked me. He jingled the bells of his fool's cap that he was playing with. 'You said yourself he refused to run off with us. We can't just throw a cloak over his head and abduct him, can we?'

'No, we can't,' I said. I looked at Estrella, whose deep, liquid eyes seemed to tell me that we were all being fools. 'But we might buy him.'

This suggestion seemed to shock Maram – and everyone else – as much as it did me. And Maram called out, 'What? What are you saying?'

'If the priests have been asking after him,' I said, 'he is in great danger here. It would be for the best.'

'But doesn't he hate emptying bloody basins for that damn Mangus?'

'He *does* hate his servitude, yes,' I said. 'But I think there is something he loves greater than his hate.'

'Ah, I don't understand. Do you mean, then, that we should buy him as our *slave*?'

'Only until we've left Hesperu. Only until he comes to trust us. Then we shall tell him all, and free him.'

It seemed a dark and desperate deed, but then we had reached the end of our quest to find ourselves in a dark and desperate place. None of us could think of a better plan. And so Liljana finally said, 'All right then, but please let me handle the negotiations.'

Later that morning we returned to Mangus's house, and Maram disappeared into Mangus's healing chamber to have his dressing changed. After Mangus had finished, he left Bemossed to clean up while he met with Kane, Liljana, Maram and me in the atrium. It was there, with flowers perfuming the air and water bubbling from the fountain, that Liljana proposed buying Bemossed.

'We're only poor players,' she told Mangus, 'but we could give you one of our horses for him.'

As she spoke, the sounds of Bemossed tidying up beyond the open door to the healing chamber suddenly quieted. And Mangus said, 'But what would I want with a horse? And why would you want to buy a Hajarim?'

He knew well enough the answer to his question. As Liljana started to say something about all the dirty tasks involved with a traveling troupe's constantly making and breaking camp, Mangus held up his hand to interrupt her.

'Mother Magda,' he intoned as his face fell stern, 'I know there is talk about Bemossed in the village. But it is only idle talk. The villagers are only simple folk, and know nothing of the art of healing.'

'Are you saying that Bemossed is of no help to you?'

Mangus ran a finger along one of his coils of white hair. He pulled at the cuff of his tunic. I sensed his great interest in dealing with Liljana. But it must have occurred to him that if he insisted that Bemossed was of little value, he could ask only a small price for him.

'Bemossed,' he said, 'is a *great* help to me. No one has ever kept our house so clean My wife and I are very fond of him.'

'But is he of no help in *healing*?'

Mangus looked at Maram and Kane, and then back at Liljana. 'I did not say that. He helps in ways that you wouldn't understand.'

'Is he a healer, then?'

'*Bemossed*?'

Liljana sidled over to Maram and grasped his arm. She said, 'Garath felt sure that Bemossed laid his hand upon him. The people of the village have told of such layings-on of hands as well.'

Mangus now ran his finger along the collar of his crimson tunic as if the atrium had suddenly grown too hot. He said, 'You should know that this is an unusual situation and that we have the sanction of the Kallimun. Before my slave touches anyone, he is purified.'

'Then he *is* a healer?'

'No, certainly not. He does help me, but only as a bandage draws out pus.'

'You were right,' Liljana said, 'I *don't* understand.'

Mangus drew himself up straight and with all his dignity told her, 'Festering sores such as Garath's are caused by demons attacking the body. Bemossed is one of the few born able to draw out these demons.'

'Into his *own* body?' Liljana asked.

Just then Bemossed came out of the chamber bearing a soiled basin. He did not look at me as he crossed the atrium then exited by way of the back door.

'He is Hajarim,' Mangus said, as if that explained everything. 'And so you must understand, as these demon-drawers are quite rare, that my slave is very precious to me.'

Indeed, he was. Although Liljana stood there haggling with Mangus for most of the next hour, she was able to whittle down the unbelievable price that Mangus asked for Bemossed only to a slightly less staggering sum:

Forty ounces of gold!

I cried out this number in the silence of my mind. Who had so much money? I thought that selling Bemossed might very well put an end to Mangus's life as a healer – which might be exactly what he wanted. Perhaps he intended to retire to a small estate by the sea or to flee Hesperu altogether.

Forty ounces of gold!

Liljana finally threw up her hands in disgust. She looked at me as apologizing for failing to move Mangus.

Then I reached into my pocket and drew forth a little bit of metal and stone that was more than precious to me. It was the ring of a Valari lord: heavy silver set with four large, brilliant diamonds. On the field of the Raaswash, in sight of the opposing armies of Ishka and Mesh, my father had put it on my finger to honor me for completing the quest to find the Lightstone. Since his death, however, I had not dared to wear it.

'This,' I said, showing Mangus the ring, 'is surely worth forty gold pieces.'

His eyes narrowed as he examined it. 'Even if the stones are real, what would I do with a diamond ring?'

Because my throat hurt and I could not speak just then, it

was Liljana who answered for me: 'You could sell it, if you wished.'

'*You* can sell it, if you wish,' he told her. 'I haven't the time, but in Kharun, which is only thirty miles up the road, there are jewelers and gem sellers. Why don't you return here when you have the sum that we've agreed upon?'

Although he smiled at us in a kindly way, his face returned to its usual stern lines, and he indicated that he would argue with us no further. We had no choice then but to return to our camp, and this we did.

'Forty ounces of gold!' I shouted as I stood by the fire that Daj tended. I held the ring in the flat of my hand as I stared at it. 'How can I trade this for gold? Am I a *diamond* seller?'

Diamond sellers were destitute warriors or knights who sold their rings against the law of all the Valari kingdoms, and so brought upon themselves and their families everlasting shame. The worst of thieves were those who waylaid traveling knights for the treasure that they wore or despoiled fallen warriors of their glittering armor, and these were counted as diamond sellers, too.

Kane came over to me and snatched the ring from my hand. His eyes flared with impatience but with compassion, too. He said to me, 'If you can't sell it, then I shall, eh? All right?'

I could not look at him as I nodded my head.

Atara, who sat by the fire as she repaired one of her arrows, said, 'The ring of a Valari lord might be recognized as such even in this land. I would hate for one of the jewelers here to give us away.'

'So,' Kane said, making a fist around the ring. 'Then I'll chisel the damn diamonds out of it.'

True to his word, he went off to break my ring apart. I could not bear the sound of his hammer beating against iron, and iron cutting open silver. After Kane had finished this evil work, he came over and said, 'Will you ride with me to Khaurn?'

'No,' I told him, 'you go with Liljana. It will be better if I remain here.'

I watched as Kane and Liljana saddled their horses. It seemed utterly mad to me that they were setting out with the diamonds of my ring to get gold to buy a slave.

They rode away after that. And so, at the edge of the peaceful village of Jhamrul, in a fallow field where voles burrowed and larks sang, we waited all that day and most of the next for them to return. We all gave thanks when we saw their horses cantering back up the lane. With the afternoon sun dropping toward the hills in the west, they dismounted and Liljana showed me a leather purse full of forty jangling gold coins.

'I've never haggled so hard,' she told me. 'I wanted sixty pieces, but with the sack of Avrian, diamonds are flooding the markets just now. I was lucky to get forty.'

'All right,' I said, 'then let us go back to Mangus and hope that he hasn't changed his mind.'

'If he has,' Kane growled out, gripping a knife beneath his cloak, 'we'll change it back for him.'

Mangus, however, proved true to his word. After we met once again in his atrium and gave him the gold, he counted out the coins, then said, 'I can't tell you how hard it is for me to sell my slave. But it is for the best.'

I thought that he might be speaking truly. I sensed in him a surprising fondness for Bemossed, and more, his fear for him, as if he dreaded that the Red Priests might return and take Bemossed away to a much worse fate than he would find with us.

He called Bemossed to him then. Bemossed came into the atrium bearing a tied-up cloth that contained his few possessions: a spare tunic, an owl's feather, an old tooth and the like – or so Mangus told us. Mangus prepared a paper attesting to Bemossed's sale. He invited his wife and the other slaves of his household to bid farewell to him. They all seemed sad to see him go, though I noted that none of them clasped his hand or embraced him.

'Perhaps your wanderings will bring you back here someday,' Mangus said to Bemossed. 'But wherever you go, may the grace of the Dragon go with you.'

As we made our way to the front door, the cold, dead eyes chiselled into the bust of Morjin seemed to watch our every movement. Bemossed walked like a condemned man, with his gaze cast down upon the ground. So it was that we made the Maitreya our slave.

36

It was too late in the day to break camp and resume our travel, and so we returned to our cart and settled in to enjoying the delicious dinner that Liljana prepared. She cooked us ham and maize-bread, green beans in butter and cucumbers sliced up in sour cream and mint. For dessert we had a rice pudding sweetened with honey, cloves and cinnamon. She determined to welcome Bemossed into our company with foods that might nourish his body, and a camaraderie of like souls. She amazed him by giving a piece of bread directly into his hand. He looked upon her, I sensed, as the mother whom he could hardly remember. It must have been hard for him to reconcile his obvious warm feelings toward her – and toward Maram, Atara, Estrella and Daj – with his bitterness at me for buying him and bearing him away against his will.

That evening, I borrowed Master Juwain's gelding and gave Bemossed his first riding lesson. As soon as we could, we would set out to recross the north of Hesperu, abandoning the cart when we reached the mountains. Bemossed would need to learn his way with horses. This, I saw, might prove no easy task. Although he had no trouble gentling the gelding with long strokes of his hand, he nearly refused to mount the beast. As he put it, 'How is it that men think that they can make slaves of a noble creature and compel him to bear a great weight upon his back?'

These were the greatest number of words that he had spoken to me since the morning in the meadow. After I compelled *him* to place his feet in the horse's stirrups, he spoke to me only a little and only at need, responding to my questions or commands with quick, quiet utterances. He never failed to be polite. A score of years as a slave had taught him the ways of respect, and it seemed to me that he used this acquiescent manner not so much to placate me as to pierce me with a spear of guilt over what I had done to him. That he already knew me so well chagrined me, even as it made me believe that he truly *was* the one whom we had sought for so long.

He did not, however, carry this revenge to my companions. Neither did he befriend them, at least not at first. In the morning, when we drove our cart out of Jhamrul back toward the Ghurlan Road, he sat beside Estrella on the seat with me in near silence. He seemed to listen to the thump of the horses' hooves and the grinding of the cart's wheels – and to Maram's booming voice as he held forth with Master Juwain and the others, riding ahead of us. Once, Liljana dropped back to ask Bemossed the name of some strange vegetables growing in a field off to the side of the road, and he chatted with her pleasantly enough. And, later that afternoon, Maram got him to laugh with a recitation of 'A Second Chakra Man'. Bemossed seemed to bear a great fondness for Maram, and asked him more than once if his wound might be getting better. I felt him, though, restraining his deeper affections, for Maram and the rest of us, as a man might clamp down his hand upon a cut vein. Beginning with his parents, I thought, he had lost too much in his life to want to risk losing more.

We made a good few miles that day beneath a clear, hot sky, covering nearly half the distance back toward Orun. Our plan was to recross the Iona River, and then to lose ourselves on forest roads and country lanes, cutting the Senta Road well to the north of Nubur, where we could hardly explain to Goro and Vasul how we had suspiciously transformed ourselves from pilgrims into a troupe of players. We said nothing of this plan to Bemossed. Given time, I was sure that we could win him to our purpose. But for now, as Liljana advised, he must get used to us, and we to him.

If he remained a mystery to us, then he must have found many things about us to be more than strange. He surely wondered why Kane insisted on surrounding our camp with a fence of old logs and brush, and more, that he remained awake all night, prowling about like a great cat listening to every sound in the woods around us. Master Juwain, in various conversations, betrayed his great erudition about a great number of things, including the healing arts. I could almost hear Bemossed asking himself how a reader of tarot cards and horoscopes had come by such knowledge. I think he puzzled as well over the obvious fact that Daj had been born of Hesperu. When Maram brought up the matter of the Avrian crucifixions, Daj turned toward the north and said, 'They always promised that if there was another rebellion, they would nail everyone up on crosses instead of selling them as slaves.'

Atara, I sensed, seemed a marvel to him – and possibly much more. After dinner that evening she asked him for help in changing her blindfold. He brought a pot of warm water to her, and cloth for bathing as well. In the light of an almost full moon, he watched as she sat on an old log and washed her face. The hideousness of her scarred eye hollows did not repel him; rather it aroused in him a blazing compassion. He could scarcely control the quavering of his voice as he said to her: 'Is it true that in being blinded you gained the second sight?'

'I gained *something*,' she said to him. 'At times, my sight is clearer, now.'

'But what do you *see*? I heard you telling fortunes in the square. You promised the widow, Luyu, that she would find happiness and love.'

'I said that she *could* find these things. There is always a way. Always a path.'

'Truly? And can you see this path when you look at someone?'
'Sometimes.'

'As you can see other paths, through meadows or woods? I've never heard of a blind woman who can see everything.'

'Not everything, Bemossed. I can't see you.'

This, I thought, should have given me great hope, for Atara had told us that the Maitreya always remained veiled in shadow to her, and so she could not describe the lineaments of his face.

'Here,' she said to him, 'come closer.'

She bade him to kneel down on the ground in front of the log, and he reluctantly did as she asked. Then she reached out toward him, fumbling through naked air until she found his face. She traced her fingers across his forehead and along the line of his curly black hair. She pressed lightly upon his closed eyelids, then touched his fine nose and flaring cheekbones. She let her palm rest upon his bearded jaw. She smiled, then told him, 'I think you must be as beautiful as Luyu said you were.'

Atara's words seemed to stun him. He gazed at her for a long moment before calling out softly, 'She said that . . . about a slave?'

'She has eyes,' Atara said sadly. 'She is a woman, and a widow at that.'

'Yes, but she should not even have been looking at a Hajarim.'
Atara smiled again and said, 'If I still had eyes, what would I

567

see when I looked at you? *Not* a Hajarim. There are no such ones in our company.'

And with that, she found his hand and took hold of it. She brought it up to her face. He needed only the slightest encouragement to touch the golden hair of her eyebrows and then let his fingertips come to rest in the empty spaces beneath. She sat on her log while he knelt before her, face to face, for what seemed almost forever. I heard their breaths rise and fall in perfect rhythm with each other. Then a deep desire that she usually kept hidden poured out of her like a stream of glowing white iron. I could not tell if it was longing or lust or love – or perhaps all three. I did not know if Bemossed could feel her burning passion for life as I did, like a white-hot sword thrust through my belly. He was like a man discovering a new land of beauty and wonder. He kept touching his fingertips to her eye hollows, oblivious of time, oblivious of me. I doubted if he purposed to inflame my jealousy; I doubted as well that he would have acted otherwise solely because it distressed me.

In truth, I sensed much in his encounter with Atara that distressed *him*. His fingers and hands began trembling, and he seemed barely able to contain his own blazing passions. If the sun shone all day and all night, I thought, it would incinerate everything that it touched. I felt him again clamping down on the desire that surged through him, this time closing off his heart. After resting his hand upon her cheek, he finally broke off touching her altogether. He wrapped a new blindfold for her, and tied it around her head. Then he went off to help Estrella comb the mud out of the horses' coats.

Later that night, before bed, I stood with Atara in the moonlight. As it had been for most of the miles since the Skadarak, she still seemed totally blind. I said to her, 'Maram's wound is no better – do *you* feel anything, where Bemossed touched you?'

She rested her fingers on her blindfold and laughed out, 'I think *you* feel something that you needn't. You've no cause for worry on this account.'

'I'm not worried,' I told her.

She reached out to grasp my hand as when I had first met her and we sat together beneath the stars. She said to me, 'Bemossed would be an easy man to love, I think, but never as I do you. He is like the brother I never had.'

She kissed me on the lips, lightly, and then went off to sleep inside the cart with Liljana and Estrella. I lay down by the fire, staring up for hours at the silver moon and the bright arrays of stars. A single question burned through my mind deep into my soul: Why did it seem to be Bemossed's fate to heal, in love and light, while mine drove me on to strike my sword into others and slay?

In the morning we set out again to the east. The road led slightly downhill, toward the low country around the Iona River. As I drove the cart, Bemossed sat on the seat opposite me, with Estrella in between. For hours, he said nothing. He tried not to look at Atara, riding along on her roan mare ahead of us, or at me. He stared out at the fields of cotton and the rice bogs, and the occasional stretches of forest, and I wondered if his service to various masters had ever taken him through this steamy country. I felt him brooding over matters that he would not speak of. I sensed in him an anguish of the soul which, strangely, he seemed to cherish and hold onto, as he did other dark moods and sensations. I thought he was too much at home inside himself with all the colors of his feelings: the blue of his awe and sorrow for the world; the violet of his unfulfilled desire; the red of his great anger toward me.

For most of his life, I thought, he had necessarily looked to himself alone for any succor or understanding. But with his touching of Atara, some deep drive to trust others seemed to open inside him. As the miles passed behind us that long, hot day, I sensed him finding a deep accord with Estrella, and she with him. He spoke to her of little things, which she smiled at or commented upon with a flutter of her fingers or an arching of her eyebrows. And she seemed to speak to him. And not just *to* him but *of* him: her lovely, open face shone as brightly as any mirror, reflecting the glories of his soul that she found within him. Without being conscious of this talent, I thought, she showed me Bemossed's kindness, his compassion, generosity, fire and an otherworldly grace.

But there were darker things, too: stubbornness, jealousy, and an excruciating sensitivity to other people and to the world. He carried deep in his eyes intimations of despair and doom. I sensed that he felt flawed in a fundamental way. Then, too, I think he feared the long, dark night of the spirit when he found himself cast out into the deadness of the world and could not find his way back to his secret land. It came to me, as I saw him touching his fingers to Estrella's throat and his eyes grew bright and fey, that he sought this abidance through healing. And at least a part of

569

this primeval urge to make things whole he directed at me. This amazed me: that despite his ire, despite his dread of my wrath and my fury for vengeance upon my enemies, he still wished to restore me to my best self and to bring out in me only the good, the beautiful and the true.

We made camp that night in a clearing in a wood to the south of the road not five miles from Orun. While Liljana and Estrella began preparing dinner, Kane galloped off to scout ahead and ensure that we might make the river crossing without running into King Arsu's army marching down the road from Avrian. He returned two hours later to a bowl of stew that Liljana had kept warm for him. Between bites of steaming okra, maize and beef, he told us, 'The army hasn't passed yet, but it's expected any day. We'll do well to be up early tomorrow and cross over the Black Bridge as soon as they open it for taking tolls.'

I might have hoped that Kane would join us in retiring early, taking a little rest, if not sleep. Instead, he set up on the side of the cart a painted wooden target. He took out the seven knives that he had ordered from the smith in Ramlan. They were each long and tapered to a fine point, perfectly balanced and razor-sharp. He stood on bracken-covered ground oblivious of the mosquitoes that came out and whined through the semi-darkness; he hurled his knives spinning through the air, trying to fit as many as he could into the small, white circle at the center of the target. The small moon above the trees cast but little light for him to make out the target's rings. How he worked such magic remained to me a mystery. Warriors of Mesh cast lances at targets, and used knives to cut meat or other men, but we rarely learned this art that Kane now displayed with such great determination and virtuosity.

Later, Liljana brewed up some tea for us, and for Kane, some thick Khevaju coffee which Bemossed brought to him steaming in his cup. Everyone except Kane retired soon after that. He took long slow sips of his dark drink in between his target practice. I tried to fall asleep to the thunk, thunk, thunk of steel driving into wood. In watching Kane all ashimmer in the moonlight, in looking over at Bemossed stretched out in a troubled stillness by the fire, I brooded over the mystery of men. Would the brilliance of our spirits someday lift us up toward the stars? Or would our inborn flaws drive deep through our hearts, dividing us against ourselves and letting in the darkness?

It was in that strange time between darkness and day that I

awoke to a sense that something was wrong. Mosquitoes whined about me without pity; frogs croaked from some water deeper in the woods. A faint light suffused the trees and undergrowth, while the fire had burnt out completely. I sat up to take stock of Master Juwain, Maram and Daj sleeping near me. Over by the fence surrounding our encampment, unbelievably, Kane seemed to be sleeping, too. But Bemossed was nowhere to be seen.

My first thought upon noting this shamed me: that he and Atara had stolen off into the woods together. My second thought frightened me, for I feared that Bemossed had run away. As quickly as I could, I stepped over to Kane and bent down to shake him awake. This proved harder than I would have supposed. When Kane finally opened his eyes in a burst of consciousness, though, he whipped himself into motion, sliding out a dagger and nearly disembowelling me before I moved aside and shouted at him: 'Kane! It is only me – Valashu!'

'Val!' he shouted back. 'Val – what happened?'

Our cries aroused our companions. Maram and Master Juwain came over to us in a hurry; a few moments later, the door to the cart opened, and Atara came out with her unstrung bow in her hand. She joined us by the fence, and so did Estrella and Liljana. Kane rubbed at his eyes and said, 'I don't know what happened.'

When I told of how I had found him, Maram upbraided Kane, saying, 'You fell asleep, *that's* what happened. You, the invincible Kane, the ever-watchful, the ever-waking: you finally closed your damn eyes like any other human being and –'

'So,' Kane growled out. He sliced his dagger in the air inches from Maram's throat as if to silence him. 'I never just *fall* asleep.'

Liljana noticed Kane's cup dropped down onto the forest floor near the fence. A residue of coffee stained its insides. She picked up the cup and sniffed at it. Then she said to Kane, 'I remember Bemossed bringing you your coffee. He must have slipped a soporific into it.'

'One of your sleeping potions, then? You should be more careful, Liljana.'

'*You* should be careful,' she told him. 'Of what you say. I've kept my medicines safe enough, and so has Master Juwain.'

She went on to say that she detected a faint, bittersweet odor of some botanical emanating from the cup, but it was neither that of mandrake or poppy or anything else familiar to her. 'But many plants here in Hesperu are strange to me. It seems likely that

571

Bemossed must have stolen a soporific from Mangus before we left Jhamrul.'

'So,' Kane said, hurling the cup down to the ground, 'I should have smelled it, too.'

And I, I thought, should have turned my mind toward suspecting that Bemossed might be planning an escape, for I had surely known it in my heart. And then Atara reminded both me and Kane: 'This is no time for recriminations. Bemossed is gone – what shall we do?'

'I'll go after him,' Kane said simply, moving toward the cart to gather up some things. 'He can't have gotten very far.'

'I'll go, too,' I told him.

'And I,' Maram said.

'No,' Kane commanded him. 'It won't do for all of us to go running across the countryside getting lost. Stay here and guard the others. I'll hunt *this* rabbit best alone.'

After he had packed his horse's saddlebags with food, water and other necessities, he led the beast toward some broken undergrowth beyond our camp. He found Bemossed's track easily enough. It led off toward the south, through the woods.

A few moments later, he disappeared into the wall of green and left us there wondering what to do. Liljana immediately impressed Daj and Estrella into helping her prepare breakfast. Eating good food together, I thought, was her answer to a great many problems.

We waited there in the clearing through the long hours of the morning as the sun drove the dew from the grasses and other vegetation, and heated up the air. I listened to the birds chirping and some chittering squirrels fighting in the branches high overhead. After a while, I took out my flute and played a few songs. I watched as Liljana sewed up a rip in Maram's fool's costume and Master Juwain read from the *Saganom Elu*. Daj showed Estrella a game that he had invented with Master Juwain's tarot cards. The day wore on.

By late afternoon, I grew concerned. It seemed that Kane's 'rabbit' had gotten much farther than Kane had supposed – either that or Kane had run into some sort of trouble. When evening darkened the trees and the mosquitoes came out in blood-sucking clouds, I could not bring myself to eat very much. I stood at Kane's post by the heap of logs peering through the nearly blackened woods. I listened for the sound of Kane's horse swishing through the undergrowth; I watched the stars whirl slowly about the sky, and I waited.

I slept only a little that night, when Maram relieved me for a few hours. The new day found me back at my vigil. Because of my tiredness, I was slow to act when I heard at least four horses clopping along the road hidden by the swath of trees. I commanded Maram and Daj to gather up Altaru and Fire, and our other mounts, and lead them off into the forest. This they did. And just in time, for a few moments later, six soldiers wearing a yellow livery marked with many small, red dragons burst into the clearing. They bore lances, sheathed swords and small, bossed shields. It seemed that they had espied our cart's tracks in the soft earth leading off the road and had followed them here.

'Have you any chickens, pigs or goats?' their grizzled sergeant called out to us.

They were, as we discovered, a foraging party sent into the countryside to find food for King Arsu's army, which had finally marched and was nearing Orun. One of the soldiers rode over to our three packhorses and sized them up with a practiced eye. He offered his opinion that they could be put to work in the army's baggage train – or at least slaughtered and cut up for food. It horrified me to learn that these soldiers of King Arsu ate horse meat. I prayed that Maram and Daj would keep Altaru from whinnying out a challenge from wherever they had hidden him in the woods. And our other horses, too. And then the sergeant took pity on us, saying to his man: 'How are these players to pull their cart without horses?'

He dismounted and walked about our encampment. He went over to the cart, where Kane's target hung. He noted the seven knives stuck into it. He pulled one of them free, then backed off a dozen paces. As he squinted, he flung the knife at the target. It struck the painted wood butt end first, and sprang back into the air with clang of steel before striking the ground.

'Knives,' he laughed out, shaking his head. Then he rested his hand on the stacked brush near our wagon and said, 'You don't need such protections any more – haven't you heard? The errants have all been crucified and won't be waylaying travelers any more.'

He seemed quite proud of his accomplishments up in Avrian, and so did his men. Without asking our leave, he opened up the cart's back door to look within. I wanted badly to push him aside and take out my sword, which I had hidden beneath some bolts off cloth. The captain and his men wore only the thinnest of scale armor beneath their livery. I thought that I might be able to cut all of them apart as one of their butchers might section a requisitioned horse.

But Liljana was cleverer than I and possessed of greater restraint. She found a ham, and presented it to the sergeant, saying, 'I'm sure everyone is thanking you for making the land safe. We would ask you to breakfast but we must soon be on our way. But please consider that we have taken meat together.'

The sergeant smiled at this, and so did his men. I was sure that they would devour the ham before they had gone five more miles. Then, at need, they could tell their quartermaster truthfully that they had been our guests instead of confiscators of supplies they did not share.

We all breathed easier to see the soldiers ride off as they had come. When I thought it safe, I called for Maram and Daj to bring the horses back into the clearing. I explained what had happened, then said, 'It seems that the army will encamp in Orun tonight, and so it's not safe for us to go on.'

'It's clearly not safe for us to remain here, either,' Maram said. He sighed, then added, 'And I was hoping to have that ham for dinner.'

We all had greater concerns than missing victuals. We worried that Bemossed or Kane might have encountered other soldiers fanning out along the river. Perhaps Bemossed lay dead or dying in some stinking rice bog with a spear wound though his belly; perhaps Kane had been cut off from returning or had been captured.

The passing hours heaped worry upon worry like a growing stack of lead weights upon our chests. When evening came and still Kane remained absent, the long night wreaked upon us an excrutiating dread that slowly tightened like the turning of a torturer's screw around our skulls. None of us slept very well. We awoke at dawn to whining mosquitoes, aching heads and a wall of mist that clung to the greenery of the woods. I knew that we could not bear to remain another day in this place, waiting and doing nothing.

In silence, I brought forth Alkaladur to begin my morning sword practice. The rising sun warmed the woods only a little, and did not burn off the mist. And then, after a couple hours, I heard the noise of a horse clopping along the road. The noise came closer as the horse obviously turned into the woods straight toward us. A few moments later, Kane's horse broke from the mist, and I saw Kane sitting grimly upon his back. A rope tied to the horse's saddle trailed behind a few yards and pulled upon the bound body of Bemossed. I had to blink my eyes, to make sure it really *was*

Bemossed, staggering along behind Kane and half-hidden in the mist. Mud caked his curly hair and covered his face, arms and his tunic. His bare legs seemed to have been cut by thorns, and streaks of blood had washed away some of the mud staining them. He bled from his chest, as well. There, the irons that Kane had locked around his arms and back had abraded his tunic and opened up his flesh. I ground my teeth in horror at this sight; I had sent Kane after the Maitreya – or at least a great, free spirit – and he had brought him back to us in chains.

I rushed forward and swung my sword at the rope, parting it like air. I placed my hand upon Bemossed's back, but he shook me off, insisting upon walking into our encampment of his own power. I shouted at Kane: 'Unlock him! You had no need to put chains upon him!'

'No need!' Kane growled at me. He came inside our brushwork fortifications and dismounted. He sat Bemossed down upon a log. He gripped the chain pinioning Bemossed's arms against his chest, and he shook Bemossed and snapped at me, 'So, what do you know of need? *This* rabbit ran faster and farther than I could have guessed. And when I finally caught him, he fought me like a trapped rat. There was no other way to bring him back, and so I'm not sorry for that.'

'Well, he *is* back,' I said, 'so unlock him.'

'No – he'll just try to run away again.'

'Unlock him, Kane!'

Kane shoved his savage face closer to mine and glared at me. But then I glared at him, and flung all his fury back at him, and something more. Finally, he looked away from me and muttered, 'Unlock him yourself, if you want.'

He brought forth a key and slapped it into my hand. Then he stalked off toward the fire as he called out, 'Maram! Where's that damn brandy you've been hiding away?'

After I had taken the chains off Bemossed, Liljana came forward with some tea for him to drink. But he refused to take it. All he seemed able to say was: 'Leave me alone.'

'But you have to drink *something*,' Liljana said. 'And eat some breakfast, too. And we have to get you cleaned up! Daj, go fetch some water from the stream and put it to boil so that –'

'Leave me alone!' Bemossed shouted at her.

The force of will that poured out of him stunned me. I stood gripping the bloody chains that I had taken off him. Atara, waiting nearby, turned her blindfolded face toward him with a look of great concern. Master Juwain paused in making ready the needle and thread and other gleaming instruments he might need to tend to Bemossed's wounds. Estrella knelt down on the muddy ground by Bemossed's feet. It amazed me that he allowed her to take hold of his hand.

'I'm sorry it came to this,' I said to him. 'Sorry, too, that we had to take you with us. But Taras is right – it couldn't be helped.'

Bemossed stared at me then. The hurt in his soft brown eyes wounded me deeper than any accusation could have.

'It is for the best,' I told him. 'I know you don't understand.'

'*You*,' he finally said to me, 'don't understand. You speak to me of freedom – and then you make me your slave! You can put me in chains or cut out my tongue or crucify me, but you are more of a slave than I!'

His words shocked me, but I knew exactly what he meant. So, I thought, did Atara and Maram, and everyone else. I said to him, 'We didn't mean to keep you a slave. As to our eyes, truly, you are not. We hoped you would come to trust us and then –'

'You think what you did makes me *trust* you?'

He looked at me with such a deep searching of his soul that I could not bear it. Something broke inside me then. I turned toward Kane and rattled the chains in the air. I called out, 'No, not this way – this cannot be the way!'

Kane said nothing as he stared at me through the fire's hot flames.

I flung the chains to the ground. I turned back to Bemossed and told him, 'All right – you are free, then!'

He smiled sadly at this as he rubbed his wounded chest. 'Free of the irons, and I suppose I should thank you for that. But still free to go only where you make me to go.'

'No, you misunderstand me,' I told him. 'You are *free*. We will make out a deed of manumission.'

His eyes locked onto mine. 'Truly?'

'Truly,' I told him.

I held out my hand for him to grasp, but before he could act, Kane stalked over from the fire and knocked his forearm against mine. He growled at me, 'What are you doing?'

'As I said,' glancing at Bemossed, 'I'm giving him his freedom.'

'No, you can't.'

'You're right, I can't,' I said. 'I can't give him what he already possesses. Men are born free, and free they remain.'

'Do you think so?'

576

'We don't make slaves of men, Kane!'

Kane bent down to pick up the chains on the ground, and now he shook them at me. 'We do what we *have* to do, eh? There was no other choice.'

'No, this is wrong,' I said, striking my fist into the chains. 'There must be another way.'

'Just letting him go, then?' Kane hurled the chains spinning toward the cart, which they struck with a jangle of iron links and dented wood. 'I *won't* let him go – go off to be captured or killed by the bloody Red Priests! Do you know how far I've come to find him?'

The dark flame burning up his eyes told of a journey across the stars and across the ages. I did not know how I could put it out.

'The Beast murdered Godavanni!' he shouted in anguish. 'He caused Issayu to jump from a tower onto the rocks of the sea! I won't let him take this one! I won't *lose* him, do you understand?'

So saying, he whipped free his sword from its sheath and faced me. I clenched my fingers around the black jade of my sword's hilt. The line between anguish and madness, I knew, was thinner than Alkaladur's flaming edge.

At the same moment that his hand darted out to grasp hold of my sword arm, my hand locked onto his. We stood there in the quiet woods in the misty morning, pulling at each other and testing each other's strength.

'Kane!' Liljana shouted. 'You let go of him – let go right now!'

But Kane, I thought, as his black eyes burned into mine, would never let go if that meant freeing my arm so that I might strike out at him.

'Val! You let go, too!'

'No!' I shouted.

'Val, please,' Master Juwain said to me. 'Let go so we can make sense of this!'

If *I* let go, I knew that Kane might strike his sword into me.

'Val!' Atara called out. 'Let him go!'

Just then Estrella darted forward, and ducked beneath Kane's and my locked arms. She squeezed her slender body between us as she pushed one hand against Kane's chest and the other against mine. There came a moment when the fire filling up Kane's eyes cooled, slightly. I let go of my sword, and heard it strike the earth. Then I let go of Kane's arm and told him, 'Kill me, if you must, but you *will* let Bemossed go free!'

As Liljana stepped forward to pull Estrella away from us, I waited to see what Kane would do. He stood staring at me in wonder, and my heart raced in great surging pulses. His eyes grew hot and wild – but no wilder, I thought, than my own. His breath steamed from his lips with a bitterness that I could almost taste. He hated, I knew, but his wrath slowly boiled away beneath the blaze of an even greater thing.

'So, Val,' he said to me. He sheathed his sword and then bent to pick up mine. He pressed it into my hand. 'Valashu Elahad. I *will* let Bemossed go, will I? Ha – I suppose I will! But what then? Are we to let one man go free, only to watch the whole of Ea become enslaved?'

Bemossed, I thought, had heard a great deal that we had not intended for him to hear, at least not yet. He had seen the flaming of my sword's silustria. If he told of this to anyone, the Red Priests would surely find out and try to hunt us down. It didn't matter. If he went off on his own, it would be the end of everything anyway.

And so, after taking a long, deep breath, I began to explain who we really were and why we had come to Hesperu. I could not give a full accounting of our journeys and trials, for there was too much to tell. But I gave him our names and the lands of our births; I said that Master Matai, of the Brotherhoods, had pointed us toward the Haraland of Hesperu in our quest for the Maitreya.

'Thank you . . . Valashu,' Bemossed said to me at last. He gazed at me for at least a full minute. 'Thank you for trusting me. But there is still much that makes me confused.'

He picked off a little of the mud encrusting his arm and shot me a troubled look. And I said to him, 'Speak, then. We haven't much time.'

He nodded his head, then forced out: 'You say that this Master Matai and the oracle at Senta led you to me. But I know nothing of the Maitreya.'

His face, at that moment, was open and full of puzzlement. I sensed no guile in him. I remembered lines of the verse that Master Juwain had told to me:

The Shining One
In innocence sleeps . . . .

'You know yourself,' I said to him. 'You know what is within you.'

'But how can *that* lead you to the Maitreya?'

I exchanged a quick look with Master Juwain. Although it seemed impossible, Bemossed obviously had no idea of why we had sought him out.

Master Juwain said to him, 'I'm afraid you don't understand. *You* are the Maitreya. At least we have good reason to believe you might be.'

Bemossed stared at Master Juwain and me as if we had eaten poisoned mushrooms and fallen completely mad.

'*I*?' he called out at last. 'You think *I* am the Maitreya? The great Shining One? Do you know *nothing*?'

'We know what we have heard,' I said, thinking of the golden songs that rang throughout Senta's caverns. 'We know what has been prophesied, and what we have seen.'

'What have you seen, then? What have you heard? Have your wanderings kept you ignorant of all that has happened? Haven't you *heard* that Lord Morjin has been proclaimed as the Maitreya?'

It took me a moment before the tightening of my throat allowed my fury to pour out of me: '*Morjin*? That cursed Crucifier? You think *Morjin* is the Maitreya?'

Bemossed looked at my sword, which I still clutched in my hand. He gasped in dread as blue flames erupted from the silustria and writhed in swirls all along its length. I quickly slid the blade back into its scabbard, which extinguished this little bit of hellfire.

'You hate him, don't you?' he said to me.

The only answer that I could summon then was a single word: 'Yes.'

'Many do,' he said. 'But it is his priests who are evil, not he.'

I drew in a breath of moist air and said, 'Do you really think so?'

He looked down at his dirty, scratched hands, then gazed off into the misty forest. 'I know almost nothing of the Dark Lands, but too much of my land. I was born into great injustice, and things have grown only worse. The Kallimun priests, with King Arsu's consent, *torture* Hesperu. They torture the whole world. They have made of everything a foul disease. All in Lord Morjin's name – but against his will.'

I looked at Master Juwain, who could hear nothing in his ruined ear because of Morjin's will. I looked at Liljana, who could not smile. Then I looked at Bemossed and asked him, 'Why do you think the Red Priests act without Morjin's consent?'

He shrugged his shoulders and told us, 'The Master – Mangus –

always said that men cannot bear perfection, and so out of envy will do their best to sully and destroy it.'

At this, Kane growled out, 'But Mangus seemed on good enough terms with the Kallimun. He spoke well of the damn Red Priests!'

'So it is everywhere now,' Bemossed sighed out. 'So it must be. In the village square or within the hearing of others, one must say one thing. But in one's house among family, and in the privacy of the heart, one says another.'

'But what do *you* say?' I asked him. 'Do you believe that Morjin is *perfect*?'

'If he is the Maitreya, he must be,' he said simply. 'I have read and reread the *Darakul Elu*. Everything in Lord Morjin's words speaks of his desire for perfection.'

I ground my teeth at this and said, 'Desire or not, why should you think that he has succeeded and he isn't the poisoned well that his priests draw all their evil from?'

'Because in the Black Book,' he told me, 'especially in its heart, in the *Songs of Light*, I have felt such love. And because . . .'

His voice died off into the little sounds of the woods. And I said to him, 'Yes?'

He waved his hand at an oak tree at the edge of the clearing, then reached down to touch a broken fern that we had trampled under. And he said, 'Because the world cannot be a cruel jest. The One created it as a gift to us and not a torment. Soon Lord Morjin will rule over all lands, even the Dark ones. If he was evil, then evil would prevail, not just in enslavements or crucifixions of the unfortunate, but with everyone – and everywhere, forever. The One could never allow this to be.'

Master Juwain, who had more liking for philosophical arguments than I did, said to Bemossed: 'If the One could never permit this, and the Red Dragon is but the One's eyes and hands, then how can the Dragon permit his priests to do what they do, in his name?'

'Because,' he said simply, 'Lord Morjin's priests have defiled his good name and all that he is. But he *is* the Maitreya. And so when he comes into his power, he will come into Hesperu, and into all lands. He will purge the evil from his priesthood, and restore the world.'

I could not bear any longer to hear such things. And so I stared at Bemossed and said, 'It was Morjin who crucified my mother.'

'No, that cannot be. One of his priests, perhaps, acting upon his own –'

'Bemossed!' I shouted. I motioned for Daj to lead Atara over to us. I lay my hand upon her face and said, 'Look at her! Morjin did this to her!'

'No, no,' he murmured as he gazed at her. 'No, no.'

I grabbed onto his hand and pulled him so that he looked back at me. I said, 'He is the Red Dragon, the Lord of Lies. He is the Great Beast. It was Morjin, with his own hands, who took her eyes!'

I told him of how we had gone into Argattha to gain the Lightstone, and of how Morjin had tortured Master Juwain, Ymiru and Atara. I knew that he heard the truth of what I said. His fingers grasped at mine as his whole body began to tremble and he wept without restraint.

Then he asked Atara, 'Is it as Valashu has said?'

'It is worse,' she told him.

'I'm sorry,' he said to her. He took hold of her with his free hand. 'The Dragon took *your* eyes, and yet it is I who have been blind.'

'You've nothing to be sorry about,' she told him.

'I don't know – perhaps I *shouldn't* have run away.'

He stood up to face her, and he lay his hands over her temples, where the white bandage pressed her golden hair. He looked at her with great gentleness, even as something hard and hurtful knotted up inside him.

And she said to him, 'We had hoped . . .'

He took his hands away from her and shook his head sadly. 'I cannot be the one you hope me to be.'

'But we had heard that you healed a great lord's daughter. When she was near to death. You laid your hands upon her and –'

'No, you don't understand,' he said. 'I can heal no one. It is not as you must think.'

'How is it, then?'

Bemossed held his hand up to the sun's rays burning down through the thinning mist. He said, 'A spectacle's lens gathers light and strengthens it, but in itself illuminates nothing. I am such a lens, and nothing more. There are times . . . when everything is utterly clear. Then there is light – there is always *light*, but some-times it shines so brilliantly. Within it is everything. The design for all things, in their wholeness, in their being, in their joy. This *light* is such a joy. It is that which touches those I lay my hands upon, not I. But when *I* am utterly clear, I touch upon it, for a moment. It is like touching the One itself. It is like . . . the whole world is

581

beautiful and can never be full of ugliness or hurt again. Then, and only then, I am perfect. Then it all passes through me, like lightning, and sometimes people are healed. They call this a miracle.'

He fell silent, and we gazed at him in utter silence. At last Master Juwain said to him, 'So it would be with the Maitreya.'

'But so it is with many people,' Bemossed said.

'No, not *many* – your gift is quite rare.'

'Surely it is not. Surely many others can do as I do. They just don't speak of it.'

He went on to say that once he had lived in the south, near Khevaju, and had known of three young healers who had disappeared into the Kallimun fortress there.

'Everyone is afraid to appear as different, and who can blame them?'

'In the Free Kingdoms,' Master Juwain said, 'people have no such fear, and yet I know of no one able to heal as you do.'

Bemossed smiled sadly at this and said, 'If they do not fear the Kallimun, then they fear themselves. That which they will not touch. Surely, no man or woman exists who cannot be open to what shines from the One?'

'If that is true,' Master Juwain said, 'then what is the Maitreya?'

Bemossed shrugged his shoulders and said, 'He is not the lens, but the light.'

The two of them contended in a like manner for a while. I joined in this argument, and so did Maram and Liljana. We could not quite convince Bemossed that he might be the Maitreya; we could not quite convince ourselves. But there still seemed no better course than to take him away from Hesperu. And so I finally said to him, 'You now know what we feared to tell you, and with good reason. What will you do? Will come with us?'

Bemossed picked another scab of mud off his skin, and then looked off into the forest. He said, 'This is my land. As cruel as it is, as cruel as it has been to me, it is still my home.'

'Then come back to it,' I said. 'In strength, after we've stopped Morjin. You can do nothing for your people, now.'

'I don't know,' he said. 'There was Taimu, the miller's son, whose leg was shattered almost beyond repair. There was Ysanna, who was only a breath away from dying.'

'In the lands we must pass through,' I told him, 'you will find no lack of people who are ailing or close to death.'

'I don't know,' he said, looking up at the sky.

582

Master Juwain gripped a pair of tweezers in his hand, and said to him, 'Whatever you are, whatever your gift might be, I believe that the Grandmaster of my order might be able to help bring it forth in all its glory. With the aid of the gelstei we call the seven openers. Then you might be able to claim control of the Lightstone, even across a thousand miles. Think what a lens that would be!'

I felt Bemossed's heart quicken, and his eyes brightened. But he shook his head as if he couldn't believe what Master Juwain had said might be possible.

'I don't know,' he said again. 'I just don't know.'

He stared at the mad colors of the cart as he seemed to listen to the *weet-trit-weet* of a swallow singing from the branch of a nearby tree. Then he looked at me and asked, 'Why have you kept the minstrel hidden all these days?'

I started to give the usual excuse about Thierraval's shyness and retiring ways, but Bemossed's hurt look reminded me that I must try to be truthful with him in all things. And so I said, 'The minstrel's real name is Alphanderry. And he is not as other men.'

'What is wrong with him?' Bemossed asked.

'Nothing is *wrong*,' I told him. I sensed in him a strange dread burning through his belly. So I asked him, 'What is wrong with you?'

'Only that I feared you had done something to the minstrel. As I supposed you wished to do to me.'

'What do you mean?'

He shrugged his shoulders and smiled at me. 'Because you are from the Dark Lands, as I thought of them, I supposed you wanted to use me in some evil rite. It is said that demons there castrate men against their will and make of them women for their pleasure, and do even worse things.'

I stared at him in disbelief.

'I have been marked,' he said, touching the black cross tattooed into his forehead. 'In any case, people have always singled me out. I see the way they look at me. I know there is something about me they can't bear. And so who better to choose for a strange rite?'

I wanted to laugh at this almost as much as I wanted to weep. Instead, I asked Maram to open the door to the cart. Then I called for Alphanderry to come out and make Bemossed's acquaintance.

From twenty yards away, seemingly attired in rich velvets and wool, Alphanderry appeared much as any other man. But as he came closer, the colors of his skin and curly hair seemed to grow ever more vivid and almost too real. When he closed the distance and stood next to the log upon which Bemossed sat, he fairly glowed. His large eyes filled with light – and so did his lips, cheeks and forehead.

'Bemossed,' he said, bowing, 'it is my pleasure.'

Bemossed stared at him in wonder. He said to him, 'They call me the Maitreya, but it is *you* who shines!'

Alphanderry laughed at this in a rich music that poured from his throat. He seemed to look deep into Bemossed's being as if layers of flesh were as nothing to him.

'Who *are* you?' Bemossed asked him.

'Hoy – who are *you*? The Maitreya, they say. Well, we can only hope.'

It came time to tell of the Timpum, those strange, luminous beings that shimmered through all of Ea's vilds. Were they really the children of the Galadin or seeds of light that the Galadin had bestowed upon the earth? And could these seeds somehow blossom into a human being whose substance seemed pure radiance? We didn't know. All that we could explain to Bemossed was that Flick had somehow become very much like our old friend, Alphanderry.

'*What* are you?' Bemossed asked him.

Alphanderry's warm, wide smile invited friendship, even intimacy. Bemossed gathered up his courage and reached out to take hold of Alphanderry. With his delight of touching of hand to hand, he was like a child with a new game. But it was still impossible to apprehend Alphanderry in this way. Bemossed's hand passed right through him as if he had thrust it into a pool of glimmering water.

He almost fell off his log then. And he said to Alphanderry, 'If you are made of light, *you* must be the Maitreya.'

'The Maitreya?' Alphanderry said. 'Hoy – I am a minstrel.'

'But –'

'You are made of light, too. Everything is. I heard you tell Valashu this.'

'But –'

'I am not here to argue,' Alphanderry said, 'but to sing. What shall I sing of?'

He didn't wait for an answer, but only smiled as he intoned:

> *The Shining One*
> *In innocence sleeps,*
> *Inside his heart*
> *Angel fire sleeps,*
> *And when he wakes*
> *The fire leaps.*

About the Maitreya
One thing is known:
That to himself
He always is known
When the moment comes
To claim the Lightstone.

Alphanderry stopped singing and looked at Bemossed. And he asked him, 'What will it take, I wonder, to wake you up?'

And with that, he vanished into nothingness.

An astonished Bemossed stood up, looked around and asked, 'Where did he go?'

'I don't know,' I told him.

I stared at the cross shining from his forehead, and I couldn't help remembering my mother's arms stretched out and her hands nailed to a piece of wood.

Where does the light go, I wondered, *when the light goes out?*

Bemossed stared back at me, at the lightning bolt scar cut into *my* forehead, and the deeper wound cut into my eyes. I never told him, with words, how desperately I needed him by my side in the final battles that soon must be fought. He knew it even so. A lovely light came into his eyes as he smiled me. I felt my heart quicken and my breath whispering like a cool wind even as the old pain in my chest died away.

'Valashu,' he said, holding out his hand to me. 'I have decided: I will come with you as far as the Brotherhood's school, and perhaps farther.'

We clasped hands then and stood there smiling at each other. In him I sensed much of Karshur's strength, Yarashan's verve and Asaru's grace and goodness. He was like the brother I no longer had.

'And I,' I told him, 'will go with you, even to the end of all things.'

After that he clasped hands with each of the others as we welcomed him into our company. It grieved me only a little to see him embrace Atara and kiss her lips. Then Kane shocked him, coming up to crush Bemossed's slender body to him and kissing *him*. And he growled out, 'When you ran, I fell mad like a rabid dog. Will you forgive me?'

'Will you forgive *me* for biting you?'

They laughed together then, Bemossed's gentle tones as warm as a summer rain and Kane's voice breaking from him like thunder. It was a happy moment, full of soaring spirits and hope.

It took most of the next two hours for Liljana to help clean up Bemossed and Master Juwain finally to tend his wounds. After we had broken camp and everything was packed away, I hitched Altaru to the cart and patted his neck as I told him, 'All right, old friend. Let's see if we can find our way back home.'

But this, it seemed, was not to be. Just as we were setting out, I heard an unwelcome noise through the trees, and quickly drawing closer. From the direction of the road came the beat of horses' hooves against stone. Then soldiers burst into the clearing again, and this time there were many more of them.

37

At the head of these armed men rode Lord Rodas, who was now in command of this district's magicians, alchemists, dancers, augurers and courtesans – and traveling troupes such as ours. It seemed that he had grown in power in the days since he had extorted silver from us on our crossing of the Black Bridge. Upon seeing this scrawny New Lord in his silks and gold embroidery, I gathered that he had been successful in a scheme to slander Lord Olum and see him ruined. He made his way toward our cart as if he had been elevated to lordship over all the Haralanders, and not just a few ragged outcasts. His six hirelings in their hideous purple and yellow livery accompanied him as before, but so did twenty of King Arsu's men-at-arms. They wore weapon-scarred bronze armor and bore shields and lances that looked well-used. It seemed that Lord Rodas had begged King Arsu to detach this company in his charge in order to 'escort' us to the army's encampment just outside of Orun.

Lord Rodas's gaze swept from the cart to Bemossed, now wearing a fresh tunic that hid most of his scrapes and cuts. Lord Rodas said to me: 'I see you've acquired this man since our last meeting. You must be doing well, though with the price of slaves falling so low, I suppose even *poor* players such as yourselves can afford one, if only a Hajarim.'

He brought out a purse full of jangling coins and bounced them in his hand.

'The King has asked to see you, and has given me coin in pledge of your performance,' he told us.

'We *are* honored that King Arsu requests this,' I said, feeling the sweat running down my sides, 'but our way lies opposite from Orun.'

'It is not the King's *request*,' Lord Rodas told me, 'but his *command*. And mine. As it is also my command that your way not take you out of the Haraland. Now, come! The King is returning to his encampment, and we must prepare for his arrival.'

I eyed the twenty soldiers sitting on top of their horses. Unless we were willing to fight them all and managed to kill them to the last man, we had no choice but to go with Lord Rodas into the very last place in Hesperu that we wished to go.

I nodded at Kane then, and he nodded back his affirmation that a battle at this time would be too great a chance.

And so, with ten of the soldiers riding behind us, and ten more with Lord Rodas and his hirelings out in front, we made our way onto the Ghurlan Road. A stiff wind rose up to blow away the mist from the walls of trees lining our way. The birds nesting there chirped and sang in the peace of the late morning. Bemossed sat with me on the seat of the cart, and appeared to be listening to them – or perhaps to the drumbeat of his heart. The grinding of the cart's wheels turning over worn stone reminded me that time itself was grinding on and on, and pulling us inexorably toward our fate.

By the time we passed through the rice bogs and finally reached Orun, the sun burned up the blue sky like a gout of Galda fire flung up by a catapult. We turned south onto the great road running along the Iona River. King Arsu's army had encamped in some pasturage off to the right of the road a couple miles outside of the city. Their hundreds of tents spread out in neat arrays like a little city of its own across fields of grass, all churned-up and muddy from the tramp of many horses' hooves and the boots of thousands of men.

Upon seeing this, Maram nudged his horse up close to me and muttered, 'Into the belly of the beast, once again – oh, too bad, too bad!'

'It will be all right,' I told him. 'We've only to perform as we have a dozen times already. And then we'll find a way to go on.'

'Do you think so? I'm afraid that this will be our *last* performance.'

'One way or the other,' I said, smiling, 'the last.'

'Don't jest, please. I can't believe that we were stupid enough to pose as players.'

'But it was *your* idea.'

'I know, I know,' he muttered. 'My stupid, stupid idea.'

Lord Rodas led us down through the lanes formed by the many

rows of tents. Outside them stood King Arsu's soldiers, cleaning their armor or sharpening their spears – or roasting meats over little fires, playing dice, or swatting at flies and grumbling, as soldiers do. They cast us curious looks as we passed by. I gazed back at them with an even greater curiosity, which I tried to conceal. My eyes drank in the length of their spears and the size of their shields: rounds of thinnish-looking wood that I did not think would hold up very well beneath the cut and sweep of steel kalamas. I looked for the weak places in their fish-scaled armor; I watched a few companies of these battle-worn Hesperuks at drill, standing too close to each other as they locked shields in a dense block of men many ranks deep bristling with iron spear points. It seemed that it would be hard to attack such an armored block – almost as hard as it would be for them to maneuver. I noted, however, that all of King Arsu's men seemed to move to a fierce and relentless discipline.

At last we came to the camp's center: a great square formed by the soldiers' tents with the pavilions of King Angand and Arch Uttam standing on either side of King Arsu's pavilion, to the south. Smaller tents of prominent commanders were arrayed nearby. Many banners flapped in the strong wind. A pole flying a bright yellow one emblazoned with a great red dragon had been planted in the earth just outside of King Arsu's pavilion: a vast, billowing monstrosity of purple silk sewn with gold. King Angand's pavilion was of sky blue, as was the field of the banner displaying his emblem: a white heart with wings. Of all the Dragon kings, only King Angand had kept his family's ancient arms, because only he had possessed the foresight to make alliance with Morjin freely, instead of being forced to swear fealty to him.

Across the square from King Arsu's pavilion, vendors from Orun had arrived to set up carts, stalls and small tents of their own. Most of these were food sellers, offering fresh fruits, tarts and various roasted meats. The Harlanders were fond of a strong-tasting riverfish called the katouj. It seemed we couldn't go ten yards without passing some old woman frying up this foul-smelling fish in pan of sizzling oil. The Haralanders ate it piping hot, on slices of salted bread slathered with a hot greenish sauce that looked like toad slime. It occurred to me that a people who could consume such fare could endure almost anything.

As we moved through the square, I counted scarcely two hundred of Orun's citizens standing about eating with the soldiers. If this had been anywhere in Mesh – or in Ishka, Taron or Kaash – the whole city would have turned out to greet the realm's warriors.

But most of the soldiers that King Arsu had summoned for the assault upon Avrian were levies from the south. These darker, shorter men looked upon the Haralanders with contempt, even as the Haralanders did them, though of course in secret. The few Haraland contingents of *this* army, as I soon learned, were those who had proved themselves again and again in fanatical devotion to their king.

The arrogance of all the soldiers hung in the air like a charge before a thunderstorm. They bullied their way to the front of the food queues or charged about on their horses so that people had to leap out of their way to keep from being trampled. I thought that King Arsu had been wise to recruit mostly Haraland men for the army that had invaded Surrapam five hundred miles to the north – what better way of removing the most resentful and bellicose of his subjects without having to nail them to crosses?

Lord Rodas led us to a place reserved for us in the center of the line of carts. Here gathered the performers summoned to show their skills to King Arsu and King Angand. Lord Rodas commanded us to await the arrival of the King, who was off at the local Kallimun school to consecrate a great new statue of Morjin. The captain of the twenty soldiers in Lord Rodas's charge informed him that his men had completed their escort and had better things to do than to watch over a troupe of ragged players. Without waiting for Lord Rodas's consent, they rode off toward their tents, leaving Lord Rodas and his hirelings as our guards.

Lord Rodas, with a false largesse, bought us all servings of katouj, which we forced down with false smiles of gratitude. Although it seemed that many people in the encampment had turned their gazes upon us, common sense told me that we attracted no more attention than we should have expected as heralded players. Even so, Maram fell so nervous that he could hardly eat – for him, a rare affliction. He stood next to me, fairly gagging on the green katouj as he grumbled, 'Why is everyone watching us?'

He caught Daj staring at a mounted knight across the square, and murmured to him, 'What's the matter with you? Keep your eyes down!'

But it seemed that Daj could not help staring at this knight, for a surge of hatred washed through him, and he stood trembling like a cat waiting to fight. I came over to him and wrapped my arm around him as I whispered, 'What *is* the matter?'

And he whispered back, 'That man killed my father and my brothers. He sold my mother and sisters into slavery. And me.'

I bowed my head at this. His suffering, I realized, burned no less terribly than did my own.

The knight whom he had been regarding, I sensed, took too great an interest in us. On top of a snow-white stallion, he rode slowly along the rows of soldiers kneeling down in front of the tents as they awaited their king. He seemed to be searching the ranks for any sign of disorder, or indeed of displeasure, in any of these men who had been honored to attend the day's celebrations. He gripped in his fist a long lance, with which he pointed here or there, as if to chasten individual soldiers to hide the boredom in their eyes or sit up straighter. His bronze fish scales had been polished to a blinding sheen, as had his helm, crested with green peacock feathers. His golden surcoat showed a half-sized red dragon that proclaimed him as a lord of some importance. He wore a blood-red cape. Many of the townsfolk from Orun could not bear his gaze and turned away from him. He guided his horse over to the foodsellers' stalls, casting men and women dark looks as if he suspected them of disloyalty to the King or even of being assassins. And all the while, with dartings of his dark eyes, he kept glancing at Daj and me and the others of our company – and particularly at Bemossed.

At last he worked his way over to us. Lord Rodas, who had dismounted, saluted this man and called out, 'Lord Mansarian – this is the troupe I told you about! Here we have Kalinda, the fortune teller, and Mother Magda and Garath the Fool.'

Lord Rodas presented each of us in turn, and Lord Mansarian stared at each of us, in turn. He seemed tall, for a Hesperuk, and thick in his limbs and body. His face was like a hammer, all blunt and scarred, and his eyes drove into each of us like nails. As his gaze fell upon me, I thought that I had never seen a harder-looking man, not even in Argattha.

'Arajun,' he said, staring down at me. His voice came out all hoarse and raspy, like a wheeze of ill wind. The scars seaming his heavily bearded throat suggested that he had been badly wounded there. 'Arajun, the flute player – is that right?'

'He pipes like a bird,' said Lord Rodas, who had never heard me play. I saw that Lord Rodas had begun to sweat, whether from the hot katouj sauce or the sun or his fear, it was hard to say.

'And you, Jaiyu,' Lord Mansarian said to Daj. 'You are of the Haraland, are you not?'

Daj nodded his head as he kept his gaze on Lord Mansarian's boots.

'Where in the Haraland, then?'

'Ghurlan,' Daj said, naming the one large city in the north that had never rebelled against King Arsu. It pained him not at all, I sensed, to tell this lie.

'And how did you come to be with this troupe?'

'My mother died in childbirth,' he lied again. 'When my father passed on, too, Teodorik and Mother Magda adopted me into their troupe and took me into other lands.'

Lord Mansarian nodded his head at this as he stared at Master Juwain and Liljana. I gave thanks that he appeared not to recognize Daj, who had been very young when Lord Mansarian's men had enslaved him.

Then Lord Rodas gathered up his courage and pointed at Liljana as he told Lord Mansarian, 'Are you still looking for healers? As you can see, there are none with this troupe, and certainly no young ones – just an old potionist.'

I felt Liljana restraining her ire at being called old. I felt, too, Lord Mansarian fighting very hard not to look at Bemossed, even as Bemossed struggled to keep his eyes cast down upon the ground.

Lord Mansarian sat on his horse above us, and I sensed within him a great turmoil of anguish and hate. He seemed to keep locked inside his heart some fearful thing that he did not want anyone to see. The tension between him and Bemossed grew tighter and tighter, like that of a great weight pulling on a grappling hook buried in his chest. At last his eyes stabbed into Bemossed, and he stared at him. Then he pointed his lance at him and called out, 'Lord Rodas! The King will arrive soon, and it would be best if he did not have to look upon this Hajarim. Keep him out of sight!'

'Yes, my Lord!' Lord Rodas called back, bowing so deep that he practically scraped the ground. It seemed he had forgotten that he, himself, had been made a lord.

Without another word, Lord Mansarian looked away from Bemossed, reined his horse around and continued his patrol.

'A great man,' Lord Rodas called out a little too loudly. 'And a great Haralander, too.'

'What is his rank?' I asked Lord Rodas. 'He must be a great lord.'

'Stupid flutist – can you be so *ignorant*?' he barked at me. He was one of those cowards whose fear too easily transformed into ill-use of those whom he considered beneath him. 'Lord Mansarian commands the Crimson Companies!'

He went on to tell something of Lord Mansarian's fearful past. Some years before, it seemed, when King Arsu had sworn fealty to Morjin, Lord Mansarian had taken up arms against the King in protest, along with other Haralanders. He had fought with great cunning and savagery, killing many. At last, however, the Red Priests had found a way to his heart, and they persuaded him to turn traitor to the rebellion – and to pledge his undying loyalty to King Arsu. King Arsu had then tested him, in many ways and in many places. Lord Mansarian always proved himself, and more, like many converts to a new cause, strove to serve his king with zealousness. He requested permission to form a force of other Haraland nobles and knights who opposed the rebellion.

These two hundred men – they were called the Crimson Companies, after the red capes they wore – soon wreaked a bloody terror upon their kith and kin. They hunted down rebels through every part of the Haraland. When they drove the last of them behind Avrian's walls, King Arsu had then led the main body of his southern army in siege against the city. After it finally fell, he gave the surviving errants to Lord Mansarian and the Crimson Companies for justice. It was Lord Mansarian who had suggested and taken charge of crucifying them all along the Avrian Road.

'The Red Capes did their work well,' Lord Rodas told us, 'as you will see if I decide that your troupe should try its fortunes up around Avrian. The errants' corpses are to be left on their crosses until they rot and the vultures pick clean their bones.'

I turned to watch Lord Mansarian riding along the lines of kneeling soldiers as he stabbed his lance at them. There was a coldness about him, as if the evil of his dreadful deeds had turned him to stone.

Lord Rodas went on, 'It is said that now the King will have him hunt down those who have taken false oaths of loyalty – as well as counterfeiters, enchanters, false healers, and the like.'

At the mention of the word 'healer', I tried not to look at Bemossed, standing next to me. Lord Rodas turned away, saying, 'See that your Hajarim removes himself from sight, as Lord Mansarian commanded!'

Lord Rodas scowled and strutted off, leaving us under the supervision of his hirelings.

I walked with Bemossed over to the cart. In a low voice, I said to him, 'This Lord Mansarian recognized you?'

'Yes,' he said.

'And you recognized him.'

'Yes,' he said again, nodding his head. 'The lord who brought his daughter to the Master to be healed – it was Lord Mansarian.'

And with that, he went inside the cart and shut the door. Could it be, I wondered, that the pitiless Lord Mansarian might be protecting Bemossed out of gratitude for curing his child? Or was he only waiting to betray both Bemossed and our company to the King at a key moment for his own gain? I watched Lord Mansarian all stiff and stonelike on his great horse, but he did not look back at us.

My other friends came over to me, and we all stood in front of the cart looking at each other. Maram bit at his moustache and then said, 'Ah, I need good quaff of brandy.'

'Well?' I said, looking at him. 'Are you waiting for me to try to stop you?'

'I wish that was my only obstacle. Haven't you heard? King Arsu has banned all spirits from his encampment. It's said that soon he'll ban them throughout his realm.'

I thought that Maram might try to steal off and drink in secret. But it seemed that he had other plans.

'Ah, Mother Magda,' he said to Liljana. 'O great keeper of our company's coins! I don't suppose you have a few silver pieces to spare?'

Liljana shot him a quizzical look and asked, 'What for?'

'I thought I would make the acquaintance of the ladies in that tent.'

He smiled as he pointed at the nearby tent of some courtesans.

Liljana stared at him with such scorn that any other man would have reddened with shame.

But Maram, being Maram, only threw up his hands and said, 'Well, I had to try, didn't I? As I think I shall try my charm, since I haven't anything better. It has sufficed before.'

He took a step toward the courtesans' tent, and I held out my arm to stop him. I said, 'Don't you remember what happened with Jezi Yaga?'

'Do I *remember*? I do, I do, my friend, and it is precisely that memory that moves me. I've learned too well, ah, just how fragile I really am. And so, since I've likely only a few hours left on earth, I don't want to spend all of them waiting for this king to arrive while I stare at his ugly soldiers.'

He broke away from me and strode off toward the tent. One of Lord Rodas's hirelings moved to intercept him. But when he discovered that Maram did not intend to flee, he let him go. The young tough in his ill-fitting livery might have no sympathy for love of freedom, but he certainly understood well enough raw lust.

A short while later there came a commotion from the western part of the encampment, and someone cried out, 'The King! The King is coming!'

I looked towards the lines of soldiers in front of the tents there. The lines were broken, I saw, for no one stood or knelt to block the very wide center lane leading into the square. Down this lane rode a company of fifty of King Arsu's knights in burnished bronze armor, bearing blue plumes upon their helms and blue capes upon their shoulders. Their shields and surcoats showed quarter-sized red dragons. Then came the smaller escort of King Angand, whose knights bore their own individual arms: black boar's heads, golden eagles, red lions rampant, and the like. Their armor, being partly of steel plate, shone brilliantly. King Angand rode at their center. Although he seemed a smallish man, his renown was vast; in all the realms of the south, no other king had done such great deeds in war or possessed so fine an army. His strange emblem – the white, winged heart – gleamed from the banner that one of his knights bore and from the silken surcoat covering his own chest. His great ease with his mount hinted at a lifetime of long, hard marches and battle.

The same could not be said of King Arsu. To begin with, he rode no horse. Indeed, he did not ride at all, if that meant guiding the beast that bore him. Rather, he sat within a sort of canopied and gilded fort perched on the back of an elephant. Until that moment, I had wondered if the drawings that I had seen in books might be pure figments. But this huge beast was as real as the earth that shook beneath its treelike, driving legs. Its swaying nose, seven feet long, hung down from a fearsome face festooned with two great curving tusks that could have impaled a man and left him hanging high in the air. It was said that the Hesperuks captured elephants in the wild, in the south, and then armored them and trained them for battle. If true, then I hoped never to meet such a raging mountain of flesh at work. Strangely, its handler – a small man sitting on the elephant's neck in front of the King – controlled it with the well-timed tappings of a little stick.

King Arsu seemed himself an elephantine man. As the elephant stepped and swayed, the layers of fat beneath King Arsu's bronze armor seemed to flow and swell out one portion or another, and spill out over the neck in a cascade of fleshy chins. Despite the armor, I could see that he was no fighting king. So huge were his

595

arms and labored his motions that he would have difficulty wielding a sword or drawing a bow. No spatter of blood, I thought, had ever marked the bright yellow surcoat that ballooned over him. This silken fabric, of course, showed the three-quarter sized red dragon that Morjin made all his subject kings to bear. Perhaps wisely, though, Morjin had left King Arsu the one glorious trapping of the Hesperuk monarchs: a great, flowing cloak sewn with ten thousand parrot feathers, in brilliant colors of red, yellow, green and blue. King Arsu's golden crown – set with three great emeralds – seemed almost dull in comparison to this fantastic garment.

The two kings and their guard entered the square and made their way toward King Arsu's pavilion, where a raised dais, covered in a silken canopy, had been built. Five heavy chairs had been set out upon it. I wondered that his army should burden itself hauling the supplies needed to construct such a box, but it seemed that King Arsu's soldiers never traveled without a good supply of wood.

King Arsu came down from his kneeling elephant, and with a great groaning effort, managed to climb the few steps leading up to the box. He wheezed as he stood behind the long table at its front. Then he settled his great bulk down into the centermost and largest of the chairs: an ornate work of teak and gold encrusted with gems. A short, dark woman perhaps thirty years old came out of the pavilion behind the dais and sat down on the chair to his left. Her name, I learned, was Lida: the King's cousin and consort, who went everywhere that King Arsu went, even to war. An old man wearing the red robe of a priest of the Kallimun claimed the chair to King Arsu's right. I overheard someone call him Arch Uttam: the highest of all Hesperuk's priests and the most terrible. His flesh seemed to cling like a tight glove to his skull. King Angand sat next to him, at one end of the dais, while Lord Mansarian came up and took the chair beside Lida at the other end.

A silence now fell over the square. King Arsu gazed dismissively at the bowls of apples and the pitchers of lemon squash and various nectars set out on the table. Then a slave hurried up to bring him a goblet full of mother's milk sweetened with honey, his preferred drink. He sipped from it, and then looked out to address the hundreds of people assembled there. His voice seemed incongruent with his massive form, for it came out of his throat all high and squeaky, like that of a mouse: 'Soldiers of Hesperu! Citizens of Orun! We are met today to celebrate our victory – as well as Lady Lida's birthday, only two days hence!'

He turned toward Lida, and the two small, piglike eyes embedded in his fleshy face seemed to warm happily. Then he looked back out over the square and announced: 'We are told that we shall have entertainments! Dancers and singers – and the finest traveling troupe in all the north! So sit and enjoy yourselves! The most valorous of soldiers that a king was ever honored to lead have more than earned this day's revelries!'

His words, I thought, fairly shrieked with bravado and insincerity. And yet his many soldiers looked upon him with a real reverence lighting up their faces. Their king had once again led them to victory. He had bestowed upon them honors, loot and captured women. More than this, however, he had given them great purpose. From the sheer heat of enthusiasm that passed from soldier to soldier like a flame, I knew that they believed utterly in the crusade on which King Arsu led them. Surely, in the war that must soon come, they would die fighting with great fervor for King Arsu – and for their King of Kings whom they called Morjin.

'Has everyone eaten?' King Arsu called out. 'Good! Good! Then Arch Uttam will lead us in a recitation, and then our sport will begin!'

As Arch Uttam stood up from his chair, so did everyone else assembled around the muddy grass – even King Arsu. A dozen Red Priests dressed in flowing scarlet robes now entered the square and positioned themselves among the soldiers at intervals of forty paces. They looked toward Arch Uttam to begin reciting from the *Darakul Elu*. This he did, without having even to open the black book that he clutched in his veiny, cadaverous hands. In a grinding, unpleasant voice he intoned a long passage that he had committed to memory, as he had many others of this dreadful book:

'Warriors who carry within their hearts the ineffable flame of the One, who bear inside their souls the seeds of angels – go forth to victory against those who have turned away from the Light! Face death with courage, and you yourselves will never truly die! Master your fear! Make sacrifice of your blood that others may know greater life! Be strong and take dominion over the weak . . .'

Arch Uttam spoke on and on in a like way for what seemed forever. I noticed that many of the soldiers in their ranks raised up their eyes toward him as they moved their lips in echo of the words that he recited.

At last, he finished. Then he beckoned toward two of his priests standing off in front of Arch Uttam's pavilion. They held between them a young woman perhaps of an age with Atara. She wore a tunic of lamb's wool as white as snow. They had to help her walk out into the square in front of the box, for her glazed eyes suggested that they had given her some sort of potion that robbed her of her will. Her head kept nodding forward toward her chest. Arch Uttam came down from the dais then. A third priest stepped forward to give him a bowl fashioned from a human skull while a fourth priest handed him a knife.

'No,' I whispered, 'it cannot be!'

It nearly killed me that I could not move or cry out in protest, but only stand there raging silently. I wanted to gouge out my own eyes. Then one of the priests clamped his fist in the woman's hair, and pulled back her head, exposing her throat. With a quick, practiced motion, Arch Uttam sliced his knife across it, even as he positioned the bowl to catch the blood that pumped out of her. It did not take very long for the woman to die. More priests appeared holding up a bier trimmed in satin and gold. They laid her gently upon it. Arch Uttam stood above her, raising high the blood-filled bowl for all to see.

'A virgin with all her life to live,' he called out, 'has freely given her life so that we might be stronger! An innocent girl who in her sacrifice has become the greatest of warriors! We bear her body away to lie in glory. But she will live on, forever, in us! *This* is the Way of the Dragon!'

So saying, he put the bowl of bone to his lips. I watched in horror as he took a few sips of living blood, *his* preferred drink. Then he passed the bowl to the priest nearest him, who likewise drank from it, and so it went with other priests until the bowl had been emptied.

I did not want to believe what I had seen. I bowed my head in shame. Atara stood next to me stricken as well. Estrella buried her face in Liljana's side as she began weeping without restraint. Kane stared out into the square as his hand convulsed in a death grip and he muttered, 'So, damn them forever – so, so.'

All the soldiers and townsfolk of Orun bowed their heads as well, not in shame but to honor this young woman, whose name was Yismi. I overheard an old woman say that Yismi's betrothed, Olas, had been killed in the siege of Avrian, and that she would now find happiness in joining him in death.

After that, Arch Uttam returned to the dais and sat back down. So did everyone else. And then King Arsu signalled for the entertainments to begin.

From out of nowhere, it seemed, Lord Rodas hurried up to us. He seemed to have taken no more notice of Yismi's sacrifice than he would a chicken slaughtered for supper. I contemplated setting my hands around his neck and breaking it. Instead I looked down at the ground as he called out, 'Where is that fool who calls himself Garath? Well, we still have time. You are to go last, after the pairs from Avrian, but you should be ready all the same.'

We retired one by one to our cart, where we donned our costumes in Bemossed's silent company. Then we stood together outside and watched as forty youths from the nearby Kallimun school paraded out into the square. They wore golden tunics gathered in with bright red sashes. After forming up facing the King on the very spot where Yismi had been put to the knife, the priest leading them motioned with his hand for them to bow to King Arsu. Then the priest cast them a stern look and motioned for them to begin singing.

They sang like angels. Their voices rang out high and sweet – too sweet and too high for youths who were almost men. I had never heard quite such a lovely pitch and tone pouring from male throats before. But then, in the Morning Mountains, no one would ever think to geld a boy like a horse just to preserve the beauty of his voice. It shocked me to learn that many of these youths had not only submitted to their castration without complaint but had actually volunteered to be mutilated, 'offering up their manhood to the Dragon,' as they put it.

The father of one of these youths stood nearby beaming proudly, even as my father once had when I had competed with the sword at tournaments. I overheard him say to his wife: 'Who would ever have dreamed that our Dyrian would sing for the King?'

And another man a few paces away exclaimed, 'What a day this is! What great days are to come!'

I sensed in them the same passion that stirred many of those throughout King Arsu's realm: a great dream for the future, in the coming Kariad and the march into the Age of Light. But with their longing for a better world came a great fear as well, for they dreaded being left behind in the glorious crusade that Morjin led. And so they were willing to sacrifice the most precious of things to see this dream made real: not only their freedom and their children's wholeness, but their very lives.

The youths sang five songs, and it seemed that they strove for a purity of voice like that of the Galadin. Then they cleared the square for dancers wearing bright green silks and little cymbals on their fingers. I watched them gyrate, leap and jangle in front of King Arsu's box for a while. They were quite skilled in the *maracheel* and other traditional dances of Hesperu. After they had finished and knelt gasping for breath, King Arsu cast out gold coins to them with his own hand. Then they ran off happily, clanging their little cymbals and whooping with joy.

It came time for the pairs from Avrian to entertain the King. But before his soldiers could bring them out, a lathered horse bearing a blue-caped rider galloped down the center lane into the square. He drew up in front of the King's box. He dismounted and bowed to King Arsu, who beckoned him forward, up upon the dais. I watched as this messenger, or so he seemed, bent low and cupped his hands around King Arsu's ear. King Arsu nodded his head and smiled. Then the messenger hurried off the dais. He gathered up his horse's reins and disappeared into the throng of soldiers standing about guarding King Arsu.

King Arsu held up his hand as he cried out in his whipsaw of a voice: 'We have had great tidings! King Orunjan has journeyed from Uskudar at our invitation, and is even now journeying up from Khevaju. A master priest sent by Lord Morjin rides with him: the renowned Haar Igasho. We are to meet soon, in a conclave of kings such as has not been held for an entire age!'

This news caused the hundreds of soldiers and townsfolk gathered around the square to let out a great cheer. It caused *me* to want to retrieve my sword and cut down every Kallimun priest that I could before falling upon Arch Uttam. If Haar Igasho had gained renown, it was only through betraying our own people and bringing shame upon all the Valari. I wanted to slay him for the atrocities visited upon Mesh almost as badly as I burned to cut down Morjin. Prince Salmelu of Ishka: this was who Igasho had once been, before resentment and poisoned pride led him to try to put an arrow in my back. Ra Igasho he had been called at our last meeting, after he had been made a full priest of the Kallimun. And now it seemed that Morjin had elevated him once more in reward for helping to crucify my grandmother and mother. I could only wonder why Morjin had sent *Haar* Igasho into Hesperu. It must be, I thought, that Morjin wished to warn the priests of King Arsu's realm to look for us in case we journeyed this way. And to aid them in identifying us and hunting us down.

I traded a quick, dark look with Kane and then Liljana. Our circumstances, already perilous, had suddenly grown deadly.

I tried to think of how we might possibly slip away from under

Lord Rodas's watchful eyes and steal out of the encampment. No means of escape suggested themselves to me. It seemed that we must somehow get through the day and hope that we could ride fast and far before Haar Igasho met up with King Arsu and Arch Uttam.

The next 'entertainment' made it difficult to get through half an hour. Lord Mansarian's men, in their blood-red capes, brought out the first of the pairs from Avrian: two naked men, among the last of the captive errants. Lord Mansarian had kept these defeated rebels alive in order to inspire the Haralanders along the road down to Gethun and Khevaju. Lord Mansarian's soldiers gave each of them a razor-sharp short sword, then quickly backed away. These two men, once brothers in arms, were to fight each other to the death. If they refused this final degradation, or turned upon the soldiers guarding them, their children held hostage would be crucified.

I forced myself to look out into the square, for I wished to gauge the Hesperuks' skill with weapons. The combat was bloody and quick; in only a few moments, the taller of the two men lay fallen on the muddy grass, disembowelled and nearly decapitated. The soldiers drawn up in their ranks cheered with gusto as they had for the young singers. I hated them for that. I thought that I would never understand human beings. Perhaps we would do better simply to free Angra Mainyu from Damoom, and then to perish down to the last man, woman and child in a holocaust of flame.

Three more pairs of men Lord Mansarian's soldiers brought out to fight for the pleasure of the King, pair by pair, until four men survived the first round of this deadly competition. Then they paired off these men together, and made them slay each other in another vicious round, until only two remained. These two – now bloodied and barely able to stand up – faced each other in the final combat. A rumor going around the square had it that they were best of friends, but I had no way of confirming that. If friends they truly were, then they fought with a rare passion to rend and slay. Lord Mansarian had promised the sole survivor his freedom. At last, only one of them stood, looking down over the body of his opponent. He cast his sword upon the bloody grass. He bowed his head. Then Lord Mansarian's soldiers closed in upon him to grab his arms and take him away to be crucified. He would find his freedom from his errors in excruciating agony over several days, as so many had before him.

Now Lord Rodas paced back and forth with a nervousness eating at him. Just as he was readying himself to charge into the courtesans' tent and call out once more for Garath the Fool, Maram marched out of it. He came straight over to us. His face, I saw, had fallen a sickly white as if he had met up with a ghost.

'What's wrong?' I whispered to him.

'Ah, nothing,' he whispered back. He looked over at Lord Rodas, who fairly clung to him like a tick. 'Nothing I can tell you now.'

'Was it the girl?' I said, remembering what Arch Uttam had done to Yismi.

'Ah . . . what girl?'

I stared at him as I shook my head. I did not know whether to rage or give thanks that Maram's pursuits had spared him witnessing Yismi's murder.

'What's that?' Lord Rodas snapped at us as he rushed over. His angry eyes took in the traveling tunic that Maram wore. 'Fool of a fool! I told you to be ready – and now we'll have to keep the King waiting.'

'Be at ease!' Maram snapped back at him. 'Or you'll give yourself apoplexy. No one is going to keep anyone waiting!'

So saying, he cast me a troubled look and hurried to go inside the cart. We moved it out into the center of the square then, facing it toward King Arsu's box. Kane, barechested and wearing his billowing silk pants, hung his painted target from its side. By the time he had made ready his chains, the cart's door flew open and Maram burst out into the square.

Then it was our turn to perform for the King.

38

How Maram had donned his costume and painted his face so quickly, I didn't know. He immediately managed to trip over Kane's chain and nearly landed face first in a mound of horse droppings. It was farce at its crudest, yet it made everyone laugh. After the horror of the sword fights, I thought, no less Yismi's butchery, the people in the square needed whatever relief they could find.

Maram himself took no pleasure in his performance. Some great fear burned through his bouncing belly, and he could not tell me what it was. It did not keep him, however, from shimmying about in mockery of the *maracheel* dancers, and making everyone laugh all the more.

Although we had improvised our way across the Haraland, we had always set the rhythm and routines of our show ourselves. It was not to be that way this day. Without warning, as Estrella joined Maram in a silly pantomime, a seemingly jovial King Arsu held up his hand and called out to them: 'Enough! Enough for now, good Garath! Let us see what else your troupe has prepared for us.'

He turned toward his left, where the Lady Lida sat pretending amusement at Maram's and Estrella's antics. Her dark, sharp face, I thought, hid her true sentiments as if covered with a veil. It disturbed me that she kept stealing quick glances at Liljana, who waited by the side of the cart with the rest of us.

'My Lady,' King Arsu said to Lida, 'since it is your birthday, what would you most like of this troupe?'

Lida didn't hesitate to answer him. She spoke in a sweet and perfectly controlled voice as she told him, 'My lord, I would like a love potion, that my ardor for my king always inflames me as it does now, even when I am ugly and old.'

Her words pleased King Arsu greatly, and I felt a flush of pride wash through him. It seemed that he could not get enough flattery, just as he had a nearly bottomless thirst for sugared drinks.

'Dear one,' he said to her, 'you will never be less than beautiful, and as for growing old, is it not written that those of impassioned blood will enjoy the eternal youth of the angels?'

His quote from the *Darkakul Elu* elicited a quick nod of Arch Uttam's skull-like head. He gazed at King Arsu as if noting down his every word. His umber eyes, though smoldering with a cruel intelligence, seemed utterly dead.

'My Lord,' Arch Uttam said to King Arsu, correcting him, 'it is written that they will enjoy the *everlasting* youth of the angels.'

King Arsu waved his hand at this as he might bat away a fly. Even so, I felt a flicker of fear burn through him. Then he told Lida, 'You shall certainly have your potion.'

He called out his command to Liljana then. She went inside the cart, and then hurried back out holding a blue-glassed vial full of a dark liquid. She stepped forward toward the dais, where one of the King's men moved to take it from her. But Lida stayed him, and came down from the dais to take the potion from Liljana herself. I watched as she turned her face to whisper something in Liljana's ear, and Liljana likewise spoke back to her.

As Lida returned to her place, Liljana walked back to us. I wondered what she had said to her, for she fairly beamed with a new hope.

And then King Arsu pointed at Atara and said, 'Kalinda, Teller of Fortunes – come forward and let us hear of our fate!'

He smiled if expecting the usual promises of love, children and a happy future. Atara did not disappoint him. With Daj leading her forward by one hand, she clutched in her other the glass sphere that we had bought in Ramlan. Despite her blindfold, she appeared to gaze into it deeply. Then she lifted up her face toward King Arsu's box.

'My Lord!' she called out. 'I see for you the fulfillment of your greatest desire. You will gain that which you have sought all your life.'

King Arsu smiled hugely to hear this. It was, however, scryer talk, and therefore likely double-edged in its meaning. King Arsu seemed not to realize this. Likely he had never encountered a true scryer before, as all the women of that order had long since been purged from his realm.

'The fulfillment of our greatest desire,' King Arsu repeated. 'That is well. But we have many desires. It would be hard to tell which one is the greatest.'

His answer caused Arch Uttam to look at him with scorn. And then King Arsu hastened to call down to Atara: 'Tell us then of victory! Tell us of our army, which will soon march forth on the great crusade!'

King Arsu looked out at his hundreds of soldiers assembled in the square.

Atara fell silent. I felt my heart quicken its painful beats as something stabbed into me. Then Atara drew in a deep breath and called out:

'I see an ocean of grass, covered with armies of men. I cannot count the number of spears gleaming in the sun. The shields of the army of Sunguru shine like thousands of mirrors; the men of Uskudar stand there, too, like ebony pillars. Your army, King Arsu, gathers at their center. And you, on top of an elephant draped in armor, at the center of it. Your enemies stand before you. It will be said ever after that they had no hope of prevailing against such an invincible force. And then fate will find you, and everyone assembled there that day. It will be the greatest battle fought in all the ages of Ea. And you will gain the greatest victory of your life.'

She stopped speaking and stood there facing King Arsu. A terrible strangeness shivered up my spine like the chill of the winter wind. I feared with all my soul that Atara had told King Arsu the truth.

King Arsu turned directly toward Atara. At last, he put down his goblet of honeyed milk and clapped his puffy hands together. He called out, '*That*, Fortune Teller, was a great one indeed. And it deserves a great reward.'

And with that, he reached into his purse and cast a handful of gold coins at her. Daj retrieved them from the grass. After Atara had bowed to the King, Daj took her by the hand once again and led her back to our cart.

Next to Arch Uttam, King Angand sat quietly gazing out at Atara. Although a stew of strong sentiments bubbled inside him, his brown face remained stonelike. His dark, almond eyes gleamed with cunning, but betrayed none of his thoughts. I had never known a man harder to read. Did he pay any mind at all to Atara's prophecy? And what had he made of the messenger's news, that King Orunjan, his old enemy, would soon meet up with King Arsu and himself in conclave? Did he dwell at all upon the great irony that Morjin had put an end to the incessant wars of the south by leading the Dragon Kingdoms straight toward a final war that would consume all of Ea?

He finally broke his silence, turning to King Arsu to say: 'It would seem that our fates are linked together. But that is the future. Why don't we return to the present and witness the skills of the strongman?'

I sensed that he hated almost everything about his enforced rapprochement with King Arsu and the bloodthirsty Arch Uttam, and wished to remove himself from their presence as soon as he could.

King Arsu nodded at this, and called out to Kane: 'Taras – is that your name? Why don't you show us what you can do?'

What Kane could do, I thought, as his eyes deepened into black pools, would be to grab up his sword and charge King Arsu's box, cutting down any guard who stood in the way. And then to cut short the reigns of Morjin's two greatest kings and one of his most valued priests before other guards came to kill him.

Instead, he gathered up his chains and positioned himself in front of King Arsu's box. Then Arch Uttam wagged his bony finger at him as he addressed King Arsu: 'I'm sure this man is as strong as everyone says. I'm sure we would all like to see him break his chains, but is this wise? It might give the slaves bad ideas.'

Something ugly in his voice grated as if the whole world irritated him. I watched as he forced a thin smile upon his face. I thought for a moment that he might be joking, although he did not seem capable of any sort of levity.

King Arsu took him seriously enough. He sipped some of his sweetened milk as he seemed to consider what Arch Uttam had seemed to offer as a suggestion. Then he said to Kane, 'You are a juggler as well, aren't you? Well, then, juggle for us, good Taras.'

He waved his hand at him as if that settled the matter. Then Daj brought out a little basket filled with Kane's seven colored balls. For a while Kane entertained King Arsu and the other luminaries in the box – and the soldiers and townspeople, too – with the blur of his hands and a stream of leather-covered spheres. He sent them high up into the air on a rainbow arc, and then whirled about in a full circle, catching them with perfect timing and passing them even lower and faster as the balls flowed in an unbroken streak of crimson and orange, indigo and violet. I thought it likely that no one present in the square had ever seen such juggling.

At last, though, everyone grew tired of this amusement, as

people do. And so Kane put his balls away, and went about performing feats of prestidigitation. I had never come across anyone so skilled at this sleight of hand. He dared to ask Lady Lida for a gold coin, and then made it vanish into thin air. After showing Lady Lida his naked palm, he made a fist and blew on it. When he opened his hand again, *two* gold coins gleamed there.

'Marvelous!' Lady Lida said, clapping her hands together.

'Marvelous?' Arch Uttam said. He tried to make himself smile again. 'Let us hope it is not *sorcerous*.'

I never learned how Kane worked this magic, and he never told me. Although I found some measure of wonder in it, as did Lady Lida and King Arsu, it seemed only to bore Arch Uttam. He stared at Kane with his soulless eyes as he steepled his thin fingers beneath his chin; something about Kane seemed to vex him. It was the King's prerogative to command entertainments, but that didn't stop Arch Uttam from rudely speaking out.

'I'm sure we have all had enough of this man's tricks,' he said. He turned to look down his thin nose at Kane. 'We have heard, player, that your skill with knives is something to be seen.'

Kane could not keep his old hate from burning through him. He growled out, 'Even as was yours, priest.'

Arch Uttam sat staring at Kane as if he could not believe what he had just heard. Finally, he barked at Kane: 'What was that?'

Kane smiled his savage smile, showing his long white teeth. And then, to Maram's horror, and mine, he said, 'Today, I only cast my knives at a wooden target. But you put yours through that girl's throat with a precision we all must wonder at. She couldn't have suffered much, eh? Who else has such skill but a high priest of the Kallimun?'

Kane managed to say this without obvious sarcasm but only the greatest seeming sincerity. Even so, he walked a knife blade's edge between condemnation of Arch Uttam and compliment. A fool such as Maram might be able to get away with such wordplay, but Kane was Kane. Arch Uttam stared at him again, and his eyes finally came alive with hate.

'You revere Lord Morjin's priests, do you?' he said to Kane.

'Even as I do Morjin himself,' Kane said. 'What would the world be without him and the truest of his servants?'

With many eyes now gazing upon Arch Uttam in witness of this singular interchange, it seemed that he had no choice but to interpret Kane's words as praise. But I felt the poison in his voice as he snapped at Kane: 'The world will be a paradise when we all *do* serve him truly. As you may serve him now by showing us what is possible through years of discipline and great concentration.'

Kane bowed his head at this. Then he beckoned toward Estrella, standing with the rest of us by the cart. She walked toward him bearing a velvet-covered tray on which sat seven gleaming knives. It was her job to hold the tray up to Kane as he plucked up the knives one by one and hurled them at the target. And again, to retrieve the knives and stand many paces farther back as Kane repeated a remarkable feat: planting six of the knives in a perfect hexagram around the edge of the innermost circle while the seventh knife transfixed its center.

Arch Uttam stared at the target, and for the moment seemed disinclined to speak.

King Angand, however, clapped his hands and said to Kane, 'If you could learn such skill with the sword, we would be glad to have you ride with our army.'

'And ours,' King Arsu said. 'There are always errants to deal with.'

'Yes,' Arch Uttam said to Kane. He smiled at him. 'Then *you* could put steel through flesh instead of wood.'

I prayed that Kane would let Arch Uttam have the final word in this deadly duel forming up between them. For at least ten of my heart's beats, Kane did not say anything, and he did not move.

And then he growled out to him, 'I'm just a simple player, eh? Throwing knives is one thing; facing swords in the heat of battle is another. As you have said, Arch Uttam, I can only hope to master my fear. And someday, by the One's grace, to witness the defeat of those who have turned away from the Light.'

He bowed then, not so much to Arch Uttam or King Arsu, but to the sun burning like a circle of white-hot steel above their silk-covered box. Without another word, he turned about and walked back toward the cart.

'What is *wrong* with you?' I whispered to him as he moved up close to me.

'So, Morjin is wrong,' he muttered. He cast a quick, killing look at Arch Uttam. 'It's wrong that the Beast himself isn't here instead of his lackey. Then I'd put a knife into each of his damn eyes!'

We hoped to end our performance with Alphanderry singing a few songs. King Arsu agreed with this plan, and waved his hand at the cart's door as if commanding it to open. When Estrella walked over and turned the handle to let out the mysterious minstrel known as Thierraval, everyone around the square fell silent. They watched as Alphanderry positioned himself in front of King Arsu's box – but not *too* near it. Then Kane took up his mandolet, and Estrella and I our flutes, and we all gathered together to play for the King.

Three songs we gave to King Arsu and his companions, and to the many soldiers looking on and listening in wonder. For we made, I thought, a wondrous music – or rather Alphanderry did. While Kane and I, with Estrella, summoned out of our instruments ancient melodies, Alphanderry sang out with the much finer instrument of his voice. No words poured forth from his golden throat, not even those of the Galadin. The perfect tones that his lips shaped and shaded had something of the form of words, and something of their meaning, too, but seemed to go far beyond them and touch upon that deep, resounding place in which words had their source. It was a true magic that he worked that day. His songs pierced the hearts of all who listened. Each person in the square, I thought, heard in them what he most wished to hear: yearning for love or exaltation of war; chants pealing out like bells and hymns to life and lamentations of the dead. Even as I breathed into my flute and played to accompany Alphanderry's marvelous singing, I couldn't help thinking of the astonished look in Yismi's eyes as Arch Uttam had sliced his knife across her throat. So it was, I sensed, with many of those who listened to Alphanderry. Something in his brilliant voice seemed rip through the thin veil that separated life from death, and the earth from the starry heavens. By the time he finished the last of his songs, many people were weeping and many more stared at him as if they could not believe what they had just heard.

In the vast silence that came over the square, as King Arsu and King Angand stared at Alphanderry stunned and unable to speak, Alphanderry bowed his head to them and quickly returned to the cart. Estrella walked over with him to shut the door. Then she came back over to where Kane and I stood in front of King Arsu's box, and we made our bow together.

At last, King Arsu returned to himself. He smiled at us even as a thunder of applause rang out from around the square. He reached for his purse with its golden coins. But then Arch Uttam stopped him, laying his bony hand on King Arsu's arm. He raised his other hand to silence the soldiers who were shouting, clapping and calling for Thierraval to come back out of the cart to sing for them again.

Now the air fell so deathly still that I could hear the flies buzzing around the foodsellers' stalls. Arch Uttam's scabrous eyes looked from Kane to Estrella to me, then settled upon the cart. He looked at King Arsu. And then, in a bone-chilling voice, he called out: 'There is error here.'

Hundreds of people seemed horrified to hear this. Hundreds of pairs of eyes now turned their heat upon us. I sensed Kane readying himself to respond to Arch Uttam's dreaded accusation. I shook my head slightly to warn him to say nothing.

And then I called up to the box: 'What error, Arch Uttam?'

The High Priest of the Kallimun of Hesperu stared down at me. His knife-like eyes fairly cut open the scar marking my forehead. Something about me, too, seemed to vex him.

'Do you really not know, flute-player?' he asked me.

'We have only played the ancient songs,' I said to him.

'But do you not know that many of them have been proscribed?'

He waited like a spider watching for a butterfly to become ensnared in its web. As it happened, I did *not* know this, but I did not want to betray my naivety. And so I said to him, 'We are only players who have traveled far and performed mostly in small villages. It might be that we haven't learned of everything that has been proscribed.'

'Ignorance of the law is no excuse for violating it,' he said to me.

'Indeed it is not,' I said, sweating beneath the sun as much his hateful gaze. 'And that is why we have striven to play only the classics that would be acceptable. But since we don't have your keen discernment as to which songs fall into error, perhaps we have chosen unwisely.'

My words did not mollify him. He only stared at me and said, 'Then it is upon me to enlighten you. Which songs would you choose, if King Arsu should command you to play for us again?'

It now seemed that there could be no escaping Arch Uttam's web. I glanced over by the cart, where Maram shook his head as if he had given up the last of his hope.

And I said to him, 'The *Song of the Sun* is full of beautiful music.'

And Arch Uttam snapped his head at this as he told me: 'That which is beauty becomes ugliness when it lapses into error. And so the *Song of the Sun* has been proscribed.'

'But what about the *Gest of Nodin and Yurieth*? That is a simple love song.'

'It may be simple,' Arch Uttam said. 'But it has also been proscribed.'

I did not need to ask him about my favorite verse, the *Song of Kalkamesh and Telemesh*, which told of the crusade to liberate the Lightstone after Morjin had first stolen it late in the Age of Swords.

610

As we would soon learn, that epic was first on the proscribed list. And so I asked Arch Uttam, 'Has the *Lay of the Lightstone* also been proscribed?'

'Proscribed? No. But one may sing it only with changes made to the old verses that reflect the Lightstone's true history. And Lord Morjin's place in that history.'

Changes, I thought. *Lies, and more lies.*

I said to Arch Uttam, 'And the *Lord of Light*?'

'It is the same with that work, especially so.'

I gave up trying to find any traditional song, epic or poem that Arch Uttam would approve. I glanced quickly at Daj and said, 'What, then, of the *Gest of Eleikar and Ayeshtan*?'

Arch Uttam frowned at this. He obviously hated that I had named a work with which he was unfamiliar. I sensed, too, that without words to provoke his scorn and cognizance, he had failed to identify the melodies of Alphanderry's three songs.

'I'm sure that I have never heard of that work,' he said. 'And sure that I don't wish to.'

'But is it on the proscribed list?'

'*All* works,' he told me, 'that have not been approved have been proscribed. That is the new edict. You should know that.'

It nearly killed me to bow my head to him and say politely, 'Then in the future we will make sure that all the words to our songs are approved. If we are in doubt, we will play only pure music, for its own sake.'

This failed to mollify him as well. His frown deepened as he stared at me and announced, '*Nothing* must ever be done for its own sake. Not a walk in the sunshine or the smelling of a flower's fragrance. *Especially* the making of music. It arouses too many passions. And all passion, as it is written, must be directed toward one purpose, and one purpose only. It disappoints me that you seem not to know this. It is a grave error.'

I felt a lust for violence stir inside Lord Mansarian and many of the soldiers standing about. When Arch Uttam spoke of a grave error, they could expect to see blood.

I prepared to run over to the cart and retrieve my sword so that I could make a last fight of things. I would not stand to be scourged and have the meat shredded from my bones – to say nothing of being crucified. Nor would I abide watching Estrella and Kane being tortured likewise, if Arch Uttam should include them in the correction of the error of playing a few lovely songs.

I do not know how things would have gone for us if Lady Lida hadn't caught King Arsu's ear and said, 'Who of us hasn't made errors from time to time? Who of us hasn't lapsed into enjoying a beautiful sunset just because it is beautiful? These players tried to give us a fine music, and in their ignorance chose their songs foolishly. I am no priest, of course, but are these players' errors really so very bad?'

Arch Uttam stared at her as if he wished to nail *her* to a cross, and only awaited the chance.

Just before Arch Uttam responded to this, Lida resumed speaking to King Arsu. The King held up his hand to silence Arch Uttam. He seemed utterly taken with Lida; she communicated things to him with a few murmured words, a pressure of her hand against his wrist and the imploring look in her eyes.

Then King Arsu turned to Arch Uttam, and for the first time that day, took on something of the aspect of a true king: 'We must take into account that these players are practically strangers in our land, and should be treated with the hospitality for which Hesperu is famed. Is it generous to construe their errors according to the strictest possible interpretation of what we know of error? Must we fear the goodness of our hearts and the forgiveness that Lord Morjin has taught us? We know well that we can be stern, at need – who has not lost a beloved companion in this last war? Who has not exulted in the sight of the Avrians crucified for their defiance? But this is a day of celebration: of our victory and our cousin's birthday, and therefore of life. Can we not celebrate the gift of our lives in realizing that all who live are subject to error? Surely these players have made errors, but surely they are no worse than Errors Minor.'

King Arsu, I thought, having completed a successful campaign, was in a great good humor. He practically *willed* Arch Uttam to bow before his magnanimity.

But a High Priest of the Kallimun will bow before no one – except the Red Dragon himself. And so, in an icy voice, Arch Uttam said to King Arsu: 'You are a great king who has led Hesperu to victory in great battles. And we can all give thanks that you have devoted yourself to the study of war and the ordering of Hesperu's empire, won in the Red Dragon's name. But there other battles that must be fought, and it is your very great devotion to final victory that has necessarily kept you from studying the deeper ways of error. It is to free you to fulfill your purpose that the Red Dragon, in his compassion, has sent his priests to aid you. And that is all that I would ask of you today, that you let them, for that is *my* purpose.'

King Arsu's high spirits seemed to plummet. He could not gainsay

Arch Uttam without defying Morjin himself. And so he told Arch Uttam: 'It is upon you, of course, to decide the nature of these players' error. But let us say that they have made only an Error Minor. Shouldn't it be enough that they correct it by forfeiting their prize to the Kallimun school here? And that they be commanded to memorize the list of permitted works and the changes that have been made to them?'

Now it was Arch Uttam's turn to seethe with ire. Almost everyone listening to their debate, I thought, found King Arsu's judgment to be reasonable. Arch Uttam could not gainsay King Arsu without undermining his authority and thus ruining his effectiveness in leading Morjin's armies to triumph. And so it seemed that he had no choice except to be merciful toward us.

He gazed down from the box at Kane, Estrella and me. And he told us, 'As King Arsu has suggested, let it be. Are you willing to forfeit your prize?'

Over by the foodsellers' stalls, Lord Rodas stood with his six toughs waiting to hear how I would reply. His indignation bubbled out into the air like boiling oil.

'Yes,' I said, answering for all of us.

'And are you willing to memorize the changes in the songs that you may sing?'

'Yes,' I said, looking down at the grass.

'Very well,' he snapped out. 'Then your errors will be corrected.'

I felt the muscles along my throat begin to relax, as of the tension slowly easing on a piece of bent steel. And then Arch Uttam pointed at the cart and said, 'Let us make sure the minstrel understands this, too. Bring him to me.'

Kane flashed me a quick, dangerous look. Then he shook his head and said to Arch Uttam, 'Thierraval always keeps to himself after a performance. It is his way.'

'Excluding oneself from others is also an error,' Arch Uttam said. 'Therefore your minstrel will have a different way today. Go fetch him.'

But Kane only glared at Arch Uttam, and did not move.

Arch Uttam finally looked away from him. He turned his anger on Estrella, the smallest and youngest of our company. He pointed at the cart and commanded her: 'Go open that door, right now, girl! Or do you wish to stand in defiance of one of Lord Morjin's priests, which is defiance of Lord Morjin himself?'

Estrella had no choice but to carry out Arch Uttam's command. She ran over to the cart and opened its door. After looking inside, she turned toward Arch Uttam and shook her head. With quick motions of her hands and a look of puzzlement on her open, expressive face, she made it clear to Arch Uttam, and everyone else, that Thierraval was not inside the cart.

'What?' Arch Uttam cried out. He glared at Estrella. 'What are you saying, mime? Speak in words!'

'She cannot speak,' Kane growled out. 'She is mute.'

'Mute, you say?'

'As silent as the sky. But her meaning is plain enough: You won't find Thierraval inside the cart. As I told you, he always vanishes after a performance.'

'What trick is this, juggler?'

'No trick at all, priest. You might say it is part of our act.'

Arch Uttam drew himself up stiffly and sneered at Kane as if he refused to bandy words with a lowly player. He whipped about, turning to face Lord Mansarian. He pointed at the cart as he called out, 'Go bring me that minstrel!'

Lord Mansarian bowed his head to him. He threw back his red cape, drew his sword and came down from the box. After hurrying across the square, he brushed Estrella aside. He practically leaped up into the cart. I heard him banging about inside as if striking his sword's pommel against the cart's floor and walls. I could only guess at Lord Mansarian's reaction in coming face to face with Bemossed hiding there, and Bemossed's response to this search. I commanded my arms and legs not to move; if I could have stilled my racing heart, I would have.

And then Lord Mansarian stepped out of the cart and closed the door. He called up to Arch Uttam: 'The minstrel is not inside.'

I could not keep my breath from bursting out in a rush of relief.

And then Arch Uttam called down to Lord Mansarian: 'What? Are you *sure* he is not hiding there? It must be a trick: a false bottom to their wagon. A false wall.'

'No, I tested for that. The minstrel must be elsewhere.'

Arch Uttam stared at our cart as if he might order it chopped to splinters with axes. Then he stared at Lord Mansarian. When this grim-faced Crucifier, famed for ferreting out errants from hiding places in their houses, declared that no minstrel hid inside it, even a high priest of the Kallimun had to accept this.

At last, Arch Uttam said, 'The minstrel must have slipped away somehow when we were discussing these players' errors. It would seem that they are adept at sleight of word as well as prestidigitation.'

He looked past the food-sellers' stalls and the courtesans' pavilion at the many rows of tents of the army's encampment. He cast his gaze down upon Estrella and said, 'Tell me where he went! You must know.'

But Estrella only held out her hands as her eyes grew wide with mystification and she shook her head.

'Speak!' he commanded her. 'Do not mock me any more!'

Kane's voice rolled out like a dark thunder as he called up to Arch Uttam: 'She cannot speak any more than you can fly!'

Arch Uttam seemed ready to order Kane put to death on the spot. He snapped out, 'You mock me, too. You say the girl cannot speak. We shall see. Lord Mansarian!'

He commanded this butcher to take hold of Estrella, and bring her forward. Although Lord Mansarian may have stood in debt to Bemossed, he did not extend his gratitude to Estrella. I watched helplessly as he did Arch Uttam's bidding. He escorted Estrella up the steps of the box and over to Arch Uttam so that they stood between the priest and King Arsu. Lord Mansarian clamped his bronze-shod arm across Estrella's trembling body so that she could not flee. Her dark, wild eyes found out mine as if pleading with me not to let anyone harm her.

'Don't be afraid,' Arch Uttam said to her as he rose up from his chair. 'For the true of heart there is nothing ever to fear.'

King Arsu's guards did not like anyone outside his entourage to approach very close to him, not even a weaponless young girl. King Arsu seemed not to like this course of events either. He said to Arch Uttam: 'Can we not get on with the celebrations?'

'We must always celebrate truth,' Arch Uttam said in a deadly calm voice. He placed his fingertips on Estrella's jaw to tilt her face up toward him. 'I think this girl has something of the look of the Sung. And the look of defiance.'

Next to Arch Uttam, still sitting at the edge of the box, King Angand looked on with interest. He seemed to question whether Estrella might really have had her origins in the people of Sunguru.

And then Lady Lida touched King Arsu's arm and said, 'If the girl really can't speak, then she can't be held accountable for defiance.'

Before King Arsu could say anything, Arch Uttam barked out: 'Lord Mansarian! If this girl has dared to play us all false, do you think that *you* could make her speak?'

'Yes, Arch Uttam,' he said as his arm tightened across Estrella's slender chest. His scarred face seemed as empty of life as a steel mask. 'Thumbscrews would loosen her tongue, if it was stuck. A little fire applied in the right places would make her sing.'

I traded a quick look with Kane. I could see his black eyes, like mine, looking for a way out of the violence moving toward us like a fog of blood.

Arch Uttam smiled at Lord Mansarian. He seemed to be testing him; I sensed that this had become a ritual with them: the High Priest of Hesperu trying to make sure of the devotion of a once-noble man who had gone from being a rebel to Hesperu's greatest murderer.

'I might prefer a flaying,' Arch Uttam told Lord Mansarian. 'But even you, I think, might have difficulty peeling the skin off a girl.'

If Arch Uttam was trying to frighten Estrella into speaking, then he failed. Or perhaps he was still trying to find some act or abomination so utterly cruel that Lord Mansarian would refuse to carry it out.

'I could take the skin off her hand,' Lord Mansarian said, 'like a glove.'

I noticed Lida's fingers moving against King Arsu's wrist, and King Arsu suddenly called out: 'This is no day for torturing children!'

Arch Uttam only smiled at this. He said to Lord Mansarian, 'You yourself once resisted the truth, did you not?'

'Even as I resisted Lord Morjin,' Lord Mansarian said.

'And you did this of your own will, did you not?'

'Freely, I did.'

'And so who was to blame for the torments you suffered?'

'Only myself,' Lord Mansarian said. He let his eyes look down upon Estrella. 'But there can be no resisting the Red Dragon's *power*. It is perfect – and glorious.'

I sensed the sincerity in his voice, as well a deep loathing of himself. Clearly he blamed himself, and not Morjin, for whatever evil had befallen him.

'Perfect and glorious!' Arch Uttam called out as he caressed Estrella's face. '*That*, Lord Mansarian, is a perfect characterization of Lord Morjin and all that he puts his hand to.'

His bony fingers now touched beneath Estrella's jaw and felt down along her delicate throat. He used them to force apart her jaws. He positioned her so that the sun streaming through the box's silk covering illumined her open mouth. He grabbed up a cloth and used it to take hold of her tongue. Then he pulled it out as he rudely stuck his fingers down her throat until she coughed and gagged.

As it happened, he had once been a healer of some reputation. And this former healer who now hunted down healers in the Red Dragon's name, loudly announced: 'There is nothing wrong with this girl, in her body, that keeps her from speaking. And so there must be something wrong in her mind: some error of thought.'

He let go of her, even as Lord Mansarian maintained his hold. He wiped his fingers with the cloth. Then he continued: 'All errors of thought can be corrected with right thoughts. And no thought can be more perfect than that of Lord Morjin himself.'

Arch Uttam bent down and brought his horrible face up close to Estrella's. I could almost smell his foul, bloody breath as he said to her with a false kindness: 'Do not be afraid, girl. Close your eyes. Hold the image of Lord Morjin inside you. Concentrate on it! Let it blaze like the sun! The Red Dragon will burn away your muteness more surely than Lord Mansarian's fire.'

Arch Uttam then pressed his palm against Estrella's forehead as if to sear this image into her.

I stood there with Kane on the grass of the square looking up at the box at Arch Uttam, Lord Mansarian and Estrella. I felt *my* hand aching to grasp the hilt of my sword. I felt my heart aching as well. At last, Estrella opened her eyes and stared at Arch Uttam. She could not hide her contempt for him, or her fear.

'Well, girl?' Arch Uttam asked. 'Does Lord Morjin live inside you?'

Estrella slowly nodded her head. She could not tell him that Morjin, who had taken her speech in the first place, would always dwell inside her like a snake wrapping its coils around her throat.

'Speak, then!' Arch Uttam commanded her. 'Speak now!'

But Estrella only shook her head and held out her hands helplessly.

'Speak, damn you, brat!'

Tears welled up in her eyes.

And then Kane shouted up to the box: 'If the girl is ever healed, it will only be through the Maitreya!'

'She is as whole as you or I!' Arch Uttam shouted back at him.

'No – she is mute and has been so for years!'

'You,' Arch Uttam said, pointing down at Kane, 'lie.'

Arch Uttam made a fist as if to control the trembling of his fingers. And then he added, 'And therefore you are guilty of sedition as well.'

Around the square, many people looked upon this scene intently but did not say anything. I saw Lida gripping King Arsu's hand in silence.

King Arsu said, 'Before crucifying them, we would like to know the truth of things.'

'Indeed,' Arch Uttam said. 'The juggler and the girl must be put to the test.'

Lida's hand tightened around King Arsu's hand, and the King told Arch Uttam, 'It is too fine a day for more torture.'

Arch Uttam considered this. 'If not torture, then a trial – a trial of arms.'

Kane's black eyes gleamed at this. So did mine. I imagined King Arsu sending out Lord Mansarian or some champion to fight Kane sword to sword.

But Arch Uttam, it seemed, imagined other things. He plucked an apple from the bowl of fruit on the long table in front of him. Without warning, he hurled it straight at Kane's face. Kane snatched it out of the air and stood looking at Arch Uttam with loathing.

Then Arch Uttam explained the nature of the trial that he had in mind: Estrella was to go down to the cart and stand before the target with the apple balanced on top of her head. Kane must then throw the knife at the apple.

'If the juggler misses,' Arch Uttam announced, 'it is only because his bad conscience spoils his aim, and we shall know that he is lying. Likewise if he strikes the girl.'

What must it be like, I wondered, to feel so superior to others that one could torment, maim or kill them at will?

I hoped that Lida might somehow persuade King Arsu to put a stop to this barbaric trial. But the King seemed to take a great interest in Arch Uttam's proposal, as he did in all cruel and bizarre things. I watched him pull his hand away from Lida.

'And if he strikes the apple?' King Arsu asked Arch Uttam.

With reluctance, Arch Uttam forced out, 'Then we shall know that he is telling the truth.'

'Let be so,' King Arsu said. 'If the juggler strikes the apple, there is no error, and they will be free to go.'

He pointed down at the cart. 'Put the girl in her place.'

Lord Mansarian now escorted Estrella back down to the cart. He stood her up with her back to the target, facing Kane, and then backed away. Kane stalked forward, squeezing the apple in his hand. He touched her cheek, kissed her brow. Then he set the apple gently on top of Estrella's head. After grabbing up two

618

throwing knives, one in either hand, he returned to his place in front of the target.

I overheard one of the soldiers say, 'Why *two* knives? Doesn't he know that Arch Uttam will never give him a second chance?'

A second soldier next to him shrugged his shoulders and said, 'Maybe the other knife balances him.'

This was true. Kane would strive for every advantage in this evil trial that Arch Uttam had forced upon him. But I knew that Kane had a deeper reason: if he missed, the second knife would be for Arch Uttam.

I now walked over to the foodsellers' stalls with my friends, so that we would not distract Kane by standing too near the cart. I wondered if Bemossed knew what was about to happen as he dwelled in the darkness inside it.

Out in the square, Kane looked at nothing except the apple perched on top of Estrella's head. She stood almost perfectly still, fixing her gaze upon him. I sensed no fear in her – at least no fear of Kane. Although her face remained quiet and serious, she seemed to be smiling at him from some place deep inside herself.

I knew that Kane could split the apple. He would not let his love for Estrella ruin his aim.

And then, before he could raise back his arm, Arch Uttam cried out: 'We have all seen this man's skill; at this distance, casting the knife will be no trial. Therefore, let the distance be doubled.'

King Arsu, with Lida pulling on his elbow, looked at him as if he thought this last condition was cruelly unfair. Lord Mansarian looked at Arch Uttam this way, too – and so did half a hundred nobles and soldiers. But Arch Uttam would not be defeated a second time that day.

'*This* is written,' he called out. '"*We must always double and redouble our efforts to prove ourselves worthy of the journey toward the One.*" Let the juggler prove himself to us. Lord Mansarian!'

He issued a command to Lord Mansarian, who borrowed a spear from one of his red-caped soldiers. He then walked over to where Estrella stood in front of the cart. With hardly a glance at her, he began counting out paces as he stepped out toward Kane and then continued counting until he reached a place on the grass twice Kane's distance from the target. There he stuck the spear into the grass, down into the loamy earth. Kane was to stand behind the spear, facing Estrella.

After Kane had taken his place at this new mark, Lord Mansarian once more retreated nearer to King Arsu's box.

Again, Kane fixed the whole of his awareness on the apple gleaming a bright crimson on top of Estrella's head. Arch Uttam had set for him an impossible distance, better suited to archery than the casting of a foot-long knife. Maram stood on one side of me muttering, 'Ah, too bad, too bad!' while Daj waited on the other side almost weeping. Even Atara seemed terrified by the future now about to fall upon us in a whirring of steel. I felt my heart pounding wildly. I did not think that even Kane could make such a throw.

Neither, it seemed, did anyone else. From his chair up in the box, King Angand said to Arch Uttam, 'It is too far and too windy. This is no true trial of arms. No man who ever lived could make such a throw.'

But Arch Uttam only scoffed at this. 'They're magicians, aren't they? They made the minstrel disappear – maybe they can make the wind stop, too.'

While Estrella waited for Kane to make ready, she closed her eyes as if she could not bear to look at him. I felt her enter into an immense, inner stillness. All at once, the splendidly colored banners flapping above the pavilions of King Arsu and King Angand drooped down and the wind suddenly died. Kane's eyes blazed brightly. And then, with a suddenness that astonished everyone, his arm drew back and whipped forward with a blinding speed. The knife flashed through the air in a whirl of bright steel almost impossible to see. Its point drove straight through the apple's center, pinning the apple to the target. Then, and only then, Estrella opened her eyes and smiled at Kane.

'He did it!' Maram cried out, clapping me on the shoulder. 'Oh, my lord – he really did it!'

Kane's great feat caused hundreds of soldiers to draw their swords and strike their pommels against their shields in a tumult of acclaim. Even Lord Mansarian bowed his head to Kane. But Arch Uttam only cast him a hateful look. He stood by his chair up in the box waiting for the thunder of celebration to die down.

'The juggler got lucky,' he finally called out with a sickening peevishness. 'And luck is no part of a true trial.'

'A trial is a trial,' King Angand said.

'*This* trial,' Arch Uttam said, 'is not over. Let the distance be doubled again!'

So saying, he grabbed up a second apple from the bowl. Again, he hurled it out toward Kane. But almost before the apple left his hand, Kane cast his second knife, left-handed, straight at the apple.

The knife struck it in midair, and the greater weight of its steel carried the apple back toward Arch Uttam so that the knife buried itself quivering in the table with the apple transfixed upon its blade.

'Was that luck, too, priest?' Kane called to him. He grinned like a wolf, showing his long, white teeth.

Arch Uttam stared at the knife planted in the table as if he couldn't believe what he had just seen. I, myself, had always thought that striking a moving target in the air was impossible.

With a great sigh and groan, King Arsu heaved himself up from his chair. He looked straight at Arch Uttam and said, 'The trial is over. The juggler and the mime are deemed to have told the truth and shall be free to perform where they will, even as *we* have said.'

At this, Estrella ran forward toward Kane and leaped into his arms. She wept and laughed silently, all at once. And then the wind began blowing fiercely again.

'Sire!' a voice called out. This came from Lord Rodas, who began advancing across the square toward King Arsu's box. It seemed that we might not be so very free, after all. 'Sire, my players have forfeited their prize in payment of their error, but what about *my* portion of it?'

Now Lady Lida stood up, too, and whispered something in King Arsu's ear. And King Arsu pointed at Lord Rodas as he called down to Lord Mansarian: 'There is something vexing about this New Lord and his insistence on gaining gold. Take him to be questioned, and his men, too.'

Lord Mansarian hurried forward to carry out this command. He grabbed the outraged Lord Rodas's arm, while other knights of his red-caped company closed in upon Lord Rodas's six hirelings and escorted them from the square. It seemed that we really were free.

Then Arch Uttam cast us one final, poisonous look that promised death, and stalked off toward his pavilion. We hurried over to the cart, which we began making ready for the next leg of our journey, out of Hesperu and into the vast, forested miles of the mountains that lay beyond.

39

We left the army's encampment as quickly as we could without giving the impression that we were fleeing from it. When we reached the Avrian Road, we turned north toward Orun, only two miles away. We soon stopped at the edge of a cotton field. I opened the cart's door so that Bemossed could finally come out of his prison and join us in the sunlight. He embraced Estrella and ran his hand through her curly hair as he told her, 'I knew that Kane would not cut off a single lock.'

He embraced Kane, too, and stood there as if wondering what we would do next.

Although I wanted to unhitch Altaru and gallop back through Orun and across the Black Bridge to escape the men who had almost murdered us, I felt the need for council even more. And so I called for everyone to gather close by the cart.

'Liljana,' I said, looking at this stout woman who had kept her calm through the whole of our ordeal. 'You seemed almost familiar with Lady Lida, and she saved us, more than once. Why?'

Liljana nodded her head into the gusting wind. And she said simply, 'Lida is Maitriche Telu.'

This news surprised all of us, especially Master Juwain. He said to Liljana, 'I had thought that King Arsu's grandfather, King Taitu, had destroyed the Hesperuk Maitriche Telu.'

'I had thought this, too,' Liljana said. 'But it seems that at least one sanctuary must have remained undiscovered.'

'And in all those years, they have sent you no communication?'

'They wouldn't know how, or whom to send word to. You see, even within the Maitriche Telu, we have our secrets – and so we survive.'

For the course of two long quests across Ea, Liljana had told us very little of the ancient Sisterhood that she led. And now, she would explain only that the Maitriche Telu was composed of secret sanctuaries in all lands. The sisters of individual sanctuaries knew each other and the identity of their mistresses only, and the mistresses each reported to a single matriarch in charge of several sanctuaries, and so on. This gave great protection in case any sanctuary was discovered and its sisters tortured, for they could betray only the next highest sister in the net that connected them to the great sanctuary in Tria and the Materix herself. But if enough knots in this net were destroyed, it could also leave them isolated and ignorant of the workings of their own order.

'But then how did you recognize Lida?' Master Juwain asked.

'There are signs we use,' Liljana said. 'Secret signs that others see as normal expressions and gestures. It is its own language.'

I bowed my head to this woman whom I had come to respect more than almost any other. I asked her, 'Can Lida help us, then? It will go badly for us if Arch Uttam sends assassins after us or if King Arsu changes his mind.'

Liljana shook her head at this. 'Lida has only so much influence over King Arsu. As for Arch Uttam, she lives in mortal peril of him.'

'*We* are ourselves in mortal peril,' Maram said. He looked about the field as if Arch Uttam's spies might be hiding among the white, wind-whipped bolls of cotton. 'We must go on as quickly as we can. That traitor Salmelu, who now calls himself Haar Igasho, is riding toward King Arsu's encampment.'

'We know,' I said to him. 'While you were in the courtesans' tent, King Arsu announced that King Orunjan was coming to a conclave along with a master priest.'

'He did?' Maram said. 'But did he also tell that Morjin rode with them?'

'What?' I said, looking down the road toward the south. 'Morjin? Here, in Hesperu? How do you know?'

'Ah, I don't *really* know,' Maram admitted. 'But while I was with the courtesans, King Arsu's messenger came into the tent for a little comfort after his hard ride, or so he said. He liked to talk, that man did. He said that Morjin rode with King Orunjun in secret. Well, very soon, I think, it will be a secret that is no secret that Morjin has come to Hesperu – to meet with the other kings to plan the conquest of Eanna, if not the whole damn world.'

Now I stared hard at the road's gray paving stones as if they might tell me if my enemy was pounding down them toward us.

I said to Maram: 'Surely it can't be Morjin, himself. Surely it must be the third droghul that Atara told of.'

At this, Atara turned her blindfolded face toward me and said, 'I assumed he was a droghul, but I can't *see* that, Val. The one who comes – it *could* be Morjin.'

I waited while a farmer plodded along with a wagon full of manure, and I let him pass by. Then I drew forth my sword and pointed it down the road. Its silvery blade seemed to burn with a blue fire but gave little light. If Morjin himself had come from Argattha, he would surely bear the Lightstone with him, wouldn't he? And so wouldn't my sword flare in resonance with the golden cup as it once had?

Master Juwain saw the thrust of my reasoning, which hadn't changed since the first droghul had pursued us across the plains of the Wendrush. He said to me, 'I'm afraid you can't use your sword as a test this way any more, Val.'

I watched as the flames running along Alkaladur's length grew hotter. I said to Atara, 'If we knew it was really Morjin, I could wait for him and put an end to things, here and now. And the rest of you could take Bemossed to safety.'

I looked at Kane as if to ask if he would give up everything for this final vengeance; his eyes burned with a dark fire of their own, and I saw that he dwelled with death.

'But we don't even know if Bemossed *is* the Maitreya!' Maram said. 'And without you and Kane with us, we'll never live to reach home!'

Master Juwain nodded his head at this and said, 'There are other considerations as well. If you kill Morjin and fail to reclaim the Lightstone, it will pass to Arch Uttam or King Arsu. Or to another high priest if Morjin has left it in Argattha. In the end, one of these would become a new Red Dragon. And complete Morjin's conquest in his name.'

'Not if Bemossed could keep *him* from using the Lightstone,' I said.

'But could he? Would he?' Master Juwain said to me. 'Maram is right: if you throw your life away this way, Bemossed might not live to contest anyone for the Lightstone.'

'That is a chance we'll have to take!'

'Indeed? But on whose behalf must we take it? Yours? The dead who are buried on the Culhadosh Commons? Or the living, in all lands?'

'No one can see all ends,' I said. 'We have such a rare *chance*!'

At this Atara came over to me and grasped my hand. In a clear voice, she told me, 'If you and Kane go after the one who pursues us, I see your deaths.'

Atara's face turned toward me as she tried to fight back her fear, and I saw our deaths, too. And I said, 'I don't care!'

'No, Val,' she said to me as her hand tightened around mine. 'You *must* care. And you must live.'

Master Juwain nodded his head at this. 'There is a great deal at stake here, beyond our lives or even the life of Ea.'

At that moment, Alphanderry stepped out of the shimmering air and said to me, 'I would rather sing while you play the flute than wail at your funeral.'

Bemossed, I saw, stood near the cart taking in every word of our debate. His large, luminous eyes held much doubt, and he seemed at once both restless and calm, innocent and wise.

'I have seen too much death, Valashu,' he said to me. 'Is there no other way?'

I squeezed the black jade of my sword's hilt so hard that my hand hurt. I said, 'Not so long as Morjin lives.'

'Is there no way, even for him, other than murder and war?'

I shook my head at this. 'You're a dreamer, Bemossed.'

'You have called me the Maitreya as well,' he said. 'Should I not then dwell in dreams?'

He brushed back the curls from his gentle face, which came alive with a deep light that seared into me. Then he looked from me to Kane. Something inside my fierce friend seemed to soften. And Kane said to me, 'There is a time for fighting and a time for fleeing. Even if we *could* come within striking distance of Morjin without him smelling us out, which we couldn't, what do you suppose would happen then, eh? King Arsu would send Lord Mansarian and his damn Red Capes after our companions, and they'd hunt them down.'

'Likely they will hunt us down anyway as soon King Orunjan meets up with King Arsu,' I said. 'If anyone should tell of us, Morjin will come after us with the whole of King Arsu's army.'

'That is a good argument for going quickly, as Maram has said. We will have a lead – let's keep it and lose ourselves in the mountains.'

Estrella gazed at me with a look of utter simplicity and a question in her eyes that cut into me like the keenest steel: Why kill at all unless killing was inescapably thrust upon me? She had a way, I thought, of showing me my soul.

625

'All right,' I finally said. I sheathed Alkaladur, and put it back inside the cart. 'Let us then flee, as fast as we can.'

But with our heavy cart and our horses yoked to it, we could not set anything like a rapid pace. We needed to find a wood where we could abandon the cart, and with it our disguise as players, but it would be folly to do this too close to King Arsu's army.

And so we continued our journey back up the road. The wind blew steadily out of the north, cooling the sweltering valley of the Iona River. We turned east at Orun, which stank of rotting wood and oily fish, and we crossed over the Black Bridge into the rich bottom land on the east side of the river. A few miles farther on, we left the road to strike out along back lanes more or less straight for the Khal Arrak pass through the mountains. It would be more difficult to ride cross-country through field and forest, but easier to throw off anyone who might pursue us.

Amid rice bogs and swarms of mosquitoes, we soon came upon a village of a few dozen mud huts called Tajul. We had no intention of stopping in this ugly place, but the sight of our cart, painted with such eye-popping colors, drew the curiosity of the few villagers not at work in the surrounding fields.

One of these, a thick-bodied man with a shock of curly hair and a grizzled beard, called out to us: 'Good players! Have you any medicines? My son is sick, and could use something for his pain.'

Though he might once have been tall, he stood all hunched over as if crippled with some disease; all his movements seemed to torment him. He wore a tunic of good silk, belted with a piece of thick leather chafed in a way that suggested it might once have borne a sword. He gave his name as Falco and said his son had been kicked in the belly by a mule.

Master Juwain asked him, 'Is there no healer hereabouts who can help him?'

Falco shook his head at this. 'We had a good one, Jahal, but he left our village last year.'

He spat into the street, and I suddenly knew that Jahal had not left the village of his own will, but had been taken away.

At the grave look that fell over Falco's face, Master Juwain said to him: 'I have had some practice tending our troupe's wounds. May I look in upon him?'

Though we all wanted urgently to go on, Falco said that he would be honored to offer us refreshment, and Master Juwain climbed down from his horse – and it seemed that there was no help for breaking our flight in this poor village.

Falco invited all of us to come inside his house – all of us except Bemossed, who stayed with the cart. Falco opened the door to his house, and we entered its large, single room. I immediately noted the scabbarded sword mounted above the polished teak mantle. There, bending in front of the fireplace, his eldest daughter hurried to get some water boiling for coffee.

Across the room, his son lay in bed, and his wife sat in a chair by his side, holding his hand. Falco presented her as Nela, and then smiled at his son as he said, 'And this is Taitu, named for the old king.'

Taitu, I saw, could not have been more than fifteen years old. I thought him a handsome lad, though it was hard to tell, for his smooth face was all contorted in pain. He lay flat out on his back, and wore a pair of silken trousers but no shirt. A livid bruise marked the brown skin near his navel, and his belly bulged out almost like that of a pregnant girl.

Master Juwain went over to him, and sat on the edge of the bed. He gently touched his hand to Taitu's belly, which caused Taitu to gasp in agony. Master Juwain then pushed against Taitu's skin, and Taitu's head snapped back as he let loose a terrible scream.

'Stop it!' Nela cried out, holding on to Taitu's spasming hand. 'Let him be!'

Master Juwain took his hand away and looked at Falco. And Falco said, 'He's dying, isn't he? I've told him he must prepare for death.'

I could almost feel Master Juwain's hand burning to take out his varistei and hold it to Taitu's belly. I felt the ache in his throat as his voice grew clear and deep, but held no hope: 'I'm afraid the blow fractured your son's spleen. Perhaps other organs, too. He is bleeding, inside. If there are any potions to stop it, I am unfamiliar with them.'

'But do you at least have a balm?' Nela asked us, mopping the sweat from Taitu's forehead. 'Something strong – I don't want him to suffer.'

Without a word, Liljana moved to go back outside and prepare for Taitu a tincture of poppy. But then the door suddenly opened, and Bemossed stood limned in the light pouring in from the street.

Falco stared at the black cross tattooed into Bemossed's forehead, and he called out, 'What is the Hajarim doing here?'

At first, Bemossed made no response to this, in words. He stood quietly looking down upon Taitu. I marveled at the change that

627

had come over him. His face shone like the summer sky after the wind has blown heavy clouds away.

And then, without doubt or hesitation, he said to Falco, 'I can help your boy.'

I sensed that Falco trembled to call him a liar and order him from his house. Instead, he stared at Bemossed as if dazzled by the sun.

'Let him help,' Nela said to Falco. She gazed at Bemossed as a desperate hope bloomed inside her. 'Let him try.'

'All right,' Falco finally said. He crossed the room and shut the door behind Bemossed. He looked at his daughter, and then at his wife. 'But let no one tell that we allowed a Hajarim into our house.'

Bemossed went over the side of the bed opposite Master Juwain. He smiled down upon Taitu as if to reassure the boy that everything would be all right. Then, as gently as a butterfly settling down upon a flower, he laid his hand on Taitu's belly. Taitu gave no cry of alarm, nor did he writhe in anguish at Bemossed's touch. He only gazed into Bemossed's eyes, even as Bemossed gazed at him. There came a flash, as of lightning out of a perfectly blue sky. It hung in the air above the bed in a blaze of glorre. Bemossed's hand seemed to channel this splendid fire deep into Taitu's belly. I felt a hot, surging new life stream through Taitu's insides. It seemed incredibly sweet and bright; I sensed it seeking out ruptured blood vessels and filling them up, making that which was broken beyond repair perfectly whole.

After a while, Bemossed took his hand away from Taitu and smiled at him again. We all watched in amazement as the boy's swollen belly began to shrink, like a waterskin being emptied. At the same time, he began sweating profusely; it seemed that the volume of blood filling his belly was being passed out of his skin as water.

'Mother,' Taitu said, looking up at Nela. 'It doesn't hurt any more!'

Nela tried to force out a 'thank you,' but she could barely speak against the sweet anguish choking up her throat.

'He will get better, now,' Bemossed said to her. 'Keep him in bed for the next day, and give him no food but much drink.'

Falco could not restrain the tears filling his eyes. He could not keep himself from grasping Bemossed's hand and calling out, 'You saved him! It is a miracle!'

Bemossed began to protest that all life was a miracle, and that this was only another of its workings. But Falco cut him off, saying,

'When I rode with Lord Mansarian, I heard a rumor that a Hajarim had healed his child, but I never really believed it until today.'

Falco crossed the room to the mantel and picked up the bottle of brandy that sat there. He said, 'We will drink to miracles – and my boy's life. Daughter! Fetch glasses, that we might celebrate!'

As his daughter hurried to carry out his command, I wanted to make our excuses and leave the village as quickly as we could. But something in Falco's manner stayed me. I said to him, 'You rode with the Red Capes?'

'I did,' he said. He seemed not to care whom he admitted this to. 'For two years, until we trapped a band of errants near Sagara. They deserved death for assassinating Haar Dyamian, and who was I to speak against it? But Ra Zahur, the priest who rode with our companies, demanded that we also crucify fifty men and women from Sagara, in retaliation. I *knew* the Sagarans – knew that they'd had nothing to do with the errants who murdered Haar Dyamian. And so I had to speak out.'

Falco's daughter gave out small glasses, and he filled them with banned brandy. 'To life!' he called out. He nodded at Bemossed. 'To those who bring life instead of taking it!'

Then he tossed back the brandy in one quick swallow, and refilled his glass. He waited for us to drink, too, before continuing his story.

'I've always spoken too freely, or so my Nela tells me.' He raised up his glass toward his wife. 'And so Ra Zahur recommended to Lord Mansarian that I be whipped and discharged for being too lenient with the enemy. The enemy! These were blacksmiths and potters in Sagara who were no more assassins than is my own son. They were Hesperuks, and Haralanders at that – our own countrymen, or so I said. But it didn't matter: Ra Zahur said that I should be whipped, and so I was.'

Falco downed two more glasses of brandy, and said, 'The dragon teeth tore the meat out of me, and made of me a cripple. I was lucky that Lord Mansarian took pity on me, and gave me a little gold so that I could buy some land and make a living for my family.'

Maram, who had matched Falco drink for drink, said, 'I hadn't heard that Lord Mansarian spared anyone pity.'

'Lord Mansarian is a hard man, it's true,' Falco said. 'But then, he's had a hard time of things, and few harder.'

'How so?' Maram asked, taking the bottle from Falco and refilling Falco's glass.

629

'You haven't heard? I thought everyone knew the story by now.'

With an obvious pride and longing, he recalled the days when Lord Mansarian had been the greatest warrior in the north to take up arms against the King. But finally, the King's men had hunted him down, at the estate of Lord Weru above Avrian, where Lord Mansarian had hidden his children. On the day the soldiers and priests came for him, the mother was away, seeking a healer to cure their daughter, who had the consumption. Falco gave the girl's name as Ysanna. The whole family had been thrown into a dungeon – the mother and Ysanna, too, when they returned. Then Arch Uttam came up from Gethun and ordered the children crucified before Lord Mansarian's eyes – all except Ysanna. Arch Uttam said that he had no liking to put a sick girl to death. So he gave Lord Mansarian a choice: Lord Mansarian's remaining daughter would be spared, her mother, too, if Lord Mansarian admitted the error of his ways. He had only to take the Red Dragon into his heart.

Falco seemed close to tears as he told us, 'Some say that Lord Mansarian was reborn that day. *I* say that he died, the best part of him. And if the crucifixion of his children drove the nails through his heart, what *he* did then turned him to stone. For freely, it's said, with his own hand, he crucified Lord Weru and his family – even the children. Then, with Arch Uttam and the other priests attesting the oath, he swore loyalty to King Arsu. Since then, there is no one who has slain more errants in the King's name.'

With that, he turned his head to spit into the fire.

I clapped him on the arm and said to him, 'Perhaps it's good that you no longer ride with the Red Capes.'

'Perhaps,' he muttered. 'But some of my old companions were good men, once. I know that many of them feel as I do, even if they say nothing.'

'Why do they still ride with Lord Mansarian, then?'

'What choice do they have? To desert and be hunted down? To see *their* children crucified? Then, too –'

'Yes?' I said, squeezing his arm.

'It takes more than courage to rebel. They must have at least a little hope. If a leader arose such as Lord Mansarian once was, or if Lord Mansarian, himself . . .'

His voice died off as he looked into the fire. And then he muttered, 'But, no – after what happened at Avrian, that's impossible now.'

The anguish in his voice caused Bemossed to leave Taitu's side and approach Falco. A deep understanding shone from Bemossed's face, and he looked at Falco as if he wanted to help him, too. Seeing this, Falco held up his hand and said, 'Go away, healer! I don't deserve your miracles. If you only knew what *I* have done. The truth is, whipping wasn't punishment enough for my *real* crimes.'

He took out of his pocket a single gold coin and pressed it into Bemossed's hand. Then he shuffled across the room to open the door.

'You'd better go now,' he said. He looked over at Taitu, who had now managed to sit up against the headboard of the bed. 'Thank you for saving my son's life.'

When he opened the door, however, there came a flurry of feet against muddy earth and I heard a boy's voice call out: 'The Hajarim healed Taitu! The Hajarim healed Taitu!'

I traded a quick, cutting look with Kane. Short of running after this eavesdropper and putting him to the sword – and perhaps everyone in the village – there was no way to keep the secret of what Bemossed had done.

We said farewell and hurried out to the cart. As my friends mounted their horses and Bemossed joined me on the cart's seat, a dozen villagers came out of their huts and in from the fields to watch us pass by. No one tried to stop us or even speak to us. They only stared at Bemossed, some in wonder, but some in loathing, too.

I feared for Falco, but even more for Bemossed, and us, that the Red Priests would inevitably learn of what had happened here. And so as quickly as we could, we left the clump of mud huts far behind us.

The cart's wheels ground and squeaked along the potholed road. Late in the afternoon, the farmland gave out into a rougher terrain of scrubland dotted with pools of stagnant water and bramble patches. I saw no good place to abandon the cart that would keep it hidden, and so Maram suggested that we simply burn it. But the smoke, I thought, might attract attention rather than repelling it. And so we journeyed on, into the early hours of the evening.

And then, perhaps ten or twelve miles from the village, just as it was growing dark, we came into a stretch of forest. Kane found an old path leading off the road through the trees. The horses struggled to pull the cart down this narrow, rocky strip, and it was an even harder work to get the cart off the path and cover it with a tangle of undergrowth. If anyone pursued us, the cart's tracks would certainly give it away. But at least it wouldn't stand by itself in some field like a colorful beacon announcing what we had done and where we had gone.

We took from the cart only those supplies that we would need for a long, hard ride. Liljana regretted leaving behind a large, cast iron oven that she had acquired along the way, and Maram told her that she had become spoiled. In our search across Hesperu, I thought, we all had, for we had never gone without food or suffered through a rainy night without a roof to protect us. After we had put aside our Hesperuk garb and donned tunics, trousers and traveling cloaks – and gathered up our weapons – it came time to consider one of the most daunting problems that faced us.

'Bemossed,' Kane said, pointing at the man we had bought as a slave, 'can't ride.'

Bemossed stood stroking the neck of Littlefoot, the gentlest of our horses. If he took any insult from Kane's words, he did not show it.

'He *can* ride,' I said. 'I've taught him.'

'So, one lesson only. He might be able to sit on that gelding without falling off, but he can't really *ride*.'

'He'll *have* to,' I said. 'We'll help him – there's no other choice.'

I looked at Bemossed and smiled, even though I felt heavy doubt pulling at me. I regretted that he had to take his second lesson at night, in the middle of a mosquito-infested wood, but there was no help for it.

'At least we'll have a bit of moon to light our way,' I said as I gazed up through the trees at the glowing sky.

'Perhaps it would be better,' Master Juwain said, 'if we rested and continued on at dawn.'

I shook my head at this. 'When Morjin learns that we entertained King Arsu, *he* won't rest. And neither will Lord Mansarian and the Red Capes.'

We mounted our horses then, but we did not ride very quickly, for it was dark in the forest and Bemossed had a hard time of things. I had to show him again how to set his feet in the stirrups and hold the reins. His unease communicated to Littlefoot, who nickered nervously and seemed ready to buck Bemossed off his back. It pained me, and all of us, that walking seemed the only pace that Bemossed could safely get out of Littlefoot that night. I told myself, though, that Bemossed was learning quickly and that tomorrow would be a better day. I told myself, too, that any pace at all was a good one if took us away from our enemies.

I intended to ride without much rest straight for the Khal Arrak pass, perhaps sixty miles away. After a while, however, I saw that the terrain between here and there was too rough, and would ruin the horses. Worse, Bemossed had no legs for riding. A couple of hours before dawn, when his muscles began cramping along his thighs, I looked for a good place to stop. We came to a stream cutting the road and flooding it; no one, it seemed, had ever bothered to build a bridge here. We moved off into the woods and made camp near the stream's banks. Mercifully, few mosquitoes came out to bite us, not even at daybreak, when I moved over to where Bemossed slept on a pile of leaves and shook him awake.

'Is it time already?' he asked me, yawning. 'It seems that I just closed my eyes.'

He stood with difficulty, and limped like an old man over to Liljana, who handed him a cup of hot coffee. She had arisen an hour before, taking scarcely any rest, just so that she could make him a hot meal of egg pie and maize bread.

We ate quickly as the sun filled the forest with a warm, green-tinged light. The leaves of the oaks and dogwoods about us began to glow, and many birds chirped out their songs. It did not take us long to break camp, for we had not made much of one in the first place. It was a bright day promising much sunshine, and I dared to hope that we might reach the mountains safely by the end of it.

Just as we readied to mount, though, Maram let out a cry and jumped away from his horse. He grabbed at his leg and shouted, 'It burns! It burns!'

I feared that he, too, had taken a cramp – or even that a poisonous snake had crawled into his trousers and had bitten him. He continued shouting and jumping about as if he had been dropped down onto a bed of coals, even as he pulled frantically at his trousers. Finally, he managed to undo them and pull them off over his boots. He cast them away from him. He stood there half naked, and I saw that the skin along the outside of his leg *had* been burned as if seared by the sun.

'What happened?' I cried, rushing over to him. Everyone else made a circle around us.

'It is my firestone!' he said.

Maram usually carried his red gelstei secreted in a long pocket sewn into the leg of his trousers. Now we all watched as this cast-off garment began to smoke and smolder. A few moments later, it burst into flames. It didn't take long for the fire to consume the

633

wool. In the center of the ashes, glowing brightly, the hot, crimson crystal burned against the ground.

'What did you do?' I asked him.

'Nothing!' he said. 'I haven't even *thought* of using it for a thousand miles.'

'Then what made it come alive?'

My question almost needed no answer. Even so, Master Juwain pointed at the seething firestone and said, 'It is Morjin.'

It seemed that Morjin's power over the Lightstone – and therefore over our gelstei – had grown. It seemed that we no longer needed to wield our sacred crystals in order for him to take control over them.

Daj went to fetch a spare pair of trousers from Maram's saddle-bags, and Maram dressed himself again. He stood looking down at the red gelstei, which still poured forth a ferocious heat.

'Oh, my poor flesh!' Maram said, rubbing his leg. He bent to hold his hand above the radiating firestone. 'My poor, poor crystal – how am I to hold it?'

He might as well, I thought, have tried to grasp a heated iron.

'I'm afraid you might have to abandon it,' Master Juwain said.

'Abandon my *gelstei*? No, no – I can't do that.'

'You can't carry it with you, either.'

Maram stared at the burning stone. 'It will cool – you'll see. It *must*.'

We waited a few minutes, but the firestone lost none of its torridness. Neither, it seemed, did it grow any hotter.

'We must ride,' I said to Maram. 'Ride now.'

'No, I can't leave it behind. What if some boy wandering through these woods found it? What if *Morjin* did?'

This objection persuaded all us that we could not simply leave his gelstei burning on the ground here. As we had been told, it might be the last remaining firestone on Ea.

'We won't leave it,' Kane called out. He went over to one of the packhorses and lifted off a waterskin. And emptying its contents on the ground, he went over to the stream, where he bent down to scoop into the skin handfuls of sandy mud. He laid the waterskin on the ground next to the firestone, and he used a rock from the stream to push the firestone point-first down into the opened neck of the mud-filled skin. We waited a while longer, and although the leather skin grew warm, it seemed that the firestone was not hot enough to burn through sand and consume its container.

Kane stowed it back on the horse, and he said to Maram: 'If it gets any worse, it will burn the beast and not you.'

His assurance, however, did not console Maram, or any of the rest of us. Maram said, 'I always hoped that if I faced Morjin again, I might burn him with my stone's fire. But now I'm afraid he's coming to burn *me*.'

I was afraid of this, too. I began to sweat as a familiar and dreaded sensation stabbed through my spine into my belly. It was like being devoured inside by a ravenous snake.

Maram looked straight at me then, and so did Kane and Master Juwain. Bemossed did, too. His soft eyes filled with a grave knowing as he said to me, 'This poison that Morjin put in your blood burns you and bonds you to him, doesn't it, Valashu?'

'Yes,' I said, 'it does.'

Bemossed stepped up close to me; he set his hand upon the scar on my forehead as if to cool the fever that always tormented me. 'He is drawing nearer, now, isn't he?'

I nodded my head as everyone looked at me. I felt Morjin's desire to destroy me driving through my navel, even as the point of Maram's firestone had pierced Kane's waterskin. A terrible pressure inside me bruised my organs and built hotter and hotter.

'He has found me,' I said. 'Either he or his droghul.'

'Then let us ride,' Kane said, 'and see if we can reach the mountains before him.'

There was nothing to do then but mount our horses and try to outdistance the enemy I felt pursuing us. Whether this might be a single droghul hunting by himself or Morjin riding with Lord Mansarian and two hundred Red Capes, I could not say. Neither could I tell how far behind us they might be.

'All right,' I said to Kane, 'let us ride.'

And so we set out up the road leading north, toward the great, snowcapped peaks of the Crescent Mountains that shone in the distance many miles away.

40

The horses' hooves beat a thudding tattoo against the earth as the trees along the narrow road flew by. I soon saw, however, that Bemossed could not hold this pace. Twice his foot popped out of his stirrup, which confused and angered his usually gentle horse. As we were bounding down a rough, turning stretch of road, he lost the reins altogether and in desperation threw his arms around Littlefoot's neck to hold on for his life. I called for a halt then. I waited while Bemossed collected his senses and his breath. I rode over to help him reposition himself and take up the reins again. Then I set forth at a slower pace.

I heard Maram mutter to Atara, 'Ah, but it's going to be a long day.'

For two hours we rode through the forest, until it gave out onto an expanse of farmland. The road turned toward the northwest; as the Khal Arrak lay to the northeast, we had to ride off the road to find little lanes between the fields and sometimes cut straight across them. More than one farmer shook his hoe at us and shouted curses at us for trampling his cabbages. I worried that we attracted too much attention. I felt our enemy drawing ever closer – even as the pressure inside me built ever more painful, and hotter and hotter.

'We must ride faster,' I turned to tell Bemossed. 'You must try.'

He nodded his head at this and said, 'It still seems wrong to burden this beast this way, but I will try.'

'Your horse is named Littlefoot,' I told him. 'And he is no beast but a great being who is *proud* to bear you. If you do your part, he will do his.'

He grasped his reins and patted Littlefoot's neck with a new resolve. And for the next hour of the day, beneath the hot noon sun, he managed to hold a canter without once losing his stirrups or reins.

And then we came into a torn, treeless country of poor soil that looked to have been overfarmed. Hesperu's sometimes torrential rains had eroded the slopes of the hills rising up toward the mountains. We had to cross many gullies and slips of silt and stones. This demanded skillful horsemanship, but as we were riding over a particularly broken patch of ground, Bemossed clenched his reins too tightly and caused Littlefoot to whinny and rear up. He lost his balance then and flew off onto the ground. Although he took no injury from this fall, he barely managed to roll out of the way in a frantic effort to keep Littlefoot's driving hooves from crushing him. After that, he did not want to ride anymore. I felt him, however, steeling himself to climb back into his saddle and master this difficult art.

Master Juwain, I saw, was having a hard time of things, too. The work of getting across the gullies caused him to gasp, as if drawing in breath was a strain. This surprised and worried me. He had always seemed to me as tough as tree bark. Even in the heights of the Nagarshath range of the White Mountains, where the air is the thinnest on earth, he had climbed up through a terrible terrain as if he possessed the lungs of a much younger man.

When we stopped by a stream to refill our waterskins, I saw him take out his green gelstei and stare at it. Then I finally understood. I said to him, 'It is Morjin, isn't it?'

He nodded his head, then gasped out, 'He has . . . found his way . . . again . . . into this crystal.'

Maram came up and looked at it. 'I never felt a fire so terrible as that which came out of your stone when you tried to heal me. Morjin is burning *you* with it, isn't he?'

'No . . . it isn't like . . . that,' Master Juwain said again. He waited to catch his breath. 'The varistei, I think . . . is making my blood sick. Making it so that it can't . . . hold the air I breathe in.'

Liljana stepped over to look at the beautiful emerald crystal in his hand. She said, 'Then you must get rid of it.'

'I will,' Master Juwain said, closing his hand around his crystal. 'If things get worse, I will bury it.'

I did not want to pause any longer to hold an argument. None of us, I knew, would readily abandon his gelstei. I told myself that if we could flee far enough from Morjin, he would lose whatever power he might be gaining over the stones.

'Let us ride,' I said. I looked at the mountains, now standing out sharply in stark gray and white lines perhaps only twenty-five miles away. 'Let us leave this dreadful country behind us.'

We set out again, and the terrain became even worse: rockier along the steeply cut slopes of the hills, and filled with dense vegetation in their troughs. Much grass grew here, and we saw a few herders grazing their sheep and goats upon it. But a tough, rubbery plant called hape also sprouted from the poor soil, in large patches through which the horses had a hard time driving their hooves. Littlefoot stumbled twice here, and I didn't know how Bemossed was able to keep from being thrown. Even Fire, the most sure-footed of our horses, nearly broke her leg in a tangle of hape that concealed a rocky hole.

As the sun crossed the sky's zenith and began falling toward the west in a gout of yellow fire, the air grew stiller and hotter. We sweated and prayed for any hint of wind. I wondered if Estrella might be able to summon up a breeze. But this strong, sweet girl worked hard just to keep her horse moving forward. I listened as Master Juwain gasped and wheezed, and our horses snorted out froth into the blazing afternoon. My eyes burned as if someone had pushed me face-first into an oven. My heart burned, too, and my blood which pulsed through my aching veins. And with every mile we put behind us, I felt the hateful thing that pursued us drawing closer.

At the crest of one hape-covered rise, I called for a halt. I scanned the country behind us. A haze of heat and moisture steamed off the broken hills. I could not detect anyone riding over this ground; the only things that moved were a few dozen sheep a mile away. Kane, who had dismounted, lifted up his ear from a rock on the ground, and he shook his head. He murmured, 'Nothing – not yet.'

'Atara?' I said, looking over to where she stood leaning against her horse. 'Can you see anything?'

The sickness that burned through her belly struck deep into my own. I felt smothered in a thick blackness, as if a great hand had pushed me down into a mass of stinking black mud. I saw Atara grasping at the pommel of her saddle with one hand, even as she clutched something close to her body with her other. And then she turned to show me her diamond-clear gelstei. She told me, 'I can see almost nothing – not the land which we ride over, or the hours of the rest of this day. There is only Morjin. He is here, inside this crystal. And he is *here*, in these hills, somewhere. He comes, Val – how quickly he comes!'

Bemossed moved over to help her mount her horse. I thought it strange that even totally blind, she could ride much more fluidly than he, as if she had become a living part of her fierce, beautiful mare.

We began moving again, north and east toward the break in the mountains called the Khal Arrak. Whenever we came up over a swell of ground, I looked for this pass in the folds and fissures of rock to the north. I could not quite make it out. Even so, I felt certain that we rode more or less straight toward it: my sense of dead-reckoning told me this was so. I tried to assure Maram that we were going the right way, and he made a joke of this, saying, 'I hope you're right, because if you *don't* reckon correctly, we're all dead.'

A short distance farther on the ground got better, with fewer rocks and hape plants, and more grass for grazing. There should have been many sheep in the hills hereabout, and shepherds, too. For three miles we saw none of these; however, we did come across half a dozen houses, crumbling and obviously abandoned. I wondered why everyone had left them.

Bemossed, exhausted, fairly teetered on top of his horse and said, 'I heard there was war in this district, and plague, too.'

'Oh, excellent!' Maram grumbled. 'A cursed land – and we have to ride straight through it. Is there no other way?'

I looked out at the hot green hills around us. Perhaps ten miles farther on, a band of darker green forest covered the rising ground leading up to the mountains.

'Hmmph, you'll be all right,' Atara said to Maram, joking with him. 'Just don't drink the water here, and try not to breathe the air.'

Liljana, upon hearing this, did not smile. She sat on top of her horse next to Daj as she combed her fingers through his thick hair, checking to see if he might have picked up any ticks or other vermin on our ride. Then she broke off her inspection and said, 'I wish that I did not have to breathe the same air as Morjin, anywhere on earth. He makes everything so *foul*.'

The unusual shrillness of her voice alarmed me, and I nudged Altaru over to her. We traded knowing looks, and I asked her, 'Has Morjin found his way into your gelstei, too?'

She nodded her head as she brought out her blue whale figurine. She looked at it hatefully. 'He slides himself into my mind, like a tapeworm! He is filth! He is an abomination who never should have been born! I can't tell you what he is saying to me – I can hardly tell myself.'

Her words alarmed not just me, but everyone. Kane rode over to her, and cast his eyes upon the blue gelstei. He shouted, 'Then it must be destroyed!'

'No, not yet,' Liljana murmured, closing her fingers around her crystal. 'I can still bear it.'

'Can you bear giving us away? If Morjin can see what you see, hear what you hear, then –'

'But he can't!'

'How do you know?'

'I just do. He wants only to madden me. He speaks and speaks to me, but he doesn't really know if I can hear him.'

'But how do *we* know that, eh?'

'How can you ask that? After all we've suffered together? Don't you know *me*?'

'But what if you're wrong, eh?'

Liljana thrust her hand inside her cloak as she glared at Kane. And she snapped at him, 'You'll just have to trust me!'

'So,' he growled as he glared back at her. 'So.'

Liljana usually spoke with care, so as not to upset the children with things that they didn't need to know. But now she cried out: 'It doesn't matter anyway! Morjin is tracking us, and not by my thoughts. He will run us down, and soon!'

'Did he tell you that?' I asked her.

'Yes!'

I looked up at the mountains, which seemed so close, and yet still too far away. I said to Liljana, 'Then he told you lies – we will escape him, again.'

'You tell yourself lies. We are riding so *slowly*.'

'Be quiet, woman!' Kane thundered at her. 'You worry more than Maram! And that's just what Morjin wants, eh? It's your damn gelstei! You should throw it away before *I* do!'

His large hands, it seemed, fairly trembled to rip open the folds of her cloak and seize her gelstei. And so I shouted at him: 'Kane! Morjin wants even more that we should start tearing at each other's throats!'

As I said this, the deep lines cut into his savage face smoothed out, and his eyes cooled, slightly. He turned away from Liljana. Then he brought out his black gelstei and sat on his horse staring at it.

'Damn Morjin!' he muttered. 'Damn his eyes! Damn his blood!'

He made a fist around his dark stone, and lifted his hand back behind his head as if making ready to hurl it from him. And then his whole body seemed to lose its strength. His arm fell to his side as he slumped in his saddle. He put his gelstei away. He turned to me to snarl out, 'Let's ride, damn it, while we still can!'

And so ride we did, trying to keep our hope fixed on the great rocky wall of mountains growing larger and larger in front of us. We pounded around and over grassy hills. Flies came out to bite us. Our sweat, like fire, burned in the little wounds the flies tore in our flesh.

And then we crested a good-sized hill, and the dark blanket of forest we sought for shade from the fierce sun and cover from our pursuers' eyes seemed almost close enough to touch. I thought that we might possibly reach it and vanish into its trees. Then I turned to scan the rolling ground behind us and a flash of white and red brightened the top of one of the hills. I squinted against the sun, and I could just make out a white horse bearing a bronze-armored warrior and his flowing red cape. Lord Mansarian, I remembered, rode a snow-white stallion. I knew this was he. His men galloped right behind him. There must have been at least two hundred knights of these Crimson Companies, pouring down the hillside like a stream of bronze and red. Somewhere in this frightful mass, I thought, rode priests of the Kallimun. I knew that their master rode with them as well – either he or the droghul of Morjin.

Seeing this, Maram sighed out, 'Ah, too many, too close – too bad.'

'No!' I said to him. 'We can escape them yet! Let's ride!'

I urged Altaru to a gallop; it gladdened my heart to see Bemossed push his gelding to match this pace. He and Littlefoot both seemed near to collapse, but they managed to negotiate the easy slope down the backside of the hill. Another and larger hill rose up before us. I led the way around it, through a broad, grassy trough, and I dared to hope that the sight of our enemy would inspire us to a speed great enough to leave them behind.

But it was not to be. Just as I rounded the hill, I came upon a stream cutting through a gully. Altaru jumped across it, almost without breaking stride. Just as I turned in my saddle to warn Bemossed of this unexpected obstacle, though, he seized hold of Littlefoot's reins in confusion. Littlefoot planted his hooves in the grass, stopping up short of the stream. Bemossed, completely unprepared for his horse's sudden balk, went flying headfirst from his saddle through the air. His momentum carried him clear across the stream, where he struck the ground with a sickening impact.

He threw up his hands to protect his head, and I heard bones break. It was something of a miracle that Atara's horse and those of the children, following close behind him, managed to jump the stream without trampling him.

We all gathered around Bemossed near the edge of the gully and dismounted. Bemossed stood up bravely, holding his drooping arm in his hand. He winced in pain as Master Juwain quickly examined it, but did not utter even a murmur of complaint.

'Both bones in your forearm are broken,' Master Juwain announced. 'Not badly, I think, but they must be set, and your arm wrapped.'

'Not here!' Kane growled out. 'There is no time!'

'He can't ride like this,' Master Juwain said.

'He can hardly ride as it is,' Kane snapped. 'But ride he must.'

'All right,' I said. 'Then he'll ride with me.'

I mounted Altaru, and then helped Maram and Kane as they fairly flung Bemossed up onto Altaru's back behind me. I told Bemossed to wrap his good arm around my waist and to hold on tightly. Then I whispered to my great, black stallion, 'All right, old friend, you must run quickly now – quicker than you ever have before!'

Altaru, however, although the strongest of horses and a fury of speed over short distances, had never had the wind for long races. With Bemossed's weight added to mine, Altaru sprang forward with a great surge of determination that could not last very long. We galloped for a while over the lumpy, grassy ground. The breath snorted from his huge nostrils, and I felt an agony of fire building within the great, bunching muscles of his flanks and legs. I feared that he would run so hard that his heart might burst. I wanted to weep at the valor of this great-spirited being.

I heard the horses of my companions pounding after us and Bemossed's tormented breath exploding in my ear. I felt his arm tight around my belly, but trembling with the effort to keep holding on. I knew his strength was failing, as was Altaru's. After a couple of miles, my horse's pace slowed to barely a gallop. His whole body seemed to knot and quiver with a burning agony. I did not know how he kept on running.

We came out into a bowl of thick grass surrounded by hills. In its center stood an old cottage, or rather, its ruins. It had no roof and only three good walls: the fourth wall, facing us, had crumbled in places, and its doorway lacked a door. I pointed Altaru straight toward this hole in the wall's mortared stone. And Maram cried out in protest to me:

'What are you doing? The pass lies *that* way!'

He pointed off past the right of the house.

'We won't make it – not this way!' I called back to him. 'We must make a stand, here.'

He didn't argue with me, nor did anyone else. I drew up in front of the cottage and waited as my friends joined me and dismounted. Kane and Maram helped Bemossed down from Altaru's back; then I rode him through the doorway into the cottage. Kane took charge of getting the other horses and everyone inside. I dismounted, too, and began walking around the cottage's single room. Piles of old leaves and bits of stone littered its packed-earth floor. Three of its walls, as I had thought, seemed to be in good enough repair. They stood a good seven feet high. The southern wall, however, had crumbled down to a height of four feet along much of its length. It was no castle that I had chosen for us to defend, but the best protection we could hope to find.

While Master Juwain and Liljana worked to set Bemossed's arm and wrap it, Kane unholstered his bow and began sticking arrows down into the dirt floor. So did I, and so did Maram. He moved with speed but without conviction or hope. I heard him mutter to himself, 'Ah, Maram, my old friend, this is madness – this is surely the end.'

'How many times have you said that?' I asked him, pushing an arrow down into the rain-softened earth.

'I don't know,' he grumbled. 'But sooner or later, I'll be right.'

I looked out over the crumbled section of wall for the approach of our enemy. I said, 'We survived the siege of Khaisham, didn't we?'

'By a miracle, we did. But here we have no escape tunnel.'

'Then we'll have to find a different way to escape.'

Behind us, near the cottage's north wall, Estrella tried to quiet the horses. She and Daj had tethered them to an old beam that lay on the floor there; other than it and some splinters from an old window frame, the cottage seemed to have been stripped of wood and all its furnishings.

'This is not so bad a place,' I told Maram. 'Not nearly so bad as Argattha, where we fought off a hundred men.'

'But there we had Ymiru with us, and we wore armor, too. And Atara had her other sight.'

He turned toward Atara, who was busy stringing her great horn bow. She kept her arrows in the quiver slung on her back. I felt her waiting desperately for her second sight to return.

'We will win,' I told Maram.

'Against *two hundred* knights?'

'Yes,' I said.

'How, Val?'

I looked out over the low section of the wall toward the gap in the hills to the south. And I told him, 'I don't know, but we will win.'

My words did not convince him. I wasn't sure that I could even convince myself. I saw Kane's jaws working with all the tension of a steel trap, and I sensed that even my grim-faced friend had rarely found himself in such a desperate situation.

There came a grinding snap as Master Juwain set the bones of Bemossed's arm. Bemossed gave a gasp, and his face contorted with pain. He said nothing. I saw little hope in his eyes, and I wondered if he regretted coming away with us. I felt a tightness in his throat; a sense of doom seemed to grip him in an iron-clad fist. I couldn't help thinking of what Master Matai had said about the Maitreya: that his star would burn brightly but not long.

A few moments later, Lord Mansarian rode his white stallion through the gap in the hills to the south. The green peacock feathers of his shiny bronze helm fluttered in the breeze. Four or five of his companies of Red Capes thundered behind him. Lord Mansarian led them to a point in the grassy bowl about four hundred yards away: just outside the range of our arrows. He drew up his men in long lines facing the cottage. I caught a flash of a white-haired man wearing a red robe, and I knew that this must be one of the Red Priests. Another priest – Salmelu, I guessed – sat on his horse next to a man covered from head to knee with a gray traveling cloak. I could not see if he wore armor beneath it. I could not see his face, but the acid burning my throat told me that this must be Morjin.

'Damn him!' Kane muttered. He stood next to me behind the crumbled section of wall. Damn his blood!'

Daj came up to us, and craned his head over the wall to look upon our enemy. He gripped his little sword in his hand, and he said, 'Why do they wait *there*? Why don't they surround the house?'

'Because,' I told him, 'it is easier to ride down fleeing rats than to face them cornered with no place to run.'

He immediately understood and said, 'They *want* us to flee. Well, *this* rat will kill at least one of them as they come over the walls.'

So saying, he pointed his sword at the Red Capes. I remembered how in Argattha he had used a spear to dispatch several of Morjin's wounded soldiers.

Lord Mansarian posted two men on the gentle slopes above the western and eastern sides of the cottage – no doubt to give warning in case we *should* flee.

Seeing this, Maram said, 'Why don't they just storm us and be done? What are they waiting for?'

They are waiting for our nerve to break, I thought. But I said nothing.

Maram twanged the string of his bow, and said, 'How many do you think that we can hit before they reach the house? Five? Ten?'

'Ten? Hmmph,' Atara said. 'You won't be able to shoot with any accuracy until they come within a hundred yards. And then you'll only have seconds to get off your rounds.'

'And that is my point. Even if by some miracle, we each get five of them, or even ten, that's only thirty men, which will leave –'

'Be quiet!' Kane snapped at him. 'This is no time for arithmetic!'

'Is it not?' Maram turned to look at Master Juwain wrapping Bemossed's arm in the corner as Liljana paid out a length of linen from a large roll. 'Nine of us minus nine leaves zero, which is all that will remain of the great Lightstone Traveling Troupe as soon as the damn Red Capes find their courage and charge us.'

He threw down his bow in disgust and moved over to the horses. It did not take him long to find his brandy bottle and to begin drinking straight from its glassy mouth.

'What are you doing?' Kane shouted at him. 'Get back to your post!'

'Give me a moment, damn you! I just want one more taste of brandy before I die.'

Kane stepped toward him as if intending to seize him by the neck and drag him back to the wall. But I stayed him, and said, 'Let him be.'

'But he'll drink himself senseless!'

'No, he won't,' I said. I didn't add: *Who could blame him if he did*?

I gazed out across the field at the two hundred Red Capes sitting on their mounts and pointing their spears at us. At the center of their front line, Lord Mansarian seemed to be consulting with the two priests and the gray-cloaked man I took as Morjin.

'Maram is right,' Kane said to me. 'We won't kill very many before they reach this wall.'

'Maybe we'll kill enough to drive them off,' I said.

'No – we won't. They'll come over the wall, and through the doorway,' Kane said grimly.

I gripped the hilt of my sword and said, 'I will kill anyone that tries to come through it.'

'So, you will – but it still won't be enough. Maram and I can't hold this wall by ourselves.'

'But what about me?' Daj said, pointing his sword toward our enemy. 'I can fight!'

I looked down upon this valiant young warrior, and at Atara, who stood next to him gripping her bow. How wrong it was, I thought, that Lord Mansarian and his war-hardened men should have driven to battle a blind woman and a beardless boy.

'There is a way,' I said to Kane. 'There must be a way.'

But I no longer believed this. I looked over at Bemossed, grimacing as Master Juwain fashioned a sling for his arm, and I silently raged that we had found this bright, gentle man only to have to lose him soon to our enemy's spears.

'There *is* a way!' Kane said to me. His hand shot out to lock upon my forearm, even as his eyes took hold of mine. I saw the old hate flare up inside him, even as he saw it seething in me. 'You know the way!'

'No,' I murmured. 'No.'

'Yes, this is the time – there isn't much time!'

'No, I can't.'

Kane let go of my arm to stab his fingers out toward our enemy. 'You have a sword inside you – use it!'

'I have sworn not to!'

'Use the valarda, damn it! This one time! Strike the Beast! Kill his droghul! Do it, Val!'

I looked out at the lines of mounted men in their gleaming, fish-scaled armor. I stared at the merciless Lord Mansarian and the man in gray who might be Morjin. It was Morjin, I remembered, who had nailed my mother and grandmother to planks of wood. And now he waited to murder my friends, who were the only family I had left.

Hate, the dark, destroying passion, fairly emanated from Lord Mansarian's men likes waves of heat. I felt it working at Lord Mansarian and burning up the man who must be Morjin. It howled like an enraged animal inside of Kane, and most of all, in myself. I could not escape it any more than I could the hot, humid air that hurt my lungs and stung my eyes.

'Valashu,' Bemossed said to me.

He came over and stood with me by the wall. He looked at me with his wise, brilliant eyes. Although I had said almost nothing to him of the valarda and the way that this terrible force of the soul could kill, he seemed to understand even so.

I set down my bow, and took out my sword. I no longer cared that its sacred silustria burned with fire.

There came a movement from the lines of Red Capes, and three knights rode forward to join Lord Mansarian. I guessed that they were captains receiving orders to make ready to charge us. Seeing this, Liljana stepped up to the wall and so did Master Juwain.

'Val,' Liljana said. The essential kindness of her soft, round face melted away before something fearful and furious inside her. 'If ever there was a time to use the valarda as Kane has said, this must be it.'

I stared at this woman who was like a mother to me, but I said nothing.

'Think of all those who have sacrificed so much for you to have come this far,' she said to me. 'Can't you sacrifice your vain attachment to a *principle*?'

'The only principle that *really* matters,' Maram bellowed out to me from across the room, 'is life. But you don't care about that, do you?'

Master Juwain, I thought, wanted to advise me as well. But he stood quietly, and his gray eyes flickered back and forth as if he was reading a book. He seemed to be searching for words or the right verse that would reveal the absolute truth in order to guide me – searching and searching. I felt his mind spinning like a steel discus hurled out into space.

'What will be?' Atara said to me. She had put down her bow to re-tie her blindfold so that it wouldn't come loose in battle. Her voice grew as cold as a mountaintop as she said to me, 'What will be left of the world if you don't do what you were born to do?'

Her hatred of Morjin, like ice, seemed to touch even Estrella. She walked over to Atara, and pressed Atara's hand to her face. I felt this lovely girl's dread of what soon must come, and even more, her loathing of the darkness from which none of us seemed able to escape.

'You should wait with the horses,' I said to her, pointing across the room. 'You should try to keep them calm.'

She closed her eyes as if looking inside herself for a place of calm that spears and swords could not touch.

'Valashu,' Bemossed said to me again. He held his hand out toward Alkaladur's angry red flame. 'This cannot be the way.'

I saw in my sword's fire my dead father and my brothers and the thousands of warriors who had fallen upon the Culhadosh Commons. And I shouted, 'It is the way of the world! What does it matter if I slay with a sword forged out of gelstei or the hate in my heart?'

I stared at my sword, and I could not move. I felt its point piercing my hands and my feet – and every other part of me – crucifying me to something worse than death.

And Bemossed told me, 'No good can come of this.'

'Good comes,' I called out, looking across the field, 'when warriors kill those who need killing.'

Bemossed blinked as if he could not hold the moisture filling up his eyes. He said to me, 'Even yourself, Valashu?'

'Can *you* stop it?' I said to him. 'What is a Maitreya *good* for?'

Why, I wondered, had fate chosen Bemossed as the Shining One, and not me? The answer burned along the blade that stabbed through the center of my being: because I was damned. Because I was who I was.

There came a shout from across the field, and I looked out to see a third red-robed priest leading a packhorse up between the ranks of knights toward Lord Mansarian. Something seemed to be slung over the horse's back; I hoped it was not a packet of arrows and a bow. It nearly maddened me to have to wait here to see how Lord Mansarian would attack us – and to know what I would do. I felt this uncertainty torturing not just myself, but my friends as well. The battle had not yet begun, but *the* battle raged as it always had inside each of us.

I felt this most excruciatingly in Estrella. She seemed lost in a dark cavern of pain that had no bottom or end. Her heart beat quickly and agonizingly, as if she were fleeing from a bloodthirsty beast. And then everything inside her grew utterly still as if she had plunged deep into cool waters. An image came into my mind: that of a brilliant silver lake. She opened her eyes then and looked at me. She looked at Bemossed. Her whole being gleamed like a perfect mirror. Bemossed gazed at her in wonder. He stared and stared, deep into the eyes of this glorious girl, but even more at the great shining wonder of himself.

'Look, they move!' Maram cried out. He came hurrying over to the wall to grab up his bow. 'They're coming!'

I turned to see one of Lord Mansarian's warriors ride forward bearing a white banner of truce. Then came Lord Mansarian and a line of six knights. Morjin and the three priests rode behind the knights, using them as a shield in case we should fail to honor the truce and begin shooting arrows at them.

'Why should they even *want* to parlay?' Kane snarled out. He lifted up his bow. 'So, we'll speak to them with arrows through their throats!'

'Are *we* trucebreakers, now?' I shouted at him. 'Must we commit *every* abomination?'

'The only abomination is in letting Morjin and his creatures live!'

Our enemy rode a dozen yards closer. Kane nocked an arrow to his bowstring, and so did Maram.

Just then Alphanderry appeared and stood with us behind the wall.

'Look!' Daj cried out. 'Look at Bemossed!'

As Bemossed stared at Estrella, his face shone in the onstreaming rays of the sun. Everything about him shone: his eyes, his lips, his great, throbbing heart. He stood in a shimmer of glorre. I could hardly believe what I saw. Bemossed took his arm out of his sling and cast down this bit of cloth. He smiled. His eyes grew as brilliant as the stars. He seemed to behold himself as he had always longed to be.

'Hoy!' Alphanderry sang out. '*La neshama halla!*'

Bemossed looked out at our enemy, and I felt in him no fear. He looked at the sky and the earth; he looked at me. He seemed utterly without doubt. A bright, shining hope lit his smile, and more, the sureness of triumph. I knew then that Ea had not just a dark and false king of kings, but a new Lord of Light.

'*La neshama halla jai Maitreya!*'

In the air in front of him, a plain golden cup appeared. It seemed at once to be as hard as diamond and without true substance, like light. Bemossed reached out with his bandaged arm to grasp this cup. The moment that his fingers closed around it, my sword blazed a bright glorre. Then a dazzling radiance filled up every corner of the cottage, and swelled outward and upward to illuminate the green hills around us and the deep blue of the sky. Strangely, our enemy, riding ever closer, seemed unable to perceive this splendid light.

'The gelstei!' Maram shouted. He seemed stunned as by a hammer blow to his head. He ran over to the horses, and removed his firestone from the waterskin encasing it. He held it up for us all to see. '*My* gelstei – look, it cools!'

Liljana and Master Juwain took out their gelstei then, too.

'I won't break the truce,' Maram sighed out, tucking the fire-stone down into the pocket of his trousers. He came back over to me. 'I think you Valari are right, after all. All that *really* matters is honor – to honor the glory of life. And so if I must die, I must die, too bad.'

Liljana pointed at the gray-cloaked man who rode with the three priests behind Lord Mansarian. 'I doubt if that is really Morjin. *He* wouldn't trust us to keep the truce. I was wrong, Val. Don't waste the best of yourself on him.'

'I agree,' Master Juwain told me. He seemed able to breathe more easily. 'It is likely some sort of trap.'

Atara moved up next to me, and she reached out blindly to lay her hand on my chest. And she said, 'Do what you were born to do, but not *this* murder.'

Our enemy came even closer, within the long range of our arrows, and now even Kane put down his bow. He turned to gaze at Bemossed with great dread, and yet with an intense longing, too. I knew that he wanted to weep and laugh and roar out all his wild joy of life, all at once. Finally he said to me, 'Do not use the valarda to slay. Remember the two wolves, Val. Remember who you really are.'

At this, Bemossed smiled. He held out his hand to me.

'Valashu Elahad!' someone called out from far away. The voice sounded raspy, like that of Lord Mansarian. 'Liljana Ashvaran! Maram Marshayk! Atara Ars Narmada! We know that these are your real names!'

And then a deeper, richer voice reverberated across the field. It was bright like silver and as cruel as steel. It rang with a will toward torment and vengeance, and left no doubt who in the body of men riding toward us held command. Too often, in my dreams and in my waking hours, I had trembled with loathing as I listened to the fell, deceptive, deadly voice of Morjin.

'Valashu Elahad!' the man in the gray cloak cried out to me. 'It has been too long – too long since I said farewell to your mother, and to Mesh!'

I turned away from Bemossed then. I could not take his outstretched hand. I noticed Daj staring at my fiery sword.

At a distance of two hundred yards, Lord Mansarian called for a halt and sent the knight bearing the white banner cantering toward us. He rode straight up to the cottage. He drew up in front of our wall, and said to us, 'You are offered a truce, that Lord Mansarian might discuss with you the terms of your surrender.'

'Terms!' I shouted. 'We all know the terms here: our deaths, or yours!'

The knight looked at Bemossed standing next to me. He said, 'Lord Mansarian has asked me to assure you that he will do all he can to spare the life of the Hajarim. Will you speak with him?'

Kane, standing on my other side, snarled in my ear: 'It's a trap! Don't let that Morjin thing come any closer!'

I fought to quiet the wild pounding of my heart. I remembered how Lord Mansarian had protected Bemossed at our performance for King Arsu – likely at great risk to himself. I said to Kane, 'He *might* spare him.'

'He *won't*, damn it! Don't let them close, I say!'

'No,' I whispered. 'I *want* them all as near as they can be.'

I nodded at the knight. 'All right – tell Lord Mansarian that he can approach us, and we will honor the truce.'

But the knight shook his head at this. He sat holding up the white banner, and he said, 'First, put down your bows and come out from behind that wall. My lord will not meet beneath the threat of your arrows.'

'All right,' I said again. 'We will come out – twenty yards only.'

I nodded to Kane and Maram, and we began walking toward the door. And the knight pointed at Atara, and said, 'The princess, too.'

'But she is blind!' I said.

'So are bats blind,' the knight said, 'and yet somehow they fly through the air straight as arrows. My orders are clear on this: the princess must put down her bow.'

Atara smiled coldly, and she laid her bow on top of the wall. She, too, moved over toward the door. So did Bemossed. He said to me, 'Let me come with you.'

I looked for the golden cup in his hand, but I could no longer see it. The radiance pouring out of him seemed lost to the hellish glare of the sun. I told him, 'No, you must stay here. It will be all right.'

I told the knight that we would meet with his master, and he turned to gallop back to Lord Mansarian.

I drew in a long, deep breath of burning air. I clamped my fingers around the hilt of my sword, and I tried not to look at Bemossed. Then, with Maram, Kane and Atara close behind me, I stepped through the doorway out into the brilliant sunlight.

41

My friends followed me out across the grass to a distance of twenty yards. There we waited.

Lord Mansarian and his knights, with Morjin and the priests behind them, came within a hundred yards of us, and then fifty. If they should break into a charge, or at any time draw their swords, we could beat a quick retreat back into the cottage.

At twenty yards, I called out, 'That is far enough! Come down from your horses!'

'What!' Lord Mansarian wheezed out. 'Who are you to issue commands here?'

'We are not mounted,' I told him, 'and we will not hold parlay with you speaking down to us.'

Lord Mansarian looked behind him at the man in the gray cloak. This mud-spattered traveler threw back his hood to reveal a shock of golden blond hair and a beautiful face that I knew too well. His golden eyes burned into mine. In the manner of the Grays, he had affixed to his forehead a flat, dark stone: a black gelstei. It seemed to suck at my will to resist him. He, himself, seemed to swell with an enormous will to crush anyone who stood against him. I felt a weakness run through my legs as if my body were being drained of blood.

'Lord Morjin?' Lord Mansarian said to this man.

'We will dismount,' he said. His beautiful voice pounded through the air like a great hammer. 'Let the Elahad have his way.'

His motions as he came down from his horse were sure and swift. He seemed as full of life as a young lion. I felt sure that Morjin had lost the power of illusion over me, and so he could not disguise the hideousness of his true appearance as a rotting old man – if indeed he still appeared so. I doubted this. Looking

652

at him, I suddenly doubted all that I knew to be true. I wondered, again, if he had used the Lightstone to remake himself as he had been in his body long ago. As for his soul, I thought, nothing could ever expunge its foul, terrible stench. I could not tell if he was really Morjin. Indeed, in this hateful creature who stood glaring at me, it seemed that Morjin and his droghul might have become as one.

'We demand your surrender!' he called out to me. 'Throw down all your weapons, your gesltei, too, and your lives will be spared!'

I let my hand rest on the hilt of my sword. I wondered if I could whip free my blade and charge him, and cut him down before the six dismounted knights standing near Lord Mansarian stopped me. If I cut his cloak and tunic to bloody shreds, I wondered, would I find the Lightstone secreted there?

'How long will you let us live then?' I asked him. 'Long enough for your priests to nail us to crosses?'

It shouldn't have surprised me that Arch Uttam, at Morjin's right, had found the hardiness to ride with the Red Capes in our pursuit, so great was the malice that he held for us. On the other side of Morjin stood my old enemy, Salmelu. Although he called himself Haar Igasho now, and he wore a red robe instead of armor and the emblem of a prince of Ishka, his ugliness of face and spirit were the same. He smiled at me as if my plight gave him great satisfaction.

'If you don't surrender, Elahad,' Salmelu told me, 'you *will* be crucified!'

Arch Uttam turned to cast him a venomous look. I sensed his jealousy that Salmelu had the privilege of accompanying their master.

'That is for Lord Morjin to decide,' he reminded Salmelu. 'Lord Morjin, the Merciful and Compassionate!'

He gazed at Morjin as if he did not suspect that this creature might be only a soulless droghul. I wondered, however, if he truly believed that Morjin could be the Maitreya.

'Surrender, Valashu Elahad,' Morjin called to me, 'and you have my promise that you won't be crucified. You will live as long as you can.'

The command in his voice stunned me. I thought it an abomination that he, too, possessed the gift of valarda. He poured all of his power into willing me to submit to him.

'You lie,' I said to him. I stood there sweating and fighting for breath. 'And so we will surrender only when we are dead.'

'Is it death you want so badly? Would you bring it upon your friends and everyone you encounter?' He drew in a deep breath, and then roared out: 'Ra Zahur!'

The third priest, a man as squat and hairy as an ape, struggled with the tarp that he had taken down from the packhorse. He moved with a great strength, as if he spent the hours of the day lifting stones. At last, when he had the bundle standing upright, he used a knife to slash the rope binding it. He pulled down the tarp to reveal the face and body of a boy about fourteen years old.

'Taitu!' Bemossed cried out from behind the cottage's wall. 'Why? Why?'

He came running, and although I yelled for him to go back inside, he paid me no heed. It was all I could do to catch him and hold him fast before he closed the distance toward Morjin and his filthy priests.

I stared out at Lord Mansarian, hating him as well as Morjin. Taitu, I saw, had been stripped naked, and he could not stand of his own. I thought it a miracle that the hard ride slung over the back of a bounding horse hadn't killed him outright. I sensed, though, that he didn't have long to live: the horse's backbone had crushed Taitu's organs as surely as had the mule's kick, swelling out his belly again with blood. His soft eyes had grown glassy, and he seemed to cry out silently for Bemossed to help him.

'It is said,' Arch Uttam called out, 'that the Hajarim healed this boy with a laying on of his hands. That power is the Maitreya's only, and so all who have conspired in this lie have committed an Error Mortal. The boy's father and sister have already paid the price, and even now hang on crosses in their village.'

'No!' Bemossed cried out. 'It is *you* who lie!'

'Be quiet, Hajarim!' Arch Uttam spat out. He moved over and drove his fist into Taitu's belly. He waited a long time for Taitu to finish screaming. Then he said, 'As you can see, the boy is *not* healed. But we are merciful, as always. Ra Zahur! Help him!'

While I held Bemossed fast with my arm, Ra Zahur plunged his knife into Taitu's belly, and ripped him open. A great gout of blood poured out of him, along with his ruptured organs. From the cottage behind us, I heard Liljana cry out in grief. Kane cast Morjin a look that seemed blacker than any gelstei, and I wondered if he had hidden in his pocket one of his throwing knives. Nearly two hundred yards across the field, Lord Mansarian's red-caped soldiers in their quiet, mounted lines gazed upon this horror. Surely they had seen worse crimes. As for Morjin, he watched Taitu die with all the compassion he might have held for a worm. I sensed that he cared nothing for Taitu, but took great pleasure in Bemossed's pain.

'Once,' Bemossed said to Morjin, 'I thought you *were* the Maitreya. But now I see what you are.'

Bemossed stood staring at Morjin, and a terrible sadness welled up out of him. I marveled that he seemed able to suffer great anguish and sorrow and yet remain open to the deep light that filled his eyes. I could not. I felt only acid burning a hole through my heart. Bemossed seemed to sense this, and he turned his attention toward me. I thought that he feared nothing, for himself. But for me, everything. I knew that he did not want to lose me to the dark, twisting thing ripping me open.

'No,' he murmured to me. 'Not this way.'

I gripped the hilt of my sword. I sensed Alkaladur burning in its scabbard, where I had sheathed it. If it grew as hot as a firestone, I wondered, would it melt straight through the scabbard's thin metal?

Morjin kicked his boot into Taitu's fallen body. He smiled at me. He nodded at Bemossed and asked me, 'Well, Elahad? Will you surrender and spare your friends such agony?'

I knew then that he *wanted* Bemossed to live: so that he could torture out of him the secret of how the Lightstone might be used to its fullest power. He wanted, too, for me to draw my sword.

'We will never surrender to you!' I called out. 'I told you this in Argattha!'

Morjin – or his droghul – smiled at Atara, who stood next to Kane. He told her simply, 'Surrender, and I will restore what I took from you.'

But she shook her blindfolded head, and said softly, 'Liar.'

I felt a pressure filling up my belly and pressing at my brain behind my eyes. Water, I thought, builds within a cloud until the thunder sounds and the lightning flashes to let it out. I suddenly knew that I must strike out with the valarda. Morjin – Lord Mansarian and the priests, too – stood close enough that they would feel its full force.

'Surrender,' Morjin demanded of me again, pointing toward the cottage at Estrella, 'or I will do to the girl what I let Haar Igasho and my soldiers do to your mother.'

I found myself floating in empty space as if I had been abandoned on the only world left in the universe. For a moment, everything grew cold and dark. I felt only a single thing: the terrible fire of life that tormented me. I knew then that I *loved* slaying in righteousness evil men such as Morjin. I *would* slay him, I vowed. I would thrust the bitter sword of my malice straight through him. He would die, like a worm caught in a holocaust of flame. And then there would be light again, and an infinitude of stars – and I would find peace at last.

'Morjin!' I cried out, 'you will never harm any of my friends again!'

His smile grew wider and brighter, and I knew that he would try to turn my hate against me. He would try to seize my will and make me into a ghul. I didn't care. I wanted to howl out all the rage inside me that I could not hold. I would then live as a maddened beast or a monster, but at least Morjin would be dead.

'Look at him!' I heard Arch Uttam say to Ra Zahur as he pointed at me. 'The only heir of King Shamesh, and he can't even decide what to do.'

'It was like that in Mesh,' Salmelu said. 'But you'll see, in the end he'll betray his friends as he did his own father and mother.'

Salmelu's face soured in contempt for me, and I knew that I would kill him, too, as I should have in the red circle of honor in King Hadaru's hall. I would kill all the creatures of Morjn, in their red robes and their shining armor, in all their hundreds and their thousands, in every land of the world. All those who stood against me in mockery and evil deeds, as Salmelu did, I would destroy.

No.

Molten silustria, I thought, must burn far hotter than even white-hot steel. With it, my silver sword had been forged. And with some substance infinitely hotter than this, *I* had been forged, the silver of my soul – and it flowed with a hellish fury in the center of my heart.

No, Valashu – you were born for more than murder and hate.

When I listened hard enough, and deeply enough, I could hear my mother whispering to me, for she, too, dwelled within me. She did not call for vengeance. She cried out to me only that I should live, in pride and joy, as the son whom she loved.

'Valashu,' Bemossed said to me. And once again, he held out his hand to me.

I stared at his slender palm for what seemed forever. Then finally, I took hold of it. The moment that my calloused hand touched his softer fingers, my fury to destroy brightened into a rage to live. Something dark and ugly inside me burned away in a fiery light. I felt instantly lighter, as if a great weight had been lifted from my chest. The air I breathed seemed sweet. I took a great gulp of it, and howled out, not in hate but in utter freedom: 'Morjin! I won't betray them! Not my friends! Not my father and mother, or my brothers!'

The blood cleared from my eyes, and I saw many things. I knew that if I struck Morjin dead, Lord Mansarian and the priests, too, I would only incite Lord Mansarian's men to a killing frenzy of revenge, for that was the way of the world. But there were other ways, as well. And Morjin, I suddenly sensed, *could* be defeated.

'I won't betray *you*!' I shouted at him. Kane stared at me in disbelief, for these were the strangest words that I had ever spoken. '"All men shall be as brothers" – so it is written in the *Darakul Elu*.'

Morjin glared at me in confusion. I did not recall ever seeing him so unsure of himself. 'What do you know about *that*, Elahad?'

'I know about Iojin.'

'You . . . what?'

'I know you stabbed him in the back with your own knife. And I know you loved him.'

The cloaked man standing less than twenty yards from me seemed unable to speak, and I wondered after all if he might be Morjin's droghul. He glared at me with a bottomless hate. Then he shouted, 'Be silent! You know not what you say!'

His face flushed bright red from the blood burning through him, and I suddenly knew that he had long ago poisoned *himself* with the kirax, to remind himself of what Iojin had suffered and to atone for this terrible crime.

I said to him, 'You have never gone a single day, have you, without wishing that he could live again?'

'Be silent! Damn you, Elahad!'

I remembered Kane, high on top of a mountain, telling me that there were no evil men, only evil deeds. And I said to Morjin, 'No one is damned. There is a way out.'

Now Morjin turned his terrible golden eyes and all his spite upon Bemossed.

'Let us go free,' Bemossed said to him. 'And let yourself go free.'

'Don't speak to me that way!'

Bemossed only smiled at him, in defiance, but in deep understanding, too. He fairly blazed with a deep desire that the world, and all that lived within it, should be made whole again.

'Don't look at me that way, Hajarim!'

I let go of Bemossed's hand, and grasped my sword's hilt again. And I told Morjin, 'It can all end, right here and now.'

Hot acids seemed to burn Morjin's throat, choking him, and he pointed at me as he called out to Lord Mansarian, 'Kill him! Kill the Elahad!'

Two of the knights standing near Morjin looked to Lord Mansarian in consternation. I took them as captains of the Red Capes, and I had overhead their names as Roarian and Atuan. The tall, muscular one, Atuan, nodded at Lord Mansarian. Then Lord Mansarian turned to Morjin and said, 'But, my lord, we are met here in truce!'

'How can there be truce with such as *this*?' Morjin said, hissing at me. 'Kill him, I say!'

He cannot bear it, I thought. *That which he most desires, he cannot abide.*

I saw that Morjin could withstand very well my killing fury but not my compassion. And what, after all, *was* true compassion, this valarda that connected men soul to soul? Only suffering with. Suffering each other's joys, or suffering agonies, but always being joined as one in the great experience of life. As with love, it was a force and not a feeling.

'Morjin!' I called out.

My eyes met his, and a shock of love ran through me. *Not* love for him: only a Maitreya, I thought, could possess the grace to love such a loathsome being. My love for my family, however, blazed within me like starfire. I could not contain it. I could not keep to myself the anguish of wanting to talk to them again, to cross swords with my brother, Asaru, in a friendly practice duel, and to feel my grandmother's soft, wrinkled hand on mine as we walked together through the halls of my father's castle. I wanted to smell my mother's hair again and the spice of peppermint and honey as she made for me hot tea.

'Morjin!' I cried. 'You kill too easily! Know, then, what it was like for me when you killed my family!'

I drew my sword and pointed it at him. Its silver blade flared with a brilliant flame. If the valarda was the gift of empathy, I thought, then Alkaladur was the weapon of compassion. *Not* this length of silustria, sharper than any razor, whose diamond-bright polish drove the sunlight into Morjin's eyes. But the *true* Alkaladur, wrought of a purer substance, as radiant as the stars. The Sword of Light shone within me, as yet only half-forged. All that I had suffered had gone into its making. All that my friends had suffered *with* me infused its essence as well. Even now, as Liljana, Master Juwain and the children looked on from behind the wall of the cottage, and Kane, Maram and Atara stood by my side, I felt all their courage, kindness and great will toward life. They seemed to pass these fundamental forces to me through their eyes and in their throbbing hearts, in flames of red, orange and yellow, green and blue, indigo and violet. The whole world seemed to pass its fire to me. Somehow, Bemossed seemed to weave it all together into a pure, white blaze that streaked through my sword and me straight up into the sky. Hotter and brighter, it built, until it flared a brilliant glorre. Then this perfect color gave way to a single, clear, indestructible light. And so at the last, Bemossed's love for me, no less Morjin's hate, had put into my hand the greatest weapon in the universe.

'Damn you, Elahad!'

All the fire and force of my soul I poured into this sword. Alkaladur blazed like the sun. Across the distance between us, it struck into Morjin's heart. He gasped and grabbed his chest; he raged and cursed and wept. He stared at me with his golden eyes, now wild and maddened with anguish. I almost couldn't bear it. He had told me once that the only way I would ever free myself from suffering would be to inflict even greater suffering upon another. It was not so. As I drove the Sword of Light deeper and deeper into Morjin, my agony burned through me, and all of Morjin's incredible pain, too. I thought that it might kill me. It killed *something* in Morjin. I felt him longing desperately for some impossible thing: perhaps that he and the world could somehow be different. I felt him longing for something even more. He looked at me strangely. He cringed away from me as a black, bottomless terror took hold of him. I knew then that there was one thing that he feared above all else.

'Elahad!' he screamed out to me.

He continued screaming until his voice grew hoarse. He ranted and bit his tongue, and spat out a bloody froth. He sweated; from nearly twenty yards away, I could smell his foulness and fear. He told of how he would torture me in a dozen hideous ways. The debasement of this powerful man to a snarling, suffering, craven beast stunned all of us looking on.

And then Morjin returned to himself – or perhaps he found sustenance and strength in the being of his droghul. He drew in a deep breath, and stood up straight. He wiped the blood from his mouth. He turned to Lord Mansarian, and said, 'The truce is over. You have heard the Elahad say that they will not surrender. Therefore you will attack, and kill them all.'

'All except the Hajarim,' Lord Mansarian said, looking at Bemossed.

Morjin looked at him, too. But Bemossed's bright face seemed only to drive him to a new fury. '*Especially* the Hajarim! You are to kill him outright, or deliver him, bound in chains, to me!'

'That was not what you promised!' Lord Mansarian rasped out.

Arch Uttam turned toward this grim, red-caped man in astonishment. So did Atuan and Roarian, and Lord Mansarian's other captains. It seemed that they had never dared to think that any soldier of Hesperu would openly contradict the great Red Dragon.

'You must have misunderstood me,' Morjin said to Lord Mansarian. His silver voice trembled with dismissal and undertones of threat, too.

'I misunderstood nothing,' Lord Mansarian said. 'The Hajarim was to be given to me, for whatever corrective that I might contrive.'

'He will be crucified!' Morjin snarled out. 'Alive or dead.'

'But Hajarim are never crucified!' Lord Mansarian reminded him.

'This one,' Morjin said, pointing at Bemossed, '*will* be crucified. You have my promise.'

Lord Mansarian looked at me, and I sensed that some part of my suffering over my family's death called him to remember the slaughter of his own. He met eyes with Bemossed, and I felt his intense gratitude for what this man had done. And something more. As Bemossed smiled at him, Lord Mansarian's dark, doomed soul began to sparkle with hope once again.

'No,' Lord Mansarian told Morjin.

'No? You say this to *me*?'

Morjin's ferocious will beat down upon Lord Mansarian like a battle axe. Lord Mansarian stood there sweating. But he finally found the courage to say, 'The Hajarim saved my daughter's life. And so I owe him *his* life.'

'You owe him nothing! You owe *me* everything!'

Lord Mansarian let out a long sigh, and then traded looks with Atuan. Remorse gnawed at his eyes. He seemed suddenly unable to bear Morjin's lies and spite. Then he said to him, 'All that I have done in King Arsu's service is wrong. I will not dishonor myself, ever again.'

'*You* are wrong!' Morjin shouted at him. 'All honor is to be found in loyalty: to your king, and to *his* king!'

As the tone of command reverberating through Morjin's voice grew almost too great to resist, Lord Mansarian hesitated. And Arch Uttam warned him, 'Be careful of what you say, warrior. You speak errors, Major and Mortal.'

'I speak the truth,' Lord Mansarian said. 'And I have no king.'

At this, Morjin spat on the grass in front of Lord Mansarian and told him, 'You, and all of the Crimson Companies who are gathered upon this ground today, are under King Arsu's command! And therefore mine!'

'Are they?' Lord Mansarian said, nodding at Roarian. 'Let us see about that.'

He turned and hurried over to his horse. He quickly mounted, as did Roarian and Atuan. They pointed their horses facing away from the cottage.

Now Morjin's whole body trembled as his jaws clamped together with great enough force to break his teeth. He spat again, in a spray of blood, straight at me. His face contorted with rage as he screamed, 'Damn you, Elahad!'

Then he and his priests, with the four other captains and the banner-bearer, climbed onto their mounts. They all whipped their horses to a gallop, and began a wild race with Lord Mansarian back toward the lines of Lord Mansararian's red-caped knights.

'Ah, I suppose the truce *is* over,' Maram said as he looked from Kane to me. 'What do we do now?'

'Go back,' I said. 'Let us go back inside the house.'

I placed my hand on Bemossed's shoulder to urge him to haste. But he stood facing our enemies across the field as if he would not be moved.

'You have already worked one miracle today,' I said to him. 'I know what you want, and I want it, too. But as long as Morjin lives, he'll drive men to war.'

'You do not know that, Valashu. If I held the Lightstone –'

'So,' Kane growled out to him, 'you'll hold the Lightstone only if *you* live. Which you won't if you stand here dreaming impossible dreams, eh?'

He turned back toward the cottage. So did Maram, who took Atara's hand. Then Bemossed looked down upon Taitu's body and called out, 'Wait! Let us not leave the boy here like this to be trampled by horses.'

I nodded my head, and we quickly wrapped up Taitu again in

the tarp – now his shroud. We bore him back into the cottage. Kane immediately grabbed up his bow and nocked an arrow to its string.

'They are within range,' he said as he looked out over the crumbled cottage wall.

I looked, too. Those who had come to us under the banner of truce had reached Lord Mansarian's companies. The neat lines of knights on their horses had collapsed into a chaos of men and mounts swarming around Lord Mansarian and Morjin. Angry shouts rang out across the field.

'Two hundred yards?' Atara said to Kane. 'That is too long a range. You can't be sure of hitting Morjin at that distance.'

'I'll hit *someone*,' Kane growled. 'And that will be one less to fight coming over these walls.'

'Why fight at all?' Maram said. He nodded at Estrella, who stood by the horses. 'Why don't we flee, while they argue?'

'No,' I said, shaking my head. 'If we do that, we might end their argument for them and force them to make common cause again. And we would expose our backs to them.'

'What shall we do then?'

And I told him, 'Wait.'

While the pasture rang out with shouts that grew louder and more numerous, Master Juwain examined Taitu's body to make sure that he really was dead. Estrella stood by my horse, feeding him some grain. Liljana, not knowing what else to do, went around with a waterskin so that we all might quench our thirst. Daj drank thankfully, then gripped his sword as he stood next to Maram behind the wall.

Then one of Red Capes near Morjin drew his sword and plunged it through the throat of a knight shouting at him. As if a trumpet had sounded, all the knights gathered around Morjin drew swords or brought their spears to bear. Dozens of them paired off, and began hacking or stabbing at each other. They fought fiercely as their enmity for each other drove them to a maddened melee.

'They'll kill each other for us!' Maram said.

He put his hand on Kane's bow as if to restrain him from loosing an arrow. But Kane had already come to the same conclusion, and he muttered, 'So they might.'

We all watched then as Lord Mansarian ripped free the crimson cape from his shoulders and cast it to the ground. He cried out: 'Captain Atuan! Captain Roarian! All my companions who would follow me! Let us be free!'

662

Perhaps eighty of the two hundred knights also cast off their capes. The green grass soon gleamed with a carpet of red. Those knights loyal to Lord Mansarian gathered near him, if they could. I clenched my fist to see Lord Mansarian's companions so badly outnumbered.

'Estrella!' I called out. 'Bring Altaru to the door!'

'Yes,' Maram said. '*Now* we can flee.'

'No, we can't,' I told him. I nodded at Bemossed, and said, 'Our new friend might be the Maitreya, but he *still* can't ride well enough to escape from Morjin.'

'Then what shall we do?' Maram asked.

And I told him, 'We'll fight. Kane and I will.'

'But why?'

I pointed across the grass, where horses trampled red capes with their hooves and men clashed sword to sword, trying to murder each other. The melee had now grown into a battle. I said simply, 'If Lord Mansarian can prevail, then we will live.'

'But what about *us*?' Maram said, looking at Liljana and Estrella. 'You can't just leave us undefended!'

'We won't leave you,' I told him, clapping him on the shoulder. 'Kane and I will fight better mounted. And you will guard the wall.'

I told him to fire off an arrow at any of Morjin's knights who came within thirty yards of it. After we got the horses out of the doorway, I watched as Daj helped Atara into position facing this rectangular opening. She stood with an arrow nocked to her bow's string, waiting. If anyone should try to force the doorway, Daj would direct her to loose an arrow blindly at zero range.

Then Kane and I mounted our horses. Just before we rode forward, however, I turned toward the wall in hesitation. Bemossed stood there looking at me. He told me, 'Go and do what you must, Valashu. You are a warrior. And as you have said, war is still the way of this world.'

Altaru, smelling blood and battle, drove his hoof into the earth as he let loose a great whinny. I drew my bright sword. I said to Kane, sitting on top of his big brown horse beside me, 'We've no armor, and so you will have to watch my back.'

'Ha – and you mine!'

We hardly had to touch our horses to urge them into a gallop toward the mass of men before us. Many had already fallen, and their bodies lay sprawled upon the grass, along with many bright red capes. Knights, whether fighting for Morjin or defending Lord

Mansarian, called out challenges and curses to each other as they hacked and stabbed and screamed and died. In seconds we drew within a hundred yards, and then fifty, and now I too smelled blood spraying out into the air. The wind whipped at my face, and carried to me other hateful scents. I could hardly bear these men's rage to kill each other. And then Kane and I charged straight into the heart of the madness.

A red-caped soldier spurred his horse toward me as he tried to intercept me with a spear thrust through my chest. I parried the spear with my forearm, then cut right through the bronze armor covering his belly. He cried out in agony, even as one of his companions tried to impale me, too. Him I cleaved from shoulder to side. A nearby soldier, seeing this, called out, 'The musician has a sword! Such a sword!'

Many of the men riding about now looked upon Alkaladur in astonishment and terror. My sword's silustria shone with a dazzling white light. They shrank back from it, and from me. Morjin, twenty yards away, surrounded by a wall of horses and knights fighting ferociously to protect him, looked toward me as he cried out, 'It is the Elahad! Kill him – kill him now!'

A dozen knights charged forward to carry out this command. And Lord Mansarian, off toward my left, shouted to *his* men: 'Spare the musician, the juggler, too! Protect them, if you can!'

If any of the knights who had remained loyal to Morjin still thought of Kane as just a juggler and knife-thrower, he now gave them cause to change their minds. With three blindingly quick strokes of his sword, he cut down three knights that had come too close to us, and then whirled about in his saddle to cleave the arm off a fourth knight trying to spear me through my back. His black eyes flashed with a wild joy, and for a moment met mine. Then he struck out again and again, even as my sword sliced through fish-scaled bronze as if it was leather.

'The errants are demons!' an enemy knight cried out. 'Demons from the Dark Lands!'

'They are from Hell!' another knight shouted. 'The musician's sword blazes like the sun!'

Demons Kane and I might be, I thought. But we were also something more. We had fought together in terrible battles, side by side and sword synchronizing with sword. And now, together, striking with steel and silustria in perfect rhythm, slaying in a fury of lightning cuts and thrusts, we fought as true angels of death. Our enemies gave way before us. Although they had been trained to war, they were not Valari. A few wielded their weapons with skill, but their heavy armor weighed them down and slowed their motions. It seemed they had spent too many campaigns hunting down poorly armed errants instead of sharpening their virtues against true knights. Kane and I charged at them with a practiced passion to slay, and so they fell before us and died.

Lord Mansarian used the terror that we created to deploy his knights around the mass of men protecting Morjin. They fought fiercely, pressing Morjin's men closer together. This offset their superior numbers, for soon Morjin's knights bunched together so closely that those nearest Morjin at their center could hardly wield their spears. It was possible, I saw, that through this strategem Lord Mansarian's men might actually prevail.

And then Morjin cried out to his knights, 'Move aside! I need no protection! Move, I say!'

As he had commanded, his men tried to make room for him, whipping or spurring their horses out of his way. He pushed his mount through the gaps between the horses around him, straight toward me. Then Lord Mansarian's knights tried to close in on him. He killed two of them with two quick cuts of his sword; another he stabbed through the throat. He fought with a fearful skill nearly equal to that of Kane.

'Damn him!' Kane shouted from next to me. He shook his sword at Morjin, and drops of blood went spinning through the air. 'Let's finally kill this beast!'

We urged our horses toward Morjin, even as five of his knights pressed toward us to cover his flank. Morjin turned to stare across the field at Kane and me. The black stone stuck to his forehead began glowing with a dark light. A vast, black chasm seemed to open in the ground before me. I felt it pulling at me, down through the layers of earth into death.

'Elahad!' Morjin screamed at me. 'Valari!'

And then, without warning, he unleashed a new weapon, dreadful and terrible. From deep inside his throat he let loose a sound like nothing I had ever heard. In its ear-shattering tones was something of an eagle's scream and the hyena's hideous call – and the shrieks of millions of men and women dying in torment. This cry pierced straight to the heart and turned hot blood to ice. I grasped my chest, and clung to my saddle. And all the while, Morjin cried out in a voice of death: **'Aiyiiyariii!'**

Two of Lord Mansarian's knights spurred their horses toward Morjin. He whipped about in his saddle, and directed his voice toward the first of these, who froze in terror as he gasped for breath. Then he fell from his horse, dead. Morjin now screamed at the second knight, who clutched at his throat as he choked and died, too.

'Aiyiiyariii!'

Morjin now screamed out his death voice at me. I had a sense that he could strike out this way only at one person at a time. I sensed, too, that this weapon was new to him, awkward and untested. Perhaps what I had done to him earlier had broken open his being in such a way that all his evil and hate could now be carried through the air in a hideous sound. It fell upon me like a blast of dragon fire, and nearly killed me.

'Father!' I gasped. 'Mother!

Sweat ran from every pore on my body, and I fought back the urge to vomit up blood. My heart beat with such a hard and violent pain that I thought it would burst. I wanted to drop my sword and clasp my hands over my ears. But it was my sword, I believe, that saved me. As often when I was near to death, I drew strength from it. I felt Alkaladur's bright silustria feeding into me the very life of the sun and the earth. I raised it up just in time to block a sword from slicing off the top of my head. Then Kane came forward to kill the knight who had so nearly killed me. He, too, I sensed, fought a desperate battle against Morjin's death voice, which now fell upon him.

'Val!' Kane shouted at me. 'Keep hold of your sword!'

Perhaps Alkaladur gave me the will to resist Morjin's voice; or perhaps years of battling him had inured me to the worst of its power. Whatever the cause of the new strength pouring through me, I found myself able to keep to my saddle and fight off the men who suddenly assaulted me. Seeing this, Morjin came forward to attack me with a more mundane and substantial weapon. In a fury of motion he drove his horse against mine and thrust his sword at my chest. It would have killed me if Altaru hadn't reared back, striking air with his iron-shod hooves. Morjin worked his horse around to my side and slashed at me, again and again. I didn't know how I parried his ferocious strokes. Any one of them, without the protection of my armor, might have cut me to the death. Kane moved in from the other side to help me, but Morjin – or his droghul – nearly chopped the edge of his sword through Kane's neck. I had never seen Kane lift *his* sword so slowly, so desperately, as if he were fighting his way through an icy, raging sea.

Atara had warned us that each of the droghuls we faced would be more terrible than the last, but nothing had prepared me for the power of this dreadful being. *Was* he truly a droghul, I wondered? All of Morjin's ferocity and malice poured out him in his furious sword and murderous voice. It seemed impossible that he might kill either Kane or me, or both of us, but I knew that in another few moments he would.

'Damn you, Elahad! Damn the Valariii – **Aiyiiyariii!**'

Just then Roarian and Atuan came forward with three other knights, and pressed an attack against Morjin. Two of these Morjin killed with his fell voice, but the others seemed able to bear it. They joined Kane and me in trying to cut down Morjin. This caused Morjin suddenly to alter his strategy. He shouted out: 'Haar Igasho! Ra Zahur! To me! To me! Kill the Valari for me!'

The red-robed Salmelu, who called himself by the foul name of Igasho, now rode up to us with Ra Zahur and a half dozen knights. They began slashing at us with their swords. Three of them surrounded me, and I began fighting a furious battle for my life.

'Do you see the sword I bear, Elahad?' Salmelu shouted at me. 'It is no kalama, but I will put it through you, even so!'

I shouted out, too, in a terrible frustration because I could not quickly get away from the men surrounding me. I had only a moment to see Morjin turn his horse and gather up a dozen enemy knights to act as his cover. Then they charged en masse straight toward the cottage.

A sword whirled toward my throat, and I parried it. Kane came up beside me, and killed the enemy knight nearest to me. Then he turned to cross swords with the blocky and bestial Ra Zahur.

'I *will* have my revenge!' Salmelu screamed at me. He feinted with his sword toward my face, then tried to disembowel me. 'I will have it now!'

Aiyiiyariii!

Morjin's death voice rang out from across the field. I stole a quick glance to my left, and saw one of Lord Mansarian's knights grasp hold of his head and plummet from his horse's back. Lord Mansarian, charging upon Morjin even as Morjin continued galloping toward the cottage, lowered his spear and aimed it at Morjin's chest.

'Valariii!'

Salmelu's horse and mine drove their hooves against the slick, reddened grass, fighting for purchase and advantage as they whinnied and snorted and pushed at each other. For a while we exchanged blows, each of us fighting desperately to find an opening. Salmelu seemed sure of himself – sure that his defeat in our duel two years before had been just bad luck. I knew it was not. I knew, too, that I had slain many men in the time since then, sword to sword, and that I could slay Salmelu now.

We clashed swords, once, twice, thrice; we feinted and thrust, parried and slashed. Desperation ate at Salmelu's inky eyes. Then, finally, he stabbed his sword at my throat in a lightning thrust. I moved my head aside just in time to keep from being torn open, then thrust *my* sword at his shoulder. The point of it drove in just deep enough to split the muscle and score the bone, which caused Salmelu to cry out and drop his sword. I might have finished him then if Lord Mansarian hadn't screamed out in a terrible agony. I turned to see Morjin jerk his bloody sword free from Lord Mansarian's belly. This gave Salmelu time to whip his mount about, and go galloping from the field.

'Val!' Kane shouted to me. He parried a vicious blow that Ra Zahur dealt him, then chopped his sword through Ra Zahur's neck, cutting off his head. 'We must get to the house!'

But we had no time left. Even as I drove Altaru forward and cut down the last enemy knight attacking me, Morjin resumed his charge toward the cottage. Six of his knights still covered his front. A bowstring cracked, and an arrow whined out and buried itself in one of these knight's chests – and now only five men rode with Morjin. Maram fired off another arrow with a similar result, and then there were only four. And then, before Maram could nock another arrow and aim it, the four knights and Morjin thundered right up to the cottage.

Aiyiiyariii!

'Bemossed!' I cried.

I felt Morjin's hate shriek out toward this gentle man who must be the Maitreya. I knew that he would soon kill him, either with his voice of death or with his sword. I could do nothing to stop it. I galloped back toward the cottage with Kane covering my side, and the wind burned my face. I could not believe that we had come this far only to lose Bemossed to the ravening beast who flung himself at the cottage's wall even as he continued howling out his hate.

'Val – help me!' Maram cried.

But I could not help him. I could only watch in horror as Morjin leaped off his horse and onto the top of the wall in one incredibly graceful motion. He struck down at Maram, and Maram fell, back behind the wall. Then Morjin leaped into the cottage, and the wall obscured the sight of him falling upon Bemossed and my other friends. A terrible scream split the air.

A few seconds later, Kane and I reached the cottage. We came down from our horses and ran toward the doorway. I pushed through it first, stepping over the bodies of two knights there whom Atara had killed with arrows. She stood holding her bow, with a third arrow pulled back toward her ear. I shouted at her, 'Atara, it is me!'

She immediately lowered her bow. I turned to see Maram rising up off the body of the knight who had gone over the wall before Morjin had. Maram bled from a gash on his forehead. Morjin – impossibly – lay near the knight, dead.

'What!' I cried out. I looked at Bemossed gathered with Master Juwain and Estrella over by the horses. 'What happened?'

Liljana, who stood over Morjin's body holding a sword, quickly explained things: It seemed that Maram had clashed swords with the first of the knights to assault the wall and had killed him as he tried to scale it. The second knight he had also destroyed. Morjin, though, jumping down into the cottage, had smashed the pommel of his sword into Maram's forehead, stunning him and causing him to fall. Morjin had then tried to cut down Liljana to get to Bemossed. But Daj, squatting down behind the shelter of the wall, had thrust *his* sword through Morjin's belly, straight up through Morjin's insides into his heart. It was nearly impossible to kill one of the great Elijin with a single blow, but it seemed that Daj had accomplished this great feat.

'I hid,' Daj told me. He proudly held up his bloody sword. 'As Lord Morjin forced me to do in Argattha, I hid, and then I killed him. He *is* dead, isn't he?'

I knew that he was dead, and so did everyone else. To make sure of this, however, Kane came forward and slashed down with his sword to cut off Morjin's head. He cut off the black gelstei fixed to it. He gave this stone to me. Then he clamped his fingers in Morjin's golden hair, and held up his head high above the cottage's walls for all to see.

'Death!' he roared out. 'Death to the Beast and all who follow him!'

I stood with Kane behind the wall. I looked out across the bloody, corpse-strewn field. The sight of what Kane showed everyone caused the remaining knights to cease their combats and stare at him in horror.

'It is Lord Morjin!' one of the red-caped knights cried out. 'Lord Morjin is dead!'

'Lord Morjin!' a second and a third knight cried. 'Lord Morjin!'

I took a quick count, and determined that Lord Mansarian's knights had indeed prevailed against those remaining loyal to Morjin, for only twenty-three of these red-caped knights still kept to the field on top of their horses, while some forty men now looked to Captain Atuan to command them. It seemed that Morjin's knights had no one to lead them.

'The Maitreya is dead! The Maitreya is dead!' – this call passed from one defeated knight to another.

Then Arch Uttam rode forward from as out of nowhere. He tried to rally the knights, calling out, 'Vengeance! Kill the errants, and avenge Lord Morjin!'

The red-caped knights, however, paid him no heed. Two of them turned to ride away from the cottage, and then three more. Then the rest suddenly broke, making their way across the grass toward the hills in all directions. Seeing that his cause had grown hopeless, Arch Uttam called out a curse to us, and then galloped off after them.

Captain Atuan, who had indeed now taken command, rode slowly about the field with Captain Roarian and other knights looking for survivors. He showed the vanquished mercy, for only an hour earlier, they had been his companions. Those of the wounded who wore a red cape and could still ride were put on horses, and then driven from the field; those who could not ride and would die anyway were put to the sword. Captain Atuan's own wounded he treated the same way. This proved a great problem, however, as one of these turned out to be Lord Mansarian.

'He is dying,' Atuan called out to me as he rode up to the cottage. 'He calls to the Hajarim to ease his pain before he goes on.'

Bemossed, showing no fear of Atuan's remaining knights, who had terrorized the north of Hesperu for so long, walked out of the cottage. So did we all. We crossed the field, and came to the place where Lord Mansarian lay dying on the grass. Someone had taken off his armor and cut back his underpadding. It shocked Atuan and Roarian and the other former Red Capes to see Bemossed set his hands around the terrible wound splitting open Lord Mansarian's belly. Lord Mansarian shook his head at Bemossed as if to tell him that healing him would be hopeless.

'Let me be,' his heavy voice rasped out. 'Let me thank you for saving Ysanna's life. I never thanked you, did I, Hajarim?'

670

In answer, Bemossed only smiled and looked down at him.

'I never learned your name, either. What is it?'

'I am called Bemossed.'

'Bemossed,' Lord Mansarian said, smiling back at him. 'It is a good name.'

And then, before Bemossed could work his magic upon him, he closed his eyes and died.

'It was his time,' Bemossed said, taking his hands away from Lord Mansarian. His face shone with a strange light. He seemed not at all dismayed that he had lost the chance to heal him. 'Let us bury him.'

After that, in the remaining hours of the day and late into the evening, we worked with Captain Atuan and his men digging graves for Lord Mansarian and all those who had died there. We buried poor Taitu and the vile Ra Zahur – and even the remains of the being who had called himself Morjin.

When the moon rose over the earth and cast its silver light upon the many mounds we had made upon the field, Captain Atuan bade us farewell. He stood over the grave of Lord Mansarian, and he said to us, 'We have lingered here longer than we should have, but we must go.'

I looked through the wan light at the forty battle-weary knights standing near their horses. I said to Atuan, 'But where will you go?'

'To our homes,' Atuan said. 'To gather up our families and flee into the forests. We will be hunted now.'

'So will *we* be hunted,' Maram said. 'Perhaps you should ride with us as far as the mountains.'

Atuan shook his head at this. 'I do not think that any of our former companions will come after you. They will surely ride back to King Arsu's encampment and make a report of what has happened here. You have time.'

He then told us of a secret pass through the mountains into Senta that lay closer than the Khal Arrak.

'Go back to *your* homes,' he told us, 'or wherever you will. But go carefully. I think there will be rebellion throughout the length and breadth of Ea, now that Lord Morjin is dead.'

And with that, he mounted his horse, and so did the knights who had remained loyal to Lord Mansarian. They rode off into the night, and disappeared around the curve of the hill to the south.

My friends and I stood in the moonlit graveyard in silence for a few more moments. And then Daj said to me, 'Is Lord Morjin *really* dead?'

I opened my hand to stare at the piece of black jade that Kane had cut from our enemy's forehead. It seemed to pulse with a malevolence and murmur with a soft, fell voice that cursed me even as it called to me.

'No, he is not dead,' I told Daj. 'Morjin would never have risked his life coming to Hesperu, much less pursuing Bemossed and storming the house. It was a droghul you killed.'

'He whispered a strange thing to me just before he died,' Daj informed me. 'He said: "Tell Valashu I am free."'

I closed my fist around the black jade, with its sharp facets. I walked back toward the cottage, where I found two good-sized stones. I set the black jade on the flatter of these. Then I used the other stone as a hammer to smash the fragile gelstei into pieces.

'What shall we do *now*?' Daj asked, coming over to me.

I looked at Bemossed holding Estrella's hand in the strong light raining down from the heavens, and I smiled at Daj. I told him, 'Now we will go home.'

I turned to mount Altaru and begin the long journey back toward the lands from which we had come.

42

We rode only a couple of hours after that, for we were all exhausted and the ground soon grew even hillier and more rocky. We wanted, though, to place a good few miles between us and the cottage in case any of the Red Capes *did* return. We finally made camp in a cluster of rocks above a stream flowing down from the mountains. Although the ground was almost too hard for sleeping, sleep we all did – all of us except Kane. He stood guard over us with his bow strung, watching the moonlit swells of ground below us. But nobody pursued us that night, not even in our dreams.

When morning came, the sun rose in the east, all golden and glorious. So, it seemed, with Bemossed. He moved with a new purpose, and he smiled more, as if all that he looked upon pleased him. His eyes shone with a new light. In the coming days, I looked for it to fade, but it did not.

Just before we set out for the secret pass, as Master Juwain was changing the dressing of the wound in Maram's chest that had never healed, Bemossed came over to Maram. He set his hand directly upon the raw, red wound, and Maram cried out as the salts of Bemossed's skin burned him. Bemossed left his hand there even so, for a long time. And when he took it away, Maram's flesh had been made whole again.

'Oh – oh, my Lord!' Maram shouted, pushing out his chest to the sky. 'I am healed!'

He hugged Bemossed to him in a crushing embrace, and then began dancing about the rocks half-naked. He whooped for joy, and then said to Bemossed, 'You *are* the Maitreya, truly you are, and nothing is impossible now!'

This, however, proved not to be so. Bemossed proceeded to lay his hands over Atara's face and then Estrella's throat. But even after an hour of great effort, Estrella still could not find words to speak, and Atara's eye hollows remained empty.

'I'm sorry,' Bemossed said to Atara. He bowed his head to Estrella. 'I've failed you.'

Despite Atara's disappointment, she clasped his hand and told him, 'You could never fail me. There must be many things beyond the power even of a Maitreya.'

She smiled at him, sadly and wistfully, and yet with great gladness, too. She seemed happier than she had been in a long time.

'What could be beyond the power of the Shining One?' Maram exulted as he thumped his chest and gazed at Bemossed. 'The perfect power of a perfect, perfect man!'

Bemossed blinked his dark eyes as his lips tightened with anger. He said to Maram, 'Whatever power passes through me might be perfect, but I certainly am not.'

Maram, though, only waved his hand at the sunlit rocks and the green grass all about us, and said, 'Today, *everything* is perfect!'

Bemossed rolled his eyes in exasperation, and couldn't help smiling at him. Then turned to me and said, 'You understand, don't you?'

I gazed at him, and his face gleamed with all his kindness, goodness and his bright, soaring spirit. But the deep light that filled him now also illumined his restlessness, obstinacy and his anguish of life – and all his other flaws. And the more brilliantly it shone, the clearer and sharper these flaws seemed to be.

'Give it time,' I said to him, clapping him on his shoulder. I looked from Atara to Estrella. 'My brother, Asaru, was the finest knight Mesh has ever seen, but even he didn't learn to wield a sword all in one day.'

Bemossed considered this. It was strange, I thought, that even in the depths of a dark, brooding silence, something inside him seemed to sing with light.

'Val is right,' Master Juwain said, coming up to Bemossed. 'All that I have read about the Maitreya leads me to believe that his gift must be trained like that of any other man.'

Bemossed nodded his head as his face brightened once again. 'All right, then let us leave this land and go where I might find such training.'

After that, we saddled our horses and rode until we entered the band of forest beyond the pasture country. We saw no sign of Red

Capes hunting us, or indeed, of anyone. Birds sang out from the trees in abundance, and deer browsed on the bushes, but if any people had ever dwelt here, they had many years since fled for other places. We made our way through the rugged, rising hills toward the pass that Atuan had told of. We found it only with difficulty: a sharp and treacherous break in the mountains that was more of a crack splitting naked rock than a true pass. We had to work our way through it walking our horses in single file. It snaked north and east, and it took all our care to negotiate it without any of our horses – or us – stumbling and breaking a leg. Finally, though, after a long, hard work, we came out into the great bowl of lowland where we once again looked upon the city of Senta. Great, jagged peaks rose up in a ring of white for miles around us.

Maram gazed out at the wheatfields to the south of Senta's houses and buildings, at the rocky prominence called Mount Miru. There, the opening of the Singing Caves led down into the earth. He told me, 'I would look upon this marvel. I would hear the angels sing.'

But this, too, was not to be. We held council, and we decided that going into the caverns once again might prove too dangerous.

'So,' Kane said, 'King Yulmar might not welcome us, since we left a slaughter on the caverns' doorstep the last time we came this way.'

Liljana nodded her head and added, 'We must do all that we can to slip past Senta without alerting the Kallimun's priests or their spies.'

'But we defeated the Kallimun – again!' Maram said. 'And killed the greatest monster that Morjin ever sent after us! We vanquished the Tar Harath, to say nothing of Jezi Yaga or the Skadarak. And we found the Lord of Light! We should go into the caverns to sing of our deeds!'

'Didn't you tell me,' I said to him, 'that you never wanted to go down into the earth again?'

'Ah, well, I suppose I did,' he said. He looked at Bemossed. 'But that was *then*.'

In the end, however, Maram saw the reason of our arguments, and he grudgingly accepted the need for prudence. It was, as he said, the greatest disappointment of his life. It consoled him some- what that he had Alphanderry, the greatest minstrel of the age, to sing for him in the caverns' stead.

'I'll come back,' he promised himself, looking up at Mount Miru.

'Someday, Morjin will be finally and utterly defeated, and I'll come back and make a true pilgrimage here.'

We spent most of that day crossing the tiny kingdom of Senta, or rather, skirting it, for we rode in a great circle around Senta's farmland and forests, keeping close to the mountains. We encountered only a woodcutter and a few farmers, who gave us leave to cross their fields. At the end of the day, we made camp in a wood northeast of the city, just below the pyramid mountain that had pointed our way toward Senta. We spent the next morning working our way up through the pass around this icy peak, and so we left the civilized realms of Ea's far west behind us.

We came down into the thick forest of that wild upland where no people lived. For the rest of that day and part of the next, we picked our way with great care ever downward, searching through the trees and huge rocks for the road by which we had approached Senta. Kane had an excellent memory for terrain, and so did I, and so we had no trouble finding this road, in its broken segments, or the long valley through which it led. The Valley of Death, Maram called it, for it disquieted him to wonder what had happened to the people who had once lived here. But as before, on our journey toward Hesperu, this broad, green swath through the earth proved to be just the opposite, for we took from it ripe apples and wild, golden wheat, as well as antelopes and boar and other game that sustained our lives.

It was here, during the warm, sunny days of early Ioj, that Bemossed finally learned to ride. Here, too, he began putting to the test whether we had truly dealt Morjin a significant defeat. Day after day, as we rode down the grass-filled valley, he would gaze out at the rocks and the golden-leaved aspen trees as if looking for the Lightstone's radiance in all things. Twice, as during the battle with Morjin's droghul, I saw the Lightstone appear and Bemossed reach out to grasp it. He seemed still to lack the power to make it his own and wield it as he had been born to do. We all, however, felt a change in our gelstei: Maram's firestone cooled to the temperature of warm bread, while Atara found her kristei to be suddenly lighter and almost free of taint – and so with our other crystals. We all dared to hope that Morjin might be losing his power over them.

After twelve days of easy travel, the valley grew drier as we approached the canyon that gave out onto the Red Desert. None of us wanted to recross this wasteland. Maram, especially, sought for arguments to put off this passage or avoid it altogether.

'But Bemossed is making such excellent progress *here*!' Maram said to us. 'If we go into the desert, he'll have to fight the dreadful heat, and so he won't have the wherewithal to fight Morjin.'

'But we can't just remain in this valley forever,' Liljana told him.

'Why not? There is enough game to feed us forever – and wild wheat that could be brewed into a good beer.'

Liljana, I thought, almost smiled at this. Then she said to him, 'But I haven't seen any grapes from which we could make wine, and so brandy. And courtesans there are none.'

Maram considered this. 'But we could at least wait until Ashvar, couldn't we? Or even Valte, when the desert grows a little cooler?'

'The desert *must* be cooler now than it was in Marud,' I told him. 'We must cross it as soon as we can, and you know why.'

At this, Maram raised up his hands in surrender, and said, 'All right, my friend, but if I die of heatstroke in the Tar Harath, you'll never forgive yourself.'

The next afternoon, we came down into the Dead City, half buried in the desert's swirling, reddish sands. Hundreds of miles of emptiness opened before us, to the north and east. Here grew a little ursage, rock grass and other tough plants. It was said to rain here in Segadar and the other months of winter, but we would be unlikely to see any moisture fall from the sky unless Estrella worked her magic again.

For three days, we rode east, taking water from the Yieshi wells that we came to. We saw no men or women of this tribe, not even at the easternmost well where Manoj and his family had dwelt with their little black tents and stinking goats. We speculated that he might have gone off to make war with the Zuri, but we didn't really know. We filled our waterskins almost to bursting from his well, still nearly full from the storm that Estrella had summoned. We left no coins to pay for it. As Atara reminded us, we had given the Yieshi a great deal of water, which in the desert was a hundred times more valuable than gold.

After that, we went into the Tar Harath. This immense country of sun-scorched rocks and blazing dunes proved to be not so hellishly hot as Maram had feared – which is to say that the torrid air did not quite sear our lungs or steam the flesh from our bones. But the days waxed more than hot enough to make us sweat and swear and suffer. Somehow, we bore it. Maram, who had ventured this journey in the opposite direction alone, found the grace to remark that our companionship made the miles and the days pass more easily. Then, too, as he put it, with his wounds healed, he had only to endure a more or less human measure of pain.

This grew greater and greater the deeper that we pushed into the Tar Harath. Miracles we had found in abundance all along our way, but we had no magic to keep the sun from sucking the moisture from our bodies and emptying our waterskins a little more with every passing mile. Finally, our water ran out altogether. Then Estrella took out the blue bowl that Oni had given her, and she tried to call the clouds to her from out of nowhere. She failed. We were never able to determine exactly why. Some things, it seemed, especially the ways of the wind and the human heart, would always remain a mystery.

We might have despaired then, but we did not. I reminded Maram, and myself, that on our outward passage Estrella had led us to the Vild, and she would again. So it proved to be. Our course across the drifting desert sands had held straight and true, and less than a day later we came upon the giant oak trees and olindas that grew by the greatest of magics in the middle of a wasteland. And so we entered the Loikalii's wood, parched and dust-worn but still gloriously alive.

When Maira, with Anneli and others of her small people, came to greet us, she called out in delight: 'The seekers return! With the bright one they sought! We must make a feast!'

It took two days of eating and drinking for us to consume all the succulent fruits, nuts, wines and other things that the Loikalii brought to us from their fecund woods. We rested as much as we wished, and then arose to eat, drink and sing some more. I unpacked a bottle of old brandy, bought in Hesperu, that I had been saving for many miles. As I had promised Maram, I filled our cups with this marvelous liquid, and made a toast to love. Toward the end of bringing more love into the world, Maram renewed his acquaintance with Anneli, who wanted again and again to hear the story of how Bemossed had healed his unhealable wound. At last, on the third day of our sojourn, we all gathered around Oni's magic pool that she called the Water. Bemossed had a hard time believing that I had fallen into it, only to emerge onto the banks of another much like it on another world. As we stood over it looking down into its still, silvery waters, I said to him, 'Why don't we put it to the test? Why don't you dive in and see what you can see?'

Just then the amethyst towers and golden buildings of the city called Iveram appeared from out of the pool's shimmering water.

Bemossed gasped at the wonder of it, and he said, 'No, thank you – I am a man of *this* world.'

He planted his feet on the bank of the pool and grabbed hold of my arm to steady himself, and he stared in amazement as the faces and forms of the Star People came into view. I recognized the noble Ramadar, Eva, Varjan and others of the true Valari whom I had met on their world of Givene. No words did they speak, nor could any common language pass through the water that connected our two worlds, or so I thought. I knew, however, that the Star People recognized Bemossed for who he was. Their black, brilliant eyes blazed with great rejoicing.

And then the pool shimmered like silustria, and the Star People disappeared from our sight. Through the clear water other things took shape: the great, golden astor tree, Irdrasil, and the two perfect white mountains, Telshar and Vayu that framed it in the distance. Although the Galadin of Agathad did not make themselves visible to us, I had a sense that Ashtoreth and Valoreth – and others of their order – were aware of much that occurred on Ea, and elsewhere. If they had faces like other men and women, they surely smiled to behold Bemossed and know that all of Eluru had a new Lord of Light.

After a while, the pool's radiance dimmed and its surface quieted to a sheeny silver, like that of any other still water. The Loikalii, in awe of what they had seen, turned toward Bemossed and began clapping their hands as they chanted: 'A song! A song – give us a song!'

At this, Bemossed seemed genuinely embarrassed. He said, 'I never learned many, and none worthy of such a wonder.'

Then Alphanderry came forth out of nothingness, and walked up to him. He smiled at him and said, 'Hoy, I have songs! Thousands upon thousands! If you'll give me a few notes, I shall give one to you.'

As Estrella and I took out our flutes and Kane his mandolet – and the Loikalii sucked on ripe apples or plums to prepare their throats for a songfest – Alphanderry stood by the pool looking at Bemossed strangely. And then he began singing out old verses beloved of Master Juwain and the rest of us:

> When earth alights the Golden Band,
> The darkest age will pass away;
> When angel fire illumes the land,
> The stars will show the brightest day.

679

The deathless day, the Age of Light;
Ieldra's blaze befalls the earth;
The end of war, the end of night
Awaits the last Maitreya's birth.

The Cup of Heaven in his hands,
The One's clear light in heart and eye,
He brings the healing of the land,
And opens colors in the sky.

And there, the stars, the ageless lights
For which we ache and dream and burn,
Upon the deep and dazzling heights –
Our ancient home we shall return.

The Loikalii learned most of these words, the music too, with a single recitation, for such was their gift. They insisted on singing the verses again – and again – thrice more, until they had them perfect. Then Maira arose from the grass and said to Alphanderry, 'You bring words that echo our dreams.'

'How not?' Alphanderry said. 'I am of the Forest, am I not?'

Maira smiled at this and turned to Bemossed. 'And you – we hope, we hope! – will bring the fire that heals.'

For a moment, Bemossed's eyes grew troubled as if he stared down into a dark place. Then this mood melted away before the blaze of his design. Although I sensed in him little vanity or arrogance, he also had little patience for pretended humility. Now that he knew with a surety who and what he was, he seemed to accept this with all the naturalness of a flower opening its petals to the sky.

'What I bring already is,' he said to Maira. 'The fire you speak of is spread upon the earth, but people do not see it.'

'Then you will help them to see,' Maira told him.

At this, Bemossed smiled sadly as he looked at Atara.

'You will, you *will*,' Maira said. 'And when everyone sees the world as it really is, the world will never be the same.'

Later that morning we said goodbye to Maira and the Loikalii. Oni promised to send cooling winds from out of the northwest, and so it proved to be. After we had left the woods to make our way across the drifts of red-tinged sand, we followed this steady wind, or rather it followed us. Although the days never grew really cool, as with a bright Valte afternoon in the mountains of Mesh, we found ourselves able to travel straight through from dawn to dusk. Even the heat of high noon seemed sweetly hot, as if the sun's rays penetrated our garments and flesh to fill our bodies with an ease of being and a love of light.

The sheer brilliance of the deep desert dazzled all of us. During the long hours of the days, the sand scattered the sunlight up into a perfectly blue sky. And at night, the stars came out in all their shimmering millions. Bemossed seemed almost wholly ignorant of astrology, and so I pointed out to him constellations such as the Swan and the Great Bear and others that my grandfather had once taught me. One evening, after dinner, as we sat together on the crest of a great dune, Bemossed reached up toward an array of lights named the Angels' Tears, and he said, 'I don't think those stars shine down upon Hesperu.'

'Of course they do,' I told him. 'We haven't come so far to the north that they wouldn't. It is just that these stars are faint, and the air in your land contains too much moisture, and so blocks their radiance.'

He nodded his head at this, then told me, 'It is strange: water is life, and here there is so little of it. And yet everything here is so *alive*.'

I said nothing as I gazed off at Solaru, Icesse and bright Arras, and other lights that were as old friends to me. And Bemossed continued: 'The sky here is so black – and yet the stars are so bright.'

I said nothing to this either as I found the splendid pair of lights that I had named Shavashar and Elianora.

'I don't think he can see us here,' Bemossed said to me. 'Morjin can't – and that is strange because the air in this emptiness is clearer and the light is more brilliant than I had ever imagined.'

I drew my sword and watched the starlight play upon its silvery surface. I said, 'Once, I was sure that Morjin would find his way to claim this for himself. Now, I think, it is almost free of his foulness. The others say that of their gelstei, too.'

Bemossed smiled at this. 'And you think that is because of me.'

'I know it is. With every passing mile, *you* seem ever clearer. Ever brighter, too.'

His heavy eyebrows pulled together as he said, 'But we still have so many miles to go.'

'Do you doubt that we can defeat Morjin now?'

He thought about this as the wind whipped wisps of dark sand across the gleaming dunes, and blew steadily out of the northwest, almost as from another world. The words he spoke then would remain with me for many, many miles, and all the rest of my life: 'But that is just it, Valashu. I do not wish to defeat Morjin as you do.'

During the days that followed, as we held a straight and steady course across the Tar Harath, I tried better to understand this wise, gentle and yet powerful man who had been born a slave. He seemed always willing to be open with me, even as I sensed that he always kept the worst of his sufferings and his deepest dreams to himself. Something in his essential being seemed flow like quick-silver, difficult to look upon for all its shifting brilliance, and impossible to grasp. In the end, I thought, he would remain to me a more profound mystery than life and death.

In the coming days we journeyed on past the ides of Valte into the later part of that month. As we drew farther and farther from the Loikalii's wood, the north wind gradually weakened and then died altogether. It didn't matter, for finally the desert began to cool of its own. Our long ride across it became almost pleasant.

And then we came out of the Tar Harath into the country of the Avari. On the 24th of Valte we found that break in the moun-tains sheltering the Hadr Halona. As we rode past the many tents and houses of this place of water, the Avari came out into the streets to greet us. Warriors drew their curving swords and saluted us, and they shouted out their surprise that we had returned from out of the Tar Harath. Many of them, I saw to my dismay, seemed to have been recently wounded, as evidenced by arms hanging in slings or bandaged faces. I knew without being told that the Avari had finally been driven to war, even as Sunji had feared.

We met with him later that day in his father's house by the lake when King Jovayl invited guests for a great victory feast. Some of these were elders of the tribe with whom we had sat before: Laisar, Jaidray, Barsayr and old Sarald. Maidro arrived wearing a white bandage wrapped around his head, and we cried out in gladness to greet our former companion. Arthayn accompanied him, but we waited in vain for Nuradayn to appear. And then Sunji informed us that the impulsive Nuradayn had fallen in battle.

'He survived the Tar Harath,' Sunji told us, 'only to die leading a charge against the Zuri's swords.'

'He was a brave man, and we honor him,' King Jovayl announced as he bade us sit down to the many platters of food laid out on his great white carpet. 'When he went into the Tar Harath, he was still much of a youth, and too reckless, as we all knew. But when he came out, he was a man, bold and yet balanced, and worthy of all our respect. And so we gave him a command.'

He went on to say that the deep desert was like a forge, either shaping and tempering the steel inside a man or destroying it.

'The Tar Harath has changed you, Valaysu,' he said, staring at me. 'There is something about you now, something. It is as rare as skystone, and ten times more striking. It cannot be denied.'

He nodded at Liljana, Daj, Master Juwain and paused for a long time as he looked at Maram. 'All of you. You have done a great thing, and this greatness shines for all to see.'

He lifted up a bottle of wine, and he filled each of our glasses with his own hand. Then he bowed his head toward Bemossed.

'It seems that you have found the one you sought,' he told us. 'Well, we shall see.'

Bemossed returned his bow, and said, 'What do you mean, lord?'

'My warriors have returned with me from the battle,' King Jovayl told him, 'and too many of them bear wounds beyond all help. If you are the Maitreya that Valaysu sought, you will heal them.'

He went on to recount what had happened in the desert while we made quest in faraway Hesperu. Sunji had thought that there might be war with the Zuri in the autumn, but King Jovayl had surprised him, and everyone else in the tribe, by moving against the Zuri in the heat of Soal. And more, he had surprised the Zuri. It had been the Masud's wells that Morjin's droghul had poisoned, (with the compliance of the Zuri), but it was King Jovayl who led the crusade of vengeance. He had not only made allies of the Masud and their fierce chief, Rohaj, but of the Yieshi as well. Their three armies, like the points of stabbing spears, he had co-ordinated in a vicious attack upon the Zuri, from out the west, the north and east. They worked a great slaughter upon the Zuri warriors, and they put to the sword their chief, Tatuk, and all the Red Priests who had corrupted him. Some of the Zuri women they took as wives, while others they slew – along with many children, too, for even boys ten years old tried to defend their families with lances and swords. King Jovayl had finally managed to put an end to this massacre. Then the Avari warriors, along with the Masud and the Yieshi, had driven the survivors from their homes, and they divided the Zuri's lands among the three tribes.

'The Zuri are no more,' King Jovayl announced proudly. 'We have heard that a few of their clans have begged mercy from the

Vuai, but they must be few, and they will never take back what we have claimed.'

I traded looks with Maram, who took a huge gulp of wine. It was a terrible thing that the Avari had done, but that was the way of things with the tribes of the Red Desert. With a single brilliant and ruthless campaign, King Jovayl had put an end to Morjin's hopes of conquering this vast country, at least for a time, and I should have been glad for that.

Bemossed, however, took no joy in King Jovayl's news – nor, in truth, in King Jovayl. All during the feast, he picked at his food and kept a silence. Later that night, as we took a walk by the lake, he said to me, 'Did you see the way that King Jovayl and the elders looked at me? As if I existed only to prove their prophecies and justify their crusades. Is that why I *am*?'

I gazed at the starlight reflected off the lake's black, mirrored surface. I said, 'King Jovayl has only asked for your help in healing his people, and there is nothing wrong with that.'

'Does he care about *them*?' he said.

'Of course he does – they are his warriors.'

'His warriors,' he repeated. 'Who have murdered in the name of the good.'

I let my hand fall upon my sword's hilt and said, 'So have I, Bemossed.'

'I know – I have seen you. But you did not slay women and children.'

'Is it so much better to slay a man?' I asked him. 'Slaughter is slaughter. That is war, and why I hate it. And why it must end.'

I turned to look at him through the pale light pouring down from the sky, and I told him, 'And *that* is why you are.'

The next morning, however, when King Jovayl called the wounded to his house from the dwellings across the Hadr Halona and the pastures farther out in the desert, Bemossed was loath to go among them. He remained within his room, and people said that he was not the Maitreya after all – either that, or his power had failed him. And so Master Juwain went out to tend to the stricken warriors in his place. Master Juwain had a great gift of his own for healing, and he managed to draw a lance point buried deep in the back of one of the warriors and to reset the bones of another whose arm had been badly broken. But he could do nothing for a third warrior sweating and gasping at the pain of a leg crushed when a horse had fallen upon it – nothing without his gelstei, that is. In desperation, not wanting to have to cut off the man's leg, Master Juwain finally took out his gelstei. He held it over the shattered leg. But as before with Maram, a hot green fire poured out of the crystal instead of a healing light, and struck into the man a pure agony. Seeing this, Bemossed's heart broke open. He hurried out of King Jovayl's house, and set his hand upon the man's leg, and he made it whole. Likewise, he restored a warrior named Irgayn with an infected sword wound in his belly, and young Daivayr who had suffered a dizzying blow to the back of his head, and others. At the end of the day, when this great work of healing was finished, I took him aside and said to him, 'You were kind to men you call murderers.'

Then he looked at me with a deep light running in his eyes like water, and he told me, 'Until war is ended upon this world, we are all murderers.'

We stayed one more night in King Jovayl's house, and set out at dawn to continue our desert crossing. King Jovayl commanded Sunji, Maidro, Arthayn and six other warriors to escort us to the edge of the Avari's country, and this they did. For a day we rode south along the little range of mountains, and then we turned east and travelled a good few miles farther until we came to lands claimed by the Masud. There, by a great red rock as flat at the top as a sheet of paper, we said farewell to Sunji – I hoped not forever.

'We have no plans to return this way,' I told him, 'but the wind blows where it will blow.'

'Not always,' he said, removing his cowl to smile at Estrella. We had stopped not far from that place in the barren mountains where she had found a new source of water. 'But I hope one day it blows us together again.'

'I know it will,' I told him. 'Until then, go in the light of the One.'

'*That* will be easier now,' he said, bowing his head to Bemossed. He told him, 'I never thanked you, did I, for healing Daivayr? He is my brother.'

After that we journeyed east through the sere, sun-baked land by which we had first entered the desert. We drank water from the Masud's wells, and we did not fear that they would take this as thievery. After the battle in the canyon, when Yago had cut off the second droghul's head, he had promised us that if we ever ventured into the Masud's realm again, we would be welcome.

So it proved to be. On our fourth day out from the Hadr Halona, a band of Masud warriors returning from the destruction of the Zuri espied us. At first they seemed eager for another battle, for they charged upon us in cloud of dust. But when we called out our names and that we were friends of Yago and under the protection of Rohaj, they called back that they would extend us all their hospitality. True to their word, they shared with us some dried goat meat, figs and fermented milk. Then, over the next few days, they rode with us all the way to that place where the desert ended against the great wall of the White Mountains.

We said farewell to these warriors, too, and I wondered if we really would see any of the Red Desert's fierce peoples again. It surprised me that I had come to love the desert – its brilliance and stark beauty – as much as I dreaded going up into the mountains.

Part of my disquiet, I knew, came from my memories of the monster that had so nearly killed us on our first crossing of these heights. As we worked up toward the gap where Jezi Yaga had once lived and turned wayfarers into stone, we finally caught sight of the place where she had perished. High on a shelf of rock overlooking the desert, she still stood: a great, hideous stone statue with violet eyes. Maram, with some trepidation, insisted on going up to her and laying his hands upon her face. Perhaps he wanted to reassure himself that she really was dead. He wept then, and he could not tell us why.

We all moved forward past this lonely sentinel, and we began working our way through the gap's rugged terrain. That night it grew quite cold. Master Juwain calculated that we had journeyed into Ashvar, the month of the falling leaves, which in the mountains could turn almost as frigid as winter. No snow, however, fell upon us during our passage of the gap. We rode up and up past red-leaved trees through air that steamed our breath. When we came to that place by the gap's central stream where Jezi had turned Berkuar to stone, we paused to pray for him. He stood like an immortal, still wearing the gold medallion that I had placed around his neck.

'Perhaps you should take that back,' Liljana said to me, pointing at the medallion. 'If anyone chances this way, he will likely claim it.'

'No, let it remain,' I said. 'Berkuar is entitled to keep it.'

'Then perhaps we should bury him, and let it lie with him.'

I considered this as I watched Bemossed step up to Berkuar and touch his hand to Berkuar's stony fingers. I found myself gazing at Bemossed a little too intently.

And he said to me, 'I cannot bring back the dead, Valashu.'

'I know that,' I told him. I rapped my knuckles against the trunk of a maple as I added, 'And I know it would be best to leave Berkuar just as he is, looking upon these beautiful trees. It is a kind of life, isn't it?'

After that we journeyed on into the more heavily wooded eastern reaches of the gap, and I thought more and more about life – and thus about death. Although we hadn't yet drawn very close to that dark, diseased part of the Acadian forest called the Skadarak, I knew that we could not avoid it. Our reasons for setting a course close to it remained as before. It was reason that told me we could survive it, as we had once, and yet as I contemplated going anywhere near the Skadarak's blackened and twisted trees, my disquiet built into a howling, belly-shaking dread.

So it was with my friends. In our descent of the mountains down into Acadu's cold, gray woods, Daj fell as quiet as Estrella, while Atara, Liljana and Master Juwain rode along lost in a terrible silence. And then, with our horses' hooves crunching over dead leaves, Maram finally looked at Master Juwain and said, 'At the Avari's hadrah, when you tried to use your crystal, you only proved that Morjin still has a hold on it. It must be, then, that he still has a hold on the Black Jade, and so on us.'

Master Juwain could usually summon a well-thought response to almost any statement. This time, however, he only looked at Maram as he shrugged his shoulders, then drew the hood of his cloak over his bald head.

And so I told Maram, 'He has no hold over us – at least, not our hearts.'

'But what of our gelstei?' He drew out his firestone and stared at it. 'I'm afraid of what I feel building inside this. I *am*, Val.'

'It will be all right,' I told him.

'It will *not* be all right, just because you say so.' He turned in his saddle to look back at Bemossed, riding next to the children. '*He* was supposed to take control of the Lightstone from Morjin.'

'Give it time,' I told him.

'Time,' he muttered. 'In another day, I think, we'll come to the Skadarak. Who knows, we might have entered it already.'

His deepest fears, however, and my own, proved groundless. After some more miles of riding through gray-barked trees shedding their leaves, we came to that strip of forest bordering the marshland to the south and the Skadarak to the north. I led the way straight into it. We rode on and on into a smothering stillness, and soon the sky grew thick with black clouds, and we all heard the call of a voice we dreaded above all others. But then

687

Bemossed nudged his horse up close beside me. He smiled at me, and the sun rose in that dark, dark place. Alphanderry came out of nowhere to sing us a bright, immortal song. And although the terrible voice continued murmuring its maddening tones, as it always would, we did not listen. And so we completed our passage of the Skadarak once again.

The workings of fate are strange. We had traveled all the way from Hesperu nearly a thousand miles across some of Ea's harshest and deadliest country without incident, almost as if we had gone on a holiday. Now, with only one last stretch of forest to negotiate before reaching our journey's end, Maram rejoiced that our luck had held good. But he rejoiced too soon.

The woods of Acadu, as we discovered, proved to be infested with even more Crucifiers than before, for Morjin had sent a battalion of soldiers down from Sakai to quell the unrest and exterminate the forces opposing him. We did what we could to avoid them. The trees, however, more and more barren with every mile that we pressed eastward toward winter, provided us little cover. We had trouble crossing Acadu's rivers: the great Ea and the Tir. We hoped to fall in with the Greens and gain a little protection for at least a part of our passage, but we learned that these Keepers of the Forest had concentrated their forces for a great battle up north of the minelands, where Acadu bordered Sakai. I set a course almost due east, over wet leaves and between trees that seemed as dead and gray as ghosts. Thus we made our way through the rainy and dark days of late Ashvar by ourselves.

We came close to the Nagarshath range of the White Mountains safely. And then, within a span of fifty miles, we fought two battles. In the first of these, a squadron of soldiers came upon us at the edge of a farmer's field, and they demanded that we surrender up Atara and Estrella to 'cook and provide comfort for them,' as they put it. We killed these ten Crucifiers quickly, down to the last man. Two days later, with the jagged, white-capped peaks of the mountains gleaming through the leafless trees, a band of Acadians who had gone over to Morjin tried to relieve us of our possessions – as well as our lives. We fought an arrow duel with them: Kane put a feathered shaft through their leader's eye, while Maram killed two men with arrows buried exactly in the centers of their chests. Seeing this, their companions lost heart and melted away into the forest. We all made ready to rejoice then, but we discovered that Daj had taken an arrow straight through his thigh. Remarkably, he bore this nasty wound without crying out or making any sound.

He kept his silence, too, as Master Juwain drew the arrow with great difficulty, for its barbs had caught up in Daj's tendons. Bemossed managed to heal his torn and bleeding leg with little difficulty, and within an hour, Daj could walk with little pain. I, however, suffered a stab of guilt that would not go away, for this was the first time in our travels that one of the children had been seriously wounded.

At last we came to the place where the forest's trees rose up the steep slopes of the mountains. We found the ravine by which we had come down into Acadu months before, and now we made our way up into it. The ascent was hard, for Ashvar's rains had fallen here as snow, which grew deeper and deeper the higher we climbed. It grew much colder, too. I kept watching the sky for sign that the clouds might thicken up and loose upon us a major storm.

'If it *does* snow too much or too long,' Maram said, giving voice to my thoughts, 'we could be trapped here all winter. How much food do we have left? Ten days' worth? Twenty, if we stretch it?'

'Be quiet!' Kane told him, looking about the trees of the snow-covered ravine. 'If we have to, we can always kill a few deer.'

'If any remain this high up,' Maram said, shivering. He watched his horse's breath steaming out of its nostrils.

'So, if we *really* have to,' Kane told Maram with a wicked light in his eyes, 'we could always kill *you*. I'd bet that you'd keep us in meat longer than three fat bucks, eh?'

To emphasize his point, he moved over and poked his finger into Maram's belly, still quite rotund, though considerably diminished due to the hardships of our journey. And Maram said to him, '*That* is not funny! You shouldn't joke about such things!'

Something in Kane's voice, however, caused Maram to look at him to make sure he really *was* joking. With Kane, one never quite knew.

'I'm afraid that snow or no snow,' Master Juwain said, 'we must go on. Tomorrow is the twenty-eighth of Ashvar.'

'Are you sure we're not late?' Maram asked as he pulled his cloak tighter around his throat and stamped his boots in the snow. 'It feels more like Segadar – and late Segadar at that.'

'I've kept a count of the days,' Master Juwain reassured him.

'But are you certain about the twenty-eighth? I haven't had a clear sight of the stars for half a month.'

'I am not the greatest astrologer, it's true,' Master Juwain admitted. 'But if my calculations are correct, then tomorrow the moon *will* conjunct the Seven Sisters.'

689

Again, I gazed skyward at the overlying sheet of gray above us. Who could tell where the moon would cross that night? Who could even see the sun, much less the stars?

We continued climbing up into the mountains, all the rest of that day and most of the next. One of the pack horses stumbled in the deep snow, and broke its neck on some rocks. It died before Bemossed could even attempt to help it. Later, the foot of Daj's wounded leg began to freeze, and we had to stop more than once to thaw his toes. Finally, though, we came up to a wall of rock where one of the tunnels through these mountains opened like a yawning, black mouth. With great satisfaction, Master Juwain announced that we still had hours to spare.

'The conjunction should occur late tonight,' he informed us, 'just two hours before dawn.'

'Ah, it *should* occur,' Maram agreed, 'but what if it doesn't? I wish Master Storr had given us one his gelstei so that we could unlock this damn tunnel any time we pleased.'

But Master Storr, I thought, for all his hope that our quest would end successfully, had not been willing to entrust the key to the Brotherhood's secret school to wayfarers who might be captured and might surrender up his precious gelstei to Morjin.

'If you're wrong about the date,' Maram said to Master Juwain, 'when is the next nearest motion of the stars that will open this?'

'Not until the second of Triolet. I don't think you would want to wait that long.'

'I don't want to wait another hour, much less twelve,' Maram said. 'But I suppose there's no help for it?'

If Bemossed had doubted that the pool in the Loikalii's vild might provide a passage to the stars, he could not deny the magic of the tunnel. Two hours before dawn, with the sky beginning to clear, we entered this dark tube of rock. It came alive in pulses of iridescent light. As before, its workings made us sick in our stomachs and disoriented us; and as before, our focused will took us through it, out into that beautiful, sunny valley that sheltered the Brotherhood's greatest school.

This time, no trick of Master Virang or our own blindness kept the sight of it from us. We rejoiced at the cluster of gleaming stone buildings by the valley's frozen river. It took us until mid-morning to ride down through the drifts of snow and reach this haven. Abrasax and the six other masters, with all two hundred of the men who lived and studied here, came out of their dwellings and gathered in front of the great hall to greet us. When Bemossed fairly dropped off his horse, stiff and nearly frozen, Abrasax gazed at him for a long time. I sensed that he was seeing in him colors other than those of the outer world: the green of the fir trees; the sweeps of white snow; the blue sky's brilliant golden sun.

'Valashu Elahad,' Master Storr said, standing next to Abrasax, 'brings *another* stranger into our valley.'

Estrella came up to Bemossed, and took his hand. She waved her other hand about in the frigid air as if she desperately desired the gift of being able to talk to us again. But as Abrasax had said months before, her words held less power than did her eyes or her heart. She looked at Bemossed in adoration, with a perfect brilliance felt by all who stood gazing upon them. For a long moment, it was Estrella who seemed to speak, in sparkling streams and shimmering oceans deeper than any words, while Master Storr stood there struck dumb like a mute – and so it was with the other Masters of the Seven, and all the Brothers, as well as my friends and even myself.

'He is no stranger,' Abrasax said as he bowed his head to Bemossed. Then held up his long, wrinkled hand, and shouted out: 'It is he whom we've known from all our books and dreams! The quest has been completed! Valashu Elahad and his companions have found the Shining One!'

Then he cast aside all decorum and restraint, and he rushed forward to embrace Bemossed, as he did with each of us in our turn. His old face warmed with the brightest of smiles.

Even the dour old Master Storr couldn't help smiling along with him, and he called out, 'Then they have brought us the greatest gift in the world – and just in time for your birthday, Grandfather!'

All the rest of the Seven and the two hundred Brothers standing about in the snow let out a great cheer. Abrasax's attention finally turned from the miracle of Bemossed's existence to the sorry state of our clothing, mounts and our care-worn flesh. Then he commanded us to repair to the guest houses and recover from our great journey.

43

The next few days were a time of rest and restoration. We took up residence in the two guest houses by the river, and we spent whole hours bathing our worn bodies in the great cedarwood tubs that the Brothers kept full of steaming hot water. We sat with the Brothers in the great hall to take our meals: simple, sustaining foods such as beef and barley soup, lamb stews, and hot bread drenched with sweet butter. We slept as much as we liked, in good beds, swaddled in crisp cotton sheets and thick quilts stuffed with goose down. At night, it grew bitterly cold in those high mountains, and it seemed impossible that we had ever suffered through the Red Desert's inexorable heat. As well, we had a hard time imagining that there were places and things in the world that were not bright and clean and good.

Abrasax's one hundred and forty-seventh birthday arrived on the third of Segadar, and the Brothers and my companions all gathered for a great feast to celebrate it. All that day Liljana had labored in the kitchens baking chocolate and raspberry cakes, which were Abrasax's favorite. When it came time to eat them, he praised her artistry and declared that in all his long life, at this school and others, he had never tasted a confection so fine as the one Liljana baked for him. He commanded that the Brothers break out their reserve of rare teas to accompany the cakes; all present stirred into their cups an orange blossom honey from Galda that was rarer still. Its sweetness, Abrasax said, would always remind him of this evening with Liljana and the rest of our company – and, of course, with Bemossed.

We might have luxuriated thusly all winter, and fallen into indulgence or even sloth. But when Master Okuth deemed us sufficiently strong, Abrasax appointed each of us tasks: Master Juwain was to record a complete account of our journey, paying particular attention to what we had discovered in the Vild and in Senta's Singing Caves. Abrasax asked Liljana to begin imparting to the Brothers her great knowledge of herbs and poisons, as well as her many recipes for delicious foods that were unknown to them. He commanded that Daj and Estrella should receive instruction in ancient Ardik and other languages, as well as mathematics, music and the arts. When Daj complained that he would rather spend his time completing the *Gest of Eleikar and Ayeshtan*, Abrasax arranged with Master Nolashar for Daj to work this composition into his music lessons. Atara he set to caring for the horses, sheep, cows and pigs that the Brothers kept in their stables. It was hard, often dirty work, unfit for a princess, much less a great warrior of the Manslayer Society, but Atara surprised us all by looking after these animals with a love that she often found difficult to tender to human beings. Strangely, Abrasax insisted that Kane and I should spend at least three hours each day practicing with swords. And stranger still, he asked Maram to sit at a desk composing a whole new set of verses for 'A Second Chakra Man'.

Bemossed did not escape the Grandmaster's demands. Indeed, he had the hardest work of all of us, for he had to face the most terrible of enemies in a relentless combat. Each morning just after dawn, Abrasax would go into the little stone conservatory to sit with Bemossed and Master Virang, who led Bemossed in endless hours of meditation. Their labor, as I understood it, was to clear each of Bemossed's chakras so that the deep light that lived within him might rise and blaze forth, unclouded by the dark moods and sense of doom that too often grieved him. And each afternoon, in the short, sharp brightness of the winter days, Bemossed met with Master Storr to attune himself to the Cup of Ashurun. Whenever Bemossed dared to lay his hands upon it, this great work of silver gelstei glowed with a strong golden radiance and resonated with the Lightstone hundreds of miles away in Argattha. Master Storr soon determined that Bemossed *could* touch upon the True Gelstei from afar and reach with his luminous being deep into its heart. Someday, he might even master it this way, though Master Storr thought the danger to Bemossed would be very great.

Bemossed did not like to talk about this, nor would he say very much about his endless struggles with Morjin. One night, however, after a particularly brutal session of delving the Lightstone's mysteries, he took me aside and confided to me, 'Morjin will die before ever giving up the Cup of Heaven again. And he will slay.

He hates . . . so hatefully, Valashu. Far more than you do. And it is so *foul* – fouler than a corpse rotting slowly in a slaughterhouse for a thousand years. You think that you have known darkness in the Skadarak, but what lies within Morjin is blacker than any Black Jade.'

He told me then that he did not know how he could bear it.

But bear it he did, and more, he gained a great victory over Morjin. There came a day in Yaradar, just past the darkest time of the year, when we all felt our gelstei free of Morjin's taint, as of wounds drained of poison. Master Juwain ventured to use his varistei to germinate and grow some barbark seeds that he had brought out of Acadu, while Liljana pressed her blue figurine to her head and managed to speak mind to mind with one of her sisters in faroff Alonia, or so she said. Maram broke off his versifying to go out into the Valley of the Sun with his red crystal and unleash bolts of fiery lightning, just for the sheer joy of it. Then Kane took out his gelstei to demonstrate how the black jade had been designed to be used. It frustrated Maram for Kane to steal his fire, so to speak, but more than once, Kane kept Maram from killing himself in a great blast of rock and heat, or at least badly burning his hands. As for Atara, she did not regain her second sight. Even so, she spent what seemed entire days gazing eyeless into her clear scryer's sphere. As she told me, she did not look for things faraway in space or time, but rather concentrated all her will upon imagining them to be.

Master Storr finally deemed it safe to begin exploring the properties of Estrella's blue bowl, which Estrella gladly lent to him. He thanked her for bearing it all across Ea, and told all of us: 'You *do* have a talent for discovering gelstei. It is a pity, though, that you could not also bring me the lilastei that you say the Yaga used to turn men to stone.'

In early Triolet, with the snows falling heavy and deep, we broke our usual rhythms and routines to receive a rare winter visitor to the valley. A Brother Vipul, at great risk, had forced his way through the mountains on snow shoes to bring Abrasax important news. After Abrasax had allowed Master Juwain to use his green crystal to heal Vipul's frozen feet and had sat drinking hot cider with Vipul for most of an afternoon, Abrasax called the Brotherhood's masters into a conclave to speak with my friends and me.

We met in the conservatory that evening. Bemossed entered the room looking tired and troubled, and yet strangely happier than he had ever been. In truth, his whole being seemed to glow. We all took our places around the three low tea tables. One of the brothers came in to fill our cups with steaming tea and serve us hot lemon cakes. The many candles set ablaze in their stands cast their warm radiance on the twelve pillars holding up the domed roof. Snow plastered over the round windows to the north and west, but the southern windows let in the light of the stars.

After asking each of us to tell of the progress in the tasks appointed to us, Abrasax moved on to his purpose in calling us together. He sat straight and stern on his colorful cushion, his curly hair and beard framing his striking face in a wreath of white. Then he said to us, 'Brother Vipul has been ordered to bed, and so we will discuss his tidings in his absence. It is time, in any case, that we discussed certain things.'

With what seemed infinite patience, he bit off a piece of his cake and chewed it thoroughly before taking a long sip of tea. He looked from Estrella to Bemossed. Then he looked at the table in front of me, where I had laid the diamond that Ramadar had given me by the pool on Givene: the great gem that had once been set into my ancestor, Adar's, crown. Abrasax had asked me to show it to the Brotherhood's masters as a proof of miracles.

'I have said many times,' he told me, and the rest of my friends, 'that each of our acts, as with a stone dropped into a pool, ripples outward forever. Together on this last quest of yours, you have cast entire mountains into the waters of this world. We all worried that the risk would be too great and the goal almost impossible to achieve. And yet you forced Morjin to take great risks of his own. He spent much time and will working his three droghuls from afar. And to what end? The tribes of the Red Desert now ally themselves against him. In Hesperu, brave spirits have made rebellion again. It is said that King Arsu has recalled part of his army from Surrapam to smash it, and so we do not need to fear the conquest of Eanna and the northwest, at least not yet. Something else is said, not just in Hesperu, but in Sunguru, Uskudar and all lands: that Morjin is dead. The rumor has spread like a wildfire. The Red Dragon will now have to spend even more will to quell it. Perhaps he will even be forced out of Argattha to show himself, in Sunguru, I think, and in Karabuk. Already, in Galda, it is too late.'

He ate another bit of cake and drank some more tea. I sensed that like a minstrel working up to the end of a great epic, he revelled in making us wait for his good news.

'In Galda,' he finally told us, 'there has been another revolt, greater than the last. The Red Priests and anyone connected to the

Kallimun have been killed or driven out. A common knight named Gallagerry has claimed lordship of the land.'

He looked at me and added, 'I am told that the revolt was led by common captains of the army that you and yours so terribly defeated at the Culhadosh Commons. You count that battle as the worst moment of your life, and rightly so, but what you did there, Valashu, now engulfs the world with the force of a tidal wave, does it not?'

I noticed Bemossed smiling at me, and I remembered that false humility would not serve me. But neither would pride.

'On the day you speak of,' I reminded Abrasax, 'what I did caused the Lightstone to be lost.'

'Lost, yes, but not forsaken.' Abrasax looked across the table at Bemossed, and bowed his head to him, as did Master Storr, Master Matai and the other masters of the Brotherhood. 'Bemossed now keeps Morjin from wielding it.'

'But Bemossed cannot wield it himself.'

'No, he cannot, and that bright eventuality must likely await the day when he sets his hands upon it.'

Across the room, the Cup of Ashurun gleamed upon its stand. I found myself wishing that this work of silver gelstei was the real Lightstone. I found myself wanting to promise Bemossed that the day would surely come when he *would* lay his hands upon the true Cup of Heaven.

'We have had reports out of Argattha,' Abrasax told me. 'Morjin has broken off the excavations there. He cannot, we believe, free the Dark One without full command of the Lightstone. And so, as of *this* day, he turns his attention to more pressing matters.'

'*I* have had reports of that,' Liljana announced. 'I am told that Morjin has prepared the Kallimun to make ready assassinations all across Alonia. My sisters believe that Morjin has gained a hold over Baron Maruth of the Aquantir. They fear that he will ally himself with the Marituk tribe and let the Sarni cross the Long Wall. Such a force could conquer Iviunn and Tarlan, and then all of Alonia could be lost.'

'So it could,' Kane added. 'As for Galda, do you think that Morjin will let the revolt prevail? Ha! – he will surely send an army from Karabuk to destroy this Gallagerry and restore the Kallimun.'

'And let us not forget that the Dragon has a new weapon,' Master Juwain said. 'If he himself, as his droghuls did, commands a voice of death, then woe to anyone who tries to stand before him.'

'Not *anyone*,' Master Okuth said. His gray hair gleamed on his round, heavy head like iron. 'All of you *did* stand before him. I should think that this death voice has something to do with Morjin's fifth chakra – and your ability, all of you, to withstand it must come from the soundness of each of your chakras. As Grandfather has said, your auras have been strengthened, like an armor woven of light. We should not be surprised at this: each of you, except Bemossed, once held the Lightstone. And Bemossed is Bemossed.'

'What you say might be true,' Master Juwain told him. 'But I still would not want to face the real Red Dragon, in the flesh.'

Abrasax allowed us, as well as Master Yasul and Master Matai, to speak on in a like way for some time. Then he finally held up his hand and told us: 'We cannot delude ourselves that Morjin has been defeated, or that what you did along the way to Hesperu will bring his certain defeat. But neither should we deny that we have gained a great victory.'

Now he looked at us across the table, and bowed his head.

'*You*, all of you,' he said, 'have done this great thing. And the marvel of it is that you did it without paying back evil for evil.'

I felt a burning inside my chest, and I said, 'Almost, we did such terrible things. Too many times, it was so close.'

'And in that,' Abrasax said, 'you gained the greatest victory of all.'

'Perhaps,' I told him.

'You vanquished your murderous hate of Morjin. And more, transmuted it, like an alchemist, into a thing of the truest gold. I know of no greater feat.'

I felt my mouth pulling into a grim smile. I looked at Bemossed; Estrella sat next to him, and she seemed like a great, shining mirror perfectly reflecting the brightness of his being. This last journey, I thought, had transformed all of us.

Then I said to Abrasax, 'With the help of my friends, I did – for a moment only. A man such as Morjin might be killed, once and forever, but not my hate for him. That is one battle that must be fought again and again.'

'And now you will fight it successfully,' Abrasax told me. 'You will use your gift to bring a great light into the world. Just as, in the end, I believe that the good will triumph over all that is dark and wrong.'

I found myself tracing my finger over the diamonds set into the black jade of the hilt of my sword, which I had laid at my side by

697

the table. And I said, 'What you call the good *must* triumph. But it is no simple matter. The valarda, I know, must never be used to slay. It is a beautiful thing, like life itself. It connects heart to living heart, as light passes from star to star. It *is* pure light, in a way, and so love, for it brings into creation all that is bright and good. And yet, and yet . . .'

I paused to take a sip of tea, and I looked at Abrasax. Then I said, 'Morjin crucified my mother and grandmother, and that was the most evil thing that I have ever suffered. And yet it led to the beginning of my understanding of him, which is a good thing, yes? This burning sense of the soul that sometimes I love, and sometimes I hate above all else. With it, I saw how I might strike a kind of light into Morjin. He could not bear it, for he sees in the compassionate and the beautiful all that is weak. And so it drove him to make a mortal error. *I* did. You could say that I used a good thing to kill the droghul, which is an evil act in itself. And yet only through this evil and the slaughter of many men were we able to make our escape from Hesperu and bring Bemossed here – which you count as the greatest of good.'

Abrasax considered this as he ran his finger around the rim of his tea cup. Then he stood, and walked over to the conservatory's western wall. Into its smooth stone had been carved a yanyin: a simple circle, bisected by a sigmoid line, like the curve of a snake. Its right side was set with quartz, as white as snow. A piece of black obsidian made up the other half. I couldn't help noticing how the black part of this ancient symbol swelled like a wave into the white as if to push against it, as the white did into the black.

Abrasax touched his hand to it, and said, 'This reminds us that light and dark are inextricably interwoven in the creation of the world. So it is with good and evil.'

'Yet you speak of good's inevitable triumph,' I told him. 'As do I.'

'As you say, it is no simple matter. I believe that life will always entail suffering, even after this age is ended and the Age of Light begins. But the suffering that man makes out of pride, ignorance and hate, which we call evil, that must surely end.'

He looked across the room as if to ask Bemossed to help explicate the deepest mysteries of life. Bemossed could not help laughing at the Grandmaster's obvious expectation. After bowing his head to Master Virang and Master Matai, he looked at Abrasax and said, 'You are the scholars and philosophers, men of well-chosen and beautiful words. Who am I? A Hajarim whose only gift is to keep burning like a torch so that you don't forget to light a fire of your own.'

He smiled at me, then shrugged his shoulders as to cast off a great weight pressing upon him. Then he said, 'All right, I will try.'

He took a sip of tea, and his eyes grew sad and bright.

'I learned in the desert that water is the source and substance of all life,' he told us. 'As the One is the source of all things. It flows through us and all around us, like a river leading down to the ocean. And that bright, infinite sea is what we all long for most deeply, isn't it? We have only to plunge into the river and let it take us there. But what man or woman has the courage to do that? It seems simpler, in our thirst for water, to wade out and try to empty the river bucket by bucket. But our thirst is infinite, is it not? Who has not known merchants who have amassed gold a thousand times in excess of their needs while their slaves starve to death, or kings who slaughter tens of thousands as they press on ever to conquer new lands? Or even once-great Elijin lords such as Morjin who seek unbounded power to fill the emptiness inside them? The ways of bringing hideous wrongs into this world are themselves nearly infinite. And so the ages go on, as the river goes on, and we continue to try to stand against it or to direct its currents for our own need. Why should we be surprised when it pulls us down into the mud and muck, and drowns us? Why *can't* we be content to discover how the river will flow? If we could do that, we wouldn't have to speak of good and evil.'

In the quiet of the conservatory, we all looked at Bemossed. The candles' light brought the soft features of his face aglow. At times he seemed a plain and simple man, and at other times, something much more.

Abrasax, still standing by the symbol-carved wall, said to him, 'Why not, indeed? Might I ask, then, where this great river will carry the Maitreya?'

'That is no easier for me to determine than for anyone else,' Bemossed said. 'But for now, I will remain here, Grandfather.'

'And you, Valashu Elahad? Will you and your companions stay with us, too?'

I took hold of my sword, and stood up to work off some of the restlessness building inside me. I paced around the room, looking at the various glyphs and the crystals set into the walls. I came to where Abrasax stood by the yanyin, with its gleaming curves of black and white. I drew my sword, and for a long few moments I watched the silver blade flare with a deep glorre. Then I thrust it straight into the heart of the yanyin. Its point, almost infinitely sharp, came to a rest in the fine crack between the yanyin's white quartz and black obsidian without chipping off the slightest sliver of stone or marring the yanyin in any way.

And I said to Abrasax, and to the other masters still sitting at the table, 'No, I will return to Mesh.'

'To Mesh?' Abrasax said. 'But your own warriors turned away from you and cast you out.'

'I cast myself out. But now the river that Bemossed has spoken of is carrying me back home.'

'Are you sure?'

I looked at my bright sword, and nodded my head. 'As sure as I am of anything.'

'But to what end?'

'To the end . . . of ending Morjin's terror,' I told him. 'There are those of my people who would still follow me.'

'To war, then?'

I drew in a long breath, and I remembered the lessons that my father had once taught me. I said, 'I must strike now, while Morjin is compromised, where he is the weakest.'

'To strike with that sword?'

I lifted up Alkaladur, and pointed it toward the starlight streaming in through one of the windows. 'This sword he fears like death. But there is another sword that is not so easy to see. He fears that one even more. It remains half-forged, and I still do not know how to wield it.'

Abrasax sighed and regarded me with his deep, perceptive eyes. 'It is a dangerous path that you've chosen.'

'Have *I* chosen it, Grandfather?'

He looked at the thing of silustria and light that I held in my hand, and he said, 'When you first came here, Master Storr accused you of being of the sword. That is still true, isn't it?'

'Yes,' I told him. 'I bear two swords now, and I will use either one, or both, against Morjin.'

'Will you not content yourself to see if Bemossed can prevail against him?'

I bowed my head to my new friend. 'Bemossed will do what he can do, and I will do what I must.'

'What is it then that you hope to accomplish?'

I looked at Estrella sitting beside Daj as she calmly ate a piece of lemon cake; I looked at Maram steeling himself for yet another journey, and at Atara abiding with a deep and lightless silence.

Then I looked at Kane. I smiled and said, 'Nothing less than Morjin's utter defeat. I believe in a victory so final and complete that even the stones buried miles down in the muck of the earth will sing with joy and light.'

'Ha!' Kane suddenly shouted. His deep voice set the walls of the conservatory to ringing. 'Ha! – the stars will dance and the earth itself will sing!'

He sprang to his feet and crossed the room almost in one blinding motion. He knelt before me as he laid his calloused hand on the flat of my sword's blade.

'So – I've waited too long to hear you say that,' he told me. 'To Mesh we'll go, and then if we must, to the gates of heaven or hell!'

Abrasax sighed at this. Then he, too, dared to touch my sword. He called out into the room, 'The river might flow to the sea, but it seems that it takes many turnings to reach it.'

He asked Kane and me to go back to the tables and sit back down. Then he stepped over to the door. He opened it to ask something of a Brother Hannold who waited outside. After taking his place again next to Master Storr, he folded his hands beneath his chin as he patiently waited.

After some time, Brother Hannold entered the room bearing a dark, dust-stained bottle. Another Brother followed after him carrying a tray of tinkling glasses. Brother Hannold set one of these deep-bodied glasses in front of each of us, even as he gripped the bottle in his other hand. I guessed that it must contain one of those sweet-bitter infusions of herbs that the Brothers favored in place of more convivial drink.

Then Brother Hannold uncorked the bottle.

'Ah, brandy!' Maram said as pushed out his fat nose to sniff across the table. 'Excellent! Excellent!'

'Brandy!' Master Storr cried out. 'It cannot be!'

His liver-spotted face grew red with outrage, and Masters Matai, Okuth and Yasul also seemed disturbed by this turn of events, while Master Virang rubbed his chin in confusion.

'Brandy it is, truly,' Abrasax said. He motioned for Brother Hannold to pour a bit of this dark, fiery liquid in our glasses. 'We will drink to the success of our guests' last journey, and their future ones, as well.'

'But, Grandfather,' Master Storr said, 'we do not drink to such things! It is not our way!'

'I believe that a new age is coming, and so there will be new ways. And so tonight, just this one time, we will drink.'

'Even the children?'

Abrasax smiled at Daj and Estrella, and said, 'Yes, even the children.'

Daj's eyes gleamed as Brother Hannold poured a little brandy into his glass. It was only a fourth the amount that Maram convinced Brother Hannold to pour for him, but Daj didn't seem to mind. After Abrasax had raised his glass and proposed the toast, bidding us to follow the sacred rivers that ran through each of our hearts, Daj downed his brandy in two great gulps. Miraculously, he did not cough or choke on it, but only sat triumphantly as if he had done a great thing.

And then he called out: 'I have an ending for my story. Does anyone want to hear it?'

At that moment Alphanderry appeared in a swirl of sparkling lights, and stood over the table.

'Of course we want to hear it,' Master Storr said. He drained his glass, and then held it out for Brother Hannold to refill it. 'We might as well have a songfest to go along with our drink, since we're breaking the peace of this chamber, to say nothing of our school.'

'Ha – peace be damned!' Kane said, smiling at Daj. 'Tell us how your story ends!'

Daj smiled back at him, and said, 'Well, for a long time, I didn't think it *could* have an ending. At least not a happy one. Eleikar *must* kill the wicked king to gain his vengeance and keep his honor. And he must *not* do anything that would wound Ayeshtan's heart, so how can he even think of killing her father?'

To the little sounds of brandy being sipped and glasses tinkling, we all sat contemplating this conundrum. None of us, not even Bemossed, could find an answer for Daj.

'So – tell us, then,' Kane finally said to him.

'Well,' Daj said, smiling back at him, 'it is Eleikar, after all, who finds his way out of his dilemma. It seems that he goes off on a quest of his own. He returns to Khalind with a kind of black gelstei, more powerful even than the Black Jade. He uses it to kill the wicked king and then take him down into the land of death. There, the king meets Eleikar's family – and all the people he has murdered. They all tell him what it was like to be stolen from life. And the king understands because now *he* has been stolen from life. By Eleikar. But Eleikar uses the gelstei to bring the wicked king back to Khalind. Only he is not wicked anymore because all he can think about is how good it is to be reborn and live again.

702

And so he becomes a good king, and gives Ayeshtan to Eleikar in marriage, and everyone lives happily ever after.'

Daj finished speaking and looked at Kane proudly. He seemed utterly swept away by the words that he had spoken to us.

Then, in a kindly way, Master Storr said to him, 'You do know, lad, that the black gelstei has no power to do such things. Not even the Lightstone can be used to bring the dead back to life.'

'This is *my* story,' Daj said, staring across the table at him. 'And in Khalind, people *can* live again.'

Abrasax met eyes with me for a moment, then turned to Daj to say, 'Perhaps they can indeed. Well, I for one would like to hear the whole of this gest. Will you sing it for us?'

Daj nodded his head proudly and said, 'If Master Nolashar will accompany me.'

Master Nolashar smiled at this, and brought out his flute. He played a haunting melody, while Daj stood up and sang out verse after verse of the *Gest of Eleikar and Ayeshtan*. When he had finished, we all clapped our hands, even Alphanderry, who did so without making the slightest sound. Then he said to Daj, 'Hoy, a minstrel you are! Why don't you and I sing together – Master Nolashar, too? There are so many songs!'

Abrasax called for a little more brandy, but Maram – along with Master Storr – drank much more than a little. Master Storr finally got up from his cushion and wobbled over to Liljana. He kissed the back of her head and told her, 'I'm sorry I ever called you a witch.' Then he wobbled back to his cushion.

After that, we sat for a long time in that beautiful place, in the best of company. As the evening deepened into night, Master Nolashar played his flute, while Daj and Alphanderry stood together in the starlight, and seemed to sing the whole universe into creation. It was one of those rare times when I sensed that all things might be possible, even the impossibilities of Daj's story.

Bright days followed that night, and grew longer and longer as winter passed into spring. In Gliss, the month of the new leaves, the snow began melting from most of the lower reaches of the Valley of the Sun. My friends and I would still have to wait until Ashte before daring the passes of the eastern Nagarshath, and so we had little to do except to study and prepare ourselves for another journey – and to wait and hope.

Late one morning, on a perfectly clear day, I met with Atara, and we walked together along the path by the river just below the school's ash grove. The trees showed a greenish fuzz of new leaves, while the first dandelions and fairies' eyes pushed up through the grass in sprays of yellow and white. We found a beautiful place, and laid down two blankets on the sloping ground that looked out over the partially frozen river. Water rushed in a gleaming black torrent down the channel cut through the river's ice. The petals of the flowers all around us caught the sun's brilliant light and reflected it up into the bluest of skies.

It was warm enough that we sat comfortably with only our tunics and cloaks to cover us. After a while the sun reached its zenith, and it grew warmer still, and we cast off the gray, woolen coverings that had seen so many miles. Atara smelled like her mare, Fire, for she had spent part of the morning trimming her hooves and combing her down. We picnicked on some cheese and bread, and apple cider that the Brothers had made last fall. For a while we spoke of little things such as the fine spring weather and the health of the horses. And then we moved on to other matters.

'Will you not consider remaining here with the Brothers?' I asked her.

'No, I don't think so,' she said. 'I've promised Fire a ride across the Wendrush again. But I promise *you* that I won't slow us down.'

I looked at the clean cloth that she had wrapped around her face. I said, 'I know you won't. But has there been nothing at all? Even a hint of your second sight returning?'

'No, nothing,' she murmured, shaking her head.

'Perhaps if you remained here all summer, and sat in the conservatory with Bemossed, he might –'

'I would rather ride beneath the open sky with you.'

'But he is doing such great things,' I told her. 'One day . . .'

I let my voice fade off into the soft roar of the river. I had nearly spoken of that which Atara did not wish me to speak of.

She grasped my hand in her warm fingers and said, 'It's all right – all right for *you* to wish that he might restore me.'

'But do you never think of this now, yourself?'

'Of course I do. But of course I mustn't. What will be will be. What *is*, now, is just as it should be. In so many ways, even after this last terrible, terrible journey, I have been restored already.'

I smiled at this, and said, 'I remember that you once told me how suffering carves hollows in the soul – only to leave room for it to hold more joy.'

She pressed her palm to her blindfold, which covered hollows as deep as the caverns beneath Argattha. And she said, 'These past days, with the children safe and Bemossed so happy in becoming this shining light for everyone, *I* have been so happy, too.'

My smile deepened as I squeezed her hand in mine. I gazed at her face, wishing with a hot pain in my eyes that she could gaze back at me.

'Bemossed makes people happy,' I said.

'The Maitreya, we call him, the Lord of Light,' she said to me. 'But what does that *mean*? What light can any man summon to bring help for this terrible world? This above all, I think: that everything that *is*, is so beautiful. It all shines, here and now.'

I looked out across the river at the acres of star lilies and white fairies' eyes gleaming in the strong sunlight. In the sky, an eagle soared, a little streak of gold against icy mountains and bright blue rock. The whole valley, with its brilliant green fields and forests powdered with snow, seemed on fire.

'What you say is true,' I told her. 'And yet, somewhere in the world, right now, a bird of prey is tearing out the insides of a vole or a hare. And somewhere, a man or a woman is dying upon a cross.'

'That, too, is true,' she said, and her voice grew thick with sadness. 'But even dying, they look out upon the same sky and the same earth that we do.'

I pressed her hand to my face, and I said softly, 'But *you* do not see at all now, not even with your second sight.'

'Don't pity me,' she said, pulling her hand away from me. The old coldness seemed to fall over her face like a cloud covering the sun.

'I don't pity you. But I will not believe there is no hope.'

She smiled coldly, even as her sadness deepened. Her fingers reached into the spray of blond hairs falling over her shoulders. She managed to pluck one of them out, and she held up this gleaming, golden filament for me to see. 'One chance only, Val. One slender, slender chance exists, finer even than this, of what you hope will be. And for all our gladness at finding Bemossed and what he has accomplished, it is exactly the same chance we have of defeating Morjin, in the end.'

'I know that,' I told her. 'But even if there is only one chance in ten thousand, I will think of how we might bring his defeat, and nothing else.'

I reached out and prised the hair from her fingers. I coiled it around one of mine, then folded it into a handkerchief, which I put in my tunic's pocket. And I said, '*Almost* nothing else. If there is only one chance in all the universe of you being made whole and marrying me, I will make it be.'

She sat next to me, with the sun beating down upon her, and the essence of horse and her musky skin steamed off her garments. I listened to her deep, quick breaths. Then she said, 'You sound so sure of yourself. The tone in your words – I have never heard you speak this way.'

I felt my own breath building in my throat like a storm. I no longer doubted that I could give voice to what whispered in my heart.

'My grandfather,' I told her, 'believed that a man can make his own fate. What can a man and a *woman* together make? Everything, Atara.'

She stood up and stepped carefully down to the river's bank, where she scooped up a handful of old snow. After shaping it into a ball, she returned to the blanket. She sat holding it before her face as if it might reveal the shape of the future. At last she said, 'King Jovayl was right about you. This journey has changed you.'

I felt a bright, warm thing filling up my blood with an unbearable heat. I no longer feared letting it loose into Atara like lightning.

'Tell me that you believe in the future,' I said to her.

She squeezed her snowy ball and replied, 'Of course I do.'

I took the snow from her and cast it into the river, where the dark, churning water swept it away. I took her cold, wet hands in mine. I held them, tightly, until they warmed, and then grew hot.

'Say that you will be my wife.'

'You want my *promise*?'

'No – I want you say that it must be. That no other future *can* be.'

She sat breathing quickly, and she said, 'I *almost* believe that.'

I stared at the blindfold binding her face. My eyes felt like firestones, and I wanted to burn it away.

'Don't look at me like that!' she told me.

'How do you know how I look at you? You are blind.'

'I have never been *that* blind. I can *feel* you looking and looking . . . and loving, the way that you do, with all the fire of your sweet, sweet heart, which I want to –'

I kissed her then. I felt something inside her melt, utterly, and flow like a sweet liquor, and so I cupped my hand around the back of her neck to pull us together. Her lips crushed against mine as she threw her arms around my back and pulled on me, fiercely, as if she wanted to take every part of me inside her. From within her throat, and mine, came a deep murmur almost like a growl, and we must have sounded like animals. But we were angels, too, for we kept passing the bright, warm thing to each other in our lips and our breath and our pounding blood, back and forth, until the fire grew so brilliant and hot that we could not bear it.

At last, she pushed away from me, and sat sweating and gasping. Her breath steamed out into the cool air as she told me, 'What I *won't* make with you is a child, not here and now – not with men still dying on crosses, as you say.'

'No – that would not be right,' I agreed. 'But someday, you will bear me a child. The most beautiful, beautiful child.'

She smiled, then laughed as she took hold of my hand and squeezed it. She said, 'Oh, Val, I *do* believe you – what else can I do?'

I kissed her again, and for a longer time. Then I told her, 'When the baby comes, you will look upon him with new eyes, *I* promise you.'

'But what if we have a girl?'

'Then you will look upon her even more gladly, as will I – especially if she is as beautiful as you.'

She sat quietly for a moment as she oriented her face toward me. Then she asked, 'Do you still think I'm beautiful?'

'More beautiful than any woman I've ever seen,' I told her. 'Even Asha and Varda, all the Star People, would envy you.'

She tapped her fingers to her blindfold and said, 'They would not envy me this, I think.'

I reached out to untie her blindfold and pull it away from her. I traced my fingers beneath her brows and across the bridge of her nose, even as my eyes grew warmer and I couldn't help looking and looking. Finally I said, 'A day will come when you will take this off for good. You *will* see again, Atara.'

She grasped my hand, and pressed it over the front of her face. She said, 'But I see so much now. I see *you*.'

I listened as the eagle above us let loose its harsh, haunting cry. I said, 'Tell me what you see, then.'

'I see a man,' she said, 'who had lost everything in the world, only to gain the whole world, and more. You are larger now, somehow, inside. Like that impossible stallion you ride. Like the sun. I don't know how your skin can contain you. You are wilder – so willful and wild. And even angrier than before, and you hate Morjin no less. But it is a different force now. It does not rule you.

707

You rule, now. The man I have wanted to be with every hour and with every breath since I first laid eyes upon him: he, who almost died. I see *that* one, who somehow found a moment of compassion for the vilest of beasts, even though that beast had slaughtered all that he loved.'

'Not *all*,' I said, squeezing her hand.

'But your mother and grandmother, your beautiful brothers, they –'

'They are here,' I said, pressing her hand to my chest. 'For so long, I kept thinking of them as murdered, dead. But truly, they live.'

I knew she wanted to weep, but at that moment I felt nothing except joy, and so I held her close to me. For a while, she *did* weep, but soon her soft sobbing gave way to a deeper heaving of her belly as she began laughing with a gladness for life that she could not contain. Finally, she sat back away from me and said, 'There is such a light in you – this beautiful, beautiful light! Kane says it is like a sword; I would say like the sweetest fire. I've never known anyone to love like you, to live like you, not even Bemossed. The *passion*. It is what you were born for. Sometimes, I know, I am all ice inside, but when you touch me the way you do, I'm all water.'

She paused to draw in a deep breath, then added, 'And that is why I love you. And why I *will* marry you.'

She kissed me, and then laughed for a long time, a delightful sound, like the ringing of the river. Then I could not contain *myself*. I leaped up, and pulled her up to her feet. I wanted to throw off my tunic and let the wind cool my burning skin. I wanted to fly like flame over the mountains. Why didn't their snow, I wondered, melt when I looked at it? Why didn't Atara gasp out at the fire in my hands when I took hold of her sides? I lifted her off the blanket then. She was a tall woman, large-boned with lithe muscles like a great, tawny cat, and yet I lifted her as if she were a child, and then whirled her through the air as I began dancing about.

After I had set her down, she turned toward me and said, 'I see a bird, Val. Bigger than that eagle that called to us. Bigger even than a dragon. He is a great swan, as silvery as that sword of yours, and he flies toward the stars. Once there, he *becomes* a star: so big, so bright. And that is *my* star, whose light I cannot live without.'

For a while, we stood together on the cool grass, arm in arm. We faced the mountains to the east, over which the sun had risen only a few hours before. Beyond the Nagarshath range stretched the bright, emerald grasses of the Wendrush and the beautiful mountains of my home. And beyond that, the sea. All of Ea, it seemed, lay before us. It would have been easy to think that the whole world was ours, existing only for our pleasure, as Morjin thought of things. And the world *was* ours – but only to love as we loved each other and to protect with our last breath. I did not need to speak of this to Atara. If our marriage was to mean anything at all, it could only be that we must live for something much greater than ourselves.

I reached down to pick the first flower that I could find, and I pressed into her hand.

'Here,' I told her, 'take this as my troth.'

'A *dandelion*, Val? It is the most common of flowers.'

'Today, no flower in the world is common to me. But what would you have me give you?'

'Only this,' she said, squeezing her hand around the flower. 'You're right – it is perfect.'

'But what would you give to me?'

She sniffed the air and said, 'A star lily, I think. Their fragrance is so sweet.'

I looked about the meadow at the many flowers, and I finally espied one of these lilies, with its long, slender white petals and bright yellow center like a bit of starfire. It grew among some buttercups and fairies' eyes twenty yards away. I moved to step over to it, but Atara laid her hand on my shoulder.

'No,' she told me. 'I must give it to you.'

And with that, she fairly danced across the meadow. Without the slightest hesitation or fumbling, she reached straight down to pick this one, bright flower. She came back over to me, and wrapped my fingers around it.

'This is my troth to you,' she told me.

Then she reached out with a perfect accuracy to wipe the tears running down my face.

'We have so little time,' she said to me. 'It is so peaceful here. Let's lie together while we can. I want to feel your heart beating next to mine.'

We returned to our blankets, and threw our cloaks over our thinly clad bodies to cover us. As I held her close to me, I felt her breath upon my face. I knew that she was willing to give herself to me, utterly, as I was with her. But I knew, as well, that this glorious union must wait. I felt no bitterness in this, only an immense anticipation. She pulled me into the warmth of her breasts and her belly, and I could not tell that we were two separate beings, for our hearts beat as one.

Thus we lay for hours on that bright, perfect afternoon, and the whole world seemed to stand perfectly still. At last, however, the earth carried us into the future, as it always did. It grew cold and dark, and the stars came out like millions of tiny white flowers. For a long time, we soared among them. I listened for the voices of those who dwelled there. I did not know if the dead would ever speak to me again. The living, though, and the infinitude of beings waiting to be born, sang out only the most brilliant of songs. Atara and I sang with them, and so did our son, and our voices, like the exultations of angels, filled the night with a fiery and inextinguishable joy.

APPENDICES

Heraldry

THE NINE KINGDOMS

The shield and surcoat arms of the warriors of the Nine Kingdoms differ from those of the other lands in two respects. First, they tend to be simpler, with a single, bold charge emblazoned on a field of a single color. Second, every fighting man, from the simple warrior up through the ranks of knight, master and lord to the king himself, is entitled to bear the arms of his line.

There is no mark or insignia of service to any lord save the king. Loyalty to one's ruling king is displayed on shield borders as a field matching the color of the king's field, and a repeating motif of the king's charge. Thus, for instance, every fighting man of Ishka, from warrior to lord, will display a red shield border with white bears surrounding whatever arms have been passed down to him. With the exception of the lords of Anjo, only the kings and the royal families of the Nine Kingdoms bear unbordered shields and surcoats.

In Anjo, although a king in name still rules in Jathay, the lords of the other regions have broken away from his rule to assert their own sovereignty. Thus, for instance, Baron Yashur of Vishal bears a shield of simple green emblazoned with a white crescent moon without bordure as if he were already a king or aspiring to be one.

Once there was a time when all Valari kings bore the seven stars of the Swan Constellation on their shields as a reminder of the Elijin and Galadin to whom they owed allegiance. But by the time of the Second Lightstone Quest, only the House of Elahad has as part of its emblem the seven silver stars.

In the heraldry of the Nine Kingdoms, white and silver are used interchangeably as are silver and gold. Marks of cadence – those smaller charges that distinguish individual members of a line, house or family – are usually placed at the point of the shield.

Mesh

House of Elahad – a black field; a silver-white swan with spread wings gazes upon the seven silver-white stars of the Swan constellation

Lord Harsha – a blue field; gold lion rampant filling nearly all of it

Lord Tomavar – white field; black tower

Lord Tanu – white field; black, double-headed eagle

Lord Raasharu – gold field; blue rose

Lord Navaru – blue field; gold sunburst

Lord Juluval – gold field; three red roses

Lord Durrivar – red field; white bull

Lord Arshan – white field; three blue stars

Ishka

King Hadaru Aradar – red field; great white bear

Lord Mestivan – gold field; black dragon

Lord Nadhru – green field; three white swords, points touching upwards

Lord Solhtar – red field; gold sunburst

Athar

King Mohan – gold field; blue horse

Lagash

King Kurshan – blue field; white Tree of Life

Waas

King Sandarkan – black field; two crossed silver swords

Taron

King Waray – red field; white winged horse

Kaash

King Talanu Solaru – blue field; white snow tiger

Anjo

King Danashu – blue field; gold dragon

Duke Gorador Shurvar of Daksh – white field; red heart

Duke Rezu of Rajak – white field; green falcon

Duke Barwan of Adar – blue field; white candle
Baron Yashur of Vishal – green field; white crescent moon
Count Rodru Narvu of Yarvanu – white field; two green lions rampant
Count Atanu Tuval of Onkar – white field; red maple leaf
Baron Yuval of Natesh – black field; golden flute

FREE KINGDOMS

As in the Nine Kingdoms, the bordure pattern is that of the field
and charge of the ruling king. But in the Free Kingdoms, only
nobles and knights are permitted to display arms on their shields
and surcoats. Common soldiers wear two badges: the first, usually
on their right arm, displaying the emblems of their kings, and the
second, worn on their left arm, displaying those of whatever baron,
duke or knight to whom they have sworn allegiance.

In the houses of Free Kingdoms, excepting the ancient Five
Families of Tria from whom Alonia has drawn most of her kings,
the heraldry tends toward more complicated and geometric
patterns than in the Nine Kingdoms.

Alonia

House of Narmada – blue field; gold caduceus
House of Eriades – Field divided per bend; blue upper, white lower;
    white star on blue, blue star on white
House of Kirriland – White field; black raven
House of Hastar – Black field; two gold lions rampant
House of Marshan – white field; red star inside black circle
Baron Narcavage of Arngin – white field; red bend; black oak lower;
    black eagle upper
Baron Maruth of Aquantir – green field; gold cross; two gold arrows
    on each quadrant
Duke Ashvar of Raanan – gold field; repeating pattern of black swords
Baron Monteer of Iviendenhall – white and black checkered shield
Count Muar of Iviunn – black field; white cross of Ashtoreth
Duke Malatam of Tarlan – white field; black saltire; repeating red
    roses on white quadrants

Eanna

King Hanniban Dujar – gold field; red cross; blue lions rampant on
    each gold quadrant

Surrapan
King Kaiman – red field; white saltire; blue star at center

Thalu
King Aryaman – Black and white gyronny; white swords on four black sectors

Delu
King Santoval Marshayk – green field; two gold lions rampant facing each other

The Elyssu
King Theodor Jordan – blue field; repeating breaching silver dolphins

Nedu
King Tal – blue field; gold cross; gold eagle volant on each blue quadrant

THE DRAGON KINGDOMS

With one exception, in these lands, only Morjin himself bears his own arms: a great, red dragon on a gold field. Kings who have sworn fealty to him – King Orunjan, King Arsu – have been forced to surrender their ancient arms and display a somewhat smaller red dragon on their shields and surcoats. Kallimun priests who have been appointed to kingship or who have conquered realms in Morjin's name – King Mansul, King Yarkul, Count Ulanu – also display this emblem but are proud to do so.

Nobles serving these kings bear slightly smaller dragons, and the knights serving them bear yet smaller ones. Common soldiers wear a yellow livery displaying a repeating pattern of very small red dragons.

King Angand of Sunguru, as an ally of Morjin, bears his family's arms as does any free king.

The kings of Hesperu and Uskudar have been allowed to retain their family crests as a mark of their kingship, though they have surrendered their arms.

Sunguru

King Angand – blue field; white heart with wings

Uskudar

King Orunjan – gold field; ¾ red dragon

Karabuk

King Mansul – gold field; ¾ red dragon

Hesperu

King Arsu – gold field; ¾ red dragon

Galda

King Yarkul – gold field; ¾ red dragon

Yarkona

Count Ulanu – gold field; ½ red dragon

The Gelstei

THE GOLD

The history of the gold gelstei, called the Lightstone, is shrouded in mystery. Most people believe the legend of Elahad: that this Valari king of the Star People made the Lightstone and brought it to earth. Some of the Brotherhoods, however, teach that the Elijin or the Galadin made the Lightstone. Some teach that the mythical Ieldra, who are like gods, made the Lightstone millions of years earlier. A few hold that the Lightstone may be a transcendental, increate object from before the beginning of time, and as such, much as the One or the universe itself, has always existed and always will. Also, there are people who believe that this golden cup, the greatest of the gelstei, was made in Ea during the great Age of Law.

The Lightstone is the image of solar light, the sun, and hence of divine intelligence. It is made into the shape of a plain golden cup because 'it holds the whole universe inside'. Upon being activated by a powerful enough being, the gold begins to turn clear like a crystal and to radiate light like the sun. As it connects with the infinite power of the universe, the One, it radiates light like that of ten thousand suns. Ultimately, its light is pure, clear and infinite – the light of pure consciousness. The light inside light, the light inside all things that *is* all things. The Lightstone quickens consciousness in itself, the power of consciousness to enfold itself and form up as matter and thus evolve into infinite possibilities. It enables certain human beings to channel and magnify this power. Its power is infinitely greater than that of the red gelstei, the firestones. Indeed, the Lightstone gives power over the other gelstei, the green, purple, blue and white, the black and perhaps the silver

– and potentially over all matter, energy, space and time. The final secret of the Lightstone is that, as the very consciousness and substance of the universe itself, it is found within each human being, interwoven and interfused with each separate soul. To quote from the *Saganom Elu*, it is 'the perfect jewel within the lotus found inside the human heart'.

The Lightstone has many specific powers, and each person finds in it a reflection of himself. Those seeking healing are healed. In some, it recalls their true nature and origins as Star People; others, in their lust for immortality, find only the hell of endless life. Some – such as Morjin or Angra Mainyu – it blinds with its terrible and beautiful light. Its potential to be misused by such maddened beings is vast: ultimately it has the power to blow up the sun and destroy the stars, perhaps the whole universe itself.

Used properly, the Lightstone can quicken the evolution of all beings. In its light, Star People may transcend to their higher angelic natures while angels evolve into archangels. And the Galadin themselves, in the act of creation only, may use the Lightstone to create whole new universes.

The Lightstone is activated at once by individual consciousness, the collective unconscious and the energies of the stars. It also becomes somewhat active at certain key times, such as when the Seven Sisters are rising in the sky. Its most transcendental powers manifest when it is in the presence of an enlightened being and/or when the earth enters the Golden Band.

It is not known if there are many Lightstones throughout the universe, or only one that somehow appears at the same time in different places. One of the greatest mysteries of the Lightstone is that on Ea, only a human man, woman or child can use it for its best and highest purpose: to bring the sacred light to others and awaken each being to his angelic nature. Neither the Elijin nor the Galadin, the archangels, possess this special resonance. And only a very few of the Star People do.

These rare beings are the Maitreyas who come forth every few millennia or so to share their enlightenment with the world. They have cast off all illusion and apprehend the One in all things and all things as manifestations of the One. Thus they are the deadly enemies of Morjin and the Dark Angel, and other Lords of the Lie.

The Greater
Gelstei

THE SILVER

The silver gelstei is made of a marvelous substance called silustria. The crystal resembles pure silver, but is brighter, reflecting even more light. Depending on how forged, the silver gelstei can be much harder than diamond.

The silver gelstei is the stone of reflection, and thus of the soul, for the soul is that part of man that reflects the light of the universe. The silver reflects and magnifies the powers of the soul, including, in its lower emanations, those of mind: logic, deduction, calculation, awareness, ordinary memory, judgment and insight. It can confer upon those who wield it holistic vision: the ability to see whole patterns and reach astonishing conclusions from only a few details or clues. Its higher emanations allow one to see how the individual soul must align itself with the universal soul to achieve the unfolding of fate.

In its reflective qualities, the silver gelstei may be used as a shield against various energies: vital, mental, or physical. In other ages, it has been shaped into arms and armor, such as swords, mail shirts and actual shields. Although not giving power *over* another, in body or in mind, the silver can be used to quicken the working of another's mind, and is thus a great pedagogical tool leading to knowledge and laying bare truth. A sword made of silver gelstei can cut through all things physical as the mind cuts through ignorance and darkness.

In its fundamental composition, the silver is very much like the gold gelstei, and is one of the two noble stones.

THE WHITE

These stones are called the white, but in appearance are usually clear, like diamonds. During the Age of Law, many of them were cast into the form of crystal balls to be used by scryers, and are thus often called 'scryers' spheres'.

These are the stones of far-seeing: of perceiving events distant in either space or time. They are sometimes used by remembrancers to uncover the secrets of the past. The kristei, as they are called, have helped the master healers of the Brotherhoods read the auras of the sick that they might be brought back to strength and health.

THE BLUE

The blue gelstei, or blestei, have been fabricated on Ea at least as far back as the Age of the Mother. These crystals range in color from a deep cobalt to a bright, lapis blue. They have been cast into many forms: amulets, cups, figurines, rings and others.

The blue gelstei quicken and deepen all kinds of knowing and communication. They are an aid to mindspeakers and truthsayers, and confer a greater sensitivity to music, poetry, painting, languages and dreams.

THE GREEN

Other than the Lightstone itself, these are the oldest of the gelstei. Many books of the *Saganom Elu* tell of how the Star People brought twelve of the green stones with them to Ea. The varistei look like beautiful emeralds; they are usually cast – or grown – in the shape of baguettes or astragals, and range in size from that of a pin or bead to great jewels nearly a foot in length.

The green gelstei resonate with the vital fires of plants and animals, and of the earth. They are the stones of healing and can be used to quicken and strengthen life and lengthen its span. As the purple gelstei can be used to mold crystals and other inanimate substances into new shapes, the green gelstei have powers over the forms of living things. In the Lost Ages, it was said that masters of the varistei used them to create new races of man (and sometimes monsters) but this art is thought to be long since lost.

These crystals confer great vitality on those who use them in harmony with nature; they can open the body's chakras and awaken the kundalini fire so the whole body and soul vibrate at a higher level of being.

THE RED

The red gelstei – also called tuaoi stones or firestones – are blood-red crystals like rubies in appearance and color. They are often cast into baguettes at least a foot in length, though during the Age of Law much larger ones were made. The greatest ever fabricated was the hundred-foot Eluli's Spire, mounted on top of the Tower of the Sun. It was said to cast its fiery light up into the heavens as a beacon calling out to the Star People to return to earth.

The firestones quicken, channel and control the physical energies. They draw upon the sun's rays, as well as the earth's magnetic and telluric currents, to generate beams of light, lightning, heat or fire. They are thought to be the most dangerous of the gelstei; it is said that a great pyramid of red gelstei unleashed a terrible lightning that split asunder the world of Iviunn and destroyed its star.

THE BLACK

The black gelstei, or baalstei, are black crystals like obsidian. Many are cast into the shape of eyes, either flattened or rounded like large marbles. They devour light and are the stones of negation.

Many believe them to be evil stones, but they were created for a great good purpose: to control the awesome lightning of the firestones. Theirs is the power to damp the fires of material things, both living and living crystals such as the gelstei. Used properly, they can negate the working of all the other kinds of gelstei except the silver and the gold, over which they have no power.

Their power over living things *is* most often put to evil purpose. The Kallimun priests and other servants of Morjin such as the Grays have wielded them as weapons to attack people physically, mentally and spiritually, literally sucking away their vital energies and will. Thus the black stones can be used to cause disease, degeneration and death.

It is believed that that baalstei might be potentially more dangerous than even the firestones. For in the *Beginnings* is told of an utterly black place that is at once the negation of all things and paradoxically also their source. Out of this place may come the fire and light of the universe itself. It is said that the Baaloch, Angra Mainyu, before he was imprisoned on the world of Damoom, used a great black gelstei to destroy whole suns in his war of rebellion against the Galadin and the rule of the Ieldra.

THE PURPLE

The lilastei are the stones of shaping and making. They are a bright violet in hue, and are cast into crystals of a great variety of shapes and sizes. Their power is unlocking the light locked up in matter so that matter might be changed, molded and transformed. Thus the lilastei are sometimes called the alchemists' stones, according to the alchemists' age-old dream of transmuting baser matter into true gold, and casting true gold into a new Lightstone.

The purple gelstei's greatest effects are on crystals of all sorts: but mostly those in metal and rocks. It can unlock the crystals in these substances so that they might be more easily worked. Or they can be used to grow crystals of great size and beauty; they are the stone shapers and stone growers spoken of in legend. It is said that Kalkamesh used a lilastei in forging the silustria of the Bright Sword, Alkaladur.

Some believe the potential power of the purple gelstei to be very great and perhaps very perilous. Lilastei have been known to 'freeze' water into an alternate crystal called shatar, which is clear and as hard as quartz. Some fear that these gelstei might be used thus to crystallize the water in the sea and so destroy all life on earth. The stone masters of old, who probed the mysteries of the lilastei too deeply, are said to have accidentally turned themselves *into* stone, but most believe this to be only a cautionary tale out of legend.

THE SEVEN OPENERS

If man's purpose is seen as in progressing to the orders of the Star People, Elijin and Galadin, then the seven stones known as the openers might fairly be called greater gelstei. Indeed, there are those of the Great White Brotherhood and the Green Brotherhood who revered them in this way. For, with much study and work, the openers each activate one of the body's chakras: the energy centers known as wheels of light. As the chakras are opened, from the base of the spine to the crown of the head, so is opened a pathway for the fires of life to reconnect to the heavens in a great burst of lightning called the angel's fire. Only then can a man or a woman undertake the advanced work necessary for advancement to the higher orders.

The openers are each small, clear stones the color of their respective chakras. They are easily mistaken for gemstones.

THE FIRST (also called bloodstones)
These are a clear, deep red in color, like rubies. The first stones open the chakra of the physical body and activate the vital energies.

THE SECOND (also called passion stones or old gold)
These gelstei are gold-orange in color and are sometimes mistaken for amber. The second stones open the chakra of the emotional body and activate the currents of sensation and feeling.

THE THIRD (also called sun stones)
The third stones are clear and bright yellow, like citrine; they open the third chakra of the mental body and activate the mind.

THE FOURTH (also called dream stones or heart stones)
These beautiful stones – clear and pure green in color like emeralds – open the heart chakra. Thus they open one's second feeling, a truer and deeper sense than the emotions of the second chakra. The fourth stones work upon the astral body and activate the dreamer.

THE FIFTH (also called soul stones)
Bright blue in color like sapphires, the fifth stones open the chakra of the etheric body and activate the intuitive knower, or the soul.

THE SIXTH (also called angel eyes)
The sixth stones are bright purple like amethyst. They open the chakra of the celestial body located just above and between the eyes. Thus their more common name: theirs is the power of activating one's second sight. Indeed, these gelstei activate the seer in the realm of light, and open one to the powers of scrying, visualization and deep insight.

THE SEVENTH (also called clear crowns or true diamonds)

One of the rarest of the gelstei, the seventh stones are clear and bright as diamonds. Indeed, some say they are nothing more than perfect diamonds, without flaw or taint of color. These stones open the chakra of the ketheric body and free the spirit for reunion with the One.

THE LESSER GELSTEI

During the Age of Law, hundreds of kinds of gelstei were made for purposes ranging from the commonplace to the sublime. Few of these have survived the passage of the centuries. Some of those that have are:

GLOWSTONES

Also called glowglobes, these stones are cast into solid, round shapes resembling opals of various sizes – some quite huge. They give a soft and beautiful light. Those of lesser quality must be frequently refired beneath the sun, while those of the highest quality drink in even the faintest candlelight, hold it and give back in a steady illumination.

SLEEP STONES

A gelstei of many shifting and swirling colors, the sleep stones have a calming effect on the human nervous system. They look something like agates.

WARDERS

Usually blood-red in color and opaque, like carnelians, these stones deflect or 'ward-off' psychic energies directed at a person. This includes thoughts, emotions, curses – and even the debilitating energy drain of the black gelstei. One who wears a warder can be rendered invisible to scryers and opaque to mindspeakers.

LOVE STONES

Often called true amber and sometimes mistaken for the second stones of the openers, these gelstei partake of some of their properties. They are specific to arousing feelings of infatuation and love; sometimes love stones are ground into a powder and made into potions to achieve the same end. They are soft stones and look much like amber.

WISH STONES

These little stones – they look something like white pearls – help the wearer remember his dreams and visions of the future; they activate the will to manifest these visualizations.

DRAGON BONES

Of a translucent, old ivory in color, the dragon bones strengthen the life fires and quicken one's courage – and all too often one's wrath.

HOT SLATE

A dark, gray, opaque stone of considerable size – hot slate is usually cast into yard-long bricks – this gelstei is related in powers and purpose, if not form, to the glowstones. It absorbs heat directly from the air and radiates it back over a period of hours or days.

MUSIC MARBLES

Often called song stones, these gelstei of variegated, swirling hues record and play music, both of the human voice and all instruments. They are very rare.

TOUCH STONES

These are related to the song stones and have a similar appearance. However, they record and play emotions and tactile sensations instead of music. A man or a woman, upon touching one of these gelstei, will leave a trace of emotions that a sensitive can read from contact with the stone.

THOUGHT STONES

This is the third stone in this family and is almost indistinguishable from the others. It absorbs and holds one's thoughts as a cotton garment might retain the smell of perfume or sweat. The ability to read back these thoughts from touching this gelstei is not nearly so rare as that of mindspeaking itself.

Books of the Saganom Elu

Beginnings
Sources
Chronicles
Journeys
Book of Stones
Book of Water
Book of Wind
Book of Fire
Tragedies
Book of Remembrance
Sarojin
Baladin
Averin
Souls
Songs
Meditations

Mendelin
Ananke
Commentaries
Book of Stars
Book of Ages
Peoples
Healings
Laws
Battles
Progressions
Book of Dreams
Idylls
Visions
Valkariad
Trian Prophecies
The Eschaton

The Ages of Ea

The Lost Ages (18,000 – 12,000 years ago)
The Age of the Mother (12,000 – 9,000 years ago)
The Age of the Sword (9,000 – 6,000 years ago)
The Age of Law (6,000 – 3,000 years ago)
The Age of the Dragon (3,000 years ago to the present)

The Months of the Year

Yaradar	Marud
Viradar	Soal
Triolet	Ioj
Gliss	Valte
Ashte	Ashvar
Soldru	Segadar